Beyond the Beginning

by

Kenneth J. M. MacLean

SECOND EDITION

Beyond the Beginning by Kenneth James Michael MacLean

Copyright ©by Kenneth J. M. MacLean

ISBN: 9780979430442 Library of Congress Control Number: 2009932073

Cover Image Credit:

NASA/JPL-Caltech and The Hubble Heritage Team (STScI/AURA)

Beyond the Beginning is the third book in the Potentials of Consciousness series.

Also by K.J.M. MacLean: *The Vibrational Universe*

Distributed by: Baker & Taylor, Ingram Book Group

The Big Picture is an imprint of: Loving Healing Press

Loving Healing Press

Contact the author at www.kjmaclean.com

Contents

"Grau, teurer Freund, ist alle Theorie
Und grun des Lebens goldner Baum"
— Goethe

"My dear friend, all theory is gray
Life's golden tree alone is green"

Deep within the fabric of the cosmos, the completion of a 16 billion year cycle is imminent. Even within the illustrious civilization of the Twelve Galaxies, only a few of the greatest minds even suspect such a thing.

Soon all eyes will turn toward earth, for it will be a primary player in the universal drama that is, even as you read these words, now unfolding. Two young people, both social misfits, are to play prominent roles in this cosmic drama.

We must therefore begin our narrative with their story...

1

ROBERT and Rachel Frankel had one child, a son. Even at the age of 4 he was tall and gangly. Not awkward exactly, but not graceful either. He had a head of curlicues that stuck out as if pulled by static electricity. He looked a bit clownish but they didn't care. It was a minor blemish.

John was a very strong, intelligent, and immensely curious boy. That became evident one day when Robert Frankel walked downstairs into his tool room, intent on getting a Phillips head screwdriver. Robert heard noises from inside. He leaned against the doorwall, peeking inside. John stood on a chair. With his arms outstretched the boy lifted the heavy toolbox and brought it down to another chair he had placed alongside. He clambered awkwardly off the chair. John rested his elbows upon it and studied the toolbox. Robert watched as he figured out latch and hinges. The boy slowly opened the cover, his eyes widening with delight at what lay inside. His little hands fished around and found a hammer. John grabbed the handle with both hands. He stood back on the chair and pounded down a protruding nail on his old worktable.

He then found a file. Robert saw his son grab the file and start to pound on something. The boy flinched, for his little hands had been roughed up by the tool's serrated plane. The child then placed the file alongside the edge of the worktable and began sawing back and forth. To his delight a few wood shavings were removed. John howled with glee and began sawing madly. Wood shavings were flying about everywhere. The little boy was laughing and giggling like mad.

"Hold on there son. You're going to wreck my table!"

Robert took John in his arms and congratulated him. "That was a good job, son. Maybe one day you'll build something."

"Yeth," John said.

Robert whistled a happy tune as he carried John up to the living room.

John was always getting into things. He was constantly climbing on chairs and knocking stuff off the shelves in his zeal to find out about his environment. Rachel had to keep her good candle holders, dishes, and other fragile knick knacks out of his reach. She sometimes complained that her house looked like a locker room. But she never was much of a housekeeper. Rachel Frankel was entirely too much interested in her career to care that much.

"Hey dad, why is the sky blue? Why is the sun yellow? Why is it light and then dark? Why does the top stay up when it spins?" These and many more questions spilled from his lips every day. Robert and Rachel were so glad when he learned to read, for now they could point to a book. "Here, read this," became their mantra.

Sometimes it was hard to find books that were comprehensible to a child. They spent hours explaining the fundamentals of physics and astronomy as best they could to his 6-year-old mind. Robert realized that science really didn't have a perfect grasp of the world around them. When Robert tried to explain gravity he could only point out that a larger object had more gravitational attraction.

"But why Dad?" John asked.

Robert scratched his head and consulted his textbooks, but he wasn't really sure and neither were the texts.

John learned at an early age that grown-ups didn't have all the answers. That fueled his curiosity even more.

Robert was proud of his son and imagined great things for him. Perhaps an architect, or a scientist. Something big anyway. Robert made plans to save enough to send him to the best schools. So what if the kid wasn't too coordinated? It's brains, not brawn, that make for success in this world.

The Frankel's lived at 337 Magnolia Drive, in an old two story wood and brownstone house a couple of miles from the Carleton University campus. Carleton was known as the Harvard of the Midwest to its residents in Midland, Illinois, population 97,000. Midland is a college town surrounded by farmland. Their neighborhood had tall elm trees that in summer provided a thick canopy across the asphalt street. It was in an older section of town. Its residents were mostly academics or retired executives from the Chicago area. Most people moved to the college town because of its friendliness, atmosphere, and rich cultural life. There were only three children on the block, all older than John. As the child grew up he learned to entertain himself. He grew comfortable being alone.

"Now we are 6 and clever as clever. I want to be 6 now forever and ever." Robert was up in John's room reading to his son just before bedtime, from *Now We Are Six*.

"I like that dad. Say it again."

Robert repeated the cute turn of phrase. He liked it too. It had an innocent cheerfulness, something he saw in his son's eyes all the time. It reminded him of something he had lost.

But that didn't matter right now. When Robert Frankel was with his son he could open his heart and feel young again. Reading to him just before bed was the highlight of his day.

John laughed delightedly. "Again, daddy."

Robert repeated it over and over, each time watching his son gurgle with laughter.

"I'm clever too daddy!" John said joyfully.

"Yes you are son. I love you very much."

"I love you too dad."

"OK son, time for bed." Robert folded up the book, switched off the light, and looked back into the room. The child's curly little head was on the pillow and he was half asleep already.

Robert walked down the stairs and saw Rachel in the living room, reading a book. There was a little tension in their relationship these days, but not at this moment. Robert walked up to her chair, tossed her book away and pulled her up to him.

"I love you too, Rachel."

Surprised but pleased, she kissed him.

"Time for bed dear."

Tonight, at least, all was well in the Frankel family.

By the age of six John had learned to ride a bike. Being the adventurous sort he was always going places his mom told him he couldn't. She was afraid for him. But John was guided by a stronger beacon: his unflagging curiosity. One day John was a mile or so from home in a strange neighborhood. He saw a little girl sitting on the porch steps in front of a big, old-style house. He stopped his bike on the sidewalk and looked at her. She had raven-black hair and there was something very interesting about her. Maybe he should talk to her and find out who she was.

"Hi," he said.

She did not respond.

To John this was curious. When you said hi to someone they were supposed to say hi back.

He pedaled his bike slowly up the front walk to get a closer look at her. John noticed her lips were red.

"My mom says you're not supposed to wear lipstick until you get older."

The little girl looked him squarely in the eyes and John had to pedal backward. For a brief instant he sensed an overwhelming presence. Something touched him in every cell of his body. Then the feeling was gone. The strange girl regarded him for a few more moments. Then she dismissed him from her awareness and resumed inspection of the rock she had in her hands.

"Why are your lips so red?" John asked. "What's your name?"

"Shutup."

John was confused. He innocently repeated his question.

The girl reached down and grabbed a handful of sand and pebbles. She threw it into his face.

"Ow! That hurts!" John had gotten something in his eyes and they began to water. "Hey, you're not very nice!"

She didn't answer.

John was upset and angry. He turned his bike around and rode home, tears rolling down his face.

When the boy got home he told his father about the girl.

"Where were you son?"

"I don't know. I just got on my bike and rode around."

"Did you go past a traffic light?"

"Yes."

"John!" Rachel exclaimed. "I told you never to go past the light. It's too dangerous."

Robert sighed. "That's OK son." He was secretly proud of the boy's adventurous spirit. "What did the house look like?"

"It was real big. It was brown I think and white on top and had a dark porch on it. That's where the girl was sitting."

"Mike Walters' place," he said to Rachel. They had been sitting in the living room reading.

"John, please don't ride so far," Rachel said. "You might get hurt." She didn't care what Robert said. Her son was too little to be riding around in traffic even though he was taller and stronger than anyone his age.

" I won't I promise mom," John said. "Do you know who she is?"

Rachel looked at her husband. "Isn't that the girl they adopted before Debra went off?"

"Yes, that's right. I believe her name is Genevieve. Sounds like a holy terror."

"Stay away from there son," Robert said.

John couldn't stay away. Every day after school he would ride over but she did not reappear until a week later. He saw her lying out on the grass with her hands behind her head.

"Hi," he said.

"Oh it's you again."

"You want to play?"

"Why don't you go find some boys to play with?"

"I don't know any boys except the ones in school. They don't like me."

"Tough."

She was maddening but he liked her anyway.

About two months later he spotted her at school, trudging in from the snow. She stomped her boots and tugged off her coat. She was boyish looking and different from all the other girls. Maybe that's why he liked her. A fellow weirdo.

"Did you walk all the way?"

"Yeah."

"That must be at least two miles."

She just shrugged and started to walk away. Suddenly she turned back and faced him.

"You can come over today after school if you want." Then she was gone.

After dinner John rode his bike in the snow. He didn't tell his mom where he was going, waiting until she went upstairs to her study. He knew she was having trouble with her book. If he didn't call attention to himself she would soon forget about him.

From his first floor study just off the hallway, Robert glanced up from his computer. He saw his son pulling on his winter coat, and he smiled.

Mom and Dad are weird sometimes, John thought as he pulled away from the house. They told him completely different things.

He had a tough time seeing anything in the dark. His bike wheels slipped often on the icy sidewalks but finally John reached her house. He rapped the big lions-head knocker.

The door opened into a foyer tiled with thick flagstones and lighted by a single dim bulb. "Take off your shoes," the girl said. She led him down a darkened hallway into a large, carpeted living room with a huge fireplace. A fire blazed. As John approached he saw a stocky man with a large head, glasses, and thick black hair seated in one of the armchairs. The man was reading a magazine.

The man glanced at the new arrival. "So this is your little friend," he said to the girl.

Friend? John didn't think throwing sand in his face qualified.

He sat down on the sofa next to her, across from the man. There was a book on the side table. John already knew how to read so he sounded out the words as best he could: "Linguistics, a Modern Approach." Wow. He didn't understand the meaning of the title. Is this something she read for fun? Probably her dad's book.

The girl beside him was silent, looking into the fire. John looked around, feeling uncomfortable. He liked the big living room but thought it had a sort of unloved feeling.

Just then a thin woman dressed for the cold entered softly from the hallway. She wore a winter coat with its hood pulled up over her head and a scarf on top. On her feet were black furry boots. She spoke timidly. "I'm finished for the day Mister Walters." John thought that she spoke with a funny accent.

"Very well Magdelana."

Magdelena smiled briefly at the girl, then hurried out. John heard the front door close softly.

"What's your name?" John asked.

"Genevieve."

"Where's your mom?"

"She's gone."

John nodded to the man in the chair. "Is that your dad?"

"Yes."

She always answered his questions literally, but did not elaborate.

"Who was that lady?"

"She's our housekeeper."

"What's a housekeeper?"

The girl sighed. "She cooks and cleans and watches me when dad's not here."

"Oh." John didn't really understand. There was silence, broken only by the occasional rustling of the magazine.

"My dad's a science writer," John said hopefully. Genevieve did not respond. The man in the armchair grunted but did not look up.

He tried again. "Lots of snow today."

Nothing.

John sighed. If this was her home life it was unlike any he had ever heard of.

John tried to draw her out but she seemed uncomfortable with his questions. After half an hour he got up to leave.

"See you. Nice meeting you Mr. Walters." The man moved the magazine and mumbled an acknowledgment. John let himself out.

He navigated his bike over the slippery sidewalks. There was something sterile and unfriendly about the house and the people in it.

Then why, he asked himself, did he like the girl so much?

2

ONE day a funny looking creature came into the Full Moon, a bookstore run by Mats Karlsson. Mats was a burly 6-footer with a head of thinning blond hair. He stood at the counter, chatting with a customer. The other man suddenly turned his head to stare at the new arrival. His eyebrows raised in curiosity.

Mats had seen a lot of odd people in his bookstore but this guy was most curious. The fellow was very short and wore a gold colored habit, or cloak, with long sleeves. A hood came way out from his head. Mats couldn't see his shoes and his eyes looked like they were glowing. Oh boy, another weirdo.

Mats was known around town for his ability to get his hands on rare and out of print books (and other outlandish stuff. He had once procured a monkey's tooth for someone who wore it around his neck as a good luck charm). Mats had his own little personal network of people across the country who scoured used bookstores. They kept an eye on anything unusual and he paid them well for their services.

Mats leaned over the counter. "What can I do for you?"

"I wanthhh to ssssshell thisssssh book."

The little creature was very nervous. Mats thought he looked out of place even in his unusual bookstore.

Mats grabbed the book from two small, leathery hands which seemed to have too many digits.

Mats looked the book over carefully, judging its worth. It had a dark blue cloth cover and was written in hieroglyphics. No author or title. It felt alive almost. Mats sighed and wondered how he was going to get rid of this one. Maybe he should just tell this weirdo to take a hike. An impulse told him to accept the book. Mats always followed his hunches. It was unusual and Mats liked unusual things.

"All right, I'll give you twenty dollars for it. No more, mind you."

Mats held a thick hairy forearm over the counter, offering his hand. "What's your name? I'm Mats."

The little man jumped back, frightened.

Mats shook his head. He thought that maybe it was time to get out of this business. "Do you want to sell the book or not?" He was getting impatient and there was another customer waiting. The little guy seemed to be almost on the verge of panic.

"Twenty dollarshhh," he said softly.

Mats handed over a $20 bill. The fellow looked like he had never seen one before. He passed his hand over it as if expecting Mr. Jackson to perform a magic trick. Then he turned abruptly and sort of glided out of the store.

"Who was that dude?" said a teenage boy. "Looked like something out of Star Wars. Hey, you got any books on love potions?"

Just another day at the Full Moon bookstore, Mats Karlsson proprietor.

John's fascination with Genevieve continued even though she gave him little reason to like her. Aloof and alone, she traveled the hallways at school without companionship. John had never seen her initiate a conversation with another student. He knew that she was smart, and without question the most unusual person he had ever seen. Compared to her he was normal. It gave him comfort to know there was someone even weirder than him.

John knew she must have a personality, but even when they were alone she refused to talk about herself. Sometimes (when she thought he wasn't looking) she would glance at him sharply, as if measuring him. On these occasions he would raise his eyebrows and say "Yes?" But she just gave him her terse smile, the corners of her mouth slightly upraised. "Oh nothing."

One time he asked her about her mom.

"I don't know who my mom is." She spoke without emotion. "Dad says I'm adopted."

John didn't understand how a person couldn't know their own mother, or care. He knew that she wouldn't discuss the matter further. Genevieve was a challenge, a riddle that needed to be solved.

John went over to the Walters' for an hour or so almost every day after dinner, weather permitting. Genevieve's dad was either in his library or out in the armchair reading his magazines or looking at his laptop. She said he never went anywhere.

"Not even to a movie?"

"Nope. Says he's got more important things to do."

"Does he watch TV?"

"We don't have a TV."

Genevieve liked to play chess and taught John how to play. It was fun. John was able to almost immediately recognize patterns in the movement and position of the pieces on the big wooden board. The pieces were cool too, cleverly sculpted from stone. They had felt on the bottom to protect the playing surface. John liked the heavy feel of them and the sound each made when he plunked it down on his chosen square.

Genevieve won all the games at first. John soon caught up with her, his good memory allowing him to play several moves ahead. He studied some games by the masters and got so he could beat Genevieve most of the time. It was the only thing they did together that he was better at than she.

One time when he beat her she got mad. "I don't understand why you made that play!" She was exasperated. John had taken her rook and then her queen after what appeared to be two senseless sacrifices. "How did you do it?"

John thought for a moment. "I'm not sure. It just seemed like the right thing to do."

"See, you don't really know what you're doing. If you did you'd be able to explain it."

Mr. Walters observed the play. "The boy plays intuitively as well as logically."

Intrigued, Mr. Walters challenged John to a game, and then another one, until Genevieve got mad.

"Dad, he's MY friend!" she pouted.

After that Mr. Walters didn't want to play anymore. Even after two games John had learned a lot from him, enough to know that he was a really smart man. John thought he might even be smarter than his own dad.

Gradually Genevieve thawed toward John and allowed him to become her friend. That summer John spent quite a lot of time bike riding with her.

His parents still discouraged their son from seeing so much of Genevieve Walters. "There's something wrong with her," Robert said. "She's as strange as her father."

"Yes son," Rachel affirmed. "Find some other friends. Expand your social horizons."

John did not want to expand his social horizons. Genevieve was quite enough entertainment for him. That afternoon she had been fearless. They were riding in the city park by the river with its narrow cement trails. Genevieve treated it like an obstacle course, darting on and off the road between trees and park benches. When they came out of the park she went fast down the hill with no hands, running the stop sign. John was afraid she would kill herself.

She would sometimes taunt him. "What's the matter, you scared? Boys aren't supposed to be scared." John just shrugged. He didn't feel the need to respond.

John and Genevieve felt no compunction about riding their bikes around town. The Frankel house on Magnolia Street was over a mile from the Walters house on Traver. Both were in older academic neighborhoods about two miles south of the city's center.

Genevieve enjoyed riding alone in Old Town with its brick covered streets. She liked the historical district with its shops, theater, and natural history museum. There was something about people that fascinated her even though she didn't understand them or know how to talk to them. On Saturday mornings she would get up at 5:30 and hang out at the farmer's market. She watched the people, never becoming part of the scene. She was content to observe from a distance. Then she would ride over to the Frankel's around 8 and knock on the side door.

"Can John come out and play?"

When Robert opened the door he'd frown at the unusual looking girl. "I'll see if he's finished breakfast." When Rachel came to the door she'd just say, "I'll go get John."

Never was she invited inside the house. This did not bother her, for she knew not of love. She was used to being treated with indifference and even scorn. There were only two people in her life she talked to. Magdelena felt sorry for the child and made it a point every day to ask her about her day, and counsel her when she could. Genevieve, always reticent, never felt the need to volunteer much of anything. And of course there was John. John was the only person on earth she felt comfortable with. He was the only one who smiled at her and who seemed genuinely interested in her.

John was always glad to see his friend even though he could feel the wall she placed between them. It didn't matter to him what they did. In the winters after homework he'd ride over and they'd sit by the fire and play board games, or chess. John liked Mr. Walters' big library. When he could get permission he entered as often as he could, always under the watchful eye of Genevieve's gruff and taciturn father.

When the weather was good the two would ride their bikes. They explored the city, always led by Genevieve's sense of adventure.

John remembered one time he and Genevieve rode way, way out of town until they got to the dirt road by the railroad tracks. The road was freshly graded and covered with little stones. It had a sharp downhill turn and their bike wheels kept sliding out of control on the pebbles. Genevieve dared him to see who could ride faster around the curve. John declined. She looked straight at him with a little sarcastic smile she used only with him. He could never figure out what she was thinking or feeling in those moments and he could never understand why she always faced him directly. It was like she was testing him or something.

John laughed. "Go ahead if you want."

Genevieve pedaled the bike to the top of the incline and took off quickly. When she hit the curve she placed her left foot down for balance and turned the handlebar almost 90 degrees. She began to slide off the road but at the last minute the bike grabbed and she went shooting around it. John was amazed.

He rode carefully around the curve and saw Genevieve at the bottom. She had her hands over her eyes and stood with her bicycle. He was about to say something to her but something kept him silent. She stood there for a few minutes without moving. Then her hands went to her sides and she took four or five deep breaths. She opened her eyes and turned her bike around to face him. For the second time she looked directly into his eyes and John felt himself being probed. Genevieve sort of...expanded herself. Not physically, but mentally. It was powerful enough that he knew it wasn't his imagination. Suddenly the feeling was gone and she was just Genevieve again. She smiled cheerfully at him.

John was amazed. His friend never expressed emotion, at least not to him. He wondered how she did that trick of making herself bigger. It was really cool. He wanted to be able to do it too. There was definitely something special about this girl, something mysterious. He'd hang out with her forever until he discovered what it was.

"Hi John," she said brightly.

"Hi Genevieve. Would you tell me please what that was all about?"

"No John, I won't. I don't understand it myself. But I feel a lot better now."

"Did you find something down there?"

"No." She pointed to her head. "I found something up here." She gave him a girlish toss of her head and raced up the curve. She looked different to John now, more like...like a girl. He never thought of Genevieve as a girl, she was just his friend. More like his best friend, his only friend.

All the way home Genevieve chattered to him. He had never seen her so animated before. For the next two or three days she was a lot friendlier to him.

One warm early June day just after John's 11th birthday he came home from school with a letter in his pocket. His teacher had pulled him aside after school and told him he would be promoted an extra grade.

Robert and Rachel were thrilled when they read the letter.

"It says here that you'll be in the seventh grade instead of the sixth grade next term and go to Carleton Junior High," Robert said. He was very proud of his son. "Is that all right with you John?"

"Yeah I guess." John didn't care one way or the other. He loved learning new things but school was a slow and boring way of doing it. The sooner it was over the better.

"It also says that when you reach the tenth grade you'll be placed in an accelerated program of college prepatory study." Robert spoke with satisfaction.

Rachel was just as proud as her husband of John's accomplishments but she was worried about John being with older children. After John went upstairs to his room she talked to her husband. "Maybe we shouldn't Robert. Studies have shown that younger kids don't learn as well if they're in class with older kids. There can also be psychological problems."

Robert dismissed her fears with a wave of his hand. "John is really smart. He's tall for his age and strong. He'll know how to handle it."

Rachel's fears were warranted. That fall, a bully from the ninth grade attacked John on the playground and gave him a bloody nose. Rachel was incensed and wanted to go right to the principal. Robert nixed that. "It's about time we taught this kid to defend himself."

"No Robert, none of that." Rachel did not want John to learn aggressiveness. Her son was even-tempered. She didn't want that trained out of him.

"Rachel, it's different for boys. John has to nip this in the bud or every kid on the playground is going to come looking for him. Let's send him to Matsumoto."

Rachel brightened. The Frankel's knew the martial arts instructor from their mutual attendance at the monthly Midland City Council public hearings. He had impressed them as an intelligent and cultured person. "Good idea! Matsumoto is a good teacher. John can learn about a new culture as well."

Hideki Matsumoto was known as a cultivated man who emphasized the spiritual aspects of martial arts and respect for opponents. Rachel knew that over the years he had rejected several students who had refused to learn discipline and control.

It was settled. John began taking judo classes once a week.

After a few months of martial arts classes it was evident that John was very strong but clumsy. His long legs were thin and he was easily knocked off balance. Matsumoto worked with him with little success. Occasionally John could overpower even older boys with his strength. More often than not he was out of position.

"It's my big feet."

Sensei Matsumoto pointed to his own feet, which were very large. "The size of one's body is not relevant. To be successful one must cease all self-limiting thought. Do you understand John?"

"Yes Sensei."

John worked on his movement, practicing over and over. Most of the other boys would out-quick him.

One day, during competition, John got thrown to the mat seven consecutive times. He was getting his ass kicked by everyone and his body was sore from the pummeling it was taking. John faced his next opponent and bowed. The boy was older and solidly built. He was one of the best fighters in class.

John tried to grasp on to the front of his judogi for a hip throw but the boy quickly stepped around. He placed his hand on John's shoulder and his foot behind John's ankle and shoved hard. John crumpled to the mat, the wind knocked out of him. He was about ready to cry. He wanted to get on his bike and go home.

From his prone position on the mat John looked up and saw the other boy's contempt. His opponent was taunting him. John Frankel was slow to anger but now he was getting really hot. He had reached the end of his rope but he couldn't let it end like this. John took a few moments and steadied himself inside, breathing deeply in and out. He decided to concentrate very hard and eliminate all extraneous thoughts, as sensei had told them over and over. "Focus completely upon the task at hand. Clear your mind and decide exactly what the end result should be. When you act do not hesitate but move quickly and decisively."

John got up and stood tall, facing his opponent. They both bowed again. John could see the other boy moving in for the kill. At that moment John's head cleared and he felt totally relaxed. He saw the other boy moving toward him in slow motion. John had time to think about exactly what he wanted to do. He bent his knees and placed his right hand between his opponent's legs. Unflexing, he grabbed a handful of cloth with his left and lifted the boy completely over his head. John smashed him to the mat with all the force he could muster. The whole thing had taken only a few seconds. For John it was like being in a trance. The noises of the gym had disappeared, there was a perfect silence surrounding him. John stared down at the unmoving boy on the mat.

Suddenly he came out of it. He heard an explosion of sound and activity.

Sensei bent over and examined the boy. "He'll be all right. Just stunned."

The boy came to, moaning. "I feel like every bone in my body is broken." He looked at John. "Lucky throw. I'll get you next time." Then he winced in pain.

"You had better go over and sit down son."

Matsumoto gestured to John. "Where did you learn that, John? I do not teach that move here. It is for advanced students only."

"I don't know. I just did it."

The older man regarded his student curiously. "Come with me."

Sensei led John up to the front desk. He bent over and opened a drawer, fishing inside for something.

John noticed a picture on the desk. It was a younger version of Sensei, holding a trophy. On the wall behind was a banner in Japanese characters.

Sensei looked up and handed John a piece of paper. He spoke quietly. "John, what you did was remarkable. To attain the state of perfect peace, to move like the snake and strike quickly. What you achieved was an altered state of consciousness."

John was intrigued. "What's that?"

"An altered state of consciousness enables the fighter to easily accomplish difficult tasks which before were impossible." Sensei looked the boy directly in the eyes and noticed the bright intelligence behind them. "You cannot have had prior knowledge of the move you made on your opponent. Yet you were able to access a hidden knowledge that made you very powerful."

"But I did know it Sensei! I knew just what to do. It was easy."

Sensei smiled broadly. "Precisely. An altered state of consciousness brings a sudden leap in ability."

"Wow. How do I do it again?"

Sensei grinned. "You have asked the correct question John. The trick is to do so at will. For thousands of years men have attempted to formulate the procedures for such states without success."

John saw Sensei's attention turn inward. "I too experienced such a state in meditation. I have never been able to duplicate it."

After a few moments Matsumoto smiled sagely and gestured toward the piece of paper in John's hand. "On that list are books which may guide you in your quest. I read them when I lived in Japan. The English translations are good." Of course an 11-year-old child could not fully understand the material. An inner voice told him that this boy was unusual and might benefit from the information.

John looked at the list.

- *Techniques For Meditation*, Yu Shao-Chen.

- *The Space Beyond Time*, Kageyasu Sumitimo.

- *A Wrinkle in Time*, Madeline l'Engle.

"What's this one doing here?" John asked. He had already read it.

Hideki Matsumoto smiled and winked. "My favorite."

John glanced once more at the photograph on the desk.

"My finest moment. Kyoto Invitational, twenty years ago. The next year I foolishly broke my leg in three places, playing at kickboxing. The bone never healed correctly and I was finished competitively."

His brow darkened for a moment.

John noticed a photograph of a beautiful Japanese woman in an exquisite kimono. Her face was painted white. She had red lipstick and black hair.

Sensei's countenance cleared and he smiled at the picture. "My wife. With such a woman it is not possible to be sad." Then he turned and looked into the boy's eyes, regaining his complete attention. "Take from these books what you can and reread them when you are older. The material in them can be understood on many levels of consciousness." He realized he was talking to John as an adult. It did not seem inappropriate. "If you ever have any questions please come down to see me."

John spoke sincerely. "Thank you Sensei. I may take you up on that."

John bowed in appreciation, cleaned up, and left by the back entrance. As he turned toward his bike he saw through the closing door that the boy he had thrown was back at it.

Over the next two months John tried to duplicate the altered state of consciousness. It eluded him just as Sensei said it would. He tried to read some of the books on the list but found them heavy going. He tried meditating but it did nothing for his eleven-year-old psyche, even though he understood the concept.

Gradually he lost interest in his judo classes. Despite encouragement from Sensei he made little progress. One day after class he apprehensively told Sensei that he did not want to continue.

To John's surprise Sensei smiled. "You are wise, son. I do not think your future is in martial arts."

On the playground a few of the older kids still liked to bully him and he couldn't understand why. When he asked mom about it she told him that there was an innocence about him that the tougher kids seemed attracted to. "Don't ever lose that, son," she said with a tear in her eye. "I don't care what your father says. A man who doesn't know his heart can't succeed in life."

That didn't really help him much so he walked up to one of his tormentors one day on recess.

"Whaddaya want, Frankel?" said Ricky Davis. Ricky was two grades ahead of him, taller than John, and beefy.

"Why do you like to pick on me?" John said innocently.

Ricky laughed and said he was like a nail that needed to be hammered down. "You stick out Frankel. Sometimes I just want to punch ya."

John shook his head and walked away. He understood that he was different in a way completely unknown to him. Fortunately John had learned enough from his martial arts classes to fend off older kids like Ricky. Eventually they learned to find easier marks.

The next summer John and Genevieve were riding their bikes in Old Town. Genevieve said, "Lets go see the whorehouse."

John didn't know what she was talking about. He followed her to a seedy and dirty block of the city on a street that dead-ended at the river. Genevieve pulled up across the street and pointed to a flashing sign that said "Girls, Girls, Girls."

"There it is," she said.

John looked puzzled. "That's a whorehouse?"

"Of course silly. That's where you can go to have sex if you're a man. But you have to pay."

"You pay for sex?" John was astonished.

Genevieve stared at him as if he was retarded. "Don't you know anything?"

John knew a lot about sex. He found a book in Mr. Walters' library called the Kama Sutra. It showed men and women doing it in all sorts of positions.

"Where do women go for sex?" John asked.

"Women can get sex anytime they want." Genevieve spoke smugly. "We don't have to pay. Men come to us."

She gave John an unfathomable look. He looked at her thin, wiry body. He couldn't imagine having sex with any girl, least of all Genevieve.

As they began to peddle away they heard a voice behind them. "Hey kids! Want to score?"

John was all for leaving but as usual Genevieve wanted to investigate. She turned her bike around and John followed her lead. "Score what?" Her head was cocked to one side.

"I got some really good meth here kid. You got any money?"

Genevieve backed off. The man was scruffy looking and he had a weird look in his eyes. "I just took a hit 15 minutes ago. I feel more like I do now than when I first got here."

"Huh?" said John.

Genevieve backpedaled and they turned their bikes and got out of there just as fast as 12-year-old legs could pedal.

When they reached a safe spot they stopped. "What did that guy say?" John asked.

"Uh...he said...uh..."

John smiled. Genevieve always had an answer for everything and he wondered what she'd come up with. She saw his teasing grin and drew herself up, her chin in the air. Her logical mind could make no sense of the words. "He said he feels good right now."

"Because of the drugs," she added smugly.

"Oh so that's what it was." John replied skeptically, the smile still on his face.

Genevieve whirled her bike around and pedaled furiously all the way home. John laughed loudly behind her the whole way. For once he'd gotten the better of her.

From then on it was a standing joke between them.

Carleton University has a very strong academic reputation. Even so, the school's membership in the highly competitive Midwest Conference also generates a fervent city-wide interest in athletics. Many of Midland's intellectuals – who make up a significant portion of the population – criticized what they felt was an unwarranted emphasis on sports. They felt that the university would be better advised to spend their money on improved educational facilities. Yet most of these die-hard academics were secretly proud when their teams did well. Almost all of them overwhelmingly supported Carleton's recent football stadium seating expansion.

John caught a little of this athletic fervor when the university's basketball team won the conference championship. As school began that fall he looked for an opportunity to play. Some of the guys would bike over to Greg Ortwell's house for pickup games. Greg had a driveway that opened up to a big three car garage so there was lots of space. The public courts were always occupied by high school and college kids. Greg's dad bought an expensive rim and backboard set for his son's junior high friends. One day after class Greg approached him.

"Hey Frankel, you want to come over and play with us?"

John was surprised but pleased. "Uh, yeah Greg. I'll play."

"Good! We start right at 5 and play until 6. Make sure you're on time."

At first the other guys wanted John on their team because of his height. After a time they realized he couldn't hold on to the ball. He often dropped passes thrown to him, enabling the other team to recover and score a quick basket.

"What's wrong with you Frankel?" Greg asked him.

"Hit him in a bad spot, right in the hands," said Gene Watson. Gene's father owned a store that sold athletic equipment and he could get used basketballs for free. All the guys liked Gene because no matter what game they played he always had stuff to hand out.

"Hold your hand out," Greg said.

John placed his hand against the other boy's hand.

"Look at that, Frankel," Greg said. "You got hands as small as a girl."

John saw that it was true. He was much taller than Greg but his fingers only came up to the next to last digit of Greg's hand. John smiled good-naturedly. "You're right!"

Greg was disgusted with John's lack of competitive spirit. "Frankel, you're worthless. You don't even care."

John shrugged. "Are we going to play or not?"

"Hang onta the ball next time," Greg grumbled.

But John couldn't hang onto the ball no matter how hard he tried. His hands just weren't big enough. After a couple of weeks nobody wanted him to play anymore. John didn't mind. It wasn't much fun for him anyway.

The following spring John transferred his athletic interest from basketball to baseball. He had no interest in soccer because of his big clumsy feet. There were two baseball diamonds at the school and he joined some of the informal pickup games after classes. In baseball it didn't matter how big your hands were because you wore a glove.

Genevieve liked baseball too and was good enough to play with the guys even though all of her hits were singles. If John was the tallest in his class Genevieve was the fastest runner, boy or girl, below the high school level. She was skinny and couldn't hit the ball very far. She made up for it with her speed on the bases and in the field, and her competitive fire. The guys put her in the outfield where she ran down balls that would normally be hits.

Genevieve was tough as nails. John found that out a couple weeks later at one of the diamonds at Midland East Junior High. The games usually began friendly enough but after a while the competition often heated up. Genevieve loved it and showed her mettle during two remarkable incidents that afternoon.

After hitting a single Genevieve tried to stretch it into a double. She barreled into second base with her feet up in the air. She kicked Ricky Davis, who was covering the base and attempting to tag her out. The ball fell out of his glove and he grunted in pain. Ricky lost his balance and fell awkwardly to the ground. Ricky swore. He slammed his glove in the dirt and picked up the ball in his left hand.

"Safe!" Genevieve exclaimed, rising to her feet with her arms in the air.

Ricky got up, angry, and pinned her with his eyes. "I don't care if you're a girl. If you ever do that again I'll kill ya."

Genevieve stood on the base and returned his gaze. To John, standing at home plate, she looked like a little terrier confronting a German shepherd. He was afraid for her. His heart was pounding like a laboring boiler in the bowels of the Titanic.

"Oh yeah, you want to try?" Genevieve said it so softly almost no one heard. All activity halted. The players turned their attention to the drama being enacted on second base.

For a split second John thought Ricky was going to punch her lights out. He clenched his right fist and took a small step forward. Then his eyes widened and the ball fell to the ground. "You heard me." He spoke gruffly but all the air had gone out of him. The boys glanced at each other, shocked. Ricky Davis was a grade ahead of John and known as a tough guy. Nobody wanted to mess with him.

"Ricky's scared of her, I saw it!" Greg muttered to himself. John was flabbergasted. The whole thing hadn't lasted more than 15 seconds but after that when Genevieve ran the bases they all kept their mouths shut no matter what she did.

John knew he was valuable because of his strength, even though he made some mistakes in the field. He would either strike out or get a home run. Whenever he hit the ball it went a long way. When he messed up in the field some of the guys would rag on him, especially Kenny. "Hey dumbass!" he would scream loudly, a cigarette dangling from his fingers. "Catch the fuckin' ball don't play with it!" Kenny didn't like John because he thought John was lazy. Kenny could hit the ball a ton and field well. He was almost as fast as Genevieve.

John hated it when Kenny was on his team. Everything that came out of his mouth was a variation on "dumbass." John knew that Kenny's father was a construction worker. There were stories of child abuse in the Miller home floating around the school, but that didn't make Kenny any easier to take. John eventually found a way to shut Kenny up: ignore him. Eventually even Kenny learned that he wasn't going to get a rise out of John.

After the game the guys were milling around when a girl came over from the parking lot and spoke to Genevieve.

"What's your name?"

"Genevieve."

"Hi, my name's Patricia. I'm on a girl's softball team. I've seen you play. You're as good as some of the guys. We want you to play for us."

Patricia had on a nice looking uniform, red with white lettering. She had brown hair tied back in a pony tail and wore a visor cap with the words 'Watkins Athletics' on it. Genevieve wore her usual black slacks and burgundy top. Her face and her clothing were soiled.

"I don't play in leagues," Genevieve said. "I just play for fun."

Patricia put her right hand on her hip. "Playing in a league is fun too. Besides, you get to wear these cool uniforms."

"Thanks, but I don't want to."

"Why not?"

"I just told you."

"That's not a good reason."

Patricia didn't get it, John thought. She had no idea who she was dealing with.

"It's good enough for me," Genevieve replied. She spoke with a note of finality.

The other girl got mad and she sneered. "You're just scared, that's all."

Now all the guys gathered around. Like most boys they were curious to see if a fight would develop. A grin of anticipation slowly spread over Ricky Davis' face.

Ricky saw Genevieve return Patricia's stare with a slightly taunting smile. They were standing about two feet apart and the other girl was bigger. Patricia got so mad she shoved Genevieve hard onto the ground, then stood triumphantly over her.

Genevieve calmly got up. To Ricky it looked like she was just going to walk away. Suddenly her right foot shot out in a karate kick and caught the other girl in the abdomen. As Patricia crumpled to the ground Genevieve stepped in and slapped her hard in the face. Patricia began to cry.

"Don't ever do that again," Genevieve said softly. She calmly walked away.

Ricky Davis was impressed as hell. Most of the guys were in shock and the rest of them were in awe.

"Did you SEE that?"

"Wow, that was COOL!"

Kenny stood with a cigarette in his mouth and wondered what the kid with the red lips was going to do next. He *loved* it when somebody got their ass kicked. He had no sympathy whatsoever for the bigger girl. She got what she deserved, the dumbass rich bitch.

Greg and Gene went to see if Patricia was all right. Her breathing was labored and there was a red patch on her cheek. It looked like there was no permanent damage. Patricia's father knew something was wrong and came running over from the parking lot just behind the diamond. He checked on his daughter, then approached them.

"Who did this?" he demanded.

"Don't look at me," Gene said. "It was her."

Patricia's father went over to Genevieve. "Did you hit my daughter?"

"She hit me first." Genevieve was unapologetic.

The man's face reddened. He wanted to box the ears of this dirty, impudent girl but he controlled his temper. She was just a kid after all. "The difference is that you injured her. She just wanted to ask you to join the baseball team."

Genevieve looked calmly up at him. "If you don't want your daughter to get hurt, tell her not to attack other people when they don't do what she wants."

She said it like one grownup to another.

The boys were staring at each other in disbelief. Ricky Davis guffawed and Kenny threw his cigarette on the ground. This was better than watching his old man yell at his mom.

Patricia's dad said, "I'm going to report this to the principal. What is your name?"

Genevieve didn't reply.

"I SAID, WHAT IS YOUR NAME YOUNG LADY?"

It became obvious by her body position and demeanor that Genevieve was not going to answer him.

Patricia's dad pointed a finger in Genevieve's face. "You're in trouble, girl." Genevieve did not flinch. "You haven't heard the last of this." He turned away and led Patricia back to their car and drove away.

The boys were all speechless.

"Aren't you scared?" said one.

"I didn't do anything wrong."

"Yeah but you know adults. They can twist things around and get you in trouble."

Genevieve smiled. "Well then, I have all of you to back me up."

Another incident in the legend of Genevieve, John thought. A couple of years ago she had rescued John from a big bully on the playground, hitting him in the head in with a small rock. That was pretty amazing but this was even better.

"Well," Genevieve said, "are we going to finish our game or not?" She was standing there with her glove on just as calm as could be.

"Yeah. Lets go!" "We're going to kick your asses now!" "We got the kung-fu queen on our side!"

All the guys were cheering and clapping for her as her team took the field.

On the bike ride home John asked her how she did that kick.

"You think you're the only one who can take martial arts?"

John just shook his head. She was amazing.

The next afternoon John and Genevieve were lying side-by-side on the grass, looking up at the clouds. Genevieve said, "Sometimes I think that clouds are like people. They're always changing their minds, going in different directions."

"Yeah, you're right! I never thought of it like that."

She was silent for a couple of seconds. Then John felt her suddenly take his hand and squeeze it. He turned his head and thought he saw, for an instant, a look of love for him on her face. It wasn't the face of a 12-year-old girl, but a woman. It must have been his imagination. She was just Genevieve, his buddy.

After dinner that day Magdelena cleaned up and left the house. Genevieve saw that her father was in his library again on the first floor. This room faced out toward the street and had a big picture window. She walked up the dark wooden stairs to her room on the second floor. She looked at the walnut-paneled walls. Everything in this house is dark. The house reminded her of an old mansion she once saw in a horror movie.

There were four medium sized bedrooms in the old house. Two faced the front and two were in the back across the hall. Genevieve knew that her father had planned on a family. She knew this from remarks her father had made to her during one of their infrequent conversations. She wondered who her mother was. She hardly remembered Debra, who had left when she was only four.

Genevieve's room was in back, on the right as you came up the staircase. Dad's bedroom was on the other corner, facing front. The other two were guest rooms although Dad never had any guests.

Genevieve opened her bedroom door and was startled to see a woman sitting on her bed. A big woman with long red hair and very large, round eyes with unusually red irises. She wore a loose-fitting white robe. Her hands were tucked into the folds of the robe.

Genevieve was startled. "Who are you?"

The woman smiled lovingly at the girl. "You may call me Kjirsten." She pronounced it sheer-sten.

Genevieve pondered the woman for a second, her head cocked to one side. The redhead noticed the intensity of the girl's expression and the sharp intelligence behind her jet black eyes.

"How did you get in here?"

The older woman noticed there was no fear, only genuine curiosity. She felt an inner excitement. She did not answer the question directly, for that would only complicate matters. This young earthian girl may or may not be candidate material. She could not afford to take chances.

The woman spoke. "Genevieve, you know the location of the bookstore called the Full Moon, do you not?"

Genevieve thought the woman's speech patterns were too precise. She said nothing, nodding her head affirmatively.

"Some time ago a very important book found its way into the occult section of that bookstore." She leaned over slightly, gazing intently at the black-haired girl with the unusually red lips. "If I describe the book will you be able to locate it?"

Genevieve nodded. She had been in the bookstore many times and was a favorite of Mats. If she couldn't find it he'd tell her where to go.

Genevieve burned with curiosity about this exotic looking woman but Kjirsten's commanding presence was almost hypnotic. Genevieve found herself answering promptly and was unable to volunteer a single question.

"Very well," the woman said. She nodded her head toward the bed, indicating that Genevieve should sit beside her.

Genevieve seated herself. The big woman placed a huge hand around her slight shoulders, smiled warmly into her eyes, and began to speak. Genevieve noticed something unusual about that hand...

3

WHEN John was 13 he came down into the living room one evening. "Dad, I just had a visit from Grandpa Harold."

Robert put down his reader. "Grandpa Harold has been dead for two years."

"If he's dead, what's he doing up in my bedroom?"

Rachel and Robert were alarmed. Robert said, "I thought kids were supposed to go through this phase when they were little."

"Come upstairs and show us, dear," Rachel said.

John saw Harold standing beside the desk, just as he had left him. "Hi Grandpa Harold." He looked back and forth. "You see him don't you?"

"Uh...no son, I don't," Robert said. He was really worried now.

"I don't either John," said Rachel.

"Let me prove it to you. Grandpa, tell me some personal secret of yours that I couldn't possibly know. OK."

"Harold says that he had an affair with his secretary for almost two years. Nobody knows about it except Dad."

Robert's jaw dropped.

"Is that true, Robert? Why, he was forty years older than her."

Father turned slowly to stare at his son. "How did you know that?"

"Harold just told me." John spoke with the air of someone who states the obvious.

"Come on son, don't lie." Robert was becoming irritated. "Maybe gramma told you."

"Harold says gramma didn't know either. He says gramma isn't in the habit of telling family secrets to kids. He says please don't tell her."

Robert knew that both of these statements were true. His father had sworn him to secrecy.

John added, "Harold also says that when you played golf with him you always cheated."

"I did not!" Robert said hotly. "He..."

"Harold says you would nudge the ball with your iron to get a better lie."

"I ..."

Robert and Rachel stared at each other. Robert said, "Either this kid is going crazy or..."

Rachel finished his sentence. "Or Harold is really here."

"Harold says, 'pico sico porcupine.' What does that mean dad?"

"Oh my God," said Rachel, placing the palms of her hands on her cheeks. "Maybe we should all go in for psychiatric observation."

John didn't understand what was such a big deal.

"Son, you let us know if you see any more...ghosts, OK?"

"Is it bad that I see Grandpa Harold, dad?"

"Well son, let's say it's unusual."

"OK dad."

For the next several weeks Rachel, and especially Robert, watched their son for signs of mental instability.

"John is unusually tall for his age. Perhaps he's experiencing some thyroid dysfunction," Rachel said.

"Or an alteration of brain chemistry," Robert said, feeling a pang of worry in his solar plexus. Rachel's eyes widened, showing her concern.

Nothing unusual occurred but they decided to send John to see Dr. Patterson at the Kessinger hospital's psychiatric wing. Robert and Rachel had to fill out and sign a detailed admittance form.

Dr. Patterson interviewed John, did a lot of tests, and kept him under observation for an entire day. At 6 p.m. he called Robert's mobile. Robert put it on speaker and Rachel came close to the phone.

"Mr. Frankel? Other than an abnormal curiosity I can find nothing wrong with your son. He seems completely normal."

Robert let out a breath. "Thank you doctor."

"You mentioned that your son said he saw a ghost?"

"Yes," Robert replied. "It was very unusual. This ghost was a departed family member. He told John three things about his personal life that a 13-year-old boy couldn't possibly know."

There was a pause. "Well, your boy is only 13. If these visions persist we may have to put him on medication. But I don't believe in medicating children unless it is absolutely necessary."

"Doctor, maybe my husband and I should also come in for observation."

Patterson chuckled. "I don't think that will be necessary. You did the right thing bringing John in to see me. Let me know if he exhibits any more unusual behavior."

"We will, doctor, thank you." Rachel was greatly relieved.

"You can pick up your son now," Patterson said. "He's reading a book in the lobby."

On the way home John sat in the back seat. Rachel kept glancing back at him nervously. "Will you please stop doing that mom?" John asked. "You're making me feel like a freak."

"I'm sorry son. I'm just a little worried about you."

OK, John thought. I'm not telling them anything even if I see ghosts every night. He hated it when mom looked 'concerned' because it meant a lot of extra hugs and kisses and lot of stupid questions like, "How are you doing son?" when he was perfectly all right.

That night he reviewed his experience. The ghost was cool. It looked and felt just like Grandpa Harold. One thing struck him. Talking with grandpa felt the same as at Sensei Matsumoto's two years ago when he threw his opponent to the mat. A lightness and a feeling of confidence, certainty, and well-being accompanied both experiences. During these periods he could apparently do stuff that nobody else could.

John was on the lookout for more ghosts over the next few weeks but nothing happened. This experience fueled a burning desire to know more about himself. He wondered whether Grandpa Harold was just a figment of his imagination, as dad said. If Harold wasn't real then how did he know that stuff? John kept these questions and others like it in the back of his mind. He learned not to ask dad about these things because he'd just get a scientific explanation that didn't really answer his question.

"Ghosts don't exist son," John remembered him saying. "They can possibly be explained as neural discontinuities in the chemistry of the brain..." Then dad would smile like he'd just explained the secrets of the universe in 100 words or less. John would act pleased because he didn't want to hurt dad's feelings. Mom wasn't much better. She was a philosophy professor and couldn't keep from using words like "ontology" and "epistemological." Occasionally John biked over to the Full Moon and asked around because the place was frequented by academics from Carleton. John found little satisfaction there. It seemed that adults were just as much in the dark as kids, although they covered their confusion with a lot of fancy theories.

John discovered the pool hall that spring during a biking expedition to the south side of Midland. It was located on the campus of Carleton University, on the 3rd floor of the old Carleton Union building that was used for campus events and meetings. John thought pool halls were in red light districts. He was glad this one was respectable so Robert and Rachel wouldn't get upset.

The room had an old brown linoleum floor and big arched windows. It was lit by long grey metal fluorescent light fixtures which hung from a very high ceiling. The place was heated with old style radiators, just like at home. The room contained 18 tables. He learned later that a lot of pool tournaments were played here.

Students occupied most of the tables. There were a few serious players, mostly men who congregated in a special marked off section in the spacious L-shaped room. Dirty magazines lay on a shelf. John heard some quiet cussing. A man threw down some money on the green felt and challenged another player to make a trick shot. A blind guy in back with sunglasses sold cues. At the counter sat a middle-aged man with sallow skin, a scraggly black goatee, and a chest that sort of caved in. He took one look at John and said, "You want a table? There's four free right now. Its $20 an hour."

"OK." John looked up and saw the sign: "No minors allowed."

"Table 8." The man gave him a case with the pool balls for that table. He marked something in a ledger with a broken pencil.

The case was heavy but John carried it easily. He found his table and unloaded the balls, each of which hit the table with a satisfying thud. Against the far wall he saw a rack with a bunch of cheap cues. John grabbed one, taking it back to his table and rolling it flat like he'd seen one of the other guys do. The damn thing was warped. He put some chalk on the tip and smacked the balls as hard as he could. To his delight one of them rolled into a pocket.

After a couple of minutes an older guy came up to him. "Wanna play?"

"Sure," John said. "I don't know how to play anything though."

"That's OK. I'll show you."

"I'm John."

"Freddy."

Freddy was as tall as John's 6' 2". He wore baggy pants and had a scraggly beard and brown hair. Freddy said that his father was a used car salesman and used to play semi-pro.

"Are you a student?" John asked

"No. But they let anyone come in here as long as they have money and don't make any trouble."

"Who's that guy at the counter?" John nodded his head at the nervous looking man who repeatedly placed his fingers to his lips. "He looks like he needs a cigarette."

Freddy laughed. "Jack had to give it up a couple of years ago. Lung cancer. That's what makes him so grouchy all the time."

Freddy showed John how to break the balls and how to apply some basic English. He showed him how to "get position." This meant always keeping the cue ball in a spot that was easy to make the next shot. Freddy showed him how important it was to think several shots ahead. He called it "running the table." Since there were 15 balls you had to think 15 moves ahead. John liked that because it reminded him of chess and because pool is a game you can play standing still. John didn't have to compete with anyone else. All he had to do was pocket the balls on the table. The size of your hands didn't matter either.

Freddy was patient with him. John's pattern recognition skills helped him to figure out where he was going.

"How many times have you played?" Freddy asked him.

"This is my first time."

"Really?" Freddy was impressed. The kid learned quickly.

Freddy had a case that contained his cue, in two pieces. One of the pieces had a grooved thread sticking out of one end, which fitted the smaller piece. Freddy's cue was deep blue with ornamental silver markings on the handle.

"Your cue is really cool," John said.

Freddie smiled and gave it a pat. "My baby. Let's play a game of 8 ball."

"OK, but you have to show me the rules."

They played a few games and then Freddy taught John the rules of straight pool and 9 ball. He gave John tips on what English to apply to the ball.

After half an hour another boy came up to them, carrying a case of balls.

"Hey Kenny," Freddy said. "This is John."

Holy shit. It was Kenny, the hothead he used to play pickup baseball with.

Kenny spoke gruffly. "I know who he is. Whatever happened to that skinny girl you used to hang out with?"

"I still hang around with her. She doesn't like pool."

Kenny laughed.

John saw that Freddy and Kenny were going to play at another table. He thanked Freddy for his advice. John liked him. There was no reason to help a beginner but he had done it anyway.

"Can I watch you guys play for a while?" John asked. "I might get some tips."

Kenny was pleased. He liked to show off.

"You'd do better to go to that table over there," Freddy said. "Bob Dillinger is playing. He won the Midland Open last year. Kenny and I are pretty well-matched but we have a lot of holes in our game."

"That's OK," John said. "I'll just watch you guys if you don't mind."

Kenny spoke sharply. "Stay out of the way."

John carried his case up to the counter and paid. "Not bad, kid," Jack said. "I was watchin' ya." As John turned away he spoke with a smirk. "How old are you? 14?"

John flushed. "I..."

"Don't worry about it kid. If you don't cause trouble I'll let ya come back."

John smiled sheepishly. "I'm going to watch Freddy and Kenny if you don't mind."

Jack snorted when he heard Kenny's name. He waved his hand in the air to indicate that it was OK.

John walked over to table 10 where Kenny and Freddie had already agreed to play straight pool up to 100. Ten feet above the floor wires had been hung that went by every table, stretching from one end of the huge room to the other. On the wires were little wooden disks that you could move to count points. When somebody made a shot their opponent would reach up with the cue and slide over one of the counters to record a pocketed ball. John liked to hear the "click" as one of the disks struck another. To the players it meant success.

John watched as Freddy carefully maneuvered himself around the table, always trying to control the cue ball to allow for an easy shot the next time. When he did miss he put the cue ball on the rail so Kenny couldn't get a good shot.

"Goddamit Freddy, you coulda left me something to shoot at," Kenny complained. He missed and slammed the end of the cue stick on the floor.

John watched for a while, noticing that Freddy was calm and composed and made most of his shots. Freddy improved his play whereas Kenny complained a lot and tried to show off to John. Kenny gradually played worse and worse. There was a lesson there somewhere.

Freddy won the game 100 – 77. John thought it was time to go.

"When do you play?" he said to Freddy.

"Almost every day if I can get a table."

John liked the pool hall and played at least once a week, especially during the winter. Often he would see Freddy there. He even got Freddy to give him a few lessons. John liked to sound the older boy out. Freddy seemed to enjoy being a mentor to someone.

In early July, just before his 14th birthday, Genevieve led John on an adventure. This series of events would connect both of them to a minor player in a much larger game.

Genevieve rapped on the Frankel's side door at 9 on a Saturday morning. John stepped onto the driveway and saw her standing with her bike, ready to take off immediately.

"John, we have to go on a bike trip today," Genevieve said matter-of-factly. "Look. I have a small foldup tent in this nylon sack. Here's a small backpack with food." The backpack and tent were attached to a lightweight metal contraption that fit around the shoulders and strapped to the body, resting on the back.

John smiled to himself. He noticed that the rig was much too big for her small frame. "We do?"

John could tell by her tone of voice and her expression that she expected him to comply. When she wanted to get his attention she would stand two feet in front of him and gaze directly up into his eyes. At these times John would feel an almost hypnotic compulsion to do as she wished. It didn't feel weird or anything but he wondered how she did it.

"Yes." Genevieve spoke in authoritative tones. "Tell your parents we might not be home for dinner."

John protested. "My mom and dad will be worried," John protested.

Genevieve looked up at his 6' 5" from her 5' 4". "You don't have to come if you don't want." She smirked.

John blanched. Sometimes his friend regarded him as just a big baby. "It's not fair. Your dad doesn't care what you do. If you don't show up for dinner tonight he probably won't even notice. My mom and dad will have a fit."

Genevieve shrugged.

"Why do we need all that stuff?" John said.

"We need food and a tent in case it rains and we have to camp."

Now John was really alarmed. "You mean we'll be gone all night?"

"I didn't think you were coming."

"I didn't say that!" John was frustrated. He wanted to go. But ever since his visit to Dr. Patterson last year Rachel and Robert had attempted to keep a tighter rein on his activities. They thought he was fragile or something. It was irritating but there wasn't anything he could do except try to act "normal," whatever that was.

"Then shutup and go tell your parents." Genevieve spoke impatiently. He could tell what she was thinking. "C'mon John, stop whining."

John picked up on that thought right away. "They're not home. They went to the nursery to buy some plants for the garden."

Genevieve stomped her foot. "Do I have to tell you everything? Go write them a note."

John grinned. He had gotten a rise out of her. He walked inside, scribbled a hasty note, and left it on the kitchen counter.

"Who's going to carry the backpack?" John asked innocently as he reappeared through the side door and onto the driveway. Genevieve had leaned the rig against the house.

She didn't say anything, just pedaled away.

John shrugged. Genevieve knew he was coming. She knew that logically he was bigger and should carry the pack. It was simple. He had made a big deal about it. He smiled, easily hoisted the rig, and took off after her. It didn't weigh much but he suspected he was going to have sore shoulders tomorrow. Fortunately the thing had shoulder pads built in to the straps.

Midland was located in the upper middle of the state. The college town was surrounded by farmland. They rode south out of town past Carleton University. After half an hour or so they were in the countryside.

"Where are we going?" John asked.

"You'll see." Genevieve kept pedaling and didn't turn her head.

It was a warm summer day in early July. The land was green and the fragrant air was full of life. They were on a secondary road and traffic was light.

An hour later Genevieve stopped and pulled her bike over to the side of the road. There was a small stand of trees close by. "I have to pee."

John followed, grinning. "So do I. I think I'll go behind those bushes."

Genevieve did not rise to the bait. She just walked in the opposite direction into the small clump of trees.

They stopped twice more to drink water and eat a little something from the backpack. By early afternoon they reached a small town. John saw the sign: "Welcome to Hanford Pop. 3,567."

Genevieve took them through the town and then along a dirt road. They rode past two farmhouses and a large white-fenced section with horses to a ranch house sitting in a little cul-de-sac at the end of the road. The house had a well cultivated vegetable plot and was surrounded by herb and flower gardens. At the back, John could see a large extension had been added to the existing structure.

Genevieve walked up to the door and knocked lightly, as if she was expected.

An older woman with white hair answered the door and smiled. "Are you Genevieve?"

"Yes ma'am."

Genevieve knew how to be polite when it suited her, John thought.

"Is this your friend?"

John noticed the woman had piercing blue eyes and stood very straight. She seemed to pulsate with energy. The woman stepped out onto the porch. She shut the gray painted screen door and inspected him carefully. She didn't look *at* him so much as *around* him. He thought it was weird. After a couple of minutes she let her breath out. "Come in."

They walked into a comfortable living room filled with books.

"Almost as bad as your father," John muttered.

"She's a scientist," Genevieve explained. "And a psychic. She needs lots of books." She frowned. "My dad doesn't ever do anything with his."

"A psychic?" John was beginning to suspect he had got himself in a lot of hot water over something that might be completely nutty. "Your father is a scientist!" John was annoyed. "Why didn't we just talk to him?"

"You didn't have to come."

John rarely got angry but he was beginning to feel pretty hot right now. He had just spent five hours on a bike. His legs were exhausted and his shoulders were sore.

"So I'm supposed to tell mom and dad I rode 80 miles to see a psychic?"

"Tell them anything you like."

Genevieve turned to face him. She looked him straight in the eyes and the old woman did the same. John felt like a specimen being inspected by alien beings from the planet Meepzorp. Were those rays coming out of the old lady's eyes?

Under their gaze he felt his anger slowly melting away.

Genevieve seemed…different. She was always reserved, always going her own way. Now she seemed as old as the woman beside her. They both studied him for several minutes.

"Come with me John."

The woman led John to the back of the house and opened a door, flipping on the light switch. To his amazement he saw a fully equipped scientific laboratory. At the far end of the large room he saw some instruments upon a large table with a polished black marble top. The devices were connected to a very large monitor.

"Will you please stand in the center of the room by the two painted lines?" the woman asked. She didn't wait for his agreement but guided him to the proper position.

"What am I supposed to do?" John asked.

"Just stand quietly and let me observe you." The woman spoke efficiently, reminding John of the family doctor who was used to dealing with patients. He still felt irritated but was fascinated by the equipment.

"It'll take a few minutes to tune the instruments," the woman said.

John thought it odd that she had not introduced herself.

She began fiddling. "Aha."

Genevieve stood off to the side. She approached the monitor at the older woman's exclamation.

John felt like a lab animal. He knew he could just walk out of the place but his curiosity got the better of him. Maybe if he stayed a while longer he'd get some answers.

John stood there for several minutes. He made a careful inspection of the room. Finally the old woman spoke curtly. "Finished. Thank you John."

From across the room John saw the woman and Genevieve deep in conversation. The woman pointed once or twice to the monitor display, as if explaining something. He saw Genevieve nod a couple of times.

John didn't get it. What was he doing here? The whole thing was a joke. He was disappointed in Genevieve. He knew she was off on one of her impulsive adventures, but this time it made no sense at all.

John was just about to walk over to the pair when he noticed Genevieve smile at the woman. John saw an angelic look on her face. It was weird. And yet John felt relieved. Sometimes he worried about his logical and often emotionless friend.

The absurdity of his situation struck him. "Who are you, what are those instruments, and what did you do to me?"

"The equipment is used to measure the human energy field. I took a snapshot of yours," the woman said.

"Human energy field?" Oh no. He knew what dad would say about that. A load of crap. "There's no such thing."

"It's too complicated to explain right now," the woman said.

So he wasn't going to get any answers. Time to go. He turned and strode quickly outside to the bike. Genevieve followed him.

"Where are you going?" she asked.

"Home," he said. "If I ride fast maybe..." He stopped and got out his phone. It was past 4 now. He'd never make it back to the house before it got dark.

"We have to stay here for the night silly," Genevieve said. "We can't go riding around in the dark."

"Yeah." John was disgusted.

"You can sleep in the guest room," the woman said.

Neither the woman, nor Genevieve, thought it odd that two fourteen-year-olds of the opposite sex would sleep together in the same room. If Rachel knew she'd have a fit and so would Robert. It wasn't as if his parents were Puritans. But neither of them cared much for Genevieve. They'd been urging him to find other friends for years now. John shrugged mentally. If it was OK with Genevieve it was OK with him. He had the slightest sexual interest whatsoever in his skinny friend anyway.

They sat down to a dinner of soy protein, vegetables, and fruit. John wondered if the woman had any hamburgers. He was a little intimidated by her so he just ate what was on his plate. She hadn't even told them her name. After the dishes were cleared the woman left the room, leaving John and Genevieve at the table.

John was tired. "I don't understand why I had to lug the tent around all day if we were coming here. We could have found shelter under some trees if it rained."

"Because I don't like getting rained on," Genevieve said.

John looked at his mobile. "The forecast was for partly cloudy."

"Forecasts are unreliable."

John shrugged. It was typical Genevieve and the only explanation he would get from her. "Who is this woman and how did you find her?"

"She's someone my father used to know. Worked with him on some top secret project."

John didn't pursue the matter. Anything to do with Michael Walters was a mystery. The reserved, distant man hadn't said more than three complete sentences in a row to John in all the time he'd known him. He knew Genevieve knew the woman's identity but wouldn't tell him. Damn these Walters'! Like father like daughter.

Thinking about Genevieve's father reminded him of mom and dad. They were probably having a cow right now. "I need to call home."

Rachel was worried and Robert was angry. "Young man, you tell me where you are right now so I can come get you."

"I don't know where we are dad." He was going to add, 'It's all Genevieve's fault,' but he didn't. "I'll be home tomorrow for dinner."

"You're in big trouble," Robert said.

"Oh John are you all right?" his mom asked.

"Of course I'm all right! Why wouldn't I be all right?"

"I'm worried about you."

John was irritated. "I took a little bike ride mom. Get over it."

"Don't talk that way to your mother!" Robert shouted. "I'll..."

John broke the connection.

He walked into the living room and inspected the bookshelves. There were texts on microbiology, mathematics, and philosophy. An entire wall was devoted to romances, some detective fiction, and an extensive science fiction collection. "Almost as good as the Full Moon," John remarked, impressed. He found a novel by Robert Forward and eagerly began to read.

After a couple of hours darkness fell. John couldn't keep his eyes open any more. He put down his book and trundled to the bedroom. The room was sparsely furnished with two single beds and a small table between them, upon which sat a large lamp. John took the single bed nearest the door. The other bed sat against the opposite wall under the single window. To his surprise Genevieve followed him in and sat on the bed opposite. John took his pants and shirt off in the dusky half light, intending to sleep in his underwear. He dimly perceived Genevieve looking at him and got red-faced.

"What are you looking at?" he said.

"Nothing."

Just as he was dropping off to sleep she spoke. "John?"

"What?"

Her voice was softer, more feminine. She sat up in the bed with the sheet covering her. In the dark he couldn't see the expression on her face.

"Nothing."

When John woke up there were voices coming from the kitchen. He stumbled into his clothes and wondered what was for breakfast. "Vegetables, tofu, and fruit." John sighed. He didn't really expect bacon and eggs but his stomach was telling him it would be a great idea.

It was apparent that Genevieve and the woman had been talking for quite some time. He was sore and just wanted to get on the road. If the weather was good maybe the fresh air would make him forget about this place.

At 7:30 they hopped on their bikes and began the trip back to Midland. John's shoulders were painful but not so much as his legs. He wondered whether Genevieve felt any discomfort. She was ahead of him on the road pedaling, as always, without effort. Sometimes he thought she was an android but he wasn't going to let her see him struggle. He caught up and passed her, taking over the lead.

During one of their rest stops John asked her again why they had come. She didn't answer. Sometimes he couldn't understand why he liked Genevieve at all. Soon he would pay for his blind trust.

They got home around 1 p.m. Genevieve insisted on riding over with him. As soon as they walked in the side door Robert exploded when he saw the thin black-haired girl with the red lips. "Oh so it's you, is it? I should have suspected you'd be involved in this."

"She didn't have anything to do with it," John said. "It was my idea." His legs were shaking from fatigue after riding 120 miles in less than 24 hours. He ignored the pain, keeping his face expressionless.

"Where did you go?" Robert demanded.

John could see Genevieve was about to tell him everything.

"We took a real long bike ride dad. We camped out. Then we rode back. It was fun."

"We almost called the police!" Dad was ranting now. John knew that he just had to look bored and say as little as possible.

"You're grounded," Robert concluded angrily.

When their interview was over John walked with Genevieve to the driveway to get her bike. He was hobbling but she seemed as fresh as a cool breeze.

"Why did you lie to your dad?" she asked. "It was all my idea."

John shrugged. "I don't know."

She smiled shyly up at him. "Thanks."

Then she was off in a whirlwind of jet black hair.

4

Three years later...

Jᴏʜɴ Frankel was a weirdo, always had been, probably always would be. He was just on a different wavelength from anyone else. At Midland East High School all the kids could feel it. He didn't have to say anything. Even in a crowded hallway people could detect him by some kind of osmosis of the air.

"Hey Frankel! Stick your finger in a light socket?" That was Jeremy, the class clown.

"Frankel you dick! Help me with my math homework?" That was Ja'Quan, the big lineman on the football team. John often tutored some of the kids in the athletic department in math and science so they could keep their grades up. Midland East prided itself on its high academic standards, unlike the school across town. John waved his assent.

"Oh Fraaaankellllll! Here I am sweetie pie," exclaimed Jessica, the girl who loved to tease him. The kids weren't hostile toward him, not like when he was in grade school. There was an understanding that John Frankel was weird but special, as if they knew something about him that he didn't even know and were trying to get him to notice.

"OK Ja'Quan. Come to Masterson's study hall at 4."

Ja'Quan raised his hand in acknowledgment.

John Frankel was very good at math. He found the patterns in numbers interesting. His pattern recognition skills made him good at the symbolic arrangement and logical order that mathematics offered. But John Frankel's mind was far more wide-ranging. His was a quest for the nature of ultimate reality. Deep inside he knew that it could not be found in mathematics, science, art, music, or any of the classes he had taken so far. It wasn't in any of the books he had devoured in his 16 years on the planet.

Now a junior, John Frankel's parents were constantly despairing of his "inability to concentrate." They didn't understand that he was searching for something no school could provide. He didn't even know himself what he was looking for but he would recognize it when he found it.

After 7th period he passed Genevieve in the hallway. She had big eyes for him lately even though she had known him practically all his life. Genevieve was now a sophomore but they were almost the same age. John was one year ahead of everyone else, which meant he was one year younger than everyone in his class. Which meant he got teased a lot. But he'd gotten used to it. John Frankel was weird, but weird in a good-natured way.

"Hi John!" she said brightly.

"Hi Genny."

"Don't call me that!"

"Why not? It suits you."

"I'm Genevieve to you, you big moron."

He liked that Genevieve was feisty and knew her own mind. And she was really smart.

"All right, what do you want? I got to get to old man Masterson's and help the guys with their math."

"I found a really unusual book at The Full Moon," she said sweetly.

John brightened. "Yeah? What is it?"

"It's about meditation I think," Genevieve said.

"Gimme a break. I hate meditation. I've already got a couple from Sensei Matsumoto I never finished."

"Yeah? Well you're going to love this one. It's got really cool symbols and some fascinating imagery."

He was intrigued; she saw it on his face.

"So John, why don't you come over at 7 and I'll show it to you." She spoke coquettishly. "Unless you're going to get all lovey-dovey with Ja'Quan."

"You're insufferable," John said. "I don't know why I put up with you." Lately she'd been deliberately trying to provoke him for some unknown reason.

"Because you like me that's why." Genevieve looked directly into his eyes and smiled.

"I'm not going there," John replied.

They both knew he had a crush on Kathleen, the gorgeous cello player in the classical quartet. John couldn't care less about classical music but he sure did dig Kathleen.

Genevieve was looking at him strangely.

"Earth to John. Earth to John! I'm right here. I just asked you a question."

"Huh?"

"You're calling me insufferable?"

"Jeezzus Genevieve, what is it?"

"If you come over at 7 I'll show you the book. Otherwise I swear I'm going to burn it. Mats said it was the only copy he's ever seen."

John loved the Full Moon, one of his favorite city haunts. The Full Moon was a large rambling place. Three stories of crowded bookstacks in a converted old frat house.

"All right, all right. At 7 then."

Genevieve flounced off.

He couldn't for the life of him figure out what her game was. It seemed she wanted to be his girlfriend. Maybe her heightened interest stemmed from his attention to Kathleen.

John snorted to himself. Fat chance he'd ever get anywhere with Kathleen Summers but it was fun to fantasize about her anyway. John Frankel the hero rescuing the damsel in distress. He'd probably get there just in time to see her carried off by fifty other guys. He started down the long corridor leading to the stairwell, lost in thought. John had unknowingly reached the stairwell and was about to blindly take a stair. He was startled to feel his body being shoved against the blue railing.

"Hey idiot! Watch where you're going."

One of the kids had lunged over to help him. John didn't even recognize who it was. "Thanks. Forgot where I was."

His rescuer walked away. John heard him mutter to himself. "Weird John Frankel, does all his sleeping standing up."

He was going to be late for Ja'Quan.

After his tutoring session John headed over to the Full Moon for some reading material. The Full Moon was the coolest bookstore in town. The place was owned and operated by Mats Karlsson, a middle aged Swede who was into the esoteric and the paranormal. John thought that the store was a reflection of Mats himself: A little run down but fundamentally sound.

John approached the Full Moon in the chilly late afternoon air. He stopped to look up at the painted mural across the front of the store. The painting was 10 feet wide and 6 feet high with a gigantic full moon overlooking a castle on an ocean shore. It exuded an energy of excitement, mystery, and new worlds. It was a city landmark that attracted walk-by traffic and curious tourists. Mats never said who painted it.

John parked his bike at the bike stand in front and shoved open the thick blue door, which opened easily on well greased hinges. Mats stood at a long oak counter, chatting with his patrons. A bunch of other people sat on small tables in a small cafe, drinking and eating.

John walked to the science fiction section, browsing for a while. He loved the place because Mats never pushed anyone to buy.

Suddenly he remembered Genevieve's book and his appointment at 7. The clock on the wall said it was 7:10 already.

John swore. It would be just like her to burn the book. He busted out of the aisle and almost ran over a lady with a cup of coffee. He made the stairs, taking them two at a time, and raced toward the front door. He waved to Mats and bolted out the big blue door. It was dark as he ran to his bike. He hopped on and raced the two miles to the Walters.' Breathless, he rapped hard on the door but there was no answer. John raised his fist to give it a smash when a cool and collected Genevieve opened it. The momentum of his swing threw him off balance and he stumbled into the foyer, almost tripping over his own feet.

"You're late," Genevieve said. "I was just about to throw this on the fire." She placed her hand on the book, which was on a small table along with a briefcase and a few scattered papers.

John looked in to the living room and saw the blazing fire.

"Where's your Dad?"

"He's in the library as usual."

"He works at Carleton, doesn't he? Toiling in one of the university's research labs?"

"Yes. He has a high security classification from the government. He can't talk about his work to anyone, not even me."

"Dad's been a real bore lately," she added.

Lately?

John's eyes went to the book. Genevieve grabbed it before he could and swooped into the living room. At the head of the room a gigantic fireplace roared. The room contained two large sofas, three wing chairs, a writing desk, a podium, an easel, several laptops, a projector, and a rolled up movie screen. The ceiling and walls were painted in dark browns but the room was well lit with windows on two sides. This was a room for people to gather, to discuss, to make presentations, or to just relax. He had never seen anyone in it except Genevieve and her father. These Walters' are strange people. Strange but deep. It was one of John's favorite places in the whole world. He couldn't understand why Michael Walters spent so much time shut up in his dark library.

Genevieve flopped on the couch with the book in her lap. "Here it is."

The book had a dark blue cloth cover, fraying at the edges. It smelled musty as if it had been sitting on a shelf for a hundred years. John immediately noticed that the book shimmered a little. He took his eyes away and looked at it again with his peripheral vision. Yes, there it was. Like a mirage on a hot summer day. John's eyes widened.

"I found this in the arcana section at the Full Moon," Genevieve said.

John sat down next to her and inspected the book. It had no title or markings. The first page should have displayed the book's title. Instead it showed a finely detailed image of a man sitting underneath a strange looking tree in a meadow.

Surrounding his body was a spherical field of energy marked with symbols. John looked again. The man was not human. Or rather, he was humanoid. He had large floppy ears sticking out from a bald, cylindrical head. His eyes were large and perfectly circular. His nose protruded. His mouth was wide with thick lips.

John turned the pages, each of which contained symbols. He was familiar with Egyptian hieroglyphics and other runes from his perusal of the books in Michael Walters' vast library. These were completely different. The symbols definitely weren't alphanumeric. The pages were yellowed, and very thick.

"This is a manual of some sort," John said, with growing excitement. The first third of the book contained the strange pictograms, followed by a series of images of the alien man in the meadow. The next page contained a beautiful, finely etched full color image of strange blue and purple geometric patterns moving in a living mist. The image had astonishing resolution and looked even realer than a photograph.

John flipped pages randomly and saw a beautiful white marble city on a perfectly flat plain of blue glass. Another page revealed an eerily beautiful world with a purplish-black sky. A magenta sun rose over a lavender ocean onto a reddish-brown beach. This image, like the others, was alive. John suspected that these pictures were not artist's conceptions. Something told him they were representations of real places.

There were a dozen more. Some looked like earth, others were impossibly bizarre.

"You couldn't make this up," John said. "I mean, some of these places are too fantastic. Not only that but the resolution is impossibly fine." He picked up the book and inspected it, looking for any clues to its origin. He didn't find anything.

Genevieve inched closer. "I was fascinated and I thought you might be too."

John had no clue what any of the symbols meant but he felt a growing excitement within him. "You know, I just might be able to decipher these things,"

He turned his head toward his friend. "It will be a considerable challenge."

Genevieve met his eyes and they both smiled.

That night, in his room, he looked carefully at the pictures in Genevieve's book. They weren't photographs or paintings or drawings, more like unbelievably fine etchings. When he placed his attention on any of them he was gradually pulled into the scene.

John turned to the page with the white city. In minute detail it showed an immense, perfectly flat plain with no markings or imperfections. In the near distance a city of elegant white buildings stood alone. All of the structures curved gracefully to the sky, beckoning to him. The architecture was nothing like John had ever seen on earth. Every surface was subtly curved. As John concentrated upon the drawing his bedroom disappeared and his awareness began to zoom onto the plain. After a few more moments he felt himself fully present in the scene. He began to walk toward one of the buildings. The glass surface felt smooth but it yielded just a little under his weight. John stopped and looked around him. The blue plain stretched unbroken to the horizon in every direction. In the far distance he saw other splotches of white. More cities perhaps? His feet did not make the slightest sound. This world was eerily still but beautiful. John saw no signs of life anywhere and no movement, yet the place did not feel lonely or abandoned. There was purpose here, functionality. For what?

John walked up to one of the structures. It was cool to the touch, smooth and alive. It felt like a combination of hard ceramic and living skin. An opening appeared to his right. At first it was hexagonal and no more than two and one half feet in height but over 6 feet in width. Slowly the opening adjusted itself to John's body proportions. It soon shaped itself into a curved arch about 7 feet tall and 4 feet wide. John saw no machines and heard no sound whatsoever. Although he observed carefully, the process of its metamorphosis was invisible.

He was entirely present in the scene yet he felt his body in the bedroom chair as well. How was this possible?

John walked through the opening and into the building. A soft glow emanated from the walls. Inside there were no rooms and no objects, just the gracefully curved walls he observed from the outside. The floor itself was the flat, light blue floor of the plain of glass.

This place should be utterly boring but it wasn't. Impressions of the city floated through his mind...a vast network of similar cities...part of a great galactic civilization. Spaceships were landing on the blue plain, thousands of beings spilling forth from them...

Some of the buildings changed colors. The plain was green here, red there, white over there, as the people marked off the boundaries of their personal and group areas. John tried to get the body type of the builders. If the original opening was any indication they were short, wide, and low to the ground.

John realized that the more he concentrated, the deeper and deeper he could go into this vision. Wow! This civilization was old, so very old. None of the buildings had received a visitor for eons...

There was a crash and John jerked back in his chair. His attention was fully restored to the surroundings of his bedroom. A book had fallen from the desk onto the floor. John stared at the finely etched drawing on the paper. Had his experience been a daydream?

No. The impressions on his consciousness were too richly detailed and the feelings within him were too unusual for that. His entire being resonated to the eerie beauty of the place. It was as familiar now as the pool hall, or even his bedroom.

John turned to another page and gasped. He was in deep space surrounded by thousands of galaxies. To his right an immense but beautiful blue-green nebula attracted his attention. Then he was inside it. Again, a tendril of his consciousness sat in his chair but most of him was flying around inside the mist. He had never felt so free in all his life!

Another page imaged a beautiful planet with a violet sky. The entire surface was covered in water, with just a few islands here and there. Dolphin-like beings swam swiftly a few feet beneath the surface. Underneath the crystal clear water dozens and dozens of different species swam around. This time he quickly drew his attention from the image.

The etching on the last page displayed a blackened planet. The entire surface was covered by one gigantic city. Super high skyscrapers jutted against one another and walkways connected them at every level. People were screaming. Smoke rose from many of the buildings. Others were ravaged by fire and bodies were flying out of the windows.

Wow, what happened here? John placed his attention in one of the buildings and was immediately assaulted by terror. He backed out quickly but not before receiving an impression that would stay with him for the rest of his life. The etching showed the impending destruction of an entire planetary civilization, of literally hundreds of billions of people. And it could have all been prevented, if only...John jerked his thoughts away. He was being drawn in again to that horrible place. He slammed the book shut. His palms were sweating.

The planet was immensely overpopulated. An unimaginable number of people were jostling and tripping over each other, living in little apartments with no place to recreate or even breathe fresh air. Despite that there was a comforting connectedness here, a close bonding of all members of this civilization. These people depended utterly upon each other for their survival. The ambience of the planet was a feeling that "we are all in this together." John thought it might not be too bad to live here after all, but somehow it had all gone wrong. He slapped his palms on the desk and the stinging pain brought him fully back to himself. Whew! We thought earth was overcrowded!

John got up and walked around the room. His head was spinning and his heart pounded. This was clearly no ordinary book. One or two vivid daydreams, maybe, but not four in a row.

John put the book in the desk drawer and went to bed. He dreamed bizarre dreams.

After class that day John went up to his room. He threw his schoolbooks on the floor and got the mysterious book out of his drawer, placing it on his desk. The early April sun shone brightly. Even though the day was chilly he cracked a window to let in some fresh air.

His interest now was not in the pictures but the symbolic text that accompanied them. He tried to scan the symbols into his computer but nothing came out. He tried it again. The scanned image was blank

He tried scanning different pages and a couple of the full sized images toward the back of the book. All came out blank. Now his curiosity was fired. He checked the scanner and the software with a page from one of his textbooks. Everything seemed to be in order.

John was forced to painstakingly render each unique symbol by hand. Fortunately only a dozen were intricate and he was able to draw these well enough for identification. After several hours of work he had identified and compiled a four-page list of distinct symbols. He scanned the symbols into his computer and copied them into tables. He arranged them in the most sensible order he could think of. When he was done he had 129 in all. Five of the symbols were larger than the others and more intricately designed. These images seemed to belong together so he put them on a separate page.

John glanced at his computer display. It was almost dinner time. His father entered the room. "What's that you have there?"

John had the book open to the first page. Robert bent over the desk, looking at the symbols. A light began to turn on in his eyes. "That's a code."

John sometimes forgot that his father was a code cracker in his younger days. A couple of years ago he had shown John the basics and had given him a few encrypted texts to read.

"Looks a little like one of those old Soviet codes, but much more intricate," his father said.

"I've looked through the book and written down every distinct symbol I could find," John said. "I made a table of the most common ones."

Robert Frankel looked at John's table of symbols and then back at the page of hieroglyphics. "This is not a layered code designed to conceal information. Once you have deciphered the symbols the meaning will be apparent."

John was impressed. His father had made his determination after only a few minutes, whereas he had been studying it for hours.

"Do you think so?' John said, excited.

Robert studied the text again and spoke with certainty. "Yes."

John's heart skipped a beat. Was this an instruction manual? For what?

Robert slowly picked up the book and inspected it. "Where did you get this, son? It looks a little like an old alchemy text I saw once at the Carleton graduate library."

"Genevieve gave it to me. Said she found it at the Full Moon."

Robert frowned. The Walters girl again! She hadn't come around at all for over a year. He and Rachel thought that John had finally outgrown her. Well, one book did not a relationship make. As he examined the strange and unusual text he noted how like Genevieve it was. Despite his irritation, he had to admit he was fascinated by the finely-etched runes.

John took the book from his father's hands. He placed it on the desk and turned to one of the spectacular full page images at the back of the book.

John saw his father grunt and immediately turn his attention back to the symbol tables. John turned the pages to the white city. "Isn't that beautiful?" he asked, trying to draw Robert's attention into it.

"Beautiful etching," Robert murmured, staring into it for a couple of seconds.

John waited for something to happen but his father just straightened.

"Exquisite work."

"You didn't notice anything...ah, unusual?"

"I've never seen work that fine," Robert acknowledged. "Show me those symbols again."

Robert again perused John's table, ignoring the book entirely.

John turned the book to the middle section and the image of the humanoid with the field of energy surrounding his body. Several more etchings of the same scene were on the following pages. In each succeeding image the field of energy got brighter and brighter. The last picture in the series showed that the man had disappeared.

"What do you make of that?" John asked excitedly.

Robert shrugged. "I haven't the foggiest idea. Looks like something from a science fiction or fantasy book."

"Why would someone go to the trouble of writing a science fiction book in such an elaborate code?"

His father dismissed the question with a wave of his hand as if it, and the book, were unimportant. "If you have any trouble son let me have a crack at it. But don't neglect your homework. You must maintain your grades if you want to go to the best colleges."

"Yes dad." Dad had been on him since freshman year about that. It was getting old.

After Robert left John turned his attention back to the code tables. He made little progress in deciphering the symbolic text. He sat with his elbows on the desk and his head in his hands. He asked himself, What do you expect to get from this book? Immediately he recalled the time he threw the older kid to the mat at sensei Matsumoto's dojo. He had reached what Sensei called an altered state of consciousness. He remembered Sensei's exact words. "An altered state of consciousness brings a sudden leap in ability."

John teased himself with the idea that this unusual book might contain instructions for attaining such a state. Concentrating on any of the remarkable etchings effortlessly brought about a change in awareness. Someone had the knowledge to construct and print them onto these pages. He turned to the etching of the white city on the blue plain of glass. Perhaps the images were just a demonstration of some kind of technique or process for altering awareness. Like a demo for a new piece of software. He was about to eagerly dive back into the book when he noticed the clock on the wall above his desk. It was after 10 p.m. already.

"Damn. I got to get that history paper finished tonight."

John reluctantly put away the book and began to write about something he had absolutely no interest in.

The next day John came out from his 3 o'clock history class onto the parking lot. A bunch of guys were milling around on the baseball diamond. Kathleen Summers was there so he walked over.

"Hey Frankel what're you doing here?" said Greg Ortwell, a stockily built senior. "You can't play sports."

"I can't? Remember I used to play basketball with you guys."

Greg snorted. "Yeah, and you sucked. I'll bet you couldn't hit the ball out of the infield."

"The hell I couldn't."

"Hey Greg, let him have a few swings," Gene Watkins said. John knew Gene, the second baseman on the East High team. John had kept up a nodding acquaintance since their grade school and Junior High days, when they'd played some pickup baseball.

"All right Frankel!" Gene said. "We'll get Trevor to throw you a few pitches."

Trevor Jones was also on the team. He played cricket in England for a few years and could throw really fast.

John saw Kathleen sizing him up. By the look on her face she didn't think much of his chances.

"Hey Trevor, go easy on Frankel," Greg said.

John hadn't played baseball since the 8th grade. Fortunately, all he had to do was get his bat on the ball.

Most people at East High would say John Frankel was absent-minded. However, John knew that when he really needed to concentrate he could clear his mind of everything and give his full attention to a problem.

"Batter up!" Gene shouted.

It was time to step up to the plate. John awkwardly grabbed a bat, almost tripping over his own feet. Several of the guys laughed, as did Kathleen.

"All right Trevor," John said, taking a few practice swings. "Show me what you got."

John had seen a baseball training video Mats had shown to one of the kids at the store. For a lark he took a little practice last year at the batting cage at the school. It turned out to be a lot of fun. After a few sessions he was able to at least get his bat on the ball with the machine turned up at 85 mph. John remembered to plant his front foot, steady on the back foot, and shift his weight through the ball, turning into it on impact.

By now a small crowd of students had gathered. John was acutely aware of Kathleen's presence. He saw Trevor getting ready.

"Hey Frankel!" somebody shouted. "You only get three strikes!" Everybody laughed.

"Give me one practice swing," said John. "I need to get my timing." There were a few hoots but it was agreed.

Trevor wound up and fired the ball in. John swung and missed badly, way behind the ball.

"Nice swing Frankel!" somebody said. "The object is to hit the *ball,* not the air."

Kathleen was amused.

John realized that hitting in a batting cage was a lot different than hitting a real pitcher. The windup and the motion of Trevor's arm was confusing him.

"OK Frankel," someone said behind him. "You got three strikes. Let's get this over with so we can practice."

Trevor threw it in. John swung and missed again. He still wasn't catching up to the ball.

"Strike one!"

John concentrated. He'd been to a few of the school games last year, hoping to catch sight of Kathleen in the stands. He'd seen Trevor pitch once. John knew he had a good fastball and changeup but didn't throw hardly any breaking stuff. That was fortunate for him. His pattern recognition skills told him that Trevor was just going to heave the ball on a line as fast as he could.

Trevor wound up and fired a fastball. John managed to tick it with the bat.

"Good hit Frankel, you doofus!" someone said.

"Strike two!"

The next pitch John fouled off. He heard a scream behind him and saw Kathleen angrily getting up. The ball had almost hit her.

"Jerk!" she said angrily to John. Then she turned to Gene. "Why don't you guys just play ball?"

John had had enough. It wasn't going well and now he had pissed off Kathleen. He was really going to bear down, determined to at least get one out of the infield. He stopped and took a few slow, deep breaths.

"C'mon Frankel, get in the batters box!" the guys shouted. John did not heed them. He stood for a few moments, breathing, until he felt the tension begin to melt away.

John stepped back into the batter's box. "Come on Trevor, throw that thing in here!"

John concentrated his attention on Trevor and felt his remaining anxiety dissolve, replaced by a state of total relaxation. Time itself seemed to move leisurely. He saw Trevor slowly wind up. He clearly saw the ball release from his hand, flying through the air like a slowed-down instant replay. John had time to connect solidly. The ball flew on a line to left. John was strong, Abe Lincoln strong. The ball flew way over the 320 foot wall in left center and smashed against one of the bleacher seats.

"Shit!" Greg exclaimed. "Did you guys see that?"

"Nice poke Frankel!" said Gene. "Never seen a bat move that fast."

"Damn awkward swing though," Trevor said in his slightly British accent. "Never saw anyone get on one of my fast balls with such a clumsy motion." He was looking at John curiously from his position 60 feet 6 inches away on the pitcher's mound.

The guys crowded around him, even Kathleen.

"How'd you do that?" said Bill Richardson, the left fielder.

"I don't know. The ball took forever to get to me. I saw it all the way."

They were all looking at him quizzically.

"You got into the zone," Bill said. "I've been trying to do that for two years and here comes Frankel and does it on the first try." He regarded John with disgust.

"Lucky hit," somebody said.

"Do it again," said another.

"Hey Frankel, you want to try out?" Gene said a little sarcastically.

John laughed. "No way. I'll take my lucky hit and go home." He tossed the bat aside, picked up his books, and walked off toward the parking lot. He felt Kathleen's eyes on him the whole way. He wanted to look back but he knew it wouldn't be cool.

"Weird John Frankel," somebody said.

John was pleased. He had hit the crap out of the ball and showed Kathleen what he could do. Now she would know he wasn't just a nerd who could help her with trigonometry.

As he approached the bike rack he stopped short. He had once more attained a sudden leap in ability.

The day after his baseball exploits Genevieve caught up to him in the hallway at school.

"Heard about your heroism on the diamond yesterday," she said a little sarcastically. She had turned to face him directly and looked straight up into his eyes, as she always did when she wanted his complete attention.

John laughed. "Yeah. Gene asked me to try out."

She said nothing, but continued to look into his eyes.

"Oh! You want to know how I did it."

Her lips curled. She remained motionless, waiting for him to explain.

"I got into what I can only call an altered state of consciousness," he said. Her large eyes suddenly brightened. John thought he could almost see flashes of light coming from them. Why would she be so interested in that?

"Tell me," she said impatiently, stomping her foot.

"I saw the ball all the way. It was like time slowed down."

He thought he detected satisfaction in the slight smile that passed over her lips. She broke eye contact. "OK. You want to do that math homework set tonight?"

Even though Genevieve was a grade behind she was in all his science and math classes. Midland East allowed students to test into anything for which they could qualify. It never made sense to John why he had been promoted and Genevieve not.

"Do I want to? Or will I?"

"Dad's not home tonight, he's at a conference in Chicago." She knew that although John respected her father's vast academic knowledge, he gave him the creeps. "If you want to come over around 8 we can finish by 9."

"OK." It would give him a couple of hours after dinner to look at that book again.

He sat through a dull history class with his eyes on the well marked desktop. He was determined to figure out how, twice in his life, he had attained the status of a Zen master. Such a state must be duplicatable. If it was, just think what he could do.

John Frankel, the big slugger, smashing home run after home run over the left field wall. At first base he'd make all the plays, for the ball would be traveling in slow motion. After the winning home run he'd trot around the bases slowly, savoring the adulation of all the students. Kathleen would throw herself into his arms....

John sighed and looked up at Mr. Peterson, the American History instructor, droning on about the Civil War. As if anybody gives a shit about that outdated crap. Why do they still teach such worthless stuff? Dad was on him to decide on a major for college but he didn't have much interest. If his parents truly understood his ambivalence they'd be shocked. In the Frankel family, attending the best universities was a core belief. If college was anything as boring as high school he'd rather just skip the whole thing.

John came home from his study session with Genevieve and walked up the curved staircase and down the hall to his corner bedroom. The room had windows on two sides and was heated by an old-style radiator.

He studied his symbol tables fruitlessly for two hours. Dad had been little help. After looking at the book twice more Robert decided that the manuscript was undecipherable. "Like the Voynich manuscript son." Robert showed John on the computer an ancient document that had eluded the understanding of the best code crackers for decades. "Don't waste your time with it. This book is a curiosity, nothing more. You need to concentrate on your classwork."

John objected, opening the book and pointing to the image of the white city. "These etchings are not just static drawings. They draw you into them."

Robert gazed at the picture for about ten seconds and his eyes widened. "What the hell is this?"

"Isn't it cool? Now you know why I'm spending so much time with it."

Robert cut him off. "Son, what you have here is just a clever optical illusion. I've seen some skillfully designed images that are intended to mess up the neural pathways. These are probably like that."

"You didn't look long enough. If you—"

Robert's face hardened. "You're not to waste your time with this John. You need to focus your attention on your studies. Next year you'll be a senior and you need to score in the 95th percentile on the SAT's. You need all As this year and next."

Now might be a good time to tell dad that he really wasn't that interested in Harvard and Stanford. "But dad—"

Robert angrily waved a hand to indicate that the discussion was over, pointing to John's textbooks. He walked out of the room.

As a scientist his father should have jumped at the chance to investigate this phenomenon. For a split second John had seen fear in his eyes. John understood that his dad was curious only within certain parameters. For him, anything outside the boundaries of accepted science was invalid.

John flipped through the pages of the book and looked at the images of the strange looking humanoid. His body was surrounded by light. On the last image in the sequence he had disappeared from the meadow. Then it hit him: the human energy field. Wasn't that what that weird Hanford lady said she was measuring? He had read something about that. It was called the merkaba.

Deciphering the code now became the single most important thing in John's life. He thought of Genevieve. She was really smart and might be able to help.

When he called her that Saturday she begged off. "I'm sorry John, dad's got me doing some research."

John thought it sounded contrived, and that wasn't like Gen. It was odd. Genevieve had given him the book and seemed very interested in having him understand it, yet evinced no interest in it herself. He was sure she had given him the book for a reason. Genevieve never did anything by accident. She knew her own mind better than anyone he ever met.

John picked up the book and examined it, noticing again a faint shimmering coming from the cover. Or was it just his imagination?

"You're very strange, my friend," he said to it.

Rachel Frankel woke up one morning in a cold sweat. She was approaching 50 and her son would be a senior next year. Soon she would be alone with Robert for the rest of her life.

It was her fault. She had insisted on only one child. Robert had wanted to fill up the two empty bedrooms with children but she knew that the task of looking after those children would devolve to her. He would selfishly shut himself up in his study, watch C-SPAN, and go to his writers meetings. He would be oblivious to the needs of his family. He'd been doing it for the past 15 years. Maybe that was just how men were.

Rachel Frankel was honest with herself. It had suited her to limit their family to John. She admitted to herself that she was just as devoted to her career as was her husband. They were a perfect fit: two self-centered academics who had the obligatory child. She had pretended to involve herself in John's life but had just gone through the motions.

She thought of Genevieve, John's lifelong companion. Both she and Robert had rejected the girl, thinking her too emotionless and detached. But wasn't that a perfect description of herself and her husband?

Rachel picked up her phone almost unthinkingly and selected the Walters' number. While the phone rang she asked herself what her motivation was for calling the girl. A memory immediately came to the surface, of the last time Genevieve had been over to see John. Genevieve had arrived at the side door carrying her math book, obviously prepared for a study session. Rachel automatically called up the staircase. "John, Genevieve's here." When John came down to meet her the girl looked up at him and said "hi" with an easy familiarity. They both ran up the stairs side by side, racing to see who could get to the top first. She heard John laugh and the girl screech as John shoved her playfully aside and made it to the door first. "Beat ya!" Then the door slammed. These two are best buddies and have been for a long time. It was one of those obvious things she had unconsciously accepted but had never reconciled herself to. Her rocky marriage and her work made her oblivious to what had been going on right under her nose. Her reverie was interrupted by a voice.

"Hello?"

"Uh, this is Rachel Frankel. Is this Genevieve?" Rachel's heart pounded. She didn't understand why she felt so nervous.

Rachel heard the girl's intake of breath. "Uh, yes, this is Genevieve."

"I'm John's mother, but you probably know that." Rachel felt stupid. How many times had Genevieve been over to the house? The girl must know her voice.

"Yeah."

OK, Rachel thought, I'm going to have to do this all by myself. "I'm calling because...because you've known John a long time and I think it's about time I got to know you a little better." Her words were falling all over each other.

Another pause. "You never thought so before," said the voice on the other end. The girl's voice was matter-of-fact, without rancor or bitterness.

"I'm so sorry about that." Rachel was about to apologize but the girl cut her off.

"Don't worry about it Mrs. Frankel. I've learned to live in the present. I never think about the past." Left unsaid between them was the thought, *because it's too painful.* Both women understood. That understanding seemed to create a bond where there was none before.

Something inside Rachel softened. "Well then, why don't we wipe the slate clean and start over."

There was no answer. Rachel thought the girl might have hung up but she hadn't heard a click. She waited for a response, unconsciously holding her breath.

"Mrs. Frankel, I think I'd like that."

Rachel could hear the relief in the girl's voice. Her own nervousness vanished. An hour later she hung up the phone, amazed and pleased. The first half hour of their conversation had been very awkward. Rachel struggled to find common ground with the reticent girl. Mostly they talked about John. Rachel told her about her job and her own family. She explained that she had a PhD in philosophy and worked at the university. She told the girl that her husband was a popular freelance science writer who sold his pieces to blogs, magazines, and newspapers.

"I've never had a mom," Genevieve said. "My father doesn't seem too interested in what I'm doing. I've learned to take care of myself."

Of course, Rachel thought. She had lived her whole life with Michael Walters.

Despite her reluctance to talk about herself Rachel got the girl to open up a little. She was very intelligent and well-spoken, but emotionally distant. During their dialogue Rachel discovered that her own objection to the girl stemmed from a dislike of her father. She and Robert had first met Michael Walters twelve years ago at one of the monthly meetings of the University Musical Society. The man was cold and almost frighteningly remote. She felt a stab of fear in her stomach as she tried to place herself in Genevieve's shoes. To grow up with a father like that!

Rachel began to draw the girl out emotionally. By the time she hung up Rachel felt that woman and girl had made a connection. She felt a warm feeling in her heart and wondered what it would have been like to have a daughter.

"Would you like to come to dinner this Sunday?"

Rachel could almost feel the girl blush with pleasure.

"I'd like that a lot Mrs. Frankel."

"Well then, Sunday at 5 o'clock."

As she hung up the phone Rachel felt inordinately pleased with herself. She knew Robert would object, but she would cook his favorite dish. If he didn't want to participate he could eat in front of the TV.

On Sunday Genevieve came over for dinner wearing her usual black slacks and burgundy top. It was clear to John that it was all mom's idea. Dad had that "I'm tolerating this but I don't like it" look that often presaged an angry outburst. He hoped the old man would keep his temper. To John's surprise Genevieve opened up a little. Rachel seemed genuinely interested in her.

Rachel dominated the conversation at table. She asked Genevieve all sorts of questions about home, school, and her interests. Genevieve responded in multiple sentences and was very polite, which seemed to mollify Robert a little. A few times Genevieve caught John's eye and smiled as she described a few of their exploits together.

Robert questioned her closely about their bike trip to Hanford a couple of years ago. Genevieve deftly avoided discussing the old lady and her laboratory. John knew that his father had a long memory and tended to hold grudges. Fortunately, Genevieve's logical mind and her wide vocabulary impressed Robert. He began to thaw toward her a little. John suspected that mom's beef oriental didn't hurt either.

Twice during dinner he saw Genevieve and his mom exchange knowing glances, as if they shared some secret. How had that come about in less than 36 hours? It must be a girl thing.

John and Robert left the dinner table with the two females chatting. In the hallway Robert said, "Got your homework done son?"

"Uh, almost." That was the problem with advanced placement classes: extra work on the weekends. "I was going to ride over to the Full Moon before it gets dark." Mats kept the store open until 8 on Sundays and he wanted to browse through the SF section.

"Go finish it before you do anything else." Robert was insistent.

Dad was getting to be a real pain in the ass.

During the next two weeks John twice more requested Genevieve's help with the codebook and was refused. She knew more about the book than she was letting on. That made him angry because he had always been honest with her. He didn't like to get angry because it reminded him of dad. Despite their truce at the dinner table and their agreement about his education, dad fought a lot with mom these days. He could hear their muffled arguments through the closed door of Rachel's study on the opposite side of the hall. Often they'd go at it in dad's study on the first floor. Sometimes they quarreled about him but he didn't want to know anything about it. He'd put on some music and turn up the volume, drowning out the irritating voices.

As his junior year wore on Robert continued to rag on John about going to the Ivy League. The vibe in the house grew intolerable. John hardly wanted to go home anymore and spent a lot of time in the pool hall or at the Full Moon, or just riding around. A couple of times he rode by Kathleen's house on the weekends. He didn't have the guts to knock on her door. Unfortunately, his heroics on the baseball diamond hadn't softened her towards him at all. John knew he wasn't going anywhere with Kathleen, but somebody ought to tell his hormones. Every time he passed her in the hall he got the shivers. He tried to sit next to her in study hall but she was always surrounded by her girlfriends or other male admirers.

Occasionally after school he'd go over to Ja'Quan William's house and some-times stay for supper. He had become friends with the huge lineman on the football team during their informal math study sessions after school. His ability to explain complex concepts had attracted a number of students to these meetings and they had become a regular part of his routine.

The big guy had a big family. John marveled at how easily they expressed their feelings to each other. The house was noisy, with lots of jabbering and carrying on. But all of the family members were genuinely communicating with each other. They actually liked one another.

At dinner everybody talked at once. John thought it was cool. One time Ja'Quan's father looked at him. "What do you think of this family John?" The talk-ing ceased and you could hear a pin drop, all waiting expectantly for his response.

"I think it's cool. You don't hide anything from each other."

Little Rodney piped up, "That's right fool! You look like a dead president with his finger in a light socket!" The whole room burst into howls and screams of laugh-ter, but it was all good natured. At first John was shocked. After a few seconds he began to laugh as well. After that the ice had completely broken. He felt like another member of the family and was treated accordingly from then on.

John never forgot the time he asked Mr. Williams about girls. His failure to engage them was becoming frustrating. The dishes had been cleaned and put away. The family had cleared out, leaving them alone in the kitchen.

Mr. Williams looked John over. "Son, you aren't going to wow the ladies with your looks or your athletic ability. But you don't need that. You want to get a girl John, just open up to them. Express yourself and don't be phony. The great thing about women is that even the biggest jerk can find one who'll love him."

"Yeah, but how do you open up to them?" John was thinking of Kathleen. "Especially when they don't like you."

Mr. Williams laughed. "You can't be afraid to talk about yourself and express your feelings, John. You can't teach that. You just have to do it."

John thought about his father. "My dad expresses his feelings to my mom but he usually does it angrily. That doesn't get him anywhere but a fight."

Mr. Williams laughed again. "You have to be observant John. It's not all about you. It's about them too. If you want to get a girl to like you, you have to pick the right time and place. Do or say something genuine that touches her."

At this point Mrs. Williams entered the room. She came over to her husband and kissed the top of his head. He turned in his chair and looked up into her eyes. John's heart skipped a beat because a powerful feeling of love filled the kitchen. John basked in it.

"Who's the girl?" Mr. Williams asked, after his wife left the room.

John flushed. "Uh...Kathleen Summers."

For the third time Mr. Williams laughed. John didn't mind. The older man's dark, broad face expressed a genuine happiness. He was so open John thought he could see right through to his soul. John didn't know adults could be like that. He really liked it.

"I've met Kathleen," Mr. Williams said. "I don't think it's going to work between you two."

John smiled back sheepishly. "Yeah, I sorta suspected that."

"Don't worry son, there are plenty of girls out there. I have no doubt one of them is just right for you."

Yeah, John thought, but which one?

"Mrs. Frankel?"

Rachel picked up her mobile phone in the kitchen after putting the dirty dishes in the dishwasher. She was pleased to hear the voice on the other end. "Hello Genevieve!"

"Uh, I don't know how to ask you this...but..."

Rachel understood immediately that she wanted to talk about John.

"How did you guess?"

An hour later Robert entered the kitchen, opening cupboards, looking in the refrigerator for a snack. "You've been spending a lot of time on the phone lately with that girl." His voice registered disapproval.

Rachel smiled and took the phone up to her room.

Two weeks later John sat at his desk on a Saturday morning and looked out the window at the barren landscape. The leaves were off the trees and the metallic gray sky reflected his sour mood. His life sucked. His schoolwork was mind-numbingly boring. Robert and Rachel were on him every day to "excel." He wanted a girlfriend and couldn't have one. Mr. Williams' great advice about girls hadn't worked.

His mobile rang.

"John?" Genevieve sounded excited and a little nervous.

"Oh, it's you."

He could tell she froze a little on the other end. After a second she spoke shyly. "Could you come over?"

"What for?"

"Uh...I just want to talk to you for a minute."

"You're talking to me right now." What was with her lately? Genevieve was never nervous.

"I want to see you in person before I go shopping with your mom. She's trying to convince me to change my color scheme. Wants to turn me pastel or something."

Yeah, and what does that have to do with anything? Since when did Genevieve ever have an interest in clothes? She always wore the same stupid colors and outfits. With an effort John stifled himself. "I'm not doing anything right now." *Except moping.*

"All right then. I'll expect you in fifteen minutes."

John hung up and realized he'd either have to bike over there in the cold or ask Robert for his car keys. Both options pissed him off. He slammed his bedroom door, went out to the garage, and grabbed his bike. He pedaled furiously and hoped no one in the neighborhood would see his gangly legs pumping the pedals on a bike that was made for someone a lot shorter. He pedaled up the Walters' driveway and threw the bike against the side of the house. It crashed to the cement driveway.

John strode to the front door and banged on the knocker. He was *really* not in a good mood right now. Perhaps she wanted to tell him what she knew about the mysterious book.

Genevieve opened the door brightly and invited him in. John tried to keep his expression bland. He lowered his head and walked quickly through the hallway and into the big living room.

Genevieve followed him in. He sat on the couch trying to compose himself. She stood about six feet away, nervously shifting her balance from one foot to the other. "Uh John...I wondered if...if..."

That morning Rachel had encouraged her to open up a little. Their conversations had helped her to understand that she really liked John and had liked him for a long time. But she didn't know how to express her feelings to him. She wasn't sure herself what her feelings were. It was so frustrating! She suddenly blinked back a tear and turned her back to him.

John was astonished. He had never seen her cry, ever. Who was this impostor standing before him? The decisive and confident Genevieve he had always known had turned into a scared little girl.

He wondered why he had bothered to come over at all. Something of his mood must have etched his face. When Genevieve turned around and saw his expression her eyes opened briefly in dismay. She shut down. She stood rigidly now before him. Her eyes were hard, her lips a firm line. "I'm sorry I bothered you."

Now that was more like the real Genevieve. "So what did you want to see me about?"

"Nothing, dammit." He had never heard her swear before. Something was obviously bothering her but right now he didn't care. He had troubles of his own.

"So you dragged me over here for nothing? I had to ride my bike in the cold."

"Keep your voice down," she hissed. "Dad's sleeping and he doesn't feel well."

John's emotions spilled over. "Your dad's an asshole. You're not much of a friend either."

Genevieve's eyes narrowed to slits. She grabbed him by the arm and pushed him out of the living room, into the hallway, and to the front door. John's rage mounted. The last rational piece of him noticed how strong she was and how painful was her grip on his arm.

She stopped their momentum in the foyer. "Get out of here."

"Let go of me." John flung his arm out to release her grip. But he had not counted on his own strength. In horror he watched as she crashed against the wall, hitting her head against it.

Genevieve straightened and looked at him contemptuously. "Do you plan to beat me up?"

The unfairness of her accusation enraged him further. She had grabbed him first!

In the small foyer John's face was only three feet from hers, reddened by anger. For a moment Genevieve thought he might hit her.

If Genevieve could have read his mind she would have understood that he was more scared than she was. For that brief instant he saw her panicked expression and felt her fear. It shamed him and upset him even more.

Genevieve pinned him with her eyes, willing him to leave. She was now a tightly controlled ball of hostility. John felt like a guy at the bottom of the Grand Coolee dam just before it was about to burst. He knew how Ricky Davis must have felt that time playing baseball.

"I don't want to talk to you anymore. Get out of my house."

Genevieve shoved him out the door and slammed it in his face.

John stood outside the door for a few minutes in turmoil. He looked at his arm. A big red welt was forming and he couldn't believe what had just happened. He didn't understand how their conversation had escalated into conflict. He felt angry and sick inside.

A little voice in the back of his mind told him that he should go inside and apologize. He should tell her it was all an accident but he couldn't find any words. In an orgy of self pity he blamed it all on her. "Fuck you!" he yelled at the silent door, and felt a little better.

On the way home John wondered how a girl could upset him so much. No guy had ever made him so angry, not even that bully on the playground. The bully from whom Genevieve had rescued him, he reminded himself.

When John got back home he tried to calm down but it was no good. He went down to the basement to Robert's old weight set, which was gathering dust. John fired on some weights, lay down on the bench, and jerked the bar off its supports. He got back up, put more weight on, and lifted again.

Deep inside John was shocked. Never in his life had he experienced such overwhelming emotion. He felt like an automaton programmed by some evil force.

John fired on almost 300 pounds and lay back down on the bench. He knew his only release would come through physical exhaustion. He reached up, grabbed the bar, and strained to get it up off the support. What if he got it off and it crushed him? "Fuuuuuuck!" he screamed, glad that no one was home.

John got the bar off and brought it down to his chest. He mustered all his strength and slowly lifted it over his head, then brought it back down. He raised it and lowered it again, sweating profusely now. Up and down, up and down. He wanted to completely drain himself, take away all his energy so that his demon would weaken and die within him. Finally the bar could no longer be moved. It rested on his chest, pinning him to the bench. He barely had enough strength to keep it from pushing his ribs in. With one last heave John was able to shove the right side of the bar off to his left, sending the weights crashing to the floor. Paint chipped off and the bar bent a little.

John was so tired he could barely walk. He trembled with fatigue and he felt sick to his stomach. His arms felt like blobs and they hurt like hell. Dripping with sweat he dragged himself up to his room. Without cleaning up he fell exhausted onto the bed.

The next morning John felt awful. His arms were swollen and he couldn't lift them.

Rachel and Robert entered his room. "What happened between you two yesterday?" Rachel asked. "I went to pick up your friend and she looked awful. You do too."

"I don't know what happened mom. We had a fight." He felt ill and was afraid he might have done permanent damage to his arms and shoulders.

John could tell dad wanted to let him have it. Robert saw John's weakness and didn't have the heart to censure him. He had been down in the basement to replace a fuse early in the morning and had noticed the weight set and the bent bar. "You tore a lot of muscle son and you'll need to rest." Robert had done a little lifting in his time and knew what his son was feeling.

John anxiously addressed his mother. "Genevieve's OK isn't she?"

"She's very upset with you John." Her eyes widened. "You didn't hurt her? Oh John, if you touched her..."

Robert's eyes blazed. "John...you better tell us what happened right now."

Despite his nausea, John briefly went over the altercation.

"I'm disappointed in you son. It is never permissible for a man to touch a woman in anger."

John accepted his father's reprimand even though the welt on his arm had turned an ugly blue. Although his father often lost his temper with mom, John had never seen him strike her.

Rachel was more forgiving. She noticed the bruise on John's arm and had already heard about the incident from Genevieve. The girl had made it clear that John's actions were unintentional. She had honestly described her own part in the altercation although she had not addressed the reasons for it. Nevertheless, Rachel felt that John had not acted appropriately. She found herself taking the girl's part against her son.

Rachel saw John's eyes close in weariness. She herded Robert out of the bedroom.

John spent the rest of the day in bed. He slept and listened to music, trying to make sense out of why he had blown up. Most of all his arms throbbed and hurt like hell. Toward evening he fell asleep for good and didn't even come downstairs for dinner.

On Sunday his arms felt even worse. Rachel felt so sorry for him that she served him Sunday brunch in bed. While John gingerly ate with Rachel assisting, they talked. After John was finished she reached over and gently patted her son's arm. "I think Genevieve really likes you." She was testing the waters.

"Ouch! c'mon mom, that hurts," John complained.

Rachel recognized that John's pain prevented any meaningful conversation on the subject of girlfriends. She took the tray of empty dishes downstairs.

Monday was a school day and his arms were still swollen. John borrowed Robert's car and drove to school. He could barely get his books into the front seat and even had trouble with his spoon at breakfast. Hopefully Genevieve wouldn't see him today. He didn't want to talk to her and she probably didn't want to talk to him.

There were a few hoots as he walked down the hall to math class.

"Hey Frankel, what happened to you? Get hurt wrestling a math book?"

Very funny, John thought. Normally the teasing didn't bother him but today he felt like a girl with PMS.

By the end of the day John was tired and irritable. He had endured the ribbing of his schoolmates all right. But this was Monday and it was time for his tutoring session. Many of his students were athletes, along with a few clueless English and History students. Midland East required all students to take three semesters of math, including one higher level course. Those athletes who didn't make a passing grade were kicked off the team. In addition to Ja'Quan, the big lineman, there were supposed to be two others from the football team and another from the gymnastics team. Fortunately he was not responsible for their grades. If they didn't come it was no skin off his back.

John tutored primarily for the enjoyment of it and to help him understand the concepts better. He'd have to if he was going to reach the 95th percentile on the SAT's.

John walked into study hall and saw the giant already waiting, the textbook open to one of the advanced trig problem sets.

"Where's everybody?" John asked.

"I don't know but I'm ready. Let's go."

John took a desk and turned it facing the other. Ja'Quan gestured toward John's arms.

"OK Frankel, tell me what happened." Ja'Quan laid his massive forearms on the desk, leaning over and waiting for John's reply.

"I did it lifting weights."

"You? Lift weights? When did you ever do any lifting?"

"Saturday. I got really pissed, went downstairs to my Dad's old weight set."

"How much did you lift?"

"A little over 300 pounds."

The big man was amazed. "300? How many reps?"

"I don't know. Maybe 6 or 7."

"How could a skinny guy like you do 7 reps of 300 pounds?" Ja'Quan said, unbelieving.

"They say I'm strong like Abe Lincoln."

"Shit, Frankel. I can only bench 450."

John was miserable but he felt himself smiling. "Only 450?" he squeaked, looking up at the giant with the huge afro. Their eyes locked and Ja'Quan let out a huge belly laugh. John doubled over with laughter. "Only 450...." They began to pound their desks, making an enormous racket. With every exhale of breath John found his spirits lifting.

One of the teachers poked his head in the room. "Is everything OK in here?"

John and Ja'Quan just waved. They were still laughing as hard as they could. The teacher walked out muttering. "Stupid kids."

John felt great. All of that laughing was cathartic. His mental funk of recent days was gone. He was back.

"OK Ja'Quan old buddy, let's get on with some of this math...."

That night John slept deeply and dreamlessly and when he awoke Tuesday morning he felt refreshed. His arms still hurt.

That evening after dinner John called Genevieve.

"Hi John," she said.

"I don't know what to say other than I'm sorry. I—"

She cut him off. "Forget about it John. I have."

"There was something you were going to tell me before we both went nutsoid."

There was silence on the line for a moment. Was she still mad at him?

"It was nothing. Let's forget about it. Do you want to work on our lines for that stupid play tomorrow?"

Midland East had a theater program. All students had to either do public speaking or take a part in the all-school play. Both he and Genevieve decided that saying a few lines at a play was better than confronting an auditorium filled with people.

"Yeah I guess so. Why don't you come over after dinner tomorrow?"

"Dad's still not feeling up to par so I have to stay home. I want to make sure he gets some good food into him. Otherwise he'll just shut himself up in the library and drink coffee all night."

"OK. I'll come over at 7."

They read their lines in the big living room and it was OK between them again. Somehow the fight had softened them both a little toward each other. John made sure he didn't touch her. One time when they leaned over together to look at the play, he backed off and let her look alone.

"John, it's OK. It was just as much my fault as yours. I still like you. You're still my friend."

He looked at her forehead. There was a slight welt on it still. He felt like an ass. "I really do like you Gen. I'm so sorry. I can't believe I hurt a girl."

She stood right in front of him and he was forced to look up. Genevieve had a presence that affected you even when she didn't have your attention.

"On with the play!" she said cheerfully. John could see it was really all right with her and he laughed. They completed their assignment. He went home sure that all was well between them again.

For the rest of the year John had almost no time for anything but schoolwork. Rachel and Robert bore down even harder. They insisted he take two advanced placement courses the following winter term. It was either math and computer science courses or philosophy and the history of science. John thought it was a conspiracy. Both subjects reflected the primary interest of each parent. "Your grades are good son, but you need to be well-rounded." Rachel spoke seriously. "Ivy League schools like to see a balance between liberal arts and science."

John knew he was the fulcrum upon which their marriage balanced. It sucked. The thought of divorce made him feel sick so he trudged through the rest of the year, getting all A's and one B in philosophy. Every night before he went to bed he brought out the code book and looked at the remarkable etchings. Each time he was drawn into fantastic worlds that became more and more detailed. John found himself dreaming vividly and in color. When he woke up in the mornings he felt as if his conscious awareness had expanded. It was like taking a drug, but a good kind of drug.

Rachel and Robert looked over John's grades together in early June. Rachel was disappointed, hoping John might follow in her footsteps. Robert was secretly pleased because John had chosen mathematics and computer science AP classes. His plan was working to perfection. There would be more of the same for John's senior year.

The next morning Robert walked into John's bedroom unannounced. His son was at his desk, staring blankly at the wall.

"John, I think you should take a couple of summer classes. That will—

"NO."

Robert was startled and then irritated. "There's a lot of competition out there and you're at a disadvantage, coming from a small Midwest public school..."

John tuned it out. As his father droned on, one thought was uppermost in his mind: Screw the Ivy League.

Robert completed his monograph. John turned around slowly in his chair to face his father. He noticed how much weight his father carried these days and how pasty he looked. John spoke wearily. "Dad, I need a break. I need this summer vacation to unwind."

Robert sneered. "So you can play pool with the derelicts downtown?"

John said nothing. He looked steadily into his father's eyes. Robert's turned and stalked angrily out of the room.

John rose from his desk slowly and closed the door, lost in thought. Within him an excitement was slowly building. Maybe it was the constant access to the etchings that sent his consciousness outward into the universe. John knew, beyond a doubt, that something was happening out there. Something exciting and important. John felt he was to be a part of it.

5

The Eyrie

KJIRSTEN sat at the main section console surrounded by four of her five assistants. The ceiling was 100 feet above their heads and extended as far as the eye could see in every direction. It was filled with swirling purple clouds. A huge orange-red sun hung halfway over the horizon and filled the sky with pale, peach colored light. Beneath them a carpet of reddish-blue grass, almost a foot high, covered the floor. Their feet did not sink into it. Far off in the distance, animals grazed. The spectacular scenery went unnoticed by the four humanoids and the griffon. They were concentrating their attention within a huge rectangular holotank that showed a real-time image of John Frankel, seated at his desk.

This was not an ordinary image. The display showed the body of the earthian surrounded by a stupendously colored, glowing and pulsing sphere of subtle energy. The trained observers in the Eyrie had been studying the Vessel of Life for almost 5 billion years. The group knew what to look for. Candidates were in desperate need and in short supply.

Until only a year ago the earthian planet had never before graduated an Unformed Potential technician. Conditions there precluded the establishment of permanent civilizations that could sufficiently develop the capabilities of the Sphere of Consciousness. Yet somehow the present backward earthian civilization had spawned a race of physically primitive but latently powerful beings. Within the Vessel of Life, unknown potentials were activating within some of these earthians. Kjirsten studied the fascinating and complex geometries within John Frankel's sphere. She grew more and more excited. The potentials surrounding this candidate were astounding even if the probabilities of success were slim.

Kjirsten focused the display on John's computer lamp. She zoomed into its atomic structure, past the substructure of individual atoms, farther and farther, until she saw the ghostly presence of the Unformed Potential. This multidimensional substrate, or latency, existed at the boundary between matter and energy and nothingness. It is the chaotic half-reality that interfaces with every quanta within the multiverse and from which all Form arises.

Kjirsten checked her readings on the data display, which occupied the entire surface of the 6 foot by 4 foot desk. The data display showed information derived from the real-time images from the holotank. There was no doubt that the Unformed Potential was now beginning to penetrate the well-ordered atomic structure of matter itself.

Earthian scientists called it dark matter and dark energy. They postulated that it made up over 95% of the mass density of the universe. Kjirsten knew that some earthian theorists were very close to the truth. They postulated a scalar field of exotic energy that affected the visible matter and energy of planets, stars, and galaxies. If they only knew how fundamental was the relationship between the Unformed Potential and normal matter!

Kjirsten uttered a Lyran oath. What was going on out there? Why would the well-ordered structure of reality suddenly come under assault? For that is what it was. The research divisions, in their last briefing, made this very clear. If present trends continued every quanta in every universe in the All would be subjected to the effects of that...madness. Kjirsten shuddered. The ancient and fragmented station records had foretold the end of the 16 billion year Great Cycle and the beginning of another.

The phenomenon was as yet too subtle to be measured by any instruments outside the Eyrie. To those living their lives within the universes of visible matter and energy all was well, and would remain well, until the crisis came upon them. Only this research station, located beyond space and time, could have a true picture of what was now being called the Cosmic Event.

On the earthian planet the Hindu concept of time was the closest to the truth. According to Hindu cosmology the flow of Time is eternal. Creation and dissolution follow each other. Each Day of Brahma was supposed to last 4.3 billion years before the universe dissolved into the Absolute and a new cycle began. The Hindu Great Cycle was off by several billion years. The true cycle was 16 billion standard years, or 64 standard revs. A rev was the time it took a stellar system to revolve once around a typical galaxy. The All was now at the end of a 16-billion-year cycle. The life cycle in every universe and in every galaxy in the multiverse was coming to an end.

Kjirsten thought about the Eyrie and the purpose of the great research station. The Records told them of mass destruction in all of the universes after the last

Great Cycle. The All evolved like a caterpillar shedding its cocoon to a new state. The purpose of the Eyrie was to somehow prevent that destruction by studying the Unformed Potential from their advantageous position outside of space and time. But the mystery of the Unformed Potential and how it interacted with space-time was still unknown after millions of years of research. The Unformed Potential Research Group was getting close to an answer. But the end of the cycle would occur several hundred thousand standard years earlier than calculated. They had run out of time.

Kjirsten stared unseeing into the tank. The big Lyran felt the comforting pressure of Bellerophon's hand on her shoulder and smelled the acrid odor of one of his earthian cigarettes. There was nothing she could do personally about the End of Everything except to do her job as best she could. She glanced up at Bellerophon and smiled.

Kjirsten thought about the remarkable set of consciousness enhancing exercises that had allowed her to reach the Eyrie. For billions of years the technique had presented itself to any being capable of mastering it, as if under the influence of a guiding hand. But who or what was that guiding influence? Why did it not make itself known?

That book of John Frankel's for instance. Their careful monitoring of earthian events revealed that it had been brought to the Full Moon by one of the diminoti. The little creature had arrived at the bookstore through a transportal. Unfortunately, it was not possible to trace transportal movement. The little being's origin point could be anywhere within the Twelve Galaxies. Or even outside.

Not more than a handful of beings in any of the Twelve Galaxies were capable of reaching the Eyrie. Yet here was the second potential candidate from the backward earthian planet within the last five years. An analysis of John Frankel's Sphere of Consciousness showed that this one was powerful. She hoped against hope that he might somehow be their savior. That was absurd of course. An earthian movie fantasy. The forces involved here were universal in scope.

"The kid ain't doin nothing," said Davey, interrupting her thoughts. "I say we intervene right now."

"I disagree," Bellerophon countered. "If we move too early, and before the boy is ready, we'll ruin our chances."

"All indications are that the earthian will proceed as we have calculated," clicked Goliath.

"That's not good enough," Davey retorted. "Relyin' on indicators ain't going to make it. We got to act now and stop pussyfootin' around."

"Look at the definition of that sphere," Bellerophon said. "The perimeter already shows signs of firming up and he hasn't yet begun the technique."

It was true. Kjirsten recalled the incident at the baseball diamond. It was clear that the earthian had deliberately and consciously willed himself to a state of enhanced awareness, although it was not clear to him how he did it. The conscious control of one's Sphere was vitally important for all Candidates.

Kjirsten was in an agony of indecision, which went against all of her rigorous training. What to do? This earthian male was the best prospect they'd seen in the 18 standard years she'd been at the station. The situation was delicate because the candidate process could not be forced. The best technicians were always those who had found this station without help or assistance from the outside.

The griffon watched and listened as the debate flowed back and forth. Suddenly he spread his big wings and screeched. All eyes turned toward him. He said, in his squawking speech, "Leave the boy alone. He'll make it." Then he flew up into the sky and disappeared.

6

ONE cool summer day six months later John and Genevieve sat in the Walters' living room. It was nearing mid-August and school would be starting again after Labor Day.

Genevieve sat at the desk using her laptop. John lounged in one of the wing chairs across the room.

Was it his imagination or did she look different?

Their relationship had always been like brother and sister, and guys didn't notice their sisters. He took her for granted, mostly. It struck him suddenly that Genevieve was his lifelong companion, his only true friend in the whole world. He knew almost nothing about her. He looked more carefully. That tomboyish figure was no longer skinny.

"Is it my imagination or are you getting bigger?"

She turned in her chair to face him. "What do you mean?"

He put his hands over his chest.

She colored slightly.

"How come you've been so lovey-dovey toward me lately?"

"None of your business." The dolt. He's clueless. Drooling for Kathleen Summers when it was obvious that the two of them were well matched. She had taken precautions, just in case. Thank God for Magdelena, who had shown her what to do.

For the first time in his life John carefully examined his friend.

There was something almost unearthly about her appearance. Genevieve had very pale skin, almost pure white. Very large eyes with cat-like jet-black pupils gazed back at him. Fine, raven black hair fell about her shoulders, impossibly dark. A small but perfectly chiseled nose, very high cheekbones, and a delicately shaped mouth with full, red lips. If he were asked to describe her ethnic background he'd say she had Irish blood. But the coloring was all wrong. Genevieve should have blue eyes and red hair. Instead she was a contrast in black and white except for the burgundy colored lips. John teased her one time when they were kids about wearing lipstick but she had denied it with a handful of pebbles. Ears that almost came to a rounded point on top. Like a cat's. How could he have never noticed that before? The hands resting palms down on her legs were pale white against the black fabric of her slacks.

She wasn't beautiful, more like...unusual. Her facial features were perfectly symmetrical, almost too perfect for beauty. He remembered with a jolt that Genevieve had been adopted. Michael Walters was swarthy and his ex-wife, from the photograph he had seen of her, was a blonde. Genevieve couldn't possibly be a blood relative. Or could she?

Now he concentrated his attention even more deeply on his friend, sitting calmly under his gaze. She wore a light burgundy sweater tucked into black slacks. Her thin, athletic frame had filled out. For the first time he noticed the curve of hips and legs.

In her own way she was beautiful. Beautiful to him at least. John caught himself breathing in very quickly at that realization. What was it about Genevieve that felt so unique? It wasn't just physical. She possessed a countenance, a demeanor, that radiated power and strength of character.

Why had he never noticed before? Well, he had his head in the clouds, that's what everybody said.

"Where do you come from Genny?" he asked.

She turned away, embarrassed, and did not answer.

He made a mental note to try and find out.

"Come here for a minute," John said.

It was a command. Genevieve had never heard him talk to her like that before. She walked slowly over to the wing chair, standing about a foot in front of him. John's eyes were level with the sweater and its contents. He could see the curves of her pushing against it and he began to breathe rapidly.

Genevieve put her hands to her waist and began to slowly move the sweater upward. John stared open-mouthed as she pulled it completely over her head and tossed the sweater onto the floor. She took off her bra.

She looked down at him with complete concentration, as she always did, with a slightly taunting smile. He couldn't take his eyes off her and sat there like a statue, mouth agape.

"Well? You wanted to see them, here's your chance."

John couldn't move. He had seen pictures of topless women but the real thing was a sensory overload. John thought her breasts were absolutely beautiful. He wanted to tell her so but his vocal cords seemed to be cut off from his brain.

"What's the matter, you don't like them?"

John couldn't respond because he was shaking like a leaf. He had never felt this energized ever before.

He reached a finger to touch her. The feeling was indescribably delicious. She reached down, undoing the button at her waist, and her slacks fell to the ground. Then she bent her knees and pulled him down to the thick brown carpeting.

This couldn't really be happening, John thought. This was Genevieve, his buddy...

Afterward John was in a state of shock. All of his senses were intoxicated with her.

It was all wrong. Kathleen was the one in his fantasies, yet here he was with his arms around Genevieve Walters. His hands were caressing the smooth curves of her back. The feel of her against him was inexpressibly wonderful. He opened his eyes and gazed into her black ones. He looked down and saw her pure white skin next to his. She smelled fantastic. He squeezed her closer to him, kissing her forehead.

"Oh!" she said softly, and smiled.

This was a dream, John thought. In dreams if you moved too quickly you woke up. He didn't want this moment to end. So he held her gently, not even wanting to breathe. An emotional dam had burst within him, making him aware of feelings he had always had for her but never acknowledged. Kathleen was now utterly insignificant.

They had never had any long conversations in all the 10 years he had known her. Yet he always felt she was the closest person to him in the whole world. Now he was sure of it.

"Was I good?"

John was speechless. Good? There wasn't language to describe how great it was.

John raised himself on one elbow. "You were awesome. You *are* awesome." She smiled.

John ran his finger softly over her abdomen, tracing out the curves of her, and she sighed with pleasure. Well Mr. Williams, I found the right girl and she was right in front of my face all the time.

Genevieve lay back and felt his caresses, enjoying his gentle touch. Surprisingly she had enjoyed the sex. She'd thought about her and John before but wasn't sure reality would live up to her fantasies. He did not attempt to force her or go too fast. She glanced up at him and saw the love in his eyes. It melted her heart a little.

She knew there was really no need for protection, had known it since she was 13. It was part of the secret about herself she had discovered during their bike trip together to Hanford. The secret she didn't want to admit even to herself.

"You're almost too good to be true," John said.

For the first time in his life he saw pain in her eyes. Just for a brief instant. Then she smiled, a little sadly. The tender moment was broken. She sat up with her legs stretched out in front of her. John did likewise, facing her. "You were great John. I didn't know what to expect. That was about as good as I could have imagined."

John was surprised. "I didn't know you ever thought about sex."

"There's a lot you don't know about me."

"I want to know all I can," he said earnestly.

She grinned. "We're off to a good start."

"Are we boyfriend and girlfriend now?" John asked.

Genevieve put her hand to chin and pondered that for a few moments. "I don't know.... I'll have to think about it."

She saw the hang-dog look as he dropped his head in disappointment. She quickly put her arms around him and smiled. "I was just kidding you big idiot."

John brightened instantly and beamed at her.

He's just a big puppy, she thought. Did he love her? She wasn't sure. She wasn't sure what love was. It had to feel good, and this felt good. Maybe being a girl wasn't so bad after all. Something inside her was happy and glowing.

He was totally open to her. She decided she liked that, but could she open up to him in the same way? Did she even want to?

Now they both heard the sound of a car door slamming.

"Uh oh, Dad's home. Let's get our clothes on!"

The next day John walked over to Genevieve's. John banged the big lions head knocker and Genevieve opened the door. She looked up at him, smiling shyly. John realized it was totally different now. He noticed the sun on her hair, the angle of her face, her clothes, a million subtle nuances of body and demeanor he was never aware of before. She was a constantly changing sculpture. His girl.

"Can I come in?"

She turned and walked slowly from the foyer into the living room. He noticed how graceful she was and how her hair rustled slightly as she moved.

Genevieve sat down on the sofa where they had been together hundreds of times. He hesitated. She nervously patted the space beside her. "It's OK."

They both knew it was a lot more than OK. There was an electric energy between them now, pulsating. He lowered himself slowly beside her, turning his body slightly to the right to see her face. John could feel his rapid breathing. Genevieve looked nervous and a little uncomfortable. He could see she was breathing hard too.

"It's a nice day, why don't we go for a walk?" she said.

"OK."

He waited for her to rise first but she was waiting for him. They both laughed timidly.

"I'll get up first," John said. He got to his feet and held out his hand. As her hand touched his he felt a wave of electricity surge through his body. He heard her intake of breath and he almost let go of her.

He gently raised her as if she was a precious and fragile work of art. They walked out the front door and onto the sidewalk. It was a gorgeous summer day. The birds were chirping and the air smelled fragrant and full of life. John turned left and Genevieve turned right and they bumped into each other. He backed off quickly.

"Sorry, I didn't mean..."

"That's OK John. Let's walk down to Barton Street and back."

She stepped forward. John placed himself closest to the street so he could protect her from runaway cars. As they strolled slowly down the sidewalk an anxious excitement built up between them. For the first time in his life he didn't know what to say to his friend. Everything had changed profoundly.

John looked down at the girl/woman beside him and his heart swelled. Is this what it felt like to be in love? He longed to put his arm around her but he didn't know whether he should. That's stupid. Yesterday he had touched her in the most intimate places. Today it was different.

He hesitantly reached his right arm and was about to place it on her hip, but quickly withdrew. She glanced up at him reassuringly. His arm gently curved around her waist and he felt the delicious curve of her hip. He saw her smile as she looked shyly down at the ground. Suddenly the tension broke. It felt right, totally natural. He had his arm around his lady and she was content. They continued their walk in silence, reveling in the feelings that coursed between them.

When they got back to Genevieve's he felt like a boy on his first date, bringing his girlfriend home to the stern father. Standing outside the front door he handed her into the foyer.

John smiled. "Thank you for the walk. It felt great."

"It was great," she said.

There didn't seem to be anything else to say. She slowly closed the door.

John turned a little to face the street and stood unmoving on the porch for several minutes, staring into space.

From inside Genevieve saw John through the small window panel. His mouth was slightly open. She knew he was mesmerized with her, thinking only of her. It filled her with a sense of wonder but also a little fear. She had never, in her entire life, been the exclusive object of anyone's attention. She had never been loved. It was an almost overpowering feeling. She watched as he slowly turned and walked off the porch and down the street.

John began the walk home in a daze. A feeling of expanding warmth coursed through his heart. He began to walk faster and faster, feeling more and more excited. By the time he reached the door of the Frankel house on Magnolia Street he was positively exhilarated. His heart was bursting with joy. He had found a whole new aspect to his life.

That night Robert said, "What's with you son?"

"Uh, nothing dad. Feeling cheerful I guess." Robert looked at Rachel and then back at John. "There's something else. Come on, out with it."

"Well, if you must know, I'm happy because Genevieve said she'd be my girl-friend."

"I thought you had the hots for that violinist," Robert said. "Besides, Genevieve's a tomboy."

"Not any more." Well, maybe a little bit. But it didn't matter.

John knew that dad didn't get it. He glanced up and saw his mother's look of total understanding. John's eyes widened. "How...how..." he stammered. She knew. She knew everything.

Rachel walked over to her son. She put her hands on his chest and looked up into his eyes. He was now at least 5 inches over 6 feet and was growing into manhood. She was almost sad to see the boy leave and the man emerge. She was so proud of him. She knew he was gentle, strong, and wise; she could just feel it. Whoever got him was going to be a lucky woman.

John didn't need to ask her any questions. Rachel's smile and her demeanor indicated her approval and her love for him.

He bent down and kissed the top of her head. "Thanks mom, you're so cool."

That was music to Rachel's ears. To be called 'cool' by her son! It was some-thing every parent longed for. In her heart she was happy and relieved. She had not lost him.

John was almost 17 now and growing more and more independent. But he didn't seem to have any focus. She had been worrying about his future and his career. From offhand remarks he had made to her, she suspected he had no interest in university. This was shocking to her. John was brilliant and it would be a shame to waste such a fine mind. Her worst fears saw her son in a dead-end job, with no future. Maybe the Walters girl would help him get his focus. She was a straight A student and her father was one of the most respected researchers at Carleton.

Robert said, "Am I missing something?"

"Yes dear. I'll tell you about it when we go to bed."

Robert turned to his son. "Just don't get her pregnant for God's sake."

More words of wisdom from his sensitive and understanding father, John thought. "Thanks dad, I won't."

The next day John stopped at the school. The halls were still empty during the sum-mer break. His footsteps echoed on the dark brown linoleum. The place smelled like the floors had been mopped with a disinfectant.

Genevieve did volunteer work at East High, mostly tutoring summer school freshman and sophomores in math. He spotted her at her locker. "Hi Gen!"

John was still buzzed from their walk yesterday. Last night he had meant to work on the code but he couldn't think of anything but her. The memory of her drove away all attempts at reason. He was still amazed at the feelings she had un-leashed in him.

"Oh, hi John."

Is that all? John was disappointed. He had expected at least a cheerful greeting and maybe even a kiss. He wanted to feel some part of her against him once more.

"Is there something wrong?"

"No, nothing."

She was back to her usual aloofness toward him as if the events of the past two days had never occurred. As always, her eyes met his with complete attention. Behind those eyes that special feeling was gone.

"Can we talk tonight? I've got an algebra student that doesn't seem to get it."

"Sure." John shuffled his feet, hoping for something more. Genevieve turned and walked into one of the classrooms.

As John walked back down the hall he tried to figure it all out. "I guess I just don't understand girls."

John's pace quickened. He walked out of the front door and got onto his bike, pedaling rapidly to the pool hall on the Carleton campus. Freddy would be there. He was three years older.

Freddy was no help at all. "Girls? I've had five girlfriends and it didn't work out with any of them. I don't even bother anymore."

"Yeah, but I really like this one."

"Sorry John, I got no help for you. C'mon, let's play. I'll show you a new shot I just learned."

They played for two hours and John gradually got into it. On the way home he realized he hadn't thought of Genevieve for at least an hour.

After dinner he felt even better. He told himself that he wasn't going to let a girl get him down, no matter how much he liked her.

They were all around the table in the kitchen when his phone rang. It was Genevieve. "Could you call me back in thirty seconds? Thanks."

He walked upstairs to his room, but not before he heard Robert laugh. "Girl trouble already! Hasn't even been 48 hours yet."

Rachel frowned.

His mobile rang. "Gen?"

"Hi John."

"Uh, I'm not sure what we need to talk about."

"I'm not sure either."

She wasn't helping at all. It was back to her usual terse responses. "Uh, I just wondered if anything had changed between us."

"Not that I know of."

It was weird. He was doing the girl thing and she was doing the guy thing. "Do you still like me?"

"Of course I still like you! Why would you say that?"

"Never mind. I just thought that after yesterday..."

She cut him off. "Look John, something really nice happened but that doesn't mean we have to get married. I mean, I like you but I'm not going to sleep with you every day if that's what you're thinking."

Funny she should say that. That's exactly what he was thinking.

"Are you still there?" she asked.

"Yeah, sorry." He tried to keep the disappointment out of his voice. "You're right. I guess we'll just continue on the same as before."

John heard her sigh of relief. "John, I...I don't feel like I really know how to be a girl anyway."

Huh? He didn't get what she meant. "What are you talking about? You're beautiful!"

"Typical boy. I'm talking about my feelings and you're talking about my body."

Oh for God's sake. He had a lot more feelings than she did. Now she was using them as a club to beat him over the head. John was smart enough not to tell her that. Something of Mr. Williams' advice had sunk in.

"Sorry, I guess I don't know what you mean when you say you don't know how to be a girl. You're the most amazing girl I've ever met."

Genevieve ignored that. "All the other girls think I'm weird. They all wear strange clothes and makeup and jewelry and I don't do any of that stuff. They're always talking about boys and I'm just not interested in the same things. Sometimes I feel like I'm a hundred years old when I'm around them. I've never had a mother and I don't know how a girl is supposed to be."

That was the most revealing speech John had ever heard from her. "That's OK. Just be you. I liked you before we had sex and I'll like you even if I never get to touch you again." He paused. "But I sure would like to."

She laughed uproariously. "Oh John, you're so funny sometimes. I like you too. Let's just be like we always were."

"OK."

Now she was cheerful. "Good. I thought I was going to have to be a 'girlfriend' and I really don't feel comfortable with that." Genevieve said the word like it was a disease.

John received a glimmering of comprehension. "I think I get it. You see the other guys and girls and you don't want to be limited by what they do."

"That's right. I'm so glad you understand."

John felt better too. He didn't want to be like the other kids either. "We'll just be weird together."

"Good! See you tomorrow? I want to go to the lake and do some swimming."

That sounded good to him because he could see her in her swim suit. If he couldn't go to bed with her at least he could see her half naked.

"OK. I'll call you tomorrow morning."

For the rest of their summer vacation they just hung out as usual. Genevieve began to open up to him a little more but not anything like those two magical mid-August days.

During the next two weeks John tackled the code book again but got nowhere. Help was needed. The most obvious candidate was Mr. Walters. John had been in that library of his, which probably contained thousands of books on every conceivable subject. The only problem was that the guy was cold and intimidating. Michael Walters scared the crap out of him. He would approach him anyway because he just had to solve the mystery of that book. While he was there he'd ask him about Genevieve.

Two days later John left Rachel and Genevieve chatting at the kitchen table and drove over to the Walters' in Robert's car. A feeling of dread sat heavily in the pit of his stomach. He remembered the time several years ago when Mr. Walters caught him taking a book down from one of the library shelves.

"What are you doing in here?"

He was 10 at the time. John whirled around, frightened. The book fell from his hands to the floor with its binding bent backwards.

"Now see what you've done!" Walters' swarthy face was creased in planes of anger as he scooped the precious book from the floor. He smoothed its pages and replaced it reverently on the shelf.

"Uh, sorry sir..."

"You're not to enter this room except when I'm here and only after getting my permission. Is that understood?"

John gulped. "Yes sir."

Wow. One sentence and he was Michael Walters' slave forever. Did he always speak like this to Genevieve? John wondered how she could take it.

John stopped at the traffic light. In all the years he'd known Genevieve she had almost never talked about herself or volunteered any information about herself. John realized with a shock that his friend had deliberately withheld anything that would lead to a discovery of her origins.

Why would she do that? Was there something about her she didn't want anyone to know? If so, why? Despite his fear of her father John was determined to get some answers.

John parked the car in the turnaround and let himself in the back door, heading for the sanctum sanctorum. The big oak door was slightly ajar. The swarthy face of Michael Walters was visible at his desk. John knocked quietly.

"Yes?"

"Can I come in for a second sir?"

"Oh it's you John. Come on in."

John entered his favorite place other than the stacks at the Full Moon. He surveyed the bookshelved walls, all four of them stacked from floor to ceiling. The big room was lit only by a single ceiling fixture and smelled of stale coffee and old cigarette smoke. An overflowing ashtray spilled a few cigarette butts upon the polished wood surface of the desk. The walls behind the bookshelves were covered with dark paneling. The floor had the same dark brown carpeting as in the living room. Other than the single window to the left of the desk, every single inch from floor to ceiling held a book. He knew he didn't have much time so he waded right in.

"I would like to start by asking you a few questions about Genevieve sir." John spoke hesitantly, not looking directly at the somewhat forbidding countenance of the older man.

"What's there to ask?" Walters was slightly irritated. "You've known her since you were a child."

John gulped. "Yes that's true. But I don't know anything *about* her. For instance, where was she born? Who were her parents? She doesn't look anything like either of you."

Michael Walters took off his glasses. John heard the soft double-click as he folded them up and placed them gently upon the desk. He raised his head and gave John his undivided attention. For a few moments the older man scrutinized him, discerning hidden intent. "OK John. My first wife and I couldn't have children. We decided to adopt. Or rather, she decided to. As you know, our marriage didn't work out and I was left with Genevieve to take care of. I have done the best I could with her. I know I haven't been a good father to her. My relationships with the opposite sex have been ...well... rather strained."

John felt uncomfortable. He didn't want to pry into Michael Walters' personal life. He felt that the conversation was detouring off the purpose. John wanted to make the older man feel more at ease.

"I understand, sir. I think she turned out well though, don't you think? My questions are about her background. You must have noticed there is something distinctive about her appearance and demeanor. The almost red lips and pure white skin, for instance. Her completely black hair and pupils. Her features are almost too fine, like they were sculpted or drafted on a CAD program. She's just *different*, but not like any other different I've ever seen. She's...well...almost unearthly."

As John recited his little monologue Michael Walters sat up straighter and straighter in his chair. The swarthy man's eyes locked on his and betrayed a sense of alarm.

"John," he said very quietly. "You haven't been poking around in my desk have you?"

There was a subtle but implied threat in the question and John's heart began to pound. Again he understood exactly what happened to Ricky Davis at that baseball game. Just like Genevieve, this man exuded an aura of tremendous power.

"No sir. And I've never gone in here but with your permission, as you requested."

Walters questioned John with his eyes, then relaxed.

"All right then. Genevieve was adopted before my wife and I moved to Midland. We were married as graduate students at a university in another state. We found her in an orphanage, abandoned by her parents. She was the most unusual child both of us had ever seen. My wife wanted her right away, and the orphanage people were relieved. They were afraid that because of her unusual appearance no one would take her."

It was a good story, John thought. Mr. Walters was reciting it like a prepared speech. "You don't happen to know who her parents were do you sir?"

Michael Walters eyes flashed anger for a moment. "No John. The people at the orphanage are too busy trying to find homes for abandoned children without conducting genealogy surveys and private investigations on top of it."

John smiled. Mr. Walters had a very well-hidden sense of humor, very droll, just like Genevieve. Was his story just a smokescreen? Could father and daughter really be related?

He inspected the man across the desk. A wide swarthy face with high cheekbones. Thick, coarse black hair and a wide jaw. Deep set eyes with bushy brows that came almost together at the bottom of his forehead. Dark skin for a white guy. The hair is right, and the cheekbones, but the rest?

"Thank you sir. I wondered, can I get in here tomorrow night to look at your linguistics shelf? There's a book I'm studying with a code I can't crack. Dad isn't interested."

Michael Walters was intrigued. His protective cloak vanished when John changed the subject. "Why don't you bring the book over here tomorrow after dinner?" He paused. "Genevieve is taking some meals with you now, is that correct?" The corners of Walters' mouth turned up slightly in a little man-to-man smile that said, "I know you've been sleeping with her."

John flushed nervously, giving himself away. He felt like running out of the room. His curiosity kept him in the chair.

"I'll bring it over around 7 tomorrow, how's that?"

"That will be fine."

Walters picked up his glasses and began perusing the document on his monitor screen. John was forgotten.

John let himself out. In the evening cool he reviewed what had occurred during the interview. The man was definitely hiding something. John mulled over his responses and decided that he was going to look a little deeper into this story.

During the drive home John thought about the book and Genevieve's indifference toward it. When he described to her the amazing images and his experiences with them, she had just shrugged. "That's nice."

"That's nice?"

"I told you the book was interesting."

From that time forward she hadn't said another word about it.

Genevieve's curiosity almost matched his own. Why would she dismiss something so extraordinary?

John recognized that he understood hardly anything about the people that were closest to him. Were they all just mysterious or did he have some gigantic character flaw?

HONK!!!

Shit! He had just run a red light and almost got run over by a furniture truck.

John spent the rest of the drive home trying to concoct a plan for finding out about Genevieve's past.

Precisely at 7 the next evening John knocked on the closed library door.

"Come in."

John entered and placed the book on the desk. Mr. Walters put on his glasses and studied it for a few seconds. A slight upturn at the mouth told John he recognized something. "Have you seen this before, sir?"

Mr. Walters didn't answer. Instead, he lifted the book and inspected the front and back covers. He rested it in both hands for a moment and leafed through the pages. Then he placed the book on the desk.

"Well John. What do you make of it?"

"I think it's a manual sir."

"What else have you gleaned from your study of the book?"

John was a little uncomfortable. He felt like a student undergoing an examination. "At first I thought it was just a really cool book that showed some really interesting places and descriptions of them. Like a fantasy or science fiction novel. Now I'm beginning to think that the book is an instruction set for attaining altered states of awareness. The drawings are the author's impressions of, I don't know, various places. He has apparently experienced them using an unknown protocol." John held the book up, face open toward the desk. "The more I look at these drawings the more I am drawn into them. If this really is a manual I'm fired up to decipher the code and try it for myself."

Mr. Walters said nothing. John could see he was listening intently.

"There are 124 textual symbols and 5 that are completely different from the others. Genevieve gave me this book months ago but I haven't been able to make much progress on decoding it. I copied each symbol as accurately as I could and put them into tables."

Michael Walters' eyes widened a little. "I believe you're on the right track."

"You can tell all that by leafing through a few pages?"

"I am familiar with such books." He pointed to the shelf of esoteric and metaphysical volumes.

John waved his hands at the crowded walls and their row upon row of books. "You've read all these? There must be several thousand in your library."

"Almost all of them."

"If you could tell me what you make of this code, sir, I'd appreciate it." John placed some printouts with his tables of symbols on the dark oak desktop.

"There are four tables here which show where every symbol appears, the line numbers, page numbers, the number of times it appears on each page and in the entire text. These tables represent my best guesses as to the combinations of symbols which might represent concepts. I still have not been able to make sense out of them."

Michael Walters carefully perused the data. "This is excellent work, John. The reason you have not been able to make sense of the symbols is because you have been treating them as alphanumeric. Each of these symbols represents a separate idea or a thing; somewhat similar to the ideograms of Chinese. In English, for example, we have a clearly delineated alphabet which can be combined in a variety of ways to form words. The words then represent concepts."

"I'm kicking myself because I should have thought of that."

Mr. Walters leaned back in his chair, softening a little. "This is your first book of arcana. I have studied dozens of alchemy, metaphysical, magick and other sacred texts. And several linguistics textbooks. I have quite a bit more experience than you." He smiled.

"Now John, we have to determine whether these symbols represent things for which we have a point of reference. If not, I'm afraid that the text will be untranslatable."

John muttered to himself. "Hadn't thought of that either."

Mr. Walters smiled again. John had seen him smile twice now in ten seconds. That's twice more than in the last ten years. The man's thick swarthy face with the deep set eyes and bushy eyebrows gave him the appearance of a Neanderthal. It was amazing that a head like that could contain such a broad intelligence.

Walters studied the text for a couple of minutes, then pointed to a symbol of a funny looking figure with a handle that seemed to close in on itself in a very odd fashion.

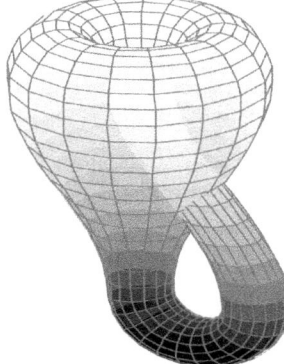

"That looks a little like a Klein bottle," Walters said.

John was trying to look sideways at the book on Walters' desk. "A Klein bottle?"

"A closed surface with no interior and only one surface. An ant could crawl around on the inside and the outside of it and never come to an edge. You could place a symbol on it, move it around, and it would appear backwards in the same place. That's because the handle doesn't intersect the surface of the bottle even though it is impossible to show that in the diagram."

John moved the book closer so he could see. As he looked at the symbol his awareness seemed to twist, or rotate, in a funny way. He could see how the handle could return into the bottle without meeting the bottle's surface..."Holy shit!"

"In order to understand the figure, take a piece of paper and roll it up so one edge meets the other in a cylinder. Now make the two opposite holes come together, while twisting the cylinder."

John tried it with a piece of scrap paper from the older man's desk.

"I can't."

"That's correct John," the older man said indulgently. "An extra dimension is required to perform the second operation successfully."

"I don't understand why something so improbable is included in the text. What's it doing in there?"

Walters frowned. He went up to one of the shelves and brought down a book. He looked in it briefly and came back to the desk. "In order to understand the symbol it is necessary to radically shift your reference points. In this context that symbol probably represents changing one's frame of reference or focus of attention."

"Cool!" John beamed at the man behind the desk. For the first time he recognized that this cold and sterile person was actually a real human being. Someone with a deep and vast understanding.

"Mr. Walters, thank you so much. Your information has given me a base from which to proceed." John found himself speaking as precisely as the man across from him. "I thought my study of these symbols was fruitless but I was just working from the wrong orientation."

"Yes. When fundamental assumptions change a whole new data set can result."

At that moment John understood that he had far more in common with this man than with his own father. Robert Frankel was brilliant but limited to his own sphere. This man had a deep and wide ranging intelligence. There was a power within him, an inner strength that John felt very strongly.

"Mr. Walters, I .... I want to say that.... I think we have a lot in common."

John saw the man's eyes briefly fill with tears. He realized with a jolt that Michael Walters was terribly lonely. What vast, unexplored depths lie between those brows? John wanted desperately to talk to this man and draw him out. He wanted to pick his brain and find out what made him tick. There was something deep and wise within him that was yearning to come out into the open.

The older man looked across the desk at the son he never had. If only.... He had to stop there or he would sink into the depressions that had occasionally resulted in bouts of drug and alcohol abuse. It hadn't worked out with his ex-wife or his daughter. But maybe this child of his acquaintance could be an outlet for him. He had so much to give but no one to give it to.

"John, why don't we make regular appointments to talk about the book, or anything else you'd like to discuss?"

John was thrilled. "I'd like that very much sir. I have a million questions I want to ask you."

Michael Walters leaned back in his chair with a deep sigh of contentment. "Well then, how about every Friday at 7 p.m.? If you have homework or are busy we can reschedule. I'm flexible." He looked at his schedule. "We can have our first appointment two weeks from this coming Friday."

John was genuinely pleased and interested. After all this was the father of his best friend and he didn't know a thing about him. Besides, school had begun again. If he had any questions he could zip over and consult the Oracle. John had a feeling this guy had the answers to everything.

John got up and offered his hand. "Let's shake on it."

The man and the boy clasped hands and smiled.

After John had gone Michael Walters got up from his chair and walked outside. For some reason unknown to him there was a warm feeling within him. Even though he would only talk with John briefly once a week he felt a renewed sense of satisfaction about his life. He knew he would look forward to these appointments and they would be the highlight of his week.

He had blown it with Debra and his daughter, and indeed with every woman he had ever been interested in.

Perhaps the boy would be different.

7

During the next four days John shut himself up in his room and worked on deciphering the symbols. He ignored his homework. Mr. Walters' suggestions had led to tentative translations for almost half of the pictograms. He also discovered that a pictogram could have a different meaning depending on which other pictograms surrounded it. This was a cool way to transmit information!

One evening after dinner Robert poked his head in the door and entered without knocking.

Robert saw John's books piled on the floor and his desk littered with papers covered in symbols. "You're going to get that homework done aren't you son?"

John jumped out of his chair and banged his knee on the desk. "For God's sake dad you scared the crap out of me!" Why couldn't Robert respect his privacy?

Robert's face was a study in irritation.

Oh no, here it comes. Another Lecture About Higher Education.

"I think you're spending entirely too much time with that stupid book."

John ignored him as cheerfully as he could through the pain. Sometimes that worked and the old man would just go away. Gingerly, he reseated himself and resumed his study.

"Don't ignore me. I asked you a question!"

No you didn't. You expressed your disapproval. Sighing, John turned slowly in his swivel chair and faced his father.

"Don't give me that. You'll show a little respect for your father."

You have to earn respect before you can demand respect, John thought. He didn't say it. He looked calmly at his father, waiting for him to make the next move.

This made Robert even more angry. His father strode across the room and took the codebook and John's papers off the desk.

"Get your homework done first, do you understand? You need top grades to get into the best schools."

Since when don't I have good grades, John wanted to say. His father was being totally irrational. He said nothing.

Robert reached down. He grabbed the pile of class books from the floor and slammed them down on the desk, almost knocking over his laptop. "This is where you should be concentrating your attention."

John stared at the textbooks which were lying about on his desktop. "American History, 1865–1945." "Biology, Science of Life." "Probability and Statistics for Mathematicians and Scientists." "Discrete Mathematical Structures for Computer Science." He had little interest in any of them right now, especially the first two.

Robert shook John roughly by the shoulder. "Wake up before it's too late! I'm going to confiscate that crazy code book if you don't start shaping up." Robert stalked out of the room, leaving the door open.

John got up, walked to the door, and closed it.

Dad must have had another argument with mom. The home scene was getting more and more brutal. Robert was obviously dissatisfied with his marriage and mom was depressed about it. Neither of them knew how to make it better. If he ever had kids he'd treat them with more respect.

I'll take mom any day over dad, John thought. Underneath her intellectual exterior she was warm and loving. Dad was smart but he didn't seem to know himself or have any desire to.

John shoved the school books off the desk. He thought better of it and placed them in a neat little pile at the end. If the old man barged in again it would look like he'd completed the homework. He grabbed the code book, retrieved his papers, and tried to regain his focus.

As the school term unfolded John felt more and more disillusioned with the educational process. All of his classes were boring, especially the two advanced placement classes. Robert and Rachel had insisted. He groaned inwardly at the extra work involved. Mr. Barta, the Comp Sci teacher, had already assigned a difficult computer lab. Fortunately Genevieve was in this class and they'd be able to team up.

Genevieve hadn't said much to him for the past three weeks, noticing his complete immersion in the code translation. She had been invited to dinner every Wednesday at the Frankel's. Once, as John looked up abstractly, his mind on the code, she had smiled approvingly at him.

Rachel saw that smile and was pleased, interpreting it as a sign of affection for her son. She thought the two were perfectly matched. But they were too young to be having sex. She had cautioned Genevieve against it.

John sat at his desk on the Monday afternoon before his first scheduled appointment with Mr. Walters. It was amazing that in one short week Mr. Walters had become his mentor. Dad wouldn't know the answers to any of the questions that burned in his soul. He wouldn't even care, but Mr. Walters would. There was more love for him from the sterile recluse in that dark lonely house than from his own father.

A car horn outside brought John's attention back to the present. The codebook was open to the first image of the weird guy in the meadow. Why were these images only printed on one side of the paper? Idly, he flipped through a couple of the pages and understood. With growing excitement he returned to the first image and placed all of the relevant pages between his thumb and forefinger. He rapidly released them and saw a movie. Like an expanding balloon, the odd looking man became surrounded by a faint little sphere of light which grew larger and brighter. In the last image, the man was gone.

Where did he go? On impulse John went to the end of the book that contained the fascinating etchings. There were 32 of them including the beautiful, deserted porcelain city with its flat blue surface. It finally dawned on him that the book described a process whereby one could change the vibration of the field of energy around the body. When that happened...you went someplace.

With this new orientation John began to rapidly understand the symbols in his table. In a couple of hours he had his first translation of the book.

The manual outlined a series of mental protocols combined with a series of complex breathing techniques.

Breathing techniques were a part of yoga and almost all forms of meditation. But this was far more sophisticated. The mental protocols detailed the composition of something he translated as the Sphere of Consciousness. Inside this...thing... were templates that could be activated to attain altered states of awareness. It was like a vehicle for consciousness that could take you to different dimensions. Everybody had one apparently.

John shook his head. This material was way beyond him, or anything he had ever heard about in science fiction or fantasy. It was fantastic.

John picked up the book and examined it again. It didn't have a title, a printing date, an ISBN number, or even an author's name. There was nothing in the book that could give any clue to its origins. There was something else odd.

The blue cloth cover was fraying at the edges and the corners of the book were pushed in. It smelled musty, like it had been lying around on a shelf forever. You couldn't fake that.

The paper smelled the same way but it was completely unwrinkled. That didn't fit. An old book like this, the pages should be bent or crinkled and torn or smudged in places.

He felt the paper. It was yellowed but perfectly smooth. The coloring was unvarying throughout the page. Paper should not age so uniformly. After careful inspection of every page, his suspicion was verified. Each page was exactly the same. Not only that but the paper was unusually thick and did not feel like paper at all.

The symbols were all printed with impossibly fine resolution. He got a magnifying glass out of his desk drawer and examined one of the symbols. Under magnification John could barely make out an infinitesimally small dot. How could such a microscopic thing be printed? It couldn't, not even on the best printers. The symbol came into greater focus whenever he looked at it, just as the etchings did. It was alive!

It was impossible to print on any paper with such fine resolution, John decided. In his zeal to discover the book's meaning he had overlooked the obvious.

He looked up at the clock, which read 20 minutes after midnight. John closed the book and got ready for bed.

The next day John stopped Trevor Jones in the hall. "Trev, your dad is a librarian, right?"

"More than that. He runs the graduate library at Carleton. If you called him a librarian to his face he might give you a smack."

"I have a really old book that I got from the Full Moon, written in hieroglyphics. It has weird symbols and drawings. There's no title, no author, or anyplace to find out where it came from."

Trevor raised his eyebrows. "All books printed in the United States have a title page in front that identifies the author, publisher, date of publication, and the ISBN number."

"Maybe it wasn't printed in the United States," John offered.

"Any book in print must have a title page of some sort." Trevor spoke confidently.

John slammed his fist into his palm. "Right! That's why this one is so weird. It's really old but there should at least be an author's name. I wondered whether I could ask your dad a few questions about it."

Trevor smiled. How many times had he seen his father's eyes widen in excitement just anticipating a rare book? "Are you kidding? Dad would walk ten miles to see an unusual book. You can bring it over one night this week after dinner. I'll ring you tonight and let you know. Give me your number."

"That would be great. I'll be waiting for your call. Thanks!"

John liked the blond-haired pitcher for the East High baseball team. Trevor Devon Jones was always straight with him. He didn't get into any of the teasing and bantering so common with most guys.

All through the evening John waited for his phone to ring, but the only call they got was for Rachel. She was working hard on her latest book.

Finally, around 10, Trevor called.

"John, Trevor here. Dad says you can bring the book over after dinner tomorrow. 7-ish. Is that all right?"

"7 it is. Now I have to get your address. Never been to your house."

"Right! We're at 2135 Kingsley, on the south side close to campus. It's a dark blue house with a black metal gate."

The next day John couldn't wait for 7 o'clock. He sat through his classes without paying attention and got caught with his pants down by Old Man Masterson on a biology question. "Frankel! Where is the left occipital parietal suture?"

"Huh?" There were a few smirks and giggles. John didn't care.

"That's a point off your final exam Frankel," the white haired disciplinarian barked. "In my class you had better pay attention."

What a dickhead! Compared to Masterson his dad was a saint.

After school John wolfed down dinner and raced through his homework. He got the keys from Robert with a minimum of effort and drove over to Trevor's. The house was huge with a long blacktopped driveway that led to a gigantic four car garage. John parked in a large turnaround. He walked to the front along a path which, in warmer weather, would be surrounded by flower gardens. Standing at an enormous wooden door, he hit the doorbell. John expected to see a butler with white gloves, but he was greeted by Trevor.

"Hello John, come in. Father is with someone now but is anxious to see your book."

Trevor led him into a large foyer with a marble floor and high ceilings. They passed through a large, tastefully decorated living room painted in dark blue with white woodwork. Trevor directed him into a bright, well appointed library with dark green carpeting. The walls were painted in a rich, deep gold paint. The windows were stained glass. Books lined the walls but unlike the Walters' library it was bright and cheerful. The light coming into the room made fascinating patterns on the carpet. The office was beautiful and probably conducive to noble thoughts.

John was impressed so far. Clearly, the Jones' were wealthy but not ostentatious. Everything he had seen so far was of very high quality, but understated. "Dad will be in in a minute."

While they waited Trevor explained to John about his family. "The Jones family came originally from Welsch Flintshire. In 1853, William Jones left the lead mines and ventured across the ocean to the gold mines in Ballarat, Australia. He made a tidy fortune. He returned to England two years later and prudently invested his money in Shares. He moved to London and set himself up in fine style. William was ostracized by the rest of the hard working Jones clan. But his descendants, without the least sign of embarrassment, have enjoyed the fruits of his adventuring spirit."

John smiled. "I have no idea where the Frankel's come from."

Just then Mr. Jones came out of a small room in the back with another man, who saw himself out. He seated himself at a large cherrywood desk with a computer on it. The top of the desk had a few books and a neat stack of papers, covered by a beautifully carved crystal dove. He rose briefly to shake John's hand. "I'm Dalton Jones."

"John Frankel."

Mr. Jones was dressed in dark, well tailored pants and a light colored and tailored shirt. He looked comfortable and relaxed. John liked him immediately.

"Well John. Let's have a look at that book."

With a small magnifying glass Mr. Jones made a careful but interested inspection. John didn't tell him his suspicions about the paper or the dynamic nature of the symbols and etchings. He wanted to test this man's power of observation and his knowledge of books.

"Just as you say, John, there are no identifying pages. The cover looks old, as well as the paper." He paused for a moment and felt one of the pages. "The paper in this book is odd. It is very thick, unwrinkled, and shows no signs of wear."

Bingo.

Mr. Jones became more and more animated as he continued his examination. Finally he put down his glass and folded his hands underneath his chin.

"John, this is one of the most unusual books I have ever seen. I have to admit that I am very excited. Not only is the paper...unusual, but the detail of the text and images is astonishing. The printing resembles more a sophisticated electronic process." He shook his head in admiration and bewilderment. "I would like to take it to one of my friends in forensics in the Midland police department. He knows a gentleman who runs an independent materials analysis laboratory. My friend says this gentleman sometimes does sensitive work for the department. He also works for other researchers. This man will vouch for his integrity and confidentiality."

He looked hopefully at John. "Would you be willing to let me have the book for a couple of days? I'll return it by the weekend."

"Certainly sir." John said. Dalton Jones knew his business and he seemed to be a man of good character.

"Thank you very much for your help, Mr. Jones." John and Trevor walked out of the library and into the hallway. As they turned left out of the library, John noticed that the hallway continued into the house for at least another 120 feet. At the end it segued into a beautiful staircase up to the second floor. This place was a mansion!

"Thanks Trevor, I really appreciate it."

"Not a problem," said Trevor, and let John out.

The next two days passed by very slowly. On Friday, Trevor met him in the hallway.

"Dad wants you to come over right after school, if you can. He found something about your book. I've rarely seen him this excited."

"I'll be there between 4:30 and 5."

When he rang the bell at 4:45 a girl about 12 years of age opened the door. "Are you John?" she asked.

John nodded. The girl was well made and seemed sure of herself. There was good breeding in this family.

"Come in then." She announced him and showed him into the library.

Mr. Jones got right to the point, tapping his finger on the cover of John's book.

"John, we had Jim Sievers analyze this book. Understand that his reputation for accuracy is unquestioned. But what he found is astonishing and frankly not believable. The cloth cover and the cardboard are completely normal. But the material of the paper is a substance that is entirely unknown to him."

John's eyes widened in surprise.

"Not only that, but there is no glue in the binding. Somehow the pages hold together. We cannot determine how."

"But..."

"Let me explain," Dalton Jones interrupted. "There are a number of methodologies that can be used to identify a substance. We tried chemical, atomic emission and atomic absorption spectrometry, mass spectrometry, neutron activation, and X-ray fluorescence analysis with absolutely no results." Jones shook his head in disbelief.

"The material is chemically inert. Not even the strongest acids had any effect on it. It was impossible to burn. We placed it in a kiln and raised the temperature to 2000 degrees Fahrenheit with no effect. We bombarded it with radiation. Nothing we did even touched the stuff. The substance does not generate a spectrograph. It is completely unidentifiable. Sievers was personally insulted, for he was able to ascertain no positive information whatsoever from his analysis. It's the most astounding thing I've ever seen. I was personally present for most of the testing."

He showed John a neat little square cut out of the bottom right of the last page, which was blank. "I'm sorry, we had to take a small sample." John saw the slight flush on the older man's face.

Mr. Jones took out his wallet and carefully removed the square from between a folded piece of paper. "It took a lot of persuasion from Jim Sievers to acquiesce to that little sample. To despoil a book is a crime, particularly one so unusual. But Sievers' analysis clearly shows that this book cannot not be a book at all! In the interests of scientific investigation I reluctantly agreed to let Sievers continue his research. But I insisted on cutting the little square myself and getting your permission."

John looked his question.

"The substance cuts like ordinary paper. That's what upset Sievers so much. It's impossible."

He handed John the square of paper. "There is the remaining bit from your book, John."

It was unmarked.

"I wonder if you will allow me to keep this sample. I'd like to continue to try and identify it. Anomalies such as this don't sit well with me. I have a well ordered life and a well ordered mind. I intend to solve this riddle."

"Sure," John said. "If you need any more samples, just let me know."

John took the book. When he got home he immediately called Genevieve with the news. Oddly, she wasn't surprised. "That's interesting," was all she said.

"Interesting? Are you kidding?" John was flabbergasted at his friend's lack of enthusiasm. He hadn't seen much of his girlfriend for weeks, other than her appearance on Wednesdays at dinner. She was consciously avoiding him. Over the years he had learned not to press her. She would just clam up and become distant. So he said goodbye and assigned her behavior to that mysterious and unfathomable subject called 'women.'

On Friday at 7 p.m. John knocked tentatively on Michael Walters' library door for their first appointment. He had a list of three items he wanted to talk about.

"Is there such a thing as a human energy field? Some call it the merkaba. This book says there is and that it exists independently of the body. My father says it's all nonsense."

"Scientifically the idea is absurd. But my own research experience indicates the possibility of it." When John asked him to explain he clammed up. "I am unable to tell you anything further due to the classified nature of that research."

John shrugged. He knew he would get nowhere pursuing the subject. Like daughter, like father.

John showed the older man his Cliff Notes translation of the mysterious book. 'It's a manual, sir. A manual for altered states of consciousness."

They spent the next hour discussing and firming up John's translation. Upon that swarthy face John noticed a slight smile, like sunlight seeping through a heavy cloud cover. Underneath that passive exterior John felt that the older man was enjoying himself immensely.

"You are on the right track John. But I can go no further for the reasons I've given." John couldn't get over the feeling that Mr. Walters had already cracked the code and knew exactly what it said. He decided to change the subject.

"My parents are ragging me to go to Harvard but frankly sir, I'm getting a little tired of school."

Michael Walters frowned. "You may not want to hear this John, but I recommend a university education. You can get away from home and meet new people. You'll have lots of different opportunities for new experiences."

John was disappointed, but what answer could he reasonably expect? The man across the desk was an academic. "Where did you go to school, Mr. Walters?"

"I received a PhD from Michigan in molecular biology, and later, a second PhD in physics from CalTech. Although I am pretty much a recluse now, in my younger days I was a real hell-raiser."

Mr. Walters a hell-raiser? John didn't believe it until he related a few of his experiences.

The last item on John's agenda was the subject of his daughter. He expressed his sentiments about Genevieve. "I've been going with your daughter for a little while now. If I can be totally honest, I really love her. She's the deepest person I've ever met besides you. But she won't open up to me. She won't talk about herself. It's frustrating. Any ideas?"

Mr. Walters sighed. "I'm no use to you there John. I don't know my daughter very well. I don't know anyone very well because I've never bothered to find out about people. But now, I think, I... I think I'd like to start. I'm beginning to discover that true satisfaction can't be found only in the pursuit of knowledge." He stared out into space for a few moments.

"That might not seem like a big revelation to you but it sure is to me. Although it has been a fascinating journey, I know now I have been a fool. I've been looking for satisfaction in my library and my research and missing out on life."

Michael Walters took off his glasses and rubbed his eyes. John was quiet and sat very still. The older man was unburdening himself. John felt honored to be the recipient. No one had ever confided in him before.

"John, I've never been able to have a decent relationship with a woman. It's just never worked out for me. But when I see you with Genevieve sometimes my heart just breaks. The kind of love you have for her I have never been able to feel. I've been watching you John. You're a very admirable person. I'm learning a lot from you. I see how open you are with my daughter. I would like to be the same way."

John was astounded. "*You* want to learn from *me*?"

Mr. Walters smiled. "Yes John. We can learn from each other."

"Don't look so astonished boy! Just because you've lived 45 years does not mean you have done so successfully."

They were silent with their own thoughts for a time. John finally said, "I'll have to ask Genevieve what she wants to do. If she wants to get out of here after she graduates next year then I'm gone. I'm going to stick around until she finishes high school even though my parents won't like it." He had been postponing that confrontation for the past several weeks.

"I'm really not sure what I'm going to do with my life," John admitted.

Mr. Walters smiled again. "When you figure it out tell me."

During the next two months John was able to complete his translation of the code. There were five sections or stages for a technique that appeared to be a manual for a transformation of consciousness. The first two sections involved breathing and meditation. The next two sections were about activating the Sphere of Consciousness. The fifth stage was out of his depth so he dispensed with it. He printed up his English translation for the first four stages.

As John read his printouts he got excited. The 'sphere of consciousness' was some sort of invisible shell surrounding a human being that affected the body and interfaced with a universal energy field. This shell contained templates that could be activated by precisely targeted thought impulses. If he had translated it correctly the 'sphere of consciousness' was capable of doing some pretty amazing things. John's rational mind told him that it was just a cool science fiction or fantasy story. No rational person could take it seriously. Yet a feeling of inner excitement pervaded his being.

The next step was to actually try it. If it was crap then he'd have a good laugh at himself and give the book to Dalton Jones.

Two weeks after his first meeting with John, Michael Walters called Rachel Frankel.

"Hello Rachel. This is Michael Walters."

"Oh...hello Michael! What can I do for you?" Now here was a shot out of the blue. They hadn't spoken more than a dozen times in the past ten years. To Rachel the man's voice seemed softer and warmer. He sounded apologetic.

Michael explained, hesitantly, that it was about time they renewed their acquaintance. "After all, John and Genevieve have been best friends for years now."

Robert came into the kitchen and saw his wife's startled expression. "Who's that?"

Rachel covered her phone with her hand "It's Michael Walters! He wants to renew our acquaintance."

Robert laughed sarcastically. "What acquaintance?"

Rachel smiled. "Just what I was thinking." She uncovered the phone. "Perhaps you could come over to dinner on Wednesday. You probably know that Genevieve has been eating over once a week. You could join her." Rachel didn't know if the recluse had any idea where his daughter was on Wednesday evening. Or any evening.

On the other end of the line Michael Walters felt a rush of anxiety in the pit of his stomach. He hadn't socialized in so long he didn't remember how to talk to people. He tried to sound confident and happy. "I'd like that, if it wouldn't be too much trouble."

"No trouble at all. Why don't you come around 6 and we'll have dinner at 7. That will give us time to talk." She'd make a goulash that would simmer happily on the stove. They'd have wine and a salad that could be prepared beforehand.

And so it came to pass that the Walters' were regular guests at the Frankel's one evening a week.

Late one Saturday morning just before Christmas Robert, John, and Rachel were in the living room,. The doorbell rang and the front door opened, letting in a blast of cold air. Michael Walters stomped the snow off his shoes and came striding in.

"I hope I'm not interrupting anything?"

Walters carried a briefcase from which he took a sheaf of papers. He tossed them onto the short legged table in front of the couch. The title page read, "Study Program for John Frankel, B.S. M.S."

"What's this?" Robert inquired.

John leafed through the document and saw carefully printed lists of courses and books. The last paper had a list of names.

"It's your study program," he said to John. "You can complete it right here at Carleton. It's an accelerated 4 to 5 year program of intensive study. At the end you will achieve a Master's Degree if your thesis is accepted. I have talked to all the Department Heads and have gotten their provisional approval." He looked at Rachel. "Final approval is dependent on John's SAT scores. Some of the faculty are still doubtful even though John's grades are satisfactory."

At first Robert was shocked. His plans for John were set. There was now enough money to pay for classes and accommodation for three years at an Ivy League school. If John received a scholarship he would not have to work and would be able to devote full attention to his studies. Now here was Michael Walters suggesting that John attend Carleton! Robert was inclined to perceive it as a slap in the face. But Walters would have had no idea of his plans for John. Unless John already told him.

John picked up the document and looked at the list of courses, and a whole bunch of books that sounded really interesting. "This is much more interesting than boring old school texts. It almost makes me *want* to hit the books again."

Walters smiled. "There are plenty of boring texts in there, I'm afraid. I've spiced up the lot. This is not a standard Masters program. It's personalized specifically for you."

John placed the papers carefully back upon the table and began to consider his options. Michael Walters had waltzed in here like a knight in shining armor, presenting him with an opportunity that fit perfectly with his stated preferences. Clearly, Walters had listened carefully to every word he'd spoken. He had taken him seriously. This hard and taciturn man had blossomed into a true friend. John could tell by his slight smile of satisfaction that Michael Walters had taken this surprise action as his personal gift to him.

Robert bent over the document. Despite himself he too became excited about the program and the book list. "I've read some of these...but the rest...why, this could easily be extended to a Doctor of Philosophy program."

Rachel came over. She sat on the couch with John and Robert. Rachel was secretly pleased. She had agreed with Robert that John should attend an Ivy League school but she didn't want him to leave home. He was the buffer between Robert and herself. She loved her son and wanted to be near him. Walters' proposal was help from an unexpected direction.

"Yes," said Walters, looking at Robert and Rachel. "I have been talking with John and have learned his areas of interest. The entire program could be modified for a doctorate in linguistics, mathematics, or computer science, depending on John's preferences."

Michael Walters leaned back on the sofa. He felt inordinately pleased with himself. The three Frankels were not only appreciative of his efforts but openly admiring. It had been a long time since he felt so much love. No, it had been a long time since he felt *any* love.

Robert understood that Walters was offering John an education at least as good as he could get at an elite university.

"I would like to offer my services as John's faculty advisor," Waters offered.

"Accepted." John said it quickly, without thinking.

Uh-oh, what have I gotten myself into? Four to five more years of school! Rachel and Robert wouldn't let him go back on his word now. Glancing up at Michael Walters, he felt it might be OK.

"Will I be able to study with you sir?"

Walters smiled. The planes of his face cracked open to reveal just a little of the man inside. "I think that could be arranged." Yes, he could help this boy. Together they would fly through the material and he could unburden himself of the vast knowledge he had accumulated over the past 25 years. With his help the boy could complete the Masters program in four years. If he had the intelligence and the desire. It would also keep Robert and Rachel off John's back.

Michael Walters saw a little of himself in the Frankel boy. Mainly he wanted to interact with someone he was beginning to admit a genuine fondness for. Although he was well respected at work his natural off-putting demeanor discouraged others from seeking him out. For the totality of his career up till now, that's just the way he wanted it. John would be his guinea pig. If he could successfully tutor the boy without ruffling his feathers then perhaps he could open up to his colleagues as well. He would know more about the boy and through him, about people in general.

Walters interrupted his musings and returned his attention to the tableau in front of him. The Frankels were all three bent over his document, their heads almost touching as they commented on it.

The eyes of Michael Walters teared briefly as he observed the easy familiarity each had with the other. It was something he had never experienced in his entire life.

Robert finished his inspection of the document and nodded his approval. Rachel almost jumped for joy. The Frankels looked toward Michael Walters expectantly.

"John would have to choose a major," he said. "Apologies to you Rachel, but I would not recommend philosophy. I have weighted the program toward linguistics and mathematics. You could choose your interests from a great variety of sub-disciplines. You might possibly even use your book decoding as your Masters thesis. It's dicey. I'll talk to Jane Arnold about that. She's the head of the Linguistics Department."

John thought for a moment. "Linguistics sounds good. I've always wanted to learn French and Spanish. A minor in math or algorithms maybe. I've a head for it."

While the others discussed the program Robert had a selfish thought. If John attended classes here they would save an awful lot of money set aside for his education at Harvard. Rachel and he could do some traveling. Maybe a change of scenery would be beneficial for their marriage. Rachel's lack of interest in sex had left him feeling frustrated and unwanted. Robert glanced down at his growing paunch. It was embarrassing. In his college years he had been on the track team, long distance. He couldn't even run to the corner now without collapsing.

Robert Frankel looked over at his son. The boy needed to get some exercise as well.

Robert interrupted the flow of conversation and turned to John. "I just had a thought, not to change the subject. You need to include an exercise regimen in this program. I don't want you turning out like Walters here, hiding out in the library."

Walters grabbed the document and pointed to the Appendix. "Thirty minutes per day at least 3 days a week must be spent in some kind of vigorous exercise that breaks a sweat. An overloaded mind coupled with a flabby body may lead to anxiety or even illness."

Robert clapped his hands. "That's very good Walters! John, do you want to go running with me or are you ashamed to be seen around town with your old man?"

John couldn't imagine running with his father, or at all. He was diplomatic. "I'll consider it. I've been doing a little weight lifting but I'm thinking of joining the table tennis group Bill Richardson is getting together at school. He's taking lessons and says it's helping his quickness and coordination for baseball."

"Table tennis?" Robert spoke sarcastically. "What the hell's that?"

"I'll tell you later dad."

Robert turned his attention back to Michael Walters. "What are YOU going to do about exercise?"

"I've already started," Walters replied. "My last checkup revealed a few problems and I am determined to overcome them. I'm trying to stop smoking and drinking coffee. I've started walking half a mile every day after dinner. I'm going to begin jogging once my body gets used to the activity. My goal is to be able to run 3 miles without stopping before the year is out."

"Excellent. Maybe we could go out together once in a while. We'll leave John to his *table tennis*."

"I'd like that," Walters replied.

There was a pause in the conversation. Robert looked at his watch. "Why don't you stay for lunch Michael?"

Michael Walters brightened some more. "I'd like that," he repeated.

John no longer had time to test out the technique in the codebook. School-work, the upcoming senior SAT's, and his fascination with Michael Walters were uppermost in his mind and occupied all of his free time.

Rachel looked forward to Wednesday's when the Walters' came for dinner. She once again found joy in her kitchen and the preparation of good food. Their family was getting bigger. Maybe John and Gen would get married and have chil-dren. Then she'd have grandkids to do for. Despite her choice of career over family, the longing for grandkids and family connections was strong within her.

Genevieve was overjoyed to see her father at table and was delighted to see his occasional smile. She had time to observe him during these get togethers and realized how solid and emotionally distant he was. Was she like that too? It was not an appealing thought.

Robert reluctantly accepted John's choice of a girlfriend. Something about her had always rubbed him the wrong way. Her skin was too pale, her lips too red, and her features too fine. She was...artificial. She was cold and aloof like her father. Her only saving grace was her intelligence and the good manners she had somehow picked up. He held her at gaze as she talked to Rachel across the table from him. The girl was definitely too small-town for John. She had reeled him in, but it might be better for John to get out of Midland and see a different part of the world. John should play the field and get to know other women.

Robert was having second thoughts about this program of Michael Walters. If he sent John out of town he'd graduate with a pedigreed diploma. And most important, Genevieve would have to stay in Midland for another year until she finished high school. Then the relationship might fall apart. He'd have to spend his nest-egg but he was planning to spend it anyway. The vacation with his wife could wait.

9

The Eyrie

K JIRSTEN continued to follow John's movements. She was frustrated. The intervention of Michael Walters had sidetracked John's attention. The boy's focus was now on the irrelevancy of the earthian study program and the exploration of the older man's mind.

She uttered a Lyran oath. Neither the boy nor the man had a clue about the big wide galaxy and its influence on the present earthian civilization. All of Michael Walters' knowledge was fragmented, a grasping at windmills.

The Denebians, Sirians, Arcturans, Vegans, Pleiadians, and particularly the Orions had been active on the planet within the last 1,000 years. They had begun to push the earthians along in their development. Nevertheless, earthian science, philosophy, and medicine were barbaric. Their ignorance of the Vessel of Life was appalling. But something spectacular was occurring on this primitive planet, an evolutionary leap in consciousness. So far this had manifested only among a tiny minority of the population. But it was spreading rapidly. The Frankel boy had the potential to be one of the best ever and the situation was getting more and more desperate.

From her vantage point at the edge of the all-that-is she had seen John's translation of the planted book. It was sufficient. He had only scratched the surface of the symbolic text but it would be enough. Now she had to hope that his interest would be rekindled. She knew how she could nudge him a little.

10

GENEVIEVE was weird. A lot weirder than him. John walked into her room on a cold Wednesday afternoon in early April of his senior year. There was a peculiar shimmering in the air of the room around her body. The air smelled fresh like after a summer rain. She sat in a chair in the middle of the room, a look of complete well-being on her face. "Hi John!" she said cheerfully.

"What're you doing?"

"Oh, just thinking that's all." She smiled, gave him a wink, and flounced out of the room.

Thinking?

A lightbulb went off in his head. That crazy book he had translated talked about a "sphere of consciousness" that supposedly surrounded every person. Could Genevieve know about that? She had turned him on to the book. Was she doing the technique? He had lost interest in that stuff.

Since that wonderful time last August he had tried to get her to talk about herself. "I want to find out a little more about you," he said to her one day, trying to draw her out.

"Not much to tell; you've been my friend since childhood." That was as much as he could get out of her.

John asked Rachel if Genevieve could sleep over in his room, expecting a flat refusal. Rachel offered little objection. For once she overruled her husband.

"They're too young to be sleeping together," Robert protested. "You said it yourself. She's not right for John. At school they all think she's a weirdo." He was marshaling arguments that didn't make sense even to himself, trying to justify his gut feeling about the Walters girl.

Rachel snorted. "It's obvious he loves her, I can see it in his eyes and the way he treats her. They've been friends since childhood and they understand each other. Besides, they're already having sex." Genevieve had told her that during one of their talks.

Robert's eyes widened. "They are? I thought it was only that one time."

Rachel looked scornfully at her husband. "I've known it for months. I told you last summer but you wouldn't listen."

"Damn kid," Robert grumbled. Another point against Genevieve, using sex to entrap his son. Women had all the advantages in that department. Then he remembered one fine evening spent in the back of an old Chevy when he was only 17. That little fact undermined his argument and added to his upset. He felt as if the train had already left the station with Genevieve and John on board.

Robert was frustrated. "I don't want those kids having sex down the hall from us." Rachel caught the double meaning but decided to ignore the jibe. She didn't like the idea either but she was a realist. "John and Genevieve are 17. If they are going to have sex it's better to keep an eye on them. That way we can exercise a little parental guidance. Michael Walters is useless."

Robert had to admit his wife was right.

And so Genevieve began to spend one or two nights each week at the Frankel's.

"I'm no good at loving or sex," she said on her first night in his bed.

John had learned not to contradict her when she made self-deprecating sexual statements. Her femininity was a sore spot with her. John couldn't understand why. He thought at first she might be gay, but she was great in bed. Her body responded enthusiastically to his touch. He had to go slow with her and pay attention to her every subtle gesture though. He was no great lover but was very motivated to do a good job. John thought she was absolutely beautiful and a total turn-on.

Genevieve was confused at John's constant and enthusiastic reaction to her body.

"I don't get it. We both have two arms and two legs and a pair of tits. Mine are just bigger than yours. You seem to get turned on whether I have my clothes on or off."

John just shrugged. "What can I say? There's some kind of magnetic attraction that draws me to you." It was true. A lot of girls were better looking than Genevieve, but not for him. It was her unusualness that drew him to her. For him there could never be another girl.

After several weeks Genevieve learned to enjoy his sexual interest because it was always accompanied by respect and admiration. She admitted that sex felt wonderful. But he was always touching her and she wasn't sure that his interest wasn't primarily motivated just by sex.

John continued his tutoring because it helped to hone his skills for the upcoming SATs. He had to score in the 95th percentile to do Michael Walters' program and receive his mentoring. Robert was worthless.

On the first day of classes of his senior year John was walking out of the building when George Krewalt approached him.

"John, can I have a word with you?"

The other students scattered quickly. The assistant principal was a hard-ass and no one liked him. "Uh, sure."

"Last year you did some very helpful math tutoring for athletes. Would you be willing to hold a general study session in math after classes? Anyone who wanted could come."

The man was pressuring him but John liked the idea. He could be the Michael Walters to his fellow students. "Sure, that would work for me."

So once a week after dinner and before the school closed he would hold an open work session. The first two were supervised by William Baldrige, head of the East High math department. He gave his enthusiastic approval. The sessions were popular because John had his father's gift of easy expression. The kids were happy because they were under a lot of pressure from their parents to achieve. The teachers were only too happy to receive competent help. They were well paid but parental and administrative demands were high. Carleton University has a national reputation for scholastic excellence. Midland East is a feeder school to the university. It is rated in the top five percent nationally for high schools every year and wanted to stay there.

After the first semester grades and test scores in mathematics were up twenty percent. Some of that increase was attributed to the open sessions. John didn't know it but he was becoming quite popular with the school administration and with many parents in the community.

During one of these sessions he became reacquainted with Ja'Quan Williams, the big lineman on the football team. The assistant principal introduced him to John at the beginning of a crowded session one evening during the end of the fall term. "John, meet your new assistant."

The big man grinned ear to ear as he shook John's hand. His huge afro bobbed up and down. "I did it," he said proudly. "I worked every problem in that advanced placement calc book we studied last semester. Now I'm ready to strut my stuff."

John was impressed and welcomed the help. "Can you still bench 450?"

"470 now, little man." Ja'Quan pointed at John's curly head of hair. "Get a *real* afro, white boy." They both laughed and got to work.

During the rest of the term Ja'Quan became even more popular, if that was possible. The big man's combination of intellectual and athletic prowess, his impressive physique, and his friendly nature made him an almost unanimous choice for senior class president. Some of that popularity rubbed off on John. The relationship with his peers changed subtly. The teasing he had endured since junior high ended.

The following week John experimented with the first set of instructions of the technique from the codebook.

He mentioned this to Genevieve and her eyes lit up for a second. "Good luck." She would say nothing further. John shrugged and let the matter drop.

He memorized the complicated breathing patterns for both stages and the mental exercises for the second stage and printed them out. The mental exercises were cool. The codebook identified areas in the merkaba that could be activated. The breathing, along with the mental exercises, was supposed to do that. First you had to master stage one.

John did what Genevieve did. He sat on the chair in front of his desk with his feet flat on the floor and did the breathing exercises.

Nothing happened.

He tried it several more times. Other than feeling a bit more peaceful and calm, it was a load of crap. But what did he expect? The book was obviously written by a lunatic. Or someone with an overactive imagination. John persisted because he didn't want to give up after all the work he put in.

As the days went by with no noticeable improvement John became frustrated and disappointed. The translation was correct, he was sure of it. Fuck it. The end of his senior term was quickly approaching. That meant the SATs, final exams, and the prom.

Final approval for the special Masters program of Michael Walters depended utterly on his scores on the senior SAT's. Robert was threatening to send him away to university whether he liked it or not. If he didn't ace the exam he would have a huge fight with his father.

Michael Walters said, "If you don't get all A's and at least 1500 on your SATs I'm afraid the Department heads will nix the whole thing." 1600 on the SATs was a perfect score.

He'd take Genevieve to the prom, of course. John thought about skipping it but mom had already mentioned the idea of making a prom dress for Genevieve. Surprisingly, Genevieve told him she wanted to go.

"I didn't think you liked to socialize."

"I don't. But if I go with you this year I'll have an excuse not to go next year." She smiled ruefully. "One prom per lifetime is enough for me."

John laughed and agreed wholeheartedly.

"Time for dinner!" Rachel yelled from downstairs. John and Genevieve were working on a term paper for old man Masterson. They had started the paper only an hour ago and were almost done.

"How's it coming there Gen?"

"Just got to finish up the last section. Let's get down to dinner. We don't want to keep your mom waiting."

They trudged on down to the kitchen. Even though the house was old, Rachel's kitchen was not. A gigantic gas range/oven with a big vent that went out of the ceiling occupied the center of the room. From the ceiling hung big metal bands filled with cooking pots and utensils. There were plenty of cabinets for storage. Off to the side Rachel put her mother's cherry hutch that held her precious china, crystal, and family heirlooms. The large counters contained an assortment of food processors, blenders, and other helpful kitchen gadgets. On the other side of the room sat a massive oak table with bench seating.

Robert began fishing around in a pot. "What's this? Smells delicious."

Rachel slapped his hand. "Get out of there Robert. This is supposed to be a surprise."

They all got seated and Rachel brought over the dishes. "A five course dinner tonight. I hope you're hungry."

"Wow, we're getting the red carpet treatment," John said. "What's the occasion?"

Rachel glanced over at Genevieve. "Oh, I don't know. I just felt like cooking. I'm trying to finish that book on ethics and I just couldn't concentrate anymore."

"Hooray for ethics!" said John.

They had a great dinner and everyone chatted happily. Even Robert got into the happy vibe, John noticed. Probably nothing politically unpalatable occurred today. He hated it when dad lectured on current events because other opinions were quickly shot down. His father always backed his statements with an impressive array of facts and statistics. But his prosing stifled the atmosphere in the room. Rachel hated it too but she never said anything. They both knew objections would lead to an argument.

Rachel noticed that Genevieve sat silently. She never volunteered anything unless asked, and that often reluctantly. Rachel could see something was bothering the girl.

After everything was in the dishwasher and the kitchen cleaned up Rachel spoke to her. "What's the matter sweetheart?"

Genevieve looked up at Rachel. "I was just feeling a little...I don't know." She was sad. Rachel had never seen her like this.

"Let's go up and talk. The men can fend for themselves down here."

They went up to Rachel's study.

Rachel said, "What are you going to wear to the prom?"

"I thought I'd just get something off the rack. You know, one of those places where you can rent dresses."

"Oh dear no. Let me make you something."

"You're a seamstress too?"

"Yes. My mother taught me. She always said you had to have something to fall back on."

"Making a dress is a lot of work. Are you sure you want to do it? I can just get dad to give me some money."

"I would be happy to. I haven't done any dressmaking in a couple of years and I don't want to get too rusty. Take that stuff off and let me get your measurements."

Genevieve brightened. "OK."

She took off the top and her slacks and stood in her underwear. Rachel noticed the black top and the burgundy slacks. She picked up the pants. Good label, and nicely tailored. I wonder where she bought her clothes and where she got the money for such expensive stuff. Probably from Michael. He had been a horrible father but now he was turning about a little.

Rachel looked Genevieve up and down critically.

"Dear Genevieve, I know just the thing for you." She rubbed her hands with glee. "But I'd like to show you off in pastels. Brighten you up a bit."

"Please Mrs. Frankel. No pastels. And not too ostentatious. I prefer the classic style."

"Call me Rachel, dear." Rachel thought for a moment. "I have it. This dress will be as classic as it gets. I'll concoct a black dress with a silver ribbon around the waist. Then, a pair of burgundy heels. A string of pearls around your neck and my old diamond heart pin just below the shoulder."

Genevieve smiled, then sighed.

"What's the matter dear?"

"I was just thinking how great it would have been to have a mother. I'm not so good at the girl stuff." Tears began to well up in her eyes. "Just having you take care of me tonight has been a real treat."

Rachel gazed at Genevieve with affectionate regard. This could have been the daughter she never had. She thought of all the wasted years and what they could have done together. Rachel considered how this little girl had had to negotiate herself through the trials of becoming a woman all alone. She thought of Michael Walters. The man is a complete introvert. Totally incapable and unprepared to deal with a daughter. Why had he adopted her anyway?

Tears began to run down Genevieve's cheeks. She threw herself into Rachel's arms and both women began to cry. After a short time Genevieve raised her head and looked up at the taller woman. A smile slowly spread over both faces. There was now an implicit understanding between them: mother and daughter. They burst into laughter, dancing and stomping across the room like a couple of children, holding hands. Finally, exhausted, they had to sit down. After a few moments Rachel spoke. "Come daughter. Let's take your measurements for that dress."

She got out her tape measure and began carefully measuring thigh, waist, hips, arms and bosom.

"This dress will take all of my skill to make but I'm up for it." She looked carefully again at the girl/woman in front of her. Pure black hair and eyes, with the whitest skin she had ever seen. The burgundy lips, the delicately chiseled features, and the unusually shaped ears. Unusual but striking. How to show off this unusual girl to her best?

Genevieve smiled. "What will it look like dear Rachel?"

"It's going to be a surprise but I guarantee you'll love it."

The women walked down the stairs together and headed for the direction of the living room. John and Robert were shouting at each other. Rachel stood behind Genevieve a few feet outside the door. Robert was leafing through some papers. Their presence was not noticed.

"I've applied to Princeton, Stanford, Yale, Harvard, Berkeley, Michigan, Wisconsin, and Virginia. Or you can do that program Michael Walters put together for you. But you're going to start university next fall."

"I'm not going to start until next year. I want to spend more time with Genny."

Robert was infuriated. He didn't know which was worse. His son's arrogance or his infatuation with that Walters girl. He decided the girl was the greater evil.

"So it's Genny is it? Since when did a girl stop you from doing what's best for you?"

"You don't know what's best for me, dad. What worked for you doesn't work for me."

Robert sneered. "What do you plan on doing for the next year? Maybe get a job at a hardware store? Or spend all your days studying that stupid book you seem so obsessed with?"

"I don't know what I'm going to do dad. I'll play it by ear. I do know one thing. Whatever I do is going to have to feel right to me."

Robert calmed a little and tried a different tack. "Look son. You don't have to spin your wheels here in Midland. You've got a great start to your education. Now it's time to continue while you're on a roll. You can go to Harvard or somewhere out of Midland and spend my money. See the world a little. It'll be fun. If her grades are good enough Genevieve can follow you up next year."

Wow, John thought. He doesn't even know she's never gotten anything but A's. "She's smarter than I am dad. She'll have no trouble."

"There, you're all set." Robert was smug.

"No way. I'm not leaving her here. Besides, I need a break from school."

Robert exploded. "A break from school!! What the hell is that? I didn't save my whole life to send you to Harvard for nothing! I'll not have a son of mine waste his life over some stupid girl."

Rachel and Genevieve stood, breathless, just outside the open door. Rachel's hands tightened on Genevieve's shoulders.

John shouted into his father's face. "SHE'S NOT STUPID. I LOVE HER AND I'M NOT LEAVING HER. DO YOU GET IT NOW?"

For the first time in his life Robert Frankel wanted to hit his son. "What the hell would you know about love, boy? You're just a 17-year-old kid!!" Robert expressed his own frustrations. "You just like having sex with her!"

"Of course I do. It's not just that. I love her as a person not as a job description. That's something you have never understood. If you did, your relationship with mom would be a lot better. Genevieve is brilliant and tough as nails. She's honest and independent. She's the most admirable person I've ever met in my life. If I stick with her I can't go wrong. I just thank God every day that she likes me."

Genevieve's heart pounded in her chest. She was thrilled. John really did love her. He stood up to his father and defended her. She was so happy she couldn't contain herself. To get a new mom and now this. She bolted from Rachel's embrace and threw herself into John's arms.

Robert stood with his mouth half open. The light of understanding suddenly filled his awareness.

Robert Frankel was an intemperate man, and stubborn, but he was not a fool. What his son had said was true. He hadn't really looked at his wife in years. For him, she was just a wife. He had never reached the true Rachel behind the facade he had made up for her.

Robert saw his wife staring at him from just beyond the door. A look of despair, and then hope, flooded his face. He held out his hand to her. "Rachel...I...."

Rachel Frankel came slowly up to him. "Robert, we can both learn something from what happened here. It's not just you. It's me too."

Robert gazed down at his wife and saw her as he had when first they met at university over 25 years ago. By God. The old Rachel is still in there; the only woman he had ever loved. He placed his hands on her hips and looked her up and down, admiringly. Intelligent, warm, and still a very attractive woman at 48. He realized how lucky he was. With a look of despair he searched his wife's eyes and found an answering response. He had been holding his breath and let it out in a long sigh.

Rachel saw his relief. John had somehow reached inside her husband to a place where she had not been able to go. His son had thrown him a line. She saw the old Robert peeking out and tears began to run freely down her cheeks.

Robert knew he had to say something, make a reach to her. "Come Rachel, let's go upstairs. We have a lot of things to discuss."

11

IT was now prom night, and the end of John's senior term. Exams were over. John had gotten all A's and 1550 on his SAT's. He lost 50 points on the writing section but he didn't care about that.

John waited for Rachel to finish dressing Genevieve. It wasn't like Gen to take so long over clothes. He had never seen her in a dress since he had known her. Always she wore black and burgundy slacks and tops. The girls at school used to tease her about it until they realized she didn't give a shit.

John smiled to himself.

Things had changed forever at the Frankel household since the night he had the fight with Robert. Genevieve had begun to call Rachel "mom." Mom and dad were spending the evenings talking, hashing over the issues that had separated them and trying to find common ground. They realized that they still loved each other. Now it was just a matter of tying that thread of love into their lives again. They refused to see a marriage counselor. John thought that was wise. Two people as smart as Rachel and Robert should be able to work out their own path.

Time passed slowly. John grew more and more impatient standing out in the hallway by the front door. They only had twenty minutes to drive over to the school.

He heard female laughter and a door closing.

John was just about to yell for them to get a move on when he caught sight of Genevieve slowly coming down the C-shaped staircase. She wore a long, square cut black silk dress with sleeves that reached to just above the elbow. A beautiful burgundy ribbon edged in silver held the dress tightly to her waist. Around her neck she wore a string of real pearls. A beautiful diamond heart sparkled just below her right shoulder. On her feet were dainty, dark burgundy shoes with low heels.

His inhaled breath stuck in his throat. He stared. The blood was pounding in his head. His heart thumped loudly as he watched her descend the staircase. She approached him and said, "You look like a deer in the headlights."

"Uh .... Uh...."

At the top of the stairs a big wide grin spread over Rachel's face. Success!

Genevieve spoke brightly. "Are we going to the prom or are you going to continue to do your deer imitation?"

Still no movement from John. He couldn't believe his eyes.

She waved her hand in front of his face.

"Oh! Yeah .... Uh...I've been waiting for you guys forever. We had better leave now or we'll be late."

Genevieve looked directly at him with a big smile, quite pleased with herself. "It's customary to actually get in motion if you want to go somewhere." Her smile broadened. John had never seen her this happy before. Someone brought the sun down into this little hallway.

"Uh.... Right." He moved quickly away to the front door and was about to open it when Rachel spoke. "It's also customary when you go on a date to take your date with you."

"Right," said John. He smiled sheepishly. He walked back to her and offered his arm. "Sorry."

"No offense taken."

He walked with her to the front door, carefully opened it, and directed her through it.

Rachel ran down the stairs and looked out the window to see how her daughter would do. She had carefully instructed Genevieve exactly how to behave this night. Prom night was going to be old-school. "Just try it," Rachel told her. "You might like it." She was to wait before every door and allow him to open it. She was not to sit until he had moved a chair for her. She was not to let herself into or out of the car, but to wait for him to hand her in and out. She was to walk gracefully and regally. She was to understand that she was quintessentially a lady. None of this "I'm not good at the girl stuff."

Half an hour earlier Rachel had turned her around to face the full length mirror.

Genevieve gasped. "Is that really me?"

Rachel laughed with pleasure. "Yes it's you. What do you think?"

Genevieve was amazed. She touched the pearls around her neck and felt the luxuriant fabric of her silk dress. She saw how cleverly it had been crafted to cling to her. She looked herself over critically in the mirror. She looked...not beautiful exactly, but *different*. Exotic even. Completely different from all the other girls. She understood a little bit better why people responded to her the way they did.

Her very fine facial features and her cat-like ears made her look other-worldly. She had never really looked at herself before. *Probably because I've always thought that there was something fundamentally wrong with me.*

She turned from side to side. The dress was a magnificent creation and she was magnificent in it. Suddenly, she laughed out loud. For the first time in her life she felt totally good about being female.

"I do look great don't I mom?" *It felt so good to say that!* "Thank you so much."

"Oh Gen, you're ravishing. Just wait till all the guys see you. God, they all think you're some kind of tomboy freak. You have to tell me all about it, you promise?"

"I promise."

Now Rachel saw her student pause on the grass beside the car. John was about to let himself in on the other side when he realized his gaffe. Genevieve waited with perfect composure for him to open the door. She extended her arm and he handed her in, then closed the door for her. He raced around the front of the car and hopped in the driver's seat. He said something to her and she smiled. John's face lit up like a Christmas tree.

Rachel was glad to be alive this day.

Genevieve and John walked past the open gym doors that had been transformed for the prom. They saw a big bandstand, lots of tables, and lights and decorations everywhere. Lots of people were milling about. The band had just finished playing a tune and was discussing the next one. Genevieve's heels clicked on the hardwood floor. A few heads turned to see who had just entered.

Gene Watkins, Trevor Jones, and Bill Parkinson stood around with their dates at the back. They were hoping for refills of the alcoholic punch that sat on one of the tables along the side.

"Well, would you look at that," said a voice behind them. Bill, Trevor, and Gene glanced over, then looked again.

"Damn," said Bill with feeling. "Is that Genevieve Walters?"

"Wow! Who's that goofy imbecile with her?" Gene said.

"Frankel of course," said Trevor. "They've been pretty thick for a while now."

"He looks like a giraffe with an electric shock," Karen Ackerman said. She was Bill's date.

Trevor laughed. "Poor Frankel. That hair of his ruins the air of elegance provided by the tux."

Nina Shaloob smiled. She was Trevor's date, a short girl with dark olive skin and black hair. Nina loved the precision of his speech and his unaffected manner. Like her Moroccan family, Trevor's family had come to these shores from another country. He never fell into the carelessness of American slang to be popular.

Heather Simmons felt irritation. She glanced down at her own outfit, a green strapless gown with gold trimming and puffy sleeves. She had tried to emphasize her small bosom by tying the dress above the waist. Instead of looking at her, her date was all gaga over the robot. Heather had to admit that the dress was beautiful though. This observation increased her annoyance.

"What a stupid looking dress," Heather said. "It looks like something some-body would wear in one of those old movies."

"C'mon Heather," Gene complained. "Be cool."

"Unusual dress," Nina said. "I like it." She was one of Genevieve's few friends in the school. She could not understand the subtle hostility most of the girls felt toward her.

Bill looked on as John handed Genevieve into a chair. "I didn't know it was still OK to do that stuff."

Karen turned to Bill and smiled. "Yeah, it's still OK."

"Hard to believe that's Genevieve Walters," Gene said.

Heather spoke sharply. "You can put a nice dress on a robot but it's still a robot underneath." Gene shook his head. What was with her tonight?

A small crowd of girls gathered around John and Genevieve. They couldn't believe that the junior had come to the prom in such a dress. They were prepared to be hostile. Ja'Quan, from his vantage point on stage, saw the potential confrontation and moved to defuse it. He spoke to LaShawnda Price. "Girl, get over there and help out my friend Frankel." LaShawnda wore a white low necked dress and two inch heels. Her hair was coifed African style and she had huge silver earrings. She strode over to the group. She was almost as tall as John and all eyes turned to her. She met those eyes with a challenge, daring anyone to utter a hostile word. Then she smiled and the tension broke a little.

LaShawnda spoke to Genevieve. "Nice dress." It's simple, classic lines with no frills were completely different from anything the other girls wore. But it worked. "Where did you get it?"

"John's mother made it for me."

"Is it silk?"

"Yes."

"Those pearls are beautiful." She wished she had a necklace like that.

"Would you like to try them on?" Genevieve asked.

Lashawnda spoke eagerly. "Oh could I, just for a second?"

Genevieve undid the clasp and handed over the pearls. LaShawnda carefully put them round her neck but couldn't close the clasp.

The other girls stood around, not sure what the girlfriend of the class president was doing here. One of them looked toward the stage and saw Ja'Quan observing. Everyone looked at each other and shrugged.

"Here, let me help." Genevieve had to stand on a chair to complete her task.

"They look wonderful against your skin," Genevieve said.

LaShawnda went over to a mirror and admired herself. "They're so beautiful. There *is* a difference between fake and real." She preened back and forth a little, trying to catch a glimpse of herself from as many angles as possible.

"Thank you," LaShawnda said gratefully.

Genevieve gracefully retrieved and restored the pearls around her own neck. LaShawnda returned to the stage, receiving a big smile of thanks from Ja'Quan. "Whatever IT is, you got it," he told her. She laughed in appreciation.

John noticed that Genevieve was completely herself, unaffected, and friendly. He had never seen her act like this before in front of people.

Genevieve's nervousness had completely disappeared. She felt a powerful strength and calmness within her as the other girls looked her over. She realized that she didn't care anymore what they thought. It was freeing. Love me or hate me, it's your choice. She smiled. One of the girls smiled back and the tension was completely broken.

Genevieve understood suddenly that she had been walking around the school for years with a chip on her shoulder. A thought came to her with unexpected clarity. Maybe it was that vibe to which others had negatively responded.

"That *is* a nice dress," the girl said. Genevieve recognized her as one of the cheerleaders for the football team.

"Thanks." Genevieve replied softly. She could feel the girls warming up to her a bit. A few of the guys were stealing glances at her out of the corners of their eyes, trying not to offend their dates. She giggled to herself. This was fun! It was going just as Rachel had predicted.

John was forgotten in the bustle around Genevieve. He didn't mind even though he heard a few disparaging remarks about beauty and the beast. Some of the more cynical girls expected her to go up to the head table and flaunt herself in front of the queen. But Genevieve and John stayed at the back. The two misfits drank it all in and were actually enjoying themselves.

A short time later the group around them dispersed. John asked Genevieve if he could get her something. She asked for some bottled water and a few hors d'ouvres. On the way John received a few slaps on the back from the guys and some heartfelt male praise. "Good," he thought. "Maybe I won't be weird John anymore." Then he realized it was too late! He had already graduated.

The band began to play a slow number and John asked Genevieve to dance. She accepted and raised her hand for him to take. He took her gently in his arms. She smiled up at him and rested her head against his shoulder as they both swayed softly to the music. When it was over he offered her his arm. They both began to walk slowly back to their table. There was a powerful chemistry between them; the other dancers felt it. John received a few smiles and acknowledgments in return as they reached their table. John was thrilled. He and Genevieve had finally gotten that old feeling back.

At that moment the prom queen approached them from the side. John and Genevieve turned to see who it was.

"If it isn't Genevieve Walters," said Melissa Danridge. She wore a lavender dress and a crown, representing her status for this night. Melissa was a lovely blonde, one of the most popular girls in the school.

"Hello Melissa," Genevieve said.

Ken Saunders, her date, could feel the bad vibes. He tried to nudge her away. "Come my queen. It is time to go back to your court."

Genevieve subtly acknowledged his gesture, giving silent approval.

"What are you doing here?" Melissa said scornfully to Genevieve. "Hello weird John Frankel."

A crowd began to form around them.

Genevieve did not reply, looking calmly and steadily into Melissa's eyes. Around her she exuded an almost electric energy. Those closest to her unconsciously backed off a step in response. John remembered what happened to Ricky Davis and that girl on the baseball diamond. He tried to intervene but she looked him off.

Melissa was upset. She felt that Genevieve was trying to usurp her position. Ken looked at Genevieve with silent entreaty. "Please don't say anything," he seemed to say.

After a few moments Melissa saw that she was not going to get a response. "Come on, Ken. Let's get out of this rabble and back to the aristocracy." She turned on her heel and dragged him along with her.

John came round and put his hands gently on Genevieve's shoulders. He whispered to her. "You were great." She leaned back against him, tilted her head, and smiled up at him. His hands went around her waist. Everyone who had seen the altercation was completely silent. The band played on, the voices of the revelers could be heard all around them, the clink of glasses and feet hitting the floor. In their circle all was peaceful. They sat quietly back in their seats.

John was blown away by the whole thing. He couldn't believe this was the ironic and sarcastic girl he had known almost his whole life. She was surprising him now with new aspects of herself.

The rest of the night passed by joyfully for both of them. Ja'Quan, the class president, gave a hilarious speech in which he comically tarred and feathered the assistant principal and several of the teachers. John knew the big man had realized his dream. He would be attending Princeton in the fall and John was pleased for him. After the speech John walked up to the stage. The two shook hands warmly.

"Thanks for your help John," Ja'Quan said. John could feel the love.

"You would have done it on your own," John said truthfully.

"Yeah. But I've learned from football that the hardest way isn't always the best way." Ja'Quan said this with a wink.

After that the two introverts decided to leave.

"I had a good time tonight," Genevieve said after John drove them back to the house on Magnolia.

"I did too." John was hoping to take her immediately up to his bed.

As they walked in the door Rachel ran down the stairs. "How did it go tonight, dear?"

Genevieve went off with her into the living room, chatting.

John groaned and stomped up to his room, disgusted that Rachel had ruined the denouement to his evening.

12

THE summer after graduation John spent a lot of time with Michael Walters in the evenings, going over his program of study. He wanted to get the old man off his back and get his Masters degree as quickly as possible.

During the day he and Genevieve would hang out. In the evenings she'd sometimes sit with them in the library or go off in the used car her father procured for her. A couple of like-minded girls from the high school would go with her. The prom had made her a lot more popular. Sometimes she'd go downstairs and watch a movie by herself.

During their study sessions Michael Walters went through each textbook for the upcoming semester. He explained the important concepts so well that John understood the material without ever having attended a class. Walters read math and physics textbooks as easily as children's stories. John began to pick up on his vast knowledge and his way of looking at the symbols. He learned how to think conceptually about mathematics and physics. Soon he was able to glance at a group of equations and understand their meaning. This helped him out enormously with the physics and linguistics texts.

"Isn't this cheating?" John said one hot, late August evening as they sat at the older man's big desk in the library.

Michael Walters laughed. It was the first time John had ever seen him let go. "No John. The acquisition of knowledge is always appropriate."

John was glad because his mentor was going to save him hundreds of hours of drudgery over the next four years. He would breeze through the program.

In September Genevieve entered her senior year at East High. She had refused all offers of academic promotion. She elected, for reasons unknown to John, to remain with kids her own age.

John got a part time lab technician job at one of the Carleton optical research labs, courtesy of Michael Walters. This allowed him to work in the mornings and early afternoon and make some money. He scheduled all of his classes after 1 p.m. He hardly ever needed to go. His lab partner at work was a good looking guy named Jimmy Callaghan. Callaghan had hands with long narrow fingers. He performed all the sensitive set up work. Some of the optical equipment they used needed fine tuning and Jimmy was the man for that. John's job was to keep the experiment within the designed parameters. The work was boring but it was John's first real paying job. He wanted to do it well. Jimmy was in his early 20s. He had graduated from East High three years ago and was now a junior at Carleton with a knack for electronics.

Jimmy was excellent at his job when he chose to work. Unfortunately Jimmy was not a self-starter. He only busied himself when he thought the boss might look in. Supposedly Jimmy and John had equal status and were paid accordingly. John had assigned himself the responsibility for their work. Once past the set-up stage Jimmy chattered constantly, interrupting John's concentration. Most of the time Jimmy complained about his girlfriend.

"Who's your girlfriend?" John asked this one day to stop his whining.

"Kathleen Summers."

Holy shit! His old flame.

"Does she still play the cello?"

"Yeah that's part of the problem...." Blah, blah, blah. John didn't want to hear it.

"All right boys," Dr. Jackson, the lab director said. "Break's over. You can stop talking about girls now and get to work. Make sure you guys carefully observe and take good notes. We wasted two days last week because *both* of you were out of the room at the wrong time."

"Woops," Jimmy said. They both got busy.

On Friday John went to the high school on lunch hour. He had continued the tutoring sessions and needed to talk with George Krewalt about the material they would be covering for the remainder of the semester. It was an exciting time, for the SAT scores for all of the students had just come in the day before. Some of the teachers were talking about one test result in awed tones. John stopped one of them. "What's going on?"

"One of our students got a better than perfect score on the SAT's. 820 and 820."

1640! 800 was as high as you could get on any section. This year's test had four bonus questions.

"Who got it?" John asked.

"Nobody knows yet."

The scores were supposed to be confidential but sometimes the principal of a school would be notified of a really high test result.

"Apparently Swindell blabbed to one of the administrators and now it's all over the school."

Earlier that day the students had been in physics class, each one receiving their test results in an envelope. There were excited yelps and disappointed groans as everyone examined their printouts. "Hey I got a 720 reading.... 560 math, not good enough...oh Karen you got it made now – 710 and 680..."

Genevieve opened her envelope and looked at the results. She quickly crumpled up the paper and tossed it into the wastebasket in the corner.

"What'd you get?"

"Pretty good," was all she'd say.

"If it was so good then why did she throw it away," somebody said.

Mrs. Dalton, the physics teacher, was curious. After class ended and everybody filed out she fished the crumpled piece of paper from the wastebasket. It read: Genevieve Walters Math 820, Writing and Language 820.

Within two hours almost everyone in the school knew.

When John heard about it he was only mildly surprised. He had always suspected she was smarter than him. Last year he had gotten 800 Math and 750 Writing and Language, the highest combined scores in the school.

John noticed that Genevieve spent almost no time on her schoolwork. He'd come home after the day's activities and ask her if she wanted help. She'd inevitably say, "Got it done already." After a few months of this John began to suspect that she had never needed any help and that their homework sessions for the past two years had been more for his benefit than hers. He could tell she was bored with everything related to school. She seemed to be waiting for him to do something but she never told him what it was. Every time he brought up her family, or the orphanage, she clammed up. She and Michael Walters had some deep dark secret they weren't telling anybody.

One Monday afternoon in the spring of Genevieve's senior year John had an experience that changed his life forever.

During the evenings John made it a habit to exercise, usually a little lifting, and he would then practice the first and second stage breathing techniques from the code book. Just for kicks, he'd routinely work through the protocols that supposedly enhanced awareness of the "sphere of consciousness" described in the book. John felt no changes in himself. He kept doing the exercises to wind down from work and remove the annoying voice of Jimmy Callaghan from his mind.

That day John sat quietly in his bedroom with the windows open. The fresh spring air with its scents of new life awakening rustled the curtains and gently feathered his skin. The peaceful sounds of birds chirping made him smile. As he practiced the routines he began to feel calm and serene. His body felt light and almost detached from his awareness.

The book was in front of him and open to the image of the guy in the meadow. He wondered what it would be like to sit beside that fellow with the big ears, in that meadow. Probably birds there too. He continued into the second stage with absolutely no expectations. Then the room around him and the things in it began to shimmer slightly. John began to get a feeling for this place. A completely different world, with a different vibe, a different smell, a different...

The wall disappeared.

Something fuzzy and indistinct appeared before him, like a scene in a movie before the camera focused.

John was back in his chair. Little beads of cold sweat ran from his forehead. His breathing was rapid and he felt the pounding of his heart.

John stood up and pounded on the wall, satisfying himself it was really there.

Must have been his imagination! Walls just didn't dissolve into thin air. But this one did.

"Try it again," he muttered to himself. He was too afraid to repeat the experience. Shaking, he sat on the bed and lowered his head to the pillow. After a while he got up. He went downstairs and lifted for an hour, trying to shake off what had happened.

The fear was gone now, replaced by a feeling of well-being. The after-effects of the technique? Just the result of lifting of course. He always felt better after that.

That night after dinner Genevieve spoke to him. "Did something happen to you today? You look different."

John was curious. "Describe precisely in what way I'm different."

She looked straight into his eyes and probed him in that unusual way she had done since childhood. "You seem...a little bigger, a little calmer, a little more ... confident I guess. I'm not sure exactly." She gazed at him curiously, a little smile at the corners of her mouth. John could see she was excited and expectant.

"I'm working on something," he said.

It was like Genevieve that she did not question him further. She could read him perfectly and knew there was something he wasn't ready to tell her yet.

"OK John," was all she said.

It was several weeks before John decided to try the technique again. Mainly because it had scared the living shit out of him. Imagine, dear reader, sitting in your favorite chair in the familiar confines of your bedroom. You're looking out the window toward the backyard. Then the room and the backyard simply vanish.

It was bullshit of course. A temporary hallucination. But there was only one problem. He knew that it had really happened.

In early June, just before his 19th birthday, John wrestled with the weight set for half an hour. He went upstairs and showered. Then he sat at his desk with the printouts in front of him. The stage one procedure he now knew by heart. After 20 minutes of the complex patterned breathing he was able to achieve a state of total calm. His body felt as light as air. It no longer felt like something separate from his awareness.

During the second stage John noticed a feeling of being outside the flow of time. This was accompanied by a sense of complete well-being. It was exactly the same sensation he had experienced at the plate, and at the dojo, just before he had made a leap in ability.

Slowly John became aware of a cocoon of energy surrounding him. At first it was very faint. Using the mental exercises and continuing the patterned breathing, it became more and more real. As it did the feeling of well-being became more and more pronounced. His body, once so solid, disappeared into this spherical energy field.

With a feeling of wonder John glanced at the book. It was open to the first image. His intent was to be there in the meadow underneath the tree. The desk, the walls, and everything in the room began to shimmer but John didn't panic this time. With growing excitement he could feel what would come next.

Then he remembered he had forgotten to lock the door. Rachel was home. If she came in here now she would totally freak. He wanted to get out of his chair and lock the door.

The familiar reality of his bedroom faded out. It was too late. He was committed.

At that moment John entered a zone of blackness containing chaotic energy patterns. Then he was out. He saw a meadow and someone walking along a trail. The scene was fading in and out like a camera trying to focus. John intuitively understood that he was the camera.

Now the meadow came sharply into view along with the strange looking tree. A man just like the one in the image stood twenty feet away. He wore a close-fitting cloth toga, tied with a belt around his waist. The man put his hand to his forehead as if searching for something in the distance. Just as he was about to step forward the man turned suddenly to stare at John, as if noticing something completely out of place.

The man started and stepped back a couple of paces. He reached into his toga. John was just as startled. He was afraid the man might have a gun or a sword. Instead the man turned and walked quickly up the trail and out of sight.

John felt his body seated on the side of a small, grassy hill. This grass was bluish-green and had small cilia attached to it. John looked up into the cloudless sky. Something was wrong. The sun was too big and it was the wrong color. The sun of earth was yellow but the light from this sun was a beautiful gold. The sky was a peculiar greenish blue. The air smelled very thick and sweet as if perfumed. John dug his hand into the hill, expecting to see dirt. Underneath the carpet of the strange grass was a very hard, unyielding surface that felt like clay.

If this was a dream it was by far the realest dream he ever had.

Was this just a projection of consciousness or the real thing? Was his body still sitting in the chair in his room?

In his mind John saw himself at his desk. Suddenly the scene before him shimmered and faded. He was back in his bedroom with a tremendous feeling of well-being. John was so excited he couldn't wait to tell Gen.

Downstairs, Rachel cooked and thought. She had sent Genevieve out to the market for a few dinner things but she hadn't returned. Robert was underfoot tasting her sauce, opening covered pots, and offering unneeded suggestions.

"You're just like a cat dear, always getting in the way," she said with a smile.

"Oops, sorry honey. I promised I wouldn't make a nuisance of myself in the kitchen. Everything smells so good." He gave his wife a friendly pat on the butt.

"Where is that girl?" Rachel said, a little irritated. "I need that cream for the béchamel, and those shrimp."

Genevieve graduated a week ago and she hadn't even gone to the prom. Rachel asked her about it, hoping to see her once more in the dress she had created. But Genevieve had been firm. "I went last year."

Rachel knew that it was futile to question her further. She was growing fonder of her new daughter but Genevieve's reserve was sometimes irritating. Especially on personal issues. Genevieve simply would not talk about herself or her past. Rachel knew it bothered John too.

Robert made Genevieve apply to a few schools. With her grades and scores she could literally go anywhere. It was clear that Genevieve was not interested in academia. Oddly enough, Michael Walters had done nothing to encourage her. He didn't seem to care.

That Michael Walters was a strange bird, even stranger than his daughter. He emanated a feeling of suppressed power. Sometimes he scared her with the intensity of his emotions. Maybe that's why Genevieve was so reticent. He'd probably frightened her to death during childhood.

John wandered into the kitchen and opened a pot of marinating mushrooms. "Smells good mom!"

"Get your hands out of there. You're as bad as your father."

Robert met John's glance. "I think we'd better get out of here."

Robert directed John into his study. John could feel he was about to have one of those 'man-to-man' talks.

"All right son," Robert said. "You can live with us if you'd like. Genevieve can move in even. But starting in the fall you pay room and board."

"OK dad." Talking to his father was much easier now that he and Rachel had settled their differences. He wouldn't even have considered staying otherwise. He'd saved almost every penny from work over the past year and it came to a nice little nest egg. He would have enough for a down payment on an apartment and several months' rent if he decided to move out.

A few minutes later Genevieve walked into the study. She started to say something but stopped and looked at him intently. Her face was a combination of excitement and seriousness.

"John, we have to talk."

"Do we ever. I can't wait to tell you what happened to me today."

"I know John."

She smiled a deep, deep smile and he felt her expand outward to touch him. She had never looked at him with this much feeling. Her face was aglow.

"John, my love, let's go to the park. There's something I have to tell you."

Robert stared. What the hell was this all about? John and Genevieve exited his study, talking excitedly.

Robert shrugged. He went upstairs and put on his running clothes.

13

The Eyrie

B ELLEROPHON sat at the console, monitoring the progress of John Frankel. Kjirsten had instructed that someone should keep an eye on the earthian during his every waking moment. The boy was in his bedroom and Bellerophon saw his Sphere activate. "Well, would you look at the kid. He's finally doing it."

Bellerophon picked up his headset and notified his boss immediately. Now it would be possible to assist the boy, just as Kjirsten had assisted the girl ten years ago. Fortunately an earthian was available for the job. Immersion within the psychic environment of the earthian planet was not a pleasant experience.

14

GENEVIEVE drove them out to Delhi park by the Midland River. She was radiant, glowing with excitement. John felt eager with anticipation and a little nervous. Whenever he tried to speak she just pressed her finger to her lips.

Genevieve parked and led him to a grove of trees by the river. John put his back up against a big oak, facing her.

"Now John, I'm going to tell you about myself." She paused, collecting her thoughts. "I almost don't know where to begin."

"Let's start with your appearance. Your skin is unusually white, for instance. Robert has remarked more than once that it looks like you came out of a mold."

Her eyes widened. John could see she was worried and afraid.

Genevieve decided that only the blunt truth was appropriate.

"John, your father is not far off. I am the result of an exotic experiment in gene alteration." Her eyes scanned his face anxiously.

So that was it. Her father had been engaged in some highly classified research in the past. Could that research have involved Genevieve? It didn't matter. He was crazy about her, always would be.

She saw it, felt it.

Genevieve was joyful. "I was so afraid you'd be revolted."

"You need to tell me everything."

"OK. But I only understand it partially myself. You and I are inextricably tied together."

"Just the way I want it," John said.

She smiled. "And I too, my love."

John's heart leaped. She had never said that before.

"I don't have any memories of my early childhood. I suppose that's not surprising, many people don't. But I have certain abilities that you may have noticed. One of them is the ability to control the field of energy surrounding my body. You have probably experienced a little of that lately."

"You know what I've been doing then?"

"Of course."

Before John could reply she launched into a long explanation.

"Twenty years ago my father, Michael Walters, was part of a top secret human cloning project. As you know, Carleton specializes in molecular biology research and is recognized internationally as one of the top university research departments in that area. Two guys from the Advanced Technology Office of DARPA came to recruit a team of researchers for their project. Dad and five others got the red carpet treatment. They were throwing money around like candy and showed them all kinds of stuff to impress them. Dad says that there are certain hidden programs within the bowels of the military and the intelligence community. He called them special access programs. These programs are far ahead of their civilian counterparts. When Dad and his team saw the technology everybody was really excited. The team members didn't want to work for the military but the prospect of doing cutting edge research overcame their objections. A year later the team discovered the program's true intent: to create a Super Soldier who could survive under extreme conditions and be programmed to always follow orders. Eventually everyone quit. They were told that to speak of the work would result in extremely undesirable consequences. Everyone associated with the project has never spoken a word about it."

Genevieve looked away for a second and gathered herself.

"Here is where it gets weird John. Remember that bike trip we took to Hanford?"

"Yeah. We saw that white-haired tofu-eating lady."

"Her name is Hazel Morningside. She is – or was – a molecular biologist. She was part of Dad's team."

"I wondered why she had that lab in the back of her house."

"I found out most of this during a talk we had before you woke up. It was one of the reasons I went to see her. To confirm what I suspected about my origins. Fortunately Hazel couldn't live with the idea that such an unusual girl was running around completely oblivious of her origins. When I found out the truth I was really mad at her and dad. Hazel swore me to secrecy. She said that if I told my father he would have to report it and they'd both be in big trouble.

"Dad's group began working with an entirely new and exotic technology. It was light years beyond anything Hazel had ever seen or read about in the literature. I was their first and only experiment. The team was able to program certain of my physical features: the pale white skin and pure black coloring, the red lips, and the cat-like ears. I was a...biological prototype.

"Hazel said that the equipment was so advanced it was scary. She described it to me but I didn't understand most of it. Apparently they were able to image, target, and manipulate specific genes and sequences.

"Don't ask me how it was done. There are only three people who have any specific knowledge of that. Dr. Hazel Morningside, my father, and Debra O'Neill, my biological mother. Debra was the team leader. Hazel said that Debra volunteered to donate her eggs and carry the fertilized egg to term. Dad donated his sperm."

John was confused. "Masterson said that gene splicing and cloning works with unfertilized eggs."

Genevieve shrugged. "Hazel said that this technology was totally different. Apparently they worked directly with a fertilized egg and were able to alter its gene structure even after it was inserted into the mother."

She paused and spoke carefully. "John, Hazel told me that these...devices...were utterly fantastic. She suspected that...that..."

"Yes?"

"That the stuff couldn't possibly have been developed on earth."

John felt a bolt of energy through his body and he sat upright. Yes. Like the codebook with its indestructible pages and it's fantastic etchings.

Genevieve must have read his mind. "Of course I know about Dalton Jones' experiments with your book."

"Damn." John wondered where she got her information. Then it hit him. Michael Walters, who else?

"What was all that fancy equipment in Hazel's lab?"

"That stuff was developed by Darryl Hansen, a young researcher and their contact with the military. It was one of the things the DARPA guys used to impress their recruits. That's what Hansen told Hazel anyway. According to her this guy was only 20 years old and he knew things no 20-year-old could possibly know. At a meeting they had in DC, Hansen brought in some equipment that he said measured the biofield around the human body. He set the equipment up in this gigantic lab. Each team member in their turn stood in the middle of the room just like you did at Hazel's. The other researchers observed from behind a screened-off area along the far wall where all the equipment was. John, everybody absolutely freaked out. Hazel said my dad almost had a heart attack."

She paused for a moment.

"Tell me!"

"I'll tell you just the way Hazel told it to me. Apparently the equipment generated an extremely subtle field of energy that illuminated the biofield. Debra took her place as the guinea pig and the others watched. When Hansen activated the equipment they saw her standing in the middle of a sphere of light that surrounded Debra's body. Its diameter was about three feet or so above the head to three feet or so below the feet. Like that diagram of DaVinci's. Hazel could see thousands of complicated geometric patterns of light that all interacted with each other. They all went into the body and its various organs."

"You're not making this up are you? It's a great story but unbelievable."

"Just let me finish. After I'm done you can decide what you're going to do."

"All right."

"At first Hazel thought it was just a clever simulation. You know, attract the new employees with a lot of bling. When she looked closer she could see that the patterns of energy were dynamic. They were too sophisticated and complex to be merely algorithmic. The patterns changed so often that they looked alive. She concluded it was a legitimate real-time simulation of Debra's living body."

"Wow."

"Yeah, wow," Genevieve agreed. "Hanson told them that in their work the team would need to view and learn the body's energy configurations. Manipulation of specific templates, as he called them, accelerated the alteration of cellular structure. According to Hazel, Hanson didn't seem to think it was a big deal. She said he looked bored during the entire demonstration."

John shook his head in amazement. But Genevieve wasn't through yet. "There's more?"

She nodded. "The purpose of that demonstration was to get the team's attention, and it sure did. Hazel and the rest of the team were told what they were supposed to do, and the parameters of their research. There was to be a test run. If the team was successful they would have access to more of the technology. It took them a long time to get up to speed. After a year or so they discovered the real purpose of the research and everybody quit. But not before my mother gave birth to me."

"If the biofield equipment was classified how did Hazel get hold of it for her lab?"

"I'm not sure. I think she just took it. The gene altering devices were jealously guarded but the biofield analysis equipment, apparently, is not sensitive technology. Hazel said it was like taking towels from a hotel."

John smiled a goofy smile as if to say, "Is that weird or what?" She laughed. If it weren't for his own recent experience he would have a hard time believing it.

"There's one more important thing," Genevieve said. "Hazel says that this guy Hansen was...strange. She said there was something odd about his appearance and the way he spoke. She said his eyes were very large and round but there was something else. After a few minutes she figured it out." She paused.

"He had six fingers on each hand."

"Six fingers?"

"Yeah. Hazel said Hansen kept his hands in his pockets or clasped together behind his back the whole time. But something dropped on the floor by his feet and he picked it up. Hazel said she never would have seen it unless she had been looking right at him." Genevieve didn't tell John about Kjirsten and her visit to her. That would come later.

"Jezzis." For a minute he was lost in thought, trying to digest what he had learned. "Your father told me he adopted you."

"That's what he told me too."

"You're kidding."

"Nope. He thinks I don't know."

What a crazy family these Walters' are, John thought. Her father's story about adopting Genevieve was a pile of crap. John was disappointed. A little of the luster had worn off his conception of Michael Walters.

"Don't ever tell him I know or insinuate in any way that we know. He'd go bananas."

"Don't you think it would be better to clear the air?"

"No! Dad's coming out of his shell nicely. I don't want anything to interfere with that. If we told him now it might sock him right back into his old depression."

"You're very forgiving. If that happened to me I'd never speak to the bastard again."

She shrugged. "Dad couldn't say anything about it so he didn't. He made a mistake born out of a natural curiosity. You would have done the same."

John was about to object but he realized she was right. He had a lot in common with Michael Walters.

"I bear no grudges for my father, John. It's not like I've been such a great daughter to him."

"OK." John looked at Genevieve closely. "You look like a human being, not a genetic experiment."

"That's what blew the team away. The gene altering technology is flawless. It's why they all quit. The technology was going to be perverted."

John sat thoughtfully for a moment. He heard the rustle of water from the river and felt the warm breeze on his face.

Genevieve smiled. "I want to thank you for your part in drawing me out of my shell, love. Just as you have my father. We are both very grateful."

John's heart leaped again. That's the second time she called him 'love'.

Her smile widened. "John, I think I might love you."

John was thrilled and basked in her smile.

"Gen, wait till I tell you what happened to me." He launched into a detailed explanation when she held up her hand. "I know."

"You know?"

"Remember, I gave you that book."

John stared. "You mean you've experienced the altered states of consciousness?"

"Yes John."

He had a million questions but she stopped him again. "You have passed the first test, the activation of the Sphere of Consciousness. You have already progressed through the first two stages of the technique and partially into the third. Soon, if I get permission, and if you can handle it, I will guide you through to the end of the fourth stage."

"*You* will?"

"Yes John. I will."

Certain things were beginning to make sense. Clearly, she had already translated the code and knew how to use it. "Why have you been so unwilling to help me?"

"Because you absolutely have to be able to get the first two stages on your own," Genevieve said. "I was so much hoping you'd be able to do it. We weren't sure."

"We?"

Genevieve laughed but did not elaborate.

"And then what will happen?"

"I can't tell you. You have to experience it. All I can say is, there's something really huge going on out there in the universe. It's something no one on earth has a clue about. You have a chance to be a part of it. If you are capable."

It sounded mysterious and exciting. John wanted in. "Who do you get permission from?"

"From...a friend. You might call her my superior officer."

"Superior officer?" John was astonished. "Does it have something to do with your dad's research, or the military?"

"Nothing like that John."

"You're not an alien or an ET are you?" He asked this quite seriously.

She laughed. "I'm just as human as you are, love." Then she sobered. "I have it from the highest authority that you have the potential to be one of the best."

"The best? At what?"

"Hopefully you'll find out very soon."

A man in an expensive and carefully tailored black suit and designer shoes approached Mats Karlsson, who was manning the front counter at the Full Moon. He was of medium height with hair cut close to his head. Mats could tell right away that the guy was in training. All of his movements were precise and controlled.

"Looking for something in the martial arts?" Mats asked.

The man was a little startled. "No....uh....I was inquiring about a certain book. I'm told that you're a man who can procure such things."

The man's face was expressionless like a guy at a poker table. "I've been known to get things from time to time. For a fee."

The man smiled faintly. "Of course."

Both men sized each other up for a few moments.

"If you'll describe the book, sir, I'll tell you whether it's possible." Mats decided he didn't like this guy. But he was always nice to customers even if they were jerks.

"The book has a dark blue cloth cover, fraying around the edges. The paper is unusually thick, perfectly smooth, and yellowed. It is written in some symbolic language. There is no title or author name anywhere."

Mats laughed. "I usually need a little more information than that."

The man looked steadily at Mats with a coldness of gaze that made him shiver involuntarily.

"Not according to our information."

Mats smiled. In his younger days he had played rugby and had done some time for car theft. He was not to be intimidated. Still, the man before him exuded a sterile emotionlessness. It chilled his bones a little. Mats recalled that such a book had come into his possession years ago. It had been sold to him by an odd looking little guy in a cloak with bright eyes. Mats remembered how strangely the fellow had accepted payment, as if he had never seen money before. Wait a minute. Genevieve Walters had bought that book from him. Genevieve's father worked at one of the university research labs.

"That'll be hard to find," Mats said. "I'll charge you a finder's fee if I locate it. I need $100 unrefundable up front. $100 more if I locate it."

The man pulled out a billfold and handed him a crisp $100 bill. To Mats it felt like the currency had never been handled before.

"You can reach me here. Ask for Gary. When can I expect to hear from you?"

"Give me two weeks. If I can't dig it up by then I never will."

The man walked out, got into a black sedan, and drove away.

One day a few weeks later Rachel came home early to do some cooking. She thought she heard a noise up in John's bedroom.

She walked up the staircase and into the hallway. There was something in the atmosphere of the house. A turbulence in the air, like before a rainstorm. Curious, she walked slowly to the end of the hallway and stood in front of John's bedroom door. There was no sound. Yet something unusual was going on in there.

She knocked on the door. "John? Can I have a word with you?" No response. The turbulence was gone. Curiosity got the better of her. She tried to poke her head in the door but it was locked. "John?"

Rachel shook her head. She went downstairs and looked in the garage. Genevieve's car was there. Both bikes were still in their racks so they hadn't gone riding. Maybe they went out for a walk. She was about to walk back down to the kitchen when she heard voices coming from upstairs.

A few hours before, Genevieve told John to skip work. She was insistent on showing him something. It had to be this morning so John phoned in to the lab and took the day off. He listened as Jimmy complained about the extra work he'd have to do. "Just cover for me. There's nothing happening anyway until tomorrow."

"All right but you better be here on time," Jimmy whined. John took the phone away from his ear. "I have to take Kathleen's cat to the vet and I might be a little late. That really sucks, I hate cats and I have to get him into the carrier and my asthma..."

John interrupted. "Thanks Jimmy. See you tomorrow."

Genevieve giggled. "Is he always like that?"

John looked his disgust. "Yeah. But he's good at his job at least. For some reason Kathleen likes him."

Genevieve knew a little about Kathleen Summers from high school. Kathleen would be attracted to someone good looking but weak. Someone she could bend to her will. Hidden behind that beautiful exterior was a cast iron bitch. Poor Jimmy!

"John, if you're willing and able, I'm going to take you entirely through the technique."

John was excited. Then he frowned. "I don't know if I understand this technique well enough yet. So far I've just used the images in the book to guide me. What happens if you don't know your destination precisely?"

"You do a blue jaunt. And I don't want to know what that's like."

"A blue jaunt?"

"From an old science fiction story by Alfred Bester. A blue jaunt is when you send your consciousness to a non-defined destination. I imagine you could translate underneath a mile of rock, or into a wall, or something like that. It might even cause a breakup of your entire field of consciousness." She shivered. "That's why I need to guide you today." John saw her regarding him with a powerful sadness.

Genevieve recovered her spirits. "First I want to check your translation of the material."

John got his printouts from the desk drawer. Genevieve retrieved a sheaf of papers from a small briefcase and placed them upon the desk. The cover page was dark blue inscribed with a symbol of a white sphere of light surrounded by a multicolored mist.

"Wow! What's that?"

The document looked official and exuded an energy that spoke of other worlds. Reverently he brought his hand over to touch it. His eyes met Genevieve's, wide with wonder and curiosity.

"Gen..."

She smiled, a secret smile that spoke of adventure and mystery. Genevieve meticulously checked John's translation for the first section and the second section. John saw that the document had the symbols on one page and an English translation on the facing page.

Genevieve slowly closed the manual and turned her head. "This translation is correct in every particular. You didn't have any, ah, *help*, did you?"

"I asked your father a couple of questions..."

She waved her hand impatiently. "I don't mean that kind of help."

"What other kind is there?"

She said nothing, gazing intently into his eyes. Then she smiled and shook her head in admiration. To have translated it all by himself! Not even she could have done that.

John pointed to the document. "Gen, is there a translation in there for the fifth section? The first four were unbelievable enough. I couldn't make much sense of the last one."

Genevieve hastily closed the document and placed it back in the briefcase. The container sealed itself. The material simply flowed together seamlessly. There were no latches, hinges, or any way to open it.

"Where did you get that thing?"

With her foot, Genevieve shoved it under the desk out of sight. "I'll take you through the steps of the technique and show you how to control your sphere of consciousness during the last two stages. As you become more and more experienced with it you'll understand more and more. The only reason I know more than you is because I've done it longer."

"Is this the big thing you told me about in the park?"

"No John. It's just a little baby step."

Genevieve made John go through the breathing patterns for stage one and stage two, satisfying herself he was doing them correctly. Then they both did the first two stages. Genevieve checked John after this. With her enhanced awareness she could see that his merkaba was primed and ready to go.

"That is very good John. Now we're going to go through the third and fourth stage protocols which enable initiates to become aware of and control the merkaba. Here is where almost everyone fails the test. Anyone can learn to breathe correctly. The merkaba protocols have been mastered by only the tiniest few."

John's attention had to the room. He now felt a little intimidated. "What makes you think I'm so special?"

"My...superior officer says you have great potential. Don't worry John, there's no danger. You either fail or succeed spectacularly."

Kjirsten had assured her that John's book and her manual contained tried and true information. The merkaba protocols had been developed and tested over hundreds of millions of years. Her own experience bore that out. She shivered a little inside. If anything should happen to him now that...what? Now that she loved him. It felt wonderful but made her feel vulnerable. She felt she wasn't in complete control of her life anymore. A part of her was now with him. To be so intimately tied to another, to be so strongly affected by another's actions! She didn't know if she liked that.

Her heart fluttered and she wiped a tear from her eye. Why did everything human have to have two sides? Why couldn't there just be happiness without sadness?

Genevieve made sure John understood everything he was supposed to do in the last two stages. She placed her chair back to back with his. "Now we're going to do all four stages from the beginning," she explained. "I'll help you get through the final two stages." *If you are able to.*

"I'll expand my merkaba to encompass yours. Don't freak out. It'll feel strange at first, like someone is trying to steal your soul. If you just let it happen it will be an amazing experience. I can only guide and direct. You must be able to control your own sphere of consciousness."

John nodded.

"Are you ready?" she asked.

"Ready, Captain Walters."

"We'll be translating our sphere of consciousness out of the earth environment and into the vibrational pathways. But first we'll have to pass through the zone of chaos surrounding the earth. It'll be a little freaky as you probably know already, but don't panic. Let me guide you. OK?"

John nodded, feeling like an astronaut perched on top of a gigantic rocket, waiting for the big explosion.

"Let's start."

They sat back to back and began the breathing exercises. John felt a wonderful feeling of peace as his body detached itself from his awareness. John could feel Genevieve waiting for him but he didn't rush it. Then, stage two was attained. There was a feeling of expanded consciousness as he became aware of the full extent of his energy field. Also a really cool feeling of detaching from the flow of time. He was totally in the zone. It was just like at the baseball diamond and at judo. But that was just temporary. This was something that would hopefully be under his control.

John felt her presence. She was *inside* his consciousness. It felt indescribably wonderful and intimate. He almost jumped out of the chair but she caught him with a thought. "Relax." He *felt* it, felt her all around him. Wow! He got so excited he lost the connection and they had to start over.

"How....?"

She smiled. "John, what you've just experienced is just the beginning. If we can get through the whole thing it will blow you away. The only way to progress is to actually do it all the way through."

"Aye-aye, captain."

She giggled. "You're funny."

"Most people don't think so."

"I do."

They began again. John gradually became aware of a sphere of light with himself in the middle. The feeling of his body disappeared. This time, as John felt her mingle with him, he just enjoyed it. Slowly a picture formed in his mind, but it was so much more than that. Senses he didn't even imagine he had opened up to him. The room shimmered and faded out. Then a blackness; bizarre energy patterns impressing themselves upon their combined consciousness, and they were through. John experienced directly how Genevieve used the protocols to negotiate the zone of chaos. He noted it for future reference.

A feeling of well being coursed through him. John became aware of an exciting smorgasbord of exotic realities on the edge of his consciousness. Here, a beautiful, open-air multistoried marble temple in the middle of a desert with a sapphire oasis nearby...A world of forests...a misty, multicolored reality of light...and hundreds more, all inviting him to come and play. John felt himself gently guided back.

Genevieve led him to a world with a purple-black sky filled with stars. Overhead, a gigantic moon filled a quarter of the sky. They were seated back to back on a beach. The water reflected a million points of light from the sky and the pale silvery moonlight.

Both stood up to get a better look. John took Genevieve's hand and squeezed it. "Wow."

"Look, John," she said. From below the horizon a blazing pinpoint of light, slowly ascending, flooded the beach with a pale yellow-orange light and made a trail across the water. The sky brightened and a humid breeze with unusual smells filled his nostrils. Not a sound could be heard except for the wind in their faces. There were no birds, insects, or trees. Yet it was astonishingly beautiful.

"I love this place," Genevieve said.

"It's incredible. But is it real? Are we just daydreaming?" He felt his body. "It *feels* solid enough. Is it really us, here in this place?"

"What is reality John? If you wake up sweating from a vivid dream, is that any less 'real' than reality? Reality is what you perceive. It's all a matter of what you're consciousness is tuned into. Right now we are focused here so this is what we experience."

"Where is this place?"

"I don't know precisely where we are by conventional time/space coordinates. That's not how the system works. Maybe it's at the other end of the universe. All I know is how to get here and how to get back."

John remembered some of the things he had felt on the way, and how she guided him.

"Did we travel in a wormhole or use some gateway or portal? How did we get here exactly?" There didn't seem to be any spatial movement during their journey. Things just faded into and out of his awareness, like H.G. Wells on his time machine.

"I'm not completely sure. All I know is that consciousness can tune itself to whatever frequency it wants. That's the power of the technique, and the power of the merkaba. The universal medium carries an infinite sea of vibration. It's possible to 'dial in' to different places, like adjusting a radio to a particular program. The programs can be totally different but they're all available, depending on the sensitivity of your tuner. The key is getting the entire sphere of consciousness resonating to the destination. That's what the book showed us. It's magical. You never get tired of it."

"So the merkaba contains the body too."

Genevieve nudged him with her elbow. "It would appear so."

John looked at her. She was so beautiful in this strange but wonderful place. Daydream or not he could smell the sweet, dense air. A warm breeze brushed against his cheek. He could feel her hand in his and her hair rustling against his arm.

"Just open up and feel this place," she said. They stood there, soaking it in. This planet had an entirely different "feel" to it.

They returned the same way they had come. This time Genevieve didn't have to guide him so much. The vibe of earth was so familiar that the pair soon found their bedroom shimmering into existence around them. John felt his body in the chair, precisely as it had been (how long?) ago.

He looked at the clock on the wall. It read 11:35, exactly as it had just before they left.

"Gen, no time has elapsed on the clock. Explain that."

She shrugged her shoulders. "I can't John."

"If the experience was real then time should have elapsed."

He looked down and saw several grains of coarse lavender-colored sand at his feet. They were bigger than the ones on the Lake Victoria beach. John knew he hadn't had anything in his pockets that could have fallen out.

"I believe you." He reached down to pick one up and inspected it critically. "I have to believe the evidence of my own eyes I guess."

Genevieve smiled, pleased that their first attempt with the technique had been so successful. "Oh John, I'm so excited. I have someone I can share this with now. It makes me feel so wonderful."

There was a knock on the door. "John?" It was Rachel.

"Hi mom," they both said.

Rachel was astounded. "Have you been in here all this time? I came up here a minute ago and no one was here!"

"Are you sure?" John asked.

Rachel could feel something in the air again. "I think so."

"Well, here we are," John said. "What's for dinner tonight?"

"Paella for the main course. Soup to begin, a salad, and herbed bread. Chocolate mousse for dessert."

"Can I help?" asked Genevieve.

"I'd love that daughter." The two women walked downstairs, chatting.

For the time being, Rachel forgot all about her question.

That night John was still exhilarated by the experience. "How did you know where to go?"

"I have experimented a lot. It took me a long time to reach stage two. I just couldn't open up enough and I had no one to help me. The first time I shimmered out it scared me and I didn't try again for a long time."

"When did you start this?"

"One day I had an argument with Dad. I needed to calm down so I went to my room. When I opened the door someone was waiting for me."

John raised his eyebrows. Genevieve laughed.

"I was only 13 years old at the time. When I opened the door I saw a beautiful red-haired lady sitting on my bed. She made me go to the Full Moon and buy that book. I thought I was hallucinating or something because the woman had no means of transportation. She just...showed up like we did at that beach today. The next day

I saw her again. 'Close the door,' she said. 'I have something to show you.' For the next few days she came to my room every day after school. She answered all my questions and showed me how to use the protocols presented in the book."

John's curiosity was kindled and he fired a barrage of questions. "You mean this lady just appeared in your room, like magic? Who is she? Where is she from? How did she know you were using the book? Is she an ET? Why did she come?"

Genevieve put her hands up in front of her face to fend him off. "You'll get to meet her. But you'll have to discover how by yourself."

"By myself? That's not fair. If this magic lady helped you why won't she help me?"

"Because, because..." Genevieve was never hesitant in her speech but now she fumbled for words. "Remember I told you something big is happening out there? Well, you and I have a chance to be a part of it. Especially you."

"Me? I don't even know what it is!" Genevieve still was not telling him everything.

"Let's just say that if you continue on your present course you'll find something very exciting. You'll meet this lady. When you do she'll answer all of your questions."

Even though John insisted Genevieve wouldn't enlighten him further. "Practice for a while with the technique until you can do it in your sleep. I've given you all the instruction you need."

"Does your father know about all this?"

"I think he does. I used him to translate a lot of the symbols for me. He may have even tried it. I know for sure he hasn't been successful."

"How can you know that?"

"People who use this technique become subtly different, if you know what you're looking for. I've always had unusual abilities so it's not so obvious with me. You're already starting to change." She smiled. "I've been monitoring you since the day you rode up to me on your bike."

"Yeah I remember that. You threw stones in my face."

"You were impertinent."

They both laughed.

"Should we tell Rachel and Robert?" John asked.

"I think Rachel is getting suspicious. She asked me all sorts of questions while we were cooking dinner. What could I say? No one would believe it who hasn't experienced it."

Genevieve pondered for a moment. "I think Rachel could handle it. But not Robert."

John guffawed. Dad would probably call Dr. Patterson and have them both committed.

"I only have one more question. Who wrote that book?"

Genevieve looked a little confused. "John, I don't honestly know. The red-headed lady told me exactly where to go in the Full Moon to find it. 'It's on the second floor face down on the shelf on the back stack at the far right,' she said. That's exactly where I found it. You know how dark it is back there in the arcana section. It was glowing a little so I bought it. I have no idea who wrote it or where it came from."

"All right. I'll practice and see what happens."

At a classified underground installation somewhere in the US

"Is there any authorized activity at coordinates 2437, 8898, 1004 ...Midland, Illinois?" someone asked.

"I'll check."

"Nope. There are several classified research labs at Carleton University though."

"We detected a disturbance in the psi field at these precise coordinates. 11:35 a.m. this morning."

"We'll look into it."

An agent was dispatched and returned with the following short report:

"The location of the disturbance was pinpointed at 337 Magnolia Drive. The residence of Robert and Rachel Frankel. No anomalous activity observed. Family residence. One child, John, lab assistant. Live-in girlfriend."

"Unacceptable," said the supervisor. "Determine identity of live-in girlfriend. The agent responsible for this report is demoted one step in rank."

Another agent was dispatched. Report returned:

"Live-in girl friend is named Genevieve Walters. Father Michael. Lives at 1009 Traver in Midland, close to Carleton campus. Security clearance, category 4. Formerly associated with the Invincible Soldier project. Michael Walters resigned from project and reassigned to independent research. Records show Genevieve adopted. Parents unknown."

The report was considered.

"Send someone out to monitor the area. Reports are to be sent once per week."

Mats never heard back from "Gary," or whatever his name was. He made a note to speak to Genevieve Walters if she came in.

A week later Genevieve did come in. But she wasn't a kid anymore, by the gods!

"Didn't you buy an odd-looking book from me a few years ago?" Mats asked her. "One with a dark blue cover and no title?"

"Yes. I gave it to my boyfriend as a present."

"Some guy in a suit came around last week looking for it. Looked like somebody from the government."

"Really? What could the government want with a musty old book?"

"Beats me. I thought I'd let you know."

Genevieve thanked him and left.

Mats was satisfied. The girl knew nothing. Gary could go to hell. He'd palm him off with a couple of very passable substitutes.

A week after that Gary showed up. "What have you got for me?"

Mats showed him three books. All were old with cloth covers. All three had titles.

"None of these are the one I'm looking for."

"I'm sorry sir. These were the ones that seemed the best fit for your request."

The man paused for just a split second, mulling over Mats' response. "Do you mind if I look through your store? I've got some time on my hands today."

Mats gestured expansively. "The place is yours. Ask if you need any help."

For the next several hours Mats was busy and didn't have time for anything but business. Amidst the usual socializing and schmoozing with the stand-arounds, he had actually made two big sales.

As Gary walked by Mats' eye caught a glint of light off something the man held in his hands. It had a small display panel but Mats could not identify the thing.

"Find anything?" He noticed Gary was wearing the same nicely tailored suit as before.

Gary quickly pocketed the device. "Just a few books. Nothing that really interested me."

I wonder what he's been doing in here for the past four hours. Mats was unable to resist a little dig. "Sorry I couldn't help you sir." The man's sharp look expressed a broader understanding of the situation than Mats felt comfortable with.

After Gary drove off in the same black sedan, Mats asked around. "Did any of you notice a guy in a nice suit wandering around?"

"Yeah, I did," said a girl, a destitute young graduate student. "I was reading in the stacks on the second floor. I noticed him walking back and forth. He probably covered every foot of the store on that level."

"Didn't take anything did he?" Mats joked.

"Not that I saw." She smiled.

"Did you see him with any kind of gadget?"

"Didn't notice. Too engrossed in my book."

"Are you going to buy that book?"

"Don't need to, I finished it ten minutes ago. Thanks Mats." She walked out.

Mats hoped he'd seen the last of Gary; there was something weird about that guy. Then he reconsidered. There's something weird about everyone who comes in here, including me! Gary fits right in.

Mats laughed out loud, startling a woman with a cup of coffee in her hand.

It was dark and getting colder when John drove Genevieve's car over to the Walters' house on Traver Street. He knocked on the lion's head knocker.

It was time for his daily appointment with Michael Walters. John had a math textbook under his arm and a voice recorder in his pocket. John had begun to record the sessions with his mentor so that he could refer back to them at test time. He was also burning with curiosity to see how much his advisor knew about the codebook. Did Genevieve's father know anything about the remarkable technique he had experienced with Genevieve yesterday? He was about to let himself in to the house when the man himself answered the door. "Hi John!"

Michael Walters looked very cheerful. The two men walked into the living room. A woman was standing with her back to them, facing the fire.

"John, I would like you to meet Alicia. Alicia, meet John. He's the young man I've been telling you about."

The woman turned and held out her hand.

"Hello John." She smiled warmly. John confronted a small, plain looking woman with red hair and a few freckles around her eyes. She exuded warmth and friendliness.

Mr. Walters was seeing someone! "Hello Alicia."

John noticed that the woman was slightly taken aback by his height and the curly hair that stuck out from his head, but she said nothing. Point for her.

"Well sir, I suppose we can cancel our appointment for today," John suggested. "I can see that you are pleasantly occupied. I'll let myself out."

"Don't do that John. Alicia was just leaving. We've had a very nice dinner but she has to get up early tomorrow."

"Yes." She smiled up at him sweetly. "But I really don't want to leave."

Michael Walters blushed. "I wish you wouldn't. Maybe you should stay."

"Remember our agreement dear."

Walters reluctantly let her go and seated himself at the front desk right in front of the window.

"Don't you want to go into the library?" John asked.

"No. It's more cheerful in here."

John's eyebrows lifted. More cheerful indeed! That's what he had always thought.

"Alicia is thinking about doing a little redecorating," Walters said. "Says this brown carpeting has to go and the wall color lightened up. A couple more windows to let in more of the sunlight."

"I've always thought the same," John replied. Things had apparently gotten quite serious.

John dragged a chair over to the desk and they had their session. Afterward John broached the subject of the code book.

"Sir, I've deciphered the code in that book. With Genevieve's help it has led me on a journey that I hardly believe now ever happened, even though it seemed totally real at the time."

"Ahhh," Walters said. "You have progressed further than I thought."

"So you know all about it?"

"Yes. Theoretically at least, because I helped my daughter decipher that code. My daughter claims to have had some very vivid, ah, experiences with the material. I don't place a lot of validity in what she has told me."

"So you've never tried the procedures outlined the book?" John was curious. This man had a mind that encompassed so much.

"I fooled around with it a bit but never got any concrete results. I'm familiar with the research into paranormal phenomenon but I'm a scientist at heart. I believe in the tangible, the concrete, and the observable."

Hmmm, just like dad. This man had limitations after all.

Walters stopped for a moment slowly to wipe his glasses, lost in thought.

"Can you tell me a little about your involvement in that Invincible Soldier project?" John asked.

Michael Walters blanched. "I am not at liberty to discuss anything about that." The older man's eyes hardened and he introverted, lost in remembrance.

"Sorry sir."

John let Michael Walters be alone with his thoughts.

After a minute he broke the silence. "Mr. Walters, Genevieve and I have been on a most remarkable journey. At least I think we have. Twice now I've reached an altered state of consciousness. I have had experiences that cannot logically have occurred, yet are so real that I can't deny them. Each time I have reached such a state of well-being I felt like a holy man in an Indian book on mysticism."

Walters replied quickly. "John, I can't help you with that. At least not yet. The symbology in the book is detailed and internally consistent. However, all of my attempts to interface with a so-called universal medium have been fruitless. I have, I think, translated the document correctly."

John was a little disappointed. Confirmation from such a knowledgeable source would have gone a long way toward relieving his doubts. The more he thought about his little adventure with Genevieve yesterday, the more he was convinced that he had hallucinated the whole thing.

Walters sighed. "An independent research team I was a part of did some cutting edge work investigating the biofield. Those investigations, while not rigorous enough for my taste and completely out of the mainstream, did pique my curiosity. That's as far as I have gone with it."

He paused and gazed at John. Walters' eyes were sort of unfocused, as if he were looking around John's body. "I have observed changes in you as I have in Genevieve. As a result, I have been wrestling with some of the ideas we came up with for several years. I am finally coming to believe in their worth."

"You can see changes in me?"

"Definitely. I have concluded that the procedures outlined in that book of yours are just an extension of our research."

"The research you can't tell me anything about."

The older man was unapologetic. "That's right John. I'm sorry."

John decided that further probing would be useless. "Do you know who wrote that book?"

"No John, I do not." At John's questioning look he said, "Really. I have no clue."

"All right. What changes have you seen in Genevieve? She claims to have worked with these procedures off and on for several years."

A look of pain crossed the older man's face but he would not answer the question directly. "Genevieve is, shall we say, unusual physically and well above the norm mentally. I'm sure you've noticed that over the years."

"Yes." John waited silently, trying to draw the other man out.

"She has, like me, not allowed herself to believe fully in anything positive. I blame myself for that. I was her father and her only reference point in her formative years. I'm afraid I have discouraged her and even harshly criticized her."

The older man took off his glasses and rubbed his eyes. "I just hope I haven't started too late to salvage something from my life." Walters' Neanderthal-like face was creased into lines of despair. Then he smiled.

"Tonight, Alicia and I talked about some wonderful things." He stopped and looked directly at the young man beside him. "For so many years I was a failure with women. This time I hope it will be different."

Then Michael Walters, surprising himself and John, hesitantly and with great difficulty divulged his role in the project that had resulted in Genevieve's birth. Afterward he hung his head. "Now I have also broken faith with my former employers. That completes the circle of lies that has been my life."

He seemed about ready to burst into tears. "I've lived with this filthy secret for so long it has become a cancer. I am truly sorry for all the pain I've caused my daughter. And everyone else."

John couldn't stand to see anyone in so much anguish.

"Genevieve knows all about it," he blurted.

Oh shit! He had promised Genevieve never to mention her knowledge of her father's work.

John watched anxiously as Walters' face ran the gamut of emotions. First shock, then anger, then remorse. Finally, after several minutes, relief.

"How long has she known?"

"About six years."

"And she's still talking to me," he murmured.

"She loves you sir."

Hope flashed in Michael Walters' eyes. "Yes, perhaps I can make a new beginning. Perhaps my life can have a happy ending after all."

John smiled. "I'm sure it can, sir." John was honored that this man of such enormous intelligence had chosen to confide in him.

"I'm sorry I lied to you John. I felt I had no choice."

"I understand completely." He was glad Walters had divulged his secret. His high opinion of his mentor was restored. He had lied to the people closest to him. But he had come clean, even though it had been difficult.

John smiled. "So! When will we see you and Alicia over for dinner?"

Mr. Walters brightened considerably.

"How about this Wednesday, as usual?"

"Great! I'll tell Rachel."

John and Genevieve decided to move out of the house and get an apartment. They chose a nice new unit close to the university and John's work. Rachel was disappointed. The young couple agreed to stay until the end of the summer term of the following year.

Robert and Rachel made travel plans. They would splurge a little and use some of the money reserved for John's education. Rachel was on sabbatical until the following fall and Robert could write anywhere. It would be Europe for a month and some skiing, followed by three weeks in the Caribbean. Robert hoped to get a nice tan and show off his new figure. He had lost almost 25 pounds by rigorously following his exercise program. He was back in shape, looking good, and feeling good. There were contingency plans for more vacationing. It was possible that the house would be empty for three months.

John's parents said goodbye a week later on a cold November morning. John wondered what he and Genevieve were going to eat. Neither of them knew how to cook anything but macaroni and cheese, or toast. They were going to suffer from culinary deprivation!

Genevieve was excited to have the whole place to themselves, undisturbed. Even though she accepted the idea of getting their own place, she was going to miss the big house. She wanted one just like it for her own.

After graduation Genevieve had found employment at East High. She taught mathematics and science classes part time for the advanced placement classes. The school was prepared to offer her a job as a full time teacher. All she needed was a teaching certificate, but Genevieve didn't want to be tied down to a full time job. The idea of taking boring education classes did not appeal to her.

She decided to follow the program her father had developed for John except that her M.S. would be in physics. So Genevieve divided her time between the high school and the university but was tied to neither. Now they had two income streams. John bought a used car with his savings. There were now four cars in the household and only two places in the garage. He had to walk to the curb every morning in the freezing cold and scrape his windshield, but that was a lot better than asking the old man for his car keys, or borrowing Genevieve's.

John got a call at the lab two weeks before Christmas. "Mr. Frankel?" (People were calling him *Mister* Frankel nowadays. That must mean he was grown up). "You'd better come home, there's been a break-in. The police are at your house right now."

A break-in? John couldn't figure out what anyone wanted in their house. The only valuables were Rachel's china and crystal. Some jewelry maybe. He drove quickly over to the house but could see nothing amiss other than an overturned chair and some papers that had been spilled from Robert's desk in his study.

"One of your neighbors saw a man she didn't recognize, jiggling with the lock."

Probably Mrs. Parsifal, the old widow who lived next door.

"She said she saw him rummaging through things from her bedroom window."

"Merry Christmas," John muttered.

The police officer told John to look over the house and make a list of any stolen items.

John spent the next hour making a careful inspection but could find nothing missing. It was a mystery.

"Looks like they were searching for something they never found," the policeman said.

"It does look that way. I can't figure out what they'd be looking for."

"We'll keep the file open for now. Let us know if anything turns up missing," the officer said.

Two days later John discovered that the codebook was gone.

15

A T first John was really angry at Dalton Jones. He must have told someone. Or
maybe it was that Sievers guy who had the materials lab. John called Trevor's
father. Dalton Jones assured John he had not said a word to anyone about the book.
"I've had Jim Sievers doing some more work on the sample, but that is all."

"Do you think Sievers blabbed to anyone?" John asked.

"I can't imagine he would. I'll have a word with him."

After John hung up he began to calm down. He'd already translated the thing;
it had served its purpose. He wondered how a burglar could have known about
the book and why anyone would think it valuable. The police had no clues. The
only people who knew of the book's existence were himself, Genevieve, his parents,
Michael Walters, and Mats Karlsson. He'd have a talk with Mats tomorrow.

The next evening after dinner John stopped off at the Full Moon.

"John Frankel!" Mats exclaimed as John stomped the snow off his shoes at the
front door. "Just the man I wanted to see."

"Yeah, and I need to ask you a question."

Mats put a beefy arm around him and led him into a corner. "Putting on some
muscle. Been lifting?"

"Yeah, just for fun."

"John, something funny happened a few weeks ago. A guy in a suit came in
here inquiring after a book. It was the one Genevieve Walters bought for you some
time ago. Dark blue cloth cover. Do you remember it?"

"Yes. Somebody broke into my house yesterday and stole it. I was going to ask
if you told anyone about it."

"I'll be damned. I thought I led him astray but I guess not."

"No way to be sure he took it. What did this guy look like?"

"A government type," Mats replied. "Athletic. Sort of emotionless. Well dressed, closely shaved hair, medium height. Called himself Gary."

John thought for a moment. "I've never seen a guy like that."

"I thought you might want to know."

"Thanks Mats. Got any light reading?"

"Are you a paying customer?" Mats said with a twinkle in his eye.

"Today I am." John smiled.

"Then come right this way, sir."

John spent an hour or so in the Full Moon and chatted with Mats a little. He bought three books. *The Collected Works of Jane Austen* for Rachel. For himself, two science fiction novels. He hated reading books on digital devices. Hardcopy was best.

John went home to practice the technique. He secretly hoped that Genevieve's mysterious red-haired lady would be sitting on his bed. Genevieve clearly knew a whole lot more stuff than he did. Her suggestions about "something big" happening just fired him up because she never exaggerated.

John remembered what Genevieve said about getting a vision in your mind and the feeling of it. The images in the last section of the book were probably provided as an aid, so that a student could avoid a blue jaunt. Well, too bad. The book wasn't here anymore.

John sat in the chair before his desk, getting a precise picture of exactly where he wanted to be. He remembered a book he read as a child that described a peaceful world of villages and friendly people in a fairy-like realm. It was a fantasy book for children but it had evoked a strong feeling within him. He remembered the impressions he received during his jaunt with Genevieve. There were worlds out there to be explored; lots of them. If there was a matching reality somewhere in the universe it should at least be safe. How much harm could there be in a peaceful village?

If there wasn't anything he would just come back.

John dug his old watch out of the desk, strapped it on, and synchronized it with the clock on the wall. If the trip was real, then clock and watch should show the passage of time.

John was excited but a bit apprehensive as he began the technique.

The steps were becoming more and more clear in his mind and heart. First the feeling of peace and the detachment of awareness from the physical body. Then, in stage two, the definition and awareness of the inner sphere. This phase began the expansion of awareness outward, past the confines of the body. In this and the next stage, the ability to use the merkaba protocols became vital. These were far more than mere mental exercises. They were an ingenious set of processes for changing the focus of the initiate from the confining and limiting senses of the body to the

Vessel of Life itself. According to the book the sphere of consciousness contained an inner sphere and an outer sphere. The inner sphere went approximately three feet past the body. The outer sphere went out to thirty feet or so. Activating that sphere was where all the action was. That was what Genevieve had taught him to do in her lesson a few weeks ago. In stage four, the most important step, the definition of the entire sphere of consciousness was necessary.

John had the same experience as last time with Genevieve. He became aware of the outer sphere and experienced an awesome feeling of power and well-being as well as a feeling of being outside the flow of time. The bedroom began to shimmer and fade as his merkaba charged up its vibrational resonance. Just before his room faded out John noted the clock face on his bedroom wall. It said 7:54.

In stage four, the vibrational signature of the entire sphere of consciousness must be altered to match that of the destination. John kept his vision firmly in his mind. Now he perceived the blackness of the zone of chaos around the earth. He emerged into a space filled with misty, golden-white light. Fleeting glimpses and sensations of worlds to explore appeared within the window of his perception. He could choose from a fascinating and seemingly endless collection. Delusion or not, it was awesome!

A peaceful village, a river, and people talking took form in his consciousness. "That looks good," John said to himself.

The landscape began to focus. Now it was sharp and clear. John found himself sitting on a hillside overlooking a pastoral village of small rounded huts.

His translation to this world had been effortless. The day was cloudless. An intensely yellow-white sun was visible in a light blue sky, about twice as large as seen from earth. Birds were chirping and the trees around him were in full bloom. It was very hot and dry. The air smelled funny but it was breathable. "Pretty close to earth," he said. He looked down at his body and pinched himself. "Feels real." He wore blue jeans, a light blue solid colored cotton shirt, and athletic shoes.

John checked his watch. The display read 7:54. So, no time had elapsed during the translation process.

John began to whistle a tune as he walked down the hill to the village. The feel of his shoes striking the ground, the heat, and all of the other sensations of his body felt perfectly normal. There was no way to tell if he was dreaming or hallucinating.

The village consisted of several dozen one story huts arranged in a circle around a large, grass covered open space. As he approached he saw that a number of the villagers were gathered in a group. They were talking in a language John had never heard before. Strangely, he understood everything they were saying.

"...Jem has prepared a great feast for the celebration...."

"Yes. The girls from Bildagol will be coming as well..."

The people were short, the tallest of them coming no higher than his shoulder. They were finely formed, with dark complexions. Like elves. All of them wore thin, brightly colored clothing. There were no women in this gathering.

One of the men noticed John and spoke to him.

"Good day stranger! Where came you?"

John smiled. "From the valley." John had seen a large valley some miles away in his vision.

"Stay for the feast!" another said. "All are welcome."

John bowed in acknowledgment.

The speaker seemed pleased. "Fine manners for a valley dweller," the man remarked. "Although he is oddly attired."

John's clothing was drawing attention, and also his height. "The latest mode."

He felt entirely at home. There was no threat or premonition of danger.

John realized he had entered an experience that was an exact match to the vision he held and the feeling he had generated. What would have happened if he had a different vision? Was it possible to go to a dangerous place? He didn't want to think about materializing in one of the burning buildings on that overcrowded planet of death.

John walked slowly through the village, nodding to those he passed. He encountered a trail. After some minutes he came to a little rise and a grove of trees. Sweat poured down his face; his clothes felt sticky. He was not dressed for the weather.

Although really pumped, John thought it was time to go back. The experiment must be considered a success. It did not have a dream-like feeling. To his senses it was indistinguishable from his waking earth reality.

His old analog watch read 8:27. The second hand moved normally.

As a further test John took a stick and poked the skin along the inside of his forearm, drawing a little blood. He sat down beside one of the trees and leaned his back against it. He went carefully through the technique. The vibration of earth was easy to attain and the picture of his room was crystal clear in his mind. The now familiar feeling of excitement and well-being flooded him again. As it did the grass and the trees around him began to shimmer and fade. He encountered another chaotic zone around this world which he negotiated easily. He re-emerged into the misty, golden-white space of possibility. What was this place? Was it hyperspace, or a wormhole? It felt fantastic, whatever it was. Through the misty light he glimpsed other, tantalizing possibilities appearing and disappearing from his perception. John kept his mind focused on his bedroom. One danger in this consciousness-altering travel was getting detoured along the way. His room came gradually into focus and he found himself sitting in his chair. He was back.

John looked down at his arm. A tiny drop of blood had formed around the cut.

The clock on the bedroom wall read 7:54.

The display on his watch read 8:47.

"This is too weird." The watch traveled with him, so its display made sense. Why would the bedroom clock remain unaffected?

So he had hallucinated after all. The blood on his arm could have been self inflicted right after he came back. Yet if that were so, the wall clock should have changed the tiniest little bit. John checked underneath his fingernails. They were clean. He had forgotten to take the stick he had used to cut himself. Damn! That might have been further evidence of the reality of his experience.

John's head was spinning. He stomped downstairs and lifted for a while. After about an hour he felt tired and relaxed. He took a shower and flopped on the bed, intending to wait up for Genevieve. He was asleep within five minutes.

Two weeks later John got up early on a Sunday morning, taking care not to disturb Genevieve. It was cold and snowy. He would lift some weights and go down to the pool hall until lunch. Maybe Freddy would be there. John was just about to go downstairs to the weight set when he heard a couple of car doors slamming.

The doorbell rang.

For a moment he was tempted to just ignore it but the thing rang again, insistently.

John opened the door. Outside stood a guy in a black suit carrying a briefcase. The suit was flanked by two other men with shaved heads.

"What do you guys want at 8 a.m. on a Sunday morning?"

"We'd like to have a word with you Mr. Frankel."

John thought a moment. He was never going to get rid of these guys by ignoring them. "All right. Come on in."

John sat down in his easy chair. The suit sat on the sofa, in front of the table strewn with books and Robert's magazines. The other two stood behind the sofa, flanking him on left and right.

The guy on the sofa took something from his briefcase and slammed it onto the table.

"What do you know about this?"

It was his book, minus the cover.

"That's my book you've got there!" John exclaimed. "It was stolen last month from my house. How did you get it?"

"We want to know what you know about this book," the suit demanded.

"You didn't answer my question."

"Don't play games with us John Frankel."

"Are you Gary?"

The man was extremely well trained and did not react in any way, yet John knew that the fellow in front of him was indeed Gary.

Gary pointed to the book. "We want to know where you got this book and anything you know about its contents. We represent the government of the United States. We're asking you to do your duty as an American citizen and help your country."

John flared. "Is it the policy of the government of the United States to break into people's houses and steal things?"

Gary almost let his emotions betray him. The idiot they had sent into the house had a key for the side door lock and the deadbolt. He had been instructed to leave the house precisely as he found it. The probable location of the book in the subject's second floor bedroom was known. But no, he had to go rummaging around and make his presence known.

"It is when the national security of the United States is involved." Gary spoke flatly, without apology. "You haven't answered my question."

John sighed. "The book was purchased at the Full Moon bookstore by my girlfriend a few years ago."

Gary smiled to himself. The kid didn't know it but he had just implicated one Mats Karlsson. He'd have to have a word with that gentleman. And get his money back.

"John, this is a national security issue. We have reason to believe that this book contains important information that could be vital to the interests of the United States. It is written in symbolic code. We would like to know the full extent of your knowledge of it."

John smiled. "Let me get this straight. At the NSA you have the most brilliant code crackers on the planet. But you've come all the way out here on a Sunday morning to ask a 20-year-old kid?"

Gary allowed himself the tiniest chuckle, feeling a certain affinity for this subject.

"Let me explain," Gary said. "We first found out about the unknown substance of the pages of your book from Jim Sievers, a materials analyst who has a laboratory in Research Park. We know that the substance is indestructible. At first we thought the code might be an instruction manual, like a textbook, about the composition of this material." Gary picked up the book and held it in the air. "I don't have to tell you the military advantage we'd have if we could figure out how to shield our tanks, ships, aircraft, and personnel with this stuff. We'd be indestructible."

John hadn't thought of that. He didn't like the idea of *any* government having that kind of advantage, even his own.

"It turns out that the code has little or no relation to the material at all. It's some kind of meditation." Gary threw the book on the table in disgust. "Is that correct?"

"Yes, that's right."

"We want you to tell us exactly what this meditation does. We want to see your translation of it."

John was surprised. "You already know what's in the code. You've cracked it."

"Yes we do, John Frankel." *Or we think we do.* "However, the information is written symbolically and is open to interpretation. Our success rate with the material has not been very high even though we've put some of our best people on it. Those who do master the procedures quit on us. We are certain that you, and possibly your girlfriend, have been able to...ah...interact successfully with a non-local medium. Those who do allow them to achieve abilities that would be very helpful to your government. And very dangerous if it got into the wrong hands." Gary knew he was treading into dangerous territory. The existence of the Unity Field and its properties was a very closely guarded secret. To think that a college kid in some hick town had discovered its secrets was something his superiors had no tolerance for.

"Leave my girlfriend out of it, OK?" John was alarmed. How much did these guys know of their activities?

Gary gave him a hard look. "She's in it whether she likes it or not. As are you."

John stiffened but tried to keep the anger he felt off his face. "Will you excuse me? I need to get a glass of water."

While he filled his glass in the kitchen John composed his thoughts. Gary had walked in here like he owned the place. He had already admitted his complicity in the break-in. What could he do about it? Not much. Better to cooperate than fight these guys. They had the might of the State on their side. He took a drink and walked back into the living room. The bodyguards were motionless but John could tell they were aware of his every movement.

"To the best of my knowledge," John said, "the book describes a conscious meditation that results in altered states of consciousness. It can be used to access other... uh...places."

The man looked expectantly at John.

"Have you experienced these altered states?" Gary knew he had because they knew how to monitor the Unity Field. They just didn't know how to use it.

"Yes I have."

"In your estimation, can the information in this book be used for remote viewing over long distances?"

"Remote viewing?"

Gary explained impatiently. "Remote viewing is psychic information procurement. It has been scientifically validated as an assist to intelligence gathering. Over the years our, ah, competitors, especially the Chinese and the Russians, have been able to radically improve their accuracy rates into the 90th percentile. We think they may have copies of this book or something like it. As a result it has been impossible to protect our sensitive military and important hi-tech electronic and technological know-how. The power of the mind, John Frankel, is not deterred by fences, shielding, or even encryption. To make a long story short, we are now at a severe disadvantage. The Stargate Project was our attempt to duplicate the successes of our enemies. But we were only able to attain accuracy into the 55th percentile. We'd be better off shooting darts blindfolded. We're in the dark here, John. We need your help."

"Why are you guys so interested in this airy-fairy stuff?"

Gary's face was set in hard planes as he looked John straight in the eye. "It's not airy-fairy, John Frankel. You know it."

John hadn't a clue what to do. He decided his best course of action was to tell the truth. "In my work with this material I have not pursued that line of investigation. My best guess would be that it can."

The agent felt relief because his mission was now half accomplished. He also was alarmed.

"John Frankel," he said slowly, "do you know who wrote this book?"

"No sir, I do not."

"Do you know how to destroy this book? If it fell into the wrong hands..."

"No. I'm sorry. You guys already know the tests that Sievers did on it."

Gary paused for a moment. "Would you be willing to help us train a group of people in this...meditation, or whatever you call it? As a favor to your government and in the interest of protecting the American people from an attack by a hostile country?"

John thought this was completely irrational. The meditation induced a feeling of well-being, not hostility. He wanted to get rid of Gary before they woke up Genevieve.

"I will write up a full report of my translation of the text along with my interpretation of what it means. I will include in my report everything I have experienced in my work with this information. You can then decide for yourself how to use the data." John spread his hands. "That's the best I can do."

"You'll have to leave the book with me for the next few days."

"We know where it is."

The written translation from the subject was essential along with his cooperation. Later, they could enlist the subject and his girlfriend for personal instruction, if that became necessary. He had accomplished both parts of his mission. His superiors would be pleased.

John figured that in writing the report he could clarify his thinking in regard to the material and gain some new insights. Maybe he could make some progress on decoding that elusive fifth section.

Gary picked up one of the magazines from the table and began idly leafing through it. "Your responses have been satisfactory, John Frankel," he said finally. "When can we expect your report?"

"I'll have it ready for you by the end of the week. Shall I email it?"

Gary was horrified. "Insecure transmission. Write out your report in longhand. Drive it personally over to the Federal building downtown. Place the report in a plain white envelope addressed to Gary, Federal Building, Suite 102-B, Midland. Hand it to the receptionist. He'll know what to do with it."

John nodded his assent.

Gary got up. Immediately the other two moved to flank him. He was almost through the door when he turned and spoke formally. "The government of the United States thanks you for your cooperation." John stood by the front door watching the sedan drive away.

"You handled that well John." Genevieve stood at the top of the stairs in her robe.

"You heard the whole thing?"

"From the hallway."

"I think the guy's sincere. Just a little misguided."

"I think he's pretty paranoid." She walked down the stairs and plopped into the wing chair. "What should we do about this?"

John thought for a moment.

"Nothing. I intend to write a full and genuine report. I believe that no possible harm can come to anyone who studies this material. In order to be successful with it you have to transcend the current paradigm of conflict and hatred. If that's the case I'd like everyone in the government to work with it. Maybe it will change the world for the better."

Genevieve brightened. "You're right! Wouldn't that be great?"

John went downstairs to lift weights. Later he took Genevieve to the pool hall and taught her how to play 8-ball. She was a natural.

During the next three days John wrote the report he had promised. He dropped it and the book off to the receptionist at the front desk of the Federal building.

As he walked out, John turned around and inspected the structure. The Federal Building was a fortress. It could probably withstand a bombing attack.

John came home from the lab one day in early March. Suitcases were in the front hall. Robert and Rachel were talking in the kitchen.

Rachel gave him a big hug. "Let me look at you." She stood back and looked appreciatively at him. "You're different."

Robert agreed. "Yes son, you're looking strikingly good."

"I'm starting to fill out more. The weightlifting is helping."

"It's not that so much." Robert studied him. "You're bigger. I mean, you feel bigger. I mean...I don't know what I mean. You're different in a good way."

John was pleased. "It's that book dad. It has the most incredible information in it. I have been practicing with it for months now."

"What is it dear?" Rachel asked. "If it can do such good things for you I want some too."

"Let's discuss it after dinner," John said, hoping that Rachel would want to cook tonight. They were both sick of their own pathetic attempts at food preparation. When they finally got a place of their own one of them would have to learn how to cook.

Rachel spoke firmly. "Let's get takeout tonight. I've been spoiled these past three months."

Over dinner, John explained what he'd been doing with the technique. He left out the wild bits and talked about the calming effect of the breathing exercises.

""It sounds difficult." Robert listened with only half an ear. New-agey stuff bored him.

"It's not. It's a piece of cake actually, especially now that I understand the purpose. I'll show you the technique just as the book described. Want to try?"

Robert begged off. Rachel said, "I'm game." John looked at his father. "Dad, you have to be completely silent and unobtrusive."

"I'll go into the living room and read. I'll just observe from in there."

"Ok mom." John moved two chairs out into the center of the kitchen floor. "Sit in the chair with your feet flat on the floor and your hands in a comfortable position. Or you can do it lying flat on the floor."

Rachel objected. "I always thought it was important to meditate in a certain position."

"That isn't true with this meditation. Like a lot of things, we focus on the ritual and miss the point of the exercise. The point is to feel as physically comfortable as you can."

"In that case, let's go into the living room. I'd like to lie down on the carpet with my head on a couple of pillows."

When Rachel was comfortable John explained the general theory of the technique and showed her how to breathe properly.

"Breathe deeply from the abdomen. Fill the lungs on the inbreath and completely release the breath on the exhale." He showed her how to use the body like a bellows to suck in air and to allow prana to flow into the chakras. He went through the specific breathing instructions for stage one and gave her a copy of the printout for the first stage. When she was ready, he talked her through the procedure. After half an hour or so Rachel suddenly sat up. "John! I felt it."

"Felt what?" Robert and John said together.

"I'm not sure how to explain it. For an instant I felt totally peaceful, serene even. It felt good."

John smiled. "You got it mom, right on the first try. It took me months! How did your body feel?"

"I didn't even know it was there." Rachel was astonished. "This is much better than yoga."

"Wow. You nutted it right off the bat."

Rachel laughed. "Nutted it?"

"Guy talk," Robert said. John got excited. "Mom, you only went the first step. There's so much more."

Rachel's eyes opened wide. "I feel like a kid again, opening a present. Let's do more of this tomorrow."

"Mom."

"What?"

"Go look at yourself in the mirror." Robert looked at John. He noticed it too. Rachel walked to the big full length mirror on the wall in the hallway. "Look at your face," John said.

It was *soft,* and glowing a little from the inside. "This is a lot better than face creams."

"How did this happen?" Rachel asked.

"I don't know mom. It sure does make you feel and look better doesn't it?"

Rachel was amazed. "All this from half an hour of breathing!"

"The pattern of the breathing is complex but ingenious. Somehow it opens your chakras and the prana just flows in. That's the best I can explain it."

Robert was skeptical. "Looks like she's back to normal now."

Rachel looked again. The glow was gone.

"Tomorrow after dinner. We'll do it again OK?"

"Sure."

John worked with Rachel for the next couple of weeks on the technique. He was curious to see whether it would work on someone who knew nothing about the theory behind it. If Rachel could benefit from the technique then maybe a lot of other people could too. He would have something to offer his fellow human beings and might have a positive influence in the world.

Robert watched skeptically as John worked with Rachel. He did not participate but carefully noted everything his son said. He memorized the breathing patterns.

John eventually got Rachel through the breathing exercises of the second stage, to the point where her smaller sphere was primed for activation. "Oh John, this feels so good!" Rachel would say.

"Do you see or feel anything different about yourself?" He was interested to know if his mother now had a greater awareness of her merkaba.

"I feel bigger, lighter somehow."

When John pressed her to continue she was having none of it. "But mom, there's a lot more you can do with this technique."

"Like what?" she asked, curious.

John was stumped for a second. He certainly couldn't tell her about the rest! "Well, you can feel even better."

"My life is great right now."

John understood that the technique must be presented to others as a commonplace self-help, stress-relieving meditation. 99.9% of the population would have no interest in the other stages anyway. Even if he could get them to believe it was possible. That made him feel better because he could talk easily to others about it. He wanted no more of the "Weird John Frankel" crap.

Rachel would spend twenty minutes each day with it. She told John she was feeling more relaxed, confident, and happy. She looked ten years younger.

Robert actually complained to her about it. "If you get any younger you'll get propositioned by your male students."

"Might be fun," she teased.

Robert wasn't really mad. Not at all.

Bill Richardson called John on Friday just after work.

"Hey Frankel. We finally got a space to play table tennis. You still interested?"

John had forgotten all about that. "Uh, yeah, I am. I've been doing some lifting but I need some aerobics too."

Last week John went out with Robert for a jog but had to stop after a couple of blocks. He couldn't even keep up with his 52-year-old father. That was a little embarrassing but he hated running.

"We got some guys from the university. Me, you, Gene, and two other guys from the high school. Gene's dad agreed to get two professional quality tables. He's letting us use space in that old warehouse he moved out of a couple of years ago. If there's enough interest he figures he can make some money distributing equipment."

"That's great! When do we play?"

"We finally got the league forming up. There are some good players so we'll have to practice."

John didn't want to devote too much time to table tennis. Like pool, it would just be a hobby.

"I can practice twice a week with you guys for two hours. I'm real busy right now so that's all I can do."

"That's OK," Bill said. He knew John was in school and working as well. "Even if you don't join the league you can just play with me and Gene." Gene Watkins was Bill's buddy from their days on the East High baseball team.

They agreed to begin play the following Tuesday from 8 p.m. until 10 p.m. To most people (like Robert) table tennis was a pathetic game called "ping pong" where two people stood still and bounced a ball. The game Bill and Gene wanted to play had the ball going over 100 mph and emphasized speed and quickness. It was just what he needed to get his sorry ass in shape.

16

O N Monday night John watched Rachel do the technique. She was an expert now on the first stage and the breathing for the second stage. After that he went upstairs to take another look at the symbols he had copied from the code book.

There were still seven unknown symbols in the fifth section. One of these stood out. It had a bunch of concentric circles with a tiny dot on the outermost one. When you looked into that symbol in the actual codebook the concentric circles got bigger, and there were more and more of them.

John began the technique with the symbol clear in his mind. As his outer sphere energized, the room around him began to shimmer and he felt a surge of joy flood through his entire being. He negotiated the zone of chaos around the earth and found himself floating within the golden white mist. Within the mist were impressions, images, and feelings that impinged upon his consciousness, then melted back into the potential. John felt a sense of limitless possibility coupled with a feeling of excitement and well-being. This state of consciousness felt perfectly real even though he could not see his physical body.

John concentrated on the symbol in his mind. Within the mist, the symbol appeared. It began to vibrate as if it were alive and responsive to his thoughts.

He formed the question, "What does this symbol mean? Show me it's precise function in the greatest detail possible."

The concentric circles in front of him expanded and slowly he zoomed into the center of it. The circles had become rings, zooming past him more and more rapidly like the starfield screensaver on his computer. In just a few seconds, millions of them had disappeared from his peripheral vision. Despite the rapidity of their passing he knew precisely how many there were and his position within them.

John was sure the symbol was acting as a guide. As long as it was present there was no danger of a blue jaunt.

Now the rapidity of his progress accelerated. The rings flashed past faster and faster until they were no longer distinguishable. John was in a tunnel of light, growing brighter and brighter.

There must be some way to stop this headlong plunge, but how?

John reached for something to hold on to and thought of Genevieve. Immediately, the blur of light softened and individual rings again became distinguishable. The rapidity of their passing slowed dramatically and he stopped within a ring about 1/3 of the way out from the center. (How do you express 1/3 of infinity? John just knew it, that's all.)

The reality around him burst into billions of colors. He was surrounded by a gang of little childlike beings, laughing and giggling.

"Ooooooh. Look, [dark dark blue]."

John had entered an astonishing world of intensely bright and variegated color, each one having its own unique feeling.

A question popped into his mind: "Who are you?"

He was bombarded by more sensory experience than he had ever dreamed possible, but John did not feel overwhelmed. The color palette was far greater than the 24 million on his computer monitor screen. The colors shifted constantly so the place had a different feeling in every instant. Even the pastels had an intensity far greater than the colors of earth, which were pale and wan by comparison. This world was a living, breathing riot of color and feeling. It was exhilarating.

John knew that he was not upon the surface of any planet. He couldn't see or feel his human body but it didn't matter. There was a feeling that all was well. Here there were no defined forms, no solid objects, no sky, no ground, no sun, moon, and stars. Nevertheless, it was remarkably beautiful.

The others waited for him to respond in some way. Just like on earth he was lost in a daydream!

"Where am I?" he said.

Giggles and laughter. "You're here of course! Where did you think you were?" More laughter.

One very bright yellow being hovered close. "I am [goldenrod]"

Another beautiful light blue being came up. "I am [bright turquoise]"

Soon all of them were identifying themselves to him, trying to merge with him. He could feel the consciousness of each one. They felt incredibly light, ephemeral, and joyful.

"Ooooooh, this one is so dark." That was [goldenrod].

The creatures around him were brightly colored. One color always dominated but that color was generated from billions of others. Evidently he appeared to them as very dark blue.

The author is not capable of describing such a reality in words. The only analogy that can be made is to imagine every molecule of air having a different color and feeling, all of it different shades of wonderful.

"C'mon, lets play," [goldenrod] said. "Yeah!" said the others. They dashed off to play a game of hide and seek. The little light beings would hide behind cloud banks of light and try to blend in, or change their coloring scheme as much as possible to match the surrounding environment. John did not participate. He just reveled in how wonderful he felt. The patterns of color and sensation were beautiful and unbelievably complex. His intellectual pattern recognition skills were pitifully inadequate to identify even the simplest configurations. Here he must feel his way.

It seemed to these creatures of light that [dark, dark blue] was holding back. The others began to tease him (nothing new here, John thought).

"You are hesitant, [dark dark blue]. Come join us!"

Genevieve might really like this place, he thought.

The thought of Genevieve brought another brightly colored being to him. This one was a bright orange. "Let us mingle together," [it/he/she?] said coquettishly. "First you have to catch me!" [bright orange] squealed with delight and raced away. John chased [bright orange], seeing and feeling the billions of subtle colors he was moving through. Suddenly [bright orange] stopped and was inside him. "Oh my God."

He could feel every nuance of [it/his/her] being as [bright orange] changed its coloring inside him. The polarized concepts of "male" and "female" were inappropriate in this place, but it was an ingrained habit of thought.

Every feeling here seemed magnified a billion times but all of it felt positive. Yes, that was it. On earth there was just as much negative as positive in the environment.

After an instant [bright orange] was out.

"Oh!" she said. "You are so very [intense/powerful/poignant]." She was awed and he could feel it. Soon the others gathered around him. "Why do you not play with us?" they asked.

"You feel like little children," he said.

They laughed. "Of course we are!"

"Aren't you?" a lightly colored brown being asked. "Do you not play as well?" said another.

"Where I come from the children play and the adults work."

"Why do not the [adults] play?"

"Because they are often too tired," John explained.

All of them exchanged looks of puzzlement.

"What is [tired]?" they asked.

"Tired is when your body wears down because of overexertion. Then you need rest."

"What is [wears down]? What is [overexertion]? What is [rest]?" All of the bright little beings clamored for answers at the same time.

After attempting to explain he realized they had no concept of tired, or anything negative. These beings knew only joy. Suddenly John understood.

"Of course!" he said. "There is only fun here."

"Yeah!" they said. "Let's play!"

Over the next (what felt like to John) days and weeks he played and played and played and never got tired. He felt just like a little kid again. Every little care and worry was gone. John barely recalled his original purpose for coming. The translation of the symbol of concentric circles was less important now. The powerful sensations he was feeling overwhelmed his intellectual function. Or, perhaps, his intellect was fully occupied in trying to figure out this new experience.

He merged with many of the brightly colored creatures of light. Each time felt the most excruciating, intense pleasure. None of them could merge with [dark dark blue] for more than a few moments.

Once goldenrod asked him, "Why are you so [dark/intense/wise]?"

John felt that now would be a good time to get his question answered. He brought the concentric circle symbol to the forefront of his mind. He indicated one of the smaller circles toward the center. "I believe I am here."

All of them immediately understood. John was astonished. He thought they were a bunch of mental lightweights.

"How do you know of this?"

They all had a great laugh at that one. "How do we know?!" one of them asked. "The [symbol for All] is known throughout the all-that-is."

John felt stupid. These beings completely understood what he had so painstakingly translated from the book.

They began to probe him.

"[dark dark blue] is from the outermost edge," a pale pink being said.

For just a moment all of them were in awe. "Wow!" bright turquoise said.

But these creatures could not be serious for more than a few moments. "Let's play!"

They were off. Goldenrod stayed behind. "Let us merge again." As they melded John was turned inside out in a most agreeable way. He understood now that his body was almost pure light in this universe. They separated. John said, "Let me envelop you, dear Goldenrod." John gently surrounded and pleasured [it/him/her]. It was fantastic, incredible, wonderful. Goldenrod shuddered with ecstasy. He had barely touched [it/him/her].

"Oh!" Goldenrod said, and snuggled up to him. Soon another came, and another, and another. In this ephemeral world it was possible to pleasure multiple partners. They spent some time in enjoying each other. John was in indescribable bliss. Here, there was no "bored." Here, there was no "coming down from the high." There was just an infinity of positive feeling. He had, by now, experienced billions of colors and sensations but had never felt the same way twice. It was too good to be true. But it *was* true.

There was no need to sleep and no desire to either.

Goldenrod "introduced" him to all of the others but he lost count of them. They played a myriad of games and altered the environment to suit. John was not as good as the others in changing the colors but he was able to show them how to make things "solid." Solid was an idea that had never occurred to their light and carefree personalities. John pushed and shoved a bunch of light together and fashioned it into a mountain. Then he made a plain of green "grass" with "trees" and "rocks." He made caves in the mountain, and meadows, and rivers, and lakes, and sandy beaches. They were all astonished. The little beings didn't understand how they could have failed to think of such a delicious thing. [dark dark blue] had opened up a whole new set of possible experiences! All of them were very creative and soon had the hang of it. They invented game after game and played them. They made up different rules and played again.

When they were not playing [dark dark blue] showed them through pictures in his mind what his world looked like. He identified each and every different life form, landscape, and object he could think of. The little creatures of light were astonished by the variety. [dark dark blue] was too, always having taken his planet for granted. As he continued to think of more and more and more things his friends wanted to visit.

"Is it possible for you to visit me on earth?" [dark dark blue] asked.

"None of us have ever even been close to the dot on the outer edge," [bright turquoise] said.

"Why do you call it the dot on outer edge?" [dark dark blue] asked.

They were astonished at his question.

The symbol appeared before him. All of the little light creatures now combined to form a single intelligence.

"The universe is composed of superposed layered realities. There is no limit to the number of layers. All realities coexist within each other. All are accessible to those like yourself who have discovered the secret of consciousness alteration. The symbol of concentric rings is just a helpful metaphor. Toward the center there is less density or organization. Toward the outer edge there is more. Beyond the furthermost ring is what you might call a special zone of chaos. We perceive that you have not yet encountered it but believe you soon will. This area is the womb of creation, the incubator of what-will-be."

"Why does my universe look so much different than this one?" [dark dark blue] asked.

"One cannot build a great ocean liner before one learns to construct all of its simpler components. The evolution of thought starts out as very general, then gets more and more complex. Somewhat like your Euclid who started with 5 postulates. He developed simple constructs at first, then used those to generate more sophisticated theorems.

"All that is proceeds from that which has gone before. Everything in existence must draw on the energy and constructs from that which has been previously built. You call this concept evolution. It is the idea upon which the All itself has been constructed."

[dark dark blue] pondered. "Who or what created the universal medium?"

"That we do not know. It has always been and always will be. It is a pure potential, from which all things come forth."

As time passed [dark dark blue] became more accustomed to his environment. He was taught how to change his coloring. This allowed him to experience the world of light from different perspectives. [dark dark blue] invented more games and played them.

In time [dark blue] learned to manipulate individual "pixels" of light in the most subtle fashion. [he/she/it] was able to change the patterns of the world to suit [his] every whim. He made light creations and built a personal temple many stories high, with walkways and staircases and magnificent views. He created plains of grass and oceans of watery light and immersed himself in them. [dark blue] discovered that creating here was effortless, for the light seemed insubstantial and easily manipulated. The only limitation was his own imagination. Experiencing here was constantly exhilarating. [dark blue's] intellectual function was still finding it hard to accept. The others ooohed and ahhhhed at his constructions, for he was much better at "solid" than they.

[dark blue] noticed that as he changed his coloring from within, the light around him responded differently. He learned from [light brown] and [goldenrod] to allow others to alter his coloring. At first [dark blue] was hesitant. When he allowed [goldenrod] to gently change him it felt so good that he was soon participating much more fully with the others.

As time passed [blue] noticed that it was becoming easier for the others to merge with him as well.

One "day" [sunflower] said "[blue], why have you come to us?"

[blue] began to think. [blue] hardly remembered, or cared about, anything except the dynamics of the ever changing light. [blue] looked at himself and saw waves of tiny particles of brilliant color, interweaving within themselves and forming an overall impression of blueness. [blue] consciously changed [his] coloring and felt a fresh breeze of new feeling inside [him].

Dimly, [blue] remembered a planet called earth and a [female?] he was attached to there. But then the one called [ebony] wanted to mingle and [blue] forgot all about it.

One day as [light blue] played a presence came into its mind.

"John," it said.

"I do not understand. I am [light blue]."

"John," the presence said. A picture of the planet earth spun in the mind of [light blue].

"Do you remember?" A picture of the one called "Genevieve" formed before [light blue]. [he] remembered the delicious feelings connected with [her]. [light blue] began to ponder. This was an activity not understood by the others. Something akin to it only occurred for them when it was necessary or desirable to become a single intelligence. But [light blue] was different and had brought them many unusual and wonderful experiences, so they left him alone.

For a time [light blue] thought hard. [His] intellectual function was almost gone. The attempt to concentrate on anything for more than an instant was now very difficult.

Let's see, there is the playing, and the mingling, the colors, and the infinite variety of sensation. There is also something else. Something [he] is capable of but had not touched in quite a while.

[blue] began to think of the planet spinning before him. He noticed the whiteness surrounding it. Yes, the clouds. Clouds! [He] observed the blue on the surface. Water. It was a dark blue, just like [he] was.

[dark blue] began to remember and began to slowly reconnect with the fullness of himself. There were land masses and mountains on the planet, which he had showed the others. And there were males and females. And there was work, and tired, and happiness, and sadness. [dark blue] became very confused, for such a place seemed contradictory and impossible.

[dark blue] thought for a long time and did not play the games. [beautiful violet] came to mingle. [dark blue] said, "I am pondering."

"What is pondering?"

[dark dark blue] tried to explain. "It is somewhat like deciding upon a landscape for playing 'solid.' Except deeper."

"I do not understand deeper," [beautiful violet] said. "But that is all right [dark dark blue], for we love you any way you decide to be."

Her sweet innocence touched him. It reminded him of his dearest Genevieve. Genevieve!

In an explosion of awareness he was John again. All of the others noticed immediately. They all gathered around.

"Is it time to return to your world on the outer edge?" [goldenrod] asked.

"Yes dear ones, it is." John felt like an ancient sage speaking to a group of innocents. But he knew these children could combine to form a much vaster intelligence. They just didn't want to most of the time.

"I have so much enjoyed my visit. Let us plan to play again."

"Yeah!" They all said. "Thank you for your game of solid!"

They were off.

John felt a sense of deep satisfaction. He had learned so much, experienced so much joy, and couldn't wait to get back and tell Genevieve.

He began the breathing exercises.... wait a minute. He hadn't breathed in what seemed like a couple of years. So what should he do? Orienting himself toward a state of consciousness that in this reality seemed effortless. From this place of playfulness he was able to easily reach the place beyond time. He connected to the golden-white substance of the universal medium.

At first it was very difficult to reestablish within him the vibration of earth because he had not experienced it in so long. He had to fully define the vibration of the destination so John reconnected with his intellectual function. Gradually, it became easier to hold the vision and regain the feeling of earth. He kept the image of his room and Genevieve in front of him. He was eventually rewarded with the shimmering and fading out of the present environment. John reached out and probed the universal medium. Within its fabric were vibrational trails, like airline routes marked on a map. It was fascinating to reach out along a branch and get a feeling for another world he might become a part of. The feeling of adventure and excitement was palpable.

John remembered the symbol of concentric rings. He let it guide him back to the outermost ring and the dot on the edge of it. Why did the earth have a special marking?

Slowly now, the dot grew larger. John encountered a chaotic but eerily beautiful riot of energy that Genevieve called earth's zone of chaos. He had almost forgotten. The world of light also had a similar zone but it was lighter and far easier to negotiate. John made it through and his room began to take form. First fuzzily, then more clearly, he found himself in his body and the room stopped shimmering.

He was back, sitting in the chair with his hands in his lap. John felt full of joy and childlike playfulness, for part of him was [dark dark blue] and would remain so forever. He wanted to get up and dance a jig, tease Genevieve, knock over a few chairs, and go outside and throw snowballs.

The clock face read 6:45. Exactly the same time he had left. Once again, no time had elapsed on earth. Yet he had spent the equivalent of several subjective years in the universe of light.

That was impossible. One couldn't arrive and leave at the same time! John walked clumsily to his computer. He confirmed that the date and time was indeed the same as his departure.

He was far too happy to worry. He had learned and practiced feeling joyful for so long it had become a habit. It was one he did not ever want to break.

John stood and almost tripped over his own feet. His body felt very heavy and awkward, as if he were encased in a suit of armor. It was thirsty and told him it desired to eliminate unneeded substances. The concepts were almost foreign to him, but he recalled the appropriate place for such activities. The bathroom.

He laughed. The bathroom? It was something John had forgotten to show the little light beings. He was sure they would have found it hilarious.

John considered the objects on his desk. He remembered "work," and "lab," and "Jimmy," and "school." Suddenly he experienced something shocking: a negative thought accompanied by an uncomfortable feeling.

This planet earth was engulfed in an ocean of thought. Yes. Fear, anxiety, scarcity, competition, worry, and hatred. These were very strange to his new orientation. He wondered whether he would be able to block them out.

John worked on that for a while. The more attention he paid to blocking them the more he found himself resonating to them. There was something backwards about that.

He didn't feel so good anymore. The feeling of pure joy was leaving and John experienced sadness. Sadness? His new friends would never understand; he barely could himself.

John stumbled into the bathroom. He inspected his human body in the mirror. It looked and felt ludicrous. His body of light was beautiful and subtly changed in every instant. But this gross and ugly thing! The absurd hair flying out in all directions, like a drunken clown. The long arms and legs and small hands. His cock hanging down and his knee joints and elbows sticking out. His big feet.

John began to laugh. He laughed and laughed and howled like a madman, naked in the bathroom. For a second it seemed as though [goldenrod] was there with him. From the sublime to the ridiculous. If they saw him now they'd lock him up.

John was adjusting his thinking to earth quite nicely. That made him laugh some more.

He opened the door and saw Genevieve walking down the hall toward him. She stopped and stared.

"John! Where have you been?"

They spent the evening and half the night talking. It took quite a while for John to adjust to his body, and hers too. But then his hands touched her soft skin and he saw the beauty of her. He understood that joy could be found anywhere. To experience happiness in the world of light was effortless. But in this world of tremendous polarity the experience was more poignant and far, far deeper.

He had forgotten how good it could be right here on earth. Like a man home from a very long journey, he began to appreciate the comforts of home once more. That night he made love to Genevieve so gently and so passionately she said it was the best ever.

17

THE days and weeks passed. The feeling of joy from the universe of light faded but did not completely go away. The first day back at work was a disaster. John made a calculation error in a critical experiment that ruined a complete testing cycle. Dr. Jackson was furious. John knew that Dr. J's optical work was out of the mainstream and that his funding was tenuous. Ostensibly he was working on optical calculating devices, but the work had branched off into a new and exciting area. Right now Jackson was designing a complex new optical microscope that could penetrate (hopefully) clearly into the quantum level. John's screw-up had cost the project a week of productive work, and made him feel miserable. Jimmy teased him about it unmercifully.

John was amazed that years of bliss could so quickly fade away. His experiences with the technique were sensitizing him more and more to negative thoughts. Negative emotion followed almost immediately after. John didn't like this development at all. His experiences with the technique were awesome but sometimes he wished that he'd never found the material.

Genevieve felt the same way.

"It's like the lady in that baseball movie we saw with Mats last summer," John said to her that night. "What did she say? 'The world is a simple place for those not cursed with self-awareness.'"

Genevieve laughed. "That's about it. But we can never go back now John."

Two months later John decided to test the technique during athletic competition. He was practicing with Gene and Bill in the crumbling old Watkins Athletics warehouse building, which was slated for demolition in the fall. Bill and Gene had cleaned out a 40 by 30 foot space, swept the cement floor, and installed a table.

They would play best two out of three matches while the third guy rested. John had lost all his matches as usual. The game of table tennis placed a premium on quickness and fast reaction times. John enjoyed playing, but "Frankel the Slow" was unable to keep up with the competition. His only talent was hitting the ball hard. When he got hold of one not even Gene could return it. John was tolerated because some of the really good players hit over 100 mph. He gave them a taste of what could be expected in real competition.

John was now able to complete to the middle of stage two of the technique in less than the 20 minutes between matches. He walked with his chair out of the view of Bill and Gene and placed his chair behind some empty boxes.

"Where are you going, John?' Gene asked.

"Goin' back there to pull his pud probably," Bill joked.

When it was his turn to play Bill shouted. "C'mon Frankel, get your butt over here!" John got up and walked toward the table. Bill had unexpectedly beaten Gene 2 games to 1. John saw him standing at the far end of the table, brimming with confidence.

"C'mon Frankel, I got you easy." Bill was tall but very quick and had good strokes. He could hit his forehand with speed from anywhere with lots of topspin, producing a looping shot that would jump off the table like a scared rabbit. When John hit to his backhand Bill would just block it and wait for the opportunity to smash with his forehand.

John walked up to the table feeling "in the zone." He took a few quick steps up and down to loosen up. He spun the paddle in his hand and crouched down, ready to serve.

Bill snorted. "A lot of good that'll do ya Frankel."

John served a short backspin serve to Bill's backhand. Bill softly pushed the ball back over the net, but so close to the net on John's side that he couldn't attack. After a few exchanges Bill had manipulated John out of position on the left side of the table. John was forced to put his ball high enough where Bill could crush it with his forehand. As the ball bounced on Bill's side of the table John saw his opponent move his feet and get ready for the kill. If things held to form Bill would smash the ball by him crosscourt on his forehand side, to the right side of the table. Strangely, Bill seemed to be moving in slow motion. John had time to move his feet, get set, and punch the ball down the right side of the table for a winner.

Bill looked at him sharply. To his perception John had moved lightning quick. "How'd you do that John?"

Behind him Gene spoke. "I saw the whole thing. Great footwork. Anticipated your shot, man. You got to get more game. That forehand loop of yours is too predictable."

"Oh yeah?" Bill said. "Wait'll I kick your ass with it again."

"IF you can beat Frankel," Gene replied.

"Serve!" Bill said to John. "You just got lucky."

John was elated. He had done this twice before, but uncomprehendingly. Could he maintain it? The key was not to go out of control and lose the feeling from the technique.

He was most successful when his attention was on simply playing and having fun. Intellectual analysis wrecked it. Any negative emotion brought him out of it immediately. John won the match 2 games to 1. Bill sat down and grumped. "John, you don't have that much game. I musta played really bad."

Gene snorted. "Sore loser. Watch how I take care of Frankel. You might learn something."

Gene had always dominated the play between them. In two months John had won the occasional game, but never a match.

Gene was short and stocky but very fast. He played Asian style with the paddle held between his first two fingers. This style allowed incredible speed from the forehand and backhand side. Gene had already won a couple of local tournaments. His enthusiasm for the game was rapidly replacing his love for baseball.

"I can beat you in pool," John said to himself.

"What was that?" Gene was preparing to serve.

"I said I can beat you in pool."

"What the hell does that have to do with anything? Prepare to get annihilated."

John laughed. He felt really good. it didn't matter to him if he won or lost.

Gene served.

John could never figure out what spin he had on the ball. Gene would make a bunch of gyrations with his paddle and his body. The ball would come out of nowhere, sometimes close to the net, sometimes a rocket deep to the far corner. Normally Gene got half his points on John's inability to make a proper return.

John saw Gene slowly wind up, saw the ball in the air, saw Gene turn on it and flick his wrist in a sideswiping motion. John easily pushed it back to his backhand. He lined up Gene's return and put the ball away crosscourt to his forehand.

Gene looked confused. "What's got into you today?"

Bill hooted. "What's the matter Watkins? Losing your touch?"

Gene gave Bill the finger.

"C'mon," John said confidently. "See how it feels to play from behind for once."

"All right John, you asked for it." Normally Gene only needed to play John at half speed, working on his footwork and positioning, or practicing a new shot.

Now Gene's serves were even more confusing and he moved with amazing quickness. He's really good, John thought. He almost felt like a cheater. No matter how Gene bore down, no matter how hard he hit the ball, or with what spin or placement, John was there. It was effortless. He could hear Bill behind him shouting. "Great shot John!...nice footwork...what a move!"

John won both games, 11 - 4 and 11 - 2. It was total domination, even though John did not have a good serve and Gene could get on it quickly. The only points John lost occurred when he put his own serve into the net.

Gene was flabbergasted.

They both looked at him. "What you just did isn't possible," Bill said. "You're not that good. Gene is one of the best players in the city and you crushed him. What the hell is going on?"

John was thrilled. The technique had undergone a rigorous examination and had passed the test with flying colors.

"OK boys," he said. "Let's talk."

They sat down on an old bench. John told them about the codebook and the technique. He briefly described the first two stages that got you into the zone.

"Can you show us how to do it?" Gene asked. "It sounds like something out of a movie or a science fiction book."

"You were always a weird one Frankel," Bill said. "It'd be just like you to come up with something like this."

John explained that the purpose wasn't to get better at something, but to attain an enhanced state of consciousness. "The zone is really an altered state of awareness," John explained. "It occurs in the middle of the second stage of this procedure." He explained a little bit about the human energy field and how specific use of the breath aligned the energy within it. Very briefly he went over the mental protocols for enabling it. "Once you complete the procedure you can't focus too much on the goal or you'll lose it. It's counter-intuitive."

Bill shook his head. "Too intellectual for me. I don't see it."

Gene was interested and spoke to Bill. "Remember that time John hit the homer off Trevor?"

"Yeah! You almost killed Kathleen Summers with a foul ball. That bitch! I was laughing all the way home after practice."

"Did you do that on purpose then?" Bill asked.

"No. I only just got the instruction book and hadn't figured out any of it yet."

John turned to Gene.

"If you come a half hour early I'll work with you on it before we start playing. But remember, it has taken me years of practice and you might not see results for a while." Then John remembered how fast Rachel had caught on. "On the other hand, you might get it quick. You're a fast learner."

"Anybody that can go from a nobody to beating me 2 and 0 has got something. I can see making a couple of lucky shots, but you did it for two games in a row. You were everywhere." Gene rubbed his chin. "But I didn't *see* you moving any faster. It's not like you were a blur or anything. You were just *there*, no matter how fast I hit it or where hit it. I don't get it."

"I'm not sure I do either. You can't argue with success." John paused. "I have to tell you that my purpose for learning this stuff has nothing to do with sports. Both you guys know I'm no athlete. The only reason I play at all is to get some exercise. I don't really care whether I win or lose. Competitive people will have a hard time with this, I think. They won't have the proper orientation."

Gene thought about that for a few moments.

"I think I get what you're saying. I'll just look at it as something to calm me down before a match. Sometimes I get so juiced I want to hit everything as hard as I can. Then I fuck my game up."

Bill interrupted. "OK guys, we aint in class. I'm up."

John had lost the feeling now and was busier than a one-legged butt kicker trying to keep up with Bill and Gene. Both of them unmercifully kicked his ass for the rest of the session.

John laughed and threatened to do the technique again for the last match with Bill.

"Oooooh," Bill said. "I'm scared."

A year and a half after Genevieve's graduation from high school she and John still lived at the Frankel house on Magnolia Drive.

Rachel had tried over and over to convince John not to leave, without success. But one word from Genevieve and the matter was settled. "Please John, can we stay? I so much like this old house."

"OK sweetheart. I'll keep giving dad a check every month for room and board."

"You don't have to do that son," Rachel said quickly.

"Yes he does," Robert said. "A deal is a deal. Besides, they get home cooked meals in the bargain."

"But I *like* to cook Robert!" Rachel didn't want anything spoiling her plans.

"Irrelevant. John's education fund is now most of our retirement and I'm not going to touch any more of that. I want to get a new TV set and audio equipment. We can replace that crummy old doorwall to the back porch with a new one. The roof needs fixing. All that costs money."

Rachel looked at Genevieve. "Does he always do just what you say?"

"Pretty much."

Rachel felt envious but said nothing.

A couple of weeks later John found a rectangular object wrapped in brown paper on the second shelf in his bedroom, above his desk. He unwrapped the package and found the code book inside. John didn't have to ask who had brought the book back or how they got inside the house. The old cover was gone, replaced by a new one.

He threw the book back on the shelf.

18

Alnilam, Orion Sector – 4 million years ago

ON Telek-Hath, capital planet of the Orion sector, Salat Toor sat suspended twenty feet above the floor reading a message disk. Toor was the 2,123,567th incarnation of the ruler of the Orion High Council. Through the transparent walls a riot of stars were visible. Directly in his line of vision a beautiful pattern of lights invited his attention. The luminance shone bright, then dim, in complex geometries and colors. Toor had his engineers build it especially for his entertainment. The dynamic tapestries was supposed to stimulated thought and inspire him to fresh and original viewpoints.

The galaxy was old beyond belief, and stale. Over the past 4 billion years, relationships between the sectors had become long established. Cultures had stagnated, oscillating between well-defined parameters. Galactic social scientists had been predicting political, economic, and cultural trends successfully now for almost a billion years.

Toor read the disk over again. Interesting things were happening on an obscure little water planet in the Desert. Orion maintained several bases there, but only because everyone else did. There were silly legends of treasure, or some great secret the planet was supposed to hold. After millions of years of searching nothing out of the ordinary had ever been found.

Holovids of the place showed a startling species count, with many contrasting ecosystems and climates beautifully integrated within the unusual planet. None of the galactic exobiologists and geologists could figure out how it all came together.

There was something distinctly odd about the feel of the planet and its surrounding space. Many galactics had trouble staying on the surface for more than a few days. The planet's magnetic field had a strange configuration, but that did not explain the anomalies.

Now this.

According to the report, genetic analysis of the most recent humanoid civilization showed remarkable attributes. Within their DNA were structures not seen anywhere else in the galaxy. Their function was unknown. Geneticists and exobiologists speculated that the new biology was a result of galactic interaction with the native humanoids over the past few million years. Orion scientists concluded that a new genotype was being born. One which included pieces from every culture that had ever interacted with the species.

This was unusual indeed.

If there was one thing well understood in the galaxy, it was the subject of biology and genetics. It was even possible to alter genetic structure for cosmetic purposes. Toor himself had had his earlobes lengthened in the current style.

He fingered the large, intricately designed earrings he had chosen for today. They had been shaped to resemble the famous Ptellehk star cluster. That reminded him of his latest concubine, a beauty with very shapely legs.

As Toor perused the report something suggested itself to him. These humanoids closely resembled Orions. If they had unusual abilities, perhaps they could be useful.

Salat Toor the 2,123,567th envisioned a grand plan which would take millions of years to come to fruition. A plan to restore the glory of Orion lost when Bakel Toor, his lamented ancestor, had agreed (admittedly under much pressure) to decentralize galactic politics.

What a waste. It was hoped at the time that abandonment of hierarchical societal organizations would breathe some fresh air into a stagnant galaxy. All it had done was fragment and isolate cultures so they became even more rigid than before. Orion had lost its preeminent influence within the society of Galaxy Six and thus within the Twelve as well. Once a powerful and respected decision making body, the Galactic High Council was now a figurehead. And his own influence at the head of it was reduced to nothing.

Salat Toor began to draft a policy document outlining his thoughts with regard to the earthians, as they were called. It would be music to the ears of the Traditionalist factions within Orion society.

The glory of Orion would be restored...

19

Jᴏʜɴ now had two "students," Rachel and Gene.

Rachel learned very quickly. After nine or ten sessions she had the routine down to her satisfaction. Rachel wanted nothing more than a feeling of serenity and happiness, which required mastery of stage one. Gene needed to also master the complicated second stage breathing patterns and the first two sets of mental exercises to reach 'the zone.'

The mental exercises were actually sophisticated protocols couched within a series of clever visualizations that directly manipulated the inner sphere of consciousness. These visualizations might be likened to a golfer who imagines himself lining up a shot. He or she visualizes swinging effortlessly and watching the ball fall into the hole. Their genius lay in the fact that the protocols worked even if you had no clue about the human energy field. The ingenious breathing exercises did all that.

The following Tuesday John worked with Gene before their practice session. He explained the breathing patterns and the exercises.

The next time they met, on Friday, John handed Gene a printout of the procedure. John went over the theory again. He monitored Gene through the first few steps. Gene felt funny and thought it was kind of stupid so they didn't make much progress. The following Tuesday Gene walked in with his printout and shook it in John's face.

"Frankel, this stuff is amazing."

"You mean you tried it already?"

"Hell yes! I got a tournament coming up next month and I need all the help I can get. When I first sat down with this stuff I felt like an ass. I couldn't believe I was doing it. I even locked my door so my dog couldn't get in. Then I just said, 'The hell with it. Either it'll work or it's all horseshit.' So I started. The first few times nothing happened. Or almost nothing. At the end I felt a little better I guess. The next time I went halfway through and felt really calm. That's not a good thing for me because when I play I feed off my emotions. But it still felt kinda good. So yesterday I decided to go through the whole thing. It was like being outside just before a thunderstorm. There was a feeling of stillness, but I just knew something big could explode at any time. Damn John, I can't describe what it was like. I loved that feeling of power. I felt like there was something explosive waiting for me if I could only get my hands on it. I want to know how to tap into that. Because if I can, I'm going to blow them all away. I'm gonna kick all their asses, especially Cunningham and Wang. Cunningham especially, that prick. He just toys with me, gives me those little smiles after he hits one by me. Fuck him, I want to crush him."

"You've gotten stage one and reached partially into stage two already Gene." John was amazed at his rapid progress. "When you fully nail stage two you'll get to what I call the space beyond time. You'll feel an amazing positive energy fill your entire body. That's where I was when I beat you guys last week. That feeling of power and explosiveness is your connection with the energy of your personal sphere of consciousness."

Gene had a strange look on his face. John couldn't tell whether it was one of awe or disbelief.

"Apparently you can also use it to enhance your athletic ability. When I beat you guys last week I knew I could reach anything you hit and get it back. Time slowed down for me. It was really cool."

Gene looked at John with new respect. "Amazing. I'd say you were full of shit except for the fact that you kicked my ass. I can't argue with that." Gene rubbed his chin. "So you can use this...energy, anyway you want? It'll do anything you tell it? Can I use it to get girls?"

John laughed. "All I know is that the procedure makes me feel more confident. Maybe girls respond to guys who are sure of themselves. The only way to find out for certain is to keep doing it and see what happens."

Gene was pleased. "OK John, there's just enough time before Bill comes. Leave me alone." John walked away and Gene began the procedure.

John decided to do so as well.

Bill walked in. "OK you two weirdo's, let's play. I'm working on my backhand loop and I need to practice." John and Gene ignored him. After a minute John got up. Bill stared at Gene, sitting in his chair with his eyes closed. A couple of minutes later Gene rose from his seat. Bill noticed that John's face was composed and he looked really relaxed. Gene moved like a stalking tiger.

"Hey what's going on here!" Bill was a little intimidated, especially by Gene.

John smiled. "Let's play. You and Gene start."

At first Gene was unstoppable, emanating a sense of power and agility that psyched Bill out and drove him right off the ball.

John heard sensei Matsumoto once say, "In Chinese *wushu*, you hit with your *eyes*." Sensei's feet had remained in position, his body slightly forward. With only his intent he unleashed a powerful stream of energy which literally pushed John backward so that he stumbled and almost fell.

John didn't know if Gene played any better, but he sure was having an effect on Bill. After 3 or 4 minutes Gene stopped after winning a point. "It's wearing off." Soon Gene was back to normal, beating Bill 2 games to 1. Now it was John's turn.

The same thing happened as last time. John crushed Gene 11–4 and 11–3.

Gene watched John closely the whole time, almost not even playing. From John he felt a sense of contained and controlled potential, like being around high tension wires. John had a slight smile on his face the whole time. Frankel wasn't breathing hard or efforting in any way. He was just *there*.

"You got the zone again Frankel," Bill observed.

"Wow," Gene said. "I want to get where you are."

"Practice makes perfect," John said.

After practice John entered the living room at 337 Magnolia. He said hi softly to Genevieve, who was watching a Kurosawa movie with Rachel and Robert. He went upstairs to his room and reviewed what happened.

For over an hour he'd been able to maintain stage two until he began to doubt his ability to sustain it.

Gene was able to pick up on this stuff with almost no instruction. The same for Rachel.

In all four cases, including Genevieve and himself, the technique led to uniformly positive results.

John remembered what Gary had told him. "Those who master the procedures quit on us." He wondered whether they had experienced positive results as well. If so, then perhaps the technique was intimate to human consciousness and the design of the human body.

The next step was to figure out why the effect was temporary. The best way to do that was during practice. The pressure of competition would test his ability to maintain correct focus.

He showered, got something to eat, and went back up into the bedroom. Genevieve was still engrossed in her movie. He knew she and Robert would probably engage in a lengthy discussion of it afterward.

He flopped on the bed and thought about his adventures so far. There were four of them: the trip to the valley with the weird-looking human, the journey to Genevieve's planet, his own trip to the small village, and [goldenrod's] universe of light beings. Every one was as realistic as real life. John recalled the "map" of energy he had dimly perceived on his return trip from the universe of light. From that location there were many imprints or impressions in the universal fabric. These imprints or energy tracks went off in all directions. It was a sort of three dimensional vibrational trail map that indicated someone(s) had traveled to or from there.

Does the earth have similar pathways around it? That would mean there are others practicing the technique! Maybe there was a meeting place, or a favorite spot to hang out. It would be really cool to meet others who had figured this out. Fellow weirdos who knew about the technique and had the intelligence and ability to use it. Such people would probably have special abilities. They might be expanded humans who could band together and make a difference in the world. Excited, John resolved to find the answer right away. He placed his chair so that it faced the red plastic clock hanging on the wall to the right of his desk.

John proceeded through the technique. He paid special attention to the procedures the book had outlined for stages three and four. The first two stages affected the inner sphere; the last two stages enabled the practitioner's awareness of the outer sphere of consciousness. During stage three, John's awareness of himself slowly expanded beyond the confines of his physical body to a radius of almost 30 feet in all directions. The perception of his body disappeared and he felt himself as a multicolored being of light. It was as the book described: the body and the merkaba were aspects of the same thing. As the practitioner altered his vibrational frequency the solidity of the body seemed to merge into the outer sphere of consciousness. Now his bedroom began to shimmer and his perception of it faded. The room was replaced by a golden white mist. The code book described it as the "universal medium."

Stage four required the precise vibrational identification of the target. Unless the entire sphere of consciousness resonated to the destination, nothing happened. In stage three the outer sphere of consciousness was primed. In this stage full activation occurred. The universal medium contained the vibrational footprint or signature for everything in existence. Once fully linked with it, it was possible to send one's awareness anywhere.

As his sphere of consciousness accelerated its vibration, a beautiful deep blue light surrounded it. John knew this was the signal for a successful "launch."

John noted all this in passing as he negotiated the zone of chaos. He found himself above the earth, suspended within the peculiar golden-white light of the universal medium. The now familiar feeling of complete well-being filled his consciousness. The universal medium appeared as a misty-like ocean of sensation and feeling.

"What do you want to do? What exciting place do you want to go to?" It seemed to say. "All worlds are reachable, just ask and I will take you there. In this state of being there can be no possibility of danger."

With the enhanced perception John turned his attention to earth. Were there vibrational trails around the earth? He perceived dozens of energetic pathways right away. Three were from his own recent journeys and one from the combined excursion with Genevieve. The others were Genevieve's. Each pathway had its own vibrational signature, like a pheromone trail, identifying the being who made it.

There were no others. The field around earth was empty. John probed further. Nothing.

Several of Genevieve's trails led to some place he couldn't identify. John brought the concentric rings icon up in his mind. The little light beings called it the guide symbol. Like a GPS receiver it indicated his present position at the tiny dot tangent to the outermost ring. Earth. Genevieve's trails led to a tiny dot outside the rings. There were tiny trails of energy moving out from it. Billions of them, leading to every ring in the symbol.

What's this? He moved toward it.

John abruptly found himself in a vast open room filled with workstations. Row after row of them extended farther than the eye could see in all directions, in a beautiful honeycomb pattern. An operator sat at each station.

John looked down, gasped, and screamed.

Below him was an ocean, and he was going to fall in! Vertigo assailed him and he closed his eyes tightly.

After a few seconds John realized he was safe. His feet were suspended a millimeter above the water. Deep sea waves rolled underneath him. The ocean smelled alive. He heard the sound of the water and the cry of birds. A salty breeze blew over his face and the sun was in his eyes. The sun? Above him, a hundred feet or so on the "ceiling," John saw a beautiful blue sky scudded with clouds and a small but warm sun. He conquered his fear and stood transfixed. The operators, millions of them, were buried in their consoles. When John looked down into the ocean again he became drawn into it just as he had from the drawings in the book. There were creatures down there...

"Holy shit!"

John lifted his eyes from the floor and tried to find the horizon but could not. This space was thousands, maybe millions, of miles wide. On earth the curvature of the planet provided built in limitation to sight. Here there was no restriction.

"Welcome John Frankel," someone said behind him. "We've been expecting you."

20

The Eyrie

JOHN whirled. The speaker was a short, funny looking man dressed in an ill-fitting 1950s checkerboard flannel shirt with short sleeves. He wore baggy pants tied carelessly with a belt and old-style red sneakers with big white tops and shoelaces. A cigarette dangled from his mouth. He looked like Wally from that old Leave it to Beaver TV show.

"Huh?"

"Surprised aren't you! Good! We planned it that way. Now if you'll just come with me."

"Wait a minute. Who are you? What is this place? How do you know my name?"

Wally did not answer but walked quickly toward a shabby little room a few hundred feet away. John hurried to catch up, keeping his eyes as much as possible off the floor. He spun Wally around. "Who are you and what is this place?"

"Rude bastard aren't you?"

John was insistent and repeated his demand.

"Typical male earthian," Wally said. "If you'll just come to the waiting area my friends will explain everything."

As they approached the doorway John observed a shabby room with stained and fly-speckled window glass and ugly green walls. The dirty floor was made of cheap linoleum with interlocking black and green squares.

John was disgusted. "Doesn't anyone ever clean this place?"

Wally dragged on his cigarette. A trail of ash fell from it and disappeared into the water.

John gulped. He closed his eyes again and steadied himself. Disgusted with the faint-hearted new arrival, his guide crossed the threshold into the dingy room and deposited himself on an old grey metal desk. His big red tennis shoes swung back and forth just above the floor.

John entered the room. A big creature resembling a cross between a dragon, an eagle, and a lion was sitting in the middle of the space. One of those mythological beings —

"A griffon. Congratulations," it said. "Since you're so big on names you can call me Ivan."

"Ivan?"

"Anything wrong with that, earth human male?" He (or she) spread its wings and was about to jump off the floor at John. It had long sharp claws, a powerful jaw, and a sharp beak. Sitting on its haunches, it was about six feet tall.

"The better to eat you with, my dear," it leered. John jumped back.

"Just kidding kid. Have a seat."

John was only too glad to get out of the water. He walked in and sat down on an old style metal chair with four wheels, armrests, and brown nylon upholstering on the seat. The dirty floor was worn ragged from the battered chair but it had the satisfying property of solidity. John's stomach ceased to feel like the inside of a blender. The room was lit by cheap fluorescent bulbs. Half of them were burnt out. The room smelled like stale tobacco and the griffon.

Wally waved at a very short but powerful humanoid. "Meet my friend Davey." John stared. The man had legs as thick as an oak tree and a massive bald head like a piece of granite. Davey had a huge barrel chest, gigantic hands, and light blue metallic-like skin. The light glinted off it in fascinating patterns.

"And Goliath."

"Goliath" was an ugly insect-like creature at least seven and a half feet tall. The thing looked like a praying mantis with a large triangular head, yellow eyes, powerful mandibles, and two antennae sticking out from the front of its head.

"His real name is Mxyxtlpyktlykk, or something like that," Wally explained helpfully.

Mxyxtlpyktlykk wore a top hat upon his carapaced head. Every time the ungainly creature moved he would have to hold it down with one of his four pincer-like hands.

Mxyxtlpyktlykk spoke in a strange clicking language using his jaw and his arms. When his arms rubbed together it activated little spikes protruding from its forearms.

"The latest mode," Ivan translated. "Don't be frightened by Goliath. He's good natured, just like a teddy bear. Except when you piss him off."

They all laughed. Davey's booming bass almost shattered one of the windows. Mxyxtlpyktlykk clicked again and his hat fell off. When he reached down to pick it up it sounded like the Tin Man in the Wizard of Oz.

John laughed. "What is this place?" He looked at Wally, who tossed the butt of his cigarette onto the floor and twisted it with the ball of his white topped tennis shoe. "And who are you? Can I call you Wally? Are you all nuts? Where's the Beaver?"

John felt he had entered an insane asylum.

The man frowned. "I am Bellerophon, earthian. You have a lot of nerve calling me Wally. You look like a Bozo who just stuck his finger in a toaster! And we aren't crazy. Earthians are crazy."

John didn't know how to respond to this quick-witted riposte. He just stood there observing the strange creatures and tried to make sense of an experience for which he had almost no reference points.

They looked him over silently for several minutes. John got the feeling he was being probed.

"OK," Bellerophon said. "Come with me."

John was nervous. "Where are we going?"

"To meet the boss. It's an honor so show some respect."

"I thought you were going to explain everything?"

"I lied."

The strange crew led John out of the stuffy room and across the "floor," which was making him seasick again. They arrived at a section of the gigantic facility that contained a large workstation and six smaller ones arranged in a hexagonal pattern around it.

"He's all yours," Bellerophon said to thin air.

Davey gave John a look that said, "You ain't going to cut it."

Ivan flew up over their heads and disappeared into the clouds, knocking Mxyxtlpyktlykk's hat off again.

John was really irritated. "Will someone please explain what's going on here?"

The ocean underneath his feet vanished, replaced by a seamless black floor. John sighed with relief and a soft voice answered him.

"Come over here John." He turned and saw a very tall woman standing about 15 feet away. She wore a white, one piece, loose fitting garment and had a head of spectacularly red hair, untied, that flowed to her waist. She had intensely blue eyes and her skin was bright white, of a color not possible in earth genetics. A few little freckles were artfully placed along each of her cheekbones, as if someone had painted them with a paint-by-numbers kit. She stood majestically, with perfect posture that seemed effortless. John straightened and pushed his shoulders back. He approached slowly and stood facing her about three feet away. The woman's head was almost level with his.

She held out her hand. "I am Kjirsten." John took the hand and lightly brushed the top of it with his lips. It was elegantly shaped and much larger than his own, with very long delicate fingers. There were six on each hand.

"You are very gallant," she said.

John blushed slightly. He didn't know why he'd done that and wasn't sure whether he had committed a social faux pas. The woman reassured him with a smile.

"Now John Frankel, I will show you what we are about here."

"Please," John interrupted. He tried to take the irritation he was feeling out of his voice. "Will you tell me who those clowns I just met are, and their function here? They seem more at home in a circus."

The woman laughed. "Those are my assistants. They were just having a little fun with you."

John looked his question.

"They probed you and gave the OK to continue."

John was about to ask another question. She raised her hand. Her demeanor said, "Enough."

John was impressed. This was clearly a person used to command. It showed in her regal bearing and in her movements.

Kjirsten walked over to the central workstation, which consisted of a desk about six feet in width and four in length. A flat panel display covered its surface. Behind the desk and resting upon a platform level with the desktop was a large cubic display tank. A cordless headset lay upon the desktop. In front of the desk floated two legless chairs.

"What do you think this is?" the woman said, drawing John's attention to the tank.

John peered into the tank. It contained the same image formerly projected within the room. Glowing faintly in the middle of the 3D display was the guide symbol. One of the concentric rings was highlighted. He felt himself hovering over a vast ocean, with the wind in his face and spray from the big waves hitting him in the face. He was going to fall in! He felt dizzy and looked away. "Ahhh!"

He opened his eyes to find the big redhead studying him clinically.

OK dorkus. You fell for it twice. Just bring your attention back to this gorgeous lady.

John steadied himself. "It looks like a representation of another planet. I've got a book with a bunch of etchings that work just like that. The technology to project this representation is more sophisticated than anything I'd ever imagined." John saw symbols scrolling down the flat panel screen as well, clearly linked to the 3 dimensional display. He couldn't figure out their meaning even though a number of them were similar to the ones in his book.

She nodded. "What is your assessment of this room?"

John observed the console operators in their uncountable millions. "Looks like a gigantic research station."

The redhead smiled. "It's much more than that. Try again."

John thought for a moment. No, it was too immense to be plausible.

The woman read his expression. "Go on," she encouraged.

"All of the rings in that symbol represent a real universe. And you can see them all from here."

"That is very good John Frankel. We did not expect an earthian to be able to even comprehend such concepts."

"This room must be millions of square miles in area. The number of universes must be practically infinite." John was wide-eyed.

"The room you see here is just a metaphor. It is presented in this way for your understanding. It's important that you comprehend as best you can what we're doing here. I'll explain in more detail later."

"Exactly how many universes are there?"

Kjirsten smiled. "Oh, how earthian of you! The number is too big to have any meaning."

Even John's unquenchable curiosity was overwhelmed. He spent a few moments trying to get himself together. The enormity of it astonished him.

"This facility is billions of your years old," Kjirsten said. "The knowledge it uses is ancient and universally known. The devices you see here are assists to consciousness for physical beings. They are activated by the impulses of thought, which are captured and amplified by the headsets."

John wanted to ask her about how the headset could amplify a thought but she began to speak. Her voice had a power and authority that made him want to pay attention. "Before I begin my presentation, a little background. Your planet is situated within one of the spiral arms of Galaxy 6, in a local association called the Twelve Galaxies. The Twelve are located within what your scientists refer to as the Virgo Supercluster of galaxies. This supercluster is one of over 10 million such clusters in your universe. The Twelve Galaxies are physically connected by a linked set of transport devices. We call them transportals. Transportals use an ancient technology that harnesses the power of thought. Stepping into one translates a person instantly from one place to another. No one knows who built them or where they came from, or how to create more of them. Transportals are invisible and are really not devices at all as physical beings understand them. They are little nodes in space and can only be activated by someone who knows their exact location."

"So the galaxy *is* full of ETs!" John cried. "Just like in the movies."

The big woman regarded him indulgently. "Yes John. The Twelve Galaxies are teeming with intelligent life. But each galaxy has a different ... culture."

John felt like a little kid before this woman even though she couldn't be much older than he was. The abrasive treatment he had received from that gang of lunatics had vanished. He was intensely curious.

"If the technology of this station is the same as the transportals, why can't you manufacture more of them?" John asked.

"The transportals are on a level of understanding well beyond ours. Whoever made them knew how to program the underlying fabric of space itself."

"Cool!" John blurted, and felt stupid.

The big redhead smiled. John thought it was a great smile and he relaxed a little.

"None of the transportals can reach this place. Neither can it be reached physically, in spacecraft."

"Why not?"

"Because this facility is outside of time and space. It is a little bubble of organization in the midst of...disorganization. The only way to get here is through the consciousness altering technique."

Kjirsten sat on one of the floating chairs and put on the headset. It had a thin, flexible black substance that curled over the top of the head and ended in two soft pads that pressed gently against the temples. The headset molded itself to the shape of her skull. As soon as the pads touched the redhead's temples a thin membrane of energy emerged. It covered the top of her head with glowing, pulsing light.

"That thing is awesome." He took a seat beside her and the chair molded itself to the contours of his body.

Kjirsten smiled. "You need the headsets to get into the system. In order for the device to work properly you have to be trained in the basic station protocols. You also have to be registered into the system."

It was time to give this rookie the standard orientation speech. It was boring but hopefully this earthian male would be worth her time.

John could almost see her thoughts interact with the pulsing light surrounding her head. "I want to learn how to use one of those!"

Kjirsten's eyebrows went up slightly and the corners of her mouth turned up. John felt like an obstreperous child so he shut his grille.

John noticed a change in the pulsating light around Kjirsten's head. At that moment the concentric rings symbol appeared by itself in the display tank. It was suspended within a golden-white mist. "This symbol is embedded within the universal substance and serves to orient consciousness to its position within the structure of reality. To our human intelligence it appears as a series of concentric rings. That is just a heuristic representation of something multi-dimensional." She pointed to the display.

"Each universe within the All is represented by one of the rings. Each universe is self-contained with its own unique physics. Each universe and everything in it is resonating within its own vibrational range. Everything in that universe is therefore somewhere within that bandwidth of vibration. In order for consciousness to be aware of a universe it must be tuned to it. Tuning in to one station means that you automatically dial out all of the others. This is the principle upon which the entirety of existence is organized."

"I already know about that," John said. "It was in a book I got from my girlfriend."

Kjirsten glanced sharply at John. Almost everyone who found their way here arrived in a state of total confusion. In addition, he had been roughed up a little by her entourage. This rookie appeared to be rock-solid and even a little cocky. Well, she had a big surprise for him later on.

"Yes, we know about your girlfriend."

Suddenly John understood. "Are you the lady who helped Genevieve with the technique?"

Kjirsten smiled and turned back to the console. John had his answer. The big woman moved smoothly and gracefully, with no wasted motion. Compared to her, he was Rodan.

"Now I want to show you the power of the system," she said. "Let's examine the lamp sitting on your desk in your earthian bedroom." She directed John's attention back to the big tank, which displayed the outermost ring within the guide symbol. The ring collapsed into itself and appeared as a dimpled sphere, somewhat like an apple.

The display zoomed-in to a spot on the apple's skin. John saw clusters of galaxies whoosh past until the Milky Way galaxy came into view. Then they zoomed into the solar system, to earth, to Midland, and into his bedroom.

"Holy shit."

"Got it!" Kjirsten exclaimed.

The lamp on his desk was centered in the big display tank. Next to it sat his computer and printer. A pile of books, disks, papers, and assorted junk he was too lazy to put away lay haphazardly in front of the lamp. The lamp stand was of brass with a series of smooth beveled curves. A white lamp shade rested precariously on the bulb. That's right. I broke the holder a couple months ago. Maybe it really was his lamp.

"Do you agree that this is the lamp that sits on your desk?"

"Looks like it. How do I know it's not just a representation?"

Just then a breeze from a partially opened window rustled the papers. A squirrel chittered on the tree outside.

"OK I believe you. That squirrel wakes me up almost every morning."

John noticed something interesting in passing. The red seconds indicator on the clock above his desk was moving. John didn't have time to ponder this for more than an instant.

"With these devices we have the ability to zoom in to all universes and observe anything. That in itself is helpful, but there's something else much more important. Watch."

The lamp blurred. It was now just a smear that blended into other smears that used to be his desk and the objects on it. Then the scene slowly faded out. The display showed a chaotic scramble of energy.

Kjirsten turned to John. "We are now in an undefined zone between the lamp and...the rest of existence."

"The zone of chaos!" John exclaimed.

"That's right John. If you refer to chaos as dynamically changing possibility. Every object, every life form, every planet, galaxy, and universe has one. The zone of chaos occurs on the barrier between any *thing* and the universal medium from which it comes forth."

Kjirsten continued. "These undefined zones are vitally necessary because they provide the potential for evolution and growth."

John had a million questions. "But..."

Kjirsten held up her big hand in a commanding gesture. "We're getting off the subject. I have something specific I need to show you and I don't have all day."

John's feathers were a little ruffled but he didn't want to look whiny in front of this big amazon woman.

"The next thing I want to show you may seem startling." Kjirsten turned back to the console and once more brought up the lamp. "Let's zoom into the lamp as far as we can go."

The display zoomed rapidly inward. John felt his stomach wrench uncomfortably. After several minutes the inward spiraling movement began to slow down and eventually it stopped.

"These devices are assists to consciousness. We've magnified as far as we can go, right down to the level of thought itself."

The tank display showed a solid, completely homogeneous substance.

"What is that?" John asked.

"Bingo," Kjirsten said. "The 64 billion dollar question." She looked at John expectantly, as if he was a star pupil who might come up with a brilliant insight.

"Why do we see something solid?"

"Why indeed?" she said, looking intently into his eyes.

They were both silent for a few moments. Kjirsten kept her eyes on John, who had no answer. He felt that he had failed a test.

She turned back to the tank. "We cannot observe finer than the level of thought. Just as your optical microscopes are limited by the wavelength of light and are unable to see clearly into what you call the quantum level. Apparently the universal medium is finer even than thought itself – as you can see. One of the reasons for the existence of this research station and our work here is to determine the nature of the universal medium. If we can we will have understood the ultimate nature of reality. And probably ourselves as well."

"Cool!" was all John could say. If only school was as good as this. These concepts didn't even exist in the minds of any of his instructors. Except maybe for Michael Walters.

Something was in the back of his mind. "Wait a minute. The pages of that book I have look an awful lot like this." In the display, the solid, homogeneous substance of the universal medium had a smooth, golden color.

Kjirsten frowned. "Yes, we know about your book. Whoever manufactured and wrote it knows a lot more than we do."

"I know a guy who will be very happy to hear what you just said." John was thinking of Jim Sievers, who had the materials analysis lab.

Kjirsten chuckled. "We have been following that poor fellow. The tools he has are far too limited to even come close to understanding it."

John changed the subject. He looked around at the gigantic space and the millions (or billions) of console operators. "Are all of these people really here? Or is this some kind of holographic representation?"

Kjirsten smiled. "Good guess." She put on the headset. Suddenly, most of the console operators disappeared. "Just another metaphor to help you understand how big this place is. And how large a scale we're operating on."

Even without the enhancements the place looked pretty big.

"I've only met five of you so far," John teased. "Are you like the Wizard of Oz? Pay no attention to the man, er, lady, behind the curtain!"

Kjirsten laughed. "No John. We have uncounted billions of researchers and visitors here from every part of the All. There are as many forms of intelligent life as there are environments that have been created for them. All of us are observing and studying from our particular physical or mental orientation." She waved her hand. "What you see here is only one of the sectors within the humanoid section of this facility."

John noticed the beautiful honeycomb layout and how the sides of each cell served as a hallway. Each one was about 100 feet in length and 10 feet wide. In the middle of each hallway a yellow circle was drawn... John's train of thought was interrupted as Kjirsten began to speak again.

"John, the All is so big no human can even grasp it conceptually. Oh, it's so wonderful!" Her large, intensely blue eyes sparkled with suppressed excitement and her skin seemed to glow with energy. Kjirsten's face was heart shaped. She had very high cheekbones, a delicately shaped nose, and a small mouth. A face you wouldn't see on earth, John decided. The eyes were too large and round and they sparkled like sapphires. The cheekbones were a little too high. Even so her face had perfect symmetry. Her skin was flawless, without the slightest blemish, like an airbrushed photo. The woman had continued and he jerked his attention back to her words.

"...this place has been my home for a long time. It's so amazing working here. Beings from literally everywhere can meet, exchange ideas, share experiences, and party. It's the ultimate community."

"Party?" John said.

"Oh yeah. Parties here make yours on earth seem dull."

"What do you do here that's so exciting?"

She smiled devilishly. "Just remember what you experienced in that world of light."

John inspected her figure closely. Kjirsten had long legs, big hands and big feet, but they were in proportion to her frame. John always had a fascination with colors. Kjirsten's was every bit as distinctive as Genevieve's.

"John, you have no idea of the variety of life out there. It's practically infinite. Living and working here is the most incredible experience imaginable. This community of beings is as vast as the All itself."

John caught some of Kjirsten's excitement.

Kjirsten leaned over the workstation surface, reading the symbols. John noticed how wide her shoulders were, like a swimmer's, and how her red hair fell in great waves around her body. When she moved it caught the light in fascinating patterns. It shimmered here and glowed there. Her skin was so smooth and creamy it blended perfectly with the dress. The woman was exotic and beautiful. There was something different about her physicality that could not be explained just by her features.

She was more *evolved,* more refined than he in every aspect. People from earth looked coarse and crude by comparison. John had detected the difference between them immediately, making him a little self conscious.

Barbarians at the gate, he thought. Visigoths attacking the splendor of Rome.

He was about to ask her where she came from when suddenly the huge display tank exploded into a chaos of swirling, interacting, indefinable riot of energy.

Kjirsten straightened. "Here is what I really want to show you. It's the main reason for our discussion."

Kjirsten's lips widened in a faint grin. She directed John's attention into the tank. "A special zone lies between the organized quanta of all universes in existence and the pure potential of the universal medium. It is a vast, undefined realm, the crucible of creation itself. It is called the Unformed Potential." She stood back and watched the earthian, studying him clinically.

The stuff, if you could call it that, was indescribable. It was a ghastly, roiling unreality that appeared to John as entirely random. Strange clouds, tendrils, shapes, and specters came almost into being but with never enough strength to actually become recognizable as anything definite. John likened it to a bizarre dream. It was something utterly impossible for the intellect to grasp. He began to feel disoriented.

"It's nightmarish," John said, staring into the bizarre half-reality. His pattern recognition skills were useless. This stuff was totally psychotic. He quickly looked away to get his bearings.

"This display is only a simulation of the real thing. Otherwise..."

"Otherwise what?"

"Interaction of any kind with the Unformed Potential causes insanity."

John gulped. He believed it.

Kjirsten tweaked the display. "What's all that new stuff coming in?" There seemed to be an influx of the bizarreness into the fabric of space.

Kjirsten glanced quickly at him from her position at the console. This earthian male is very perceptive to have recognized that so quickly. "We don't know. But we do know that the influx has been getting stronger."

John's head was spinning. He tried not to look into the tank but felt a compulsion to do so. Like something grossly deformed, it had an eerie attraction. His mind was still trying to grasp it, to make sense out of it. He felt himself slipping over a precipice...

"Watch it John!!" Kjirsten snapped. The force of her intent jolted his head back.

John was horrified. "What the hell is that garbage?" The half-formed randomness was worse than his most grotesque dream. A nightmare was at least comprehensible! The Unformed Potential was the embodiment of insanity itself but he couldn't keep his gaze away. A suffocating blanket of depression surrounded his mind. He put his hands to his head. Suddenly there was a tremendous slap on the side of his face.

"Damn!" John rose abruptly from his chair. Something was running down his cheek. Blood.

"What did you do that for?" He reached out to slap her hand away but withdrew. John would never again touch a woman in anger. He had learned his lesson. Fortunately her blow had broken the spell of madness within his mind.

Kjirsten's breathing was rapid and her face was flushed. She said nothing. Her eyes searched the earthian's face.

"Thank you." John calmed a little and reseated himself beside her. The suffocating feeling was gone but his jaw hurt like hell. In addition to the blood, John's cheek was beginning to swell.

Kjirsten was shocked. She had panicked and hit him as hard as she could. For the first time in 15 years she had broken her training! A high caste Lyran female was never allowed to show emotion to a male not known personally to her.

After a couple of minutes John felt a little better. "Uh, I think I'm ready to continue." His voice sounded like it was coming out of a swimming pool. She had made no effort to assist him, nor did she offer an apology.

"Are you sure?"

"Sort of." His head felt a size bigger than normal from all the data he was assimilating. The pain in his jaw hindered his concentration. A part of his mind still recoiled from the grotesqueness in the display tank. Fortunately the simulation was no longer running. The tank now displayed its default: a pleasant, misty fog that soothed the senses.

She gazed at him very intently, measuring him. "Now John, I really want you to understand this next."

He sighed. "Fire away."

"You just got a look at a simulation of the Unformed Potential. The Unformed Potential is subtly present in the interstices of existence. It is a latency from which all Form arises." She looked directly at John and spoke carefully. "Outside the walls of this research station is the zone of chaos at the end of existence. Our mission is to study it."

John was appalled. "You're joking, right? Study *that*? When you know it causes insanity?"

"Yes. It is of critical importance to understand what is happening in the Unformed Potential." Despite her training she added anxiously, "Before it's too late." For the second time in five minutes she had violated her training. What was it about this rookie that made her want to tell him everything?

"Too late?"

"I'm sorry John. I shouldn't have said that. Normally we don't divulge what I'm about to say until much later. However, now that I've begun, I might as well tell you."

She regarded John in the same way Genevieve often did. Kjirsten looked directly at him and psychically probed him. Satisfied, she continued. "There's something going on out there that has us all very concerned. I've already said that the Unformed Potential is present at the interface between the universal medium and all matter and energy in every universe. You see John, normally the Unformed Potential acts like a buffer between the universal medium and the material universe. It contains the potentials for all universes in the All, and supplies the potential energy for expansion and growth of manifested physical substance. Unfortunately the chaos of the Unformed Potential has begun, ever so slightly, to seep into the well-ordered structure of matter and energy. If this continues at its present rate the chaotic properties that all physical systems exhibit will increase in strength. This will lead to a breakdown of the bonds that hold matter and energy together. What happened to you in that simulation is child's play in comparison to what all life forms in every universe will potentially be subjected to."

John gulped. The feeling that his mind was melting came upon him again, unbidden. He shook his head vigorously, tearing his thoughts away from it. "You are seriously scaring the shit out of me."

"I'm sorry John. It's the truth." *Yes, but you didn't have to tell him like that.*

John wrestled with this for a few moments. "It sounds unreal. There's no evidence whatsoever that anything is wrong with the universe."

"Not yet," she snapped. A look of irritation crossed her features, which she quickly smoothed over. It was definitely time to return to Skjelgaard for another training session.

"Here, at the end of creation, is the perfect place to clearly observe and understand the workings of universal forces. What eventually happens to physical reality is first evident here. I'm afraid that what I've told you is the literal truth."

John said nothing. Her story was bizarre. But this alien woman was completely self-assured and frighteningly intelligent. Her almost military bearing and air of command told him she was not one to put up with nonsense. The truly strange thing was his own presence in this place.

Kjirsten broke their reverie and spoke cheerfully. "All right John. We've been talking too much. Are you game for a little experiment that might make this presentation a little more real to you?"

Kjirsten changed moods as quickly as Genevieve. John wondered what she could possibly show him next. Despite feeling tired, he was curious.

She saw his interest. "We'll run another Unformed Potential simulation."

John jerked back.

"Don't worry! This simulation is much milder than the one you saw before." Much milder indeed! She would set the program to level one this time, instead of level three. She ought not to have done that. The impulse to test this rookie had overcome her better judgment and now he had a bruised jaw to show for it.

A badge of honor, she thought. She had put her mark on this earthian male and it thrilled her for some irrational reason.

"Let's place a test thought into that potential and see what happens. You do the honors. Think of something and make it crystal clear in your mind. Project it into the tank."

John was afraid. He didn't want to look again.

"All you have to do is seed the tank. Don't focus into it, just contact it gently. Observe with your peripheral vision."

John needed a safe subject. He thought of Genevieve and focused that thought into the swirling...stuff. He turned away quickly and looked out of the corners of his eyes.

The figure of Genevieve smiled and said "Hi John." Then her features changed. She morphed into a raven, then a black panther, then a monster with huge fangs and one bloody red eye. The monster was shredded from the inside as if by the hands of someone gone berserk. It became a black and white mist with a little red spot in the middle. Eventually all traces of her merged into the chaos. "Holy shit. What was that?"

"It's trying to organize, to become *something*. The Unformed Potential wants to go from a state of *un*order to a state of order. A single thought isn't powerful enough to organize it, so it gets torn apart."

"Infinite entropy." He tried seeding it again with the same thought image of Genevieve. This time she morphed into a black, oily blob that gradually disappeared into the bizarreness.

"I put the same thought image of Genevieve into that junk," John said. "How come it turned out different?"

Kjirsten smiled. "You may have thought you seeded the Unformed Potential in exactly the same way. But you didn't. No two thoughts are identical. The Unformed Potential is so sensitive to tiny differences that it will evolve along an entirely different path."

John recalled something from one of his mathematics classes. *Sensitive dependence on initial conditions.* Scientists had discovered that physical systems were non-linear and dynamical. Chaos theory. Attractors.

He spoke of this.

"That's right John!" KJirsten said, as to a very bright student. "Every thought projected into the Unformed Potential acts as an attracting basin. At least for a little while. The persistence of phenomena within the Unformed Potential has been increasing. We suspect that the Unformed Potential is trying to self-organize."

She regarded him quizzically, as if expecting another revelation. John didn't know what to make of her statement.

"There's just a couple more things I want to show you," she said hopefully. "Are you still game?"

"OK. But no more of this Unformed Potential stuff." He put his hand on his swollen jaw. "It's turning me inside out and I've got a terrific headache."

"Very well," Kjirsten said. "It only remains to briefly discuss the uniqueness of the earthian planet. If you are to, ah, associate with us, you will have to gain a more balanced perspective about the universe outside your isolated little world."

"What do you mean? Earth is a planet just like any other."

Kjirsten wanted to laugh out loud but restrained herself. "No John. Your planet is not like any other. In fact, it is radically different from any other planet in the universe. Recall that it has its own separate little dot in the symbol for All. As a result, many eyes are following the activities going on there. The popularity of your little orb is getting downright cultish around here, and in many other places as well. There are many more beings than you would ever imagine who know the score of the latest Cubs game."

John laughed. "That is absurd."

"I, and all of my assistants, are earthian experts. That is how Bell was able to understand your 'Wally' sarcasm. By the way, I want to congratulate you on being able to understand this far. Most can...most students have to do this in three or four sessions." She smiled at him appreciatively.

This made John feel pretty good. She'd been treating him like a big sister would to a little kid brother, but whenever she got near him his pulse started racing. *Maybe she doesn't think I'm so dorky after all.*

"Tell me again why earth is so special," John said. "Our telescopes show us an infinite universe. Our planet is just a tiny speck within an insignificant galaxy."

"That's just because you don't have the right perspective You're too close to the action. You haven't yet been far enough out in space to see the complete picture. Furthermore, the history of your planet – and it is a long one – shows a pattern of tremendous growth that always ends in disaster. Periodically, life on your planet is destroyed. Almost always by natural catastrophe, and occasionally by war. Currently, you are in another remarkable growth cycle, one of the largest ever recorded."

She displayed a graph on the desktop. It had letters beginning with "T" at the bottom of the y-axis, all the way up to "A" at the top. John noticed that the spaces between the horizontal lines of the graph decreased as it went up, indicating a logarithmic progression.

"What's that spike?" John said. He pointed to a large one that was marked "463C."

Kjirsten switched to another data set. "The civilization you call Atlantis, which was inundated in a very large seismic shift of your planet's crust. The number indicates the 463rd spike of the third highest magnitude. The spikes measure disturbances in the universal medium and presage a period of intense activity in the planetary consciousness. Spikes usually are coincident with a great period of positive growth and/or turmoil. They are always associated with events that change the course of history on your planet, depending on their magnitude." She looked thoughtful.

"And they also eventually reflect, somehow, events in the All as well. It's as if your little planet acts as a buffer for the rest of us, absorbing a psychic shockwave and transmitting a pulse of transformational energy."

John was amazed. "You mean other planets don't have histories like ours?"

She laughed. "No John. Life on your planet has arisen and been destroyed many, many times. The fossil record that exists today only shows evidence of the last two civilizations. Almost all traces of the others have been wiped out."

He could only shake his head in disbelief. "That's crazy."

The graph before him fascinated him however. He scrolled it back, looking for an "A" spike. Kjirsten showed him how to increase the rate of progression. Suddenly he saw a huge spike. It was marked "23A."

"What's this one?" They were both at the console and she bent over next to him. He could feel her hair falling all over his body. She smelled sweet and exotic. John had to jerk his attention back to the display.

"That is a famous incident in the history of your planet, approximately 65 million planetary standard years ago. After a long golden age, two factions began to war. An asteroid was diverted and struck the planet, destroying almost all life upon it. The Records indicate great concern during this period that your world might die. However, the earthian planet has an amazing resiliency. Life recovered its footing, remarkably, at the very same evolutionary point. Your history records this as the end of the age of dinosaurs, but dinosaurs were only incidental."

"Incidental?"

"Dinosaurs were not native to your planet, John. They were imported, as, er, zoo animals. At that time, the entire humanoid population of your planet was less than eighty thousand."

"You mean you have records of the true history of earth?"

"Well, the history of earth as we have recorded it. Much of the history of your planet as presented in your textbooks is fictional. Much of your cosmological speculation is as well."

"Such as?"

"From the character of the light that reaches your optical telescopes, your astronomers conclude correctly that the universe is expanding, that the galaxies are rapidly moving away from each other. From this they have concluded that galaxies have always been moving away from each other since the beginning of time, and that the universe will end cold and lifeless."

Red-shift, John thought. As the galaxies move away from us, the wavelength of the light from them becomes longer. The longer wavelengths of light are at the red end of the visible spectrum. Michael Walters had told him that the current cosmology indicated a flat universe that would expand forever.

"That is not the case at all," Kjirsten said. "The galaxies always move relative to each other, but maintain a harmonious relationship. What appears as an expanding universe to your eyes is actually a cyclical relationship, related to the Great Cycle."

"So you're saying the universe isn't flat, but closed."

Kjirsten turned her head a little to the side, as if listening to something through the headset. She stood, and John followed suit. They were in front of the console about three feet apart.

"OK John, let's wrap this up. I've talked here far longer than I expected to. Are there any more questions?"

"The thing about earth being observed by everyone. That sounds weird to me."

Kjirsten took the headset off and placed it on the workstation. "Earthians tend to be polarized in their thinking and that makes for a lot of drama and interest. On earth, little bumps become magnified into big problems very quickly. Your planet is a like a gigantic soap-opera."

"So we're some kind of freak show?" John said testily.

She laughed. "Earth has been the butt of many universal jokes. The armpit of the universe, things like that. But everyone recognizes there are powerful, universal forces at work there which are not completely understood. Earth is a very, very special place, even though no one really wants to live there. Every one of you on earth is...respected for what you are doing. Every one of you has a fan club."

"Oh bollocks!" John said, just like Trevor Jones.

"It's true. I told you it was like a soap-opera! You are only 8 billion. Although that is a fantastic number for such a small planet, it is very minuscule indeed compared to those who are watching you." She hesitated. "I'm your number one fan, John."

John stood dumbfounded, unable to say anything for a while. It was too much. Even though his head hurt he felt he was in the middle of a weird dream.

"Either what you've told me is profound truth or it's a load of crap. Right now I'm inclined to believe the latter. I'm sorry, but I'm not sure whether I'm in a dream or whether you're even real."

Kjirsten looked at him intently. "Is this real?" She stepped forward, pressing her body next to his. She put one hand at the back of his head and kissed him, deeply, passionately. John was overwhelmed. He lost his balance but she steadied him easily with an arm around his lower back. No, John thought, this was all wrong...but she was determined. Finally she let him go and he lost his balance again, tumbling to the floor. She had both hands on her hips and pinned him with her eyes. "Was *that* real?" she demanded. "Am I *real* enough for you now?"

As John stood up she began to giggle.

He looked down at the erection sticking out of his pants.

"Shit!" He tried to cover it up while she laughed uproariously.

"You better put that thing away."

John couldn't help it. He found himself laughing and fell to the floor again. After a couple of minutes he got up and saw her looking at him intently.

"I'm sorry, John Frankel. I should not have done that. I am not allowed to get personally involved with candidates...but I couldn't help myself." She sighed to herself. Three times now she had violated one of the most fundamental rules of the Lyran Hyallben. The Hyallben is the strict code of honor that governs all members of the elite caste of women who rule Lyran society.

"Neither could I."

"Then it's all right?"

John nodded. Then he frowned. "Candidate?"

"I'll tell you about it the next time you come. I gave you the entire spiel in one session and you're tired now. Go back to your life. I'll communicate with you when it's time for our next appointment."

"How will I know?"

"Look for red." She turned and walked away.

To her back he said loudly, "Will I have to deal with those weirdos again?"

"Squawk!" said Ivan, reappearing from the clouds. "Watch your mouth or I'll poop on you!"

John scurried into the filthy interview room from which he had emerged what seemed like a week ago. It took longer than usual to get himself together enough to do the technique. Besides the bruise on his cheek he had Kjirsten's fragrance all over him. He hoped he wouldn't meet Genevieve right away.

He quieted his mind with a little breathing and then went through the technique. In a few moments his room shimmered into existence.

He was back. There was always a transitional period before he felt himself fully present in his body. He sat in the chair for a few minutes adjusting to the earth reality.

The clock above his desk now read 9:58 but it had displayed 9:27 just before shimmering out. How did 31 minutes get added on this time?

Just then he heard a knock and Genevieve walked in. "Hi John!"

She was so beautiful. John instantly forgot about clocks and Kjirsten. He stared nervously, fidgeting in his chair.

"What's the matter! You look like you never saw me before! You..."

She came closer and sniffed. "So you've seen Kjirsten."

John was crushed. "I'm sorry." He wanted to tell her she was everything and Kjirsten was nothing. He couldn't get the words out. He must have looked comical because she began to giggle.

Genevieve looked him straight in the eyes. "Get up," she commanded.

He struggled awkwardly to his feet and opened his mouth to speak. She came into his arms and raised her head. "Kiss me." He felt her next to him and his heart leaped for joy. He kissed her so tenderly and passionately that when it was over she gasped.

"I forgive you," she said in awed tones. Sometimes John's intense feelings for her were overwhelming. She knew he loved her with a depth of feeling that she still could not fully return. "You don't have to say anything sweetheart. That kiss said it all."

John saw it was all right and he was happy again. Within a half hour he had kissed the two most beautiful women in the universe! Not bad for weird John Frankel.

They talked for several hours about John's experiences, sitting on the bed. John explained his bruised cheek and Genevieve's eyebrows raised. "Not like her. Not like her at all. She's always been a cool one." The corners of her mouth turned up slightly. With some kind of feminine divination she gave him a look that said, "She's got the hots for you."

Silently, John had to agree.

Genevieve answered a number of his questions about Kjirsten's presentation. "I got the lecture, same as you."

It turned out that Genevieve had known Kjirsten for over eight years. "Met her when I first learned about the technique, as I told you before."

"You mean you've been going there for eight years?" The stuff he didn't know about her would probably fill a book. "Why didn't you tell me?"

"Because, as I keep saying, you had to get it on your own. But that's the last time I'll say that." Genevieve's eyes were full of admiration. "Oh John, I'm so proud of you. I didn't think it was possible for anyone to do what you did all by yourself."

John swelled with pride. He *loved* it when Genevieve praised him. It gave him goose bumps all over. "You did it too," he said agreeably.

"Yeah, but I had a lot more help. Dad did most of the translating work for me and Kjirsten helped with the rest."

John didn't believe a word of it. She was a lot smarter than he; but he soaked up her appreciation like a cat lapping up milk.

"I'm still impressed," he said. "And I love you."

"I know."

In the Eyrie, Kjirsten contemplated her interview with John Frankel. The earthian male had an effect on her like no other man she had ever met.

It was impossible for a female of her status to associate with one of the earthians unless strictly on a professional basis. Earthians were considered barbarians, and for good reason. Their genetics were a mongrelization. Their bloodlines were periodically destroyed by natural and artificial planetary catastrophes. They were not worthy of even a cursory mention within galactic geneaology. Their bodies were crude and splotchy. Their lives were short. Most of the time their biology malfunctioned. Only for a very few years could any of them pass even minimal galactic standards of human beauty and fitness.

Nevertheless, the earthian Frankel possessed a raw, untapped psychic power that she felt immediately. Perhaps there was something to the theory that the earthian species was mutating rapidly into a dynamic force for galactic change.

Besides, she rationalized, her life was here. Only five times during the past 18 years had she visited her home planet of Skjelgaard, and then only for the periodic retraining necessary to maintain her status within Lyran society. The traditions and mores of that society still held strong within her. But her new life here must supersede it in almost every respect.

She admitted to herself her interest in the earthian male John Frankel. Even though, compared to Lyran males, he was a physical weakling.

Yes, she was interested. Very interested.

21

THE next several days seemed unreal to John as he tried to assimilate the information given to him in the Eyrie. More so even than usual he was in a contemplative mood. The mundane problems of the lab and the normal routines of life now seemed ridiculous in comparison.

John jumped in his car and drove over to the pool hall. He climbed the worn concrete stairs to the second floor.

"Hey Jack, give me some balls."

Jack handed him the heavy case in his usual surly manner. "Table 8." Jack looked even more desperate for a cigarette today than usual.

John spotted Freddy and walked over to his table.

"John! How the hell are you?"

"A little confused today my friend. I need some advice."

"*You* need advice from *me*?"

"I'm afraid so. When you're done, come over."

Freddy was playing 9-ball with some guy he'd never seen before. John moved his tray over to table 8 and played by himself. The feel of the cue in his hand was comforting. The sound of the balls going into the leather pockets was music to his ears. Normalcy. Stability. That was good after his experience in the Eyrie.

Today the big room was almost full. Some of the guys were dilettantes like John but most of them were serious players. Two of them were standing at the back, b.s.ing with an old guy who sold cues. In front, Jack handed a case of balls to a new arrival. John hit the 14 ball in the corner as hard as he could. The smack of the ball made him feel good. After an hour of play he walked over to Freddy's table, which stood along the side wall by a huge casement window.

"Hey Freddy, do you think human nature is positive or negative?"

"What??"

The other guy gave him a look that said, "What kind of a nut are you?"

"Do you think people are basically good, or evil? Is life designed to be a positive experience or a negative one?"

Freddy paused, baffled. But he knew a little bit about what made John Frankel tick. Freddy thought for a minute. "I don't think about stuff like that John. But if I had to choose one way or the other I'd say that people aren't so bad once you get to know them." He glanced at the other player and smirked. "Even Kenny."

"Who's your friend?" John asked.

"John, this is Roger Krosky. Roger, John Frankel."

Krosky seemed uncomfortable. He was about medium height, muscular, with a big barrel chest, a thick neck, and a mat of brown hair. He had his cue in his case and was closing the latch. "What do you think?" John asked him.

"I think you're crazy." Roger Krosky had a high pitched voice, almost feminine, incongruous with his football build. John had to stifle a laugh.

"Why?"

"Because nobody asks questions like that in a pool hall," Krosky responded.

John laughed out loud. A player at the adjacent table, bending over a shot, straightened. "Shutup will ya?"

John ignored him. "How old are you?" John asked Krosky, toning his voice down.

"25, what about it?" Roger was belligerent.

"You've lived for 25 years on planet earth and you've never asked yourself what you're doing here? That's like playing a football game without a playbook or without studying the other team's tendencies. It's like entering a tournament without practicing."

Roger Krosky was startled. "I don't know. Never thought about it I guess."

John waited expectantly but said nothing, encouraging a response. "I guess I agree with Freddy. I might even get to like a wierdo like you." He regarded John with distaste. "But I doubt it."

John laughed again. People were looking at him but he didn't care. He pounded Freddy on the back. Roger was staring at him like a master chef at undercooked salmon.

"Thanks for being you," John said cheerfully. He got his balls, paid his bill, and walked out. Amazing what a chat with a friend will do.

On the way out John heard Roger say, "That guy is your friend?"

"Weird John Frankel they used to call him in high school," Freddy replied. "Still is, I guess. Strange guy but I like him anyway."

That night Alicia and Michael Walters came over for dinner. After dessert everyone was about to leave the table when Walters ceremoniously pulled a little felt box from his pocket. He took Alicia's hand. "Alicia Hartwell, will you do me the honor of becoming my wife?"

At first Alicia was shocked. Clearly, this was a surprise.

"Yes!" she squeaked.

With a smile of deep satisfaction, the former recluse slowly handed her the box. "Please accept this insignificant token as a small indication of my appreciation." Alicia opened the box and gasped. "Michael, it's....magnificent." Alicia pulled out a ring with a thin gold band and a large diamond set in an elegant hexagonal pattern with tiny clamps to hold it in place.

Rachel was pleased. Robert was impressed. Genevieve smiled.

Alicia put the ring carefully on her finger, admiring it from all angles. She was beaming.

Michael Walters felt that he had just enacted the denouement of a really good play. Except this was for real. As he inspected the glowing face of his new fiancée a warm glow spread to every cell in his body. It was something he had never felt since childhood.

John looked over at the man he still considered his mentor. "Congratulations."

Now everyone spoke at once. Robert pounded him on the back, loudly expressing his approval. Rachel put her arms around Alicia and babbled about the beautiful ring and how happy she was for her.

Genevieve looked at her father. "Nice going dad!"

Michael Walters grabbed his daughter and gave her a big hug. He told her how much he loved her. "Let's go into the living room." Genevieve led him away.

Robert, Alicia, and Rachel followed the couple into the living room. John was left alone at the table. Funny how Genevieve never wanted to talk about their own relationship. Oh well. I'll take her any way I can get her.

John kept looking for red.

That was supposed to be the signal for him to go back to the Eyrie. For the first couple of weeks he paid close attention but soon forgot all about it. He was in his life again.

John and Genevieve went to the wedding of Michael Walters and Alicia Hartwell. Alicia wanted a child and to John's surprise, Mr. Walters had agreed.

"I've been shut up all my life, alone," he said at one of their tutoring sessions. "Now it's time for me to live. I've never properly taken care of anyone and I feel I'm the worse for it. Now I'm ready for a family."

Talk about a change in personality. The man was hardly ever in the library anymore.

John was completing the third year of his program. Genevieve was in her second year at university. They both took classes year round with a short break in August.

The work seemed irrelevant to her and she did it with boring ease. John hardly ever attended class because he didn't need to. Michael Walters basically gave him the entire course in a few intensive study sessions and answered all his questions. They spent the rest of their time talking and bullshitting.

John felt Genevieve was still waiting for him to do something. What was it this time?

After practice in the old warehouse one hot July evening John, Bill, and Gene stood around talking. Gene had continued his work with the technique and was now able to stay in the zone for almost half an hour at a time. John wanted to teach Gene more of the technique but Gene was satisfied with his progress. He had no wish to explore further. John was a little surprised. Surely Gene could see that what he had accomplished so far was just the beginning of something much grander?

"You've reached a pretty stable platform somewhere in stage two. But there's a lot more to it."

"I'm using this to get more game. That's all I care about."

Bill wanted no part of it. Gene and John could beat him at will even though John, who was not naturally athletic, had surpassed him in a very short time. John couldn't understand it.

"It's too weird for me. It's cheating."

"Cheating?" John was astonished. "It's a totally natural process. Is working at your game cheating? Is sports psychology cheating? Is taking supplements cheating? I never hear you complain about any of that."

Bill was obstinate. "You guys do whatever you want. I'm not learning any weirdo stuff. I'll stick with the tried and true."

"But it's mostly just breathing! What's more tried and true than that? If you think breathing is cheating then try stopping. By your definition you're cheating every time you suck wind."

"I don't care," Bill said. "My dad always taught me to do things right. He's a marine and got the medal of honor. What you're doing isn't right."

John was exasperated. "What you're saying isn't logical Bill. Think about it. We're breathing and doing some mental exercises. That's it. Tell me one thing that's not right about that."

Bill refused to discuss it any further.

John gave up. It was incomprehensible. How could anyone not want to improve themselves in something they were obviously interested in?

For the billionth time John realized he was different. He was beginning to see how a person's beliefs could limit their progress. A belief, after all, is just a set of rules about something. Rules are limitations. So all beliefs must be self-limiting. Religions, political philosophies, "common sense," and tradition were all constraints on thought and action. The trick is not to get stuck in any one set of rules.

The next morning John woke up tired and didn't want to get out of bed, but it was a Tuesday. Time for work. And Jimmy. John imagined his lab partner as an ugly boil, which he lanced with a red hot needle. Goo be gone. That didn't stop the hands of the clock from their inexorable movement forward.

In the shower he had a happy thought. "I'll use the technique and just pop in to the lab. Why go to the trouble of driving over?" Although his workspace in the Physics building on campus was as familiar to him as his own bedroom, John was not successful.

That night he asked Genevieve about it. "I don't know John. I've never been able to do it either." She shrugged. "Kjirsten tried to explain it to me once but I don't think even she understands it."

A couple of weeks later John went to the lab as usual on Monday morning. The room was dark and the door was locked. He walked down the hall to Dr. Jackson's office. It too was locked and dark inside. He walked back up the hall the other way to the Administrative section. "Anyone seen Dr. Jackson?"

A woman with a name tag that read "Patricia Owen" explained. "Dr. Jackson's funding was abruptly cut last Friday evening. No explanation given."

John was shocked. Jackson could be a prick sometimes but he was an honest researcher.

"Do you know where he is?"

Patricia turned and spoke to someone behind her. "He went home last Friday and no one's seen or heard from him since. Do you want his number?"

"Please."

John went home and called. He got the answering machine: "This is Mark Jackson. Due to circumstances beyond my control I am no longer employed by Carleton University. I have accepted a job offer on the west coast and will be leaving Sunday evening. If you have an urgent message please leave it at the tone. This number is valid until the 30th."

That was it. If Dr. Jackson no longer had a job then neither did he. It was pretty mysterious. They owed him two weeks pay! He'd get Michael Walters on it. That guy had connections all over the university community.

That afternoon his mobile rang. John was sticky and sweating like a pig from a heavy lifting session and needed desperately to get in the shower. "Yeah what is it?" he said crossly.

"Is this John Frankel, formerly lab assistant to Dr. Mark Jackson?"

"Yes!"

"This is Katrina Lazlo from the astronomy department. You have been reassigned to Dr. Peter Marlowe. Please report for work tomorrow at 6 a.m. Go to room 307 in the Astro building. Dr. Marlowe will be waiting for you."

"Pretty early isn't it?" John complained. "I'm going to be worthless at 6 in the morning."

"So will Marlowe," she said dryly. "He'll have been up all night."

"What about the two weeks I'm owed for already?"

"Don't sweat it kid. Your check's been waiting for you in the physics department." Click.

"Duh." He hadn't even thought to ask for it.

At 6 the next morning he met Peter Marlowe. Both of them looked like shit. Marlowe was a short, immensely fat man with thick horn-rimmed glasses and disheveled brown hair. He wore old fashioned leather shoes and a plain white cotton shirt. His baggy pants with an enormous waistline were held up by suspenders. The man was about five feet tall and five feet wide. Mr. Five-by-five! Just like Jimmy Rushing, the jazz and blues singer.

"Good morning John," Marlowe said, holding out a pudgy hand. "I've heard good things about you from Jackson in optics. Said you were good with computers and data analysis. That's exactly what I need you for. We're trying to identify red shift quasars and other unusual objects from a new predictive model we're putting together using a number of different sky survey databases. It's mostly an analysis of previous observations. But we also have to actually identify anything we find with real observations. So we have to survey a lot. Anyway, I know that doesn't mean much to you now. Your job will be to organize the data we've generated each night and enter it in the proper format into the software. I'll show you how to do that. Later I'll have you doing pattern analysis using several algorithms I've developed."

The fat man took off his glasses and wiped some sweat from his forehead. "Going to be a hot one today." John almost laughed. Marlowe looked like a cartoon character. His round, expressive face and his thick glasses made him look a little like a spherical Mr. Magoo.

Marlowe peered up at John as if seeing him for the first time. "You're a tree."

John burst out laughing. Marlowe's expressive face was an open book to the inside of him. John liked him immediately.

"I'm sorry Doctor," John said. He yawned. "It's too early for me. I hope you don't plan on having me come in at 6 every morning."

"No, dash it, I don't." Marlowe waddled over to the desk. "Here's your machine. All you have to do is retrieve the data from the server each morning and shove it into our tables. There's a write up in a file called DATAENTRY.TXT in the main directory. Later on we'll show you what we're doing and what we're looking for. That's when you might actually be useful to us. For now you're just a flunky."

Marlowe glanced at his new assistant, testing his reaction. John was too tired to be insulted.

"When you're done just hit the 'send' button," Marlowe said. "All I ask is that you finish by 6 p.m. Sometimes I like to come in early."

John's new boss showed him the software and what he was expected to do.

"Looks pretty boring sir," John said.

"Dashed right son. Bloody boring. I sure as hell don't want to do it. That's why I imported you." He looked up at John again. "Are you an ent?"

John laughed. "No sir. But at 6 in the morning my brain is operating as slow as one."

"All right...Frankel?...Frankel. I want you to get on this software as soon as possible. I'll be sending you notes every day that should help you to get an understanding of what we're doing."

Dr. Marlowe paused for a moment. "Unless you're a bloody moron. Which I'm hoping you're not."

"Why not get someone more familiar with astronomy?" John inquired.

"Dashed good idea son. Couldn't find anyone. Budget constraints. You're already on the payroll. Best fit. You're it. Don't let me down." The little fat man fired his words like machine gun bullets and John almost laughed again. Marlowe's enormously chubby face clearly reflected his hope and frustration.

He showed John some articles to read for background information. Astronomers had, over the years, made many surveys of the sky and had digitized their images into databases. John understood that the project was a predictive model that used sophisticated data mining operations. It was very computer intensive and very theoretical. Well, he knew a bit about algorithms and data analysis.

"We're probably not going to see each other very much. I work nights but we've got email. If it's an emergency, text me on 45573." Marlowe held out his pudgy hand, the stumpy fingers wiggling in their impatience to accept John's hand. Mr. Piggly Wiggly. "Welcome aboard," said John's new boss.

John put his hand to his mouth as Peter Marlowe turned and waddled his enormous bulk out of the room. He looked like a pregnant penguin with his feet toeing out acutely. The belt around his waist vibrated from the rolls of fat like a hula hoop.

It took John a couple of weeks to figure out what Marlowe's data sets were all about. There was a ton of data, keeping him busy until 4 every afternoon.

John liked the fact that he could work alone and had the freedom to organize his day in any way he chose. He simply went into Marlowe's office sometime before 9 a.m., downloaded the data sets, and got busy. He left any time his work was complete. The job suited his loner personality very well. Sometimes he even showed up at class.

One morning at 9 a.m. John arrived at the office. Marlowe's great fanny was balanced precariously on a wheeled chair. More of it was off than on. John smiled, choking back a laugh. "Chairs are a damned nuisance," Marlowe said with profound irritation. "I've got a special one made for me in the lab but this one here is for a midget."

Man and chair resembled a hippopotamus sitting on a postage stamp.

"Dashed fine work you're doing John," Marlowe said. "Very pleased. If this keeps up and we have anything useful to publish, your name will appear. At the bottom of course."

"Thank you sir!" John was genuinely pleased. If he got a name for himself it would mean more money. Even though he liked the old house on Magnolia Street John wanted a place of his own. That required a hefty down payment. Genevieve now wanted to live in a house and refused to even consider an apartment. And what the ladies want, they get. John was pretty sure that formula was the basis for success in many relationships between men and women.

Alicia and Michael Walters were married so they no longer came around for dinner as often. Alicia was still busy redecorating and Michael was putting together a room for the baby.

Robert and Rachel planned to travel some more during the upcoming winter. They were getting along quite nicely now. It was a good thing because he was not going to live in this house under the old regime.

He and Genevieve were in some sort of stasis, just marking time. She had always expected something from him, something which was apparently still unfulfilled. Her studies bored her. Her work was satisfying but not challenging. John couldn't figure it out. She was the smartest person he had ever seen and could easily find intellectually exciting work. She hadn't bothered.

She was too deep even for him, but it didn't matter. He thanked God for her every day.

Then one day it all changed.

John drove to work one early fall morning and got stuck behind a truck carrying lumber. Irritating red flags fluttered in his windshield the whole way. Stupid one lane roads, they ought to widen it. When he got to his desk in Marlowe's office, a birthday card in bold red lettering sat next to Marlowe's computer.

"HAPPY 50th DR. MARLOWE," it read.

On the way home he had to stop at every red light. When Genevieve came home she was wearing black slacks with a bright red blouse and a red ribbon in her hair.

"You look great," he said.

She just smiled.

Genevieve almost never acknowledged his compliments even though they were heartfelt. John noticed her coloring again: the pale white skin, red lips, and intense black eyes, eyebrows, and hair. Her delicate features and bone structure. Every time they went out together heads would turn and John knew they weren't looking at him. She exuded a presence around her that was much larger than her body. Genevieve was the most unusual person, male or female, he had ever met. That included Kjirsten and even that stupid griffon.

The next day John and Genevieve had lunch together. They made a practice to eat together at least twice during the workweek. During the school year they sometimes hardly ever saw each other, even in the evenings. She often worked at the high school after hours. She tutored teachers in the science and math departments, and did computer work for the school.

They liked to eat at Gratzi's, an Italian restaurant in Old Town. John was already seated when Genevieve walked in wearing red slacks. John seated her, a habit he had maintained all through their relationship.

John reached for his napkin. Red.

Something clicked: "Look for red."

"Genevieve, would you like to take a little trip with me this evening?"

"Where to?"

"To see that redhead. Kjirsten said something about being a candidate. I've been thinking it over and I think I want to do it, whatever it is."

"You're sure you're not going back just so you can kiss her again?" she teased.

John flushed. "Well, she didn't give me much choice. She..."

"It's all right John. I'm sorry." She was looking at him with that commanding presence of hers. She held his attention for a moment, then smiled.

"I've been waiting my whole life for you to take me there."

So that was it. That thing he was supposed to do! It must involve Kjirsten and the research station at the end of nowhere.

"Is today Tuesday?" she asked.

"Tuesday?"

"Tuesday is Robert and Rachel's night out."

He snapped his fingers. "Right. Tuesday! Yes, it's Tuesday today."

She smiled excitedly, like a little kid about to open a long hoped for birthday present. "I can't wait!"

That evening John and Genevieve placed their chairs back to back, in the middle of their bedroom. Genevieve was charged. Every one of her actions seemed purposeful and animated.

"Let me guide this time," John said.

They both went through their personal routines. John felt the back of her head against him and a wave of well being coursed through him. Now, as separate personalities, they both activated their spheres of consciousness. The two merkabas pulsed with energy. John felt the consciousness of his beloved blend with his.

John remembered the vibrational impressions around the earth that led to the Eyrie. Genevieve allowed John to lead, picking up on his vision and sensations of the Eyrie.

Now their bedroom shimmered and faded away. The concentric rings symbol appeared around them as a guide and confirmation of their vibrational position within the All. The Eyrie appeared within their perception, coming into focus as they adjusted their consciousness to the correct vibrational frequencies. There. The familiar feeling of "reality." John and Genevieve arrived sitting back to back near the main console in Kjirsten's section of the facility.

John noticed that their journey seemed to take longer than their first together, probably because he was less experienced.

"Good job love," said Genevieve.

John looked around. No ocean at his feet, thank God. The crazy "assistants" as well as the fly-specked room were both gone. Six walls rose from the floor, sectioning off their cell from the rest of the honeycomb. John heard voices and activity around them but could see none of it. After a few moments they heard footsteps.

John turned and saw Kjirsten walking toward them in her white full length robe. Kjirsten stood before them, towering over Genevieve and looking into her eyes.

Genevieve smirked. "Hello Kjirsten."

It was obvious to him they had known each other for some time.

"Welcome Genevieve."

They both giggled. "Well, here we finally are," Kjirsten said cheerfully.

Genevieve sighed happily and with obvious relief. "Yes. We made it."

Kjirsten spoke in official tones. "You have successfully brought the candidate John Frankel. Well done and congratulations."

Genevieve bowed. "Thank you."

John was confused. "You mean you two are in this together?" The two women exchanged meaningful glances, but did not answer.

"Where's Davey and the rest?" John asked. "Where's that lunatic griffon?"

As if on cue a bubble of light appeared to John's right. The griffon emerged, flapping his wings and drenching John with water.

"That's Ivan to you, kid." Ivan had something wriggling in his beak, which he noisily chewed and swallowed. "Love those quillfish but you have to be careful with them." Ivan shook his huge wings a second time, spraying John again. "Oh sorry. Didn't see you there."

"OK you made your point," said John, wiping his face. The water tasted musky but not unpleasant, like nothing on earth.

Ivan looked at Kjirsten. "This earthian male is a candidate?" He squawked skeptically.

"You should know that. You OKed him."

"I'm having second thoughts." SQUAWK!!!!

Four other small spheres materialized with the heads of the others. Bellerophon had a cigarette dangling from his mouth. Ash fell on to the floor and his bubble was filling up with smoke. He looked a little like Jack at the pool hall except that Jack never actually got one of the obnoxious things in his mouth.

"Must you smoke?" said Kjirsten.

"Always!" Bellerophon threw his cigarette to the floor and they all winked out.

"Would you *please* explain the function of those jokers?" John asked.

Kjirsten spoke formally. "My assistants and I are part of the universe-wide project to determine the nature of the Unformed Potential and its effect upon physical reality. You experienced a simulation the last time you were here."

It was something he could never forget. Then it hit him. Those idiots were actually *out there*. In that insanity.

"How in hell..."

Kjirsten and Genevieve smiled. They both spoke soothingly. "It's not as bad as you think."

John was stunned. "Wait a minute. You're not suggesting that I'm a candidate for *that*?"

The two women glanced at each other. Kjirsten said, "Let me handle this." She looked at him challengingly. "Both of us are out there all the time."

Her comments had their intended effect. John's male pride was pricked.

He couldn't even think how much courage and discipline it would take. The simulation was horrible enough. The real thing was probably a lot worse. It would be the equivalent of lowering himself into a vat of molten metal. Instant doom.

He glanced up at Genevieve, who was gazing at him impassively.

John inventoried himself. Do I have what it takes? Looking deep inside himself John realized he didn't. Not by a long shot.

Blood rushed to his face. He couldn't do it. He was a coward. Never in his life did he feel so ashamed. He slouched in one of the floating chairs, his eyes on the floor.

Genevieve saw John caving in and her happiness turned to horror. Kjirsten had blown it. She was about to rush to him when Kjirsten barked at him. "John Frankel!"

"What." His shoulders were still slumped in apathy.

"On your feet!"

The strength of her intention was incredible. Automatically he felt his body rise out of the chair, but his eyes were still on the floor.

"Look at me!"

John slowly raised his eyes to the beautiful woman in front of him. She locked her eyes to his. "Now John Frankel, it is time to shake off this disgusting self-pity." Kjirsten's voice assumed a warmer tone. An encouraging tone.

John Frankel did not know it but the woman before him was a past master in the handling of men. She had been trained for it since the age of 6 by the great Lyran matriarch, Doren Amundsen. Amundsen was a descendant of the most famous bloodline in the Lyran sector.

John felt her encouragement, tinged with just the right amount of contempt. Her demeanor said, "A woman can do it but you can't?"

Self pity! Kjirsten was right. "I just can't believe you can go out in that...horror," John said. "Or even *want* to."

Kjirsten saw that John was finding an inner strength. This one was incredibly sensitive. He was completely unlike the earthian female who had progressed, workmanlike, through every level of her training without incident or drama. At first Kjirsten thought that John's reaction was from weakness. But she felt a power within him. There was something about John Frankel that excited her. It was even more exciting not to know what it was.

This one might make it. Out of the thousands she had personally instructed, and only the sixth in 18 years.

She had seen the pattern over and over. The idealistic desire to become one of the elite Unformed Potential technicians was quickly destroyed once a candidate actually confronted the terrible unreality of the Unformed Potential. Then the process became a salvaging of pride. Candidates would go through the motions, knowing deep inside they would never make it. Kjirsten had learned to recognize the signs immediately, shunting such candidates to instructors in other divisions.

"That's because, John Frankel, you have not been trained." Her voice was even warmer now and more encouraging, inspiring him with confidence. The note of challenge in her tone was gone.

Yes, maybe he could do it...

"Our training program is rigorous, step-by-step. The protocols have been rigorously tested and validated."

In that case, maybe it would be much easier than he thought. Then his gaze unlocked from Kjirsten's and he caught a glimpse of an Unformed Potential simulation running in one of the tanks. John began to quail again, but righted himself quickly. He sure wasn't going to let these beautiful ladies think poorly of him.

Kjirsten noticed John's demeanor. Better and better, she thought. Now she made the final thrust.

"To be selected as a candidate is an honor so prestigious, your name will be known throughout the All."

"It will?" John brightened considerably.

Genevieve let out her breath in a loud whoosh. She smiled, and Kjirsten smiled back.

"We both hope that you will be able to join us," Kjirsten said.

This one *had* to accept. Surviving a level three exposure on the first try was like successfully performing a 3½ twisting flip from a 60 foot board on the first jump. Of course she practically had to kill him afterwards. But it was still impressive.

The smile she now gave him was one that a woman gives a man she admires. Her attention filled him with a sense of pride and self satisfaction. John's conversion was complete.

Kjirsten smiled to herself in victory even though she was a little disappointed. Men are so predictable, even this one. She had teased herself with the idea that earthian males might be different.

"Who are these strange assistants of yours? And what's up with that griffon?" John now spoke much more cheerfully.

"All of us are volunteers. My assistants have passed the training. They have been selected for their mental toughness, their intelligence, and their courage. Above all they have demonstrated their ability to control their sphere of consciousness. If you can't hold your sphere of consciousness together, or if you seed the Unformed Potential too strongly...." Kjirsten flicked her hand across her neck to indicate "it's all over for you."

John digested that for a few moments.

"Ivan – the griffon – is our most productive team member. He is able to stay out longer and gather more useful data than anyone else in this entire sector."

John wanted to ask her why he was such a prick. Instead he said, "What is Unformed Potential work? It seems insane to study something that is unanalyzable."

"The Eyrie itself is a mystery. It was discovered long ago by a lone adventurer from the outer universes who wanted to go to the edge of existence and see if anything lay on the 'other side.' This entity found a peculiar bubble of stability within the instability. From there it was built up into a very sophisticated research and monitoring station."

"So this place has always been here?" John asked.

"As far as we know," Kjirsten said.

She pointed to the main console display tank, which now showed the Eyrie within the Unformed Potential. The perimeter of the enclosure was alive. In every instant it was being pressured into disorganization.

John tried looking into the tank at the insanity beyond the sphere for about twenty seconds. He had to pull his attention away. The pit of his stomach felt like a lava lamp. His palms were sweaty and his heart was racing.

Now he re-revised his opinion of everyone here. They were all lunatics.

"If you're willing, and you pass the training, you'll be working with them on an exciting project."

"You've got to be kidding."

"She's not kidding John," Genevieve said. She had been beside him all along, but so quietly he forgot she was there.

John turned to face her. "What's your part in all this Gen?"

"She's my fifth assistant," Kjirsten said.

Oh.

Things were beginning to clear up a lot. Compared to her work here, job and college would seem mundane indeed.

John placed his attention back into the tank.

No good. It made him dizzy and sick. "How can anyone even look long enough at this stuff to see any relationships?"

"That's what the training is all about," Genevieve said. Her voice expressed hope and encouragement.

John said nothing for a minute, thinking. He had come here with the intention to apply for candidate status. That was until he discovered the exact nature of their work. It was not only insane, but impossible. Kjirsten had hinted that he was some kind of Neo, able to penetrate the mystery of the Matrix. John knew he was no hero. Just the opposite. He could see no reason for a senseless foray into a nothingness that would tear him apart.

Kjirsten's voice interrupted his thoughts. "There's one really important thing we need to show you before you begin your training." The Lyran spoke as if the matter had already been decided.

John threw both arms out. "Hold on ladies. I haven't agreed to do anything yet."

Kjirsten was a bit irritated. Genevieve said, "Right John. You haven't formally agreed yet. You can still back out."

John didn't like the sound of "back out."

Kjirsten thought the kid was hesitant. She hoped she wouldn't lose her bet with Ivan. The griffon had dismissed John as a wannabe. "You're wasting your time with the earthian," he had squawked. "He's a lightweight."

"He is not!" she had flared.

The griffon tilted his head and gazed at her in that way he had that said, "Don't kid yourself." She wasn't kidding herself. Or was she?

There was one more thing to show him and she didn't want to. Personal honesty and her duty demanded it.

Kjirsten grabbed the headset. "Look in the tank," she said sharply.

John saw something like a soap bubble. Contained within the delicate film, or border, were a billion points of light in complex and beautiful patterns. A couple of the simpler geometries were recognizable. The bubble was literally packed with intricate and interlocking energy patterns that were so stunning it took his breath away.

"What is that?" John asked. "It's beautiful."

"It's a sphere of consciousness," Kjirsten said. "A fully activated merkaba."

"Is that what we really look like?"

Kjirsten smiled. "Yes, John. This is an accurate, pure energy representation of an actual merkaba, taken from one of our imagers."

John stared at it with his mouth open. "I could study this thing forever and not even scratch the surface."

"It is the single most important area of research within the community even though Unformed Potential work is glamorous and gets most of the attention. The investigation of the sphere of consciousness and its potential is undertaken throughout the All. Except on earth of course, and other backward places."

John said nothing, immersing himself within the display. He tried to comprehend the astonishing beauty of it. Meridians of energy constantly cycled and recycled through the bubble, supporting incredibly intricate geometries. Kjirsten zoomed the display. John saw the smaller, brighter sphere inside the big one. The meridians were much more concentrated in the center of the sphere.

Now the display zoomed to the surface of the sphere.

"Here is the area between the sphere of consciousness and the Unformed Potential."

At first John saw a solid "surface." When the display zoomed more finely he could see little viruses attacking it, like sperm attempting desperately to penetrate an egg.

"The sphere of consciousness is highly organized," Kjirsten said. "The virtual energy of the Unformed Potential is highly unorganized. The system tries to find balance. As long as the integrity of the surface is maintained the sphere of con-sciousness suffers no damage. But if there is a breach..."

The simulation showed a tiny opening. Instantly the entropy within the bub-ble was radically increased. Within a second or two the beautiful sphere was torn to shreds.

John gulped.

"Needless to say, an individual sphere of consciousness that is breached does not have the strength to overcome the overwhelming disorder of the Unformed Potential."

John's face went ashen.

Genevieve was worried. She didn't want to fail now when he was so close. She felt that Kjirsten was going way too fast. Genevieve herself did not see that video until her fourth lesson! John is a very sensitive person. He felt everything with an intensity greater than anyone she had ever met.

"I'm sorry John. We have to show this to every potential trainee," Kjirsten was saying. "It is absolutely vital to become aware of the precise boundaries of your sphere in order to hold yourself together out there."

"And we need to go out there because..."

Kjirsten smiled. "We need to observe first hand because we'd miss too much otherwise. It turns out that immersion allows a broader and more accurate per-spective of the Unformed Potential."

She paused for a moment and debated within herself. "And frankly, many beings go into the Unformed Potential because it's a rush. Imagine yourself clinging to a rope that is dangling from an airplane flying over New York City, narrowly avoiding buildings, 1,000 feet in the air. That's about a tenth of what it feels like out there. And secondarily, there is a sort of...competition... amongst those who do this work."

"Competition?" John was interested but Genevieve snorted with disgust.

"Yes John. Competition. To see who can stay out the longest, stuff like that. When the significance of the Unformed Potential was first discovered over 100 million years ago, everyone thought just like you. It took thousands of years just to develop successful protocols for easily viewing it from the inside. Then some hot-dog got it into his head to actually go outside. He was torn to shreds, just as in the simulation." She coughed. "That shocked the community so badly that a law was passed forbidding it. Even though we know that passing laws is futile in regulating behavior. Nevertheless it was done, to impress upon beings from every universe the danger of the Unformed Potential. You have to understand John. Even though there are billions and billions of us up here we are very close knit. We love each other very deeply. The dissolution of Woah, as he was known, was so terrible that we did not recover from it for a very long time."

Kjirsten said "we" as if the memory of it were still fresh.

"It is our idea, based on observation and experimentation with the Vessel of Life, that consciousness is eternal." She took off the headset and turned to face him. "What happened to Woah was not mere physical death, for we know that consciousness is physically independent of the body. This was a true death of the spirit. A total and complete erasure of a conscious personality."

She let John contemplate that for a moment.

"What earthians call death is merely a disassociation from the body into a greater awareness of yourself. We want you to understand that the sphere of consciousness *is* the identity that you refer to as 'John Frankel.' In order for 'John Frankel' to continue to exist you must keep your sphere of consciousness intact."

She spoke quickly. "There are those who believe firmly that even if your sphere gets trashed there is something greater. This school of thought says that consciousness is a pure potential and that you can never really die. At least theoretically."

"That's comforting," John squeaked.

Genevieve burst out laughing. "Yeah. A real consolation prize!"

Despite herself Kjirsten giggled even though she was annoyed at Genevieve's frivolity. This was the most serious aspect of the entire presentation.

"Maybe I didn't do such a good job explaining that one," Kjirsten said. All three of them were laughing now.

"Hey, what about that competition? Does it still exist?" The idea of immersing himself in that madness was absurd. But John's life-long association with athletes, and his own table tennis experience, made the idea intriguing.

Genevieve frowned. "I'm afraid it does, love."

John eagerly attempted to pursue the subject but Genevieve dug her elbow into his ribs. She didn't want John going in that direction.

Kjirsten was intrigued. Almost all of the best humanoid Unformed Potential workers were male. She wondered whether this earthian male had it in him. Only the strongest and mentally toughest could grind it out for more than an hour of subjective time...but she was neglecting her duty, thinking along that line.

"After the first failure many researchers worked on developing new protocols and new simulations for testing them. Our simulations can get pretty close to the real thing, although the programs always abort before any real damage can be done. To a certain daredevil section of the community it was a challenge. It was only a matter of time before someone else made the attempt. After a struggle which lasted several minutes, he too was lost. After that it became clear that someone would eventually be successful.

"Finally, one of the great Illirian superminds from Galaxy 11 succeeded. But these beings are capable of permanently linking consciousness and are utterly dissimilar to humanoid life. Several thousand years later the first humanoids were able to immerse themselves in the Unformed Potential." She stopped for a drink of water from the glass beside her. "One of them was a Lyran," Kjirsten said proudly.

"From there it became a sport. A dangerous sport, for many tried without fully mastering the then very complex procedure. We had to organize training and competitions. Otherwise meatheads who had no business being out there would get themselves annihilated. There was one big benefit though. During the games, people began to notice an influx of energy from the Unformed Potential into Real Space. Eventually, the barrier was discovered. You'll find out about that later."

"OK. I have one more question," John said. "How do you even get out there? My understanding is that you have to have a destination firmly in mind. There's nothing out there to lock in on."

"Good question!" Kjirsten appreciated John's perspicacity. "That doesn't come up until the very last portion of the training. There's a trick to it you can't understand until you've passed the simulation training. It's very, very difficult. Only a minute percentage of those who try ever succeed."

"But it's so rewarding!" she added quickly. "The feeling of being out there – it's indescribably delicious. And somewhat addicting. If you can do it, that is."

Oh.

These people were either totally nuts or really profound. John was having a hard time understanding Genevieve's participation in such a nutty thing. Then he remembered her adventurous spirit, and all of the crazy things she did as a kid.

"One last thing to tell you John," Kjirsten said. "There is a difference between projection of consciousness and actual immersion. In projection your body stays behind, as in a dream. In immersion the entire sphere of consciousness is activated and fully present. That also means the inner sphere that contains the body's energy. That's what we're doing when we enter the Unformed Potential. It's what you do when you engage in the translation process using the standard consciousness altering protocols."

Kjirsten ran out of words. John said nothing, lost in thought. The conversation reached a dead zone.

"Sooooo John, what do you think?" said Genevieve innocently, after a few silent minutes had passed.

"Think about what?"

"About helping us."

"Look, I'm nothing. I can't even look at that stuff for 15 seconds without losing it. I can't see why you're going through so much effort."

Suddenly the whole thing seemed ridiculous. "OK, I've decided. Forget it!"

He tried to rise but Kjirsten held her arm across his chest. "We are all agreed, John Frankel." Kjirsten held him in his seat. She was enormously strong and apparently was determined to get his agreement. "Your participation in this project is necessary. You just *have* to say yes." This time there was no coaxing, challenging, or guile behind her words. John could feel her sincerity. More important he could sense her belief in him. He also detected a faint sense of desperation. John stole a look at Genevieve, who was also looking a little grave. If she thought it was important it really must be. He trusted Genevieve more than anyone.

What disturbed him was the fact that these two beautiful ladies had successfully mastered the training. What kind of toughness was required to expose yourself to that primeval madness? John's respect for Genevieve increased a hundredfold. This smallish, delicate creature beside him had courage enough for a hundred men.

John thought for a long time. Kjirsten and Genevieve sat silently with him, unmoving.

John slowly shook his head back and forth. "I just don't know."

His response angered Kjirsten. *Make up your mind, earthian male!* Again she recognized that she had completely lost it with this earthian man. But the requirements of a Lyran matriarch seemed irrelevant when compared to the issue at hand. No excuse of course. She would have quite a bit of explaining to do when she returned to Skjelgaard and Doren Amundsen.

"Let me try to explain this so you'll get it," she snapped. "There are countless numbers of beings who would love to be able to do this work. It is an honor to even be selected for candidate status. To fail the training is not a stigma, but a tribute to greatness. To pass the training is...to be esteemed throughout the All. To work inside the Unformed Potential is an act of ultimate courage. If you fail you don't just lose your body, you may even lose your soul. But the rewards are commensurate with the risk. You can't know the incredible benefits unless you actually do it."

John was quiet again for a long time. The women once more waited patiently. He began to think about the work he might be doing if he passed the training. *If he passed the training.* It could be exciting...working with the energies of creation itself and learning more about the fundamental nature of the universe! It might be interesting to be a hero for a change. All his life he had been in the background, watching others get the glory.

Ultimately, John made his decision just like any 21-year-old male might have. He wanted to show Kjirsten he wasn't just a geeky guy. Most of all he wanted to prove his mettle to Genevieve. If the current situation were the norm he'd be spending a lot of time working with the women. A slow smile spread over his features.

He faced Kjirsten but could not completely block the mischief he was feeling.

"Ladies, I cannot tell a lie. The idea of working in the Unformed Potential seems senseless to me. The only reason I'm agreeing is that it would be fun to be around both of you a lot. Some unbalanced part of me thinks the work itself might be exciting. But the attraction of you both is just overwhelming." John swooned playfully.

Kjirsten's eyes were level with his and he saw her good-natured disgust.

"Males!" was all she would say.

Genevieve shook her head. The look she gave him said, "We're discussing the fate of the universe and all you can think of is sex?" She glanced at Kjirsten. "They're so...*predictable*, aren't they?"

Kjirsten stood up with her hand on her hip. "You're *sure* you want to do this? This is a first: a prospective candidate who has no respect for anything except his cock."

John guffawed. "Lighten up a little sweetheart."

Kjirsten's lips formed a straight line. John saw a glint of fire and steel in her eyes.

"OK, OK! Just kidding!" John spoke as seriously as he could. "I'm absolutely sure I want to do this crazy work, whatever it is. I am ready to become a valuable team member to the best of my ability."

Kjirsten softened. "All right then." She clapped her hands together. "Davey!"

Davey's head popped in, then his whole body. The light flickered off his metallic blue skin. "Dammit, I was in the middle of a promising..." Then he noticed John. "Oh, it's you," he said with genuine disgust. "You mean you pulled me out for *this?*"

"Come my friend," Kjirsten said. "A new candidate! It is time to begin his training."

Davey smiled. "For you I'll do it."

He grabbed John's arm. "C'mon."

The look on John's face was comical. "But...but..."

"No buts!" Kjirsten exclaimed.

Davey dragged him down the hall. "We're not off to a good start here, rook."

Genevieve and Kjirsten slapped hands. "It worked!" Genevieve said.

"Of course! Men are such beasts," Kjirsten replied.

Their eyes locked and both of them burst into laughter. John could hear it all the way down the hall.

"Where are we going?" John said. He was panicked at the idea of this roughhouse in charge of his training. Davey didn't answer. On the way, John examined his "guide." Davey was no more than 5 feet tall. He had enormously thick and well-muscled legs and arms, and a massive head with prominent supra-orbital ridges. He had wide thick feet tapering at the heel and with three equal sized stubby toes. His hands were slabs with short, thick fingers. His blue skin was his most remarkable characteristic. Even though he was a foot and half shorter Davey muscled John down the hallway like a recalcitrant piece of pasta. John thought this creature could probably snap his neck like a piece of spaghetti. If he could reach it.

In the middle of the hallway Davey stopped before one of the ubiquitous consoles and put on a headset. Twenty seconds later a cylindrically shaped vehicle with rounded edges appeared from around the corner. It floated a couple of millimeters off the floor and came to rest inside a yellow colored circle painted in the middle of the floor. "Pickup station," Davey said. "Anytime you want a car find one of the consoles."

They got in. John was very nervous. "Where are we going?"

"To one of the Unformed Potential training areas reserved for humanoid life forms."

John's stomach felt leaden just like his first day of school. He had a sinking feeling that the instruction would not be to his liking.

The car moved swiftly through a dimly lit hexagonal cell of apartments. Davey said, "These are living quarters."

"People stay here full time?"

"Sure do! I'm one of 'em. I'm addicted to this work and to the people here."

Uh-oh, John thought. This guy sounds like a fanatic.

After several minutes the car emerged into a well lit, noisy area with lots of very large rooms. None of them had doors. The entrances were all egg-shaped. The rooms contained row after row of the standard consoles with no walls or separating panels between them.

Davey walked John into one of the rooms. "These are the training areas. You'll be in here. This area is one of many reserved for first flight students." John saw creatures of every description. The only common denominator was two or more arms, two legs, and a head. As soon as the students in the crowded room spotted Davey they shouted. "Technician Davey! Hello sir! A privilege sir!" There were dozens of students milling around the blue man, jabbering excitedly.

John was surprised. His gruff instructor didn't seem like anything special to him.

Davey acknowledged the greetings and spoke with several of the students. One or two cursory glances were thrown John's way. Otherwise he was ignored.

Davey motioned John to a floating chair in front of one the standard consoles against the wall and close to the entrance. These consoles each had a small table with a headset and a 7-button panel sitting directly in front of one of the large display tanks. There was no flat panel data display. This console was one of twelve that were isolated from the others.

"We don't use the data displays here," Davey said dismissively. "Only in the research divisions."

The other students saw Davey teaching John personally. Eyebrows, or their equivalent, went up all over the room.

Davey gestured to a manual sitting on the console table. "This is your homework. In here are the standard protocols for surviving immersion in the Unformed Potential. You must memorize them and know them better than your dick. They are your best friends. Failure to follow even one of them out there will result in your immediate dissolution." Davey's voice was hard and commanding. The other students were now looking his way.

John gulped. He wasn't into military-style training regimens. If they were going to operate like that he was getting out fast.

The manual had a blue cover inscribed with a symbol of a white sphere of light surrounded by a multicolored mist. It looked remarkably like the one Genevieve had brought to his room when she checked his translation of the code. John flipped through the pages, trying to get a quick understanding of the material. There were 37 pages of instructions, all written in symbols just like those in his codebook.

"Rookie, this manual is not to leave your desk. Under no circumstances are you to translate out of here with one. Violation will result in your permanent ban from this facility. Do you understand?"

"Yes. Ah...sir."

John had a thought. He'd like to practice these routines at home and get a head start. "Before we begin I'd like to study this manual."

This rookie is bailing already, Davey thought. He'd seen it so many times. He wanted to get the simulation going and test the kid right away. It was standard procedure. However, the overarching rule was that no one could be pressured in this work. "All right," he grunted.

The stocky blue man looked around the busy training room and saw a number of students clamoring for his attention. Davey sighed. Teaching wasn't his strong suit but it was a duty all field workers must perform. "As long as I'm here I might as well make myself useful." He growled to John. "Holler when you're ready to start."

John spent an hour with the manual. After finding translations for a dozen unfamiliar symbols he was able to read it with little difficulty.

The manual contained exercises for precisely identifying and controlling the periphery and the integrity of the sphere of consciousness. The beginning of the book had diagrams identifying the templates that kept the sphere defined.

It was like reading a blueprint or a schematic for a mechanical device, except that the device was himself. Nothing about breathing in here. There wasn't any air in the Unformed Potential! The manual contained 21 rigorously defined protocols that had to be learned in order. Each one built upon the one before. Each one used templates located further and further out from the center of the sphere. The manual made it clear that once mastered, a being would have the ability to consciously project and receive thought impulses to and from another so trained. Awesome!

John understood that this manual was the mysterious fifth section of his code-book.

Davey was still busy so John spent the next two hours reading the manual all the way through. By the time the blue man tapped John on the shoulder he had memorized all 21 protocols.

"I've placed you into the system. To load the first level simulation just touch the sensor."

Davey touched the small indentation at the far left of the panel, worn from constant use. A simulation of the swirling psychosis that was the Unformed Potential appeared in the display tank.

Davey picked up the headset. John opened his mouth but Davey put up his hand. "Don't ask me how it works. I don't know or care. I'm not one of those theoreticians like our fearless leader." He put the headset over John's head. "All trainees hafta keep these on. When you feel yourself losing it the headset will communicate with the simulation and abort the program."

John felt a soft pulsing of energy on his temples. "Is there a light around my head?" he asked eagerly, turning away from the tank and screwing his eyes upward.

"No rook, there ain't no light." Davey was disgusted. "And there won't be until ya learn how to operate them without messin' everyone else up. All you can do right now is call a transport. If you can make it past the first level I'll show ya how to use them." Davey knew that wasn't true. He didn't feel like spending time showing the rook something he could learn from one of the students.

"Now look in the tank." John decided to just plunge in. For ten seconds or so it was all right. Then he began to see nightmarish formations in the chaos. A city of burning skyscrapers, explosions, smoke, people screaming, bodies flying, mutilated corpses. A feeling of paranoia seized his mind. John screamed unwittingly and backed out.

Heads turned in the training area. John heard mutters. "First-timer!" "Rookie!" "Flame-out!"

Davey chortled. "Don't mind them kid. They all did it too." He laid his heavy hand on John's arm, steadying him. After several minutes John regained his composure. He was shaking and wiped cold sweat from his forehead.

The skin on the blue man's hand was very smooth and hot. John wondered what part of the galaxy Davey came from.

"Son, the first rule in dealing with the Unformed Potential is that the predominant thoughts in your consciousness will be activated. Your attention to the potential energy of the Unformed Potential will seed it. From that seed thought, anything can happen. And I mean *anything*. I could of told ya that but you needed to experience it yourself."

John's jaw was throbbing now from cellular memory. "I was scared and thought of a world I saw being destroyed in a book I read. It was horrible."

"Happens to rookies all the time." Davey spoke unsympathetically.

"How do I keep from thinking that stuff?"

Davey snorted. John was afraid he wasn't making a very good impression.

"Discipline. When you deal with the Unformed Potential you learn real quick to clear your mind. The manual will teach you how to observe the Unformed Potential without interacting with it. You gotta make sure you don't seed it or whatever you observe will be worthless."

The blue man looked down at John, measuring him. "If you can pass the first two flights in simulation one of us'll bring you to a special training area on the skin to measure your progress. After that comes the biggie: complete immersion. That's where everybody fails. Most trainees just cave in at the very idea of it even after passing the simulator testing. Those that do make it out without killing themselves come back...different."

The hard planes of Davey's face lit up. "Being exposed directly to the Unformed Potential energy feels like you're being assaulted by an all-knowing enemy. You know that if you fail to consciously regulate even the tiniest portion of your sphere you'll be torn to pieces. Rook, you can't know how wonderful it is until you've actually experienced it. It's the ultimate high. Once you get it there is a feeling of ultimate power. You soar. I gotta admit, it's addicting." Davey was staring into the Unformed Potential simulation as if it were his lover.

"Holy shit," John muttered. "This guy is either a genius or he's totally bonkers."

Davey whirled around to face John. "What was that, *hrrlbut*?"

The blue man was intimidating, just like Kjirsten. And Genevieve too.

"Uh...I'm wondering whether you're crazy or brilliant."

Davey guffawed. He slapped John hard on the back with his thick hand, knocking the wind out of him. "That's good kid. I sometimes wonder about that myself!"

Davey continued. "If you make it past flight three and want to continue, Goliath will take over and you'll be taking short trips outside. He'll show you how to get around. He'll show you how to properly record what you're observing. The recording of activity within the Unformed Potential is the primary function of our work. That, and trying to get through the barrier. That don't concern only advanced technicians. Without us nobody would have a clue of what's goin' on. First we gotta get you so you don't freak out."

Davey pointed to the tank.

"Remember, this is a simulation program so you can't get too messed up no matter how bad you do. The randomness of the algorithms that generate the display are controlled. However, the stuff in the tank is really sensitive to thought. Just like the Unformed Potential. There are six levels of difficulty in flight one, indicated by the panel. You need to get checked out on each level before you can go on to the next. You're in the system as a level one so even if you get cocky and try the other levels they won't work."

Davey pointed to the tank. "The Unformed Potential looks like it's alive. It'll remind you of stuff in your life. It'll activate your imagination and your fears. The credo of the Unformed Potential worker is merely to observe, not add in subjective stuff. All your personal shit is just that – shit. It's worthless." Davey paused for a second. "Kid, if you don't make it it's no big deal. 99.9% of us who try, fail."

That's fine for you, John thought. But my girlfriend made it so I *have* to.

Davey was thinking the same thing.

"One more thing," Davey said. "You need to get through the two training flights mainly on your own. We found out the hard way that those who can't successfully endure the simulations have no chance of survival in the Unformed Potential. Practicing the protocols in the manual will help you get through the first two flights."

"What's the difference between flight one and flight two?" John asked.

"Flight one uses the tank here. When you have mastered the simulation program at the highest degree of difficulty you use the holospace. See that enclosure in the back?"

John saw a large spherical bubble with two monitoring stations in front. Davey leaned over and whispered into John's ear. "In there you get to confront your innermost demons. In there you are all alone, just you and the simulation program." His smile spoke volumes to John. "In there you can hardly tell the difference between the simulation and the real thing. The only difference is that the program will bail when it senses you're almost at the meltdown point."

John was feeling worse and worse. How had he gotten himself into this? He liked it a lot better before he ever found out about this place. He used to be free! Now he was expected to engage in a process that made him ill and could finish him off for good.

Davey was pushing John harder than he had ever pushed a first-timer before. The entire training regimen was designed never to place a trainee over his or her head. The process increased the degree of difficulty very gradually because this community of researchers valued each and every being beyond measure. But his instructions from the boss were explicit. Give the kid the works, right off the bat. Put the squeeze on him. Make him squirm. He felt kinda bad about it, but orders were orders. Davey knew that this kid and Genevieve were lovers. He liked Genevieve; she was tough just like him. Any guy who could handle Genevieve must have some guts, but he just didn't see it in this kid. John looked like a real meltdown.

Davey was a good-hearted fellow despite his crusty exterior. He decided to give John a break. "When you fully master each level something really good happens inside you. I can't explain it. But you feel...more you. You feel more powerful, more sure of yourself. It's a good feeling kid. If you talk to the other students they'll tell you. It's something you can't get from the standard translation protocols. It's what keeps people going through the frustrating times."

"Thanks Davey. I needed that." John felt great relief.

Davey motioned for John to start again.

At first John thought it shouldn't be too hard. He already had a couple of experiences with this stuff. But after an hour with the tank program at the beginning level, aided by advice and encouragement from Davey, he was still creating bizarre worlds.

"You know you're successful with the simulation when you can just comfortably look in the tank without causing anything to happen," Davey told him. "Keep at it and don't get discouraged." He gave John an encouraging thump on the shoulder, practically dislocating it. "Practice makes perfect. If you need me again, holler. I'll be back in an hour or so." John performed his breathing exercises to reach the state of perfect calm but nothing changed when he looked in the tank. He tried thinking of pleasant things, but that just seeded the tank. The damned stuff didn't know the difference between a positive and a negative thought. It began to morph crazily regardless.

No matter how often he cleared his mind, simply staring at the constantly changing chaos started his pattern recognition machinery. This inevitably led to a train of thought that seeded the tank.

Tears of frustration welled up in his eyes. He threw down the headset. "Fuck it. This sucks."

"OK, enough for today," Davey said from behind him. "You absolutely haveta maintain mental and emotional equilibrium to have any chance of success."

John hung his head. "I thought it was going to be easier than this."

"Chin up!" Davey barked. "You did OK for your first time."

John let that pass. He thought he did terrible. He was really angry with himself, which surprised him. Naturally even tempered, he was never one to engage in self criticism. Except in this place.

"Most candidates never make it past the first button," Davey said. "It requires tremendous control to even master the beginning level."

That made John feel a little better, but not much.

"The next time you come we'll have another go." Davey spent another hour with John showing him how to operate the console. The headsets allowed the operator's thoughts to control the display, but you had to know a lot about the construction and layout of the station to get it to work right. John soon found that even stray thoughts on the headset could lead to difficulty.

One time he attempted to bring up a schematic of the Eyrie layout when he heard a chorus of complaints from the other students. "Hey normie, quit meddling with our consoles!" said a very large, hairy, bear-like humanoid with short stubby claws on his hands and feet.

Davey calmed everyone down. "OK son, that's it. Lesson over."

John looked up at the blue man standing beside him. "Where are you from?"

Davey sat down on the float beside him. It almost groaned under his weight.

"I come from a planet in the Procyon sector of your galaxy, with specific gravity about 1.75 times that of your planet. I discovered the techniques of altered states of consciousness by accident. One day during a caravan to the dwelling of my brother in another city I saw a strange looking little fellow in a yellow cape. He sold me what I thought was a musical recording of the djilla, a flute-like instrument that I like very much. When I opened up the disk I found a bunch of interesting images and an instruction set for the consciousness altering protocols."

"Did one of the images have a guy with funny ears sitting under a tree?"

"No. Not that I remember."

"Did it have an abandoned city of white buildings in the middle of a smooth plane of glass-like material?"

Davey shook his head. "Nope."

"Did the instruction set contain symbolic language?"

Davey began to feel like a father being questioned by his overly curious son. "No. It was written in the language of the primary culture of my planet."

"What's your real name?"

Davey grinned, exposing a mouthful of large, light blue molars. "You couldn't pronounce it."

Davey rode with John back to the main area. Kjirsten and Genevieve were talking.

"Don't you guys ever do any work around here?" John joked. He had recovered his spirits a little already, thinking about how nice it would be to sleep with Genevieve tonight.

"We just got back from a field excursion," Kjirsten said. "How did you do?"

"I sucked." John felt like a little kid among giants. His relationship with the two women had altered significantly. They were the grizzled, battle-hardened veterans. He was the whiny weakling who hadn't even made it out of boot camp.

"Not bad," Davey said.

"Are you ladies done?" John said. "I'm tired and I want to get home and go to bed." He looked at Genevieve. "Hint, hint."

She laughed. "Sorry love, not tonight. Kjirsten and I still have some work to do." Genevieve looked animated and in her element.

John kissed her and walked off a little way. He sat with his back against one of the hexagonal walls of the enclosure. She'd be going out there again into that madness. It blew him away.

Even though he was exhausted, he managed to get through the technique without difficulty. John felt his energy field fire up. He connected with the universal medium and felt the familiar sense of complete well being. The Eyrie shimmered, then fuzzed out. He followed the now more discernible impression of his vibrational path back to earth. His room gradually came into focus and he found himself in one of the chairs in the middle of the room, back up against its partner. He undressed quickly and stumbled over the empty chair. John fell into bed, too tired to notice the time.

22

As always after one of his trips, the reality of life on earth was an adjustment. Part of him was still in the Eyrie, confronting the Unformed Potential. Even though his training had been unsuccessful so far, there was one benefit. In comparison, everything else seemed easy.

Today he wanted to blow off this lethargic feeling. He got on the old bike and pedaled into the office on the Carleton campus.

When John entered Peter Marlowe was there, looking tired but excited. "Ah John, there you are. Been standing here for fifteen minutes, can't sit in that blasted chair." He glanced at the offending receptacle with disgust.

John had never seen a face that so perfectly reflected what was inside. The guy would have made a great stand-up comedian.

"Dashed good job you're doing, son." John, in his study of Marlowe's model, had found a more efficient way to feed the data into the program. He had also made some tentative suggestions that led to improvement in their search algorithms. "Your background in mathematics and algorithms is going to be of use to the project. I was hoping for that when I grabbed you from the physics department."

Marlowe winked. "When I first saw you I thought you might be an idiot. You've proved me wrong."

John laughed at the good natured taunt. He stifled another laugh as his boss waddled out of the room. Mr. Five-by-five.

John was fully back in his life now and infused with some of the older man's enthusiasm. He went to work with a will.

When John was done it was well past 5. He wrote his report and put it on the server. Then he called Michael Walters and canceled their study appointment. Walters had already given him the entire semester in the first six weeks anyway. His Masters program was going so smoothly he was able to work almost full time.

A lot of his conversations with Michael Walters were of an exploratory nature. The older man gave him advanced concepts, and even presented arguments that contradicted the texts. "Never accept anything at face value, John," Walters said, "without running it through your personal filter. Just because it's written down and accepted in a university curriculum doesn't make it correct."

John found that attitude refreshing because he noticed just the opposite at Carleton. Even in the sciences, people defended their positions like junkyard dogs.

That evening after dinner John got a call.

"Marlowe here. I wanted to tell you that I won't be in for the rest of the week. I'm going to see a friend of mine in England, a doctor."

John was alarmed. "Nothing seriously wrong sir, I hope?" He really did like his boss.

Marlowe was touched; he could hear John's concern. "Nothing to worry about, dash it. But you see, I've got to take off some of this weight. Been trying for years. Tried everything in fact, but this bloke has a new approach."

"Good luck sir."

"Keep sending your reports as usual. I'll read them across the pond."

The next day there was almost nothing to do. John was able to leave the office well before noon. In his mind was a strong urge to get past the first button on that panel in the Eyrie training area. Then he could wipe that little smirk off Davey's face and justify Kjirsten's faith in him. And impress Genevieve too.

John drove home and typed in the exercises he had memorized from the manual into the laptop. Then he tried the first three or four. Five hours later he had completed all 21 and didn't even notice the passing of time. The exercises were an astonishing combination of intuitive and intellectual recognition of the merkaba. They were designed to increase awareness of the entire sphere of consciousness. The advanced protocols, from #15 to #21, were devoted solely to the definition and strengthening of the perimeter. Normally the protocols were performed with the sphere fully activated, but the manual encouraged the user to attempt perimeter recognition without it. To John's delight he was able to faintly perceive his own sphere all the way out without going through the technique first.

John was fired up to try the simulator again. He sat in his chair and went through the technique. The room began to shimmer. Like the spokes of a rotating wheel moving faster and faster, the objects in the room lost their definition. Then, pop! — the reality of his bedroom disappeared. He negotiated the zone of chaos surrounding the earth and found himself surrounded by the comforting golden-white mist of the universal medium. He brought up the guide symbol and steered himself to the tiny dot unconnected to the rest of reality. He arrived with his back to the cell wall in the Eyrie in precisely the same position as when he left. John walked around, looking for Davey. The place was deserted. Maybe everyone was sleeping. (John would discover later that the Eyrie operated on a different clock than earth.)

"Davey!" No answer. He wanted to practice right away but Davey never showed him how to call one of the transport vehicles. John walked to a console in one of the neighboring hallways and grabbed a headset, formulating his thought with crystal clear precision. "Let one of the cars come to the circle associated with this console." He walked down the hall to the yellow circle and waited. Within a minute one of the cars silently appeared.

He got in but nothing happened. There was no activating mechanism or steering wheel. The little one-seater craft with its clear, curved walls was devoid of all instrumentation.

John went back to the console and picked up the headset, clearly envisioning his destination from one of the Eyrie maps. Now it was in the system and when John reentered the vehicle it began to move. This was fun! If only we could do stuff like this on earth.

A thought intruded into his consciousness: "If all of you on earth could do this your planet would have been destroyed long ago."

That's right! But where did that thought come from?

"From me, silly." It was the car.

"Holy shit! A talking car?"

"Earthians are so primitive," it said jokingly. "By the way, you didn't have to use the headset again. Once a transport vehicle is summoned it is attuned to the thought patterns of the caller."

"Why didn't you tell me?"

"Because I wanted to see you get out again," it said impishly. "Ignorance is its own reward."

It wasn't really talking but John heard its thoughts clear as a bell. The little craft had the personality of a mischievous elf.

"Here we are," it said, stopping in the middle of the hallway within another of the yellow circles. John recognized the training room as the one he had been in earlier with Davey. He thanked the car and jumped out. It sped away without a sound.

The hallway ran for thousands of feet until it gradually curved out of sight. There were yellow circles every 300 feet or so. The hallway was a bustle of activity. John wondered how many instruction areas there were in this complex. And how many people.

John's training room was full but he was able to find the same console against the wall. A large bear-like humanoid saw him and strolled over. John recognized him from the earlier session with Davey. Thick brown hair covered his body and his head resembled nothing more than a cute teddy bear. This being stuck out a paw-like hand. "Welcome John Frankel."

"Er, thank you." John was hesitant to grab the paw and get impaled by its stubby claws.

"I'm Robinson Pihoqahiak," he said in a deep bass voice. "Most people call me Robo."

"Pleased to meet you," John said, and he was. Despite his bulk the big creature exuded cuteness. The hand contained six digits, just like Kjirsten's. The palm and fingers were padded.

Robinson was looking him over. "Never met an earthian before. Very delicate. You seem to be built around the number 5. Very unusual."

John looked around the room. Everyone he saw either had thick skin or a hard exoskeleton like Goliath. Maybe earth-style humans were a distinct minority in the galaxy.

John imitated Peter Marlowe. "Can't help it. Born that way."

Robinson's eyes went large and he suddenly bent over with laughter.

"Ho, John Frankel, I think I will like you just fine. I wasn't sure after your last visit. You messed up my simulation at a crucial moment."

"Sorry."

"If you need anything come ask me."

John was pleased to have made a new friend. "I will. You'll be easy to find."

Robinson's eyes again opened wide in surprise. Then his face crinkled in a laugh. "Ho!" he said, and walked back to his station. John saw him conversing animatedly with the others.

"I'm liking this place more and more," he said to himself. But now it was time for work.

John put on the headset and pressed the first indentation in the panel which loaded the simulation program for the beginner level. Again the swirling chaos frightened him. Soon his seed thought brought something grotesque into the tank.

Using the big tank felt as real as real life. Exactly as during his experiences using the etchings in the book, he was *there*.

"You can do it," John told himself. He cleared his mind and placed his full attention into the tank. As soon as the first pattern appeared he did not go with the thought it reminded him of. Instead he just let it go. His practice with the 21 protocols were helping.

His pattern recognition skills were not a liability now. The idea was just to observe, not follow thought trails. After two hours of work he was able to go five minutes without seeding the tank. "Good job," he told himself.

John took a break and walked out of the room and down the hallway. Students lined the walls, chatting and gesturing. A few recognized John and waved. He waved back. After some minutes John had an astonishing realization. Every one of these humanoids resembled a species on earth.

About 100 feet away, against the opposite doorway, John stared at a bird-like humanoid with vestigial wings and feathery skin. Across the hall a number of feline humanoids chatted. To his right next to the doorway of the room adjoining, a being with thick grey skin, a long trunk, and big floppy ears gestured toward another with thick crinkly skin and a pointed horn jutting from its forehead. A black and white striped humanoid with leathery skin conversed with a much smaller creature resembling a prairie dog. An enormously tall humanoid with spotted skin, a very long neck, and sticky-outy ears read one of the manuals. Next to it stood two of the mantis-like creatures, clicking away incomprehensibly.

John had always wondered how so many diverse species could evolve on one tiny little planet. Could it be that each species on earth was merely representative of the galaxy as a whole? Was earth a seeded planet, or a genetically engineered one? Fascinated, he just stood there and observed it all.

It was over an hour before John could make himself stroll back to the simulator and try again.

This time he was able to go almost ten minutes. After another hour's work he was able to cheerfully observe the maelstrom in the tank with perfect ease. John raised his hand. One of the three roving instructors assigned to the room approached the console.

"I am ready for a checkout on the first level," John said.

According to the manual, a checkout took only a few seconds. An instructor came around with an imager which showed an analysis of the simulation program. Even the slightest alteration to the substance within the tank caused the student to fail. For an experienced trainer, a glance at the imager was enough to tell whether a student had mastered the level. It was required that a student be able to coexist with the simulation for one continuous hour without seeding it. That data was available through the program and displayed on the instructor's imager.

John passed his first checkout easily. "Very good John Frankel," the instructor said. This humanoid had a head like a crocodile, with rows of flattened teeth. "You are now eligible for the second simulation button."

John was feeling cocky and exhilarated. "If they're all like this it'll be a piece of cake."

One of the students overheard him and began to laugh. "I think you'll find the other levels a little more challenging," she said.

"Yeah," someone else said. "Almost everybody who's any good gets the first one."

"All right," John said to himself. "Let's try the second level."

Now the energy in the tank was even more un-organized, more random and bizarre. The pressure on his sphere of consciousness, as it was projected into the tank, was far more intense. It felt, as Davey said, like an "all knowing enemy."

"Wow, what *is* this stuff?" he said aloud.

John backed out for a second. He cleared his mind and tried again. The chaos seemed conscious but insane. It felt like having an annoying relative constantly in your face. It was fascinating and horrifying at the same time. He was beginning to see that the Unformed Potential energy became overwhelmingly powerful only if you responded to it.

Again John projected his consciousness into the tank. Now the twisting, random energy did not seem quite so frightening. It was now possible to simply observe without judgment. He stared into the tank for minute after minute, unaware of time passing. Ghostly patterns appeared, wraith-like, then disappeared without disturbing his equilibrium. No frightening images were visible. The chaos now seemed less random, more aesthetic, a dynamically changing painting. John looked calmly now into the display and smiled. He did it! The terrifying unpredictability had changed its nature because he had changed his orientation toward it.

Davey was correct. There was a powerful feeling that came from mastering the Unformed Potential energy. It was a trial by fire that required a souping-up of your very being. John felt surer of himself and cleaner. Exposure to the Unformed Potential simulation had removed carbon deposits from the engine of his consciousness. It was a total rush.

When he raised his hand for the second level checkout most of the students just laughed. After he passed they were astonished that a first-timer could advance so quickly.

Now a bigger test.

The difficulty of the third level rose exponentially. His jaw began to hurt and he remembered the smack Kjirsten had given him...he was losing it...shit! John backed out, annoyed with himself. Again he had forgotten to apply what he had just learned. He had gotten too cocky and forgot to use the protocols.

After a few moments he steadied himself and tried again. This level required a much firmer perimeter! He could see how the levels gradually got you more and more in control of your Sphere. In time he was able to transcend the roiling chaos for an hour after immersing himself within the simulation. It was almost, dare he say it, beautiful?

John raised his hand again but this time the instructors were angry. "Just who do you think you are?" demanded a ten foot tall giraffe-like humanoid with a very long neck. John did not respond in anger or irritation. He felt fantastic. The instructor noted this and his demeanor changed to one of amazement. Glancing into his imager, he passed John without hesitation.

Every one of the students had stopped their work now and was staring at the new whiz kid.

In rapid succession John passed the fourth and fifth levels.

"That rookie can't possibly manage the sixth level," someone said. "Yes he can!" said another. The betting was on; even the instructors participated. By now the chief of training was on the scene. Word had spread throughout the humanoid sectors of the astonishing new student who was about to pass the first flight all in one session. For this approval would be needed from the highest level.

"It's never happened before!" Robinson Pihoqahiak shouted.

"Wanna bet?" said another. "I have it right here. In the past 100,000 standard years there have been thirteen candidates who passed the first 6 levels all at once."

There was an excited babble in the room. John felt fired-up, like a professional athlete during a playoff game in his home gym.

Now John pushed his finger into the rightmost indentation on the panel and the simulation program went full blast.

His guts turned to water and he almost backed out. The feel of the simulation was as of a nest of angry hornets. His consciousness was literally sucked into the tank. A trillion needles of unreality were inserted into his soul from every conceivable direction...but then something magical happened. He suddenly understood clearly that his emotional turmoil stemmed from his own resistance to this unfamiliar chaos. There was nothing inherently *bad* about the Unformed Potential. In fact, it wasn't even real! An inner voice whispered: "Let go. Let it pass through you. The Unformed Potential is a fantastic gateway to a much larger experience."

John let go, surrendering totally. His intellect screamed that it was an audacious, irrational, and dangerous thing to do. He did it anyway. As he did so a feeling of power and love flooded his consciousness. Within the artificial environment of the simulator he effortlessly maintained the integrity of his sphere. Over an hour later he reemerged, not even having felt the passage of time. He had already been passed.

At that moment Davey ran into the room. "We all heard about it kid, but I hadta see for myself." He looked John over carefully and was satisfied.

"I'll walk you back to the holospace, if you're ready."

John nodded. Everyone in the room respectfully made way. John had been transformed from a nobody who had almost refused candidate status to a minor deity. Robinson Pihoqahiak rumbled over and thanked him. "I wagered on you and have prospered considerably! Would you like to share in my winnings?"

When John discovered that Robinson's "winnings" consisted of a five-year pass to a pleasure planet of small prey animals and "beautiful" females of his species, he declined.

"We don't eat them, if that's what you're thinking. The partnering is really good," the big bear remarked amiably.

John demurred politely. "You're very kind but I don't think I'd do very well there."

Robinson looked him over carefully. "I suppose you're right." Then he brightened. "More for me!"

John and Davey stopped in front of a rounded door about twelve feet tall and six feet wide. "Are you sure you're ready son?" Davey said. There was no reason to rush. He didn't want the kid to screw up now.

John suddenly felt a little pang of fear. "I think so."

"Not good enough!" Davey barked. "You hafta be totally certain and totally committed!"

"All right!" John said. "I'm ready."

"When you walk in there you'll see a circular platform about ten feet in diameter with a railing all around. You're gonna need that railing. You'll find a red circle in the middle of the platform. As soon as you put both feet on it the simulation program will start. Don't get on until you're sure you're ready. Otherwise...it won't be good. If you get overwhelmed the simulation will sense your energy field and abort before it's too late. You can also abort by stepping out of the circle. Do you understand?"

"Yes." John noticed a human of his own genotype standing next to the observers, studying him with one of the imagers. "Who's that guy?"

"Uh, he's what an earthian might call a doctor. Just for precautions kid. Don't worry."

John's eyebrows shot up.

Davey spoke apologetically. "We've never had an earthian, other than your girlfriend, in the holospace before." The blue man didn't say it, but his attitude implied that earthian biology was a little fragile and unstable. "Earthians are a little delicate," Davey confirmed.

John shrugged it off. Davey was relieved. *The kid looks good but he has no idea what he's getting into.* He grinned to break the tension.

"We'll be monitoring your progress from the observer stations in back. Good luck son." Davey gave John a friendly smash on the back. After straightening his bruised vertebrae John stepped toward the door and it slid into the wall. A suspended walkway of the same material as the floor led into a spherical room. The room looked like an observatory without the telescope. It was about 200 feet in diameter with black walls and lighting that seemed to come from nowhere. John stepped onto the raised platform and checked his merkaba, making sure he had complete definition everywhere along it. He felt powerful, confident, and ready for anything.

As soon as John's feet hit the circle the lights in the room suddenly went out, plunging the room into complete darkness.

Then the simulation began. John was suspended in space, floating in a bizarre unreality that sucked the life from every particle of his being. He felt his soul flowing outward into a life-leeching, utterly unorganized randomness, like a highly compressed gas released into a vacuum. Hull breach! John was coming apart and instinctively stepped out of the circle. The simulation had already aborted. The lights were back on and he grabbed onto the railing. Thank God for the floor! His legs were like jelly. He felt...mutilated. Raped. Turned inside out.

Sorry, this is insane.

John stumbled against the railing and took a few deep breaths. He felt nauseous and was afraid he was going to throw up. If that was a simulation, the real thing must be unimaginable.

There was no reason to endure this. No reason at all. John began to walk unsteadily toward the door. He stopped halfway across.

What would Kjirsten and Davey say? And most important, what would Genevieve think of him? He could hear that crazy griffon now. "Told you so. The kid's a lightweight."

Fuck that. There was no need to justify any of his actions. He was almost at the door when something gnawed at the edges of his awareness. There! When that...stuff...hit him, for a nanosecond just before he panicked he had *come together*. The feeling was indescribably awesome. Under some survival instinct he had briefly realized his full potential. John basked in that feeling. For several minutes he stood there, trying to milk every last drop of it.

Outside the room, Davey stood next to the two senior instructors observing John's progress. One of the senior instructors, a very short humanoid with a face like a chipmunk, turned to his badger-faced colleague. "Thought we had a winner. Looks like another flame-out." The other nodded. "Make up your mind, rookie! Don't waste our time."

But Davey saw something. A smile slowly spread over his broad face and he clapped his thickly muscled hands. "He's got it now, boys. Watch."

The doctor looked into his imager. "Looks like the earthian held up OK."

The two official observers turned skeptically back to their imagers, which showed John's sphere of consciousness. One of them drummed his fingers on the desk impatiently as John stood unmoving on the walkway. Slowly, the four observers saw the earthian turn back and step onto the platform.

John felt the madness hit him from every conceivable direction, but this time he didn't panic. He knew there was no opponent. Just himself and his own beautiful life force. His sphere of consciousness completely energized and firmed up. John realized that the madness of the Unformed Potential energy was the primeval, formative, creative energy of the universe. He was in the womb of creation, the beginning point for every universe, every reality, every particle, every planet, every star, every galaxy, every everything in existence. Actually this stuff was *before* the beginning. It just didn't yet have a purpose. Like a mad wanderer lost in the darkness it was desperately looking for direction and guidance.

It simply did not have the seed thought around which to come together.

John was there within the roiling madness, feeling the power of his merkaba as it pulsed with light.

Finally he stepped out of the circle and the lights came on. The full meaning of "There is no opponent" was obvious now. Earth society had trained him with the concept that every action has an opposite and equal reaction. That may be true for matter and energy but not for consciousness. He, John Frankel, did not have to react to anything like an automaton. As a sovereign consciousness he could simply experience it for what it is.

John stood upon the platform for several minutes. He had never felt so good in all his life. Davey was right! The reward for this insane training was a magnificent discovery of self.

John laughed. He roared. "Hey Davey! I made it! I got it!" John felt like his old friend Ja'Quan pancaking a puny defensive lineman.

John stepped off the platform and ran across the walkway. He almost smashed against the door as it barely opened in time.

Davey wanted to give him a bear hug but John stepped away and slapped the blue man on the back as hard as he could. Davey hardly noticed. "I told ya," he said to the two instructors at the checkout station. Both were smiling. The one with the chipmunk face said, "Rookie, you pass. You are now eligible for flight three training and full immersion."

Everyone in the room cheered. Robinson came over and congratulated him. "Could you tell me how you did it?" A group gathered around John and they led him away, firing questions and chattering excitedly.

Davey shook hands with his compatriots. He called a transport cab and reported directly to Kjirsten. He was going to be the bearer of very good news.

23

Half an hour later John was still flushed with excitement. He was seated at a console in the middle of the room, surrounded by the strangest looking group of people he had ever seen. The students hung on his every word as he explained what had happened to him. Someone tapped him on the shoulder. "You're needed in your assigned sector right away. A car is outside." The students groaned; John said his goodbyes. On the way back he realized that for once he was actually popular. No "weird John" here – these guys are just as nutty as me!

This time the car said nothing. He got out in the hallway and walked toward his section. As he turned the corner the cell contained a desert simulation. His feet were walking on a hard sandy surface that did not raise any dust.

Normally the floor, walls and ceiling in this cell were programmed to reflect the mood of the persons working in the area. The first time John arrived that idiot griffon had selected an ocean planet. Most of the time the space reflected scenes from one of the group's home planets. Today, a desert scene from Davey's home world of Orodani filled the space. John walked upon dark red sand. To his left rose high cliffs, black in the distance. To his right a small mountain devoid of vegetation, painted in various shades of brown, red, and gold. Overhead a small bright blue-white sun shined in a cloudless dark purple sky. Kjirsten's group of six (now including John) had been assigned this section of the facility and were marked on all station maps. The group's function was Unformed Potential monitoring so the area was bare except for six monitoring consoles arranged in a hexagon.

John stopped when he reached the main console and looked around. The area was empty, save for an animal walking along the desert far in the background. The room simulations were awesome. Consoles and desert blended perfectly within the same space.

Needed, eh? For what? John sat down at one of the chairs and put on the headset. "Disable current imagery program," he thought into it. The floor, walls, and ceiling reappeared. John took off the headset. "Might as well go back to the training area." He heard a sound behind him.

"Pbstkzxyystck."

John whirled around in his chair. "Goliath!" The huge mantis bowed, his spindly appendages flying out in all directions. Goliath looked like a bunch of pick-up-sticks randomly tied together. From his head another of his hats fell to the floor.

John reached down to pick it up. It was a standard issue gray bowler hat like they used to wear in those old black and white movies. It had a brim about three inches wide. The hatband was bright red.

John felt a bubble of thought burst inside him. "Are you ready for some beginning Unformed Potential exploration?" The thought was accompanied by an image of Goliath within the Unformed Potential. The thought was accompanied by Goliath's sensations and feelings, and sidebands of knowledge about him and his culture and his planet. John jumped back, startled.

"How did you do that?"

"Try it on me," Goliath said.

John thought carefully about what he wanted to communicate. He sent, "Hi Goliath! You seem like a very cheerful fellow."

Goliath jumped up and down in excitement. He clicked his mandibles and rubbed the spikes on his forearms together, an erector set gone out of control. This time the hat stayed on his bony carapace.

John laughed.

"Very good John! Yes, all of my species are happy. We live together in hives and are very social. While other species busy themselves with intrigue, trade, commerce, and exploration, our highest passion is fashion." He pointed proudly to his head. "See my new hat? Do you like it?"

"It's...interesting." John sent back, smiling.

"Oh, yes. Here. I will show you the latest fashions from my planet. These holos were taken from the ball at [unpronounceable]."

Goliath sent John a collection of images of astonishing detail and intricacy. They made high definition television seem like a fuzzy black and white movie. Tall, spindly creatures with brightly painted carapaces moved about leisurely, showing off their costumes. The males wore waistcoats, cloaks, doublets, hose, and stockings. Some were wearing platform shoes with brightly colored heels. One very tall "gentleman" sported a long violet cloak, rose-lined and open, revealing a full-skirted coat of purple satin laced with pink. Underneath was a waistcoat of flowered silk. An enormous indigo cravat was tied in a complex knot around his skinny neck. His platform shoes had very high, painted heels which raised him several inches

above his counterparts. A black top hat fully four feet in height balanced precariously upon his triangular head.

John almost laughed but he didn't want to offend Goliath, who was eagerly
and excitedly pointing to this illustrious personage, or that gown, or that wig.

Jewelry by the ton hung on the females (indistinguishable from the males
anatomically, at least to John's human eyes). A few of the females wore long gowns
of brightly colored fabric. Other females painted their carapaces with a shiny metallic substance like Davey's skin, which reflected the light. All of them had elaborately
coifed wigs with hair of varying colors.

"Only the important females are allowed to wear gowns," Goliath sent cheerfully. "Here is Queen [unpronounceable], with the very latest mode direct from the
capital."

"Superb!" John sent back, a little doubtfully.

The scene resembled a cross between a costume party and the court of Louis
XIV, on stilts.

Goliath seemed to have completely forgotten about John's training. After several minutes of detailed imagery pouring into his consciousness, and discussion of
it, John was getting a little impatient. "That's great Goliath!" he sent. "Shall we continue now with the lesson?"

Goliath stopped his chatter. "But we have my dear fellow. You have now
learned to communicate properly via thought transmission, both sending and receiving. It is one of the things I must check in every new trainee. Being able to
communicate out there with your fellow technicians is crucially important. We are
now ready, I think, for an introduction to the Unformed Potential."

John was impressed. It was instruction without teaching.

"Elegantly done, Goliath!" he sent.

John knew that it was time to actually do it. How much different was the real
thing from the simulator?

"How do you get into the Unformed Potential?" John asked. "You have to be
able to match yourself to the vibration of the place you're going to. That place," he
pointed outside the walls, "has no defined vibration."

"You have anticipated my lesson," Goliath sent. "In order to enter you have
to...find a stable orientation, or a frame of reference, from which to perceive. The
only benefit your training has given you is the absolute control over your sphere of
consciousness. As you will discover, the "real" Unformed Potential is much different from the simulations."

"How do we proceed?" John asked.

"Before we attempt actual immersion I'm going to show you what's really outside this installation." Goliath called a transport and they rode along a straight, high
speed corridor at amazing speeds for about forty minutes, to the skin of the facility. When they arrived John saw a walled off corridor about 100 feet wide running
along the hull. John could barely see it curving away, slightly, in both directions.

Goliath went to a workstation and put on one of the adjustable headsets. "Stand in front of the wall, over there, about six feet away."

Goliath said, "All right John. Prepare yourself. When you're ready raise your hand."

After about ten minutes John raised his right hand. The skin blurred, becoming transparent. He stared directly into the Unformed Potential!

John was prepared for an all-out assault on his senses. What he confronted was something entirely different.

The familiar stability of three dimensional reality vanished utterly.

Here, the fabric of space was alive. It bent and expanded itself in 90 degree rotations, each one creating extra spatial dimensions that twisted and contorted his consciousness. At once he felt himself drawn into dozens, hundreds, thousands of potentially forming but geometrically bizarre spaces. Each one of them demanded his full attention.

He was lost, fading fast into a sea of infinite and fascinating potentiality...

Only his training in the simulator saved him from going over the edge. A powerful fragment of himself still held him together. But he could do no more than maintain a precarious stability, like a neophyte ice-skater.

With the little remaining awareness he had left, John Frankel saw the window panel opaque. John felt immediate relief; felt Goliath turning his body and guiding him back to a console. John sat down on a floating bench. It was similar to the one where Kjirsten and Genevieve had gotten his agreement to proceed with this schizophrenic series of experiences that left him at times groping for his sanity, and at others, discovering more and greater facets of himself.

"Are you all right John?" Goliath asked, seating himself awkwardly beside his student. The mantis' ungainly collapse into the bench amused John. He felt a little more of himself return to the present.

Goliath sent warm fuzzies into his consciousness. John felt the loving presence of his instructor as a freezing man might experience warm sunshine.

The big mantis had a special fondness for this strange earthian human. Goliath saw within John a similar easy-going personality. This personality type was very unusual among Unformed Potential field workers. Goliath was certain they made the best observers.

"Yeah I'm all right," John said. He was trying to shut down his intellect, which was madly attempting to make sense of something incomprehensible. Pieces of himself were returning from the contorted madness.

The author is not enough of a topologist to describe accurately what John Frankel experienced. The reader might get an idea by imagining the floor, ceiling, and walls of the room in which you are sitting suddenly dissolved. Imagine the familiar notions of up, down, front and back, left and right as no longer applicable. Imagine strange hyper-rotations and extensions from these directions opening to your consciousness, sucking you in without your control, on and on without limit.[1] We may give a pitiful analogy and ask the reader to envision yourself standing in a room in which every surface is covered by mirrors of all shapes and sizes, the image of yourself echoing and reechoing back and front, top and bottom and on all sides, the images combining with themselves and morphing unrecognizably.

John felt stability return. As it did, an almost irrational surge of excitement surged through his body.

"Goliath! It's...it's horrifying. And wonderful!"

"Well done John. You have come through, as you say on earth, flying your colors."

John laughed. "With flying colors, my friend."

"Very good! I am not down, or is it up? with earthianisms like the rest of our group."

John felt expansive now. "Tell me, good Goliath, why is the simulator training so different from the real thing?"

"Because we cannot hope to duplicate it," his instructor said. "We can't even describe it. You can't build something without knowing what it is. In the training we can only emphasize the vital necessity of maintaining the integrity of your sphere of consciousness at all costs. You now understand why."

"How can you hold a stable orientation in something that destroys your reality?"

"At first, the trick is perceiving with what earthians call peripheral vision, until you get oriented to it. You can't look into it, or even at it. You have to stay detached and perceive around it. It's not something you can teach or even explain very well. Once you get the hang of it, however, the Unformed Potential will begin to show itself to you. Your inner vision will open up. You will begin to see a sort of potential energy that is similar to what you are shown in the simulations. If you're good you may see patterns, or tendencies. This may help us determine how the increasing potential energy of the Unformed Potential will affect the physical reality to which it is intimately connected."

Here is where another 90% failed. If only there was some way to precisely describe and teach the process of immersion. But Goliath knew that once 'out there' you were on your own. He gazed at John with all the sympathy that an eight foot tall praying mantis could muster up.

"Any more hints?" John asked hopefully.

"No, but I thought of an earthian joke. A scientist is explaining his derivation of an important new result at a chalkboard filled with equations. The first set of

---

[1] If you draw a line on piece of paper you have a one-dimensional object. If you rotate 90 degrees, you can draw another line perpendicular to it and create a 2 dimensional square. If you now go up and down from the plane of the paper you have rotated another 90 degrees and can create a 3 dimensional cube. The square is in 2 dimensions, and when you lift the square upward you get a 3 dimensional cube. What happens if you rotate 90 degrees from the cube? You get a 4 dimensional hypercube. Try to imagine what that would look like, and then imagine another 90 degree rotation, and another, and another, and another...

equations and the end result are rigorously defined. In the middle he has written, 'Then a miracle occurs.' His friend says, 'I think you need to be a little more explicit here in step two.' That's what it's like trying to explain how to perceive the Unformed Potential. Those of us who have been successful know the beginning and ending point. But how do you get there? That is always up to the individual trainee."

John laughed nervously.

"My words cannot teach," Goliath sent. "I can only guide. You can, and should, refuse to continue any time you do not feel comfortable, John. Any uncomfortableness will be immediately projected into the potential around you, escalating your difficulties and placing you in an untenable position from which you may not recover."

John could see that Goliath was very distressed.

"I should not tell you this but I'm going to anyway. Twenty years ago, upon first passing the training, a first-timer under my supervision collapsed within the Unformed Potential and was absorbed within seconds. I do not wish that to happen to you. Besides being the most promising candidate in a very long time, I am growing fond of you."

Goliath paused for a moment, wrestling with himself.

"I am deeply sorry John. I have unburdened myself to a first-timer and that is a grievous error. But I feel it's appropriate."

The mantis looked at John curiously. This rookie had made an amazingly fast recovery from his first exposure and appeared to be as good as new.

"I want to give it another try," John said. He was feeling more and more confident. He had taken the Unformed Potential's best shot and he was still standing.

Golaith once more blurred the wall panel and John realized again the difference between theory and practice. With a superhuman effort John shut down his analytical function and turned off his curiosity circuit. Like the Enterprise playing dead, he shut down his mind completely. He was just BEING.

Within his merkaba certain templates were activated. Like a rheostat which slowly energized a light source, an inner vision awakened. Sensors he did not know he possessed encompassed and transcended the bizarre topologies of the Unformed Potential and translated it. As a light switch illuminates a dark room, John saw.

He gasped.

The Unformed Potential became a three dimensional physical space that made sense to his physical consciousness. He now had a frame of reference in which to operate.

John now saw precisely what was in the training simulators: a roiling, fuzzy, forming and unforming chaos of random potential.

He could handle that now. He was encased in a powerful vehicle of light, operated by thought, with the capability of performing any action that thought could conceive.

John Frankel began to truly understand the power, wisdom, and potential of consciousness. It was unlimited. A feeling of joy flooded through him. Even here, in this...whatever...the universal medium somehow existed. John felt a child's playfulness. He toyed with the Unformed Potential and the virtual energy within it.

John returned his awareness to his body and felt himself standing next to his instructor.

"What happened?" Goliath said.

"I have been able to stabilize the Unformed Potential so that it makes sense. I see almost exactly what was in the simulators."

"Excellent John. Is there any discomfort?"

"None at all. I feel a sense of freedom in there."

Goliath metaphorically raised his eyebrows. "Indeed! There is no feeling of pressure on the sphere perimeter?"

"Only a little. I feel like a self contained little universe, able to function at will."

Goliath stood motionless. "This is most unusual," he muttered. "Most unusual indeed!" The mantis was concerned that the earthian may be a bit delusional so he probed John thoroughly. After a few moments he was satisfied that all was well. He sent happy thoughts. "Well then John, you are doing amazingly well. Now that you have established a stable frame of reference you have a platform into which you may project your consciousness. You may enter the Unformed Potential using the standard protocols."

John saw Goliath as a beautiful being of Light. His ugly mantis body was a gorgeous set of intense vibrations in elegant and complex geometric patterns in the center of his lightbody. John understood the body's relationship to the merkaba. The body was not "solid" and the rest of the merkaba "etheric." Even though the density of energy is greatest at the center, the body and the merkaba were both made from the same stuff. The technique simply provided a vibrational re-interpretation, a re-tuning of perception. It was misleading to judge a person from their superficial body characteristics.

"Let us project together into the Unformed Potential," Goliath sent.

The room around them shimmered out. Goliath and John linked consciousness as one would tie two balls together with a piece of string.

John found himself in a constantly changing riot of shifting patterns. He felt a soft pressure on the perimeter of his sphere, exactly like being underwater.

John looked back. The Eyrie was gone!

"What's happening?" he sent to Goliath. "Where is the Eyrie? We can't be more than 10 feet from it."

"Don't worry John. We are no longer in time or space. The Eyrie, therefore, has no precise location. Neither do we. Here is where the laws of physics totally break down. We exist only as conscious entities. We are not in anything that has specific definition so there are no coordinates to describe our position."

"How do we get back?"

"The Eyrie is a bubble of stability within the chaos. One reaches it using the standard protocols."

John focused his attention on the Eyrie and began to resonate to the feel of it. His feet now felt the floor and he was back. Wow!

"Did we really go anywhere?" he said to Goliath, who was right beside him. "It feels like I never left."

Goliath chuckled. To John it looked like he was going to carve something up and eat it. "The spatial and temporal phenomena we are used to perceiving are suspended out there. I have been working with the Unformed Potential almost every day for many years. I still do not understand how or why all of us perceive it essentially the same way."

"We somehow collapse the multidimensional topologies of the potential into something that makes sense to us. If that's the case then we are only perceiving a minute fraction of the true Unformed Potential."

"Mult-dimensional topologies?" Goliath sounded confused.

"Well yeah, you know that!" John replied. "The Unformed Potential is a window into an infinity of possible ways of perceiving. You have to narrow your focus or you get sucked into a million bizarre realities. Every one of these realities, as I perceive it, has extra spatial dimensions and has the potential to become a series of interrelated universes. Just as the guide symbol shows us." John thought of the brilliant mathematician Georg Cantor. It was Cantor who first devised a method of cataloging infinities. Cantor postulated a 'countably infinite' set of numbers which could be related to other sets like it. Then he showed that the process could continue on forever. Perhaps this idea was used in the creation of a countably infinite set of experienceable universes that all stood in a defined relationship with one another. Maybe infinities could actually be organized.

John felt Golaith's amazement. "You *saw* that, my young friend?"

"Well, yeah. That's why I almost went nuts the first time."

"It's certainly a plausible explanation for the structure of the All," Goliath muttered. "The All is multi-dimensional. It makes sense that these extra dimensions would have latency in the Unformed Potential."

Goliath still had plenty of mentoring to do, but he felt their relationship subtly change. His new student might have the ability to fundamentally change the parameters of their work.

"I want to go out again," John said. He now knew what Davey felt when looking lovingly into the simulation during his first training session.

The mantis looked into the eyes of his student and saw the inner strength and self-confidence that characterized all Unformed Potential technicians. The earthian had made it! Goliath was thrilled. Like Kjirsten, he wanted to test the new whiz-kid's mettle.

They entered the bizarre world of the Unformed Potential and the Eyrie vanished once again, as if it had never been. They were both completely outside space and time. Now John discovered the overwhelming importance of the connection to his partner. The experience was totally different this time. John immediately felt the pressure on every square millimeter of his sphere as the Unformed Potential hungrily looked for something around which to organize itself. With Goliath's help John steadied himself. He felt like a serenely self-contained little universe.

Now detached and completely in control of himself, John began to notice subtle patterns in the Unformed Potential's wraith-like appearance. "Is the search for patterns in this godforsaken place the primary work of Unformed Potential technicians?" he asked Goliath.

"Yes John," the mantis replied with great love.

Goliath felt as calm and unruffled as a walk in the park.

"Our primary goal has been to penetrate the Unformed Potential and discover the source of its influx into the structure of the All. We have been unable to do so. Failing that, our duty is to gather data and report to the Unformed Potential Research Division."

"There is something missing from your explanation," John said.

"We have failed to pinpoint the source of entropy that is coming from the Unformed Potential and leaking into the ordered structure of the universes. If we can penetrate the mystery of the Unformed Potential we can determine how to stop the leakage. If it continues, physical laws will begin to break down and all life everywhere will eventually die."

"That makes no sense," John sent. "All life everywhere to die? Why create it in the first place?"

If Goliath could shrug out here he would have. "A Great Cycle occurs every 16 billion standard years. That's a long, long, long time John. In our galaxy, Galaxy 6, things have been stagnant for over a billion years."

John still wasn't convinced.

"Only fragmented records exist after the last Great Cycle. It is said that when a Great Cycle ends it results in the complete destruction of the All in order to facilitate rebirth into the new. Perhaps this is necessary. Perhaps life needs a fresh start everywhere in the All. Perhaps this results in a new, improved version of the All."

John thought of a caterpillar that turns into a butterfly. "I don't care. Nobody is going to destroy me and the ones I love!"

Goliath smiled. "I feel the same."

"All right then friend Golaith. Let's take some names and kick some asses. Nobody fucks with Galaxy 6!"

Goliath laughed so hard his transmission became clouded.

John got back to business. "Why do we search for patterns in the Unformed Potential?"

"If any one pattern ever becomes too powerful, the Unformed Potential will become seeded. If that happens it could damage the delicate order and balance of universal laws that are absolutely vital for the maintenance of life."

"Kjirsten mentioned something about a barrier. What is that?"

"The barrier is another metaphor. We use it to describe the 'place' we think is the source of the leakage of the Unformed Potential into real space."

"What if there is no source? From everything I've seen so far the Unformed Potential is a scalar. Perhaps it occupies every position in every universe at the same time."

Goliath smiled. "We have recently found something that looks like a source. We call it the barrier. That's where the others are now."

"Let's go out there!"

Goliath was impressed with his student's enthusiasm. To take a rookie there on his first immersion would be dangerous and foolish. Unless he guided him firmly.

"Don't hold back on me now Goliath. I can read all of your thoughts. It will be OK."

"All right John. Against my better judgment I'm going to accede to your request. We'll stay back and just observe for a while."

The only way to detect the barrier was to notice an increasing psychic pressure upon the sphere perimeter and follow it. Therefore, he would proceed very slowly. At the first sign that the rookie couldn't handle it, they would turn back.

To John, their progress felt like being immersed in a high-G pressure chamber with the pressure being gradually turned up. The two were being drawn in toward something massive...

"Here is where we have to halt," Goliath said. "Beyond this point one may get sucked in."

John expanded his perception. 'Behind' the barrier a gigantic, slowly rotating cloud of potential appeared before him. It disappeared into a vortex. Goliath was explaining how perilous it was to even come near it. Something about a "Roche limit" beyond which one would become irretrievably lost. He saw Ivan, Bellerophon, Kjirsten, and Davey studying it. Genevieve was absent.

The vortex called to him. It did not seem dangerous. His original exposure to the Unformed Potential now enabled him to perceive a way into the vortex. He knew how to "rotate" his awareness an extra 90 degrees and thus completely out of the 3 dimensional framework of his current perception. Within his frame of reference John activated a template in his merkaba that wasn't even in the manual. This template allowed him to safely go into a higher dimension and go "around" the barrier.

John now clearly saw a slow increase of potential as the spiraling potential disappeared from his perception. It went down into a beautiful, kaleidoscopic pattern that became finer and finer, coming forth from...what? John's curiosity impelled him to follow the trial of potential. At the edges of his consciousness voices were shouting, but John was like an eager hound who had found a scent...

"Observe, there is one who approaches."

"This is one from the outermost reality."

"How is this possible? Such a one cannot unfocus without losing its identity."

"The time is near, then."

"The time of completion!"

"Will it be able to reach our level?"

"I think not. It is not possible for the consciousness of such beings to perceive us."

"Correct. Only those in the innermost levels know of our existence."

"I'll wager it does not find us."

There was a clamoring of voices.

"You're on!" "Agreed! It is impossible!" "No it's not!" ...

Goliath and John were approaching the Unformed Potential when the others spotted them.

Kjirsten was about to censure Goliath when they all saw John *leave*. He vanished, seeming to dissolve into the event horizon of the barrier.

"John!" they called frantically. He was gone.

"We're done here. Let's get back to HQ," Kjirsten commanded.

When they were back in the Eyrie Kjirsten whirled on the giant mantis.

"Just what do you think you're doing, taking a rook out there? You've lost the best candidate in the last several thousand years!"

Goliath was calm. "I do not think John is in danger. I perceive..."

"Not in danger!" Bellerophon exploded. "We all saw him dissolve. Just like Icaron."

Goliath spoke forcefully. "No. Not like Icaron. You forget I was present at Icaron's dissolution. The integrity of his sphere was breached and he was torn to shreds. John did not lose integrity, I'm sure of that. I believe that what he did was done consciously and deliberately."

"It was stupid!" Kjirsten was very upset.

"You're just soft on him boss," Davey said. "You got way too personal. He's just a candidate who failed. We've all seen hundreds of 'em." Davey knew he was just woofin'. He had come to like the kid too.

"That's not fair, Davey! It's one thing to fail and go home. It's another to be annihilated forever." How was she going to tell Genevieve?

Ivan appeared between them. The big griffon's huge talons scraped along the floor as he steadied himself, making a sound like fingernails on a chalk board. Kjirsten covered her ears.

"Goliath's right. The kid is intact. I can almost feel him now."

Everyone was silent. The shapeshifter was a maverick, even among this group. He had the most service of any current Unformed Potential technician. When Ivan talked, people listened.

"How is that possible?" Bellerophon asked. "We all saw him disappear. He's gone."

"He's gone from our perception," Ivan said. "The kid is still in one piece. If he ever makes it back I want him to show me how he did that dimensional rotation." Ivan grunted in admiration. "The little putz has balls, I'll give him that."

Despite Kjirsten's prohibition, Goliath translated into the Unformed Potential and began searching for his student. Kjirsten let him go, hoping against hope that he'd be found.

John entered the vortex and almost immediately felt a lessening of Unformed Potential pressure. At the very bottom of the vortex John noticed a very bright point of light. It was a long, long way down.

Something told him to go back. Like an adventurer always looking over the next hill, John continued. The best way to describe what John observed is an intricate, fractal-like kaleidoscope. As he probed deeper and deeper, the patterns organized finer and more complex.

The resolution of the patterns around him eventually passed beyond his ability to perceive. John felt himself serenely floating in a calm, virtual sea. It would be great just to bask in here forever....there was no time, no space, nothing to worry about, no cares, no responsibilities, just a sense of complete fulfillment. He floated....

For the second time in John's life he became aware of a Presence. It nudged him. "John."

Oh yeah. He was John, floating [in the Unformed Potential] but with a much broader awareness.

He perceived Kjirsten, Goliath, and the rest talking about him in the Eyrie. Or was it just his imagination? Peter Marlowe was at the airport, waddling his bulk into a first class seat...Genevieve was on campus, eating her lunch...he saw Robert reading a book at the Carleton graduate library...anything he placed his attention on he could perceive. Peter Marlowe broke out his notebook and got his email. The time on the taskbar read 8:31...I wonder what would happen if I concentrated on Genevieve...and he was there, looking through the eyes of Genevieve.

She was thinking about John...his heart raced. She wanted him to make love to her tonight, to be very gentle with her, to tell her how much he loved her. Oh God I have to get back!

John reversed his progress within the vortex and returned through the Unformed Potential. He used the trick of dimensional twisting again. This time it was much easier.

John thought of Goliath and was there beside him, still looking for his student in the midst of the Unformed Potential madness.

"John! Are you all right?"

"Of course I'm all right. Is there some reason I shouldn't be?"

"John," Goliath said, "you disappeared past the event horizon. No one who has ever been lost in there has ever come back. You scared me to death. I thought I'd lost you. Come, let's go back. We've had enough adventuring for one day."

Goliath led John back to the stability of the Eyrie.

"John!!!" Kjirsten threw herself at him, giving him a bear hug. Wow is she strong.

Davey snorted. Everyone seemed upset.

Ivan appeared, squawking and flapping his great wings excitedly.

The cigarette fell from Bellerophon's lips. "Just what do you think you're doing out there rookie?" Davey was ready to turn him into a pretzel. Kjirsten's beautiful face was now chiseled in hard planes of controlled fury. Goliath was calm.

"I don't get it. What's all the fuss?"

"You damn idiot, you coulda got yourself killed," Davey said. "I'm trying to measure the increase in potential when I feel this sudden, but really powerful disturbance. I got out of there as fast as I could. I thought it was all going to blow up or something. What a waste."

Bellerophon was irritated. "If you want to get yourself torn to little bitty pieces that's your business John. The rest of us have work to do. I lost a lot of good data by your stupidity. I raced back here in a panic before I was able to complete my observations. I thought you were a goner. I don't know whether to shit or celebrate."

Ivan flapped his wings, knocking off the hat Goliath just put on his head. "Squawk!!!" he said. "I told you he was OK."

There was silence for a few minutes until Ivan spoke. "All right kid, tell us what happened." There was a chorus of affirmative shouts.

Bellerophon said, "You just dissolved. We thought you were gone, like Icaron."

"Icaron?" John asked

"The candidate I told you about who was destroyed," Goliath said.

Kjirsten whirled on him again. "You told a first-timer about Icaron? I'm beginning to seriously wonder about your judgment."

"It was an error."

"An error that probably contributed to this fiasco," she snapped.

John held up his hands. "Look guys, it was fun. I think..."

"FUN??" Bellerophon shouted. "And you thought *I* was crazy?"

"Well, it was!" John said.

Ivan appeared with a dead animal in his claws. "I told you the kid was OK," he squawked.

Ivan was about to begin feeding when Kjirsten put hands on hips. "Get that bloody thing out of here!"

Ivan raised his powerful, pointed beak. "Oh all right." The griffon winked out and reappeared a minute later. Kjirsten contemplated the bloody spot on the floor. "Males are the same no matter what species they are or what universe they come from."

"SQUWAK!" Ivan affirmed. "That's right sweetheart. You know, you're very attractive when you're angry."

"I am not angry!" Kjirsten said, clearly making a great effort to control herself. She looked like a teapot just before it tooted.

Davey put his hands roughly on John and guided him to a chair. "Tell us exactly what happened."

"And it better be good," Bellerophon said, lighting a cigarette.

"Must you smoke?" Kjirsten said rhetorically.

"Always." Bellerophon stared at John. "We're waiting."

John explained what happened to him as best he could. "During my experience I saw you guys here. I saw Genevieve, saw my boss getting on a plane, saw my Dad reading a book in the library. The funny thing is, I *was* Genevieve. I mean, I was in her body, looking out of her eyes, hearing what she was hearing, aware of everything she was thinking. It was awesome! Then the voice came and jolted me back to reality. Then I was beside Goliath again."

"The voice?" Ivan said with great interest. He leaned his big body over and leered into John's face. "Tell me about this voice."

John held his ground even though the big griffon's beak was only a foot away from his face. It smelled of blood and animal flesh. John described the voice. Ivan seemed satisfied. He moved away and smiled smugly. "The kid is good."

The rest of the group seemed to be waiting for more. John said, "That's it."

Davey didn't believe it. "A first-timer who goes past the barrier and comes back? And hears voices? I don't think so. Either John has a vivid imagination or he's just a liar." He eyes met John's, challenging him to refute his statement.

John said nothing. He always found it pointless to respond to such confrontations.

"No, he's not lying," Goliath said. "Some part of me was still with him after he entered. He must have been intact the whole time." He paused. "I believe that John was very close to a complete connection with the Unformed Potential."

This statement produced loud protests from all concerned. "A discrete consciousness cannot meld with a pure potential," Davey boomed, his bass rising above the din. "That's right in the standard protocols."

"I didn't say he did," Goliath said. "I said he was very close."

Just then another voice was heard. "Hi honey!" It was Genevieve, walking toward him with her arms outstretched. He embraced her tenderly and whispered, "I love you." She beamed up at him, then her face became etched with concern. "Are you sure you're all right? I heard what you did just now and I can't believe it."

"Never felt better in all my life," John said. "And it's perfect now that you're here. In fact, I was thinking we should go to bed. I'm tired." John made a great effort to yawn.

"Now I know you're all right," she said with a touch of playful sarcasm.

"What brings you here Genevieve?" Kjirsten asked. "You aren't scheduled for two days."

Genevieve stopped, her mouth half open.

"That's a good question." Her eyes widened and she looked at John. "You were with me just a few minutes ago weren't you? But you couldn't have been."

John grinned. "Yes I was sweetheart. That's why I made my brazen suggestion just now."

Her face turned red and her mouth opened to protest. Then she closed it and giggled. "You're going to have to tell me how you did that. I'd like to get completely inside a man's head and see what makes him tick."

"I just told you," John replied. Genevieve laughed.

Bellerophon exploded. "Would someone please tell me what they're talking about?"

Kjirsten grinned. "You weren't listening Bell. If you'll recall, John told us that he was Genevieve for a couple of seconds."

Bellerophon shook his head. Cigarette ash dropped on the floor. "I don't get it."

"You'll find out soon enough," Kjirsten said authoritatively. "The importance of this event calls for a debrief. We need to determine exactly what John experienced and whether it has any significance for our work." She nodded towards Genevieve. "It's fortunate that you're here. If what John told us is true, we may have to rethink our ideas about the Unformed Potential."

A debriefing is a group merge. They are difficult to maintain for more than a few minutes and are undertaken only when an event must be experienced truly and completely by all group members. Language is far too slow and not informative enough. With all members linked an event can be experienced with full perception, mind-to-mind. The sphere of consciousness operated (among its other capabilities) like a sophisticated hologram, recording every experience with complete accuracy.

The group gathered in a circle. It was agreed that all would meld with John. It is much more difficult to harmoniously insert oneself into a group than it is to allow the immersion. The order of merging was based upon skill level. The more already in the group, the greater the difficulty of entrance. Ivan was the last one in.

"Now John," Kjirsten said, "please take us through your experience again." John felt the awareness of all turn to him. The merge was an indescribable feeling of intimacy, trust, and curiosity.

As John relived the experience the group experienced for themselves the dimensional rotation without understanding it. They also perceived the gigantic vortex and saw that it descended without end. Everyone felt uncomfortable, even Ivan. The group became agitated like a bunch of nervous fish in a fishbowl.

Yet the vortex was not perceived as hostile by their newest member. There was something tantalizing at its end: a point of light so far down it rendered the word 'distance' meaningless.

After John completed his run through the group quickly disbanded. It was difficult for seven powerfully focused and very individualistic personalities to maintain the intimacy necessary for group consciousness for more than a few minutes.

"You sure you ain't hallucinating kid?" Davey asked skeptically.

John pointed to the walls of the Eyrie. "Everything out there could be considered a hallucination. My experience seems realer than anything I've encountered in that half-reality."

Goliath said, "I still don't understand how you went past the barrier. Does it have anything to do with what you told me after your first exposure?"

John nodded.

"Explain," Kjirsten said.

"John told me that that the Unformed Potential is actually multi-dimensional," Goliath said.

"Yes, that's right. The simulations all show the Unformed Potential with three physical dimensions. There are many more than that."

The six debriefers tried again to fathom John's experience. Even though each of them had lived it through John, none of them could get their minds around it. Except Ivan.

Other Unformed Potential technicians from adjacent cells began to join the discussion. Soon a crowd of several dozen surrounded the whiz-kid, wanting to know all about the new discovery.

"Kid, that's a pretty good trick," Ivan said. "I'll have to get a few lessons if you don't mind."

"Any time."

Ivan squawked and flicked a wing feather, brushing John's face. "Don't get too cocky kid."

"I..."

Kjirsten clapped her hands, breaking up their little dialogue.

"What exactly did you perceive, John?" Goliath inquired. "At the barrier I feel a powerful energy flow which seems to come out of nowhere. It exerts an excruciatingly painful pressure upon my sphere."

Everyone nodded at this description. All heads turned to John.

"In 4 spatial dimensions you could go inside a closed box without breaking it or opening it, just like a 3 dimensional being can see both the top and the bottom of a 2 dimensional piece of paper. I can go 'past' the barrier without going through it, and into the vortex. Therefore the vortex must be the 3 dimensional access point into an n-dimensional set of universes."

Everyone was amazed.

"That point of light I showed you is either the beginning or the end of something really awesome, I'd imagine."

"But how do you get in?" Bellerophon said. He did not understand John's "dimensional twisting" at all.

"I just sort of slide past the barrier. In 4 dimensional space, a 3 dimensional barrier isn't an impediment any more than a cover on a pot is a barrier to the contents of the pot." He showed them his mental picture of a Klein Bottle. "Consciousness isn't limited by anything except a person's imagination."

After an hour of trying to explain what he meant, John gave up. "I'm not exactly sure how I do it I guess."

The meeting broke up amidst an excited buzz of conversation. It was agreed that all present would go out once more and that John would demonstrate his new technique without actually entering the vortex. Genevieve and Kjirsten were afraid he might never come back. Ivan squawked his disgust at the two women.

At the barrier John demonstrated the dimensional rotating procedure over and over. After a half hour of subjective time no one, not even Ivan, was able to master it.

"Kid, I've got to hand it to you," Ivan told him when they were back in their assigned honeycomb within the Eyrie. "You can come play with me any time."

John thought it was high praise indeed from the shapeshifter.

Ivan spoke to Kjirsten. "If I keep practicing I think I can get it. This is going to be the most exciting challenge I've ever had."

Kjirsten was frustrated by her inability to master the new technique. She swallowed her pride and urged the griffon to proceed as quickly as possible. Ivan nodded and for once became serious. "I'll get right on it," he said, and flew off.

Kjirsten turned to John. "Did you perceive anything that might help us?"

"The influx of virtual energy is definitely coming from the vortex," John replied. "That might explain why the Unformed Potential is leaking into the material universe. But I sort of got lost in there. I didn't know what I was looking for."

"One of us will brief you. Now, the next time..."

Genevieve stomped her foot. "NO!"

"But..."

"You can't ask him to go back in there," Genevieve said.

"I just asked Ivan to. John's a member of the team now, with all that implies."

"Aren't you forgetting the first directive?" Genevieve was very angry. John had never seen her lose her temper before.

Kjirsten's face fell. "You're right. I'm sorry. I got carried away." She smiled wanly. "I've been under a lot of stress lately."

"The first directive?" John asked.

"To preserve and celebrate life in all of its forms," Kjirsten recited. Genevieve smiled up at her.

John remembered the inscription on the front of his manual. "It's not a problem. I'll happily go in there anytime. Besides, Ivan is a life form too. You can't send him in there and ban me."

"It's too dangerous." Genevieve was adamant.

John took her face in his hands and looked into her eyes. "It's not if you know how."

John saw fear for him in her eyes and he smiled. "Cheer up. This is exciting stuff. I see now why school and work has always been so boring for you." John kissed her forehead and walked over to join Davey, Bellerophon, and Goliath, who had moved off to give them some privacy.

Well, Genevieve thought to herself, *I finally got what I always wanted. But it's not working out like I thought it would.* She knew that John wasn't the problem. She was the problem. She had been able to lead him her whole life. Now John was fulfilling the potential she had always envisioned for him. He had passed her by. It was a new feeling for her. She had always been the strong one, and the smartest, in everything she had ever undertaken. It was all different now.

She gazed at John, conversing easily with Bellerophon. He looked so confident, so large-souled. It thrilled her. But she felt a little jealous. In a very short time he had gone from trainee to minor deity, completely overshadowing her. How had he done it? What sort of mind would you have to have to be able to twist out of three dimensional space? She couldn't even fathom it.

Kjirsten motioned to John. He came over to sit between her and Genevieve on the bench in front of the main console.

"First of all John, I want to congratulate you," Kjirsten said formally. "You have passed your training and will become the first successful candidate to do so in almost five years. Much more important, you have extended our work in a bold new direction."

Kjirsten regarded him passionately, her countenance a mixture of admiration and awe. Under that gaze John felt a shiver of excitement penetrate every cell in his body. "Thank you."

"Please work with Ivan and teach him the new technique, if you can. Then he can teach us. Your most important duty will be to observe the Unformed Potential activity around your planet. The phenomenon is more visible on the earthian planet than anywhere else. Report back here once a week earthian time."

John liked the idea of being independent, both here and at work. He burst out laughing, thinking of Peter Marlowe and his comically expressive face.

Kjirsten questioned him silently.

"Sorry, just thinking about my boss at work."

She shook her head in disbelief. "After my first Unformed Potential experience I was a wreck," she said to Genevieve.

"John is naturally even-tempered and good-natured," Genevieve replied. "One of the qualities that made me fall in love with him."

Kjirsten looked away quickly. John could see a few tears on her cheek.

Kjirsten sniffed, then looked back at John. She had given up all hope of maintaining her training with this man and would be roundly criticized on her next scheduled visit to Skjelgaard. Well, she might as well tell him how she felt. Lyran's were not good at holding in their emotions.

"John," she said, "this is off the subject but there's something I need to tell you. I'm glad Genevieve is here." She paused for a moment. "As a Lyran woman I am accustomed to the loyalty and love of men. I come from an ancient ruling family. In my society, I have my choice of life-mate." She stood up to her full height of almost six and a half feet and began to pace the floor. "After your first visit I realized you were the man I have been looking for my entire life. But you were already the lover of my friend. This has set up a powerful internal conflict within me." She looked directly at John. "I want you, but not at the expense of my friendship with Genevieve. So you see John, there will always be some tension in our relationship: my physical and emotional desire for you." She cleared her throat nervously.

John was amazed. He had never seen Kjirsten gaga over anything.

"Part of my training is mental and emotional control," she explained. "But sometimes, in matters of the heart..." Kjirsten turned away. Genevieve jumped up and put her arms around her. John saw that Genevieve's head didn't even reach the shoulders of the beautiful red giant. One of Kjirsten's long six fingered hands almost spanned the width of Genevieve's waist.

The women separated and Kjirsten got herself under control again.

John said, "In my society a man chooses one woman and is true to her. For me that woman is Genevieve. But I love you too, Kjirsten."

Now all three had tears in their eyes.

The three came together in a big hug. "I think it's going to work out just fine," Genevieve said. Kjirsten felt much better after unburdening herself.

As Genevieve and John prepared to leave, John suddenly had a thought. His curiosity circuit, even when operating in the background, was always enabled. "All right Kjirsten, I have a question for you. Genevieve left earth after I did. So what happens to the clock on my bedroom wall if we go back now?"

Kjirsten smiled to herself. "You tell me."

John fumbled around for an answer. "If I go back now I'd get there before Genevieve left because time never passes on earth during one of my journeys. But that sets up a potential paradox. I could meet Genevieve on earth before she left. I would have already been here and seen her after she left. But she hadn't left yet." John scratched his head. The look on his serious Abe Lincoln face was comical and totally incongruous with the crazy curly hair sticking out from his head.

Kjirsten laughed out loud and her mood lightened. "It doesn't work that way. Causality is always maintained, so you are guaranteed never to create a paradox. For example, say you left at 7:30 earthian time and that Genevieve got here at 8:46 earthian time. When you retranslate at least 1 hour and 16 minutes will have elapsed on your bedroom clock."

John looked doubtful. "What happened to the 1 hour and 16 minutes of earth time I lost?"

"Don't ask me to explain it dear," Kjirsten said. "I can't."

John and Genevieve returned immediately to their bedroom on Magnolia Street. John glanced up at the clock over his desk and noticed that it read 8:46. Right on Kjirsten. Causality was maintained. How did that work? Was there some guy with a whiteboard making sure people shuttled in and out of time without creating paradoxes? Genevieve laughed and told him to just accept it. John knew that his tenacious mind would wrestle with the problem until he got an answer.

24

THE next day John went into the office at 9, as usual. Almost before he sat down the phone rang. "John? Marlowe here."

"I thought you were going to England sir?"

"Dash it, I am in England son. Working with Langham here. Tell you about that when I get back. Just wanted to tell you that we've added to your responsibilities. In addition to your data maintenance we want you to take a look at our programming in these modules..." Marlowe explained. "I'm sending over a file on the server with the details. I want you to get on it today. Don't complain about the extra workload. Half the bloody time you just sit at your desk and fantasize."

John burst out laughing. "How did you know?"

"I was young once you know," Marlowe replied.

"What did the doctor say boss?"

"It's unbelievable. I'm dehydrated. This bloke is recommending that I drink lots of water. I'll spare you the details. He's got me drinking one gallon every day, dash it, for the next three months! If I don't bloody well go mad before then; I'm pissing every 15 minutes. Damn nuisance. Anyway, I'll be coming back on Wednesday. Going to see my brother tomorrow. Work hard."

"All right boss." Thank you Dr. Marlowe. The programming work will be interesting.

John got up and walked over to the window, thinking about the vortex he discovered last night, and the debrief. Everything he had experienced in the training and in the Unformed Potential was incredibly real. It could also be described as a very lucid dream. There was a way to check. He'd tell Michael Walters everything. He'd go through the technique right there in his library! What would Mr. W say when he disappeared right in front of him? He would bring the subject up at their next meeting on Friday. The fourth year of his program was almost upon him and he'd have to start thinking about his Masters thesis. They could talk about that and then he'd broach the subject and do his thing. John felt an electric energy go through his body.

Tomorrow he had table tennis practice. Gene was encouraging him to enter the Midland Open. It might be a lot of fun to blow away guys that should beat him easily. If he did well and went deep into the brackets it might be necessary to maintain stage two for several hours. Could it be done that long in an athletic competition? What would people say if he lost it so suddenly? He might be accused of using performance enhancing drugs.

John's pacing became faster and he was humming like a live wire.

He exploded out of the room and ran down the hallway past the gray-bearded Dr. Greiland. The wind from his passage dislodged one of the papers in his hand to the floor. In the room adjacent, two secretaries glanced at each other knowingly. "Frankel," they said as one, and laughed.

John Frankel took the steps down the stairs two at a time. He banged open the bar on the exterior door and tripped. He fell on the grass in front of the building, staining his knee. Oblivious to the stares of passers-by, he got up and took a stroll around the grounds, trying to calm himself. John walked back upstairs and began his work.

The following Friday after work and class John drove over for his meeting with Michael Walters. The brown carpeting in the living room was gone; the hardwood floor underneath sanded and finished. The room had been painted a warm gold. The sofa and chairs were reupholstered. John really liked what Alicia had done, but he had fond memories of that old carpet...

He entered the library. That at least was unchanged.

"Hi John!" Michael Walters said cheerfully.

Here was a man on the mend. The morose and intellectual persona now had cracks in it, letting out some of the inner light. Mr. W was now a thinner, lighter version of his old self. The running must be doing him some good.

"I'm going to be a father John!" Walters was unable to suppress a grin.

"Congratulations!"

"At my age no less. But it feels right." Walters took off his reading glasses and placed them on the desk. "Alicia is ecstatic. She's busy choosing colors for the baby's room. She says she wants to hear the happy laughter of children in this stuffy old house."

"When is she expecting?"

"In about six months." He looked dreamily into space. "Maybe it's actually going to work this time."

Is this the same sterile man who ignored Genevieve her whole life? "I wanted to discuss my program with you sir, and...something else, if I may, later."

Walters' eyebrows raised slightly. "Certainly John. Anything you'd like."

They went over John's fourth year studies. John pressed to use his translation of the symbolic text in his book for his Masters thesis.

"I had a hard time selling this to Jane Arnold, the department head" Walters objected. "Your book is not recognized within the academic community. There are no reference points for it. No one is going to know if you really got it right."

"That's true sir. I thought a thesis was supposed to break new ground."

Michael Walters face broke out into a wide grin. "Oh, you'd be surprised."

The older man agreed that he would test the waters again. "You need a backup thesis topic."

After a few moments of thought John reluctantly agreed.

"Now sir, I want to show you something. I want to demonstrate that this crazy book you helped me with contains some practical and very profound information."

John arranged his chair so that it was five feet or so behind the desk, giving Michael Walters a clear view. John sat facing the room's only window, sideways to the desk.

"All right sir, for the next 10 or 15 minutes I'm going to do the technique from that book of Genevieve's. Watch closely, for something remarkable will happen at the end. If you would, I'd like you to give me a detailed summary of your observations."

The other man nodded.

John began the technique. After about ten minutes he was finally ramping up on stage one. The observant and critical eyes of Michael Walters were upon him, slowing his progress. After five more minutes his merkaba began to activate. The Eyrie was in his mind and heart. The room shimmered...now he was in the zone of chaos and out, and the Eyrie slowly came into focus. He found himself sitting on the floor next to the wall where he had left the evening before. The place was dark. John saw no one. He hung around for about ten minutes, anticipating the look of surprise on Michael Walters' face. *The man is probably shitting bricks right now!*

John reemerged into the library, looking expectantly over at Michael Walters who was dutifully scrawling upon a piece of yellow notepad paper. The man looked bored.

"Well?" John said anxiously. "What did you see?"

"Nothing much. I did notice a peculiar quality to the air in the room, like a temperature inversion on a hot day. The atmosphere in the room seems refreshed, but that is purely speculative. The origin point of this phenomena seemed to come from around your body."

"You didn't notice anything...uh...unusual about me?" John was incredulous.

"Nothing unusual about your appearance. You were in the chair the entire time with your hands in your lap and your feet flat on the floor."

"I'll be damned."

"For a split instant I thought you might have flickered a bit. I couldn't say for sure."

John was extremely disappointed. Even though the clock face always showed that no time ever elapsed, the process of entering and exiting must be visible. Apparently not.

"Using this procedure I seem to be experiencing altered states of reality. I go places that seem real. I talk to people and beings I've never met before. I have experiences that are totally convincing." John yanked his chair around to face the desk and its occupant. "Now it appears that I may be hallucinating, or delusional. Yet I have experienced these...alternate realities...at least ten times. If I'm delusional I'm doing a damn good job of it!" John thought of the cut on his arm after his first solo jaunt, and the grain of sand that had fallen out of his clothing after his trip with Genevieve. "A partial enabling of this process has enabled me to play table tennis far above my normal level. I have taught it to a friend of mine and he's applied it successfully as well. I just don't understand it."

"Genevieve is able to have these experiences as well, is she not?" Walters asked.

"Yes. How did you know that?"

"I didn't. I have seen and felt that odd shimmering in the air before, on several occasions, just outside my daughter's bedroom. Afterwards Genevieve seemed much more animated and cheerful. I have noted such positive changes in your character as well these last couple of years. Your demonstration just now confirmed it."

"Did you notice something?"

"An increased...liveliness, or animation, in your demeanor."

Walters looked thoughtfully into space, as if trying to recall something.

"I remember a time several years ago when I walked into Genevieve's room unannounced. It was the middle of winter but the air smelled fresh, like a spring breeze. There seemed to be ripples in the atmosphere but they faded almost immediately. My impression was that some energy or force had been in the room. On another occasion I knocked on her door and she told me to come in. On her face was the most angelic expression I have ever seen on a human face. Again I noticed the peculiar atmospheric phenomena. I am not an excitable person so I just made a note of it."

John's foot tapped on the floor. "It appears that when I am gone, considerable subjective time elapses. When I return no time has elapsed. My body comes with me and does not seem to age, no matter how much time I spend in these other, ah, places. That is unusual because if I was daydreaming time would elapse and it would show up on the clock. Either I am undergoing a gigantic hallucination or my experiences are real." He repeated what Kjirsten told him. "The causality of time must always be maintained."

Michael Walters laughed. "You are becoming quite a metaphysician John."

John's brain was working fast. He understood now what had happened. He had reappeared in the chair a split instant after departure. The integrity of time *was* maintained. To Michael Walters' eyes, nothing had occurred except for a shimmering in the air. For him, the continuity of John's existence was unbroken.

What occurred must be relative to your frame of reference. It was impossible to determine from one frame of reference the experience of another in a different frame of reference. An objective observer would say, truthfully, that he must be hallucinating. John knew that he had a valid experience but it was impossible to prove it to anyone else. The key was to understand that the inability to prove it objectively to others did not invalidate the experience. That made him feel better.

"Thank you for your help sir," he said to Michael Walters, and left.

John drove over to the pool hall to shoot a few racks and get his mind back to reality.

John broke the balls hard and grunted with satisfaction as the cue ball smacked loudly into the pile, sending the balls flying all over the table. John lined up the 3 ball in the side. With a surge of adrenaline he hit it so hard the ball flew over the rail, almost hitting the guy at the next table.

"Sorry." John apologized and ran off to retrieve the ball, which was rolling very fast over the hard linoleum floor. It crashed against the wall twenty feet away and finally came to rest against an ancient radiator.

From the front counter Jack looked over crossly at him but said nothing. As he bent over to pick up the ball he heard a familiar voice. "How many times do I have to tell you about hitting too hard?"

"Freddy! Just the man I was looking for." John paused and frowned. "Roger Krosky isn't with you, is he?" He imitated Roger's high pitched voice. "You're a kook John Frankel!"

Freddy laughed out loud. "No John, I just came in. Nothing wrong with Roger. Pretty normal guy."

"I wasn't impressed with his perspicacity."

Freddy chuckled. "Now I gotta go look that one up. No wonder Roger didn't like you John. No one uses perspicacity in normal conversation."

John smiled. "Sorry, didn't mean to trash your friend."

"You already got a table I see. C'mon, let's play some 9-ball. I'll show you a couple of things I picked up since my last tournament." Freddy showed John how to make a *masse* shot, and the proper way to jump a ball. They played for a while and afterward went to one of the campus bars for a pitcher of beer.

"Got a sponsor now," Freddy said.

"Yeah? Who?"

"Some guy named Watkins. Owns a bunch of athletic supply stores. Cleans up selling to the high schools and Carleton; organizes leagues so he can sell his stuff."

"Yeah but why you? Why not Dillinger?" Dillinger was the best player in Midland.

"I beat him last week."

"You must be getting good."

Freddy grinned. "I'm a natural, that's what Dillinger said. Pretty good guy actually."

"What do you do for Watkins to earn your sponsorship?"

"He's got me wearing hats and tee shirts with his company name." Freddy pointed to his T-shirt with the words 'Watkins Pool and Cue' on it. "I do presentations and demos in the stores and on site and try to talk people into buying his stuff. Mostly he sells tables and cues of the major brands, but he adds on a big markup. Guy's a real businessman, I'll give him that. He could sell water pistols to an arms dealer. It's kinda boring but I'll take it if I can play almost full time."

Freddy noticed a good looking girl walk by. "Wow, look at her."

"She's OK."

"I suppose you got something better?"

John pulled out his wallet and handed him a picture of Genevieve. It was the one Rachel had taken of her just before they left for John's senior prom.

Freddy looked at John like he had never seen him before. "I thought you were gay."

John exploded. "GAY?" Heads turned to look at them. "Fuck you Freddy."

"No shit John. I thought you were, not that it matters to me." Freddy peered at the photograph again. "I've changed my mind."

"Do you get along?" Freddy said.

"Yes, really well."

Freddy's face became serious. "How do you do it?"

John thought about that for a few moments. "I don't know."

"Both my parents have been married and divorced twice. I only know how to fuck up relationships with the opposite sex."

"Have another beer," John suggested. "Women aren't everything."

Freddy laughed. "Yeah but they sure are nice."

John sat back in the booth and thought about how good it was being with Freddy in this campus bar. John rarely drank but tonight the beer tasted great. He liked the solid comfort of this booth, the smell of alcohol and cigarettes, the clink of glasses, and the sound of the occasional voice over the underlying buzz of conversation. He had just turned 22 a couple of weeks ago.

After table tennis practice the following Friday Gene spoke to John. "I entered your name in the open section of the tournament. It's tomorrow at the rec center. My father is bringing in 18 tournament tables."

The tournament!

"You don't even remember. That's typical of you John."

The next morning John dressed quickly. He put his paddle, a spare, a water bottle, a few snacks, and a towel in a little war bag. He got on his bike and rode to the rec center, wanting to arrive warmed up but not tired.

John met Gene in the front lobby. They both went into an unused office off the gym floor and did the technique. John and Gene both found the zone.

John had no rating so he was paired with another like him in a preliminary round. Sometimes bad players entered the open bracket who had no business being there. The tournament organizers tried to eliminate them quickly because none of the good players wanted to waste their time with a scrub.

The tables were lined up in a 3 by 6 grid, with little cardboard fences about 2 feet high marking the spaces for each table. John played at the back corner table away from the spectators. He won his first match easily and had to wait around for about 15 minutes for his next opponent. He went over and checked the brackets. John Frankel was seeded dead last.

The crowd was impressive, even though most of them seemed to be friends of the players. It was cool playing in front of people. John wanted to do well.

John's next opponent was a character everybody called 'wild Joe.' Joe seemed impatient to get on with the match as if he had planned on disposing of John easily.

John leisurely cleaned his paddle sponge and rearranged his sweatbands. "C'mon man, you're wasting time." Joe was banging the edge of his paddle against the table impatiently. A man with an "Event Staff" tee shirt turned his head and scowled.

Joe's first serve was a wild gyration of the body and an enormous swing of the arm, but his serve went into the net.

"0 - 1," John said.

"I know what the goddam score is," Joe barked.

John played the next ball too nonchalantly and Joe crushed it for a winner crosscourt, snorting his contempt. Despite the man's antisocial personality he was an excellent player and very aggressive. Gene told John to play defensively at first and size up the opponent's game.

Joe won the first game but John had sized him up. In the second game John anticipated every move and was there to block or redirect the other's shots. Joe rapidly became frustrated, especially after one of John's shots nicked the edge and fell off the table for a point. Wild Joe was working so hard he was getting tired. At the end of the second game Joe was cursing, stalling for time, delaying the game and making disparaging remarks about John. John hadn't even broken a sweat. So far he was maintaining the zone without effort.

John won the second game of the first match at 11- 5 and the rubber game 11–2. He won the second match two games to none.

Joe slammed his paddle on the table and glared at John. "You got lucky."

John replied courteously. "You beat yourself. I didn't play that well." The technique had not failed him!

Joe stalked off without acknowledgment. His day was over. The players to right and left nodded to John. They were glad not to have to face the abrasive player.

There were 47 entries in the open bracket because this was a regional tournament. More than likely the presence of Pavel Grigorenko had attracted a crowd of players eager to gain rating points. Grigorenko was in the top 100 in the world rankings.

John had played 2 matches and was now into the round of 32 with the good players. Gene easily beat his first opponent and caught the end of John's match. "Good job! Everybody hates wild Joe." Gene looked at the brackets. "Uh-oh, you play Simon Leavy next. He plays a backspin game and you can't be too aggressive. Lay back until you figure out how to handle the spin."

John had a lot of trouble with Leavy's slow spin game but prevailed three matches to two. He had now beaten two players he never could have touched without the technique. It proved once again that altered states of consciousness led to enhanced abilities. John was having fun. "I'm glad you entered me," he said to Gene after he had beaten the thirtieth ranked player. Gene was ranked third in the brackets.

Coming from the round of scrubs, John had played three matches and reached the round of 16. The remaining players had only gone two matches. Gene came up and slapped hands. "Saw the last set with Leavy, thought he had you. Good work."

"I just laid back and didn't try to win," John said. "I was able to get deeper into the zone that way. I don't really understand it, but it seems to work."

"You got Chen next. 2100 player. This guy's a whole different ballgame."

John and Gene both went through the technique again between matches. According to the other players, Gene looked awesome today. Quick as a cat and aggressive, he had dominated both his opponents.

John walked back to the competition and looked around the room, trying to see the merkabas of each person. He could only see a very faint glow around each body, but it might have been his imagination...

"...and at table 6, Chen Yun-Wang vs. John Frankel..." Oops! Time to play.

As the day wore on John kept winning. Chen played aggressively so John had an easier time. The enhanced awareness provided by the technique enabled him to easily get to any ball. The harder it was hit the faster were his returns. Although relatively inexperienced, he was able to defeat Chen 3 matches to 1. The technique gave him enhanced coordination and speed.

Bill Richardson came over to him after his last match. "It's not possible for you to beat the guys you beat. I'll give you wild Joe but not Simon Leavy and Chen."

John smiled. "The technique increases awareness and that leads to enhanced abilities. Gene and I already told you that."

Bill walked off. He had lost in the second round.

Was Bill right? Was he cheating?

John didn't have time to think about it. He was in the semifinals now and had moved to the most visible tables in the middle of the front row for the next match with Mike Dawson. Dawson was a formidable player who had trained at a camp run by one of the coaches of the US Olympic Team. At 2250, he was ranked a little below Gene.

John was elated. His esoteric training was proving itself at a real athletic competition. Dawson was a very aggressive player with a game similar to Chen's, but much more consistent.

Even though every game was very close, John was able to win the match surprisingly easily at 3 to 0. An unseeded and totally unknown player had made the finals!

Dawson came over to shake hands after the match. "Never seen you before."

"This is my first tournament."

Dawson was surprised. "Where do you train?"

"With Gene over there."

Dawson shook his head. "No wonder you beat me. I've never been able to get over against him."

"Hey let's go over and watch," John suggested. "He's playing Grigorenko in the semi's on table 3."

Dawson and John took a seat in the stands, a three level platform that ran the length of the tables.

Grigorenko was rated 2550 to Gene's 2380. So it was number 1 against number 2. John couldn't figure out how the number 2 played the number 1 in the semis instead of the finals, but he didn't care. Neither did the players. The competition was fierce, but everyone except wild Joe took both wins and losses in stride. All of the defeated players were watching the progress of the matches. Some of them had come from other cities and were curious about the outcome. John heard snatches of conversation about him. They were amazed that an unseeded player had advanced so far, until Dawson told them he trained with Gene.

As the match progressed John tried again to see into the merkabas off the players. The tournament was forgotten as John concentrated on Grigorenko's merkaba. Nothing happened for a while. Then, at the edge of his perception, faint meridians of energy appeared. They looked like tiny curved filaments spreading in a geometric pattern...there.

John noticed something interesting within Grigorenko's inner sphere. There were some globs, and places where the filaments were twisted and distorted. Two areas of the body were not receiving their full complement of energy. One was the right shoulder, the other was inside the body itself – the liver? Somewhere around there.

A hand shook him roughly on the shoulder. Suddenly the room burst into focus and sound.

"John! Get a move on man or you'll forfeit!" It was Gene.

"Huh?"

"John, you're up! Didn't you see the match? You were staring at us the whole time." Gene gave John a shove in the back. "Don't let me down boy! Play him like you play me."

Apparently Gene had lost. As John walked toward the table his head cleared. He saw Grigorenko, looking bored. His opponent was tall and blond with blue eyes and a handsome squarely-chiseled face.

The other tables had been cleared away to allow for better viewing. The referee's table was set up with large cards on either side of it, to announce the score.

Grigorenko spoke to John. "If you're scared to play me you can withdraw. Make up your mind quick."

It was a condescending taunt that was supposed to throw John off his game. John had never let the taunts of others bother him and he didn't now. He was in the zone. "Let's play."

In the stands a slow grin crept over Gene's face. He had seen that same smile one evening just before John annihilated him. Gene rubbed his hands in glee.

Some of the other players were about to leave. "What are you so excited about?" one of them said.

"Stick around boys. I think Grigorenko's going down."

Gene heard a chorus of protest. "No way!" "That clown's going to get killed."

"How much you want to bet?"

Gene placed a $10 bill on the seat beside him. "I got 10 bucks against all comers that Frankel beats him. Put your money where your mouth is." Soon there was a pile of paper that began to fall off the foot-wide seat. One of the players said, "I'll hold that in my duffel." Now everyone was really into the match and they settled in to watch.

John won the right to serve first. He was not a strong server. His opponents were able to quickly go on the attack, but John knew his strength was in the volley. The more aggressive the attack the more effective were his returns. He could feel his control over the perception of motion. No matter how hard or quick the ball came back he would have time to get into position.

"C'mon, serve," Grigorenko said. The referee gave John a warning. "Further delays will cost you points."

John didn't care. Winning or losing – it didn't matter now. He had been able to hold the zone all day with just a couple of refreshers. John quickly got into serving position, crouching low over the table. He stood with his right foot halfway between the end of the table and the center line. Grigorenko took the serve with his forehand and smashed it so hard down the line to his backhand that John didn't even see the ball. The ball hit the table and bounced all the way to the cardboard barrier 20 feet away.

Oops! He had been in his head, gloating. The technique didn't work if he fed his ego. Grigorenko was grinning. The expression on his face said, "This is going to be easy."

On the next serve John relaxed and found the zone again. He placed the ball to Grigorenko's backhand, as close to the net as he could. Grigorenko quickly ran behind the ball and hit another quick forehand. This time John saw it in slow motion. He stepped in and smashed the ball cross-court for a clean forehand winner.

Now it was Grigorenko's turn to be shocked. That goofball knew where his ball was going even before he did!

Out of the corner of his eye John saw Genevieve in the stands.

Grigorenko won the first game 11-9. John won the second game of the first match but lost the rubber game. So he was down 1-0 in the best 3 out of 5. Grigorenko had quickly seen that John did better against an aggressive attack, so he mixed up the power game with slow spins, cuts, and slices.

As they prepared for the second match John saw Genevieve looking at him excitedly. She was radiant, cheering when he made a point and slamming her fist on the bench seat when he missed. John felt a surge of male pride. A sense of power and joy filled his being. He was now the coiled snake, ready to strike, but also the bending reed, able to accept anything. It was an awesome feeling of absolute certainty. The match was his if he wanted it. He decided that he did.

Now with quick, effortless, and (almost!) graceful movement, he was everywhere. There was no opponent, just the dance of movement between them both. John was elated and serene, in control. The technique provided the feeling of being out of time and resulted in a sort of instantaneous anticipation. He just knew what his opponent was going to do before he did it.

Playing Simon Leavy had been a godsend. Whenever Grigorenko hit with spin John sliced it back or looped it if the ball was high enough. When Grigorenko used his power game John was just *there.* He either blocked or smashed, depending on how good he was set up. Grigorenko was really good. Smooth and fast, he played much more consistently than Gene. Their rallies would go on and on, each point hotly contested. The spectators were yelling and screaming, spurring on the two players.

John was helped by his height. The table was made for guys around 5' 8" or shorter. John had to crouch low but he could reach the ends of the table easily with short little steps. He didn't have to move as much as his opponents.

On the final point of the rubber match for the second set John served to the forehand, a little high. Grigorenko stepped in and smashed down the line to John's backhand, trying to knock the ball into John's body. John countered with a quick backhand drive cross-court. This time Grigorenko was ready and he smashed his own backhand down the line to John's forehand so fast that the spectators could barely see it. However, John was anticipating every movement before it happened. He stepped lightly over and took the ball cross-court to Grigorenko's forehand, sure he had won the point. But in an incredible athletic move the other player dived over with arm outstretched and punched the ball to John's backhand, on the opposite side of the table. It was a sure winner. John heard Genevieve's scream in slow motion and he was barely able to position his feet for a block to the middle of the table. Now Grigorenko, off-balance, could only reach out and slice the ball back. This gave John time to set up. John saw the ball dive over the net and was prepared to kill it when it grazed the net, slowing its movement. The ball bounced slowly upward and fell an inch in front of the net. Bad luck! John quickly reached in and pushed the ball back over the net to Grigorenko's forehand. They exchanged a few soft pushes, each player maneuvering for the advantage. Suddenly Grigorenko saw his chance. John had placed the ball an inch too high and the "blond bomber" smacked a hard cross-court drive to John's forehand. The rally was on again, each player hitting the ball as fiercely as possible, backing up farther and farther as the ball attained speeds of 100 mph. Grigorenko hit "loops," hard topspin shots that would literally jump high off the table. John's shots – being the less practiced player – were flatter and easier to hit back. John realized his error. He was playing to his opponent's strength. He calmed himself down. After three exchanges he noted that Grigorenko was into a rhythm of the cross-court forehand. His feet weren't moving anymore, confident he would eventually wear the unranked player down.

John's ball hit the table and Grigorenko again hit the cross-court shot. Fifteen feet away from the end of the table John moved his feet ever so slightly. He placed his back foot directly in line with the front. Just before the ball passed by his stomach John turned on it and smashed the ball so hard down the line to the backhand side that Grigorenko could only stare as it hit the table and bounced to the cardboard barrier.

Grigorenko blinked. He had only seen that shot done to him by the very best players.

In the stands, Genevieve stood with arms over her head. She clapped in appreciation and Gene roared his approval. The other players were excited. "Wow, did you see that!" "Great point!" "Maybe that stiff has a chance!"

John won the second set 2 and 1, tying the match at 1 set apiece. The other man seemed a bit deflated. It was clear that Grigorenko was indeed recovering from an injury. John saw him wince. He flexed his right shoulder and rotated it gingerly in its socket.

Still in the zone, John won the next two matches almost effortlessly.

He had beaten Grigorenko 3 matches to 1.

In the seats Gene exploded. "Pay up boys!" The player holding the money reached into his duffel and handed him a fistful of bills. The guys were astounded. No one could believe that "Grenks" would lose to a nobody, injury or no.

Gene looked at Genevieve. "Whoo! Made me a cool two hundred off my boy today!"

After the match John didn't know what to expect. He had done the impossible. Grigorenko came over and shook hands, regarding him curiously. "I'm usually pretty pissed when I lose, but there was something about the way you played. I can't describe it."

John replied graciously. "I played out of my mind. You took me too lightly." He probably had. John had snuck up on a lot of players today.

"Yeah, that's it." Grigorenko walked away, but then stopped and turned around.

"What's your name again?"

"John Frankel."

"Let's play again. You can find me at the Birmingham Table Tennis Club. Some great players there. Bring your friend if you want."

"I'll do that." John said. "See ya."

"Hey boy, you just made the best club in the state," Gene said, standing next to John. "By invitation only, and you just got invited."

John put his hand on Gene's shoulder, feeling expansive. "We'll have to do lots of practicing then."

Gene held up his winnings. "Made some jack on you today."

"You bet on me to beat that guy?"

A whoosh of black hair and Genevieve was in his arms. "You won!" she said brightly.

"You inspired me."

He suddenly felt exhausted. "Let's go home sweetheart. I'm tired and hungry."

As they walked out of the building into the parking lot he said, "Do I get a reward?"

"A reward?"

"For winning."

"You got your reward last night."

"I need another one." John placed his arm around her waist possessively.

She punched him in the ribs. "Down boy!"

That night Genevieve thought about what had happened today. She had gone to the gym just like any other normie girl and cheered on her guy. It seemed a little weird to her. Almost normal. Why had she done it?

She realized that for the first time she had someone to look up to. Someone who was actually better than she was in certain areas of life. Before she had dominated all the time and had gotten used to it. For most of her life she felt superior to everyone, because she was. That had led to her isolation. She didn't know whether she liked having to acknowledge anyone as her superior.

She realized that the relationship between her and John had altered. John was growing so fast it scared her sometimes. She kind of liked the sensation of being protected by someone stronger and wiser than herself. It was all part of her feminine side. She was becoming more receptive and a little softer. She liked it.

Genevieve looked over at the lanky man sleeping beside her and blushed a little. She thought of how John had handled her tonight, how he had been in control. The strong and sure-handed male to her more pliant feminine. She looped her arms around John's back and leaned her head against his shoulder. She fell softly asleep.

At work on Monday John thought about how weird his life was. In one version he was mild mannered John Frankel, aka weird John. He had an ordinary job, was going to college, had a girlfriend, hung out at a pool hall, lifted weights, and played table tennis pretty good.

In the other he was ten steps above a Zen master. He won tournaments he had no business even entering. He traveled to alternate universes and investigated the ultimate nature of reality with a bunch of misfits who belonged in a carnival.

Each version of himself seemed mutually exclusive. Like now, for instance. John had been able to tweak the computer code to allow for a more efficient clustering algorithm. Peter Marlowe had been delighted. His experience at the barrier, if not forgotten, was no longer occupying any of his attention. It was like it had never happened. Except for the feeling of power that was the by-product of the training regimen.

Marlowe's team had been able to identify a number of previously unknown red shift quasars. John had helped in a small way. He only knew two things about these objects: quasars were the most luminous objects in the universe; and the spectra of a quasar was much different from that of a normal star, possessing a number of strong emission lines. These two features made it possible to identify even distant quasars. John thought it was kind of cool even if it didn't have any practical application. He felt sometimes like an idiot savant. He was too detached from the project.

"Maybe it's better that way dash it," Marlowe said to him one morning as he rubbed his eyes from exhaustion. "You're just that little bit removed from the action. That keeps your ideas from becoming stale." John was skeptical.

"You're like old Prince Charlie."

"Prince Charlie?"

"Yes. When Charles was a younger man he walked into a local pub. The bartender asks him, 'What will you have?' Charlie says, 'A sherry, I think.'" Marlowe doubled over in laughter. His roly poly body, still enormously fat, jiggled like a vat of silicone gel. Marlowe saw John's confusion and waved his hand. "Never mind boy, we're all glad you're on the side."

Another incomprehensible reference. Was his boss going to have him for breakfast? A short stack perhaps? John smiled and shook his head as Marlowe waddled out of the room. A water bottle hung from his belt.

The next afternoon after class John turned on the Cubs game and suddenly thought of Trevor, his old baseball pal who had gone off to Princeton to become a star pitcher. Trevor's dad had promised to stay in touch with him about that little piece of paper from the code book. According to Kjirsten, Sievers had no chance with the stuff. John's intuition said differently.

He rang over. "Jones residence," said a smooth, British accented voice.

"May I speak with Mr. Jones?"

"May I ask who is calling please?"

"This is John Frankel."

"One moment." There was a click on the line.

"John! Dalton Jones here. How are you?"

"Just fine sir. I know it's been a long time. I wanted to check in with you about our very strange little square."

There was a pause. Through the receiver John heard fingers drumming on a desktop.

"I'll ring Jim Sievers straightaway. I'll call you right back."

Five minutes later the phone rang.

"Let me give you the location of Jim Sievers' laboratory."

Jones gave directions and a code number. "Jim will give you an hour this Saturday morning at 9 a.m. Show up on time. If you don't he might not answer the door."

Sievers' lab was located in a two story box of mostly tinted glass in the Octagon building in Research Park. John walked into the lobby and found an 11-digit display panel. He punched in "210" for the room number and the 8 digit code Dalton Jones had given him. Sievers changed it every day.

John walked up one flight of concrete steps and pressed the doorbell next to a plain, dark blue metal door with '210' painted in white. "You have to ring the bell three times, then wait," Jones had instructed.

The door was opened by a smallish, meticulously dressed man in a spotless white lab coat. His fine brown hair was neatly combed, and he wore delicate gold rimmed glasses. Sievers' hands were very fine and smooth like a woman's. This was a man used to delicate work. Sievers was inspecting him critically. "Come in." Sievers led John to a small table with a black granite top and cabinets underneath.

"I've been working with this stuff off and on for four years. I know nothing more about its internal composition now than I did then. However, there are a couple of things I can show you."

Sievers reached in and grabbed what looked like a roll of yellow parchment paper, placing on the table top. It looked exactly like the pages in his book.

"You learned how to make it!" John was excited.

Sievers frowned with disapproval. "You weren't listening."

"Uh, sorry. You said you had discovered nothing more about its composition."

Sievers relaxed. "Correct." He pointed at the parchment as if insulted by its existence. "This substance has no molecular or atomic structure. Even under the most powerful electron microscope it appears to be everywhere continuous. It can't possibly exist but it does. This substance, as far as I can tell, has an infinite density but it is as light as paper."

He flicked an edge and it began to unroll. "It is completely inert to any known analysis or energy, yet one can take a simple pair of scissors and cut it."

"How were you able to produce that roll?" John asked.

"We discovered this purely by accident." Sievers cut a small piece out of the roll and placed it into a clear container on a small raised platform. A black box was hooked up to the container and from it an impossibly thin plane of light bisected the material, passing through it edgewise. Sievers removed the material with a pair of tongs and placed it on the table top.

"Notice anything different?"

John carefully inspected the material without touching it. "Can't say that I do."

"I didn't either, until the air conditioning failed one day. We had fans going in here. When the air rustled our piece of paper..." He blew on it. A second piece, identical to the first, fluttered away.

John grabbed the new piece and compared it to the old one. "They appear to have the same thickness as the original!"

The corners of Sievers' mouth turned up in an ironic smile. "Correct. When we measured both pieces they were precisely the same. Both are as thick as the original roll." He looked questioningly at John.

"Presumably this inert substance grows?" John said.

Sievers was disgusted. It was evident to John that his sense of the order of things was disrupted by the sample.

"I can find no evidence of accumulation on the surface, or anywhere within the substance. Yet it is occurring." He looked at John again and held up the roll. "Observe that there are two new pieces. How did I make this roll?"

John thought out loud. "Well, from what you've said there are only two forces which can affect the material: a perpendicular cutting or a horizontal slicing. Therefore, either attach the pieces one on top of the other, or edgewise. I'd say edgewise because both cutting procedures began at the edge of the material."

Sievers was impressed. "Very good! You might make a decent materials analyst."

He placed the two pieces on the table surface and brought them together. As soon as contact was made they joined seamlessly together.

"No matter how many times we slice the substance it never loses its thickness. It's like the professor's bottle in 'It's a Wonderful Life.' We've made several square feet of the stuff in precisely this manner."

"How does it join together?" John asked.

Sievers smacked the table's hard surface with his open hand, startling John. "I haven't the slightest fucking idea. It's baffling. I've given up." He looked up at John, hoping for a clue. "There are times I rue the day I ever saw this stuff."

"Have you tried writing on it?" John asked. "After all, it was originally from a book."

Sievers stared at him. A first John thought the man was going to strike him. The researcher's jaw dropped.

"I mean, with a pen or a pencil," John said encouragingly.

Sievers looked exasperated. He got a pen and wrote "I AM A MYSTERY" in blue ballpoint over the two joined pieces. "Why didn't I think of that?"

"Too obvious," John said. "What happens if you wipe it?"

Sievers went into a drawer and procured a clean rag, then took some solvent from a shelf. When he wiped the surface all the ink came off. But the "paper" was inscribed in black, exactly as the symbols had been. However, the symbols in the book appeared infinitely fine in comparison to Sievers' crude lettering.

Sievers tried to remove the impressions made by the pen. No matter how hard he scrubbed he could not make a dent. "Finally some progress," he said.

"Progress?"

"This stuff is programmed to perform only a few, very specific tasks. It is inert to anything else. Like a designer atom, but much more sophisticated."

Maybe the material is responsive to the consciousness of the person handling it, like the drawings in the book that drew me into them. Sievers has been approaching the study of this stuff as if it were a material, but maybe it is programmed to respond only to certain types of thought.

Sievers regarded the material with new interest. "I'll have to change my approach."

Now it was John's turn to be impressed. This guy wasn't married to old ideas.

"Have any military or government types shown up?" John asked.

Sievers laughed. "They certainly have. I showed them the same things I showed you. They cut off part of the roll and left. I haven't heard from them since."

He looked at the clock. "Time's up. I've got several other projects I'm behind on." Sievers held out his hand. "Good meeting you. I'll keep you informed of developments." John gave him his phone number and email, and left the building.

That night he discussed it with Genevieve. "Didn't Sievers say it was everywhere continuous?" she asked.

"Yes!" John exclaimed, catching her idea. The universal medium had the same properties. Could this stuff be its physical equivalent? But how would it be fashioned? And who could make it?

Gene pressed John at their Tuesday training session to go up to Birmingham. "Let's do it before Grenks forgets about you." So on Friday they drove the 40 miles north to Birmingham. Gene remarked the well maintained roads, the large houses and lots, and the overall affluence of the place. They finally found the club in the basement of a large community center.

John and Gene were introduced to all the players. Pavel Grigorenko introduced John to his sister Svetlana.

John saw a beautifully made Russian woman with medium length blond hair and symmetric features. She was about 6' 1," between Genevieve and Kjirsten. John didn't know what to say.

"Not very bright, is he?" She was enjoying John's reaction.

"Uh, pleased to meet you." John held out his hand and she took it in a strong grasp. She had the look of a trained athlete.

John inspected both of them, standing side by side. "You have great genes."

Brother and sister laughed.

John played four matches, won two and lost two. The level of play was much higher than in the tournament. No one here had a rating below 2350. The main difference was the consistent play and the quality of the serve. A good server would use the same motion but generate completely different spins and speeds on the ball.

After the play Pavel said, "Let's go out for drinks." Gene and John agreed. Pavel led them to a sports bar with lots of wide screen TVs, a few pool tables, and plenty of places to sit. Svetlana maneuvered herself next to John. A waitress came around and Pavel ordered a pitcher.

Svetlana turned to John. "Tell me a little about yourself."

Nonplussed, John fumbled around for a response. Usually women never noticed him other than as a kind of freak. Still dressed in her shorts, John could see a pair of great looking legs up to mid thigh. She caught him looking. "Pavel says you already have a girlfriend."

John blushed.

Yup, I do, John thought, and she's the best. He couldn't stop looking anyway. Pavel and Gene were amused at John's embarrassment. The waitress came back and put down the pitcher, glancing at Gene. "I'm off in a few. Can I come and sit?" Gene said, "Sure thing!" The waitress was petite and gave him a smile before walking off to tend to another table.

"She's just my size," Gene said approvingly. He glanced over at his three companions. "Too many tall people around here."

Svetlana turned to John. "You didn't answer my question."

John tried to remember what it was but couldn't. Svetlana didn't seem to mind though. "What's your work like?"

John told her about Peter Marlowe and his part in the ongoing astronomy project. He could tell she understood nothing, but she communicated genuine interest.

"I only have a high school education," she said. "I'm an aerobics instructor and a personal trainer. There are lots of executive types around town and it's good money. I'm hoping to start my own business."

John listened intently. Svetlana was totally open to him, without the slightest inhibition. It was very refreshing to meet someone who was completely accepting of his unusual appearance right off the bat. Nothing was going to come of it so he felt OK about it.

"That's interesting," John said to himself.

Svetlana cocked her head. "What's interesting?" John decided to think out loud. "Well, there are only two women in my life who ever noticed me and both of them are highly educated. Usually the athletic girls want nothing to do with me."

She smiled again. "I do. I feel real comfortable talking to you. I usually don't with guys."

"Really?" John was surprised. "Why not?"

"I don't know...it's like either they just want to have sex right away or they're too embarrassed to even approach me."

"I was embarrassed," John pointed out.

"You're different."

John thought about that. Yep, he was different all right. Kathleen Summers once told him he was totally harmless. Maybe that was it.

"Are you married?" she asked.

John grinned. "Not yet."

Svetlana seemed satisfied. From that point on everything went smoothly. She told him about her life. "My brother and I were born in Russia. Our parents moved to the States when I was five. My father introduced us both to the game when I was seven. I have been playing for 15 years. My ranking is 2300."

Pavel overheard this. "She even beat me once."

"Twice!" Svetlana exclaimed.

Pavel laughed. "That didn't count. I was drunk."

"Then you shouldn't have played," she said firmly.

Gene's waitress, now off duty, came over to the table. Gene stood up like a gentleman and held out his hand. "Hi, I'm Gene Watkins."

"Millie Linden."

They talked easily for a while and then went to the pool tables. John showed Svetlana how to hold the cue, and some basic principles of the game. She was attentive and eager to learn. Pavel was amused and scornful. Like a true brother he couldn't understand what any guy saw in his sister, or why she'd taken such an infatuation to the goofy looking John Frankel.

After another hour John looked at the clock. "Hey Gene, it's 11:15. Let's get going."

Gene had gotten Millie's number so he was OK to take off.

"Ohhh, already?" Svetlana said. "You just got here!"

"Gotta get back to my girlfriend."

She pouted.

"I really enjoyed talking with you."

"You did?"

"Yes."

"Will I see you again?" Svetlana asked.

"Gene and I are coming up every other week."

"Good! In two weeks then."

After John got home he went into the living room. Genevieve was in her chair, reading.

As John approached he immediately noticed the remarkable difference between Genevieve and Svetlana. Genevieve felt deep, powerful, and intelligent. There was also a reserve, a feeling of holding back.

John kissed the top of her head. "Hi love."

She sniffed. "You've been to a bar. I smell perfume."

John grinned but said nothing.

Genevieve's womanly curiosity was aroused. "What's her name?"

"Svetlana."

"Svetlana! Let me guess. Grigorenko's sister."

John was amazed at her discernment. "She asked me if I was married."

"Oh?"

John leaned over and kissed the top of her head again.

"What does she look like?" Genevieve asked.

"About 6' 1," blond, athletic. She really likes me."

Genevieve slowly put her book down and stood up, smiling. "How do I stack up?"

John felt a powerful love for her overwhelm his senses. She was the most unique and wonderful person he'd ever met, including those crazy ETs at the Eyrie.

John crushed her in his arms. "She's nothing compared to you." And he meant it.

Two weeks later on a warm mid-September evening, John sat on the couch watching the Cubs game. Genevieve was on her mobile in the chair next to him. Robert and Rachel were at a movie.

Genevieve moved to sit down beside him. When he sensed her presence he immediately turned from the game and faced her, even though the Cubs were threatening to score.

"John, did you ever wonder why I never make you wear a condom?"

John couldn't follow. From baseball to condoms was too great a leap of logic.

"You told me you were using the pill," John replied. Part of his attention was still on the announcer's voice.

"I'm not using the pill John. I never have."

John's eyes widened in astonishment. She had never lied to him either.

"Then I'm either impotent or we're very lucky."

Genevieve put her hands over his and looked him straight in the eyes. "John, I am incapable of having children." She said it bitterly.

"Maybe it's me."

Now her eyes welled with tears, great big drops running down her cheeks. John's heart was ripped into little pieces. He couldn't stand to see her cry. She had only ever done it once before.

"I'm a genetic experiment, remember." She spat out the words. "Not a real woman." She lowered her head. "If you stay with me you'll never have a family."

John just sat there in shock for a moment. He noticed peripherally that the count on Crews was 3 and 2.

"Haven't you ever wondered why I never talked to you about our relationship? We've been sleeping together since I was 16. Weren't you ever curious why I never brought up marriage?"

John was totally unprepared for this. The TV told him that Crews just struck out with the bases loaded. One gone.

"I...I never asked because I didn't care. I'll take you any way I can get you. If you didn't want to talk about it I wasn't going to make you uncomfortable."

Genevieve looked up at him like a dam about to burst. Her body began to shake. He grabbed her and squeezed her against him. Her head was on his shoulder and he could feel every cell in her body spasming. She was screaming and crying like a mad woman, totally out of control. John just held on for dear life.

John didn't know what to do so he just gently rocked her back and forth. After about five minutes he began to panic; it wasn't getting any better. He was ready to call 911 but then felt her relaxing slightly. After another minute or so she had relaxed but was still making little crying and gasping sounds.

"Y-y-y-you don't c-c-care?"

She looked like a little girl desperately seeking approval. He was stunned. He told her exactly what was in his heart.

"I only know one thing Genevieve. I love you and I want to spend my whole life with you." Now tears were running down his face as well. He spoke as forcefully as he ever had in his life. "And I don't give a damn who put your genes together or whether you hatched out of an egg or came from a test tube or are the spawn of degenerate, evil space aliens."

John tenderly wiped the moisture from her cheeks with his finger.

The power and depth of his feelings snapped her out of it. In an instant she went from crying little schoolgirl to radiantly happy woman.

"Then I'm the luckiest woman on this earth," she said.

"And I'm the luckiest man."

She bounced back into her chair like nothing happened and resumed her book.

John turned back to the TV. He had just missed Wallace's grand slam and the cry of "Cubs win! Cubs win!"

25

THE following Friday night around midnight, Mats Karlsson returned to the Full Moon. He had left the old dehumidifier on in the storeroom. If it shorted the damn thing might start a fire.

Mats was careful. Although the Full Moon sometimes looked like the living room of an absent minded professor, Mats knew exactly where everything was. He meticulously maintained his old building. Last summer the cheap old wooden windows were replaced with new vinyl ones. The Full Moon didn't look like much from the outside but it was structurally sound.

He put his key in the lock and opened the door. A faint light shone from one of the stacks in back. An intruder?

He tippy-toed to the back, trying to locate the source of the light.

Mats wandered silently around the stacks for a few minutes. He turned a corner and saw a hooded figure about 4 feet tall at the end of a stack. The creature had his hands extended. In front of him was an egg-shaped volume of space about 5 feet in diameter, with clouds running through it. But they weren't clouds. The space itself was morphing! The air around the thing shimmered and glowed.

Mats caught a brief glimpse inside and it made his stomach turn. Vertigo assailed him. He crashed backwards into one of the stacks, startling the creature. "Shhhtalk ftrrblm asssshtorek!" it said (or something like that). It stepped quickly into the egg and vanished.

Mats shook his head. The space that the egg had occupied was still contorted. As he watched it reluctantly returned to its former shape. The air around it was still shimmering a little.

Slouched in a corner with his back up against a pile of books, Mats continued to stare. The area returned completely to normal and the strange illumination completely faded, leaving him in the dark.

As he recalled the glimpse into the egg, information came into his mind. A geometric network of eggs, with similar properties...connecting different worlds. By the gods, was there such a thing?

It was a portal. Just like in a science fiction book. A portal into a different dimension or reality.

Wait a minute. I've seen that creature before! Several years ago it had come in to sell him a book. A book that was bought almost immediately by one Genevieve Walters. Yes, and her boyfriend John Frankel. There had always been something special about those two, and her father too. Smart, those three, really smart.

"I haven't got the brains to figure this out," Mats muttered. He was almost out the door when he remembered his original mission. Mats walked into the storeroom and turned off the dehumidifier. He was definitely going to call on the Frankel's tomorrow.

That same Friday evening something very strange happened to John and Genevieve. John sat working at the desk in the living room, facing the picture window. Genevieve was doing research for her Advanced Placement classes at the high school.

John had thought of a much better thesis than his book translation. His pattern recognition skills, his work with Marlowe, and the codebook enabled him to develop the beginnings of a symbolic teaching language that would apply to any alphabet-based language.

Michael Walters gave it his enthusiastic approval. "You'll have no trouble selling this, John."

From upstairs came a loud crash.

"What's that?" Genevieve said, startled out of her nap. Another crash. John ran up the stairs two at a time, down the hall, and threw open the bedroom door. The atmosphere in the room was charged. To his right, a silver armadillo snuffled about on his desk. It was about two feet long and a foot high with a long prehensile snout like an elephant's. A softly glowing white light surrounded it, extending several inches beyond the outline of its body. The laptop was on the floor and the lamp had also fallen. The lampshade was crumpled and the bulb cracked in pieces.

"My laptop!" John ran over to pick it up. He was about to turn it on when the armadillo turned around on the desk.

"I am Armondo, representative of Porniarsk, the Great Avatar."

"What do you mean, representative?" John said. "Who is Porniarsk?"

"I am an – adjunct, aspect, extension – of one of those you might call the Elohim."

"The Elohim?" One part of John couldn't believe he was conversing with an armadillo. The rest of him was too fascinated to care.

"Your religions refer to them as deities, but they are known throughout creation as the builders-of-form." Armondo spoke matter-of-factly, as if reciting from a textbook.

"What's that supposed to mean?" John asked.

"We provide the programming for the things you see around you. Didn't you ever notice that the universe stays in balance? The air doesn't all of a sudden move to the other side of the room, does it? The planets stay in their orbits, don't they? Life everywhere is nurtured. You don't think the planet you're living on was created with a magic wand?"

Armondo was indignant. "Somebody has to figure out how to build this stuff!" He waved his snout around to indicate everything outside the window. "It's fine to be an idea man, but we're the guys who actually make it happen. We're universal engineers. That reminds me of a joke. There's this administrator in a hot air balloon floating above the ground..."

"What are you doing here?" John interrupted. Another lunatic in his life!

Genevieve entered the room and stood stock still.

"Porniarsk was curious about you." The creature raised itself on its hind legs and extended its snout toward John. John didn't laugh, even though it looked very cute. Armondo had a kind of noble dignity that commanded respect. "You still don't understand?" it said.

The snout rotated toward Genevieve. "This one does."

"I have no idea what you're talking about," John said.

"There is an event that you recently experienced, and which you shared with others in a...conference."

The debrief! "What does that have to do with you and your so-called Elohim?" John asked.

Genevieve replied. "On the edges of your awareness, during your run through for us, were some intelligences. You probably were not conscious of it, but I felt it."

"Correct!" said Armondo. "There were, er, bets, at how deeply and broadly you could perceive. Porniarsk lost some game points on you."

"So these Elohim, these universe builders, have a gambling disorder?"

Armondo's body moved back and forth on his tail. His pointy head rocked backward and forward. The white light surrounding him changed colors.

"He's laughing!" Genevieve exclaimed.

"Armondo is amused. That reminds me of an earthian joke." Without waiting for their approval, he launched right in, doing his best to impersonate the characters.

During this recitation, John and Genevieve stared at each other. When it was over Genevieve giggled despite her irritation.

Now Armondo was on his back with his legs in the air, his head bobbing up and down.

It was too bizarre. Wasn't it just ten minutes ago they were spending a peaceful evening together? "Would you mind telling us why you destroyed my lamp and my notebook?" John asked.

"Certainly. I was looking for something."

"That's no answer," John said.

"By the way, Porniarsk wants to see you."

"He already has," John said. "You're him."

"Not exactly. He wants to see you in person."

Genevieve stepped in. "Oh no you don't. We almost lost him last time he went off on his own."

Armondo seemed about ready to laugh again. "They look, but they do not see."

"What's that supposed to mean?" Genevieve said sharply.

"I am not to interfere." Armondo turned to John. "Look at it as an invitation. It's up to you."

Genevieve protested. "John doesn't even know how he did it. What happens if he gets lost and can't come back next time?"

"Porniarsk has something to tell you."

"What, odds on the next baseball game?"

Armondo chuckled. "John knows what I mean." Suddenly, Armondo reached up. With his snout he grabbed John's book and shimmered out.

"Hey, that's mine!" John exclaimed. He said it to empty air.

Genevieve stood with her hands on her hips. "What did Armondo mean?" John didn't answer.

"Johhhhhnnnnn. You promised me."

"I didn't! You made an assumption."

Genevieve turned quickly and left the room.

Uh-oh, John thought. I'm in for it now.

He slowly walked down the stairs, afraid she might not want to speak to him. Genevieve was in her chair, tears running down her face. John went over and put his arms around her. She was crying for the second time in a week.

"I don't want to lose you John." Her head dropped. "But I know you're going to do what you want to anyway."

He squeezed her very tightly and kissed her. "There's no danger, sweetheart. Armondo reminded me of something I'm not even sure I communicated during the debrief."

"I didn't hear anything reassuring," she said, pouting cutely. John thought she was irresistible. "I love you."

"That's another thing. I almost never tell you how much I love you."

John didn't know what to say. He waited silently.

"You're always telling me how wonderful I am," Genevieve said, sniffling. "I'm used to it. I like it. So now it's my turn."

She looked deeply into his eyes. "I love you with all my heart and soul. I think you're the perfect guy. Intelligent, warm, passionate, good natured, and very masculine. You're a fantastic lover too. Kjirsten feels it. She wants you real bad. Your new girlfriend Svetlana feels it too." She sighed. "I just want you to know how much I appreciate you. I plan to tell you that every day."

John was moved. "I'm looking forward to that."

On Saturday morning around 9, John got a call from Mats at the Full Moon. Mats had a personal relationship with many of his customers so it wasn't an intrusion. "John, I need to talk over something with you and Genevieve. Are you going to be around this morning?"

"As far as I know."

"Something really strange happened to me last night."

"You too?" John said.

There was a pause. Mats said, "I'll be right over."

About twenty minutes later they heard a knock. "Hi Mats!" Genevieve said brightly as she opened the door. Mats walked his big body over to the couch and sat down. John noticed that he still had good muscle tone.

"You been working out?" Mats said. "Looks like you put on some muscle."

Genevieve looked appreciatively. "He has."

Mats gave John a look that said 'lucky boy.' John grinned.

Genevieve looked back and forth between them. Mats put a look of boyish innocence on his face.

"What do men talk about when they're together?" she said. "Let me guess: women and sex."

"You forgot sports," Mats joked. John met his eyes and they both laughed.

"We're on the same wavelength," John said cheerfully to Mats.

"Not so hard when it only has one frequency."

Mats got serious. "John, have you ever seen a small little guy with a gold colored cloak and a hood that covers his face?"

"No. But I've seen an armadillo that calls himself Armondo and tells dirty jokes."

Mats looked up at him quizzically. "Are you serious?"

"Yup." He decided not to pull any punches with Mats. "What about your guy?"

Mats told them how he had originally received the book Genevieve bought several years ago, and his experiences last night. As he described the egg-shaped space their eyes widened.

"You said the guy disappeared after he entered the space?" Genevieve asked.

"Yup. The only people I could tell were you two. Anybody else would think I'm nuts."

"A transportal!" John cried. "Could there be one in the Full Moon?" He looked at Genevieve, astonished.

"It appears so," Genevieve said. "But why? Kjirsten never mentioned that there are transportals on earth."

"Maybe she doesn't know about them," John said.

"Unlikely. They've got observers covering every cubic inch of earthian space."

"What are you guys talking about?" Mats demanded.

Genevieve briefly described what Kjirsten had told them about the ancient galactic technology, but nothing about the technique. She knew Mats' strong interest in the bizarre but that might be going too far. As she spoke she saw Mats' jaw drop and his eyes widen in excitement.

After Genevieve finished John described their visit with Armondo. Mats looked from one to the other, trying to determine if the story was a joke. He was satisfied John was telling the truth. Their tale wasn't any more extraordinary than his. "I don't think you're giving me the whole story," Mats said.

"Should we tell him?" John asked Genevieve.

Genevieve thought for a moment. She knew the bookstore owner's wide-ranging mind and his childlike curiosity. Mats was someone who could be trusted to keep a secret. "Let's. You do the honors since you've explained it a number of times."

John proceeded to explain the book of symbols and the instructions it contained for attaining enhanced states of consciousness. He told Mats about some of their experiences with the technique. He also mentioned his experiment with Mr. Walters.

"Mr. W didn't see anything except a slight shimmering in the air," John said, glancing at Genevieve. "But it's totally real to us. I have improved my table tennis game significantly using it."

"So that's what Gary was so excited about." Mats smacked his big fist into his palm. "I noticed the same shimmering around that egg."

"Interesting," Genevieve said. "Probably some kind of energy phenomenon."

"OK," Mats said. "When do I start?" He was definitely going to step into that egg if he could ever find it again. This other stuff sounded even wilder.

"You're interested?" John asked.

"Are you kidding? Of course I am. I want to know what's inside that egg. I want to go where that little guy went last night. I want to try out this technique of yours too." Mats rubbed the scraggle of beard on his chin. "I only have one question. What is the relationship, if any, between that egg and your technique?"

John smiled. Mats could be precise when he wanted to. John often thought the big Swede pretended to be a little dumber than he really was.

"That's a good question Mats. Let's just say that" – he met Genevieve's eyes – "according to our knowledge, both are connected with, ah, a new exotic technology we don't understand very well."

"Yeah," Mats said dryly, thinking of the little alien. "And this new technology was probably developed right here in Midland. One of those new startups in the

Octagon, right?" The corners of Mats' mouth turned up slightly as if to say, 'You two still aren't coming clean.'

John smiled. "If you're successful with the technique you'll discover a lot of strange stuff. As for the transportals – the eggs – you're on your own. We've never seen one and we don't know how to use them."

The result of their discussion was that John agreed to give Mats a few lessons once a week at the Full Moon. John would go to the Full Moon on Saturday mornings and they would work in the storeroom. Mats would try to find the transportal. "For God's sake," Genevieve told Mats, "don't step into one of those things. You could be halfway across the galaxy and never find your way back."

Mats' eyes lit up. "Might be fun."

Genevieve frowned. "Your daughters might not think so." She had all the experience she wanted with negligent fathers.

Mats grinned ruefully and left.

"Another convert," John said.

Genevieve was skeptical. "We'll see whether he can do it."

For the next week it was work, work, work for John. Peter Marlowe was pressing him hard to put in more hours. On Tuesday he was in the office late at 6 p.m. Marlowe had sent him reams of data to enter and analyze. It was boring and John wanted to go home.

Peter Marlowe waddled in. John was so absorbed he didn't hear anything. "How's it going, John?" Marlowe said, sending John out of his skin.

"You scared the crap out of me!"

"Sorry old boy, nasty habit of mine. With my new physique it's easy for me to sneak up on people." John turned around. Peter Marlowe was no longer Mr. Five-by-Five. More like Mr. Five-by-Four.

Marlowe showed John his belt. "Got it on the last notch now John. Look." He removed the belt and his pants began to fall off his waist. "I've lost 105 pounds so far." The pants resembled one of those old hula hoops with some cloth attached. John couldn't believe any human being had a waist that big but he didn't laugh. He was amazed his boss had lived long enough to see his 50th birthday. Marlowe's plastic quart water bottle was in his hand.

"I'm drinking four of these every day and pissing like a ruptured water balloon. I'm starting to feel a whole lot better."

"All that because of drinking water?"

"No, of course not. I am also taking trace minerals, vitamins, amino acids, and essential fatty acids. I'm eating lots of protein. I had to get off sweets and sugar and fast food and cut way down on my carbs." He sighed. "I don't eat donuts or bagels now." Marlowe grinned. "But it's working. Mainly I drink water because I was addicted to sodas. My water bottle is a substitute for that." He stopped to take a drink. "At first I didn't think I could do it. Water tastes boring, dash it, and I've never paid any attention to nutrition at all. But the second day back from England

I drank 2½ gallons with no problem at all, and only pissed out a quart. So I was 2 gallons dehydrated. What really sold me on this program is that I only want to eat about half what I normally eat."

Marlowe looked down at his waist. "I'm shedding weight like crazy. I'm appalled that I waited so long to do something about my health."

"Better late than never boss," John said.

Marlowe walked up to the desk. "Are you almost finished?"

"Yes, in about five minutes."

"Good!" He clapped John on the back. "Things are looking up! I'm singin' in the rain today John. The world is my bloody mary."

John smiled broadly as Marlowe skipped out of the office, his great bulk swaying from side to side.

In the door he turned around. "Bright and early tomorrow John! We'll have another run for you." He waved and was gone.

That evening John sat alone with a course book in the comfortable living room at 337 Magnolia. He was pondering Genevieve's revelation that she couldn't have children, and his future with her. He had basically told her that it didn't matter. Now he wasn't so sure. Did he really want a family and children of his own?

John realized he could easily love a child that was not his "blood." They would adopt.

He slammed the book in his lap down on the end table. On Saturday he was going to the jewelry store and talk to Emile Gascard.

Friday after work Gene, Bill, and John drove up to Birmingham in Bill's car. Bill wanted to watch the play. On the phone yesterday Pavel said it would be OK. John overheard Svetlana in the background. "Is that John? Let me talk."

"Hi John! When are you guys coming up?"

"We'll be there at 7 for the start of play."

"Oh good. I want you to see me play."

"I'd like that."

"The women's competition are on tables 1 to 4."

Now, as he walked into the club, he wondered how it would turn out. As soon as she saw them Svetlana came running over. John decided that he would be friendly but not overly encouraging. Svetlana picked up on it right away. "Oh, I see you've had a talk with your girlfriend."

John grinned. "Something like that."

"I understand." Svetlana knew it wouldn't work with John, but she was physically attracted to really tall guys. She was also fascinated by the combination of John's athletic ability, his intelligence, and a certain easy-going power that seemed to emanate from him. All of the guys she knew were jocks. Her wealthy clients, most of them men, were too self-centered. "Why don't you come watch my first match? I'm up right now."

John and Bill walked over and sat on some chairs that were placed along the walls for visitors and for those who were waiting their turn to play. Gene immediately got into a match with Mike Dawson.

Svetlana was matched against a Chinese player who was ranked at 2200. As they played, he noticed Svetlana's practiced moves. She had obviously been training for a long time and reacted quickly to her opponent's shots. John wondered whether she would be interested in learning the technique. He glanced over at Bill and saw that he was all gaga. Good. Maybe Bill will fall in love or something.

Svetlana's game was like Gene's: aggressive forehand and backhand topspin. She liked to keep the pressure on and had a very good serve motion. Both John and Bill enjoyed watching her flash about the court in her shorts.

Bill was very impressed. He had lightened up a little and allowed John to show him some of the technique. Bill was here on a scouting mission, trying to figure out whether it would be worth his while to invest more time and effort in his game.

Svetlana won her first match 2 and 0.

"Did I do good?" she asked John. "Real good," John replied. "You've got a nice game."

"Who's your friend?"

"This is Bill Richardson." Bill got his long legs underneath him and stood up to shake her hand

"Hi Bill." John could tell Bill was entranced. Normally gruff and direct, he was fumbling around for words. John left them both talking and went to the tables to play.

Afterward they dropped Gene off at Sniders' sports bar to see Millie. John didn't even ask whether or how he was getting home.

On the way back John asked Bill about Svetlana.

"She's great."

John couldn't get another word out of him about her the rest of the way home.

That night as they lay reading in bed John said, "Gen, let's talk about us."

She turned to face him. "What about us?"

"I want to know what your plans are."

She slowly put down the book and turned on her side to face him. "Do you want to get married John?"

"I want to formalize our relationship. I'd love to marry but it's not a big deal if we don't. I'm asking you. Do you want to stay with me? I don't want anyone else."

She gazed at him with the most loving smile he had ever seen from her. It was answer enough. John took her in his arms...

26

O N Saturday John went to the Full Moon and showed Mats the procedures for stage one. "Practice for the rest of the week until you can do them without looking at the directions."

Mats was very excited.

"Have you found that transportal yet?" John asked.

"Nope. I've looked all over for it."

"Give me a call if you do." John had his hand on the storeroom doorknob when he remembered something Kjirsten said. "The transportal should remain in the same spot. All you have to do is look in the same place you originally found it."

After taking leave of Mats John drove over to Gascard's.

Inside, Emile Gascard told John about shape, color, clarity, and mounting. He pointed to a diamond ring with a delicate gold band and a beautiful mounting. The thin French jeweler said, '*Vraiment*, I have not lost my touch, eh?" John had to agree.

"Let's go out to dinner tonight," he said to Genevieve later that afternoon. "We'll go see 'Rashomon' at the Michigan Theater." Genevieve loved all of the Kurosawa pictures.

"Oh, that's a great idea! Where should we go to dinner?"

"I've arranged everything."

At 6:30 John dressed and came downstairs. Genevieve was still in the shower. At 7 she still had not come downstairs.

At 7:10 he heard a rustle of cloth and saw Genevieve coming slowly down the stairs, dressed in a dark blue full length satin dress with silver embroidery. Her hair was on top of her head and crowned with an intricate silver clasp. From her ears hung a set of silver earrings. She wore the pearls she had worn to the prom. Her feet were encased in a pair of dark blue heels.

"Wow, you look great."

"That's the idea!"

John drove them to Gratzi's in Old Town. Mario Gratzi, the old patriarch, himself came out to show them to a table in back. The table was covered in thick white linen. Two napkins were intricately folded at their place settings. John heard the low buzz of conversation as they walked through the crowd of diners. John seated Genevieve and they both ordered. Mario had come through with flying colors. Their waiter discretely hovered around them like a personal servant.

John knew that Genevieve understood his purpose and had dressed accordingly. During the drive to the restaurant John had felt her suppressed excitement and anticipation of what was to come. Now she was beginning to bubble over. She was radiant and couldn't stop her mouth from forming into a broad smile.

John felt it was the perfect moment. Slowly he got up from his chair and went on one knee in front of Genevieve. John felt her vibrating with excitement. Some of the other diners noticed and turned their heads to observe the scene unfolding behind them. John picked up one of her delicate hands in his. "Genevieve Walters, would you do me the honor of becoming my wife?"

Genevieve's smile now burst forth. "Yes!"

John reached into his suit coat pocket and took out a small black felt box. Silently he handed her the box and she unhinged it slowly. As the box opened she gasped. "Oh, John, it's beautiful!"

John saw her expression and was satisfied. He had genuinely surprised her. The ring's intricate mounting held a sparkling one caret diamond, representing the majority of his nest egg.

She took the ring, admired it, and handed it to him. John gently placed it upon her finger and raised the hand to his lips.

There was a clap of hands, then another, and everyone who had witnessed the proposal joined in. "Well done young man," said a distinguished older man with thick white hair. "Good job!" shouted a guy about his age. Mario himself came over and congratulated the happy couple. The old restaurateur bent over and whispered into John's ear. "That was one of the best performances I've ever seen," and gave John a wink. John nodded his head to their appreciative audience. "Thank you ladies and gentlemen, and Mario, for making this wonderful evening even more special." Mario got out his camera and took a few pictures.

"Give me your contact info and I'll send them to you."

The patrons had by now all turned about and were enjoying their dinners. John and Genevieve ate a wonderful meal and went to the movie. John could hardly keep his eyes off his fiancée the whole night, even in the darkness of the theater. Genevieve had never felt so much joy.

The next morning John joked. "We should definitely know whether we can have kids or not." He walked over to the wall by the refrigerator. "Let's mark last night on the calendar." John scratched a big X on yesterday's date.

"Silly boy." Genevieve felt a little sad. To have a child of her own...but it was not possible. John didn't seem to mind; she was deeply appreciative. He really was a wonderful man. She hoped he would make an equally wonderful husband.

That night John said, "Are you up for a little adventure? I want to go see Porniarsk."

Genevieve blanched.

"It's all right sweetheart. I want you to come with me."

"Do you think I can? I've been trained to see the barrier as something dangerous. That vortex frightens me."

"All you have to do is follow my lead. If it gets too scary we'll go back. Either both of us or none of us. We're together now forever."

She remembered last night. He would protect her. It was happening as she had hoped but never really believed. A man who was as strong and able as she, who could lead her into new territory. She didn't have to do it all by herself. It was exciting, and terrifying as well. "OK John."

"Good! I want to meet this so-called Elohim who sends crazy armadillos to wreck other people's furniture and steal their books."

Genevieve smiled. "Let's go now. We're not scheduled to check in until tomorrow, but I have a feeling Kjirsten could use our help."

They placed their chairs back to back as always and found their way to the Eyrie.

The place was crowded. Kjirsten was calling a conference.

"Barrier activity is increasing. It is clear that the Unformed Potential is now beginning to penetrate the atomic structure of matter at an increasing rate. Apparently, the Great Cycle is coming to a close faster than we anticipated! Our projections showed that we had several hundred thousand years before critical threshold. But even a tiny error in our calculations can mean thousands of years, for the Great Cycle is over 16 billion years in length.

"There have been reports from all universes of increased difficulty negotiating the universal pathways. Project leaders are assembling their best field technicians. We are coordinating a vast 'real-time' survey to determine what is best to be done. Our project is to last three sixdays. After, we will all attempt to merge in a gigantic debrief and decide what to do."

A rustle of excitement went through the group. A mass debrief!

"All of you will be given assignments, coordinated by the Barrier Project Group." She paused for emphasis. "If it gets too rough out there come in. We don't want any heroes. If you get lost we all have to go looking for you. We don't want any interruptions in the data stream. So please, think of the exalted purpose of your work and act accordingly. Remember, our team is just one of many. I'll be briefing each of you individually. Stick around until you have your assignment. Good luck!"

Genevieve whispered, "Are we still going?"

John nodded his head in the affirmative.

Genevieve was thrilled. She and her guy were going to defy the universe! She looked over at him, sitting calmly amidst the buzz of excited conversation. When they were children she sometimes thought of him as a wimp, unwilling to take risks. She realized now that his unflappableness stemmed from a deep sense of inner power and strength. She moved close and put her arms around him. John looked down and saw her looking into his eyes. On her face was a look of total trust. John was pleased and honored. It made him feel like a true man and he swelled with pride.

Kjirsten came over, her face expressionless.

"John, the Barrier Project Group wants to know what's behind the event horizon." She spoke flatly and ignored Genevieve. "Ivan confirmed the existence of a vortex but is still unable to enter it. Go and do what you can." She walked off.

"She must have changed her mind about going in," John said.

Genevieve understood her friend much better than that. "If you're ready, let's go." She knew how difficult it was for Kjirsten to make that suggestion. She also knew the Lyran's strong sense of duty.

The two earthians translated out to the barrier together. Today the pressure seemed to be particularly intense. "Rather noisy out here," Genevieve said.

"Follow me," John said. He led the way out to the barrier. John could clearly see an accretion disk of potential surrounding the event horizon.[1] He felt a massive outflow of energy pulsing and pouring out of the vortex behind the barrier. Genevieve, through John, perceived similarly. She felt something terrible and powerful and massive beyond comprehension. The vortex was the pulsing engine of creation itself, powering the entire all-that-is.

John expanded a little, enveloping her. It felt like a gentle hug. Then he *twisted* out of the familiar reference points of 3 dimensional space. Perceiving through him, Genevieve saw past the event horizon into a vast, swirling cloud of energy that emerged from and disappeared into a funnel. The funnel grew smaller and smaller until it was just a point at an infinite distance.

"How do you do that?" Genevieve asked. She now perceived the vortex as beautiful.

Genevieve was in John's hands now. She found herself reveling in the feeling of him and her together. Genevieve closed her eyes, metaphorically speaking, as John went right at the barrier. He felt her fear and backed off.

"I'm sorry, sweetheart, I just couldn't do it." Genevieve separated herself from him.

"That's OK."

"I can't believe you did this on your own."

---

[1] This is a metaphor of course. In a three-dimensional frame of reference it is the most accurate way to describe the barrier.

"Fools tread where wise men fear to go. We won't continue unless you want to."

She gathered herself. "I'm ready, but I'm going to need a little help."

John enclosed her sphere of consciousness in his. She snuggled up within him.

Now John rotated his sphere – and Genevieve's sphere within his – past the event horizon. Together they entered the vortex.

Chaos exploded all around them. It appeared to Genevieve's intellect as though they were accelerating to 'lightspeed' within a bizarre, fractal hallucination of terrifying unpredictability. The vortex was sucking them down into an infinite hole from which they could never return. Genevieve had to close down her perceptions. She felt like a kid on a rollercoaster gone out of control, just hanging on for dear life. John seemed to be enjoying the experience. Slowly she opened up, trying to perceive through him. Eventually the chaotic patterns subsided and smoothed out. They found themselves within a sort of calm sea, but still proceeding frightfully fast down the funnel. "What appears to our senses as a funnel shape is the closest 3 dimensional equivalent to something I don't understand," John told her.

To keep track of time was impossible. After several hours of subjective time they passed through the "ocean" and into a mist that grew finer and finer. Their united consciousness was expanding, merging with the mist. That's the way it seemed to Genevieve. In this place physical laws and frames of reference were suspended. The feeling of it was indescribably wonderful. "This is much farther than I went before," John said.

"Amazing, look!" John indicated the tiny point of light far below them, no closer now than it was before they entered.

"We're not making any progress," Genevieve said.

"It sure feels like we're moving towards it though, doesn't it?"

"That singularity, or whatever it is, must be impossibly far away."

"Maybe it's unreachable." John was disappointed. Genevieve said nothing, but was secretly relieved. There was no way she was going into that thing, whatever it was.

"Are you ready to go farther?" John felt like the adventurer who denies all the legends that say to enter means certain death.

"I'm ready," Genevieve replied.

The mist became finer and finer. Suddenly it disappeared and they emerged into an immense 3 dimensional bubble. John and Genevieve stood upon a circular, transparent platform approximately 100 feet in diameter. Surrounding them was an immense matrix of images. Each image occupied one spherical node in a geometric pattern that reminded John of Buckminster Fuller's Isotropic Vector Matrix. Beyond that was a background of stars, nebulae, and galaxies. They were looking into a portal to the all-that-is.

John thought of Davey. Immediately the node closest to him displayed a planet circling a bright white star, the 4th from the sun called Procyon in Galaxy 6.

Orodani! The image was displayed three dimensionally within the spherical node. "It's breathtaking," Genevieve said. John's awareness was drawn into the image just as it had done in the pages of the code book.

Genevieve spotted a brilliant, multicolored nebula. "Oh John, it's amazing. How can this place exist within the vortex?"

Before John could respond they heard a voice.

"Welcome to the control room. You made it."

Above their heads an old man with a white beard sat on a throne, holding a staff and wearing a gold crown. Golden white clouds surrounded him. John recognized his energy as identical to that of Armondo the armadillo. This must be Porniarsk himself, the Great Avatar.

Porniarsk got off his throne and strode ceremoniously toward them, in mid air, on a red carpeted pathway. "Follow me and learn the wisdom of the ages." Porniarsk stepped off the carpet onto the platform. He threw off his costume whereupon throne, crown, clouds, and red carpet disappeared.

"Hold it a second," Porniarsk said, and disappeared. John and Genevieve exchanged glances. John wanted to ask whether he was going to get his book back, and what he proposed to do about the broken laptop. But John couldn't keep his attention off the magnificence of the display surrounding him. To compare it to a planetarium would be ludicrous. Each of the nodes within the matrix was a 3 dimensional version of the images in his code book. An uncountable number of them filled the space yet all were accessible to the eye. It was an engineering miracle.

John noticed a node with a beautiful nature scene and a snow-covered mountain in the distance. Immediately the node came forward. At the speed of thought he stood upon the mountain, high above a river. John breathed in the fresh crisp air and heard the bubbling of a brook beneath his feet. The setting sun sent its golden rays over hills covered with trees painted in spectacular colors. He thought of Genevieve and she was beside him.

They soaked up the beautiful scenery for a while.

"Remember those dolphins we saw at the zoo last summer? I wonder what it would be like." Instantly Genevieve became a dolphin. She found herself in the middle of an ocean with an island nearby, cavorting with a pod of other dolphins. John followed, swimming beside her. The feel of the water on his skin was delicious. Both of them dived effortlessly under the water, twisting their powerful bodies, leaping into the air and diving into the sweet tasting water once again. "This is so much fun!" John said in dolphinese. "I wonder if real dolphins have it this good."

"Our every whim comes true immediately," Genevieve said. "I *like* it."

"OK, fun's over." Porniarsk was back, appearing as a large whale. "Go to that island over there." Soon Porniarsk, John, and Genevieve sat underneath a large tree, shading themselves from a hot yellowish-white sun.

"Let's have a bench," Porniarsk said dramatically. A bench appeared immediately.

They made themselves comfortable. "Where did you go just then?" Genevieve asked.

"I had to collect my winnings."

"Winnings?" she smirked. "This is too weird."

"Well, yeah," Porniarsk said. "I put a lot of work into those predictive algorithms! If you won the lottery you'd want to get your money wouldn't you?"

Genevieve sighed. The magic of this place was starting to wear off. Porniarsk seemed to have the personality of Dennis the Menace. She hated gamblers.

"Who are you and what is this amazing place?" John asked. "And where's my book? And, your avatar Armondo broke my laptop so you owe me a new one. Pay up!"

"Not too demanding, is he?" Porniarsk looked concerned for Genevieve. "Do you get along OK?" He was about 6 feet tall with olive skin, dark brown hair, a handlebar mustache, and big sideburns. Porniarsk was dressed like a character from the Old West.

"We came all this way to meet a little boy with a gambling disorder?" she asked John.

John laughed. "He's trying to mess with our minds."

"I don't think this guy is very bright," Genevieve said.

"Hey, that's cold." Porniarsk pouted. "I thought I was doing a good job making myself real to you."

"Is your name really Porniarsk?" John asked. "You look more like a Billy-Bob to me."

"I am Porniarsk the Great Avatar," their host said, drawing himself up. "Except I'm a lot better than a normal avatar. Avatars just sit around and look pretty and say something profound every once in a while. I can actually do things, as you'll soon see."

Porniarsk was getting under Genevieve's skin. "Why don't you just tone down the act a little."

"I guess I have to get serious, as you earthians say."

"It might help," Genevieve said.

John was relaxing. The day was cool and the fresh sea breeze smelled good as it hit his face, rustling the leaves of the trees around them.

"What do you want to know?" Porniarsk said.

"Armondo said you had a message for me," John said.

"Armondo?" He paused for a second. "Oh yeah, Armondo! He's my favorite aspect. My message is, thanks for helping me win this time. I bet that both of you would come. I was right!"

"That's what we risked our lives for?" Genevieve was fuming.

"Lighten up a little," Porniarsk said. "You made it here OK."

John and Genevieve exchanged glances.

"What is this place we're in?" John asked. "We were trying to find the singularity at the end of the vortex."

Porniarsk laughed. "Good luck with that one, bucko."

"What do you mean good luck?" John asked.

"That which you perceive as a vortex is the 3 dimensional equivalent of what you might call a feeding tube. Don't even bother trying to reach the end of it. You'll never get there."

"A feeding tube?" they both cried.

"Well yes, of course!" Porniarsk smiled smugly. He didn't elaborate.

Genevieve stomped her foot. "Tell us, you big dope."

Porniarsk backed up a step and looked at John. "Is she always like this?"

Genevieve's lips pursed and her eyes narrowed to little slits. She brought her leg back in what John recognized as one of her patented karate kicks. John placed his arm in front of her, protecting the avatar. John felt like a daddy restraining two competitive siblings.

"I don't think you two can handle it," Porniarsk said. "After all, you're just earthians."

Genevieve bristled again. "What do you mean, just earthians?" John laughed as Porniarsk placed his arms in front of him, warding her off. Clearly, the avatar rubbed his fiancée the wrong way.

"We made it this far didn't we?" she said.

The avatar apologized. "OK, OK, sorry for the insult. I'm not being a very good host."

"No you're not." Genevieve felt slightly mollified.

"You've reached the engineering section," Porniarsk said. "As Armondo told you, we are the builders-of-form. We're the engineers of the all-that-is."

"That's no answer," Genevieve said. "You sound like a politician."

Porniarsk ignored that and smiled. "From here you have instantaneous access to all of creation. Think of this place as the universe's engineering department."

"We've got something like that." John was thinking of the Eyrie.

"This is infinitely more sophisticated. Here we create the base templates and programming for everything in existence."

"Stay on the subject." Genevieve said. "We were talking about the vortex. You've got the attention span of a five-year-old."

"I do not!" Porniarsk cried. "If you want to discuss that we'll have to go back to the Control Room. That's where you first came in."

John and Genevieve nodded their assent.

"Come with me," said the avatar, leading them both back to the viewing area. All three stood once more on the clear platform inside the bubble.

"The Control Room is a multidimensional field of consciousness into which is imparted the knowledge of everything in existence," Porniarsk said. "Think of it as a multidimensional hologram that stores an infinity of data. We are in what you would call the 3 dimensional component of the engineering section." Porniarsk spoke proudly. The large, transparent viewing area resembled the cockpit of a gigantic jet fighter. Except the space was entirely empty.

"I don't see any control panels," John observed. "Or even a headset."

"That's because there are none. There are no components to this system. It is entirely thought based. It's the ultimate way to engineer anything."

"What do you mean, the 3 dimensional component?" Genevieve said.

"The All is multidimensional. Here, let me bring in a 4 dimensional component."

The space around them abruptly morphed and their bubble was now just one of a series of 3 dimensional spheres of varying sizes on the surface of a 4 dimensional sphere.

"It...it doesn't make *sense*," Genevieve said, trying to get her mind around the thing.

"Holy shit." John was amazed.

"This is what you would call a hypersphere," Porniarsk said smugly.

It was impossible for a mind used to 3 dimensions only to fully comprehend. John found it difficult to look at for more than a few seconds.

"OK! Enough!" Genevieve couldn't take it anymore.

Porniarsk chuckled and the fabric of space assumed its familiar form. Just before it did John thought he heard a chuckle echoing within it. "I shouldn't have done that but I couldn't resist."

"Are there 4 dimensional beings in 4 dimensional universes, just like us in 3 dimensions?" John asked.

Porniarsk nodded. "It's really not so different," he said mysteriously. "Just more degrees of freedom in the topological configuration space. You get used to it. It's just a different way to look at things." Porniarsk was excited now. "Let me explain. For a topological space X, the nth (ordered) configuration space of X is the set of n-tuples of pairwise distinct points in X:—"

"Oh shut up," Genevieve interrupted.

Porniarsk was indignant. "I was just getting started!"

Genevieve and John said nothing for a few minutes. John contemplated the hypersphere they had just seen. Space was obviously not an empty nothingness. Mats found that out with his transportal. But the technology needed to create a hypersphere was almost unimaginable. Maybe Porniarsk really was an avatar.

Porniarsk spoke. "Earthians, I am a very busy man. But since you enabled me to win my bet I can give you a little more time. What would you like to know?"

"You mentioned that the vortex we came through was a feeding tube," John said. "What did you mean by that?"

"I meant that there is an energy source that powers everything in the All," Porniarsk replied. "You've found the 3 dimensional component."

"Where does the energy come from?" Genevieve asked.

"That is unanswerable to your linear thinking minds," Porniarsk said. "You'd need to understand multi-dimensional topology to make any sense of it."

Genevieve snorted.

"Not even we Elohim completely understand how the system works."

"So you're not infallible!" Genevieve was pleased.

"Of course not," Porniarsk replied. "But we're damn good engineers."

"According to our friend Kjirsten, a cataclysmic cosmic event is about to unfold in our universe," Genevieve said. "Do you know anything about that and how it could possibly be prevented?"

Porniarsk chuckled. "I have been following that one, and that crowd in your Eyrie, for a long time. There's nothing you can do about it sweetheart. It's just part of a naturally occurring process in the 3 dimensional component."

Genevieve flared once more. "You seem to think it's funny! We're talking about the potential destruction of everything in the universe."

"When you've been around as long as I have sweetheart, you tend not to take things too seriously." Porniarsk was laughing now.

"I'm not your sweetheart you big jerk."

John was surprised. He'd never seen her this touchy with anyone. "Calm down, children," he said.

"Everything's going to be fine," Porniarsk replied calmly. "Take my word for it."

"I don't trust you," Genevieve said.

"Explain," John said.

"In all dynamical systems there is change and growth," the avatar replied. "Your portion of the All is almost at the end of one growth cycle and is priming itself for the next. As in all natural processes there are transitional phenomena between cycles. Don't worry. It will all work out fine."

"That's not good enough," Genevieve replied. "We have to know what's going to happen. There are uncounted trillions of lives at stake."

Porniarsk shrugged. "I am not allowed to interfere."

"You're just a clown," Genevieve said, trying to goad him into divulging more information. "You really don't know anything."

"Yes I do! I'm just not allowed to tell you because you're earthians. Your planet has a big role to play in the upcoming drama. If I told you what was going to happen it could mess things up. Just calm down sister, and relax."

Genevieve realized she wasn't going to get anything more out of Pornisrsk. "Come on John, let's get back to the Eyrie." She grabbed his hand. "We've got a lot of important work to do."

"No, wait!" Porniarsk said quickly. "I want to show you something before you go." One of the nodes from the gigantic matrix came forward onto the platform in front of them. Inside it was a brown and white cocker spaniel. A cocoon of light surrounded the dog.

"That's the most lifelike animation I've ever seen," John said. The dog wagged its tail, its eyes bright with playfulness. The animal appeared to be as solid as a real dog.

Despite her impatience Genevieve was fascinated. She reached out her hand and petted it. "Ruff!" it barked, and rubbed its head against her hand.

"I feel like I should get a stick and toss it," John joked. "What's that stuff around the dog? It looks like the inner sphere of consciousness."

"That's right," Porniarsk acknowledged. "You didn't think only human beings had them did you?"

"Never thought about it all that much." John wondered whether dogs had an outer sphere as well.

"Every living thing has one," Porniarsk said. "That's where the real engineering is."

Porniarsk pointed to the dog. "What's the difference between this cocker spaniel and a real cocker spaniel?"

"It's such a clever construct that there appears to be no difference at all." Genevieve concurred.

"Correct," Porniarsk said. "There is no difference. This dog's existence is just as valid as an earthian cocker. "

"Now wait a minute," John objected. "This is just a simulation."

Porniarsk smiled knowingly. "Remember I said that the Control Room is a multidimensional field of consciousness? Well, you can see, touch, hear, smell, and play with this dog just as you can a 'real' one. It is just as conscious as you or I."

Genevieve was shocked. "And what happens when you turn him off? He disappears back into the glop! No, I'm sorry. You can't do that with a real dog. You'll be left with a lot of blood and protoplasm. Besides, real dogs age and die. This one can't. Not only that, real animals have free will just like human beings. You can't turn them off and on like a light switch." She pointed to the cocker, who was now gamboling about on the platform. "That's just a clever animation."

"The consciousness of this dog is an extension of a universal consciousness. Just as you, John, and I are. All life, no matter what form it takes, is ultimately a focusing of consciousness. It's just like a point of light is focused with a lens from the sea of light that surrounds it." Porniarsk locked eyes with both of them. "What difference does it make what kind of physical container houses a conscious personality?"

John was utterly nonplussed. Here was an idea that should make sense given his experiences with the technique. Somehow it was just too bizarre to be believed. Or was it simply too big for his comprehension?

"I'm sorry but I'll take a rain check on that," Genevieve concluded. "Me too," John agreed.

"Rain check?" Porniarsk said.

"It means I won't reject the idea out of hand but I won't believe it either. Come back to it later," John explained.

"Give it some consideration," Porniarsk urged. "When you really understand what I've said you'll have the answer to the riddle of your Cosmic Event."

As the dog scampered about, Porniarsk left the pair alone with their thoughts. John and Genevieve sat down upon the clear circular platform, silently looking out into the vastness of the universe through the transparent walls of the bubble. The dog came up to John and curled up at his feet. John's eyes were on the constantly changing kaleidoscope of images passing around the platform.

"I don't believe it," John said.

"Me neither."

Both stole glances at the dog. The cocker wagged its tail.

After a time Porniarsk reappeared. "OK, time to finish off the lesson." The dog raised its head. It ran to the end of the platform and jumped off, vanishing into one of the nodes.

"Where did he go?" John asked.

"I don't know," Porniarsk said. "Must've found something he liked."

John and Genevieve exchanged glances. John smiled. "If we can do it so can the dog I guess."

"Pretty smart dog," Genevieve said.

"I want to know more about this control room of yours," John said.

Porniarsk smiled. "The beauty of this engineering system is that when you change the templates you get a different physical form. It makes biological engineering a breeze. Unlike earthian molecular biologists and geneticists who have to work with cellular material." Porniarsk shuddered. "I'm afraid of blood, you know. Sticky and messy."

"You design the templates that program the growth of different species?" John asked.

"That's correct," Porniarsk said proudly. "Biology follows the templates, which are all contained in the inner sphere. Just like when you build a house you need a blueprint. We have the programming for uncounted trillions of species right here in the engineering section. Every time a cocker body is made it grows off of a set of these templates. Every species has a different set. When you physically cross-breed two species you're actually altering the templates. If there is compatibility the new breed is then mirrored in the biology. That's backwards, clumsy, and slow, but it works..."

Genevieve interrupted. "Yes, but once the physical structure has been created a person is set for life. That's the role of genetics and inheritance."

"Not so fast sweetheart," Porniarsk said quickly. "Even on your primitive planet there are documented cases of so-called miracle cures, where a person inexplicably returns to health from a severe or life threatening illness. How do you think that happens? Your doctors ignore such phenomena because it doesn't fit within the agreed upon medical framework."

Genevieve spoke in mocking tones. "If you say so then of course it must be true."

"But of course!" Porniarsk agreed, puffing up.

"You embody the worst traits in a man," Genevieve shot back. "Arrogance, rudeness, and insensitivity to others."

"Yeah, but at least I get things done," Porniarsk replied. "On earth you can't even get most of 'em to take out the garbage."

Despite herself Genevieve giggled.

"Try it yourself," Porniarsk suggested to John. "All you have to do is construct a crystal clear mental image. The system will respond with the closest match."

John thought of the chittering squirrel on the tree outside his bedroom window. The space before him vibrated and the squirrel appeared before him, as lifelike as the dog.

"Cool!"

"Not bad, kid!" Porniarsk was impressed. "For an earthian."

Genevieve shot him an angry glance.

Porniarsk nodded to Genevieve. "Your turn."

Genevieve thought of Alexander, one of the neighborhood cats. Immediately Alexander – or a convincing facsimile – appeared before her in its cocoon of light. Despite her irritation with Porniarsk she was astonished.

"Why are you showing this to us?" Genevieve asked.

"To show you that there's a big wide multiverse out there and that you don't know it all." Porniarsk spoke smugly. "You call me arrogant. Earthians are not only arrogant but parochial. You think that because it doesn't exist on earth it can't happen anywhere else. Or that because it exists on earth it has to be that way everywhere."

"But you're perfect I suppose," Genevieve said with a sneer.

Porniarsk replied defensively. "I didn't say I was perfect. But I've been around a lot longer than you have."

"Just how old are you?" Genevieve asked.

"You wouldn't believe me if I told you." Porniarsk leered at her. "You should try out an older man sometime honey. We're very experienced."

Genevieve began to cock back her leg. John restrained her. "Calm down sweetheart. He's just having fun."

"A universe builder with a dirty mind," she said dismissively. "You and Armondo are perfect for each other."

"He's my aspect! What do you expect?" Porniarsk was astonished that anyone could be so obtuse.

John looked at Genevieve and shrugged. "We could look on the bright side and say that he's refreshingly different."

Genevieve smiled at that. Then she scowled and pointed her finger at Porniarsk. "I find it hard to believe this guy is an Elohim, or whatever he calls himself. He sounds more like a con man. Looks like one too."

"What were you expecting?" Porniarsk said. "I gave you the old guy with the white beard routine."

"I guess I was expecting something *grander*."

Porniarsk laughed. "What could be grander than me?"

Genevieve stuck out her tongue.

"I get it now," Porniarsk said. "You guys are looking for something like this."

He disappeared. Above them, clouds began to form in the shape of a gigantic angel with arms outstretched. The sun appeared behind the head. Light rays flowed forth in all directions. A deep sonorous voice intoned, "Welcome children. I am Porniarsk, one of the universal builders-of-form." Porniarsk appeared on the platform as an angel with beautiful wings.

"That's more like it," said Genevieve. "Better than that smart-ass anyway. Stay like that."

"I see now," Porniarsk said. "You wanted the god-thing and I just gave you a wise old man." The angel sighed. "My Old West persona has been a failure so far."

"The angel bit was very impressive," said John.

"I told you I was a good engineer," Porniarsk said. He reappeared in human form.

"That was all engineering? And the dog too? Not magic?" Genevieve shook her head. "You're destroying all my cherished myths about creation."

Porniarsk replied indignantly. "Engineering *is* magic. Any engineer will tell you that. Weren't the light rays good?"

"It's just that you're so irreverent," John said. "There's nothing sacred about all of this beauty to you. You're so flippant about it."

Porniarsk agreed. "When you get to be as old as I am you've seen it all. There's nothing to be serious about anymore. And that's good!" The avatar twirled his great moustache and then began to skip around the platform, singing a bawdy drinking song.

"He's nuts," said Genevieve to John. "I don't believe he's an avatar at all."

At the end of the platform Porniarsk suddenly stopped his dance and turned to face them. "I heard that!" He pointed his finger at Genevieve.

"You're just like the wizard of Oz," Genevieve said. "A dolt pulling a bunch of levers he doesn't even understand."

"Not so!" Porniarsk exclaimed, running toward her. "I can show you everything about both your lives from the moment of your birth. We've been following you both pretty closely ever since you mastered the protocols."

"That's not such a big deal," Genevieve replied. "We can do that at the Eyrie."

Porniarsk looked disgusted. "But we can do it a lot easier. I told you before, the control room is a window to all of existence. All I have to do is trigger "Genevieve Walters" into the system. I can find your history and your whereabouts instantly."

John had a thought that blew him away. "You mean..."

"That's right bucko. The system knows the identity and the location of every single conscious being everywhere."

For the second time in an hour John was stunned. "But...how many are there?"

"I *knew* you were going to ask that!" Porniarsk replied. "Earthians! Most demanding creatures in the universe!"

John had his mouth open but nothing came out.

"You didn't think it all happened by accident, did you?" said Porniarsk. It was clear that the avatar regarded John as slightly retarded.

"Well no, but...but..."

"But what?"

"How can you keep track of all the comings and goings? Just on earth, hundreds of people die and are born every day."

"That's right John. Fortunately I don't have to keep track. The system does it for us."

"So you didn't build it?"

Porniarsk scratched his head and looked sheepish. "No, it was already here when we arrived."

"So you *are* just a dolt," Genevieve said. She was pleased that she had gotten in the last word.

The avatar paid no heed to her. "If you could see how life grows and evolves everywhere on your planet. Not just human beings but all the myriad species and creatures on your planet. Trillions of them! It's so beautiful even I, after all these years, can't help but marvel. Then multiply that by all the planets in all of the galaxies in the universe. "

Porniarsk's eyes moistened and a tear fell to his cheek. "It's one of the real benefits working in this place." All traces of irreverence were gone now. "Life is so beautiful. Working here, it's not possible to ever be bored."

Genevieve was impressed by this speech. So was John.

"But enough of this seriousness!" Porniarsk shouted. He clapped his hands loudly and startled Genevieve. "What I want to know is, John, how did an ugly bozo like you ever find a beautiful chick like her?"

John didn't know whether to laugh or cry. Even the deities thought he was weird.

Genevieve bristled. She stood up with hands on hips. "Watch your tongue. Elohim or not, I'll put my foot in your balls."

Porniarsk backed off, a look of awe and admiration crossing his features. "Maybe it's not so bad being human after all," he mused. "Haven't explored the nuances of human sex all that much, but I can see..."

Genevieve launched herself quickly at Porniarsk but the avatar vanished.

She stomped her foot. "If I ever see that jerk again I'm going to break his neck."

"About time we were going, don't you think?" John asked.

"All right, but I need some time to cool off. I'm going back to that nice little water planet and sit down underneath that grove of trees for a while."

"I'll come with you," John said.

As they spoke, the proper node appeared like magic at the end of the platform. They both stepped in and immediately their feet hit the sand. Overhead the hot sun blazed in a light green sky. A salty sea breeze blew in their faces.

John sat down on the bench and Genevieve lay down underneath the trees a few feet away.

Porniarsk reappeared on the bench beside John, looking a little nervous. "Sorry old boy, didn't mean to offend. Rather touchy, isn't she?"

"We are with jerks like you," Genevieve said. She walked over to them. Porniarsk said nothing, watching her warily.

"There's one more thing I want to ask you before we leave," John said. "Who put the dot in the guide symbol?"

Porniarsk suddenly got up and began to sing. "Who put the dot in the dot-de-dot, who put the sham in the sham-alam-a - ding-dong..."

Genevieve kicked the avatar in the shins. "Just answer the question and stop fooling around."

Porniarsk shut up and resumed his seat.

Genevieve smiled. "There! If we ever meet again I'll know just how to handle you."

"The dot." Porniarsk's face crinkled up in thought. He fingered his great moustache. "Your planet is an ongoing experiment. That's why you have a dot all to yourself."

"An experiment?" John said.

"Can't tell you any more than that, I'm afraid."

"Why not?"

"Against the rules."

"Whose rules?"

Porniarsk smiled broadly. "If I told you I'd have to kill you."

John and Genevieve both laughed out loud. "Good one," John said.

The avatar was inordinately pleased with himself.

"Nice talking to you both." Porniarsk began to fade out.

"Hey wait a minute!" John cried. "Where's my book? You owe me for a broken laptop!"

There was no response.

John and Genevieve looked out at the beautiful water planet from their bench on the island. The air was cool and the sounds of birds filled the air. "I'd almost like to stay in this place forever," Genevieve said. "Without Porniarsk of course."

John sighed. "Yeah. No worries, and you can go anywhere and do anything you want." It reminded him a little of the universe of light.

They both felt like vacationers on their last day, knowing it was time to go home and face reality.

"How do we get back?" Genevieve finally asked.

"The same way we arrived."

She took his hand. "Let's find a nice patch of ground and prepare."

Traveling within the vortex was just as easy going "backward" as "forward."

They passed through the same gorgeous kaleidoscope of color and light as before. They reemerged abruptly into the swirling pattern of energy that marked the vortex entry point "behind" the barrier.

"Now we have to get past it," Genevieve said.

"Observe." John spoke grandly as he prepared to twist them both back through the event horizon.

"I hope you haven't picked up any bad habits from Porniarsk."

"I'd blush, but right now I can't."

"Shore up your perimeter love," John thought. "We're about to re-enter the Unformed Potential."

"Oops! Almost forgot."

John enfolded Genevieve within him. She paid careful attention to their transition past the barrier, but she only got so far and was lost. John carried her along with him. It was a virtuoso performance. Genevieve was all admiration.

There was no time left for unnecessary conversation. John and Genevieve had now reentered the Unformed Potential madness.

Soon the Eyrie floor shimmered in and felt solid beneath their feet once more.

"I feel more like I do now than when I first got here," John said.

Genevieve laughed.

They arrived in the Eyrie ahead of everyone else. One by one the barrier workers returned. The new ones introduced themselves. Kjirsten was the last to arrive.

Apparently Eyrie time was synchronous with Elohim time, for nothing seemed amiss.

"Report!" Kjirsten commanded. One by one the members gave their accounts. Fortunately the others sat in front of John and Genevieve. He had time to think. He wasn't sure whether he should give Kjirsten a precis of their adventure. Genevieve spared him the trouble. She gave a brief but accurate description of their trip.

They were all astonished and dumbfounded.

Kjirsten queried the assembled technicians. "Was anyone else able to enter the vortex?" Everyone replied in the negative. She was unwilling to fully trust observations that could not be corroborated.

"Unfortunately we still don't know anything more about what's happening." Kjirsten looked at John with a degree of disbelief.

"I guess you're right," John said. "All we have are assurances that everything will be OK."

"I don't trust Porniarsk," Genevieve said.

Kjirsten spoke to the group. "OK team, good work. Submit your written report as usual. Reassemble here at 0800."

27

MATS Karlsson's 13-year-old spoke to him one Saturday morning at breakfast. "Daaaaad, why are you spending so much time in your room? I wanted to talk to you last night."

"Sorry honey. A friend of mine showed me something really neat and I'm practicing."

"Can I practice too?"

"You wouldn't like it sweetheart. You have to sit in a chair for an hour without moving."

"Yuck. I'm going over to Patty and Karen's." She was halfway out the door when Mats shouted. "Be back by dinner OK Lena?"

"OK dad!"

He knew she'd keep her word and it made him feel good. Somehow, despite his failed marriage, the girls were turning out just fine.

Max cleaned up and drove to the Full Moon. In fifteen minutes John Frankel would arrive to teach him the second stage of the procedure. Mats paced back and forth between stacks of boxes in the crowded storeroom. He was impatient to get going. Anyone who knew him well would remark it as unusual behavior.

He loved the store and the kids but they did tie him down a bit. Mats Karlsson had a romantic, adventurous streak that needed an outlet. John's stories of adventuring sounded wild. The rational side of Mats didn't really believe it was possible to turn yourself into a rocket and blast off to other planets. But you could have a lot of fun with Virtual Reality games sitting in your chair. Maybe it was something like that.

For the past week Mats had brought up the egg-shaped space in his mind, probing it for more information. When that little fellow entered the egg Mats saw the landscape of another planet. It was an ocean world with strange looking vegetation and beautiful ships upon calm seas. A great orange-colored sun hung just over the horizon in a pale rose sky. Straight overhead a series of multicolored moons shone their pale light upon the water. The world had a different *feel* to it, and called to him strongly. In Mats' veins coursed the blood of ancient explorers, sea-going adventurers who had found the new world long before Columbus. Oh, to walk upon that shore! To meet the people who lived there! His heart sang with the lure of that beautiful place.

Several weeks of searching the back of the store had not revealed the egg. According to what John said, the transportals always remained fixed in position. Either someone turned the damned thing off or you needed a special gizmo to see it.

Mats had practiced stage one for two hours every day. He was chomping at the bit for the next part of the recipe. After each of the sessions he felt incredibly serene and powerful. His muscular body felt as light as a feather.

When John arrived Mats was ready and eager. "C'mon boy, show me that next level."

John cautioned Mats. "The technique up to the middle of stage two can be taught. That will get you poised to make the great leap. But only you can take the final step." John explained to a fidgety Mats in detail about the sphere of consciousness and the theory of vibration that had led to his experiences. "If you don't understand this nothing can happen."

After that Mats was all attention. To him, John was a likeable Nutty Professor. Yet he had a certainty and assurance that fascinated him.

John gave his friend a printout and went over the technique thoroughly. He explained how the procedures activated the two spheres of consciousness. Mats' eyes were wide with interest.

"When you successfully complete the second stage your merkaba will be much more real to you than the physical universe around you. It will be primed, awaiting full activation in stages three and four. It's totally cool Mats. You feel like you are in a powerful vehicle of energy and that you can do anything. When you get it you'll know it."

Mats let out his breath slowly. This sounded really wild, but John had a way of explaining stuff that made sense to him. His body hummed with excitement. Mats had learned to trust his gut feelings.

John paused. "Do you understand Mats?"

"Yeah, I think so."

"Good. It's all written down on the printouts I gave you. If you can make stage two I'll teach you the next two stages later. A word of warning: don't try to go past this point right now. I know you're hot to get to that world you saw in the egg, but

I don't want you to do a blue jaunt. That's when you haven't completely enabled your sphere and aligned yourself to the target. You could get lost forever and God knows what will become of you." Or you could go insane. John didn't express this thought.

Mats gulped. "This is serious stuff you're talking about John."

"Yes Mats, it is. I'm responsible now if anything happens to you."

Mats took a couple of deep breaths. "I understand John. I want to continue."

"OK then. Let's lighten up and get into it. We'll drill the procedures until you can do them without referring to the printout."

For the next hour John carefully guided Mats. By the end of their session he was able to successfully complete a practice run.

Mats sat in his chair feeling an electrical energy flowing through every part of him. "I didn't experience any spheres or anything like that, but I feel pretty good. If I never got past this point it would be worth the effort."

"That's because you have not yet mastered the mental protocols for the stage," John said. "The breathing will take you only so far. Combined with the simpler merkaba protocols it will get you into the zone. I bet a lot of people can do that. You must master the advanced protocols in order to become aware of your sphere of consciousness and activate it."

"OK John."

John was pleased. The instruction had gone very well. Maybe he had a future as a teacher.

Suddenly Mats exploded. "Odin's spear! How come nobody teaches this stuff in school?"

John guffawed. "You're joking right?"

"Well, they should. I feel smarter."

John smiled. "With this work practice doesn't make perfect. The harder you work at it the more it will elude you. There are no time limits on this thing. Just go easy and relax."

"So it's not like lifting."

John laughed. "Great reverse analogy Mats. In this stage you must let go completely. You have to just allow it to happen. You don't *do* anything. It's about *being*."

John thought of something. "I've found that if I lift beforehand, it helps. For me, feeling a little tired relaxes me even more."

Mats practiced the whole week but got nowhere. He called John on Friday and told him not to bother with the lesson tomorrow. "I understand what you mean now. I have to get it on my own. By Gungnir, it's harder than I thought."

John was sympathetic. "I have an advantage. I'm naturally mild mannered. The type A personalities will have a great deal of difficulty. They won't get it at all. You're a mixture of both, Mats. Emphasize your receptive side not your action side."

For the next month Mats did exactly that. He spent less time at the store and more time with his girls, soaking himself in feminine energy. He continued his weightlifting. Mats knew that his stocky body would quickly go to fat otherwise.

One Friday night Mats was in his room, practicing. After a while the feeling of time disappeared and a sensation of well being penetrated every cell of his body.

Then something astonishing happened. His body became gradually surrounded by a spherical, soft, golden-white light. It tingled deliciously and felt like a fresh spring breeze. Mats was so excited he jumped out of his chair.

Mats shouted to the walls of his bedroom. "Great Yggdrasill, I feel like a kid again!"

He sat back in the chair and tried once more.

Again he allowed his inner sphere to energize, but he got so excited he lost it again. "How come nobody ever told me I had one of these things?" It appeared as a faint outline to his inner sight at first, then grew more and more visible. A golden-white sphere of light surrounded his body. Inside the sphere impossibly tiny but brilliantly colored little threads of energy vibrated. Mats was so juiced he had to go outside for a walk in the brisk late October air.

Why don't I notice this sphere of light all the time? Mats placed one foot in front of the other as he stomped quickly down the sidewalk. The thing was totally invisible unless you knew how to activate it using John's crazy technique. Or maybe he was going crazy. Mats felt energized, powerful, and confident. That was just the opposite of crazy.

Mats walked until he felt a little calmer. He went back in the house and tried again, this time very slowly and deliberately.

The sphere of light made its appearance around him. He felt suspended, floating within something that felt really, really good. This is lot better than drinking! Mats was now in his own little universe. He no longer felt his body. The radius of Mats' awareness of self slowly expanded. This process is as natural as pissing, Mats thought. Why hadn't anyone discovered it before? It's so simple even a monkey could do it.

Then it happened.

In the most awesome moment ever in Mats' life, he became aware of a beautiful multicolored light almost thirty feet out from his body. He felt charged up and filled with power. Mats envisioned himself as a superhero, marching off to save the world from evil scumbags...

Someone was shaking him. Lena, Christina, and Julia were staring at him.

"Dad, could you tell us just what you were doing?" Julia said.

"Yeah. We're worried about you." Cristina spoke anxiously. "We couldn't wake you up."

"Huh?"

Lena, his youngest, explained. "Dad, you were like a statue. You were, like, *glowing.* Cris came in 10 minutes ago to ask you a question. She shook you as hard as she could but you wouldn't respond. We were going to call 911 but Maggie told us not to."

Maggie Smith, along with Don Breckenridge, ran the Full Moon with Mats. Maggie was an older woman who lived down the block. She often came over to keep Franscesca, his housekeeper, company during the evenings when Mats minded the store.

Mats had told Maggie a little of what he was doing. Thank God for her good judgment. The paramedics might have thought he was an epileptic or had gone catatonic or something. He probably would have wound up in the hospital.

"OK gang, here's the deal," Mats said. He told them about the procedure and what he was trying to accomplish in words they could understand. "So it's just like a meditation. It makes me feel wonderful when I do it. Sometimes I lose track of time. Don't worry."

"We're mad because you didn't tell us," Julia said. "We tell you everything."

The three girls, sitting on his bed, were staring at him intently with their mouths set firmly.

His mouth opened to deny it but he realized his daughters were right.

"I'm sorry girls," Mats said. "You're absolutely right. I apologize and I promise it won't happen again."

They brightened. "OK dad," Lena said. They joined hands and cried, "All for one and one for all!" That was the family motto.

At his next lesson Mats described what happened. John was amazed at Mats' rapid progress.

"You just made stage two. You were real close to the critical point."

Mats' eyes went wide. "I felt so excited I couldn't keep it together."

"That sounds right," John said, grinning. "Here's a few tricks I've learned that will help you out. I've also printed out the instructions for the final two stages."

John handed him four typed, single spaced pages. "The sole purpose of the final stages is to allow you to stabilize your merkaba without going out of control." John explained that the last two stages consisted entirely of advanced merkaba protocols. "The advanced protocols, if you do them correctly, define and enable the larger sphere. They allow the practitioner to access the universal pathways."

Mats took them reverently. "I used to read fantasy books about this sort of stuff. I had no idea it was real."

"It's real all right. At least I think it is. There's still a part of me that still isn't sure it's not a big hallucination. I'm glad you're interested Mats. I'm using you as a test subject. If it works for you I'll have even more confirmation."

"I'm happy to be your guinea pig. I want to go to that world I saw in the egg real bad." Mats had a thought.

"Aren't you worried about people misusing this? If this stuff got into the wrong hands, Odin only knows what mischief they could create."

John laughed.

"What's so funny?" Mats said.

"I just realized that can't ever happen. It's cool. The technique naturally connects you to the universal medium. When you do, you feel totally positive. The bad apples can't possibly be successful. To be successful you have to give up your badness."

John explained about Gary and the codebook. "He stole the book but gave it back. Gary told me that those who learned the technique didn't want to work with them anymore."

"Good," Mats said. "I don't like that guy."

John answered a few more of Mats' questions and was off.

28

MATS spent the next several weeks applying John's instructions, without complete success. His sphere was so big he couldn't control it.

Julia, Cris, and Lena were curious. Some of his customers noticed a subtle difference in his appearance and commented on it. Maggie noticed too.

"What is this thing you're doing Mats?" she asked him, full of curiosity. "You look younger. If it's not illegal I want some too."

Mats laughed. "It's a kind of meditation, but directed." Maggie seemed interested. "Tell you what sweetheart. If John says it's OK I'll give you a couple of lessons." Mats didn't tell Maggie or the girls about the planet he had seen in the egg. He had no intention of going any further with them than the end of the first stage.

John gave him one last lesson. "You're getting close Mats. If you can figure out how to define and control your sphere of consciousness you'll shimmer out and hit the zone of chaos." John explained how to negotiate the zone. "After you break through the zone of chaos you'll feel like you're suspended in a sea of infinite potential. To me it looks like a golden-white mist or fog. You'll see snatches of reality all around you, tantalizing places to explore." John paused for emphasis. "Always have a precise destination in your mind and in your heart before you begin the technique. You have to *feel* it. It's the feeling that vibrationally orients you to the destination."

Oh, that's no problem, Mats thought. No problem at all.

One Friday night a few weeks later Mats was home alone. The two older girls were at a slumber party, and Lena was with Francesca for the night. Girl stuff. Mats didn't even ask the girls if any boys would be there. He hoped they'd do the right thing.

Thank God for Francesca. He could just see himself explaining the female menstrual cycle to his youngest. Mats groaned at the memory of his attempt to do just that with Julia three years ago. Francesca had rescued him just in the nick of time. As he fled the room Mats heard both of them laughing. "He's trying at least," Francesca said.

Mats let her handle all that stuff now.

Mats went into the living room and closed the blinds. He didn't want any of the neighbors to see him disappear into thin air!

Mats got comfortable on the couch. He went through the technique once more. He had practiced it hundreds of times. It got you to look a slightly differ-ent way at yourself. When you did that, you were able to see and feel something that had always been there from the moment of birth. Something grand and won-derful, a fullness of being and a connection to something vast and beautiful. The best thing was, it didn't make you conceited or big-headed. Not like some of the academics in the Full Moon who liked to look down their noses at people. All this he thought in passing as he slowly charged up his merkaba.

This time Mats was successful.

He, Mats Karlsson, bookstore owner, weightlifter, beer drinker, and family man, was enlightened!

Mats let himself bask in the feeling for a while, knowing that if he continued he'd probably lose it again. He felt poised, at the brink of something big.

Within him the feeling of his destination was strong, for his Viking blood literally sang with it. It was the planet he had seen in the egg. The deep blue-green ocean, the sailing vessels upon it...Mats noticed his living room begin to shimmer.

He didn't panic this time, but kept the image he had seen in the 'egg' in the forefront of his mind and heart...a ship sailed close to shore, but such a ship as he had never seen. Her hull was made of some lightweight material, and the color! An azure blue with a filigreed prow. The beautiful blue permeated the substance, which resembled a transparent plastic. The color changed slightly in the light from the rising orange sun as the ship powered silently along on the calm water. Suddenly, the room unfocused. For a brief instant Mats was suspended in something bizarre. The zone of chaos! Odin's spear, a hallucination...but John had taught him well and he made it through. The destination, fuzzy at first, came into focus. The deck of the ship was at eye level. Mats glanced down at the water at least twenty feet below. He fell into the ocean with a great splash.

Mats didn't have time to think. He was ten feet underwater and still sinking. His butt and his feet hurt like hell from the impact. Getting his legs underneath him, Mats began to propel himself upward. It was easier than on earth but the breath had been knocked from him as he hit the water. Hurry...his lungs ached and in another second he would have to fill them...he finally broke the surface and gasped for breath. Mats watched the stern of the ship pass slowly in front of him.

"Hey! Give me a hand!" There was no answer.

Mats concluded that the vessel was unoccupied. It passed, majestic, along the clear calm water. The ship was about thirty feet long and ten feet wide. Prow and stern rose from the water and curled upward. The bow was in the shape of a mermaid and the stern was a dragon's head. She was a beautiful ship.

The buoyant water enabled Mats to float easily. He brought a finger to his lips and tasted. It was fresh, almost sweet, and scented. He looked down and almost had a heart attack. Through the water, miles deep, huge floating cities were clearly visible. There was no diminution of vision here through the water. He could see to the bottom of this impossibly deep sea just as easily as he could see the hand in front of his face. Decorated spires rose from one of the floating cities.

Mats turned to look toward shore. Fortunately land was barely a quarter mile away. Mats got on his back and began to stroke. There were no waves upon this vast ocean; the water was and serene as far as he could see. And so was the air. No movement! Any planet with an atmosphere should have some motion of the air; something about coriolis forces from the planet's rotation inducing atmospheric movement. His muscles warmed to the task and his breathing became regular. He reached land and stood upon solid ground again, facing the great sea. The shore sloped gradually outward for a hundred yards then fell off steeply, as if the ocean bed had been scooped out with a gigantic backhoe.

Mats saw five moons in a purplish-black sky. The largest of them appeared verdant, with patches of green and blue. The other four were each a different color. They were lined up in a row across the sky.

Mats looked out over the water at the rising sun. He sat down upon the shore with his feet in the cool water. A gigantic orange orb slowly inched its way up over the horizon. It eventually filled a fifth of the sky and illuminated the landscape with a soft but very pleasant pink-peach glow.

Now he turned his attention to the land, which was hilly. The ground rose almost immediately from the shoreline, and was covered with a soft, brightly colored moss.

No trees were visible. The place is gorgeous, Mats thought. As the sun rose a soft fragrant breeze touched his face. The moss reacted to the light, turning different colors and emitting a peculiar but pleasant fragrance. The air temperature was a comfortable 70 degrees or so. He had no difficulty breathing the air.

This planet felt different than earth. Mats Karlsson now understood that he stood upon the surface of another world. He didn't have a clue where he was in relation to earth, or how to get back.

Nevertheless, the urge to explore was strong. Mats set about to find a likely destination. Burrowed into the sides of the hills that rose gradually from the shore were rounded openings. Far off to his right a gigantic spire rose over the hilly landscape. Along the shore in the distance a few structures were visible. Mats made a note to investigate later, when he had some transportation. The visibility here was so good that it was not possible to determine whether the constructions were ten miles away, or a hundred.

Out of the corner of his eye Mats noticed a roiling of the air a few hundred yards to his left. He quickly retreated to the water and immersed himself, but realized it was futile. It was possible to see everything through the water just as clearly as through the air. If he could see them they could see him. Nevertheless, he stayed submerged.

A creature in a hooded, gold-colored robe emerged from an egg-shaped space. Mats saw in the roiling clouds that the little fellow was coming from the Full Moon!

The little creature carried something under one arm and scurried up the hill. It moved with the peculiar gliding motion he'd noticed that time in his store a decade ago. Was this the same guy?

Mats kept his eye on the location of the churning egg-shaped space, which looked exactly like the one he'd seen in the bookstore. All thoughts of exploration were banished for the moment. Mats got out of the water and walked purposefully toward the area, never breaking his concentration. The gravity was noticeably lighter here but the horizon was much further away. This planet must be much larger than earth. So the gravity should be greater, not less.

"You're a scientific idiot!" he said to himself. "Keep your eyes on that egg."

Mats couldn't resist testing his vertical leap. Keeping his attention on the egg (which was now returning to normal), he jumped up in the air. Wow, almost three feet! Not bad for a hulking six footer who weighed almost 240 on earth.

Mats reached the spot. It was a foot or so off the ground and about five feet in diameter, just like the one in the stacks. The area still shimmered ever so faintly. If you weren't looking for it, you'd never notice. Mats knew he was going to step into it, no matter how stupid it was. He was already lost in space anyway.

Mats entered the bubble but it didn't fit him. He stuck out.

He tried to activate it but nothing happened. Disgusted, he stepped out. Mats wanted to kick the damn thing. There was nothing to hit except a bunch of air.

The portal activated again. The space morphed and within it, just before he threw himself onto the ground, another of the creatures stepped out. It came forth from a red desert with swirling sand whipped by a strong wind. A few grains stung his face. Mats did not move a muscle. The little guy carried a bundle and without a backwards glance walked up over the same hill as had his hooded counterpart not half an hour before. Mats lay trembling on the ground, afraid of discovery. The creature seemed intent on getting somewhere fast.

What was this, a convention? He was shaking like a leaf and a little bit ashamed of himself. These portal-using dwarves were no threat to him.

Suddenly he thought of his girls.

"How long have I been here? I just promised them to be a good boy and now I'm fucking up again!"

Mats took one last look around this beautiful place. The light from the great orange sun somewhat obscured his view of the five moons now. The sky had gone from black to a bluish-orange, reflecting back onto the water.

He walked off the beach behind a small hillock and sat on a patch of green moss. The moss appeared to be one gigantic organism. When he moved over it, ripples of color reflected over the ground like a pebble dropped into a pool of water.

Mats saw the egg faintly outlined in the soft orange luminance of morning. On a hunch he walked back to the beach. Hunching over, he stepped into the dimly shimmering bubble with the Full Moon in mind. The space expanded now to encompass him and he stood up. The ocean and beach faded. Mats felt suspended. Then it was dark. Mats didn't know where he was until he heard a voice.

"OK, back in the stacks! Lights out!" It was Don, locking up.

Mats thought quickly. Let's see, he had started his adventure around eleven, which was closing time. But here it was closing again. He'd been gone over 24 hours! By the gods of Asgard, he had really messed up this time. The girls were probably frantic. Mats envisioned newspaper headlines screaming frantically about the missing owner of the famous Full Moon bookstore.

Mats heard footsteps.

Damn! It was Don's habit to walk the stacks before closing to ensure no stragglers were locked in. Mats wanted to get home quick and pretend nothing out of the ordinary had happened. He could tell everybody he fell asleep in the attic or something. Now he had to find a hiding place quick. From Don's movements he had less than a minute. But if he moved his big body would surely make a sound back here in this quiet solitude.

Then he got an inspiration: "Walk back through the portal."

Mats calmed down. It wouldn't do him any good to act like a schoolboy caught smoking in the bathroom. He scrunched down and stepped into the portal, thinking of that beautiful exotic planet and the beach. The feeling of suspension in time, then the beach came back into focus.

Well, problem solved. He'd just wait around here for half an hour, then return through the portal. Fortunately he always carried the store keys in his pocket in case of emergencies.

Mats went down to the shore and lay down. He felt the warmth of this sun, a gentle comforting heat that did not burn his skin or make him sweat. Mats left plenty of time for Don to complete his rounds and leave. Then he stepped back into the portal. Mats always had a destination in mind, just as John told him. So far it was working. This kind of travel was awesome!

The smell of the stacks hit his nostrils. He heard footsteps and saw a light come on, illuminating him. Don turned the corner and stared at him. "Mats? What are you doing here?"

"Uh...looking for a book I left back here."

Don's puzzlement showed on his face. "I didn't see you come in."

Mats smiled. "Oh, I snuck in when you weren't looking. You know how silent and graceful I can be."

Don laughed.

Mats sighed with relief. His sense of humor had gotten him out of more than one jam.

"OK Mats, I'm closing up. You know the drill."

Don looked behind him. "What's that?"

"What's what?" Mats said innocently.

"There's something funny about the air behind you."

"I don't see anything." But he did see something. A faint shimmering.

The other man shook his head. "I'm tired I guess." Don turned but Mats stopped him with a hand on his arm.

"Don," Mats said.

"Yeah?"

"Uh, what day is it today?"

Don stepped in and sniffed. "You haven't been drinking have you?"

Mats grinned. "Not yet."

"It's Friday of course."

"Friday, 11pm?"

"Of course Mats! You know we always close on time. Been doing it for ten years."

Mats tried not to let the profound relief he felt show in his face. "Uh, right. Follow me out then."

They walked to the parking lot in the cold. By force of habit Mats had done so as well, but he had no coat.

"Where's your car?" Don asked.

Mats felt stupid. "Uh, I walked." Fortunately his thick flannel shirt would protect him on this calm night. Mats turned to go. Don said, "For chrissakes, let me drop you off."

Don knew Mats never walked anywhere if he could help it. Mats liked walking about as much as a cat liked a bath.

"Curiouser and curiouser," Don said.

"What's that supposed to mean?"

"It's from Alice in Wonderland," Don said. "You know, when she starts to grow."

"I know where it's from."

"If you want a ride, hop in."

Mats hopped.

On the way Don could see that Mats was preoccupied, so he kept his mouth shut. Don couldn't get over the feeling that something extraordinary had happened to his boss. The boss' clothing had a peculiar smell. Not perfume, not sweat, but something unidentifiable. His body had a faint halo of light around it.

Don pulled in to Mats' driveway. "Thanks for the ride."

"Maybe you'll tell me about it some day," Don said.

Mats grunted, walked to the side door, and let himself in.

Mats went to the refrigerator and got a beer. He turned on his mobile and saw the date:

Friday, October 29th, 11:36 pm. How could that be? Only half an hour? He'd have to ask John.

Mats' head was spinning. He felt exhilarated and exhausted at the same time. He finished his beer and went upstairs, peeled off his clothes, took a shower, and went to bed.

As Mats drifted off to sleep something nagged at him. If the portal he went through led directly to his store, what were those two creatures carrying?

29

A t the dinner table just before the Christmas holidays, the topic of conversation shifted to Alicia and her imminent delivery. Michael Walters had taken her to the hospital that morning and Rachel eagerly anticipated good news. Robert looked forward to a promised Cuban cigar. Rachel had gotten him to agree to smoke it downstairs.

Genevieve's phone rang. She listened for a few moments. "Yes, yes, oh certainly. I'll be there right away." She looked at the dinner party. "I gotta go see dad. Alicia's having trouble."

"We'll come with," said Rachel.

"No. He's having enough trouble. Just me. He's...he says he has something very important to tell me, for my ears only."

"What are we supposed to do then?" Robert said. "I don't want to sit around here and not know what's going on. Let us go to the hospital with you. We'll stay in the lobby."

"Oh all right," Genevieve reluctantly agreed.

At the hospital Genevieve left them all in the waiting room, promising to keep them informed of developments. She walked down the hall to one of the delivery rooms. Her father stood outside the door, looking like warmed over death.

"Genevieve! Thank God you're here."

"What's happening? We're all scared to death. Is Alicia all right?"

"No she isn't. The baby is stuck and they can't do a Caesarian. It's all in God's hands now."

"Oh my God. You mean she might die?"

"They might both go. My God, Genevieve, it was just supposed to be a simple delivery...everything looked fine until an hour ago. They've got two doctors in there right now, plus one of the local midwives."

"Can we do anything?"

"Pray. Under no circumstances are we allowed to enter that room." He paced back and forth, wringing his hands. "I'm going out of my mind."

Genevieve put her arms around her father, who looked ready to have a breakdown.

She placed both her hands on his big head, which had begun to rock spasmodically from side to side. "Father!" she said in a commanding tone of voice, trying to get his attention. His eyes were glazing over. "Father!" she said again.

She slapped him hard on the cheek.

"Genevieve! You're here!"

"Yes dad, I'm here." She led him to a little bench against the wall.

"We're going to sit down and you're going to get yourself together."

"I'm sorry. I just don't know what to do. I feel so helpless."

"Feeling bad isn't going to make Alicia any better." She looked him straight in the eyes. "Now tell me what it is."

Michael Walters' eyes widened, then he hung his head. "My wife is dying and all I can think of is my personal problems." He shuddered. "My life is a waste. A fucking waste." He brought his head up and looked at Genevieve. She had never seen so much agony and grief in anyone's eyes.

"Tell me," she said. He had to get it out or something bad was going to happen. The man was on the brink of a physical collapse.

"I can't stand the lies anymore," he said. "Genevieve, it's time to tell you about your mother and myself, and how you came into this world. I know from John that you already know. But I must tell you myself."

"I've known all about it for years. The genetic engineering of me, all that stuff."

"Who told you?" Michael Walters let out his breath, explosively. "We were all sworn to secrecy on that project. It was our very lives at stake."

"Let's just say that several years ago one of the team members felt the same way as you do now. I've known the whole story since I was thirteen."

"You know that I am your biological father and Debra O'Neill is your biological mother, and that you weren't adopted?"

She nodded again.

"I'll understand if you hate me," Michael Walters said despondently.

"If I hated you I wouldn't be here."

He searched her eyes. "I've always loved you, you know. I've just never been able to tell you."

"I've never been so great in that department myself."

Michael Walters desperately needed to unburden himself to his daughter. "You were born in the lab, Genevieve. We couldn't risk a normal birth at a hospital in case something went...wrong. Debra was on the team, a brilliant researcher. She volunteered to carry the fertilized egg. We used my sperm. Debra came home to nurse you but she felt you weren't really hers, even though she carried you to term. There were so many experiments done with that...evil technology even while you were growing in the womb. Debra felt like a lab animal. For the first year of your life you were in the lab undergoing tests more than you were home. Debra couldn't take it anymore. So she left."

He looked at her much more calmly. "Debra isn't my wife, but I loved her more than anyone else in the world. I tried to make it work but the situation was out of my control. One day I came home from the lab and there was a long letter. Pages and pages, handwritten. She asked me not to look her up, that it was over between us and could never be salvaged. I have honored her request even though not a day goes by when I don't wonder what happened to her."

Genevieve said nothing. Her father began to breathe with difficulty. His face was flushed. It was obvious to her that he was fighting with something else inside.

"The remarkable thing is, our experiment worked. What I still don't get is how we did it." His eyes softened.

"You're very beautiful. I just can't get over the idea that I was interfering in the creation of life. That is something only God should have control over."

Now his eyes were intense.

"But we do have control over it Genevieve. You are the result. And by God, you're wonderful. The experiments worked to perfection! How could a bunch of bumbling fools have been responsible for the creation of something so perfect?"

His eyes were searching hers for an answer she could not give.

"This is the question that beats in my brain every time I look at you. How can we have created something even better than God?"

Genevieve was surprised. Her father had never shown any religious tendencies. His scientific training seemed to preclude such questions. She didn't know what to say.

Michael Walters stared at his daughter with admiration and awe. "You *are* better. You're brilliant, you don't get sick, and you're physically attractive beyond the norm." He placed his big hands on her shoulders. "I'm an educated man, but I do not understand how and why we were allowed to interfere in the process of the creation of life itself!" His eyes blazed.

Genevieve said nothing. She just looked at him with compassion. Michael Walters was a difficult man and had been no parent at all to her. But he was still her father.

He softened again and his eyes welled with tears. Genevieve's did too.

"Oh dad, I don't know. I just know I'm glad to be alive and I'm grateful for whatever you did."

"You are?" His eyes were searching hers intently.

"Yes. When I first found out from Hazel Morningside, I wanted to kick your teeth in. I have always felt different. The other kids treated me like a freak. If it wasn't for John and Sensei Matsumoto I probably would have gone insane. Thank God John accepts the fact that I can never have children."

Yes, Michael Walters thought, that was a strict condition placed upon their work. It was appalling. To think he had accepted it without a moment's thought! And Matsumoto, what had he to do with Genevieve other than her martial arts lessons? His face flushed. He knew nothing about his daughter. It shamed him.

That wasn't why he felt so bad. Even now, all he could think about were his own needs.

Genevieve smiled to ease the tension. She had not intended to say that, it had just come out. She had promised herself that she would never again hide her feelings from her father. John had taught her that. She had discovered it was a lot easier to live that way. She placed her hands on his head and looked deeply into his eyes.

"Whatever was done I'm now happy with it. Besides, what's not to like? As you said, I never get sick, I'm intelligent, and I have a man who loves me more than I ever thought possible. It's OK."

"You haven't answered my question!"

Genevieve smiled. Her father was like a little child asking his mother about the mysteries of life.

"I don't know dad." She paused for a moment, thinking. "Each one of us must be a little piece of God. We must all be sanctioned by God to do anything we like."

"Not good enough...daughter." He pointed to the delivery room. "Is this sanctioned as well? The pointless death of a wonderful woman and the new life inside her? The answer to that question has consumed the last twelve years of my life, even after I met Alicia. I am utterly spent, weary beyond comprehension. I give up." He sighed, a long exhale that seemed to carry a great burden along with it.

"That is why I have utterly ignored you. Every time I looked at you I felt unclean, an abomination in the eyes of God."

He paused, his face again a mask of anguish. Genevieve couldn't believe that any human being could carry so much negative emotion inside. For the first time she realized that his calm detached exterior was just a mask. A very tightly held mask that covered a roiling sea of turbulence. Now it was leaking out.

"I have been a terrible father. In fact I have been no father at all. I abandoned you, the one who needed me the most. I have failed to love you as a father should, even as one human being to another."

Michael Walters collapsed into spasms of sobbing. An intern came running over but Genevieve waved him off. She just let him cry it out.

Finally, after several minutes, he looked up.

"If you can forgive me I will be the father to you that I have always wanted to be, but never let myself be." In his eyes she saw a look of determination.

"I have been a fool. I had a wonderful daughter, a piece of myself that I could have enjoyed all these years. I swear that from now on I will never ignore my heart again. I promise to love you, my daughter, with all of my being."

Michael Walters spoke now with a conviction that melted Genevieve's heart. Like the sun shining through a rainstorm, a rainbow of light from his inner being shone forth.

"I'm looking forward to that. I have been just as guilty as you. I never bothered to be the daughter you needed. I never was interested in you either. We were a perfect match. Now we can change all that."

She held out her hand. "Deal?"

He took her hand in his tenderly. "Deal."

He hauled her to her feet and gave her a great bear hug.

"Oh!" she said.

He held her at arms length. "I see before me the beautiful person who is my daughter. The past is no more, I have transcended it. I love you."

"I love you too Dad."

He hugged her again.

Rachel, Robert, and John came running down the hall. "Any news?" Rachel said anxiously.

Genevieve said, "We've been cleaning up the past and are ready for a new beginning."

Michael's face fell as he was reminded of his wife and child. "I don't know. We aren't allowed to go in."

"Then we'll wait out here together," Robert said. He sat on his heels against the wall. "All night if necessary." They all nodded.

Two hours later the door opened. The doctor spoke wearily. "I think we're in the clear now. Mrs. Sarane here worked a miracle." Michael tried to rush inside to see his wife but was blocked from entering. "You can't go in, she's still in labor."

"She's my *wife*," Michael said angrily. The doctor eased him out the door. "She's unbelievably tired right now, and still in pain. Please. There's nothing you can do here except make things worse. Go home. As soon as we have news we'll call."

"I'm not leaving," Michael said fiercely.

"All right. But the rest of you, please go home."

Robert, Rachel, Genevieve, and John left reluctantly.

At 4 in the morning they were still up, an old movie in the player that no one was paying any attention to.

Genevieve's mobile rang. "Yes?"

"It's a girl. Eight pounds, five ounces. They're both going to make it. She'll have to stay in the hospital for a few days though." Michael Walters sounded like a man who had lost everything, then regained it at the last second.

"Thank God," Genevieve said. She gave the thumbs up signal. Rachel burst into tears. Robert heaved a great sigh of relief.

They all trooped upstairs and fell into bed.

30

Two days later Alicia left the hospital. The following Saturday Michael Walters had a party to show off his new baby and distribute some Cuban cigars. Alicia felt very tired but sat comfortably in one of the big armchairs with the baby, close to the fire.

John had never seen his mentor look so happy. He cooed over his little one continually, except when the men went downstairs to smoke.

John felt that the expensive cigar was wasted on him, but he did his bit. Michael invited some of his colleagues from the university and a dozen or so actually showed up. John was surprised. He didn't think the man had any friends at all. As John listened to the conversation he could see that Dr. Walters was well respected.

One of the men, Fred Haddick, came over to John.

"So this is the young man we've been hearing about." Mr. Haddick had the crinkly skin of an old man but a full head of white hair. He carried himself very upright, appearing to be in the peak of health.

John made small talk. "All of it good I hope."

"Actually yes. I'm a retired professor in the astronomy department. Peter Marlowe has given quite an account of your skills at data analysis and computing algorithms."

"It's my strong suit." As they talked John had the feeling the man was leading up to something. Finally Haddick said, "You don't happen to know Dalton Jones, do you?"

"Yes. I've met him a time or two. I'm acquainted with his son Trevor."

Fred Haddick seemed uninterested in Trevor. "Uh, there are rumors going around about some interesting article in Mr. Jones' possession."

John didn't know what to think of that. He had brought the book to Dalton Jones over five years ago.

"Well sir, I feel you're leading up to something here. I'm willing to be honest with you if you're honest with me. What is your purpose for asking?"

John turned up his bullshit sensor to max and looked Mr. Haddick straight in the eyes, as Genevieve had so often done with him.

"Never mind," Haddick said, and walked away.

Soon after that Genevieve yelled down the stairs. "C'mon up guys, don't be anti-social."

John was glad to leave. The men were very intellectual. The talk was about some new paper in *Physical Review Letters*. John could see Michael Walters was having a more difficult time blending in, even though he had been just like them such a short time ago. Genuinely excited about his new baby, he tried to tell the others of his metamorphosis from secluded intellectual to new and happy husband. They weren't getting it.

John walked back upstairs and looked around at the cheerful house. Such a far cry from the cold and sterile place it had been when he and Genevieve were children. He found his fiancée. "I wonder when we should get married."

Her eyes moistened and glowed a little. "John, I'm ready any time. I truly am."

"I'm going to graduate next spring. Or we can wait until you graduate the following spring."

She took his hand. "I don't want to wait that long."

"This spring then. How about June 10th?" June 10th was Genevieve's birthday.

She nodded an emphatic yes. "Oh! I want to tell Rachel right now. Can I?"

"Of course."

Genevieve found Rachel and Alicia in a crowd of women and whispered in her ear. Rachel lit up. She immediately weaved her way through the crowd to the end of the big living room. She took a mallet and banged on a little gong hanging on the wall above the fireplace.

"I have an announcement everybody!" Rachel waited until the buzz of conversation died down. "My son and Michael Walters' daughter are getting married. You're all invited to the wedding next June 10th." There were shouts of congratulations from the men and excited chattering from the women.

"This calls for another cigar!" a male voice said.

"Oh no you don't," Alicia said from her chair. "You have to stay up here and pay attention to us for a while." Everybody laughed.

"The baby will choke on all that smoke you dumbbells," Rachel muttered. Alicia and Rachel exchanged glances and they both laughed.

After everyone went home John asked Michael Walters about Fred Haddick.

"Haddick is a guy who has his fingers in a lot of pies. He's like a lot of people who have been involved in classified research. Fred has connections somewhere in the government labyrinth."

"He was asking about the codebook. Asked me if I knew Dalton Jones. Maybe he's just way behind the times. I gave that book to Dalton Jones several years ago."

Walters rubbed his chin thoughtfully.

"I'll look into it, just for curiosity's sake. Fred's been retired for fifteen years. He's always sticking his nose into something. He likes to keep busy."

As they lay in bed that night Genevieve was talkative. "John I'm so happy. Rachel and I are going to plan the wedding. All you have to do is show up. It'll be so much fun! We have to choose the reception building and the clothes for all the bridesmaids, and the menu, and Rachel's going to make me a new dress, and ..."

Genevieve jabbered on.

For just the slightest instant fear stabbed at John's heart. He could just see it now. Genevieve the harpy. "Take out the garbage honey, isn't it time to cut the grass honey, here's a list of things I want you to do around the house, honey." She would be too powerful to resist.

John snuck a glance at her without turning his head. Nothing seemed amiss. She was happy and excited. It felt right.

"...and I'm going to invite everyone I know from the high school too..."

It was going to be fine. He hoped.

31

THE weekend after Mats' adventure John went over to the Full Moon for Mats' lesson. Before he had both feet in the door Mats dragged him back to the storeroom and related his exploits.

"Any luck finding the transportal?" John asked.

"I came through the damn thing. I know where it's supposed to be but I can't see it."

"Let's go back there. I want to look for myself."

Mats found the spot. Neither he nor John could see anything.

"Have you tried turning the lights off?"

Mats slapped his head.

Sure enough, after their eyes adjusted to the darkness, they saw the very faintest shimmering in the air.

"I'll be damned," Mats said. "You wouldn't notice it unless you knew it was there."

"Ingenious," said John. "No one would ever suspect because no one would ever come back here in the dark." John wondered about the portal. He hadn't considered the possibility of a permanent warp in space. Was it possible to program a local area of space? If there was an underlying operating system to the fabric of space, then maybe it could.

"Does the portal only go one way?" John asked.

"There's only one way to find out." Mats stepped through, thinking about the beach and the clear sea with no waves in it.

Mats found himself back on the beach, the sun in the same position in the sky. John saw the scene clearly. This portal must be tuned to this place. He tried to follow immediately but it took him a while to learn to scrunch himself down before entering the portal.

Mats saw John come through. It was fascinating to watch how he materialized. First the roiling cloud stuff, then John himself. There was no fogginess of mind during these transports. You just stepped through from one place to the other. "John, it's like I never left."

"Causality is maintained," John muttered.

"What was that?"

"I'll explain it later."

John stepped back into the egg and found himself back in the stacks. Mats came through a couple of seconds later.

Mats grinned. "Just glad we did this before opening."

"It doesn't make sense," John said. "Two portals that lead back to each other. Unconnected with anyplace else."

"The creatures I saw were carrying packages," Mats said. "Both of them went up a little hill and disappeared." Then he remembered something. "One of those little guys came from a desert world. I saw it just before the portal closed. So the one on the beach can't be programmed just for the Full Moon."

John stared at Mats. "You got lucky then. Did you have your destination in mind?"

Mats gulped. "Uh yeah, fortunately. I was thinking about my girls, and whether Dan had closed up yet."

"Maybe you program your destination with a mental image, like doing the technique. How much time do we have until employees start showing up?"

"15 minutes."

"OK. Let's do some exploring."

"We'll have to work fast."

"We can spend as much time as we want," John said. He shoved Mats through the portal. (See Appendix B for world lines of Mats and John.)

John stepped through five seconds later. "Show me where those little creatures went."

On the way up the hill John explained to Mats his understanding of the continuity of time. "Amazing!" Mats said. "I can spend forever here."

The two friends walked over the treeless landscape looking for signs of another portal. The 'moss' changed colors like a hologram viewed from different angles. It would be sheer chance if they found anything. Both men were entranced by the beauty of this place. Except for a slight murmur of the great ocean behind them, there was silence.

Small plants and shrub-like outgrowths dotted the landscape. Was that a herd of animals off in the distance? Their hides changed colors. "Maybe eating the moss does that," John suggested.

Mats and John came up over the hill and saw a small circular entrance in its side. Both men ducked into a tunnel about 6 feet high and 5 feet wide. A soft orange glow like the sun came from the tunnel walls. They walked briskly on an upgrade for about an hour until Mats began to feel a waft of air on his face. "Coming to an opening."

"Thank God," John said. "My back is killing me."

John and Mats turned a sharp corner. The cave floor ended abruptly. Mats braced his hands against the side of the cave and John almost ran into him. Mats' eyes swept down into a gigantic cirque. The sides of the rock were covered with trees. About half a mile below a beautiful lake gleamed peach in the sun. The trees reached all the way to the mouth of the cave.

John peered into the distance. A small island sat in the center of the lake. Small craft were traveling to it from various points within the forest, which reached almost to the water's edge. "Look," John said. To their right an open-roofed green boxcar sat upon two raised rails.

"Looks like the same stuff as the hull of that ship," Mats said.

John inspected the setup. The wheels of the little car completely enclosed the rail. No chance of slipping off unless something broke.

"Well?" said Mats, looking at John. "There's room enough for both of us if we squeeze in."

"Just barely. This stuff is all made for people 5 feet tall."

Mats squeezed his bulk into the first half of the little car. After John got in the car took off.

"Remote controlled," John suggested.

"Hey! Maybe that ship I saw was too." Mats described the beautiful translucent blue vessel he had seen on his previous excursion.

"You didn't see anybody aboard?"

"Nope."

Their conversation was interrupted as the little vehicle began to pick up speed. The trees flew by on right and left. Every so often an opening flashed by and the path branched off. The trees changed color in soft pastels. Not quite so dramatic as the moss, but it made an interesting effect. The wind in John's face felt good. He picked up dozens of scents unfamiliar to him, all unlike any of the forests of earth.

The car steadied its speed at about 50 miles an hour and described a long, looping spiral down the sides of the cirque. It appeared that the path was making several 360 degree circuits. The car would finish precisely at the cave mouth from which they began, only a half mile lower. Once Mats fancied he saw one of the little robed creatures but he couldn't be sure.

"Mats, have you noticed any birds?" John said.

"Now that you mention it, I haven't. No insects either."

The air was clean of all airborne life even though the weather felt like spring.

As the car sped along, John began to relax into it. He felt a delicious sense of freedom knowing he could spend all the time he wanted here. No time would elapse and no one would ever know.

"This is fun!"

"Yeah. But John, this planet seems to be fully automated. Compared to earth it's underpopulated."

It took about 90 minutes for them to reach the bottom of the huge bowl. The car stopped about ten feet from the water's edge. The car was still in the forest, which was covered with the multicolored moss. They were in a large clearing of rounded gold colored huts, made with the ubiquitous building material. Five of the cars were stacked one on top of the other on a small platform next to the huts. John wondered how the cars remained in place, for there were no constraining walls to hold them. Their car made a loop and placed itself on top of the stack, freeing another to glide away, presumably back to the top of the bowl.

Mats and John got off and stretched their legs. Mats' butt was really sore and John's back was in knots.

"Let's go to that island," John said. "It seems to be a central hub for all the action."

"You're sure that we're not going to be missed back home?" Mats said.

"I'm sure."

"Let's go then." Mats walked purposefully out of the forest. John noticed that the rails went all the way down to the shoreline. "Loading dock."

"How far do you reckon it is to that island?" Mats said.

"I'd say almost 2 miles." John began to compute whether he could make it there and back. Mats jumped right in.

"Hey Mats, you think you can swim 2 miles?" John didn't want to be lugging around 240 pounds of Swede if his friend got tired.

"The gravity's lighter here, in case you hadn't noticed. It's easy swimming in this water. It's easier to move around in."

As soon as John stepped in he understood. This water had a refreshing quality and was very buoyant. As they swam John tasted it: drinkable and fresh. The water had an inner, soft glow, like everything on this world.

There were now no craft to be seen on the still water around the island. The huge sun spilled its light directly onto the surface of the lake. John could see rays of soft orange luminescence descending through its crystal clarity. The refreshing nature of the water made conversation and physical exertion comfortable. As they swam Mats told him about the floating cities underneath the great ocean he had observed on his previous excursion.

"Why can't we see the cities?" Mats asked.

"This cirque may be unconnected to the ocean."

It took them about an hour to swim out to the island, which had a very large round hut. The main hut was surrounded by five little ones. John noticed the geometry of the layout right away: a pentagon.

John and Mats walked into the large hut.

Just then they heard a voice: "Welcome, visitors."

The floor of the large enclosure was covered with the opaque, colored, plastic-like substance. John bounced up and down and discovered it was hard, but flexible. A circle had been marked out on the floor's perimeter, with smaller circles within it. Lines connected the circles at their centers.

"A very complex geometry," John said.

The Voice laughed. "Indeed it is. Come below and let us talk."

Mats pointed to the center of the circle. It had opened, revealing a platform upon which rested a little two-seater tube car. The car had seats and a bar in front for each occupant. Fortunately the car was much bigger than the tiny boxcar. The platform rested above a very long tube about 20 feet in diameter and a quarter mile deep at least.

John felt a little vertigo. The water was so clear and so deep that his vision went unimpeded for miles.

"The floating cities," Mats said.

Through the tube opening John saw large land masses floating within the crystal clear water at different levels. Each one had a different layout and architecture. Some of them were very bright and colorful, others more subdued. What he was seeing defied all the laws of physics he knew.

Mats pointed to their left. "Look at that one." John could make out buildings with colored spires upon them. Patches of green separated the structures. Parks? Agricultural areas? The floating city must be several square miles in area and at least a mile deep into the water.

"Look at that one." John pointed to a floating complex that reminded him of a carnival. Brightly and ostentatiously lit, it seemed to say, 'Come here for fun.'

"Looks like Las Vegas," John said. "Maybe gambling is a common denominator in all cultures."

"I wonder what kind of gambling you can do under water?" Mats remarked. "These people must be a lot different from us."

"Maybe they're not people."

"Intelligent fishes."

They heard a chuckle. "Place yourselves in the shuttle and see for yourself," said The Voice.

"Only one problem, and it's a pretty obvious one," Mats said to the open air. "We breathe air and you breathe water." There was no answer. "Maybe the thing is pressurized," Mats said.

John shrugged. They'd come this far, no point in backing out now. He perceived no danger.

They walked over to the shuttle and looked at each other. Mats grinned and stepped inside. John took a seat behind Mats. Instantly the craft sealed itself up. John was grateful that he didn't have to duck his head.

The thing shot away from the platform and down the tube at about a hundred miles an hour. John grabbed onto the bar in the nick of time but Mats flew backwards, crashing into him. "C'mon Mats, get out of my face," John complained.

The Voice chuckled. Both men seemed to hear it coming from the walls of their vehicle.

"Real funny," Mats mumbled, scrambling back to his seat. He grabbed tightly onto the handle like a little kid on a roller coaster.

They were making a bee-line for one of the floating cities.

"I hope we go to the casino one," Mats said. John snorted.

"I could go for a beer right now," Mats said a couple minutes later.

After a while Mats got into it. Riding in this vehicle with its transparent walls was a rush. The two men were seated at the front, not a foot away from the bow of the transparent cylindrical craft. They both felt that the water was going to come crashing in on them.

As they moved through the water (with no visible power source) John noticed how much life there was in the ocean. He counted 27 different species of water creatures. A whale with huge fins running down its sides swam alongside. It was able to generate tremendous speed through the water once it got going, and was not much slower than the tube car. The whale's skin looked like it was pixelated with tiny plankton. The plankton resembled pixels on a monitor screen. As they passed it an image formed on the side of its body: a picture of Mats and John in the tube car.

"It's saying hello."

John and Mats both waved. Clearly, the whale was intelligent.

John didn't know how the air was maintained in the car but it stayed breathable.

After a twenty minute ride the tube car approached one of the gigantic floating cities. It was enclosed in an extremely thin transparent dome.

The city's architecture was striking. Every building was a work of art, and it was gridded in a fascinating geometric pattern:

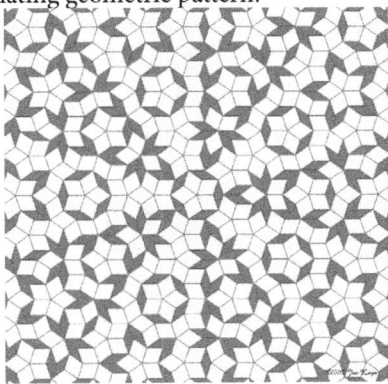

Image copyright ©2002 by Jos Leys at josleys.com. Used with permission.

"Looks like a Penrose tiling," John remarked.

The roads were colored in subtle pastels. Ramps on many levels connected the various buildings. They hung out into the air with no visible means of support. Pedestrians walked the streets and ramps in a festive mood. John had the impression everyone was on holiday.

The car drew near to a magnificent white castle decorated with very long and intricately decorated spires. The castle had dozens of turrets on many levels with green flags upon every one. Each of the flags displayed a picture of a humanoid holding a large three-pronged fork. The castle was situated in the very center of the city and rested on a green mat, probably made from the ubiquitous moss that covered the land. John was fascinated by the colors and the design of the place. Nothing clashed, every building was striking in itself but blended elegantly into the whole. The entire city was a breathtaking work of art. Mats even forgot about his desire for liquid refreshment long enough to appreciate it.

The tube car entered a little holding area on the top floor of the structure.

John and Mats stepped out into a hallway with several arched and domed ceilings at least 40 feet high. The ceilings were engraved and painted in intricate patterns and colors. The floor was tiled in browns and beautifully inlaid. On their left John saw windows, the arches of which were painted in blues, greens, and golds. The walls to their right were inlaid in complex geometric designs in various colors. Each of the arches and domes had a different theme, but some genius designer had blended them together perfectly. John's jaw dropped as he let the beauty of this place soak through him.

The two men walked about 100 yards and entered a huge open area several hundred feet square with a floor of hexagonal blue, light gray, and gold tile squares. Each of the squares had diamond patterns in the middle; each of the diamonds alternated dark green or brick red. Great marble pillars supported an arched, pale peach ceiling, elaborately and tastefully frescoed in light blue. Sculpture covered the floor, each resting upon carved pedestals of dark marble. Large transparent panels had been inserted into both walls. The panels were tinted gold and the light from them was, to John's eyes, indistinguishable from the sunlight of earth.

Like two hicks in the big city, John and Mats could only stare in awe.

Approximately 100 yards away along the far wall, someone was seated upon an intricately carved throne.

"I see that you are enjoying my little home," the voice said. The sound of his bass echoed pleasantly. He began to walk toward them.

This creature was humanoid, about seven feet tall, and had blue-green scales instead of skin. His huge feet and hands were slightly webbed from the palm to the first joint. Each digit had three joints and was twice as long as a human's. In his left hand he carried a trident.

"Just like the flags!" Mats said.

The creature smiled. "Just so."

He stopped about four feet in front of them. "I am [–]."

"I cannot pronounce your name. May I call you Neptune, the god of the sea?"

Their host seemed to be quite pleased with this appellation. "Welcome earthians, to my humble abode." Neptune waved his hands around at the lavish and tasteful elegance. There was something familiar about this place.

"You know what planet we're from?" John asked.

"Of course! We monitor all portal activity. An earthian is instantly recognizable in all but the most backward and isolated places."

John and Mats stared at each other.

"Your planet is famous throughout the universes," Neptune said. "We follow all of the important developments. You are all living in a fish bowl. Oh, and don't mind the trident. It's all a necessary part of the act."

John was forgetting his manners. "We are extremely pleased and honored to be welcomed here." John bowed to his host. Mats awkwardly followed John's lead. Mats said, "This is the most beautiful place I've ever seen."

"Do you recognize it?" Neptune said.

John snapped his fingers. "It looks an awful lot like the Imperial Hermitage Museum in St. Petersburg Russia." John recognized the décor from several photographs Robert had brought home from one of his parent's trips abroad.

"Very good! Most earthian architecture is junk, but I love the designs of that building. I have, of course, altered it to suit my tastes. Local artists have done all the frescoing, painting, and sculpting."

"Where did you get the materials to build this stuff?" Mats said.

John thought Mats had asked an excellent question. This planet seemed barren of resources.

"Some of it we get from the surface," Neptune replied. "The rest we...er...import."

"I have a million questions," John said, but was interrupted.

Their host raised an upturned hand. "First some refreshment," he commanded.

At once three females came into the room. One of them carried a silver tray with three gold and jewel-encrusted goblets. John noticed the incredible workmanship of vessels and tray. Mats stared open-mouthed at the girls. Each had scales like Neptune's, but softer and more delicate. Their scales were covered by a soft down. Each was about 6 1/2 feet tall. Their coloring varied from pale blue to aquamarine. "Wow," Mats said.

"Thank you daughters," said Neptune. "Let me introduce you to our guests, the earthians." John again couldn't pronounce the names. He determined that the older one should be Daphne, the middle one Chloe, and the younger one Diana.

Mats couldn't keep his eyes off the older one.

John nudged him with an elbow in his side. "We're guests here, remember," John hissed. "Mind your manners."

Neptune and the females seemed gratified by Mats' reaction. Daphne set the silver tray on an intricately carved table.

"Is everything here so exquisite?" John said, looking at the girls for the first time. John guessed that if these creatures were human Diana would be about 17, Chloe 19, and Daphne 20 or 21.

Neptune laughed heartily and all three of the girls giggled. "They have been anxious to meet you ever since I informed them of your pending arrival."

Slowly the girls walked forward. Mats gulped as Daphne bent down and kissed him on the head. His palms were sweating and he was breathing hard. Chloe came up to John and extended a pale blue hand, covered in soft down. He took it, and brushed it lightly to his lips. She gasped a little and smiled shyly. Diana approached John and looked challengingly into his eyes. She received the same treatment.

Neptune was amused. "It seems that feminine charms are universal." His daughters walked back to join him.

Neptune turned and said something to them in another language. The girls left the room, but not without a few backward glances. It seemed that Mats and John had also made a favorable impression.

"My eldest wanted me to tell you both that they would like to see you again."

Mats bowed. "We'd love to sir, but by Gungnir I wouldn't trust myself not to do something stupid. Maybe it would be best if we didn't."

Neptune laughed long and hard. "I believe I am coming to like you very much. You may be pleased to know that Argelainians do not share your parochial views on sex." Neptune gestured toward the tray and the glasses. "Let us partake."

The delicate goblets contained a pale pink liquid, sweet tasting and refreshing. As they drank, John asked his host how very large land masses could float within the sea without sinking to the bottom.

"I am not a physicist or a geologist. It has something to do with altering the specific gravity of the platform upon which our city rests. You may have noticed this substance before. It is translucent and is often colored for decorative purposes."

"Are your ships made from it?" Mats asked. "I thought I saw a blue one the first time I arrived."

Neptune made a gesture with his fist, a plopping motion. "Do you mean...?"

Mats colored a little but kept his tongue.

"Yes," Neptune said. "This substance is programmable. It can be made lighter than air or heavier than the marble you see on the floor. The internal structure of the material can be altered to change its density."

"Thank you," John said.

"Who are those little guys with the gold capes?" Mats asked.

"Yes, the diminoti." Neptune held his hands about 4 1/2 feet above the floor. "They are what you might call messengers. They handle sensitive communications and are good at scavenging and...er...sniffing out information. Sort of like intelligence operatives in your culture. Everyone has them. They're trusted implicitly. Once a diminoti gives his word he never breaks it."

"Are your cities in competition with each other?" John asked.

"As a matter of fact they are," Neptune replied. "Friendly, mostly, but sometimes it gets out of hand. Our people are very creative. Each city tries to outdo the other in artistry, design, and entertainment value. It works to our advantage, for each city has evolved a special theme. We all travel back and forth to sample and enjoy."

"What are the ships for?" Mats asked.

"Freighters, that's all. They convey things on the surface to collection points, and then to our cities. Our planet, like yours, is a water world. Only 20% of our surface area is dry land."

"What is the theme of your city?" John asked.

Neptune brightened. "Earth. The best of earth. Specifically, a city in the country of Russia called St. Petersburg. No one would ever have thought of it on Argelain. Although your planet is famous, it is viewed as, uh, rather backward."

"But," Neptune said hastily, "I am this planet's acknowledged expert on earth. I strive to show it in its very best aspect."

"If this castle is any indication you've done a magnificent job," John said.

"I am gratified," Neptune said. "You are the first visitor from your planet to ever come here. Earthians aren't ever found off-planet so I am anxious to show you around and get some new ideas."

Neptune preened a little. "My idea has made some of the other city lords very jealous." He scowled. "Some are even beginning to copy some of City Petersberg's designs."

John had to stifle a laugh. In some ways this guy is just like Porniarsk.

"One last question," Mats said. "Why did you say that earthians were famous throughout the universe, and that we lived in a fish bowl?"

Neptune seemed amazed at the question.

"It's amazing that you know nothing about your own planet, but on the other hand...OK. I'll try to tell you in a hundred words or less. In the first place, intelligent life throughout the universe can communicate with each other. That might seem like a novel concept to earthians but out here it's pretty well accepted. We have simple devices which we use for intra-planetary communications. There are others much more sophisticated than that, which we call transportals. Anyway, lots of these transportals have been programmed all over your planet, within it, and above it as well. Mostly they're well disguised. There are a few, like the one in the back of your store, which are placed more for convenience than reason."

"Disguised?" Mats asked. "How? And why?"

"On earth and other backward places, they have to be disguised so people don't freak out. Especially on earth because there are so many of them. A lot of them are incorporated into well known structures like pyramids and natural formations."

John was excited.

"Don't worry. You'll never find them except by accident. Like the one over the Bermuda Triangle. That's a particularly powerful trans-universal portal."

"Who set up these portals around earth?"

Neptune laughed. "Don't ask me! I'm an artist, as are all my people."

"Show me how it works," Mats said.

Neptune walked over to one of the walls. It blurred, showing the stacks in the Full Moon. When John's eyes recognized the scene his awareness was drawn into it just as in one of the Eyrie display tanks. "We can tune into any of the transportals in and around your planet and observe anything we want." The scene shifted to the Oval Office in the White House. The president presided over a cabinet meeting. John and Mats could hear every word of their conversation.

"Hey bud, what do you think you're doing?" Mats shouted.

Neptune disabled the display. "I didn't mean to offend. Nobody here is going to do anything. We don't care who wins. No one really believes what's happening on the earthian planet. It's all too bizarre and stupid."

"But fascinating," Neptune added quickly.

John changed the subject. "Where does the technology for the self-propelled tube cars come from?"

Neptune shrugged. "It has been known for eons. Just like the transportals and everything else you see around here. Once earthians aggregate their actions it will be taught to you. Maybe the next time you come I'll show you how the tube cars are fashioned."

"Get their act together," John corrected. "Not aggregate their actions."

Neptune made a note of that. "Wouldn't happen to know any good raps, would you homeslice?" he asked hopefully.

Mats laughed. "Not this Swede." John shook his head.

"Oh well. Give me a good rap any day. The stuff you call poetry is just drivel." He paused for a moment. "I have been a poor host. I apologize. I should not have slighted you or your planet. It's just that we're all tuned into events there. From our detached vantage point we see flaws which those close to the action are unable to perceive."

Neptune smiled. "I digress. The real reason I invited you here was for the Games. I also want to get an unbiased opinion from real earthians about this city I've built."

"The Games?" John queried.

"The All Cities Regional. Qualifying is tomorrow and nextday, everywhere on the planet. We'll play at the Spielplatz. Want to come?"

"Sure." Mats volunteered for both of them.

"Excellent!" said Neptune, clearly excited at the prospect. "But right now I want to take you on a tour." Three small tube cars appeared from the hallway, floating a couple feet off the floor. "These cars are programmed to follow mine." Neptune handed the earthians a glossy brochure entitled "City Petersburg – An Artist's Paradise." John leafed quickly through the pages. The booklet contained images of earthian structures and, on the facing page, their Argelainian counterparts. John read a lot of bragging about the superiority of City Petersburg's renditions. The text was in Cyrillic and in English. All residents of City Petersburg were required, as a condition of permanent citizenship, to speak fluent Russian and English. John asked about this.

"This city is about the earthian planet and specifically St. Petersburg," Neptune said. "I'm a stickler for authenticity."

They hopped in the cars and Neptune showed them every room in the castle. John was impressed. "This place is even better than the Hermitage, in some ways."

Neptune beamed. "I was hoping you'd like it. Now let's take a tour of the city."

Their host gradually raised his car to a height of 200 feet or so, allowing the earthians to appreciate the city's layout. Ten files of buildings opened out from the center, like rays of sunlight. These were interspersed with parks and other open spaces in the Penrose tiling pattern. Neptune turned his car around to face the earthians as they inspected his domain and was not disappointed in their reaction.

Mats summed up his feelings. "Maybe beautiful stuff isn't so worthless after all."

John guffawed and Neptune looked confused. John made haste to reassure his host. "From Mats, that's quite a compliment."

The little cars descended, floating ten feet above the road and three feet or so above the heads of pedestrians. The average height of the people was about seven feet, including the women. Neptune's car seemed to be an accepted fact but everyone was curious about the two visitors. John could see the pedestrians craning their necks to stare at them.

The people dressed colorfully. All seemed healthy, attractive, and well made. Is it only on earth that so many are sick? John wondered. Maybe something of Neptune's criticisms is justified.

John saw no other cars. The cavalcade turned the corner from the big castle and halted in front of a stately, peach colored building with huge arching widows and white columns. Their host showed them buildings modeled after the Mikhailovsky Palace, the Marble Palace, which looked like a beautiful pearl glinting in the light, and the Anichkov.

"I wish I had a camera," John remarked.

"Done!" Neptune handed an imager to John.

John was astonished. "Where did you get this?"

"Uh...one of our diminutive friends...picked it up for me on earth."

John realized Neptune had procured the camera before they had ever arrived, hoping that it would be asked for.

"I call this the street of palaces," Neptune said. "Although my city is modeled after St. Petersburg I have changed the location of everything to maximize its beauty. There are some real ugly places in the real St. Pete, but not here."

For another four hours they toured the rest of the city. Neptune showed them important cathedrals and buildings. The crown jewel was the Church of the Spilled Blood, a magnificent structure with beautifully colored onion domes.

"I borrowed that design to show off our city," Neptune said. "Now others have followed." He looked disgusted. "But I suppose that imitation is the sincerest form of flattery." He looked at John. "That's right isn't it?"

"Right as rain," John said. Neptune smiled and pulled out his data set. "I'll remember that one."

As they were about to go back to Neptune's castle John spotted a magnificent white columned building with lights spaced every 100 feet or so. It was surrounded by a small, deep blue lake. The reflections of the golden lights on the building and especially upon the water was magnificent. John stared, and Mats too.

"My most magnificent exterior view," Neptune said. "Got it from a photograph."

"Let's get down and look," John said. They lowered the cars and got out, standing beside a long black fence with delicate little stiles.

"A masterpiece," John said, and meant it. The sight was astoundingly beautiful.

Neptune stood behind John and placed both his webbed hands on his shoulders. After a few moments a female approached and made a grab for John's camera. He jerked back, knocking Neptune off balance. Neptune fell into the woman and John quickly reached out. With one arm he easily caught Neptune and restored him to his feet. By this time the woman was almost horizontal but Mats stepped in. He caught her in his arms and easily lifted her upright, gently placing her feet back on the ground. Both Neptune and the female were impressed. They towered over the earthians and were surprised at their physical strength.

The woman's breathing was rapid. John could tell she was excited. "You're so strong for someone so small!" she said.

The woman had very pale lavender down, large green eyes, and was very well made.

"You're as light as a feather," Mats said. She must have understood, for she bent down and kissed the top of his head. Mats practically swooned. The woman laughed and turned to Neptune. "Who are these strange creatures, sire?"

"Earthians," Neptune said.

"Earthians!" she screeched. A number of curious passersby began to stroll over.

"You don't mind do you sire?" The female grabbed Mats' hand. "Come with me my little stud."

That was the last thing John saw of Mats until the next morning. He arrived, disheveled, in their sleeping quarters in the castle. On his face was a look of awe and disbelief.

"That was the greatest sex I've ever had."

"Really? You mean we and they can do it?"

"Oh yeah. According to Mermanda (that's what I call her), sex around here is just like going shopping. You hook up with anyone you please and have fun."

"What was she like?" John said.

"Soft and curvy, just like our women. The scales on her skin are really soft and covered with fuzz. And her breasts! By Gungnir, I've never felt anything so wonderful."

John expressed his amusement in a belly laugh. It was just like Mats to find a good time, even on an alien planet halfway across the universe.

"She's a foot taller than me but I had to be very careful. These people have a very delicate bone structures. To her I was Hercules." Mats flexed his biceps. "All that weightlifting really paid off."

"Our host didn't seem to mind," John said. "Tomorrow we go to a specially prepared training area for the Games. It's an hour's ride by tube car."

The next morning Neptune assembled his entourage from the castle. The rest of the city would watch on their displays. With the displays every viewer could immerse themselves in the action, with full sensory input. According to Neptune it was almost as good as playing.

Neptune spoke proudly of his city to John and Mats just before they embarked. "The population of our city was 6,236 at the last census, taken five years ago. It is approximately 25 square miles in area, giving a population density of about 250 persons per square mile. The population of each city is a matter of pride to us. People all over the planet have carte blanche to move anywhere as long as their skill set is compatible with the city's theme as decided by its Lord. City Petersburg has been in the top 20 for the 1,357th year in a row!"

John took a picture of Neptune, his consort, Mats, and the three girls before they embarked for the Spielplatz, where the Games would be played. Mats was in front, surrounded by the girls. Daphne rested her chin on his head. Diana, the youngest, turned slightly with one hand on her hip and showed off her figure. She gave John a saucy look.

'I'll be careful with her,' he thought.

John and Mats rode with Neptune, his consort, and their attendants in a big eight-seater. Neptune's daughters rode with their attendants in a six-seater, which followed behind.

Early that morning John and Mats had heard raised voices and complaints. "Father, we want to ride with the earthians! All of us are wearing our finest costumes!" Neptune had gently but firmly denied their requests.

"Maybe he figured that your warning yesterday was valid," John said. Relief showed on Mats' face. Later, as they walked toward their cars, the girls slowed to give John and Mats a good look.

Neptune's consort had deep blue scales and green eyes. Neither men nor women had facial or body hair, but their heads were attractively shaped, not lumpy like human heads. Each female wore a distinctive gown which lent itself to her down color. The men, in fealty to Neptune, wore various shades of green.

About 40 tube cars, each with Neptune's banner marked upon its side, shot out of specially prepared slots underneath the castle. The team members had departed the previous day.

John and Mats had no idea what the Games were about so they pressed the attendants for information. John sat next to a burly gentleman who seemed friendly and talkative. According to Henry (that's what John called him) both he and Mats were world famous already. "In fact," Henry whispered, "we've already gained a lot of face for hosting you. You'll be mobbed when we get to the Spielplatz."

"What's the prize for winning?" Mats said.

"The prize is a year's free pass to all cities on the planet. You also get a personal car with the logo of the winner on it. Each team member gets a jersey announcing that you are part of the winning team. It's designed by the winner of the costume competition. You can't imagine the prestige and honor that goes with that. Everyone knows your name and you have even more cachet than a Lord, or even the King himself. At least for a little while."

"What if the weather is bad?" John asked.

Henry stared at him blankly.

"Oh! That's right, you're earthians. We don't have weather like you do on earth. We're absolutely certain to have a perfect day."

Tube cars converged from everywhere, heading toward the surface. The bottom of the platform was gaily decorated and flashed brilliantly, a homing beacon for all attendees. As they approached John saw access holes for all of the vehicles. Each was marked with a banner, one for each city. The City Petersburg entourage headed for one of the holes at the very center. "Today, at least, we are important," Henry said.

The tube cars entered and were gradually raised through the apertures and onto the surface, then sent back down to be stored. John and Mats got out after Neptune and his family but before the attendants. The earthians found themselves on a gigantic white circular walkway at least 100 yards wide. Above them the stadium stands rose at least 1,000 feet into the air. The five moons graced the sky. At this time, in the very early morning, the great orange sun was almost completely below the horizon. Two impeccably dressed men in green and white met the party and escorted them to the proper entry point. The three girls hung back and slowly surrounded John and Mats. John gave Mats a nudge and a knowing look.

Neptune and his consort acknowledged the stares and greetings of the arrivals. He noticed that the earthians were invisible and motioned for John and Mats to walk directly behind him and his consort. Meanwhile, Henry kept up a running commentary.

"Each team has 30 minutes to complete their task," he said. "Each team competes separately and against the clock. Our team finished 5th at last year's regionals and didn't make the planetary's. Only the top 3 teams make it."

Neptune's party approached a broad moving walkway which led into the stands. As they filed in, John heard a buzz of noise. He stood at the inner edge of a gigantic bowl about a half mile in diameter. A sea of faces, pennants, and gaily colored costumes met his gaze as he swept his eyes upward in a complete circle.

Henry and the other attendants rushed over to escort the women to their seats. There were escalator-like walkways which quickly motored spectators upward to the proper row. Unlike earth stadiums each seat was spacious. There was plenty of leg room and spaces to place banners, flags, food, and other accoutrements. Neptune entered with John and Mats at either side and paused for effect. Hands pointed and heads turned as the distinctive green and white banner of Neptune's party was spotted by the crowd. An excited murmur ran through the stands. John heard "earthians" more than once. Here, they were celebrities!

The walkway took them to the topmost row. John and Mats were given places of honor just behind Neptune and his consort. Neptune strategically placed his daughters to their left. The attendants flanked John and Mats. The affable Henry sat next to John. Stadium attendants hovered by Neptune and his consort, taking orders for refreshment. Soon a sumptuous (by Argelainian standards) meal had been laid, complete with flowered napkins and plenty of the refreshing pink liquid. John selected something that looked like a scallop and bit into the pink meat. It tasted sweet and dissolved in his mouth like cotton candy.

A light breeze touched John's face. This planet probably had a very small axial tilt angle and its rotation was probably much slower than that of earth. That might account for the lack of weather.

Preparations were being made to the field of play. The huge sun had advanced further over the horizon and it filled the dark blue sky with a soft peachy glow.

Even though the party was 1,000 feet in the air John had no trouble seeing the playing surface, or anywhere else in the stadium. The atmosphere here is extraordinarily clear.

(The author will forego a description of the Games, which make the Olympics look like a Sunday picnic. The Argelanian Games are a test of intellectual and physical prowess. Argelainians are accomplished geometers. A description of the Games are available here.)

After the first day of competition Neptune was worried and swore at the difficulty of the events.

Henry was amused. "Our Lord was on the competition committee three years ago urging for tougher events. Now he's got them."

To Mats' delight all in attendance partied after the competition. Bands, dances, gambling houses, art shows, poetry contests, debates, and lots more entertainment was available. This was a time for thousands to renew old acquaintances. Mats was amazed at the number of beautiful females. John noticed how proudly the men displayed the costumes of their city, each one adding a personal embellishment.

John and Mats were the center of attention almost as soon as they exited the stadium. Neptune assigned two burly attendants to watch over them, Henry being one. John spoke to Mats. "Watch yourself. The woman you want to sleep with might be the consort or daughter of an important lord."

Suddenly Daphne, Chloe, and Diana burst through the crowd and grabbed John and Mats.

John saw trouble with a capital T as Diana put her arm around him. "I thought your father told you three to stay in?" he said.

Diana stuck out her tongue. "He did. But we never listen to him if we can help it."

The three girls guided them to a series of elegant buildings. John saw many couples, and groups of three or four women and men, entering and exiting. He stopped. "These aren't sleeping quarters, are they?" he said to Diana. She was dressed to kill in a low necked silk outfit that hugged her impressive physique. "Well of course silly! It's not like we've never done it before," Chloe said. She was looking at Mats. "Three women and only two men. You guys are going to have a great time."

Daphne spoke to Mats. "We've heard through the grapevine that you're quite good."

"Help," Mats said, looking to John.

John motioned for Mats to sit down on one of the many stone benches that lined the walkway. "Ladies," John said, "all three of you are very beautiful but you are the daughters of our host. It would be bad manners for us to sleep with the children of the city king. Besides, I am engaged to another."

"Engaged?" Diana asked.

"It's when you promise yourself to another for life," John replied.

"For life? Why would you want to do that?" Chloe asked. "What if you get tired of each other?"

In response, John reached into his wallet and handed her the picture of Genevieve. He had no idea whether it would make any impression, but John did not reckon the popularity of earth in City Petersburg. Diana sucked in her breath. "She's beautiful. That hair!" Daphne and Chloe gathered around. "And that dress!" Daphne said. Soon the girls were chattering excitedly. It was decided to go immediately to the dressmakers shop and have one made for each of them. Diana decided to wear a wig to the next City dance. "I'll be all the rage," she chirped.

"Or a big flop," Chloe said disparagingly.

John sighed with relief as he and Mats walked away. "That was a close call."

"Yeah," Mats said. "But those beauties have got your picture."

"Shit!" John said. "I'll have to follow them." He was having a great time, but missing Genevieve.

Mats felt quite differently. "I'm definitely going to have some fun tonight. Ta-Ta!" John smiled as Mats walked off into the multitudes.

John chased down the girls, who had already gotten the picture duplicated three times in a large, open-air clothing shop. He retrieved his photograph. The dressmaker was as excited as the girls about Genevieve's outfit. Each of the girls discussed modifications to suit their coloring. John took the opportunity to duck out of the place. He began to tour the facilities. Like everything here, the layout was sumptuous and elegant. There were many open air dancing areas with bandshells, restaurants, art exhibitions, entertainers, open air concerts, and an athletic competition. Apparently some of the reserves who did not get into the Games during the day wanted to show what they could do. The walkways were decorated with lamps of intricate design. Each emitted a soft glow of colored light. Some of the people wore clothing and some did not. Their bodies, covered in soft protective scales, did not really need costuming. But their natural creativity and interest in geometry led to intricate and sometimes complex gowns and jewelry.

John wondered whether the fuzzy coloring of the women was evolutionary. Men were mostly a boring dark gray. Neptune's scales were green but perhaps he dyed them. Knowing the man's vanity, John did not doubt it for a second.

A very tall woman with dark blue skin wearing a thin, sleeveless garment that hung loosely around her passed near to John. The pale lavender fabric was inlaid with elegant geometric designs of silver, blue, and yellow. John stared for a moment as she walked gracefully along the white walkway. Her demeanor suggested someone fully confident in herself and interested in rendezvousing with just the right person. She caught John's eye and began to turn toward him. John walked quickly in the other direction. He wanted no temptations this night.

John walked into one of the art exhibits and saw a wealth of jewelry, paintings, and sculpture. All of it demonstrated extremely high quality. He strolled over to the jewelry section and saw hundreds of pieces. No two were the same. The work was a startling exhibition of creative imagination translated into physical form. John got out Neptune's camera and began to photograph the displays.

John picked up two delicately made pieces. A complex curved geometric pattern of gold, dark red, and blue filaments emanated from a small diamond-like point. The jeweler had placed tiny beads of white on the thin filaments. John picked them up, utterly astonished at their beauty. After close inspection of the piece he realized that the beads were not placed randomly, but formed the nodes of a polyhedron. As he rotated the objects, the filament colors and shapes combined to show a completely different aspect. Depending upon the angle from which they were viewed, the beads presented the polyhedron and its dual. They were the most utterly gorgeous pieces he had ever seen. A tear came to his eye.

A man came over and bowed slightly to John. He indicated that John should take the pieces. "You are one of the earthians are you not?"

"This is the most beautiful design and workmanship I have ever seen." The man bowed again. "I am honored to present these to you as my gift." John bowed profoundly in return to the artist. "I will present these to my lady as a special token of my love, and tell her of the great artist who created them." The man was deeply moved.

"May I take a representation of you with this imager, so that she may know the *artiste* who fashioned them?"

John got a picture of the proud designer standing next to his display case. His name sounded like Phillipe. The artist also gave John a carrying box shaped like a cupola. It was filigreed impossibly fine in a complex geometric pattern. John inspected the carrying box closely and noticed a tiny, rounded, and decorated cap on top of the cupola. The delicacy of the work was astonishing.

He took another picture of Phillipe with the digital camera. Bowing again, John left the exhibition.

The first thing he would do upon his return would be to get these set properly for Genevieve.

John couldn't wait to see her face when he showed them to her. He was also looking forward to seeing Emile Gascard's reaction when he came in with them. The proud French jeweler could have not the slightest criticism of these exquisite pieces.

Then John had a crushing thought. What if the difference in gravity between the Argelain planet and earth deformed their delicate construction? He took a picture, just in case, of the case and its contents.

John wandered about for a while, finally finding himself at the water's edge. All five moons were clearly visible in the black sky, brilliantly lit with stars. Not the desultory few stars of earth but a blazing panoply of light. This was combined with the reflection off the five moons and the pale light from the binary. It provided a silvery-blue illumination that reflected upon the water in truly breathtaking patterns. The sounds of laughter and merriment echoed behind him. Turning his attention toward land John saw lovers holding hands, heard the music and took in the dancing at two of the visible open air facilities. He smelled the light, fresh sea breeze and was filled with a sense of well-being tinged slightly with melancholy. He wished he were here with his arms around Genevieve.

John turned and walked quickly back to his apartment. Tomorrow, after the Games, he would go home. Mats or no Mats.

Early next morning as the party prepared to leave for the stadium, Mats had not yet arrived. John was embarrassed. It was poor form indeed, considering how lavishly they had been treated. Neptune had the girls firmly in hand, or so he thought. Diana gave John a wink. "Wait till you see us at the City Ball."

The attendants left the apartments and strolled grandly toward the stadium. They wore their green and white livery and proudly held the banner of City Petersburg. Hundreds of other parties joined them.

Neptune's group still drew a lot of attention. Those who hadn't yet observed the earthians desired a firsthand look. Halfway there John saw Mats tucking in his shirt and smoothing out what was left of his blond hair. Mats snuck in beside John to the laughter of all who observed. Neptune didn't seem to mind because more attention was drawn to himself and his party. His daughters had apparently circulated quite freely last night. The girls must have created quite a stir because a number of gentlemen had words for them.

As before, the competition began at sunrise. The order of play was posted on the screens. Team Petersburg was to play next to last.

Neptune groaned. "My stomach is in knots already."

John was fascinated and intrigued by the events as he watched the competition. These people were superior physically, mentally, and emotionally to his counterparts on earth. John wondered what possible purpose his planet could have in the scheme of things. From his travels so far it appeared that earth was indeed a barbarism. But if that was so, why did everyone say it was so special? Why did people here follow earth events so religiously? He shook his head. Probably just morbid curiosity.

When the competition ended people began filing out, whooping and hollering. "Let's party!" someone said. Thousands laughed and cheered.

John caught Mats' eye as they walked out. "Let's thank our host and get going."

"But I've got two lovely ladies lined up for tonight!"

John insisted. "Both of us should return through the portal at the same time."

"I'm getting used to this place," Mats said. "I like it here."

"Aren't you forgetting about your daughters? And your store?"

Mats grimaced. "You said we could live a lifetime here and return at the same moment. One more night won't matter."

"Maybe we can. But I'm no expert on time Mats, or transportals. We've already spent two days here. For all I know we may lose two days on our return."

"I promised the kids I wouldn't screw up."

"Then let's get going."

John and Mats returned to Neptune's apartments and said their good-byes. John thanked Neptune profusely for his hospitality. He told his host of his experiences the night before, and his admiration for his people and his culture. They promised to return soon. Daphne, Chloe, and Diana kissed both of them on the cheek. Diana looked especially crestfallen. Neptune's youngest definitely had a little bit of a crush on John.

"You may use my personal portal if you wish," Neptune said. "It can be tuned to the one in the bookstore."

John gratefully accepted. With Neptune and the girls watching, Mats entered the portal. Nothing happened. "Try it again," Neptune said. Mats again stepped in with no results. "That's odd."

"Maybe it's broken," Mats suggested.

"This is not a mechanical device like one of your machines on earth," Neptune explained. "It has no moving parts. Its power source comes from within the ethers. It is thought activated and has never failed."

Suddenly he snapped his fingers. "Of course! Which one of you entered first?" John and Mats thought for a minute. "It was me," Mats said.

"Then John has to go through first. Otherwise Mats will return before John left and that will set up a time paradox." (See Appendix B.)

John stepped in, the space within the portal shimmered, and John vanished. Just before he stepped through Mats looked back and gave the girls a surreptitious wink.

As he disappeared Chloe giggled. "That earthian is funny looking but I like him."

"Me too," said Daphne.

Diana was silent.

John found himself back in the stacks. Fifteen seconds later Mats appeared. John smelled the characteristic freshness of the air and observed the shimmering egg-shaped space blending back into its former shape. His body felt very heavy due to the lighter gravity on Argelain.

It was impossible to tell if they had lost any time. The lights were still out in this section of the stacks and on everywhere else, just as they had left them two days(?) previous. John was almost certain that transportal travel was identical to jaunting. Both were instantaneous methods of traversing space and should follow the same laws.

The two adventurers walked out to the front and looked at the clock. It read 7:47 a.m. "I'll be damned," John said. "Only 1 minute elapsed during our visit. And that was because of the delay both times in entering the portal."

Mats was elated. "I can go through any time I want!" He was still thinking about his two ladies and the rendezvous they had planned for later. "If I return, will any time elapse over at City Petersburg?"

"Probably not," John said. "But remember that Neptune said the transportals can be tuned to different places. We don't know how to do that. What if you step into that thing next time and you can't get back?"

Mats blanched. "By Gungnir, I never thought of that."

"Neither did I Mats. Let's not push our luck."

John slapped Mats on the back. "Lessons are over. You don't need me anymore. For God's sake, be careful!"

John returned to Magnolia Street and found Genevieve about ready to go out. She perceived at once that John had had an adventure. "John, your clothing and your skin has a most peculiar smell." She took a few breaths through her nose. "I like it. Sweet but refreshing."

"Oh my God," John said.

"What?"

He reached into his pants pocket and took out the little cupola.

"Oh John, it's beautiful."

He sneaked a look into it, expecting to find a broken mess. The earrings were intact. Phillipe had built well.

Now a broad smile spread over John's face. He placed his index finger gently under Genevieve's chin and lifted her head so that she was looking directly into his eyes. "My love," he said, "I want to present these lovely objects to you. Courtesy of Phillipe, master jewel maker of City Petersburg on planet Argelain."

He handed her the cupola. Genevieve admired it, looking carefully at the filigreed work. She raised her eyes to John in astonishment; her mouth opened in a little O. Carefully she opened the case. Her eyebrows raised abruptly upward. John heard a sharp intake of breath. For several moments she stared, unmoving. John thought she might not appreciate the objects as he had. He was about to take the case from her hand when he saw a tear rolling down her cheek. Her attention was fixed on the pieces. With trembling fingers she carefully reached in and took one out.

Genevieve placed the case on her lap and rotated the piece in the light, just as he had done yesterday evening at Phillipe's boutique. Her gaze was still riveted upon the earring, her eyes now sparkling in appreciation. Then she carefully placed it back in the case and shut the cupola. "Thank you so much! Never in my life have I seen such beautiful objects. I will treasure them as long as I live."

"I'll have Emile Gascard make them into earrings for you."

They went up to the bedroom. John explained his adventure in great detail. When he showed her the images he had taken of City Petersburg she grew more and more interested. Her eyes widened when he exhibited the shot he had taken of Neptune and the girls. Mats was in the picture with Daphne's chin on his head. Genevieve saw Diana's pose and her saucy expression. Neptune towered over all of them.

Genevieve scrutinized all three females. Diana's coloring was light blue, Chloe a darker blue, and Daphne's greenish blue. "They're all so beautiful!" She gave John a suspicious look. "Do all the women there look this good?"

John replied a little sheepishly. "Yes. That's why Mats can't wait to get back."

Genevieve hooted with laughter. "Typical Mats."

"But so do the men," John added, smiling at her. "So don't get any ideas."

Genevieve batted her eyelashes coquettishly. Her eyes returned to the image. "Who took this picture?"

"I did."

She smiled teasingly. "And who is that saucy little number on the right with the come-hither look?"

John flushed. "Diana, Neptune's youngest. I had to be careful with her. She wanted to sleep with me."

"I'll bet," Genevieve said. John could tell she was amused.

"You mean, we can do it with them?"

"That's just what I asked Mats. He said the women there are excellent lovers."

She was incredulous. "How many of them did he sleep with?"

John laughed. "I don't know, but he was gone both nights."

Genevieve perused the other photographs. "This is a beautiful planet. I love how the women dress. Their jewelry is amazing."

"You'd be a big hit because you're so small and you have all that beautiful black hair." Genevieve hadn't cut her hair for over five years and it fell halfway to her waist. "Like a China doll," he said.

She clapped her hands together in excitement. "We can go together!"

As he passed his desk on the way to bed, John saw the codebook was back in its accustomed place on the shelf. Armando must have returned it.

32

As usual after one of his adventures, John walked into the office Monday morning feeling the unreality of his mundane earthian life.

He picked up a note from Marlowe on the server: "Go over the last three weeks worth of data...." blah blah blah. He had been really into this just a couple of days ago.

John decided to check his email. What was this? Something from Gene.

John –

Been working with Bill on the technique. Going slow but he's getting it. We played on Sat and he almost beat me. Bill's not so bright but when he gets into s/g he goes for it. Anyway, he wants to bring 3 friends with him on Fri to learn the technique. That OK with you? One of these guys plays AA ball in the Carolina League. Hey maybe we're going to make a little splash with this stuff. Call me Mon night and let me know.

Guess what Bill went up to see Svetlana this weekend. Won't say a fuckin thing about it. But he told me he stopped drinking. I'll believe that when I see it. Makes me wish I had somebody. It didn't work out with me and Millie.

– Gene

Bill was the last person John ever thought would get into the technique. And now he wouldn't have to worry about Svetlana when they played up in Birmingham. He wondered what happened to Gene and Millie.

John reluctantly got the data off the server and went to work.

That Friday, John and Gene arrived at the warehouse early for practice and went through the technique. Bill didn't show with his three friends. John and Gene decided to do footwork drills for half an hour, then play best two of three games. They had just finished drilling when Bill came in.

"Sorry I'm late, Jerry's car got a flat." Bill introduced his friends to John and Gene.

"Guys, these are my table tennis buddies I was telling you about, John and Gene. This is Jerry." Bill pointed to an almost fat looking guy of middle height, prematurely balding. "He works at Johnson Builders. This here is Pat, my old drinking buddy." Pat was thin as a rail with a scraggly goatee and baggy pants. He didn't look like the talkative type to John. "Pat's a hotshot programmer at Gerlson Software." John's eyebrows raised. Gerlson was known around the U as a leading-edge company that worked in graphics. They had designed some software that was now used in the movie industry. There were rumors Gerlson also had some government contracts. You didn't work there unless you were really good.

Bill pointed to a guy with long hair tied back in a pony tail. "This is Larry Pedanik. Pitcher for the El Paso Cowboys in the Texas League."

"So what's this thing you do that's supposed to improve performance?" Larry asked.

"It'll help hitters more than pitchers," Gene replied. "It still might do you some good."

"I'm ready," Jerry said. "What do we do?"

John went into the back and got four more chairs. "Sit down and I'll go through it with you."

As Jerry moved to the chair, John noticed most of that fat was actually muscle. "Do you lift?"

Jerry laughed. "Don't have to man. I work construction."

"And drinks a lot of beer," Bill said, a little teasingly.

Jerry guffawed. "Not as much as you."

Bill waved his hands. "Not any more. Gave it up."

Jerry's mouth dropped. "Gave it up? Did you get religion or something?"

Bill grinned and turned a little red. "Hell no. I got something a lot better than that."

"Oh I get it," Jerry said. "Whoever she is, she feels sorry for you."

"We hit it right off."

"Sure you did dipshit."

"C'mon guys, let's get down to business," Larry said. "I aint got all day."

John launched right in. By now he was getting good at introducing the technique to newcomers. He explained it as a way to enhance physical performance and get in the zone. He left out most of the esoteric stuff. John presented the material as something well known even in ancient times, which was being rediscovered. He briefly discussed the merkaba, calling it a human energy field. He described its relationship to the body and went over the purpose for the breathing patterns and why it worked. In ten minutes he was done without boring everybody.

"OK guys, any questions?"

"I just want to see if it works," Jerry said. "Let's go."

"You may not notice too much after the first lesson. The real benefits are in the second stage of the process. Today, see if you can get to stage one. Later, if you're interested, Gene, Bill, or I can take you to stage two."

John led them through the technique two times. He handed each of them a printout. "If you forget here's a cheat sheet. Try to do it now on your own."

As the guys went through the routine John laughed to himself. Here we have a construction worker, a computer programmer, and a professional baseball player sitting in a warehouse meditating together. The times they are a changing.

Suddenly Jerry said, "Amazing." Then, "Wow!"

"What happened?" Gene asked.

"I got it man! Then I lost it." Larry and Pat were curious. "What did it feel like?"

"Just like John here said. I felt my body just...go away, but I was just there. I can't explain it. I'm 245 pounds and I've always been aware of my body because it's so big. It just went away."

"How'd you do?" Bill said to Pat.

"Nuthin' much happened. But maybe I'll try it again."

John thought at first that Pat was going to walk out. The man seemed to possess a naturally disinterested temperament.

Everyone had forgotten about Larry. John could see he had already made stage one. Larry appeared to be floating in his chair. John took a step over to Bill and gestured. "Look."

Bill looked at his friend, then back at John. "Do you see it?" John whispered.

"It's magic. I don't believe it." Bill had a look of pleased but surprised disbelief on his face. "This stuff works."

Larry opened his eyes. He took a deep breath and a look of determination came over his face. "I'm ready for the next phase."

"Wow," said Gene. "He's ready, isn't he John?"

"He's ready. Let me work with Larry. You guys watch the others."

Bill said, "You mind if I sit with Larry? I been having trouble getting there for more than a few minutes."

John went carefully through the stage two procedures and explained a little about the universal medium. During his explanation John achieved certainty. Athletes did not need to know about the outer sphere or the theory of vibration. He would take them to the middle of stage two. If successful, they would reach the place beyond time and be able to consciously maintain themselves in the zone.

"The most important principle in reaching the zone is letting go. When you let go, that's when you get your power."

Bill shook his head. "This stuff is deep. It goes against everything I've been taught. But I think I'm starting to see what you're talking about."

It was clear to John that Larry was a very fast learner. "Have you ever meditated before?"

"Yeah. My father taught me how when I was 13. It saved my life. I was going down the wrong road. Then my dad died of cancer when I was 17. I've been meditating at least twenty minutes a day for the last five years. It helps me get over my anger. I don't want to die young like him."

"It shows," John said. "You're by far the fastest I've ever seen."

"Faster than you?"

John laughed. "A lot faster."

Larry seemed pleased. "As a pitcher I need to maintain complete concentration. I'm the center of the action. If I do my job my team is going to win almost all the time. I've tried sports psychology till I'm sick of it. I'm hoping this stuff will be for real."

"Explain some more about letting go to get power," Bill said.

John went through it again. Larry grasped most of it right away. "OK, let me try," he said.

Meanwhile Bill and Gene were working with Pat and Jerry. After about 15 minutes Jerry stopped. "OK I got it. This is some cool shit, man," he said to Gene. "I can't believe I'm doing it. If some of my buddies on crew knew I was here they'd probably push me off a girder."

Pat was expressionless. "How you doing?" Bill asked him.

"All right I guess," he said.

They ended off twenty minutes later.

"Let's go out for a few beers," Jerry said to Bill.

"Uh, no thanks. I'm calling my girlfriend in an hour."

"Oh God," Jerry teased.

Normally Bill would have gotten angry. "You wish you had a girlfriend like mine."

Jerry didn't argue.

John handed Larry, Pat, and Jerry his printouts for the first two levels, along with his own explanation of the technique and why it worked.

Larry shook John's hand, and Gene's too. "This is going to help me I think."

"If you have any questions email me or call," John said.

"I will."

After Bill and his friends left, John turned to Gene. "You still want to play?"

"Nah." He looked pensive. "You know John, if this stuff spreads we could really make a difference."

"Yeah. There'd be a lot more guys who could beat us!"

Gene looked at his watch. "Wanna call Millie tonight. We broke up but I still haven't given up." He started out the door, then stopped. "John, when you were in school we all thought you were weird. We just didn't get it."

John grinned. "I *was* weird. You guys were right."

Gene raised his hand in a salute and left.

"I'll be damned," John muttered. He put the chairs away, locked up the old warehouse and drove home in the cold.

On Saturday John drove over to Gascard's in three inches of new snow with the little jewelry case.

"Is Emile in?"

"Emile doesn't see anyone except by appointment," the clerk said.

"He's going to want to see this. I suggest you go back and get him. I've got two exceptional pieces here that only a master could truly appreciate."

The clerk left, reluctantly. A few minutes later Emile Gascard came flying into the room, a jeweler's glass pushed up around his forehead. "What is this bother?" he said with profound irritation, glaring at John. "I am just setting a magnificent ruby."

John quietly pulled out the case and put it on the counter. Gascard gave it a quick, dismissive gesture and took a few steps out of the room. Then he stopped and slowly turned around. He approached the case carefully, like a cat sniffing around something it wasn't sure of. He reached out and picked it up, pushing the glass down over his eye.

"Where did you get this?"

John just smiled. "Open it up but be careful. The pieces are delicate."

Gascard snorted his disgust. He removed the top and gasped when he saw the pieces. Slowly he picked one up, rotating it just as Genevieve had done. He reverently replaced it. "This is the finest workmanship I have ever seen. And the design – *magnifique*. It is impossible to construct such a piece. So delicate! Such elegance! And so very *complexe*!"

"Can you make earrings out of these?"

"Perhaps. But first I want to know where you got them."

"A friend of mine I call Phillipe made them. But he's...uh...unavailable."

Gascard looked critically at John for a moment. "I cannot argue with the pieces. They are magnificent. I am honored to set them for you." He looked again at the fragile constructions and muttered, "But so very *difficile*." He looked at John. "There is not a good place to attach the hook. I will have to improvise. To destroy such work would be a crime. Give them to me and I will tell you whether it is advisable to even consider such a thing."

John nodded and gave the man his phone number. "Please phone me as soon as you make your determination."

As he walked out John smiled to himself. No way Emile Gascard admits defeat. He expected to hear from him before closing.

After John left Emile Gascard went directly to his private office and made a phone call. He spoke in French (translation provided): "Henri? Gascard. You must drop everything...no I don't care who you are seeing right now...then tell her it's an emergency! Yes. Right away. No, the back entrance! I cannot hold onto these for more than a few days...All right."

Half an hour later a black limo drove in and parked in back. A well dressed, almost foppish looking man entered the back door of Gascard's, held open by Emile. "Come, come!" Emile said impatiently. The visitor strolled languidly into the office. "My dear Emile," he said, his eyes cold steel, "you have interrupted a most pleasurable assignation." Emile understood the implied threat and quickly retrieved the case. He placed it into Henri's hands. Henri took a glass from one of the inside pockets of his dress coat and examined the cupola.

"Where did these come from?"

"The man who brought the object was evasive as to its origin. But he is known to me."

"Find out."

Henri opened the case and his eyes widened. Carefully he inspected the piece. "You have done well Emile."

"The man who brought these to you is named John Frankel, is he not? A tall fellow with curly hair?"

Emile was astonished. "Quite so." There was silence for a minute as Henri examined the piece. "Not possible," he muttered.

"Precisely. How shall I proceed?"

Henri took out a small imager and made detailed photographs. "I am going to send these to certain friends of mine. In a day, at most two, I shall have instructions."

Emile did not need to be told to hold onto the pieces as long as possible. He nodded his head to Henri and escorted him to the back door.

"Do not tell a single soul," Henri said. Emile closed the door thoughtfully. The fact that Henri had found it necessary to remind him sent a chill up Emile's spine. He would have to be discreet.

The next day Henri called. "Set the pieces, if you can, and place within each of them a small device which a courier will drop off. Do you understand Emile?"

"Perfectly, Henri."

An hour later a package arrived. In it were two white beads, to match the ones on the jewelry. Emile discerned that these two beads were slightly larger. However, he was a master jeweler and it should be child's play for him to disguise their presence.

He began by inspecting the fine, metallic threads and the placement of the beads upon them. The threads were gossamer thin and they shone as the light hit them, making them appear to be larger than they really were. These filaments are far too fragile to support even themselves. After studying the piece for half an hour it finally dawned on him. The filaments were self-supporting in an ingenious geometric pattern. To remove any of them meant the collapse of the entire structure. As long as the piece was intact, it would be as strong as tempered steel. Emile Gascard stared at the object in disbelief. He had been in the jewelry business for 40 years. The knowledge necessary to construct these pieces simply did not exist.

Gascard felt as a child before them. He was humbled by them. He knew for certain he could not have made them, galling as it was to admit it.

How could such a fragile structure stay together? He placed the piece in his delicate fingers and pressed ever so slightly. The filaments, as if they were alive, adjusted effortlessly to the pressure. He squeezed tighter, with the same results. Remarkable. Now he tested the material of the filaments. He laid his finest shaper next to a green colored filament and pressed. It bent but did not feel at all as fragile as it looked. He took his finest pliers and enclosed them around the thread. Nothing. He pressed, a little harder, and harder again. Whatever this material is, it was not at all breakable. It possessed terrific tensile strength and elastic deformation properties.

Now he turned to the problem of attaching the beads. After twenty minutes of study he was baffled again. He could detect no glues, solders, wires, or clasps. Were the beads atomically bonded to the filaments?

He put the piece down and his mouth opened in admiration. Ahhh! To learn from the master who created these! It would be so exciting, so perfect. He would build upon the techniques and create even greater masterpieces!

Emile Gascard would do his dirty work for Henri LeFleur. Then he would see about studying with this man...he was interrupted by the phone. "A man named John Frankel on the phone for you sir."

"Thank you Roberts." He switched over to the public line. "Hello Mr. Frankel."

"Have you made a determination?"

"I have determined that the fellow who made these is a genius. I tell you I must know his name...don't get alarmed Mr. Frankel. You see, I am a master. I trained under the great Etaille 40 years ago in France. But I cannot fashion these. The design is too intricate. The materials I have never seen before."

"Can you set them?"

Emile held the piece up to the light. "Yes."

"Then do so, and we will discuss their origins when I come to pick them up."

Gascard was satisfied. "Very good. I'll have them ready for you Saturday morning." That would give him plenty of time in case of difficulty. He knew now that the hook could be safely attached anywhere within the construction. He would just have to glue Henri's beads carefully and hope no one noticed.

On Saturday John picked up the earrings and presented them to Genevieve. "Look at yourself in the mirror. They were made for you." Genevieve stood in front of the full length mirror in the hallway. The pieces looked alive as the light reflected off the filaments. John saw the relationship between the curved geometry of the threads and the white beads. The polyhedron formed by the beads was inside the geometry of the filaments, and appeared to be generated from it. As the earrings rotated the shapes changed, but always in sync. Gascard had done a fine job with the setting, allowing for the symmetric twirling.

"John, these are astonishing," Genevieve said. "I don't think I ever want to take them off."

"Now you're even more beautiful, if that's possible."

Genevieve preened in front of the mirror for a few minutes, shaking her head and admiring the changing shapes and colors. John smiled. It was such a typically womanly gesture and an aspect of her feminine side that she was revealing more and more to him.

She smiled at him in the mirror. "I can't wait till June 10th."

For the next month Marlowe pushed John hard at work. The team had hit a glitch. John was once more putting in extra hours and trying to keep up with his class work. His head was spinning every night so he went down the basement and lifted for half an hour before bed every day. Somehow he found time to work on his thesis. John decided to turn it into a book. Shortcuts to Learning a Foreign Language was his tentative title. Michael Walters wanted him to publish under the University Press label and write it for academics. John wanted to appeal to the layman. He was writing the book in a conversational style. Inspired by his adventure in Argelain, he was learning French using his symbolic language.

One evening he came home around 7. "Hey Genny!"

"I'm up here!"

John ran upstairs and found Genevieve at her laptop, typing furiously. She was wearing the earrings. "Hi honey!" she said, but did not look up. He looked over her shoulder. "What are you writing?"

"A novel. About our experiences. About our life."

"Really? Do you think anyone would be interested?"

She frowned and paused for a second. "You're kidding, right?"

John realized she was right. They'd done some pretty cool things.

"As usual you're two steps ahead of me." John looked at her prose and almost immediately was drawn into the story. "That's really good."

She brightened and gave him a quick smile. "Do you think so?"

He read some more. "It's good Gen. Really good. You're a natural. You can do anything and do it better than almost anyone. I've never seen anybody learn as fast as you."

"But if it weren't for you I might not be able to do any of it," she said. "Oh John, you've drawn me out of my shell and shown me how to be myself."

He kissed her. "I don't want to disturb your creative process so I'll let you be."

As he left the room she turned immediately to her computer and began rapping the keys.

That Saturday the phone rang as he entered the living room. "Probably Mats, saying he's going to be late." It was now early February. Mats and John were scheduled to watch the Super Bowl at 6:30.

John picked up the phone. "Hey Mats, what's the excuse this time?"

"Huh?" a voice said. "Is this John Frankel?"

"Speaking."

"John, this is Larry Pedanik. A while back we did a...technique, I think you called it."

"Yeah! Larry, how are you?"

"Never better and that's why I called. I want to come back for another lesson. We've all been playing winter ball but the season's over now for us. You mind if I bring a few of the guys?"

"Uh, no! You mean from the team?"

"Yeah, and a couple guys from other teams."

"You mean people are actually interest in this stuff?"

"Are you kidding?" Larry replied. "I got 5 mph more on my fastball and my control is way better. The other guys want some. It's lonely down here in Double A. We want a shot at the Show. We all need an edge."

"Yeah sure. When do you want to do it?"

"Your next practice is Friday?"

"Friday will be OK. How many guys do you have?"

"Me and eight others."

"Wow! OK, I'll be ready. You know how to get here?"

"I'll get Bill to pick us up. See ya."

John was so excited he wanted to run up the stairs and tell Genevieve. The sound of her typing stopped him.

What was happening to his life? Things were happening so quickly, but it was all good.

As usual Mats was late and had already missed most of the first quarter. "No score," he told Mats. "You'll never guess what happened."

Mats opened a beer and stared at the TV.

"I've got nine Double A professional ballplayers coming this Friday to learn the technique."

Mats slowly turned to face John on the couch, a beer can dangling from his fingers. "Joke, right?"

"No joke."

"How'd that happen?"

"I don't know Mats. It's like magic. I guess people recognize a good thing, especially if it really works."

"That reminds me. Maggie's been burning my ear to learn the technique. OK if I show her?"

John was nonplussed. "Jeez Mats...Maggie? Are you serious?"

"It's not so hard to understand is it?" Mats puffed up a little. "She says she sees changes in me, John. Good changes."

John laughed. "OK Mats. I guess it's OK."

"I want to go back."

"Nothing stopping you," John said.

"I want to take the girls."

Now it was John's turn to face Mats. He was about to protest when he realized he couldn't find any good objections. John's mouth was half open and he closed it. The planet he called Argelain was beautiful. The people were intelligent and prosperous and he couldn't imagine any dangers there. "How are you going to get three teenage girls to sit still long enough to learn the procedure?"

Mats looked at him like he was crazy. "All I had to do was show them these pictures. After that, the mall seemed pretty tame."

"Be careful Mats. Those girls won't last one night before someone tries to sleep with them. The culture on Argelain is totally different than ours."

"Yeah, but look at it John. I'd rather have one of those intelligent, cultured guys be their first instead of some ham-handed meathead that'll just get them pregnant."

John was doubtful. He wondered how Mats had ever raised such great kids. Pure luck, most likely.

"The odds of the two species being able to bear offspring is probably remote. But Mats, you've opened up a whole new can of worms regarding sex education and the raising of children."

"I didn't do it. You did."

Now it hit him, what he had started six years ago with a funny looking book Genevieve had given to him from the Full Moon. It now seemed like several lifetimes ago. His discoveries were influencing the lives of Gene and Bill, Mats, Jerry and Pat, professional baseball players, Maggie, his mother, and even three young girls.

John shook his head. It was getting too unreal. Out of control even. Nevertheless, he sat back and watched the game with his friend until Mats' cell rang.

"Dad, come help us. We're stuck." Mats put down the phone. "Sorry John. Gotta get home."

"What is it?"

"They're having trouble with the technique."

"Let me come."

Mats was surprised. "You want to?"

"Yeah. Genevieve and I are getting married but we can never have children. I guess it's my chance to play uncle."

Mats regarded John with sympathy for a split second. "Come on then Uncle John."

That Friday John drove to practice. He became consciously aware of something he'd noticed in the back of his mind for several months now. A dark blue sedan had been following him ever since he made the turn onto Garden. He turned right at the next intersection and went out of his way. Sure enough, about 30 seconds later the sedan made the same turn.

Maybe it was the Return of Gary. John decided he was having none of the cloak and dagger stuff. If they wanted to follow him, so be it.

When he arrived Gene was already there. "Let's warm up. We probably won't get to play today."

"How'd it go with Millie?"

"We're making progress," Gene replied. "I don't know John, she's a little too possessive."

"Lots of fish in the sea," John said.

"Yeah but I really like this fish."

Ten minutes later Bill and Jerry showed up in two cars crammed with Larry and his friends.

"OK boys," Larry said. "This is the guy I was telling you about. John, and his friend Gene. They started the whole thing."

Gene was pleased to be mentioned. "Who are your friends?"

"This is Moises, Pete, Tony, Reinaldo, Carlos, Pedro, and Dave."

"You guys all play in the Texas League?"

"All except one," Carlos said. He was big, about 6' 5" and muscular. Carlos stuck out his hand toward John. "I play first base for El Paso." John shook hands. Carlos said, "Strong grip."

"Pete, Tony, and Carlos are on my team," Larry said. "Dave and Reinaldo play for Wichita. Moises plays for Tulsa. Pedro's in the Carolina League. Known him since high school."

"I'm curious," John said. "How'd you guys find out about this?"

"Easy," Carlos said. He was a friendly guy, and talkative. "We saw what happened with Larry. That guy couldn't hit the lake from a boat. Then one day all of a sudden he's got perfect control."

Pete said, "I figure it's worth some gas money. If it's all bullshit then no big damage to my wallet."

It was good enough for John. He did the same drill as before, with Gene and Bill helping. John was amazed at the change in Bill. From surly and disheveled to bright and clean in just six weeks. Maybe it was partly Svetlana. John figured he had a hand in it too.

The guys had already been prepared by Larry. John had his handouts ready and everything went smoothly. Carlos and Moises caught on right away. The other guys had a harder time of it.

Larry acknowledged John and Gene as they were all filing out. "Thanks guys. We want to come back during spring training in a couple of months. That OK?"

"Sure," John said.

John, Gene, and Bill stared at each other as if to say, "We started it, but we don't know how it's going to finish." All three of them laughed simultaneously.

"Let's go play some pool," John said. That suggestion met with unanimous agreement.

When he got home around 10:30 John found Genevieve at the desk in the living room, typing away. She already had 343 pages. That reminded him about his own book/thesis, which he was neglecting. John couldn't wait until his program was complete. The classwork was finally done and he resolved to complete the thesis in two weeks. Then his formal education would be over, thank God. He had finished the program a semester early thanks to Michael Walters. It had been a piece of cake. He hardly ever had to go to class and took his exams online.

On his way to work Monday morning John noticed another tail. John thought about asking Michael Walters to sniff around, but decided against it.

When John stepped into the office Marlowe was there. "Hi John! Long time no see. Bloody busy though, we all are."

Peter Marlowe was down to two chins now.

"Looking better," John said.

"The formula is simple John. Calories in less than calories out, you lose weight."

Marlowe stood at the desk and typed something on the keyboard. One thing good about being short, John thought. "Here's the latest data from the server. We're making progress again. In fact, we're almost there. Let me know what you come up with."

During the next two months Peter Marlowe and his colleagues completed their work. Their paper gained enthusiastic approval from the Astronomy Department. Marlowe sent it off to several academic publications, including the prestigious *Astronomical Review*.

"Only one problem with AR John. It takes months for the review process. Dash it, must be some way to speed that up." Marlowe presented the paper to John. It was titled "A Virtual Approach to the Identification of Red Shift Quasars and other Unusual Objects." At the bottom of the list of names he saw his own.

"Damn good of you Dr. Marlowe," John said.

"You made a contribution. I'm grateful."

"Looks like I'm going to be out of a job."

"We can keep you on through the winter term, until the end of April. Then our funding for this project is complete."

It was the end of February, so he had a paycheck for the next twelve weeks. What was he going to do for money after that? They were still living with Robert and Rachel, paying room and board. Expenses were minimal. He and Genevieve had a tidy little sum in the bank so he could slide for a while. John rebelled at that thought. He didn't want to be a slacker and live off Genevieve. But Genevieve was happy and wanted to stay in the old house. Thank God his parents had cleaned up their act. Rachel and Genevieve were getting along famously. Genevieve was the daughter Rachel never had. Robert had lightened up considerably, his development seemingly attendant with the weight he was shedding.

One day after dinner the four sat in the living room. Genevieve was still working on her novel and John went to work on his thesis. Rachel and Robert were reading by the fire. Rachel put down her book, lay down on the floor, and went through the procedure for stage one. Robert observed carefully. It seemed to him that her facial features had softened. She looked more feminine and youthful.

"All right, that's it," Robert said.

"That's what?" Genevieve said.

"Somebody show me how to do this stuff. I do a lot of breathing when I run but this is something different altogether."

"I'd be glad to show you dad." Genevieve had been calling Robert 'Dad' for a year now. Her father-in-law had grown to like it.

"Just the person I was going to ask," Robert said.

John smiled to himself. Over the past three years she had subtly but completely taken over management of the household. Genevieve collected a sum from Robert each month for their share of the expenses. She paid all the bills. She did the general shopping (except for Rachel's specialty food items), arranged for contractor repairs, landscaping, and snow removal. She did it so effortlessly that no one even noticed.

Robert really liked not having to worry about that stuff anymore. He had plenty of free time for writing and traveling. Rachel had time for her cooking, writing, and seamstressing. She had enjoyed making Genevieve's prom dress. After that she had received so many inquiries that her life was a constant buzz of activity. During the day Rachel taught at the university. Gourmet cooking, writing, and dress making occupied her evenings and weekends. John didn't know how she fit it all in.

As he wrote he heard Genevieve's soft voice instructing his father. John looked around the cozy living room with the fire blazing and the happy people in it. Maybe this was what family meant. It sure felt good.

33

IN early April the doorbell rang just after lunch on a cold Saturday. Rachel and Robert had left the house. Genevieve went to the door and opened it. Outside were two guys in black suits. "We would like to speak with John Frankel and his fiancée," one of them said.

John immediately appraised the situation from the couch. "Come in gentlemen."

The man on the right smiled ever so slightly and they both entered.

"Have a seat," John said, motioning to the chairs by the fireplace.

The larger of the men shook his head. "No thank you. We'll sit on the couch."

John and Genevieve took the wing chairs on either side of the fireplace, against the back wall. As he sat down John realized that his guests now commanded the room.

"We won't waste your time Mr. Frankel. You probably have a good idea why we are here." The eyes of the two visitors met and they nodded slightly to each other. "I am Martin Haliburton. This is my colleague Gyorgi Havel." Haliburton was of medium height and stocky. His partner, smallish and thin, looked Eastern European. Havel was impeccably dressed and groomed, and smelled subtly of cologne. John noticed that Havel's hands were encased in expensive leather mittens which he did not remove. He seemed unaware of their existence and wore them as if they were a part of him.

John sized up the situation. Haliburton was doing the talking but Havel was clearly in charge. The man oozed a sense of authority.

"We need your help on a matter of extreme urgency," Haliburton continued. "We are prepared to show you things which no civilian has ever been permitted to know unless they have the highest security clearances."

John's radar was on full blast now. Both he and Genevieve carefully scrutinized the two men.

"We have had you under careful observation for the past several months. We are satisfied as to your character." John's eyebrows raised. These guys are Gary, Part Two.

"A couple of years ago you cooperated with one of our agents. You seem to be a patriotic American. And most important, you are able to keep a secret. We have done a complete psychological profile of you and your fiancée and believe you can be trusted. At this point we have no choice."

John scrutinized Gyorgi Havel very closely while his partner talked. The man betrayed not the slightest physical or emotional reaction.

Haliburton continued. "We would like you and your fiancée to come with us for the weekend. It's not something that can be explained. We must demonstrate our case in person."

"Where will we be going?" John asked.

"To a facility outside the city of Chicago," Haliburton said.

John sighed. "We'd really rather not."

Haliburton and Havel sat silent and unmoving, their attention fixed on the two subjects. Their demeanor seemed to say, "We aren't going anywhere until you agree."

We're never going to get rid of these guys, John thought to himself. They were trapped by forces beyond their control just as surely as they were cornered in their own living room. But perhaps their knowledge of the technique gave them an edge. An edge Havel and Haliburton might not be aware of. John looked at Genevieve and received her silent agreement.

"All right. Give us time to write a note to my parents."

"Of course."

As John wrote Havel spoke for the first time in precise, formal English, with a slight accent. "We will return here no later than 5 p.m. tomorrow so you will not have to miss work."

John was sure that their request had something to do with the paranormal research he had discussed with Gary.

"Well then," Havel said, in a voice that was meant for everyone in the room. "Shall we leave immediately?"

They piled into a dark blue stretch limo with Illinois plates. John and Genevieve were given the spacious back area while the two men sat up front. Haliburton took the wheel. A thick plate of protective glass or plastic separated them. John was disappointed. He was hoping to ask several questions, and said so aloud.

"You will be fully briefed when we reach our destination," Haliburton said into a microphone. "If you look to your right you will see a small refrigerator. Help yourself."

The limo was spacious and well appointed. Two large seats with thick and comfortable upholstery faced each other. Tinted windows allowed for easy viewing, although there wasn't much of interest in the still wintry landscape. Genevieve opened the refrigerator and grabbed a deli sandwich. John saw cheeses, more sandwiches, soda, bottled water, beer, wine coolers, and pate with a loaf of small, thin sliced bread. He chose the water and a sandwich and they began to eat.

Havel glanced in one of his mirrors to see what they had chosen. The water, of course, and the sandwiches. Their choices accurately reflected the personality profiles of the subjects. He was satisfied.

The rest of the drive was spent in silence. John's irritation at having their weekend interrupted was subsiding as he enjoyed their comfortable surroundings. They were able to see on three sides. The limo entered the freeway and drove for about 90 minutes. Then they spent another 45 minutes on surface roads, finally entering the countryside. After half an hour or so they turned onto a dirt road, winding and twisting. The vehicle finally came to a stop in a grove of trees.

"This is it?" John asked. "There's nothing here."

Haliburton smiled. "This is it."

They piled out and walked for about 100 feet. Haliburton carried a hand held device. "Here we are." He pushed a button and a piece of the ground moved aside. A circular opening about ten feet in diameter appeared, revealing a dark stairway with soft lighting spaced every ten feet or so.

"Please hand me your mobiles," Haliburton said.

John objected and saw Havel stiffen. John shrugged. The two visitors handed over their phones to Haliburton and began to walk down the stairwell.

Three hours before Henri LaFleur was eating breakfast in his luxuriously appointed dining room. He received a call on his cell phone. It was Gerard, his personal aide. Gerard had instructions to monitor the Frankel residence and alert him to anything unusual. The earrings had served their purpose. The girl had worn them constantly. Henri couldn't blame her, for the pieces were exquisite. If there was a way to contact their maker! Such magnificent jewelry would claim enormous prices.

So far he had gotten no useful information. The Walters girl was reticent and seemed to enjoy silence and silent places. The only time she talked to the Frankel kid was at night after she had removed the delicate earrings and placed them in their case. Although the listening device was very sensitive, the resulting audio had been a frustrating mumble.

Henri enjoyed his omelet and scone. He had performed this procedure many times before and it had elicited valuable information he had used to his personal enrichment. People will pay handsomely for information. It was amazing how much data could be picked up from the wife or consort of an important man.

"Henri!" The voice on the other end was excited and impatient.

"Yes Gerard," LaFleur said languidly.

"A limo just arrived at the house, Illinois plates. Better get the car out if you want to know where they're going."

Henri picked up Gerard down the street from the Frankel house. He saw the four step into the limo. Henri shook his head. Those boys were probably black. Henri LeFleur wanted no part of that action.

Haliburton spoke into the device: "1020 and 1021 accessing with two subjects through remote entrance 12."

"Roger that."

They walked through a corridor for perhaps a quarter of a mile before coming out into an open area. The large circular room was occupied by around three dozen operators wearing small headsets, each at a console. The Eyrie! John thought.

As they passed through John Haliburton said, "Field monitoring and coordination station."

They walked out of the room down another corridor to a suite of offices.

"How big is this place?" Genevieve asked.

"One square mile," Haliburton replied.

"Holy shit!" John blurted. The stocky man smiled.

The group reached a posh office, brightly lit. Haliburton walked out of the room. Havel took a chair.

"Why did you bring us here?" Genevieve asked.

"To ask for your assistance," Havel said. He nodded to John. "You have previously helped one of our agents with a translation to a powerful psychic methodology. Since you are the originators of this procedure we would like you to personally train some of our operators."

"We could have shown you the technique in our living room," John said.

"Unsatisfactory," Havel replied quickly. "For optimum results our viewers must be instructed here, in their working environment."

Neither John nor Genevieve liked the secretive vibe in this place.

Gyorgi Havel felt their disapproval. "You have already been informed of the critical nature of our paranormal work and our subordinate position relative to our enemies."

John and Genevieve said nothing. Genevieve decided she did not like Mr. Havel at all. The sooner they could leave this place the better.

Havel's eyes became slits. "You two have no idea of the stakes involved. When you found that book and translated it, you automatically made yourself a player in a game that goes far beyond your comprehension."

"We don't want to be players," John said loudly, speaking for both of them. Havel had no idea how big the game really was!

Havel was unsympathetic. "Too bad. You're in the loop now. Live with it. Co-operate with us this weekend and then go back to your life. And don't ever breathe a word about what you see here."

Now John became angry. "You're threatening us."

"It's not a threat," Havel said. "We don't go around arranging 'accidents' for people we don't like. That stuff is for amateurs. We're a research facility. I'm just telling you this for your own good."

John shrugged and looked at his fiancée. "All right. Let's get on with it then."

"First I want to show you what we are doing here."

Havel directed them into a little four-seater golf cart and they took off. The floor was made of a hard, seamless substance that carried through the entire facility. The ceilings were about 50 feet high. The place reminded John of a gigantic small airplane hangar. It had very large rooms interspersed with corridors, some of which contained offices. They were now in a large circular area with more workstations, operators, and a ring of chairs occupied by twelve persons.

"Remote Viewing Training Area," Havel said. "Here is where we train our re-mote counter-intelligence and counter-espionage teams. The mind can go where the body cannot. However, accuracy is essential. We train within the city, where we can precisely determine the exactness of a subject's perception. This is where you will be working."

The cart moved into a gigantic room that contained a 3D holographic pro-jection. The cart stopped in the center. They were now in the middle of a busy downtown Chicago street. Pedestrians and cars moved noisily past them. John looked above and saw a sky with clouds moving slowly upon it, framed between the skyscrapers of the street.

Havel smiled. "We have imagers all over the city. We can get a real-time pro-jection of just about anywhere we want." The scene shifted to a suburban street. A man walked his dog, two kids were kicking a soccer ball, a woman filled her bird-feeder. John heard birds chirping in the tree above the feeder. A dog began to bark. "This system makes accuracy checking easy."

Havel directed the cart out of the room, down a hallway and into another area of apartments. "Living quarters," he said.

"How many people live here?" Genevieve asked.

"Almost one hundred." The cart approached a gated area. A clear Plexiglas barrier separated it from the rest of the complex.

"Research area. Restricted, so we can't go in," Havel remarked.

"What sort of research?" John asked.

"They're working on some kind of thought shield. It's far-out stuff, and the reason we brought you here."

"Explain please," John said to Havel.

"Our agent explained the situation to you when he visited your home. The Russians and the Chinese have developed a cadre of supersensitive and accurate remote viewers that can penetrate our security systems. We've stored sensitive data in every way possible but it still gets read. We've shielded and encrypted it in every way we can think of but we can't keep anything secure."

"You already know how to do the technique," Genevieve said. "My fiancée and I don't have any special abilities. I don't know what you think will happen."

"Let me show you." Havel stopped the cart in front of a workstation. He motioned for John and Genevieve to get out. "We have the ability to monitor what we call the Unity Field. It is a recent discovery. The Unity Field is a quantum substrate that pervades everything in the universe. It is extremely subtle however. For decades we've been trying to unlock its secrets. Our remote viewing operation is part of that effort. We don't know how to use it yet, but we are aware of disturbances within it. We monitor the field and mark all points of unusual activity." Havel brought up a flat, Mercatur display of the earth. John saw a bunch of bright dots scattered around the globe and a few very bright patches.

"This map shows all global Unity Field activity within the past year. You'll note the bright circles here. Four of them in China, and three more in Russia." John and Genevieve bent over to look at the display. There were three more bright circles in Europe. One in England, a smaller one in France, and one in Germany. "Now look at the map of the United States," Havel said. There was a bright circle around the DC area and another on the west coast. Another bright circle lie right smack in the middle of Midland.

"Holy shit," John said.

"That's just what we thought," Havel said dryly.

John and Genevieve straightened, looked at each other, and smiled.

"And here I thought our activities were going unnoticed," Genevieve commented.

"I need not point out that there's almost as much field activity just between you two than there are in all of our research facilities devoted to studying the subject." Havel stood straight up and confronted them. "Our previous attempts to apply the principles in the book you gave our agent did not bear fruit. We did send someone to your last instruction session. He came back not understanding much of what you said."

So there was a spy in that group of ball players! The programmer Pat? He was the only one who didn't make any progress.

"That's why we picked you up. We want you to demonstrate your technique personally to our staff."

"All right," John said. "We'll do it if you promise to leave us alone in the future."

Havel smiled briefly but made no promises.

"We're hungry," Genevieve said to Havel.

"I will have someone drive you to the cafeteria." Havel checked his chronometer. "It is almost 1800. Have dinner on us, there's no rush. Afterward you will be driven to the guest quarters. Please stay inside your room until the room chimes at

0630 tomorrow morning. You are not authorized to be outside your quarters from 2000 hours this evening until tomorrow at 0700. At 0700 a car will take you back to the cafeteria for breakfast. The demonstration will begin precisely at 0800. Please be ready."

A driver arrived in a cart and drove Havel off. Haliburton arrived a minute later and picked them up. They were driven a quarter mile to an open cafeteria with chairs and tables. Several persons who looked like maintenance workers occupied the area.

"Are you are tired as I am?" John asked Genevieve.

"Yeah. I can't wait to get out of this place."

"Neither can I. But it might be fun."

Genevieve gave him a skeptical look.

The two finished their meal silently. Haliburton sat at a table across from them but did not eat. When they were done Haliburton spoke. "Leave the implements on the table. Someone will clear them."

As they got back in the cart John could barely get his leg up and into the vehicle. He was dog-tired. Genevieve rested her head on his shoulder and closed her eyes. After a ten minute ride Haliburton showed them into a room which would pass at any good hotel. It contained a high-definition television, a small refrigerator, a shower and bath, two beds, a desk, and a small laptop computer. Haliburton exited and the opening merged with the wall. John realized they were locked in for the night. He was too tired to care. John and Genevieve were asleep almost as soon as their heads hit the pillow.

At 0630 a soft blinking light came from the walls. John stumbled into the shower and Genevieve washed her face. They ate a quick meal. John quickly typed a summary of the technique for stages one and two. He saw a 'print' key and hit it. From a small slit in the wall his hardcopy emerged. He made three dozen just in case. At 0700 the opening reappeared in the wall. Haliburton waited outside in the corridor in one of the electric carts. They got in and rode silently to a large room with curved walls in which about thirty persons were seated. Some of them were still scratching sleep from their eyes.

Havel was there. "Welcome! We're all briefed and ready to go. You have the floor."

"Give me a few more minutes," John said. "I just got up."

There were a few laughs. Havel responded impatiently. "You have less than four hours. Please show us the techniques you use in your work. We'll modify what you give us for our own purposes."

"All right. Genevieve will show the women and I'll show the men." After bodies were rearranged they went ahead. Havel posted a thick bullet-headed guard who could probably kill everyone in the room in ten seconds. John and Genevieve handed everyone a printout.

John was curious to see what kind of human being lived in an underground facility. He was betting these people were slightly nutty. He wasn't disappointed.

John had 17 men. Ten of them were just going through the motions. Clearly, not all of them were trained sensitives, as Havel had claimed. Three of them looked like Pat the computer programmer. These three had the same emotionless exterior. He kept an eye on them anyway, for the technique was so powerful that even the obtuse might get results.

John noticed that the guard had taken a chair at the back of the room and was himself going through the routine.

After an hour of practice five made it to the first level, including one of the ten he had written off. John heard an exclamation, then an oath. He turned around to see the bullet-headed man with his mouth open in astonishment. Bullet head gestured urgently to John.

When John came over he whispered, "I feel different." He spoke as if he had just announced the Second Coming of Jesus Christ.

"Explain," John said.

"My body was floating and I felt...wonderful." He seemed embarrassed to admit it.

"Good," John said. "You made it. Come over here with this group." The man moved to a seat next to a woman who seemed to be floating off her chair. "Yeah," bullet head said. "Just like that."

John grinned. "Do it again. I won't look."

Five minutes later bullet head sat there with his hands on his lap and a slow grin spreading over his face. All of a sudden he exploded. "This is better than sex!" Everybody turned to look at him.

"Hey Bobo!" somebody teased in the other group. "You finally went screwy!"

"Don't mind him, he doesn't get it." John tried to encourage the man. "People always criticize things they don't understand."

Havel had left the room an hour before and now he was back. John was sure he was observing from close by and that their session was being recorded. "How are we doing?"

Genevieve said, "I've got eight here ready for the next level." John said, "Five here plus the guard."

Havel looked at bullet head. "You abandoned your post Ruczinsky!"

John looked at Havel. "He made it to the first level." John waved his hand at the other group. "These others can work on their own if they want, but for now they can return to duty. We have 14 possibles."

Havel looked pleased. "All right. You have another—" he looked at his chronometer – "155 minutes. Then we have to return you to the surface."

As Havel walked out of the room he kicked bullet head, whose eyes opened. "If you make it we'll have to reassign you." Ruczinsky nodded his head. John could see the man had really reached a profound state of calm.

"OK ladies and gentlemen, we're going to go for stage two."

John took 30 minutes and explained the merkaba, the inner and outer spheres, and the universal field. There was a buzz of excitement in the room now that the deadwood had left, and many questions. "We know about the inner sphere," a tall black haired woman said. "I've never heard of the outer one."

John told the group a little bit about the protocols to enable definition and control of the outer sphere, and the relationship between it and the inner sphere and the body. Then he carefully went over the breathing techniques and the specific protocols for the second stage. He knew he'd have to help them individually. His work with Larry and his friends taught him the importance of absolute clarity at the outset. He carefully answered all of their questions.

"If everyone is ready let's proceed."

John and Genevieve got them going. At this stage it was more difficult to tell who would get it and who wouldn't. Sometimes, like Mats, it took months. These were trained paranormal investigators and he expected to see at least a couple make it.

At the 30 minute mark something remarkable occurred. Havel reentered the room just in time to see Ruczinsky open his eyes and smile. John turned toward the bullet head and got the shock of his life. Ruczinsky had morphed into a creature with pronounced feline characteristics. It was covered in a silvery fur and had a tail just like a cat. It had two arms, two legs, and a head.

"What the..." Havel said.

John's jaw dropped in astonishment.

The creature said, "I am from Galaxy 3, the one you call Andromeda." He rose, glided gracefully over to John, and held out a paw-like hand with a padded palm. John took it and immediately felt a pleasurable sensation throughout his body. The creature effortlessly probed John's energy field. "Yes. Yes indeed. It has finally happened." He did the same with Genevieve. "You we are particularly interested in."

All in the room were dumbfounded. Havel was the first to find his voice. "Who the hell are you? You're supposed to be Ruczinsky!"

Everyone in the room burst out laughing.

"I *am* Ruczinsky!" So saying, the creature was again the bullet head. "Although I cannot do that again for at least another rest period."

"A shape shifter!" John exclaimed. Just like Ivan.

"Yes, come to observe our friends on earth planet, in our neighboring galaxy."

"What are you blathering about?" Havel asked. "We don't concern ourselves much with you Andromedans in Galaxy 3."

"That is as may be." Ruczinsky replied smoothly. "We, however, are quite interested in developments in Galaxy 6, especially here upon the earthian planet."

John wondered about Havel's response. Did he know about ETs?

"What shall we call you?" Genevieve said.

"Ruczinsky is just fine."

"Why are you here?" Havel exploded. By now he had lost all of his smoothness and charm.

"I just told you."

"Not good enough. You can't just waltz into a top secret installation and impersonate one of our personnel."

"I can't? But you have the evidence before you." Ruczinsky tapped his bald head.

"It's unethical," Havel said.

"Unethical! And are the activities of your Orion friends over the past millennia on this planet ethical?"

Bingo! John thought. Was Havel an Orion? He looked perfectly human.

Havel prevaricated. "I wouldn't know about that. I'm just an employee."

Ruczinsky laughed. "We'll let that pass. Please, let's continue with the demonstration. That is what I have particularly come to observe."

Gradually the room calmed down and they continued the session. "Ruczinsky" abandoned his pretense as an employee and paid very close attention to John's every word. The man looked so human John could almost forget that he had transformed into a walking cat and claimed to be from another galaxy.

As he and Genevieve assisted, John could tell that this group was experienced in meditation. He mentioned that to Havel. "Yes, these are our best viewers."

John could tell that five in the group of thirteen were approaching stage two. Gradually, two of the women and one of the men opened their eyes. A look of almost angelic sweetness covered their faces. "I get it," one of them said.

"You do?" Havel asked eagerly.

The other two nodded their heads toward the first speaker.

Havel was exhilarated. "Then let us get to work right away. We will start by shielding sector A in the data encryption area." He began to walk out but noticed that no one was following.

"Come, come. There is no time to lose!"

Now the other two came alive as well.

The five looked at each other and smiled. "Come, wipe that goofy grin off your faces," Havel said imperatively. "We have a lot of work to do." Still no one moved. "Jensen! Walker! T'Munga! Muller! Willingham! Let's go!"

"You don't understand, sir," said a petite, red haired woman. "There is no way to defeat, or block, other viewers. That is totally obvious now. We've all been fools not to see it before." The others nodded their heads in agreement.

"WHAT?" Havel said. He had instantly gone from exultation to disappointment.

A thin, sandy-haired man spoke and pointed to John and Genevieve. "Sir, what we've just discovered, thanks to these people, is that any blocking thought will only draw more attention to the thing that is being protected. Like a magnet. It is the reason our installations are so transparent to other remote viewers."

Havel's jaw dropped. "So we've failed."

John received a mental communication from "Ruczinsky." "That Orion is a good actor." It was just like being out in boundary work, where you could communicate directly via thought. "Havel's Orion friends have a real need for a thought-blocking technology. He's Melet Toor, nephew to Regat Toor. The Toors have ruled in Orion for millions of years."

Havel an ET! Could it be? John began to send questions but "Ruczinsky" had closed his mind.

The redhead spoke to Havel. "Sir, if I may, there's no need for that. The Unity Field is transparent. All information is theoretically accessible to the power of the mind. Therefore, we need to radically change our priorities. It is impossible to shield or protect anything from the power of thought. It is obvious that our adversaries will be able to eventually duplicate our advances. Rather than wasting our time and energy attempting to block others from accessing our data, we need to concentrate even more heavily in research. We are still top dog in the design and manufacturing process—"

"Ruczinsky" interrupted. "This is much better than the process we have been using in our galaxy. You know, we look at you poor Troolians as rather backward. But you have managed to discover something extremely profound and valuable."

"Who asked you Ruczinsky?" Havel snapped. "Please resume your post."

"I'm sorry but I must return to my colleagues in Andromeda. First I would like to speak with these two."

Havel was completely at a loss. He understood that something profound had happened to his viewers, smiling in their chairs. But it probably bode ill for him. Damn! The Remote Viewers were all ungovernable. A necessary pain, for without them it would be impossible to win the psy-ops war. But they were unstable and untrustworthy and didn't fit in the chain of command. In his last report he had spoken confidently of success with the new method. He would be in big trouble now with Dalath Toor himself, who had personally come to earth to oversee the final strokes of the Grand Plan. His hoped for promotion would turn into a demotion... unless he could spin this new information to his advantage. He would have to come up with an angle. It would require much thought.

Melet Toor aka Gyorgi Havel stared at John and Genevieve. "You two must leave this facility by 1200. It's now 1045. Haliburton will be coming with a cart to escort you from the premises at precisely 1145. Please be ready, for you will not have authorization to remain down here past that time." Havel turned on the bullet-head. "You have exactly 60 minutes Ruczinsky, or whoever you are. Then either resume your duties or get the hell out of here." He waved his arm at the others. "To the debriefing room. Now! I want our supervisor to hear everything you just said to me."

As they filed out the little red haired woman spoke softly to Genevieve. "Thank you."

"Well how about that," Genevieve said. "Not even a thank you from Havel."

Ruczinsky' laughed. "Our Mr. Havel is an entity with very little sense of humor. We see that all too often in observing things on the other side of the pond."

John assumed he referred to the 2.9 million light year distance that separated the Milky Way from the Andromedan galaxy.

"I have a million questions," John said. "I..."

"Call me Llethrianne. First, I want to thank you for your wonderful technique. I have received more than I asked for, but surely there is more to it. You've left out the next step."

"You're very perceptive," John said. "Are you really from Andromeda?"

"Yes."

"How did you get here?"

"Through a transportal or gateway between the galaxies. There are a number of them that connect our galaxy with yours, and with others. Of course you can always do it the long way in a space vessel. Some like to spend their lives cruising around, but I'm not one of them."

"How do these transportals work? I'm curious because a friend of mine has one in the back of his store."

"You're asking the wrong fellow," Llethrianne said. "The intergalactic portals were established so long ago that no one in my galaxy remembers. We just accept their existence and have fun with them. That's something you Troolians should remember."

"Troolians?"

"That's our name for you in Galaxy 6. In our language it means something like, 'codger.' Your galaxy is much older than ours. I don't mean that in a physical sense, but in a spiritual sense. In our galaxy we are much more fun loving."

"Then why are you here?" Genevieve asked. "You could stay in your own galaxy and avoid us geriatrics."

Llethrianne laughed. "Earthians! Always so caustic! I'm here because of you."

"Give me a break," John said. "You came all the way from another galaxy just for us?"

"Sure, why not? This planet of yours seems to be attracting quite a lot of attention. We're curious. We want to know why. I've already picked up on your meditation technique; that alone was worth the trip. But we're off the subject. I asked you about the next step in the process."

"You mean you don't know?" John was amazed.

Llethrianne was silent.

John glanced at Genevieve. She shrugged as if to say, "Go ahead."

"The next step is the complete vibrational alteration of consciousness itself, allowing travel anywhere in the universe. And to different universes, as far as I can tell. We learned it from a book." John looked curiously at Llethrianne. "We thought you guys knew about this stuff."

Now it was Llethrianne's turn to be amazed. "You learned it from a *book*?"

"Yeah," John said. "That's what started the government interest in us in the first place. They stole the book a couple of years ago. Hey, I've got the thing sitting at home if you want to look at it."

Genevieve said, "There are billions of entities who know about this already and they all gather in a place we call the Eyrie. There are three in my group from this very galaxy who have been doing it for years."

John snapped his fingers. "Yeah, and they all learned about it just like we did. I asked Davey, Kjirsten, and Goliath all about it."

Llethrianne was stunned. Rumors of those with such capabilities circulated throughout the Twelve Galaxies. These tales had been uniformly discounted, for they could not be validated. Those who had supposedly attained such mastery had never been able to pass on their knowledge. To think that two Troolians from a barbaric planet had brought forth such an ingenious method! It was almost more than he could bear.

"I want to see that book."

At that moment Haliburton appeared. "I'm instructed to see you out now. You too Ruczinsky, or whatever your name is."

The trip back to the house was uneventful. This time they rode in a black sedan; apparently they were no longer in favor with the cloak and dagger set. John and Genevieve wanted to sit in the back seat and cuddle but Haliburton refused to have 'Ruczinsky' beside him in the front seat.

They arrived at the house around 4 p.m. on Sunday afternoon. Haliburton handed them their mobiles and let them out. Without a word, he turned the sedan around and left.

Ruczinsky/Llethrianne went up to the bedroom. John showed him the book. He examined the symbols and looked at some of the etchings. After several minutes he slowly closed the book and placed it on John's desk.

"Tell me, if you will, about your experiences using this technique."

John gave a brief description of what happened to him and Genevieve over the past couple of years. "Genevieve is writing a book about it, if you're interested."

"Then it's true," Llethrianne said. At their questioning looks he elaborated. "The legends within our galaxy talk of the complete mastery of consciousness, of the ability to self-transport. We have never been able to penetrate the mystery."

John almost laughed. In the thick body of 'Ruczinsky', the Andromedan's expression was incongruous.

Llethrianne stared silently at the two humans for a minute.

"It seems we have been in the dark for quite a long time." He got up and began to pace the room. "Our scientists, as you would call them, have noticed an increasing tension in the fabric of space within our galaxy. Not anything to disrupt the general routines of existence, but something of a very subtle nature." Ruczinsky raised the book in one of his meaty hands. "This book is made of a substance which we call continuous fundamental energy. It is something known to us only theoretically. We have never been able to manufacture it."

John wondered whether Llethrainne knew anything of the Unformed Potential.

"The engraving on these pages are holoportals to other locations. The knowledge to create them is unknown to us." Ruckzinsky was talking softly to himself. "Someone has written these procedures with the intention that they be used. Whoever has that advanced knowledge might also understand the nature of the physical phenomena we are observing. Surely it cannot be coincidental that this book found its way into the earthian's hands. The question is, who is this being or beings?"

"You two are the key," Ruczinsky said, fixing John and Genevieve with his eyes. For an instant John received the distinct impression of a cat about to pounce on its prey.

John laughed nervously. "I don't think so. I've already told you that three others from this galaxy have learned the technique. It wasn't from a book like this. If I recall, Goliath and Davey read it in some obscure archive on their home worlds."

"Besides," Genevieve said, "there are billions of entities from other universes who routinely travel back and forth in this way."

"Yes," John said. "But hardly any from the outer universes."

"The outer universes?"

John explained his conception of the vibrational nature of the All, the guide symbol, the Unformed Potential, and their work in the Eyrie. 'Ruczinsky's' jaw dropped.

"The guide symbol we know about. It has been a part of the civilizations of the Twelve since the beginning. Yet its true significance has been overlooked." The Andromedan spoke in tones of awe.

"You don't know it's true unless you investigate for yourself," John replied. "Don't take my word for it. I suggest you try the technique yourself. If you have any questions you can always come back and see us. If travel between galaxies is as easy as you say it is."

"I'd prefer to learn now," Ruckzinsky said. "I'd rather not stay down here any longer than I have to."

John and Genevieve spent almost two hours with the Andromedan but he was unable to precisely define his sphere of consciousness.

"You'll get it eventually," John said. "You've already made great progress."

"I'm starting to feel uncomfortable now," the Andromedan said. "Perhaps that's it. I'll try it again after I return to the Three."

The Andromedan left the room and began to walk down the stairs. John followed him. "How will you return?"

"There is a transportal in this city, in an old warehouse beyond the railroad tracks. I know how to program them."

"But that's several miles away! I thought you had to leave quickly."

By this time 'Ruczinsky' was out the door and walking swiftly down the walkway to the sidewalk. "I'll manage," he said. He began to pick up his pace. Was it John's imagination or did he glide over the pavement? With incredible swiftness he reached the corner a quarter mile away and turned out of sight.

John walked back into the house and checked his messages. "Holy shit Genevieve!"

"What is it?"

"Listen to this." John put the message on speakerphone.

"John Frankel? I hope I have the right number. I'm Jack McGrady, manager of the Tucson Cheetah's, AAA baseball club. I've got two ballplayers who have no business being here and they say you are responsible. They claim you showed them how to do some darn thing or other that got them a tryout up here. I got one boy who raised his average 155 points and a pitcher who struck out 15 his last time out. My mama didn't raise no fool but I'm willing to try anything to help my ballclub. I was wondering if you could come down here sometime and show us just what you showed them. We'll take care of the plane fare and hotel for one night. My number here is..." John jotted it down.

"You've got nothing to do at work," Genevieve said. "Except wait for Marlowe's paper to be published." That was true. He was just doing cleanup stuff now.

"What the heck. Hey, why don't I wait until the weekend? Then you can come with me."

"It's warm there!"

"Yeah! Bring your swimsuit. I want to see you mostly naked."

Genevieve snorted. "Calm down John."

John's eyes twinkled. "How about completely naked?" He started after her with his hands outstretched. She shrieked and ran out of the hallway into the living room. "Hah!" he said, cornering her. "I got you now!" But she was too quick for him. With a nice head fake she got him off balance and ran past him toward the hallway. He chased her up the stairs, taking the steps two at a time. Genevieve screamed like a little girl. She reached the top of the stairs slightly before he did. John made a grab for her. One of his hands found her right hip but she swiveled like a running back and his hand slipped off, sending him crashing into the hallway closet door. Genevieve rushed to the bedroom and slammed the door a second before John crashed into it. He heard the deadbolt click. "John! Stop it!"

"Just let me get my hands on you and I will!"

"You better calm down boy. Don't you have a phone call to make?"

John could hear her heavy breathing. He pounded on the door. "Open up or I'm coming in!"

"Get away from me you brute! Go make your phone call and we'll talk about it after." John could tell she was excited and nervous. She knew he was strong enough to break the door down. "You promise?"

"I promise."

John made up his mind. "OK."

He could hear her sigh of relief as he walked slowly downstairs. Halfway down the stairs he looked back and saw her little nose peeking out of the door. He turned around and raced back up the stairs. "John!" She smashed the door closed and locked it again. He went down the stairs again and sneaked a peek over his shoulder but the door did not move. "Oh all right," he growled. "I'll make the phone call."

John dialed and got Jack McGrady at his home. After an exchange of pleasantries John got right down to business. "Are you sure it wasn't steroids or something?"

"Son, steroids don't give you pinpoint control. You can't improve 150 points using drugs. I know these kids and they got no business doing what they did. Besides, they don't look no different. If it was steroids I'd be able to tell. They swear up and down it was what you showed 'em. If it ain't illegal I want to give it a shot."

It didn't take John long to make up his mind. Sun! Warmth! And Genevieve too. It would be a nice break. "All right. I can get on a plane Saturday morning but I want to bring my fiancée. We're both tired of the cold."

"No problem. I'll have the tickets waiting for you at the airport."

"By the way, what's your Major League affiliation?"

"Arizona Diamondbacks," McGrady responded quickly. "Good outfit."

They arranged details and John hung up. "My life is amazing. And all because of that book."

He walked back upstairs in a contemplative mood. He heard Genevieve's nervous voice inside the bedroom. "John! It's unlocked. Are you calm now?"

John opened the door and saw her standing beside the bed hefting a cardboard tube wrapper.

"Relax sweetheart. I've just been thinking about our life and how incredible it is. It would hardly be believable in a fantasy novel."

She put down her weapon. "Close the door." John reached back and kicked it shut. She took off her sweater, raised her hands over her head and gave her torso a wiggle, inviting him...

34

John and Genevieve left chilly Midland on a mid-April Saturday morning at 6:00 a.m. It was a 90 minute drive to O'Hare in Chicago. The flight was almost 4 hours. They would arrive at 11 a.m. Tucson time. There was no one to meet them at the airport but McGrady had given John detailed directions to the ballpark and arranged for a rental car. It was a dry 87 degrees on arrival. John changed into shorts before leaving the airport.

John and Genevieve got to the ballpark and found a space in the staff parking area, close to an entrance. As they walked in John could hear the crack of bat hitting ball. He smelled the warm air, heard the banter of the players as they took batting practice. The game was to start at 1:30; the stands were beginning to fill. He walked up to a door marked "Tucson Cheetah's Staff Only Entrance," and knocked.

"C'mon in."

John entered an office behind the dugout. It had a well worn painted cement floor, a couple of desks, a laptop, and a bunch of tablets. A smallish man got up and held out his hand. "You're Frankel I take it?"

"Yes sir," John said.

McGrady took in Genevieve, dressed smartly (as usual) in dark cotton slacks and a sleeveless burgundy top. "And this is your fiancée?"

"Genevieve," she said, holding out her hand.

"Pleased to meet you," McGrady said with a twinkle in his eye.

John saw a well set up older man with leathery skin and a full head of hair just beginning to turn white.

McGrady handed them two VIP passes. "Why don't you guys enjoy the game. These passes will get you free food and drinks. After, you can show us this performance enhancement thing." He gestured. "Go ahead, you can walk through the dugout. You should know two of the guys."

They walked through the office into a small corridor that led to the dugout. The other team was taking batting practice, so some of the guys were hanging around. As he walked in a voice said, "John!" It was Carlos, the big first baseman. "Hey Carlos!"

They shook hands. "This is the guy I was telling you about," Carlos explained to the other players.

"I hope you're a miracle worker. I'm 0 for 15 this season," said a small, wiry player. They were wearing white uniforms sporting a brown cheetah with green spots on it.

John spoke to Carlos. "We'll see you after the game."

They went up to the stands and were directed to seats right over the dugout. John bought hats at the concession stand to keep the sun out of their eyes. It was a nice ballpark with seating for about 10,000. He always loved the sounds and smells at a baseball game. A hotdog vendor came around and they watched batting practice, chomping away merrily.

"This is fun!" Genevieve said.

The game was high scoring and close. The home team lost to a squad from Omaha on a pinch hit double in the top of the 9th. Carlos went 2 for 4 with a home run. One of the outs he made was a hard line drive to the third baseman.

After the stadium emptied the team showered and ate. The interested players all sat in a circle in the manager's office. Besides Carlos there were seven others. Jack McGrady observed from his desk, an unreadable expression on his face.

"I want to hit like Carlos," piped the small shortstop John had seen in the dugout before the game. His name was Antonio.

Everybody laughed. John began the demonstration. "OK guys. This procedure gets you in the zone. That's the best way I can describe it. Some guys get it easily, others never do. It all depends on how open you are to it."

John kept the presentation as down-to-earth as possible, suitable for an athlete who wanted to improve his game. "If you do these first series of exercises precisely as I show you, you'll reach a state of perfect calm. That's the first step to being in the zone. Your body will feel very light, or like it's not there at all. That's a good thing because you'll have a lot more control over it.

"The second step is a little more tricky. There's a separate set of exercises after you hit stage one. I have written them down for you. After you finish the second set you'll feel like Barry Bonds or Randy Johnson. I use it myself all the time in table tennis."

Nobody got too bored so John figured it was a success. Fortunately Carlos had already prepared them a little. John was helped by the popularity of sports psychology. Almost every athlete had heard of mental exercises to enhance physical ability.

John was comfortable around athletes; he had been tutoring them since high school. He knew the lingo. His easy familiarity smoothed the way. They got into it. Two of the guys reached stage one within the first half hour. McGrady looked on silently. John wondered what was going through his mind. He had not said a word the whole time.

Suddenly Tyler, the left fielder, spoke. "Man, I feel it." Everybody stopped and looked.

"You're halfway there now," Carlos said. John had to get everybody going again. At the end of another half hour everyone made it. This had never happened before.

The vibe in the room was different; everybody could feel it. McGrady spoke for the first time. "I don't know what you're doing here son, but something good's happening." He paused. "I think."

The guys laughed.

John rubbed his hands together. "All right, now for the next step. Carlos, you can help me."

Tyler spoke to Carlos. "So this is what you do before every game."

Carlos grinned. "Yup. But it doesn't last for nine innings. Then I'm back to normal." He spoke to John. "At first they thought I was goofy. Then I went 15 for 31 so they all wanted some of what I got. I need to know how to make the zone last all game."

"We'll work on that another time," John said. "For now let's see how many of these guys we can get to the next level."

John handed out his printouts. "There are specific steps for this stage, a series of mental exercises. I can show you how to do them but in the end you're on your own. Hitting the zone is a personal thing. It's different for each person. The key is letting go." He explained, in practical language, the idea of power coming from releasing. "When you get it you'll know it. Carlos, explain a little what it's like."

Carlos told them it was like slowing down time. "I just see the ball real good. It doesn't matter how fast it is, I got time to set up and hit it. That don't mean it's always going to get through. But I almost always hit it good, unless I get anxious."

"That's right," John said. "Once you reach the zone you don't automatically stay there. But the more you do it, the easier it gets. It doesn't make you run any faster, you just anticipate a lot better. It's kind of like knowing what the pitcher is going to do before the ball even leaves his hand. At least that's how I experience it in table tennis."

"Would this stuff work for me?" McGrady asked.

Antonio responded. "Your head's too thick, skip." Some of the guys laughed. John could tell these players liked their manager.

John handed McGrady the printouts for stage one and two. "You've seen how we did the first stage. Stick around and watch. You can try it at home."

They worked for another hour. John was just about to end off when Tyler said, "Bingo!" Everybody looked up.

"Hey Brad, throw me some."

Tyler and Brad grabbed some balls and went out to the diamond.

"Warm up first Daugherty!" McGrady yelled.

Daugherty threw several pitches to get his arm loose.

"All right Brad. Give me some of that cheese, and then some sliders," Tyler said. "I want to see if this really works."

John and the guys placed themselves behind the backstop and watched the action. McGrady walked slowly out of the dugout, curious.

As the pitches came in Tyler hit them with ease. "This is amazing," he muttered. Beads of sweat formed on his face in the early evening heat. He turned to John. "It's just like Carlos said. I can see the ball perfect and adjust to it."

After about ten minutes he began to miss. "Lost it," he muttered. "Why does it go away?"

John shrugged. "I'm not sure but I guarantee you one thing. The more you do it the longer it lasts."

"Why don't you just be in the zone all the time?" somebody asked John.

"I sort of am," John said. "The more you do it the better you feel."

"OK guys enough for today," McGrady said. "We got a game tomorrow."

He turned to John. "Can you stick around for one more session tomorrow?"

John checked with Genevieve. "Sure."

McGrady looked at his watch. "It's past 6 already. Why don't we go out and get something to eat? We'll stop by the house first and pick up my wife. She never comes to day games."

"Sounds great. I'm starving," Genevieve said.

They walked out to the parking lot. The sun was setting; John hoped it would cool off. His Midwestern blood wasn't used to this heat. McGrady indicated a big, old style Cadillac. The car was in immaculate condition. "Pile in."

They entered the house, a one story ranch with a stuccoed roof. A handsome blond-haired woman put down a book and rose to meet them. "This is my wife Debra. Debra, this is John Frankel, and soon-to-be Genevieve Frankel." They shook hands.

"Debra's an intellectual, reads lots of books," McGrady said. "Only books I ever read are about baseball."

Jack McGrady told them he had been in baseball all his life. "I played minor league ball for 15 years but never made it past AA. That's OK, I would've played for nothing. Got my first coaching job in the Carolina League when I was 33. Been coaching ever since. Hope to make the big leagues one day. I will if I can develop some good players." He smiled at his wife and she smiled back. "Met her at a baseball game 15 years ago. Fell in love right on the spot."

As they chatted, John noticed that Debra kept glancing nervously at Genevieve.

"You know Debra, John here is quite a brainiac," McGrady said to his wife. "He and his fiancée have been teaching the kids a special method of concentration."

"Oh?"

"Tell her John."

Debra McGrady had the refined look and speech of someone educated. "Well ma'am, it's somewhat like meditation and it involves using the breath to concentrate life force energy in the body."

Debra McGrady was looking pale. "That's nice," she said. "Will you excuse me for a moment?" She walked out of the living room a little unsteadily.

"Is everything all right honey?" Jack said.

"I'll be fine. I just need to use the ladies room."

"That's funny," Jack said. "My wife's usually pretty level-headed. Maybe all that metaphysical talk reminded her of the old days."

"The old days?" Genevieve asked.

"Yeah. She used to work at some university doing research. Top secret stuff, or so she said."

After a few minutes Debra McGrady returned. She was dressed nicely and had fine, regular features. She still looked a little blanched. "Does anyone want a drink?" she said.

"Vermouth," McGrady said.

"Nothing for us," Genevieve said.

After Debra handed Jack his drink and resumed her seat Genevieve spoke to her. "You used to work at a university?"

"Yes, in the midwest."

"John and I both work at Carleton."

Debra McGrady choked on her martini, sending the drink and the glass to the carpet. She began coughing uncontrollably. Her husband rushed over and gave her a few slaps on the back. Genevieve went over calmly, picked up the glass, and returned with a moistened paper towel. She cleaned up the spill.

Jack got his wife calmed down. Debra leaned back on the sofa with a deep sigh. "I knew it would happen someday."

Suddenly Genevieve went white as a ghost. "No, it can't be. Oh, it can't be."

Jack and John exchanged looks of amazement.

Debra covered her face with her hands. Tears were running down her fingers. She looked up and met Genevieve's eyes for the first time. "You're Genevieve Walters aren't you?"

The two women locked gazes. Genevieve began to cry. "Mom?" she said in a quavering voice filled with anguish and astonishment. Abruptly she threw herself into Debra McGrady's arms. The two women held on to each other, crying and occasionally laughing.

John finally got it. "Holy shit," he said. "That's Genevieve's real mother!"

Jack McGrady's jaw was slowly detaching from his face. "Will someone please tell me what the hell is going on?"

John attempted to explain. "A long time ago your wife used to live in Midland, Illinois. She married Genevieve's father and had a daughter. The marriage didn't work out and the separation wasn't amicable. She left and asked that no one try to find her."

Jack was speechless. Debra and Genevieve had heads on the other's shoulder, breathing deeply, trying to control their emotions.

"Honey, you never told me about a previous marriage."

Debra disengaged from her daughter's clasp. "You never asked. One of the things I love about you." She looked happy and resigned at the same time.

"I thought I could start over, leave my old life behind."

Genevieve was a roiling cauldron of conflicting emotions. On the one hand she was thrilled to have discovered her birth mother. But Rachel was her real mother!

For John it was the last remaining piece of the puzzle regarding Genevieve's past.

Genevieve looked at Debra. "John and I know."

"Know what?" Jack asked. He was irrelevant in the tableau that was being enacted between the three of them.

Debra shrank back on the sofa, a look of guilt etched upon her face. It was clear she expected severe censure from her daughter and John.

"Don't worry, it worked out wonderfully," Genevieve said. She said it in such a way as to convey happiness, forgiveness, compassion, and understanding. They all watched as Debra's face reflected her rapidly changing emotions. Debra McGrady started several times to say something, then stopped and tried again. After a few minutes all of the air went out of her.

She placed her hands on her legs and straightened. Debra searched Genevieve's eyes carefully. "Do you really mean it?"

Genevieve nodded.

Debra burst into tears again but Genevieve knew it was OK. It was just twenty years of pent up feelings finding a release. She hugged her mother firmly and let her cry it out. The men were forgotten.

Jack McGrady was dumbfounded. His simple life had suddenly gotten horribly complicated. Jack realized that the perfect stranger on the couch across from him was now his future son-in-law. Suddenly a smile broke out on his face. "To be honest," he said to John, "you're not quite the son I had in mind. But I think I can get used to you."

"Thank you sir," John said, ever polite.

"While these women are wasting their time crying why don't you tell me all about it."

John gave Jack a capsule summary of the whole affair, leaving out Genevieve's genetically engineered origins. Jack's old school mentality would be hard pressed to accept that, no matter how much he loved his wife. He explained Debra's work as "DNA related." Jack seemed to be satisfied.

Meanwhile, the women were dabbing their faces and composing themselves. Debra looked like she had just come out of a washing machine: clean, but a little wet and wrinkled.

"I don't know about you but I'm really hungry," Jack said. "Let's go out to that fancy French bistro."

Debra was eager. "Oh! Do you mean La-Delice? Can we? Jack's idea of food is steak and potatoes," she explained to Genevieve.

"Why not?" McGrady said. "Maybe they even have a nice hunk of meat I can sink my teeth into."

"Let's go," John said. The men headed out but Debra stopped. "I couldn't possibly go in these clothes." She looked at Genevieve hopefully. "Could I Genevieve?"

"Impossible," Genevieve replied. She looked down at her pants, now slightly wrinkled. "I need to iron these. John, we left our bags in the rental car at the ballpark."

"Give us 15 minutes," Debra said. Without waiting for a response the two women ran into the bedroom together.

Jack groaned. "15 minutes. That's code for an hour at least. We might as well order pizza. I'm going to starve by the time she's ready."

"Yeah, but she'll look good I'll bet," John said.

Jack looked at him complacently. "Yes she will. She'll look damn good."

Genevieve stuck her head out into the living room. "Why don't one of you make reservations. And John, you're going to look awful silly in your shorts."

" Where am I going to find some good clothes that fit?"

"Don't worry son. I'll take care of you back here," McGrady said. "My nephew is almost as tall as you. I just got him a couple of nice suits for his birthday. You can break one of 'em in."

That night at the hotel Genevieve and John reviewed their experience. "I'm glad we told Debra to just get on with her life," Genevieve said. "It's not like we're going to have grandkids for them to visit."

"Jack was pretty relieved. All he knows is baseball. He loves his life the way it is."

"Do you think Debra can still be happy with him? When she was running away her simple life might have seemed attractive. Now I wonder."

The next day passed swiftly. The Cheetah's kicked the crap out of the Omaha team, 14-1. Carlos had 3 more hits on a 3 for 6 day. Tyler hit a double and a triple his first two times up. Then he struck out four times in a row. John could tell he was pressing. Antonio went 1 for 6.

After the game the guys who had worked with John got together in the office and complained. "I got in my zone," Antonio said. "But after two pitches I lost it. Madre de Dios, I'm glad I hit the second pitch."

Carlos guffawed. Brad said, "This technique works great for me as a pitcher because I can calm down and really concentrate. You have to be aggressive at the plate and running the bases. That's the opposite of what you're teaching us." A chorus of agreement went around the room.

"It's easier for us laid-back types," John said. "The guys who did the best with the technique are more like Carlos than Gregg." Gregg was the hotheaded catcher who had already been thrown out of a game and had no interest whatsoever in the technique.

"Carlos the cat," Antonio said. The big man smiled his approval.

"I can tell you from my personal experience with table tennis that aggressiveness defeats the technique. *Until* you master it. Then you can get as aggressive as you want. When you're first start out you need to cool it."

John again went over the idea of power being the releasing of attachment to the outcome.

"Here's how it works I think. When you're aggressive you're really focused on the goal, right? But you're also focused on not messing up. Think about it. If you were totally on the goal there would be no need for all that anger and hard work. You'd just know you could do it. It's your resistance to the goal that sets up the feeling of aggressiveness in the first place! This technique teaches you to focus on what you want, 100%, and ignore the idea of failure. That's what being in the zone means. An effortless action that leads inevitably to success."

Mouths were open, everyone was listening attentively. He was getting through.

"Being in the zone means feeling good," John said. "The better you feel the better you're going to play and the more fun you're going to have. That applies to everything in life, not just baseball."

"Wait a minute," Tyler said. "When you're aggressive you feel good too. When I'm feeling it I'm ready to kick everybody's ass. That feels great."

"That's right," Brad said.

"I'm not knocking aggressiveness," John said. "Passion is good. I'm just saying that the technique, when properly learned, eliminates *all* resistance in your game. You aren't focused on anyone else, only your game. When you focus on the opponent you take focus away from yourself. When you properly apply this technique you get to a state where there is no opponent. Just you and the joy of competing. Unless you've experienced it you can't know what I'm talking about. It works, I can tell you that."

Carlos jumped in. "Why do you guys call me 'the cat?'"

"Because you're smooth, man."

"Yeah, great swing."

"It don't look like you're trying at all."

Suddenly everybody got it. They looked at Carlos, then back at John.

Antonio spoke up. "Let's get to work."

"I'd like to sit in this time," Carlos said. "I still can't keep my big for more than an hour."

"Don't feel bad," John agreed. "Neither could I until I kept doing the technique over and over."

"Really?" Carlos said.

"Yup. Between matches I usually need to recharge. The more experienced you get the easier and faster it is to get through the routines. Ultimately you could reach a point where you didn't need the technique at all. Just a conscious decision to be there and bam! You're there."

"That's awesome," Carlos said. He regarded John as if he were some kind of minor deity.

"Remember, you're doing it. It's got nothing to do with anything outside yourself. You're connecting with the force. The more you can do that the better and better you feel about *everything*."

Carlos stuck out his hand. "I'm sure glad I met you John." John felt the love and returned it.

After 90 minutes of instruction John felt that all of the players were on their way. "I've given you the fundamentals and you've got your printouts. Now you have to master the advanced protocols for the second stage. The further along you get the more intuitive you have to be with it."

John shook hands with all the players and told them he'd be following their careers. Then he and Genevieve drove back to Jack's house to say goodbye to Debra.

"How is your father?" she asked Genevieve.

"He's a changed man. He recently re-married and he's got a new daughter. I've never seen him so happy."

Debra looked profoundly relieved. She smiled. "Thank you so much for understanding, and for giving me back an important part of my life. But please, for now, don't tell Michael. I want to do it myself." Genevieve and John agreed.

The women embraced. Debra hugged John as well. Jack and John shook hands. "Son, if what you've done this weekend turns out as good as it looks right now, you'll have done me and this organization a big favor."

"Glad to be of service," John said. "It was fun. We like your ballpark and the team." Then John winked. "But I hope you're not *too* successful."

"Why not?" McGrady asked.

"Because I'm a Cubs fan," John replied.

As they walked out the door and started their rental car, John could hear Jack's laughter.

35

A FTER they returned John got back to work on his thesis and the book based upon it. Genevieve continued with her novel.

Michael Walters was happy looking after his new wife. He was delighted with the baby even though he was losing a lot of sleep. He told John, "Amanda has opened me up even more. I feel like a kid again with a new chance at happiness."

After work Walters would insist on Alicia going off for a couple of hours to have some time to herself. Often she didn't want to.

Now it was Michael Walters who was an inspiration to John. Sometimes he felt a pang in his heart when he saw the three of them together and saw the playful innocence of little Amanda. To have a son of his own! Then he'd see Genevieve and it would be all right.

One night after dinner she caught John in one of those moments.

"Wishing you might have one of your own, my love?"

He did not try to disguise his feelings. "To have a child with you would be so great. I'd like to teach him all the stuff I know."

A look of longing crossed her features.

"Maybe what they said was a lie."

She shook her head. "It's been seven years now John, and no birth control."

John went over and hugged her. "I'm so happy we're getting married."

She brightened. "Me too."

Rachel was arranging everything for the wedding. She had begun making brides-maid dresses last fall and was almost done. Genevieve felt guilty. "Dear, you run the house. Let me take care of this for you. I enjoy it so much." Genevieve was only too happy to do so. Like John, she didn't really want a big wedding. She definitely didn't want to make all of the arrangements for one.

Rachel insisted on getting the names of even casual acquaintances from both of them. "Where are we having the reception?" Genevieve asked.

"At Roman Hall."

"Rachel!" Genevieve said. "You can fit an army in that place."

Rachel winked. "That's right dear."

"When can I see my wedding dress?"

"When it's done, daughter. On June 9th probably."

"Mother!"

John's last check would be at the end of April, in less than two weeks. He spent almost all of his time at work writing his Masters thesis with Peter Marlowe's blessing.

"I don't give a fig what you do son," his boss said to him John's first Monday back after their Arizona trip. "Just heard from AR, John. They've agreed to jury the paper by the end of the month. Looks like we've done a bang-up piece of work."

By the end of the month John had completed the thesis and handed it in to Michael Walters, who reviewed it.

"John, this is going to create quite a stir. I believe this symbolic language will have practical applications. I see no problem from Rutkowski on this one."

A week later he got a call from the department head himself. "John, I've just read your thesis. It's really quite good. I'd like to submit it for publication under the University Press label."

John was thrilled. He became more inspired than ever to write a book for the general reader based on these concepts. The challenge was to keep the manuscript accessible. "The popularity of a book is inversely proportional to the number of equations in it," Michael Walters once told him. Could he take the symbolic language and explain it simply enough for the general reader?

Meanwhile Genevieve was completing her novel. John had written one of the chapters (the best one, he thought) about his journey to the planet Argelain. Genevieve's book was all about their experiences. It was basically a romance but had lots of interesting scenes and a good plot.

She showed the manuscript around. A local publisher took a chance and distributed it to some of the local bookstores. It made enough money to warrant a second and larger run. Then a statewide distributor picked it up. Genevieve's novel began to appear in bookstores around the state in the SF sections. That spring she did a couple of book signing gigs in the Full Moon. Mats loved it because it brought in paying customers.

On June 9th Rachel unveiled the bridesmaid dresses to Genevieve and two of her friends from work. They elicited oohs and ahhhs from the women. Made of pale lavender silk, and brocaded in pale blue, with short sleeves (for the summer) and a silk sash, it was a beautiful creation. "My God, mom, you did it again," John said. "It's incredible." Tears came to Genevieve's eyes. "These patterns are wonderful!" Rachel had woven an intricate design on the fabric above the waist in front.

"I was inspired by those earrings," Rachel said. "But wait 'till you see your wedding dress."

Genevieve stamped her foot. "Oh *please* mother, may I see it now?"

Rachel smiled very smugly. "No you cannot. I'm not quite through putting the finishing touches on it. And don't you go peeking into my room."

After that everyone in the wedding party went to the church for rehearsal. Neither the Frankel's nor the Walters' were religious so it was decided to hold the ceremony in the Methodist church downtown. Robert occasionally attended church services there and was on a first name basis with the pastor.

Gene and Bill were standing up with John. Genevieve's bridesmaids stopped two blocks from the church and walked, showing off the dresses.

On the 10th, very early in the morning, Genevieve couldn't sleep so she went downstairs with her book. Her heart was pounding with excitement and nervousness. Today she was to be wed. She thought back to her fragmented family, her lonely childhood, and her experimental origins. It had all turned out so wonderfully.

She hoped she wouldn't get too nervous during the ceremony and faint. Handling a crisis situation, a piece of cake. Saying wedding vows, and tying herself to another for the rest of her life, was much more difficult...

Her musings were interrupted by soft footfalls on the stairs.

Rachel said, "Maybe it's time we look at that dress?"

"Oh yes!"

Rachel opened the door to her workroom. On a hanger was the dress, a simple but elegant concoction in white, finely brocaded down the front to the waist and hips. The dress billowed out beautifully, falling to the floor in a pool of fabric.

Genevieve looked her profound gratitude to Rachel. It was enough, more than enough. Genevieve softly walked over to the dress and fingered it.

"Try it on."

Genevieve carefully maneuvered herself into the dress. She inspected herself in the full length mirror just as she had done seven years ago for John's prom night. This was even better. Tears began to roll down her face.

Rachel quickly stepped in and wiped her cheeks. "I want to hug you but I can't."

Rachel got her out of the dress and they hugged and cried tears of joy. Rachel became anxious. "You don't plan on moving out, do you?"

Genevieve smiled. "It hasn't ever come up."

"Good. Now let's go back to sleep. It's going to be a very long day."

At 11 a.m. John and Genevieve were in the back of the big downtown church. It was over an hour before the ceremony. Already the place was crammed. John took a peek and couldn't believe his eyes. "My God sweetheart, she's invited the whole town!"

"Only 300," Rachel said.

Genevieve exploded. "Three hundred! I don't even know 30 people in the whole world."

"But I do," Rachel said. "Originally I had 350 but I had to pare down the list."

Suddenly John heard commotion and laughing. He peeked out again. Six of the guys from the Tucson Cheetah's were here. "My God, they've got a game tonight."

"Don't worry John," Rachel said. "I arranged everything with Jack McGrady."

John shook his head in amazement. "You don't even know him."

"I know him a lot better than you think."

"You're amazing mom," was all John said.

Finally it was time. John and Genevieve walked down the long aisle to the familiar strains of "Here Comes the Bride." John could see it was standing room only. The Cheetah's were standing in back. They all waved. John was inordinately pleased to have them present. He was amazed that so many people cared to attend their wedding.

Genevieve was aware of her father's arm in hers. She glanced up to see a look of complete happiness on his face. Good, maybe he's finally left the past behind. Perhaps he's even ready to hear about Debra.

Genevieve stood at the altar, her head in a whirl. Some part of her said that it was unreal, that John would never really accept her for the rest of his life, that it was all a dream. Rev. Taylor said to John, "Do you promise to love, cherish, and protect her, forsaking all others, until death do you part?" John turned to her, smiled, and melded his merkaba with hers. She almost fainted with joy. "I do," her new husband said.

Genevieve's face lit up. She threw herself into John's arms before the presentation of the ring and before the Reverend gave permission for him to kiss the bride. There were a few cheers and some clapping. She heard a whistle from the back, probably an over-enthusiastic ball player.

When it came time for her to reciprocate a surge of well being went through her. She knew it was going to be OK. She heard herself say, "I do."

"By the power vested in me, and in the presence of almighty God, I now pronounce you man and wife."

John placed the ring on her finger, looking at her adoringly the whole time. Genevieve felt like her heart was going to burst. Reverend Taylor said, "You may *now* kiss the bride" to general laughter. John gave her a deep long kiss. One of the Cheetah's gave a whoop. Somebody clapped. Soon the church broke out in cheers. Finally, bride and groom separated. They were officially husband and wife.

At the reception all of the Cheetah's gave John a big smack on the back. Antonio said, "I want one like you got." Tyler said, "I'm gonna have to rethink this whole marriage thing."

Carlos pumped his hand. "Thanks buddy. Thanks to you we're going to the bigs."

John looked around. All of Rachel's and Robert's friends were present. Mats and all of his friends and family showed up, and Genevieve's friends from work. A lot of people from the university were here. Probably acquaintances of Rachel, Michael, and Alicia. John saw Trevor Jones and a couple of his high school acquaintances. He waved to them. Suddenly Ja'Quan and LaShawnda entered the room. "John!" he bellowed. The two giants strode into the big room like they owned it. "Ja'Quan!" They embraced. John gave LaShawnda a hug too.

"You two sure look great!" John said. LaShawnda smiled.

"You do too." LaShawnda looked up at Ja'Quan. "Do you think we should try it too?"

Ja'Quan replied thoughtfully. "Maybe we should."

"I heard you made the NFL," John said to Ja'Quan.

"Yeah, but I quit. Blew out my knee and I had to hang it up. But man I was good. Got some bank too, so I'm set for life. Now I'm an assistant coach on the Princeton football team. I also teach a freshman course in African Studies. I really like it."

"That's great Ja'Quan. I always knew you'd be successful."

"Hey John!" It was Antonio. "I'm hitting .350 now but I need to ask you a question." He looked up at Ja'Quan and LaShawnda. "Wow." His face then puckered in thought for a second. "Didn't you play for Baltimore?"

"Offensive tackle," Ja'Quan said.

"Thought so."

Ja'Quan smiled. "Still tutoring John?"

"In a manner of speaking," John replied.

Antonio and John talked about the technique for a couple of minutes. Antonio said, "We all got to get on a plane pretty soon." He motioned over to the guys and they came over to shake John's hand.

"Thanks for coming guys." John shook hands with everyone. "You made my day."

"Who were those guys?"

"Players from the Tucson Cheetah's, a minor league baseball team. I taught them a performance enhancement trick."

"My boys could use some of that," Ja'Quan said. "Think you could show us?"

John realized he was going to have to write another book. He couldn't keep running around all over the country. Or could he? Maybe he could start an athletic consulting business. He didn't have a job anymore. Genevieve was making all the money with her novel starting to sell and her day job.

"Sure," John said to Ja'Quan. "For you I'll do it. I don't know how well football players will take to it though." John paused for a minute. "If you can wangle plane fare to New Jersey I can show you how it's done."

During the next six weeks John wrote a 150 page book on the technique, with detailed instructions to reach stages one and two. The first part of the book was an instruction manual. The second part of the book contained a full explanation of the universal medium, the merkaba, and how the technique brought a human being to the zone. Anyone not interested in the theory would be able to reach the state of serenity at the end of stage one. This was almost guaranteed by the ingenious breathing patterns. The last chapter had tips and suggestions for those having trouble. It was a metaphysics book masquerading as a practical manual of sports psychology. John intended it for those interested in self improvement and secondarily for athletes. John felt that the truly discerning practitioner would eventually reason that it could be taken further. He was very curious to see how many readers would come to that conclusion.

John took his manuscript to Genevieve's publisher, a small local startup called Midland Book Publishing. A man named Richard Carlysle agreed to look it over as a favor to Genevieve, who had put the company on the map in Midland.

Two days later John's mobile rang.

"This is Richard Carlysle, from Midland Book Publishing. I only have one question. Does it really work?"

"It does," John said. "I've tested the method myself and with at least twenty others."

There was a pause on the line.

"Before I publish this I want to make sure it's real." Carlysle sounded to John like a guy who was afraid of a lawsuit.

"I understand. Why don't you try it and let me know how you do? Normally I teach people personally. But if the book is any good the reader should be able to get it on his own."

"I agree. Give me a week."

Four days later John got a call around 4 in the afternoon. "Richard Carlysle. Would you be willing to come down here for a few minutes?"

John met Carlysle in his office and the man gave him a strange look.

"John, I'm not much into new age stuff or meditation. But last night I had an experience that rocked my world. I was doing the technique just like you said in the book. All of a sudden I felt this...I don't know what to call it...a feeling of intense joy. I haven't felt like that since I was a kid."

Carlysle paused. "I don't know whether it was real or not. I'm almost afraid to try it again and have it not work because I want to believe I can feel like that all the time." Carlysle looked at John beseechingly.

"Why don't you go through the technique and let's see what happens," John said. "If you get into difficulties I'll help you through it."

Richard Carlysle was a nervous, bookish, middle aged man. He fumbled with the manuscript and looked a little embarrassed. "I'm not used to doing this in front of someone. It's pretty personal."

"I understand. I've done this myself for over five years. I've taught my friends and my mother and father. The last time I did this was with a group of professional baseball players in their manager's office. Don't worry, I've seen everything."

"Wow," Carlysle said. "With baseball players?"

"Yeah. This technique can be used as a performance enhancement routine for athletes. I myself used it to win the Midland Open table tennis tournament last fall." That reminded John that he hadn't been practicing much lately. He hadn't gone up to Birmingham in months, what with the thesis and his book writing.

"OK, I'll do it," Richard said. He placed the manuscript on his lap.

"Sometimes I forget," he said apologetically. "Here goes."

After half an hour John saw he had reached stage one and was going for stage two. Carlysle stopped in the middle and consulted the book. Then he continued. John was forgotten. Soon Richard Carlysle's body was glowing with an inner light. He turned in his chair to face John, knocking the document off his lap to the floor. The hesitant and apologetic man was gone.

"OK, I'm convinced. "I feel like I could actually have a meaningful conversation with a member of the opposite sex."

Carlysle reached down and picked up John's book. "If this can work for me it can work for anyone. I'll publish your book."

That weekend on a Saturday morning John's cell rang. It was Mats. "John. Turn on the radio, NPR, right now."

John went to the old stereo and tuned to the local public radio station, recognizing George Spiegle's voice right away.

...it's the end of July and the Cheetah's still have five players hitting over .400. Carlos Fernandez, Antonio Delgado, Tyler Bateson, Richie McGuire, and Cornelius Brown. The major league affiliate of the Cheetah's, the Arizona Diamondbacks, are trying to clear their roster in order to bring these youngsters on board. Max Klesco, one of the Arizona scouts, says he's never seen anything like it:

'Reminds me of the movie The Natural. Max Mercy is describing Roy Hobbs: he hits anything he wants. Home runs, doubles, triples, just fly off his bat. That's what these guys are like.' The manager of these phenoms, Jack McGrady, doesn't claim all the credit however. 'Some new kind of performance enhancing technique, but without drugs. My son-in-law showed it to some of our kids in April and they've just been on fire the whole year."

"In Britain today, the Prime Minister said..."

"Holy shit," John said.

"Holy shit is right!" Genevieve agreed.

"They didn't mention my name in the report."

"It's only a matter of time John. McGrady has no reason to withhold your name. Even if he did the other guys on the team will blab. Besides, you just wrote a book about it."

"I hate publicity," John said. "I don't want a lot of snoops coming around here asking stupid questions."

"You know what they say: the world is a simple place for those not cursed with self awareness," Genevieve said.

"What's that supposed to mean?"

"The vast majority of people in the world out there aren't going to be interested in some kind of weird meditation technique. Even if they are, most people have a hard time following simple instructions. The technique is probably awfully difficult to master right out of a book."

"Richard Carlysle mastered it. And a bunch of dumb baseball players got it too."

"Well then," she said with a smile. "You'll just have to get used to being famous. There's always one good thing about fame."

"What's that?"

"Money usually comes with it."

Three days later Richard Carlysle called again. "I've got the proofs for your book ready. Come down and take a look."

The title would be *Performance Enhancement for Athletes and Weekend Warriors* with the subtitle "Achieve inner peace and serenity with this powerful new technique." Carlysle decided to put his own testimony on the front cover underneath the title.

"If it worked for me it will work for anyone – Richard Carlysle, Publisher."

Over the next few weeks John got a couple of emails asking for his help. He responded as best as he could. Genevieve's book was selling well and money was coming in, enough for her to quit her jobs if she wanted. She decided to keep the job at the high school and quit her university work. She liked working with the teachers and helping the kids.

NPR did a follow up story on the Cheetahs. All five were with the big club and still hitting phenomenally. A national sports network did a story on the five. Eventually John's name was mentioned. Somebody called him one afternoon.

"Is this John Frankel? I'm Pete Stuartson from SportScene, the national sports network. There are five guys on the Arizona Diamondbacks baseball team all batting over .400. They claim you taught them a foolproof way to get in the zone. Is that true?"

"If the guys say it's true then it must be true for them."

"They're all hitting close to .400 and it's the end of August! It's causing quite a stir on the team. The five players who lost their starting jobs claim it's some kind of cheating."

John said nothing.

"We want your comments for the record. I'm recording this just to let you know."

John thought carefully. "I discovered a method of relaxation that also *can* lead to performance enhancement. I make no claims for the technique, other than I have found it very useful to me. I've taught it successfully to others. The results you get are totally subjective."

"You're very careful," Stuartson said.

"I'm not looking for publicity. I wrote a book that's just been published. You can pick up a copy and see if it works for you."

"But you've caused quite a problem on the Arizona team with your method," Stuartson accused.

John sighed. "One needs to be able to distinguish between cause and effect."

"Pardon me?"

"I instructed eight of the players on the Triple A Tucson Cheetah's team. The other 31 weren't interested. Of the eight, three of the players couldn't do it. The other five you know about. What a person does with his or her life is their own decision."

"What is this technique anyway?" Stuartson asked.

"It's almost like a meditation but it can be useful to athletes. Hey, the whole thing was a happy accident. I got good results with it. Two friends of mine asked me to show them. Then a couple of his buddies, who just happened to be baseball players, used it. It's not a big conspiracy or anything."

"The reason I'm calling is because it's BIG. People just don't come from nowhere and hit .400."

"Maybe if everybody used it things would be back to normal. I don't know. Sometimes I wish I just would've kept it to myself."

"OK John Frankel," Stuartson said. "You don't sound like some kind of marketer or promoter."

"I'm just a guy who found a self-improvement technique. The only reason I wrote the book is to get people off my back. I got tired of explaining the same stuff over and over. I might make some money on the book. I hope so because I just graduated college and have been unemployed since April."

"Just to let you know, we're going to broadcast this interview on Sports Center tonight at 11. We located your high school yearbook and got a photo. You're kind of a goofy looking guy."

"Yeah, and your ears stick out from your head, fool." He learned that lingo from Rodney and Ja'Quan.

Stuartson roared with laughter. "Peace!"

His first interview was over and he thought he did OK.

Mats always watched SportScene at 11, so he'd find out whether the media trashed him.

Sure enough, at 11:15 Mats called. "John! You were on Sports Center tonight."

"Did they show my goofy high school picture?"

"Yeah. They played a conversation you had with Pete Stuartson."

"What else did they say?"

"They hyped up your technique. Said it was either inspired or a new way to cheat."

"Thanks Mats. Go to bed."

"I wish I had someone to lie next to," Mats said. "It's bad enough you don't work anymore. You also get to sleep next to that babe of yours."

"She's my wife now Mats. Goodnight."

Late in the morning, three weeks later, John got a phone call from Midland Publishing. "John, it's Rick Carlysle. I've got some good news. Your book already sold out its first run."

"You're kidding. How many did you print?"

"Three hundred. Apparently there have been news reports about some baseball team on NPR and SportScene. Now some of the new-age and self-improvement crowd are starting to buy it. I'm going to print another run of 1,000."

"That's great. How's the feedback?"

"Mostly positive so far, but that's why I called. The readers are asking for a little more detail on the exercises. I want to put out a revised edition on the next run."

John went over the text and added 35 more pages of explanations. He revised the theory part to make it even more accessible and tried to eliminate all jargon words.

Within three months the second run had sold and the third run was in the stores. It had begun to attract national attention. Three of the five hitters for the Diamondbacks all finished over the .400 batting mark. It was the first time in the Major Leagues that anyone had hit over .400 since Ted Williams had done it for Boston in 1941. It wasn't an official record because the guys had only played in the big leagues for part of the season.

One night in early October Robert had the news on. Cob Tappelle, the famous newscaster for ABC, made the following report.

A new fad is sweeping parts of the nation. Inspired by the amazing performance of five professional baseball players, weekend warriors by the hundreds are embracing a new-age health fad that some doctors say could be dangerous. The new fad is based on a book called Performance Enhancement for Athletes and Weekend Warriors. Ryan Bloger, spokesman for the American Medical Association, says that the latest health craze is completely unproven.

Ryan Bloger: "No testing has ever been performed on this activity to ensure that it is safe. The long term side effects are unknown. If the author of this procedure had any integrity, he or she would submit it immediately for review by competent health professionals. In my professional opinion, undertake this procedure at your own risk. Most certainly, consult your doctor before trying it. This applies especially to the elderly, pregnant women, and anyone already undergoing medical or psychological treatment."

Cob Tappelle: "Wynton DelMonico, a licensed psychiatrist and expert on cults, says that this procedure is reminiscent of the rituals found in some cults and secretive religious sects."

Wynton DelMonico: "The procedure seems to resemble the ritualistic mumbo-jumbo of the God's Light cult or the Raulian sect, all of which have a strict patter or procedure that must be strictly adhered to. Normally such destructive cults have charismatic and/or megalomaniac leaders who seem to be at war with society. We don't know too much about John Frankel, the originator of this procedure. But this technique has all the hallmarks of potential brainwashing."

TV shows pictures of Jonestown massacre, Waco, Bagwan Sri Rajnish, and other sects.

Cob Tappelle: "Here is Ari Flesch, Professor of Comparative Religions at Harvard University. Dr. Flesch is an expert on spirituality and gives us a final word of warning about this procedure."

Prof. Ari Flesch: "Camouflaged within a plausible format of self improvement, the techniques outlined in this book are, in my opinion, nothing more than the meandering of a quack. This book is just a come-on by another get-rich-quick spiritualist. There are far better books and regimes. I myself practice yoga. I highly recommend it for everyone."

Cob Tappelle: "In the Middle East today...."

Robert switched off the television, in total shock. The phone rang. "Yes Michael, I saw the report. I don't know what to do about it. Yes, we'll probably have TV trucks outside the house tomorrow."

John was numb. "How could they say stuff like that about such a harmless activity?"

Genevieve was angry. "They're making a mountain out of a molehill!"

Robert said, "I wish to hell I would have torn up that strange book when I first laid eyes on it."

The phone rang again. It was Rick Carlysle. "Well John, they trashed us. This is going to lead to a lot of free publicity. I'll bet we made it into 30 or 40 million households tonight that had never heard of our book before."

At first John was elated. "That's right Richard!"

"What about all of the people who now think we're dangerous criminals?" John asked. "That so-called report was a complete over-reaction. Do you think the authorities are scared by the positive potential of the technique?"

Carlysle thought for a moment. "I hadn't thought of that before, but you could be right. If enough people use our book to stay well there won't be as much need for hospital beds, treatments, and drugs. I just can't believe the medical profession feels threatened by one harmless little book."

"Neither can I," John said. "If the book sells, now we're money-grubbing leeches out to make a buck. Just like the report said."

"Yeah, they covered all the bases didn't they?" Carlysle agreed. "Unbalanced mind, dangerous procedure, quackery, and greedy rip-off artist. Remember that global pharmaceutical sales were over a trillion dollars as of 2014. The US market had about $350 billion of that. It's a lot of money."

"I've learned not to get worried about things I can't do anything about. Let's stay on an even keel, tell the truth, and not get caught up in all the drama."

"Good idea," Carlysle said. "We'll just respond based on our personal experiences with the technique. Those are positive ones."

Their phones rang constantly all night from friends, family, and a couple of local news stations. Finally the household turned them all off. Everybody went to bed.

The next morning Rachel got up and went in to work early. Robert was working on an article for *Alpha* magazine. John and Genevieve had just gotten up. Robert heard the door bell ring. It rang again, and again, and finally, continuously. He looked out into the front yard from his first floor office window. Someone stood in the bushes with their head up against the living room window. "Goddammit, that's it."

Robert ripped open the door. An excited reporter with a microphone in hand stood at the window with a cameraman behind her. Robert began to swear. He just opened the door and threw f-bombs, ignoring all questions. Finally the reporter backed off. "Who are you?" she said rudely. Robert began his four letter game again. The reporter turned off her mike in frustration. Robert's anger dissipated.

"Not bad," he thought to himself. "A good way to get rid of nosy trespassers."

The woman confronted Robert. "We'll be back." Robert smiled and started up again, following her all the way down the driveway. He wanted to make sure both her and the cameraman went away.

"Asshole," the man said.

"You're on my private property fuckstick," Robert responded. "Get the fuck out of here!" Robert's body felt strong and fit after his five mile run yesterday. He was itching for a fight.

"OK Tina, let's get in the van," said the camerman. The woman got into the passenger seat. The man sat behind the wheel.

The TV truck from channel 5 did not leave the driveway.

"We've got all day," the woman said.

This time Robert politely asked them to leave his property. The reporter folded her hands on her chest and the driver did the same. Robert immediately pulled out his mobile and called the Midland Police Department. "May I speak to Captain Kuralko. Tell him this is Robert Frankel." Robert knew Tim Kuralko from their college days on the Midland East track team.

"Tim! Robert here. Listen, we've got a TV truck trespassing on our property. Would you send a car down to take care of it? Thanks Tim, I really appreciate it."

"We're not leaving," the cameraman said.

Robert smiled smugly. About five minutes later a blue police car arrived with lights flashing, siren off.

"Not bad," the driver said. He started up the van but merely parked it out on the street beside the curb.

Robert walked back in the house and shut all the curtains.

"That's not going to be a long term solution," Genevieve said.

"No. But it sure was fun!" Robert said.

John came downstairs and got some breakfast. "I think I'll just go down and talk to them," he said calmly.

"Don't say anything," Robert advised. "They'll try to provoke you and twist your words."

"I've got some shopping to do for the house," Genevieve said. Through the side window, John saw her drive the car down the driveway. When the reporter attempted to stick a microphone in the open window, Genevieve ignored it and drove off. It was clear to him that the TV crew was going to stay until they got a statement or created some kind of a blowup.

John enjoyed his breakfast, cleaned up, and went out through the side door. He slowly approached the Channel 5 van, curious to see how the crew would react to him. A thin blond woman walked out of the truck with a microphone in hand, followed by the cameraman. She held out the mike. "You must be John Frankel. I'm Tina Brooks, city desk reporter for Channel 5 News." Tina took one look at John's crazy hair and said to herself, 'Oh goody, a real goofball. This ought to be good.' She imagined a new age cult leader or maybe an angry family of tax evaders.

John shook her hand. "Why don't you come up to the house and ask your questions." He turned and began walking back up the path to the front door. John wanted the cameraman to film the normalcy of the neighborhood and the house itself.

Behind him, Tina and the cameraman looked at each other and shrugged. Tina began a running commentary: "We have just met John Frankel, author of the controversial book *Performance Enhancement for Athletes and Weekend Warriors*. We are preparing to do an exclusive interview at his home on 337 Magnolia Street."

"Coffee or tea?" John said when they were inside.

"No thanks," Tina said. "We need to get back as soon as we can." She was disappointed. Just a normal middle class living room.

"Could we open the curtains so I can get some light?" the cameraman said.

"This is Jones Mayrand," Tina said, pointing to him.

"Why did you bring them in here?" Robert said angrily.

"This is my father, Robert Frankel. He's a writer."

"We've met," Tina said with distaste.

"Please be seated," John said. After they were comfortable John said, "Please state the purpose for your visit." John wanted to get the discussion on his ground, not out in the street.

Robert left the room.

"Tell the Channel 5 viewers about this dangerous new technique you've developed," the reporter asked.

John laughed. "Since when is breathing dangerous?"

Tina was confused. She had expected a denial, something she could feed off of. This man was too calm.

"You saw the report last night on ABC news. A number of experts pronounced your book potentially dangerous."

"You haven't answered my question."

"What question?"

"How is breathing dangerous?"

Tina was growing irritated. This interview was not turning out as expected. "What does breathing have to do with it?"

"So you haven't read the book." John was smiling.

"Look Mr. Frankel, I'm just doing my job. Recognized health experts have come out and said that your book is harmful. So why should our viewers believe you?"

"I'm not asking them to believe or disbelieve anything. If anyone is interested they can get the book and try the technique for themselves."

"Yes, Mr. Frankel," Tina said sweetly. "But we don't want people hurting themselves, do we?"

John laughed again. "It's pretty hard to hurt yourself breathing in and out."

Tina realized that the network story might have been grossly exaggerated. Although John Frankel looked a little weird, he was definitely not a megalomaniac or some cult leader. In fact, this guy was downright boring. "Is that all this is? Some kind of meditation?"

"Precisely. I don't see what the big deal is."

Tina motioned to Jones and dropped her microphone on the carpet with disgust. "What a waste of time." Just then Genevieve entered the living room, wearing nicely tailored slacks and a burgundy blouse. Tina turned around. John did the introductions. Genevieve walked gracefully forward and shook Tina's hand.

Tina was looking at one of the most composed females she had ever seen. Tina glanced down at her own clothing, now wrinkled from the van. She hated those damn seats. Her face must be a mess and her thin features probably looked haggard. But that's what happens when you get up before 5 a.m. every morning without time to dress properly. Oh well, maybe they could cut out some good footage and have a story after all.

The smile on Genevieve Frankel's face was genuine. Tina began to think she might almost like her. Not good. She had convinced Meyers to let her have Jonsey and a van. Now it would come to nothing. She would look stupid. She was hoping for a big story, a chance at promotion. She wanted to be a reader. She wanted to be on the *other* side of the camera.

As Tina and Jones trudged out (without even a thank you, Robert pointed out later), Genevieve smiled at her husband. "I think I married the right guy." John came over and gave her a big hug.

"C'mon, help me with the groceries," she said.

As they unloaded the bags and put the food away Robert hovered around, wanting to talk. "I don't understand it. She wasn't in your face like with me."

"That's because John stayed within himself and didn't allow her to get to him."

Robert accepted that and thought for a moment. "That shouldn't have anything to do with it. She's a belligerent bitch. That's what she's paid to do. How you responded to her isn't going to change her personality or her behavior."

"But it did, Dad."

Robert shook his head. "Nice job son but I think you got lucky. You can't change a person's basic nature." He turned and walked back up to his study.

"Dad's never understood people very well," John said.

However, that evening Robert appeared to be right. They all crowded around the TV at 7. Their story appeared about 5 minutes into the program.

"Our reporter Tina Brooks followed up on the sensational accusations made by Cob Tappelle last night about local author John Frankel's controversial new book."

On screen was Robert's aggressive swearing, but bleeped out. Tina's voice over said: "This is John Frankel's father, Robert. I felt in physical danger the whole time."

"That's a lie!" Robert said.

"Did you really swear at her like that?" Rachel said.

"I wasn't swearing at her. Only into the microphone to screw up her recording."

"Doesn't look like it."

Next came a picture of Genevieve driving past the microphone. "No comment from John Frankel's wife." Then the camera was inside the house for a second, showing Robert belligerently saying, "Why did you bring them in here?"

The camera then rotated to show some quartz crystals Genevieve had sitting on a cloth on one of the windowsills. Then the camera showed part of the interview with the sound off. Tina's voice over said, "The interview with John Frankel was most unsatisfactory. He told me nothing to doubt Cob Tappelle's story last night on the ABC network."

Robert smugly turned to his son. "You see what I mean?"

John and Genevieve were shocked. "That was a set-up if I ever saw one," John said.

"Clearly Tina Brooks lacks even a shred of integrity," said Genevieve.

"I'm going to call those bastards right now," Robert said.

"Please Dad, don't," John pleaded. "It's just going to encourage them even more."

"We can't just sit here and let them run all over us," Robert complained.

"What happens if we try to stop them? We become embroiled in their drama. We allow them to dictate the terms of our lives."

Robert knew his son was correct but the injustice of the situation fired his anger. "These people are liars and trespassers!" he shouted.

John felt like the roles of father and son had been reversed. "If we allow their actions to make us feel crummy we become part of the problem."

"Huh?"

"Instead of two negative people there are six negative people. We carry around those negative vibes and spread them around to others. So I say, lighten up. Be thankful for the wonderful life we have, our wonderful family, and this nice house."

Robert started to say something and stopped with his mouth half open. His anger died as suddenly as it began. "You're right dammit. You're right. Let them wallow in their cesspool." He slapped his palms down on his knees. "I'm going to finish my article."

Genevieve and Rachel smiled at John.

They talked for a while. John went up to his desk to answer his email. Every day there was more and more of it.

36

Two weeks later Richard Carlysle called to say that the third run had sold out. "Had a big spike after that ABC report. We've seen steady sales since then. You'll be getting a nice fat check."

"That's what I want to hear!"

"I've got money now, thanks to the Frankels. You and Genevieve have been the best risk I ever took." He paused. "You know, there's a lot of demand now for your book. You're becoming a national news figure. I've been telling people that we're going to arrange a book tour. I think it's time."

"OK Richard," John agreed. "As long as Genevieve comes with me."

"I've got news for you. Her book has still outsold yours, although yours is gaining fast. I want to do a dual tour. Husband and wife writing team and all that."

"OK."

"I'll arrange the whole thing," Carlysle said. "All you two have to do is show up and look pretty."

"That'll be easier for Genevieve than for me."

"That's for sure. How did a goofy guy like you get such a doll?"

"I could get rich answering that question at a dime apiece. She fell in love with my dynamic personality."

Two days later John got a call from Mats. When John

"Hey John, I want you to participate in a debate at the store. We'll have people from the medical school, the philosophy department, and some others from the university. Professor Flesch wants to come. NPR and ABC are going to send reporters."

John was shocked. ABC and NPR? "C'mon Mats. I don't want to get into that." John was angry. "You know I don't defend or apologize for my book. Otherwise I'd go crazy fending off all my critics."

"I know that John. I'm sorry. They know I'm a friend of yours. The thing just evolved, I swear. I didn't do a thing to promote it."

John smiled inwardly. Knowing Mats, he had sent out promo pieces to every university and news outlet in the country.

"Well, almost nothing," Mats conceded.

John laughed. "When is the debate scheduled?"

"This weekend, if you agree. I'm clearing out the entire front end and putting in a bunch of long tables. We'll have folding chairs for the audience. I'm hoping to get at least a hundred people. It'll be good for business." Mats was pleading.

"It'll be crowded."

"Yeah, but the media like that. More opportunity for tension to develop and something exciting to happen."

John sighed. The thing already sounded like a fait accompli. If he didn't show up it might look like he was ashamed of the material. Which he most definitely was not. "All right Mats. Just this once."

That evening John tuned in to the news and saw the advertisement for the debate. "Watch this special ABC News exclusive presentation of the debate between John Frankel and experts in the field of psychology, philosophy, and medicine. Mr. Frankel will be defending his explosive book from charges that it is thinly disguised brainwashing. *You* decide who's telling the truth! Saturday from 10 to 11 a.m., only on Channel 5 Midland."

Now John was really irritated. What a load of crap. Well, it was too late now. He'd just be honest and open and take advantage of his natural easy going nature. That's what he thought until he walked into the Full Moon that weekend and realized he'd been set up again.

When John and Genevieve walked into the Full Moon on Saturday the place was packed. Both had performed the technique before driving over to the Full Moon. John was solidly in the zone and felt ready for anything.

A little cheer went up as some of the locals recognized John. Mats met him at the door. "Uh, sorry about this John, but..." At that moment John caught a glimpse of Cob Tappelle himself. The famous anchorman was standing in the middle of the room, commanding it. "Mats, how could you?" Genevieve said. John hissed to his friend. "I'm going to set your sun for this Mats."

Genevieve entered the room behind John. Heads turned. Today she had on a pair of hip hugging dark blue slacks, a burgundy top with a feathery sash, a gold necklace, and the earrings. She found that a seat had been reserved for her, which she took gracefully.

The cameras were already rolling. Cob seemed totally in his element. John recognized the odious Professor Flesch, who gave him a slimy smile as he walked up to the long tables, which were arranged in a square. Tappelle, microphone in hand, was apparently going to be the moderator. The audience was seated on three sides surrounding the tables.

Name cards on the tables identified the participants. John took a seat next to two men he did not recognize, against the wall and facing Genevieve across the room. Cob came over to shake his hand. John saw the famous toupees. There were four of them covering what was probably an almost bald head. Cob's hairdresser had done a very good job of camouflage.

John knew he had to be careful. Cob Tappelle was a very smooth talker, famous for his incisive wit. Everyone knew the story of his unusual name. Born Cornelius Gromwich Tappelle, a childhood love for corn on the cob had given him his nickname, which he now used professionally.

John realized he was on foreign territory in the bookstore he had considered his own since childhood. Mats had screwed everything up royally. At least had the good sense to realize it. Mats stood behind the tables in front, waiting for Cob to introduce him. He looked nauseous. John gave Mats a dirty look. Mats blushed.

A crowd of people had gathered outside the store, looking in through the big front window.

A man stood by the front door with a watch. He raised and lowered his hand. The room lit up. Cob started his introduction.

"Welcome ladies and gentlemen to the Full Moon bookstore in Midland, Illinois. We are here to debate the explosive new book by Mr. John Frankel. Experts have charged that the book is exploitative and possibly even dangerous. Mr. Frankel has graciously agreed," here he turned toward John, "to explain himself so that we may all learn the truth."

John began to seethe slowly. He wasn't here at all to explain or defend himself from anything. He looked around at all the pieces so carefully arrayed on the board against him and quailed a little bit. He was clearly the pawn. Every eye around the table was turned toward him hostilely. John couldn't understand it. Was he that much of a threat? John's natural good nature began to desert him as he listened to Cob go through his carefully prepared routine.

Cob introduced Mats to the audience. The big Swede looked like an exhausted fish at the end of an expert fisherman's line. Mats threw him a look of despair and apology.

Looking around the room with his back against the far wall, John caught sight of Genevieve. On her face was a look of fierce pride and love for him. Her demeanor suggested that all was well. She raised her hand with her mobile in it, and pointed to him. John pulled out his mobile. She would help him to answer the questions, and buck him up. She was ready. And now, so was he.

John was jolted back to reality. Cob said, "And now our first question, from the noted Professor of Comparative Religion at Harvard University, Professor Ari Flesch."

Genevieve texted him.

"Before we begin, Mr. Tappelle. I will have a chance to question these distinguished gentlemen during the coming hour, will I not?"

"No, Mr. Frankel, you will not. I thought you understood the arrangements."

John smiled. "No sir. This is the first time I have heard of them."

Cob replied with a steely smile. "Perhaps next time you should come more fully prepared." Daggers shot out of the man's eyes.

"Positively simian, isn't he?" Genevieve texted and sent a picture of a little lizard crawling over a rock. John laughed.

Cob turned around, slightly irritated.

"Is something funny Mr. Frankel?" Professor Flesch asked.

John straightened in his chair to his full height, towering over the men beside him. "I'm just feeling really good right now professor."

Genevieve sent, "Real good John. You look like a man among boys."

That's right! John looked around the table and measured himself against the others. These guys are all little shrimps. With Genevieve on his side he could defeat an army of critics.

Professor Flesch began. "Is it true, Mr. Frankel, that the procedures in your book come from the ritual chanting of the God's Light cult?"

John had to admit it was a great question. If he said no he would immediately be on the defensive. But the truth was even stranger. The technique did come from a strange book – the kind of book that would immediately arouse suspicion. Could Professor Flesch possibly have inside information?

John could see a smile of victory slowly spreading over the face of his questioner. John knew he had to respond immediately. "Truth?" he texted. "Yes," Genevieve sent.

"The technique originally came from a book purchased by my wife at this very bookstore. I modified the technique to suit my own purposes."

"What was the title of this book?"

"Don't reply to him, talk to the audience," Genevieve sent quickly. Her fingers were blurs on her mobile's keyboard.

John turned and found a face in the packed bookstore, the friendly face of an elderly woman. "The book is very unusual. Originally it had a dark blue clothbound cover, fraying along the edges. It was written in a symbolic language which took me a couple of years to completely translate. As some of you may know, I have a Masters Degree in linguistics."

Surprise registered on the faces of his questioners. Apparently they had also not come so well prepared. John could tell Flesch was irritated that he had not responded directly to him.

"Good," Genevieve texted. "Talk some more about the book, your study program, how you translated the text."

John continued to speak to the elderly woman, imagining he was speaking to everyone watching on the TV. "The lithography of the book was very unusual. It was of a fineness and sharpness and detail that I had never seen before, and I've been reading books from this store since I was a child. Mats always said he couldn't wait for me to grow up to be a real paying customer."

This elicited a few chuckles among the locals in the audience, breaking the tension in the room somewhat. Cob frowned. Flesch interrupted: "Please answer the question Mr. Frankel. What was the title of the book from which you developed your so called technique?" John was stuck. He had to answer the question or appear evasive.

"Answer," Genevieve sent.

"The book had no title, no publishing information, and no ISBN number. It..."

Flesch interrupted harshly. "You developed this procedure from an unauthorized and fraudulently published book?"

"Perhaps, Mr. Flesch, you do not know that the book has been examined by Dalton Jones, a recognized manuscript authority with LIBER. Mr. Jones described it as an exciting find. The most amazing thing about the book was the paper it was written on. It was not paper at all, but a substance entirely unknown to materials analysis scientists."

With this the audience burst into excited chatter. John saw a look of irritation on the professor's face. Cob Tappelle quickly restored order. "Our next question will be from Dr. Charice Billingsley, a medical doctor known for her excellent work with cancer patients."

John was impressed. With a few simple words Tappelle had gotten off the previous subject and started a whole new thread. John thought he had won the first round with Flesch. The audience was getting interested in what he said but the excitement had been expertly defused.

Charice Billingsley wore a white smock and had dark brown hair and polished red nails. "Mr. Frankel, do you recommend this technique for the elderly, pregnant women, or those who are ill? My analysis of this technique shows me that the exercises within it can cause hyperventilation, shortness of breath, rapid heartbeat, or even arrhythmia."

Cleverly worded, John thought. He was going to respond by saying, What's harmful about breathing? She had made that answer impossible.

"Help!" he texted to Genevieve. Cob Tapelle noticed John tapping the keys but said nothing.

Genevieve's fingers moved rapidly.

"The technique involves slow controlled breathing at first and is only done to allow the flow of life force energy through the body. The ancient Hindus and Chinese called this energy prana, or chi. It has been known to every culture in history. Those who have successfully used the technique describe it as a feeling of well being. I don't claim this technique is useful for everyone. But certainly slow, controlled breathing must fit under the Hippocratic Oath: 'Do No Harm'. Also..."

Cob Tappelle interrupted him. "Mr. Frankel, you seem to have an aversion to straight answers. Please, just a yes or a no will do."

"Thank you Mr. T," John said calmly. He noticed that Cob Tappelle did not like being addressed so informally. "But I must be permitted to answer the question fully and to the best of my ability."

"Such an intelligent man ought to be able to give a simple yes or no," Cob said smoothly.

"Yes," John said. The audience laughed. "You are certainly correct." He nodded his head slightly in deferential acknowledgment to Cob Tappelle. "May I be permitted to continue?"

"Oh please do Mr. Frankel."

The audience laughed again. Many were now able to perceive that this forum was not really a debate at all. John felt that the atmosphere in the room was more like a trial. People loved trials. It probably made good television.

"Brilliant!" Genevieve texted.

Charice Billingsley asked her question again, in a more hostile manner than before. Tappelle was smooth. Even so, many in the audience were beginning to recognize that the panel members were biased against John. He detected the slightest shifting of sentiment for the underdog. Also, many in the audience were locals and so sympathetic to John. A man in the audience shouted from the back. "Just answer the question idiot." Heads turned. That gave John and Genevieve time to think of a good answer.

"If the distinguished doctor is of the opinion that slow breathing requires medical supervision, then I highly recommend it."

Some in the audience broke out into derisive laughter. Clarice Billingsley glared at John, clutching her notes tightly in both fists.

"This is no laughing matter Mr. Frankel. People a lot smarter than you have reviewed your material." She spoke passionately, holding up John's book. "They have found serious issues with it."

"I did not mean to be flippant, Dr. Billingsley. We all recognize the great work you have done and your good intentions in this forum."

"Good one John," Genevieve texted. "Her hostility toward you makes it clear her intentions are not so pure."

Billingsley was about to shoot back but Cob Tappelle quickly turned toward a very handsome and distinguished looking gentleman sitting to John's immediate right. He had white hair and wore a black pullover. Oh, oh, John thought. The heavy hitters are coming.

"Let me now introduce Chappy Osiris Brandel, president of the American Association of Psychological Studies, and winner of the prestigious McMillan Award for Therapeutic Excellence."

"Mr. Frankel, you say you translated this technique from a book of symbology. Is that correct?"

John responded immediately. "Yes sir." The man had a deep voice that commanded instant obedience.

"You have no idea who wrote the book, or its origins?"

"No sir."

"How do you know you didn't pick up a book on black magic? Or decadent spiritualism?"

This guy was a master, John thought.

One of the men across the table nodded his head in agreement at the question. Here was new tactic. John could tell it had struck a chord with some in the audience. He had to think of something immediately.

Genevieve was thrown off by the question and had no suggestions.

"Well sir, the symbology in the book was very general but its tone was uniformly positive. Most of the discussion was metaphysical in nature. It described a field of energy that I call the universal medium. Our scientists are discovering that matter and energy is connected, even across light year distances. The phenomenon known as quantum entanglement demonstrates this." He got that from one of his father's articles.

"You are not a scientist, are you Mr. Frankel?"

"No, I am not."

"Then perhaps you should stick to things you know." Brandel smiled smoothly for the camera. There were a few hoots of agreement from the audience. "The fact remains," Brandel said, "that the origin of your technique could have come from a debased or even evil source."

John knew he had to counter quickly.

"Well sir, the proof is in the pudding. If anyone wishes to read my book they may discover for themselves whether the material is positive or negative. I am a firm believer in the intelligence of the average reader. I believe we should allow others to make up their own minds without persuasion or coercion."

Chappy Osiris Brandel withdrew. John felt Brandel had made a telling point but also felt his response was a good one. No one can make you read a book.

"Not bad John," Genevieve texted. "Quick thinking."

Cob Tappelle spoke. "Our next questioner is someone who has bought your book, Mr. Frankel, and has experience with your technique. Mr. Callaghan, will you please come forward?" A thin, sallow looking man got up from the front row across from John. He took the empty seat at one of the long tables.

Oh my God, John thought, it's Jimmy from Dr. Jackson's lab!

"Jimmy?" Genevieve texted.

"My old lab partner. Chronic whiner."

"Mr. Callaghan, will you please identify yourself for the audience?"

"My name is Jimmy Callaghan. I've lived in Midland all my life. I used to work with John Frankel a few years ago."

"Would you please describe your experience with this technique?"

"It's not fair!" Genevieve texted. "We could have gotten lots of people with positive experiences."

"It really sucked. I have asthma and sometimes it gets pretty bad. So I figure, hey, I'll pick up this book. My old buddy Frankel wouldn't steer me wrong, right?" It was clear Jimmy was bitter about something. John could see he was going to blame it all on him.

"Go on," Tappelle said.

"I read through it the best I could. It had a lot of gobbledygook about life force energy and taking it into the body in certain ways. I didn't understand a lot of it but I didn't want to do the drugs anymore either. So I gave it a try. After about ten minutes my asthma got really bad and I had to go to the hospital."

"So you blame your worsening condition on this technique of Mr. Frankel, and not simply a natural deterioration from the asthma?"

"That's right."

"Thank you Mr. Callaghan."

Now the man to John's immediate left spoke up. "My name is Johnson Forsythe, director of the emergency ward at Kessinger Hospital in Midland. We treated Mr. Callaghan and found he had a severe irritation of the lung tissue, which we treated with a standard drug regimen. Normally this lung condition can be triggered in asthmatics by over exercise. That was my initial diagnosis. However, Mr. Callaghan told me all about this book and his experiences with the breathing techniques in it." He turned to John and spoke condescendingly. "You see Mr. Frankel, this is what happens when unqualified and ignorant people develop untested procedures. I would suggest that you withdraw this book from circulation. It may cause active harm to well intentioned but gullible people."

Forsythe's demeanor was that of a wise uncle to a recalcitrant child.

John spoke with as much warmth as he could muster. "Of course, in matters of medicine I must defer to competent authority. However, I must point out that lots of people have had success with this technique. If you would like sir, I can send you hundreds of unsolicited testimonials I have received via email."

"You can, of course, certify that these emails were not just made up by yourself?"

Forsythe paused for one second. He smiled. "You see John, in the medical profession we never release anything to the public unless it has been subjected to rigorous clinical testing. You can trust that your doctor is never going to give you anything that has not already been proven safe. This technique of yours fails muster on every level. It is simply something you made up and are foisting off on an unsuspecting public." He paused again and smiled avuncularly at John.

"Mr. Frankel, as scientists we don't accept that a silly technique, deciphered from an unknown and fraudulent black magic book with strange symbols, is going to do anyone any good. We can see only irreparable harm if it is continued. So I ask you again, sir. Will you, in the interest of public safety and public health, withdraw this book from circulation?"

The dénouement, John thought. It all led up to this one situation, this one question. They had maneuvered him expertly into a corner. Cob Tappelle's looked like a snake about to pounce and swallow its prey. Johnson Forsythe had cleverly not assigned Jimmy's condition to John's technique. He had practically admitted that his attack was caused by over exercise. But Forsythe was such a smooth talker no one noticed.

John could see the preponderance of agreement was all with the doctor. He wasn't going to argue the unfairness of the argument or the faulty logic of it.

"My book simply describes a technique of slow, rhythmic breathing in varying patterns. It has some mental exercises similar to sports psychology." The protocols in the book were far more sophisticated but it was the best analogy for the general public. "I would simply ask the audience whether slow, patterned breathing could be harmful to anyone, even an asthmatic. If you do consider this to be a harmful activity then I would discourage you from buying my book. I would never advocate a person doing anything he or she doesn't feel good about." John smiled. He felt relaxed, buoyed by the help from Genevieve. His voice resonated with well being.

"That's not good enough," a voice across from him said. "I have read this book of yours. You haven't demonstrated or proved that anything in your method will lead to the results you are claiming. Your so called protocols are vague. There has been no peer review of the material, no testing. This book is a menace to public health."

John spoke to Cob. "May I ask who this gentleman is?"

"I am Darby Trotter, chairman of the Department of Public Health here in Midland."

John was now sure of his ground. They had hit him with their best shot and he was still standing. He placed just a touch of amusement in his voice. "Ladies and gentlemen of the panel. You all have been asking me questions for 50 minutes. Now I think it's only fair that I should be able to ask a question of you."

Before anyone could respond John spoke again. "I look around the table and see so many distinguished faces, many of them from out of town. Tell me, why is it necessary to have 10 against 1?" John could see he had made a point with the audience. Americans always favored the underdog so it was a good play.

John had spoken to the whole room, not to anyone in particular. Cob Tappelle and a woman seated to John's extreme right responded together. Then they had to stop and figure out which one would speak.

"Good," Genevieve texted. "You have them on the defensive."

Cob Tapelle spoke. "In this matter of potential risk to public health, we feel the setting for this forum is more than fair."

It was a perfectly worded and delivered response and immediately served to defuse the sentiment generated by John's question. Despite himself John was impressed with Cob's ability. Odious as the man was, he was also a true master of his profession.

John's reaction did not go unnoticed by Cob Tappelle. *The kid has handled himself with dignity and aplomb. In the back of his mind he made a note to actually read his stupid book.*

"We have time for one more question," Cob said. "I turn now to the distinguished professor of psychiatry at Carleton University, David Griseman."

Griseman was a flabby man with a double chin.

"Mr. Frankel," he said. "Is it or is it not true that on February 21st, almost twelve years ago, you were admitted to the psychiatric wing of the Kessinger hospital here in Midland?"

John was stunned. *According to Robert, they had admitted him for one day back when he was 13. Something about seeing ghosts.*

Genevieve was no help to him here.

"I don't remember it. But it would have been when I was a child."

"A young adult."

John said nothing. He was trying to recall something...

"The admittance papers state that you were suffering from some form of dementia. I wonder, have you had any recurrence of these symptoms since then?"

John laughed, remembering his experience. "If I recall, Professor Griseman, my parents admitted me for a day. They were worried because they said I was talking to my dear departed Grandpa Harold. As I recall, my father was upset because Harold was spilling the beans about his golf game."

There were a few chuckles from the audience.

"It seems he was cheating," John added.

"You may think it's funny Mr. Frankel. I'm concerned that this technique of yours could cause mental imbalance. In many ways it is a very deep form of meditation. Combine that with the many untested mental exercises in this procedure. Abnormal or detrimental effects may result from its application."

John felt that this point was reasonable. "That's a good point, doctor. The technique does superficially resemble a deep meditation. However, the breathing and the mental exercises increase a person's conscious awareness. Any time you want to bail out you can easily do so."

John had ignored the implied hint at mental instability and found the only true datum in the man's accusations. Genevieve was thrilled. "Good job honey!" she sent.

John saw Cob checking with the director. The man was flashing two fingers.

Griseman responded immediately. "I'm genuinely concerned that someone with a history of mental instability should be writing a technique to improve mental stability. I—"

He was interrupted by Tappelle. "I'm afraid our time is up. I want to thank all of the members of the distinguished panel. I'm sorry we were not able to hear from all of you. It is clear, I think, from what we have heard today that there are serious questions about the method presented in Mr. Frankel's book. Ladies and gentlemen, you must make up your own minds as to who is really telling the truth. For ABC news, this is Cob Tappelle reporting."

The lights dimmed, the cameras stopped rolling, and the audience exploded into conversation. John heard snatches of it as he got out of his chair and walked over to Genevieve.

"That was more like a trial than a debate!"

"Frankel's a nutjob!"

All eyes were on him now. As John passed Tappelle the man stepped in front of him, forcing John to confront the famous news anchor. Tappelle held out his hand and gave John a smile of triumph. "I think we pretty much disposed of you and your book, Mr. Frankel." John wanted to wring the man's neck. He took the proffered hand and forced himself to respond politely. "That remains to be seen Mr. Tappelle."

John quickly disengaged and walked over to his wife. They embraced and he kissed the top of her head.

"C'mon honey, let's go get something to eat. I'm starving."

John and Genevieve walked out of the Full Moon hand in hand. Mats tried to get his attention but John refused to acknowledge his old friend. Despite holding himself together fairly well in there, he was really upset. Genevieve drove silently to Gratzi's, allowing him time to wind down.

John thought his performance had been a success. In a room full of predators he had kept himself in the zone except for a couple of minor slip-ups.

He closed his eyes and tried to clear his mind. His heart was beating rapidly now and he felt cold and a bit nauseous. Maybe it was a result of all of the hostile energy thrown at him. He was really shocked at the hatred that had emanated from most of those on the panel. It made no sense at all. He still didn't understand why his measly little book had upset them. It was as if he had attacked the very structure of their beliefs. Clearly, this was a coordinated effort to discredit him on a national scale.

John's mind was whirring about. His emotions were getting away from him. He decided to do the technique once again and try to calm down...

Genevieve studied her new husband, recognizing the moment they stepped out into the parking lot that he was in the middle of one of his contemplative moods. She knew that he was concentrating so hard he wouldn't even hear her speaking.

They pulled into Gratzi's. Genevieve let the engine idle. She would wait for as long as it took. After about 20 minutes John opened his eyes. "Are we here already?"

"Yes love."

"Let's go in. I'm really into some of that lasagna." John felt much better now. He was back to his old self again. Genevieve smiled and led the way.

Once they were seated she took both his hands in hers. "John, you were magnificent. I'm so proud of you."

"Couldn't have done it without you babe. I was stuck a couple of times."

"But John, the way you kept your composure! I've never seen anything like it. You were like a little bird surrounded by panthers. You were so calm, so self assured." She gazed at him adoringly.

John thought he could get used to this kind of attention all the time.

As they chatted John could see the place was filling up.

Mario came out from the kitchen to greet them. "Ah, that proposal! I'll never forget it." They chatted amiably for several minutes.

Now the place was full and the staff were a bit nonplussed. Their waiter came out to apologize in advance. "I'm sorry, but service will be slow today. We're preparing for the Saturday night crowd but it seems they're a little early."

Some of the people from the interview must have followed him over. From their table at the back of the restaurant John saw Tina Brooks walk in. She was standing on tip toes, looking around. Her gaze stopped when she saw John.

"Here comes that reporter from Channel 5," John said. Genevieve got up immediately, blocking her path to him.

That's my lady, he thought.

Tina came up to the table and stood two feet in front of Genevieve. The eyes of both women locked together. Everyone in the restaurant had turned to observe. Tina said, "Don't worry, no cameraman this time." Genevieve said nothing but continued to stare into her eyes.

Tina stepped back and dropped her gaze.

"I came to apologize. I'm sorry. I let my ambition interfere with my integrity as a reporter."

Genevieve said nothing.

John felt sorry for Tina. His wife was very intimidating when she wanted to be. A very powerful being in a smallish body. He said, "Apology accepted. Come, sit." Genevieve didn't move. "It's all right honey. Let her through." Genevieve relaxed and resumed her seat.

Tina found another chair. She sat against the wall, next to John. Fortunately she was thin or she never would have fit.

"It was awful what they did to you in there," Tina volunteered. "Like cannibals preparing a roast." She looked up at John. "I can't believe how well you handled it. My palms were sweating before Tappelle even began the introductions. I could see it was a setup from the very beginning. Did you notice the way the tables were arranged? They had you cornered." She sighed. "That's why I'm here. Anyone who could handle something like that all alone has got something, here." She placed her hand over her heart. "At first I thought you were just a publicity seeker. That's why I prepared the story the way I did. Well, my editor helped too. We thought you were a scumbag. We wanted to crush you."

Genevieve looked at John. They communicated silently, deciding to be gracious.

Tina was obviously sincere and regretted her actions. Perhaps they could make a friend.

"There must be a lot of pressure in the news business," Genevieve offered.

Tina leaned back in her chair and let go. "Oh, my, you can't imagine it. I'm up at 5 every morning. I work a city beat but I want to get into broadcasting. I'm trying to be a reader. Those are the people on camera. But really, I'm starting to wonder whether it's all worth it. I haven't gotten a good night's sleep in months."

"Did you know Tappelle was coming?" John asked.

"Are you kidding? That's all we talked about for two weeks."

"How did you convince Mats?" John asked.

"Mats?"

"The owner of the bookstore," said Genevieve.

"Oh, him. He was frothing at the mouth to have us come."

Tina regarded John closely for a minute. "I want to know whether it's safe to try the stuff in the book." She dug into her purse and came out with a copy. "I bought one before I left, along with at least three dozen others." She laughed. "You should have seen it. After you left Tappelle and the others thought they had you. Then the bookstore owner held up your book. 'I've got copies of Mr. Frankel's book right here.' You should have seen them line up. Of course a bunch of the panelists made a big fuss about money grubbing authors and greedy bookstore owners. Tappelle tried to convince the people in line not to buy it. The doctor, especially, Jackson what's-his-name, was especially insistent. A couple people left the line. The others said they were so impressed with how you did that they wanted to try it for themselves."

"I'll be damned," John said.

"I want to try it too. I'm scared after what they said."

"It's safe," Genevieve said.

Tina looked uncomfortable. "How do you know?"

"Because I learned it before John did. I bought the book several years before John ever saw it. The only difference is John did the translating entirely on his own. I had my father to help. He's a researcher at Carleton University."

Tina reached into her bag for pen and paper. "Do you mind if I take notes?" Tina realized she had an exclusive. It had happened entirely by accident.

John and Genevieve exchanged glances.

"OK," Genevieve said.

"So you both are experts in this...thing?" Tina asked.

"Yes," Genevieve said. "We sometimes do it together. It's fun."

"Why do you do it?"

"To feel better. To connect with a greater and more wonderful part of yourself."

She touched her pen to her lips. "Is there such a thing?"

Genevieve laughed. "Sometimes it doesn't seem so does it? You just have to practice the technique for a while and then you find out for yourself."

"The technique is just one of many ways of self-improvement," John said. "I make that clear in the book. I'm not some guru and I don't want to be. I hate publicity. The only reason I wrote the book was to stop people from calling and emailing me for details."

"Can you just pick up the book and do this on your own? Do you need an instructor?"

"I tell you what," John said. "Call Richard Carlysle, my publisher. He tried it all by himself. You can ask him."

"One more question," Tina said. "You don't know where the original book came from?"

"I have no idea. Do you?" he said to Genevieve.

"I picked it up in the Full Moon because it looked really old, and really interesting. I don't know its origins or who even wrote it."

John said, "Do you want to see it?"

Tina's eyes lit up. Her exclusive was going to get even better. "Right now?"

Genevieve smiled. "I think not. We want to enjoy our lunch."

"What time is it?" John said.

"12:45." A good reporter always knows the correct time, Tina thought.

"Why don't you meet us at the house at 3:30? Don't let my father see you. He wants to throw ink in your face."

3:30, Tina thought. That'll be tough to write a story and have it ready for the 5 o'clock. If she only had another half hour...but she decided not to press. Luckily she had a camera in the car. She could get pics of this mysterious book.

"OK, thanks a lot," Tina said. She rose and touched John on the shoulder. "Thanks." Tina left.

"I think we just did a good thing."

"It'll give us an ally in the media at least," Genevieve said.

"Will Robert be home at 3:30?"

Genevieve grinned. "I hope not for Tina's sake."

During dinner several people stopped by to congratulate John on his performance. As John and Genevieve walked out of the restaurant many of the diners held up copies of his book. John waved and smiled to them.

Holy shit. I'm getting famous.

John and Genevieve passed Tina in a Channel 5 car parked two doors down the street. John motioned for her to come to the front door. As they entered the house John shouted for Robert. There was no answer. "I guess we're safe."

"I hope he just didn't go out for a run," Genevieve said.

They trooped upstairs to the bedroom. John retrieved the book and dusted it off. "Here it is."

"It doesn't have a cover," Tina said.

"That's right. We had an...accident with it. The cloth cover burned off."

"You said during the debate that the pages were made of an unknown substance. Is that true?"

"It is," John said. "That's how the cover disappeared but the pages remained intact. Here, let me show you." He got a book of matches down from the top shelf which always held matches and candles in case the power went out. He flamed the match and held it to the book. Both women were startled and jumped back. The flame had no effect whatsoever on the pages. The material remained cool to the touch.

"Remarkable!" Tina said.

She picked it up and began flipping through the pages. Tina noticed the strange symbols. She couldn't believe anybody could make sense of it. "You translated this?"

"We both did," John said.

Tina shook her head. The book was open to the drawing of the white city on the flat plain of glass. Tina stared at it. The buildings had rounded surfaces and were much more beautiful than the boxlike buildings in downtown Midland. They glowed softly. That one is particularly beautiful...I wonder what it's like inside? Her feet felt the hard floor...hold it! Tina started and her hands let go of the book. It fell awkwardly to the floor. "Just what *is* that thing?"

John spoke calmly. "Did you find yourself in one of the buildings?"

"Yeah." She was starting to shake a bit.

"How did it feel?"

Tina thought back. "It was...it was...nice. Beautiful. Fascinating." She looked up at John now with wide eyes. "I guess I just got scared."

"Not to worry. The same thing happened to me."

"But what *is* it?"

"My best guess is that it's a window to another place in our universe."

"Like another planet?"

"Yes."

Tina was angry now. "So those assholes were right. It *is* a black magic book."

Genevieve was going to jump in but John replied gently. "Remember back to how you felt when you looked at the picture."

Tina began to relax. "Can I look at it again?" John handed her the book with the correct page face up.

Tina Brooks found herself in the same building, standing on a dark blue, completely level surface. That surface was not unyielding; it gave a little as she jumped up and down on it. She took off her shoes and felt the cool softness of it against her feet. She walked over and touched one of the walls. It also felt soft, cool, and comforting. The surface was a beautiful creamy white. It glowed slightly, as if waiting for something. It reminded her of the beautiful pearls her mother used to wear. The curved surfaces of the walls, as they rose higher and higher, produced a nurturing feeling of security within her. Tina began to relax. She noticed a feeling of excitement here, of possibilities, of mystery...she felt a touch on her shoulder.

"How was that?" John said.

"Really nice. It felt good." She placed the book on the desk. "So OK, it's not black magic. But it *is* magic."

"Good magic," John said. "The whole book is like that. It's really deep. It describes a method of connecting up with something that feels really good. According to the book, this good feeling is a subtle energy that fills the universe. You know, like the force in Star Wars. Except you can't use it like Darth Vader did."

Tina thought about that for a moment. In her life she hadn't noticed much of anything positive so far. "Can I take a picture of this thing?"

"Sure. Don't try to photograph the printing. It won't show up in camera memory."

"Really!" Tina snapped pictures willy-nilly. "We'll see about that."

After Tina left Genevieve spoke to John. "You'd make a great counselor. Or a diplomat. You handled her perfectly. You're so good with people."

John thought about that. He didn't have a great burning desire to interact with people but he did know how to talk to them.

"You're changing John," Genevieve said. "Growing into something I always hoped you would. And you're taking me with you."

"What is this something I'm supposed to grow into?"

Suddenly her face clouded and her eyes stared out into space. "I don't know John. It's...something about the completion of the Great Cycle. The Unformed Potential activity, it's coming to a crisis point. I'm sure of it. You're involved. We don't have much more time..."

Suddenly she threw herself into his arms and hugged him tightly. "Oh John, dearest John, I don't want anything to happen to you!"

John tried to laugh but Genevieve's fear bothered him. "Nothing's going to happen to me."

She searched his face intently. "You promise?"

"I promise."

Just as quickly as she had gotten blue she cheered. "OK then sweetheart, I'll hold you to that." She skipped out of the room and down the stairs. John heard her whistling in the living room.

"She thinks *I'm* special," he said.

37

Tʜᴀᴛ night Genevieve said, "It's time to see Kjirsten."

"It is?"

"I told her we'd come to the Eyrie every first Monday of the month. We've already missed three appointments."

The Eyrie operated on a 36 hour clock. Its "year" consisted of 72 weeks of 6 days called sixdays. One of Kjirsten's pet complaints to Genevieve was the crazy earthian calendar.

John closed the deadbolt to their bedroom. "Let's go. Rachel and Robert are already in bed."

When they arrived the place was brightly lit and crowded. Beings of every description were wandering around aimlessly. The vibe wasn't good. Kjirsten saw them and walked over.

"What's going on?" Genevieve said.

"The Unformed Potential is increasing in strength faster and faster. No one can even get out to the barrier anymore. Even routine observation and data collection is almost impossible. We're seeing the kind of potential buildup talked about in the ancient records. It's progressing a lot faster than we ever dreamed. Genevieve, the crisis could be on us at any time."

Kjirsten spread her arms apart in a helpless gesture. "It's too big, way too big. It looks like we already missed our chance. We failed!"

John and Genevieve said nothing. They were both shocked to see the confident Lyran in this mood. She looked defeated and lost.

"Some people from the research divisions are coming over to give the field group leaders a detailed briefing. Then there will be a general brief. Stick around."

John began to feel anxious. For him, the so called Cosmic Event was totally unreal, a joke. The Eyrie was just a gigantic playroom filled with cool toys. It dawned on him that what was occurring in the Unformed Potential could actually have an effect on everything. That effect could be life threatening.

It was all wrong. His experience with the technique indicated otherwise.

The Unformed Potential interfaced with all of reality. The leakage of the Unformed Potential into Real Space might infect that randomness into the well-ordered structure of existence. John shuddered to think what would happen if the walls of reality broke down. The delicate life forms within every universe would be overwhelmed with a massive increase in entropy coming from the Unformed Potential. Life everywhere would expire in a nightmarish insanity.

No, it couldn't happen. It was too stupid. The system couldn't be designed that way.

Or could it?

John began to doubt everything he had learned. Maybe the destruction of all that had gone before was a necessary cleansing, a changing of the guard to allow evolution to progress. John thought of the history of science. When the snake molts it sheds its useless skin. The beautiful butterfly evolves from the cocoon of the caterpillar, which is discarded. Periodic forest fires are needed so that the undergrowth does not choke the trees. There is ample precedent in nature for the idea that growth proceeds by destruction. "Out with the old and in with the new" seems to be the guiding principle.

Kjirsten had already explained a little bit about the galaxy and its cultures. Stagnation seemed to be the theme. After billions of years of civilization there were few new avenues left to explore. Perhaps it was time for a radical change.

John felt ill. This is not how he wanted to spend his evening. He sure as hell was not ready to die any time soon.

One of the little cars stopped in the hallway inside one of the yellow circles. A distinguished looking being in a dark blue robe emblazoned with the guide symbol strode purposefully to one of the common areas. Kjirsten and a couple dozen other team leaders joined him. Field technicians were ambling about aimlessly.

Davey, Goliath, Bellerophon, and Ivan hung out together in one of the common areas with a lot of the other technicians. Goliath spotted John and trundled over.

"What's the confab all about?" John asked.

"It looks as though we've missed our only opportunity to affect events in the Unformed Potential," Goliath said. John had learned to read the mantis' body language. The sidebands of thought from him emanated concern.

"Opportunity?" Genevieve said.

"Remember Kjirsten mentioned the mass debrief? We just completed a facility-wide Unformed Potential observation project. You two missed that. It was determined that the Unformed Potential has already reached a critical threshold. It's seeping into reality so fast that we have no hope of stopping it."

Genevieve gasped. "You mean it's begun? The end of the Great Cycle?"

"I'm afraid so," Goliath said. "From what we can conclude from our observations and our models, our window has already closed."

Bellerophon strode over, getting in on the conversation. "That's right. We blew it."

John was skeptical. "There's nothing we could have done anyway."

Davey replied belligerently. "We coulda tried to seed it in a mass merge. That woulda self-organized the stuff and prevented a buildup of entropy into the visible universes. The high muckety-mucks couldn't make up their minds about the best time to do it."

"Not quite like that my friend," Goliath said. "In order to be effective we'd have had to place our thought form into the Unformed Potential as close to the critical moment as possible. But nothing about the Unformed Potential is certain. We did the best we could. It wasn't good enough."

"We didn't even try," Davey grumbled. "Bunch of quitters."

"Do you really think you could have seeded the entire Unformed Potential?" John asked. "How would that be done?"

Bellerophon answered. "The Records indicate anecdotally that these Events occur periodically, tens of billions of years apart. The last time there *was* a successful seed. At least we think there was."

"So that means..." John flicked his hand across his throat.

"The End," Bellerophon confirmed.

"I still say we should try." Davey boomed loud enough for the conferees to hear.

"What are they talking about?" Genevieve inquired.

"The field sectors are all getting briefed by the research division," Goliath said.

"They're trying to explain how it's all hopeless and we're trying to convince them it's not," Davey said.

"Yeah, they don't really think we're that important," Bellerophon complained. "All they know is the simulation and their 'predictive algorithms' and their 'models.' To them it's just a nice little game because they've never been out there. They have never *felt* it. They look at us as some kind of fringe-element freak show."

"Except when they don't get their data," Davey growled.

The conference broke up. Kjirsten motioned everyone to look to the middle conference sector. All over the facility, gigantic tank displays, about 25 feet on each side, emerged from the floor. The thing was easily visible from each of the surrounding and crowded open sectors. The lights dimmed and a sonorous voice spoke:

"In the tank you can see the most up-to-date simulation. Thank you to our brave Unformed Potential technicians who worked non-stop for four sixdays to bring us the most comprehensive survey ever."

"About time we got some love." Davey was slightly mollified.

"As you can see, the virtual energy has already reached the critical limit and the End Time is upon us. Here is a predictive run-through from our latest modeling algorithms."

The tank showed a background of galaxies and stars. Slowly, a faint mist appeared within the fabric of space, growing more and more pronounced. The atomic structure of matter began to lose its integrity until the relationships between quanta themselves was destroyed. The universe dissolved into the Unformed Potential like kool-aid into a glass of water.

The group around John was stunned.

The presenter made it sound like a glorious return to the Godhead.

"All conscious beings will merge their personalities within a glorious Oneness. The physical shell will dissolve and consciousness will once again become pure Being, resonating only to the highest vibrations. All life everywhere will become united in bliss. I am personally looking forward with tremendous anticipation and excitement to the unfolding of this Event. All of my colleagues are as well."

"Maybe *you* are," somebody said. Nervous laughter reverberated through the group. John could hear the presenter answering questions, which were unintelligible over the babble of conversation.

"...our best guess is that we have less than one hundred years. No one knows how quickly the structure of reality can hold out against the effects of the Unformed Potential. But yes. It could be any time."

The presenter answered another shouted question. "The effects of the Unformed Potential upon physical existence will make itself apparent to everyone. We are the first to feel its effects because this station exists within the Unformed Potential itself..."

Now the questions were fired from all over. The brief sounded like an earthian press conference.

"...We think the outer universes will be affected first, and most strongly...No. You can't avoid the event by staying here. Our modeling shows that this facility will soon be under the most intense pressure from the Unformed Potential..."

"...No! Our latest models tell us that the Event will unfold gradually as the Unformed Potential asserts itself into the fabric of reality. However, the rate of its progression will increase..."

"...What will it be like? Well, those of you who have immersed yourselves in the Unformed Potential understand that better than anyone..."

After a few more inquiries the presenter finished his briefing. The tanks lowered themselves into the floor and the lights came on.

"I'm not a big believer in the We-Are-All-One crap," Davey said. "I'm me and I'll always be me."

Immediately there was nervous laughter and some strong objection.

"You weren't paying attention my Procyon friend," said a small humanoid with four arms. "Of course you'll still be you. There will just be more of you!" The being spoke cheerfully. "We will all be much more intimately a part of each other. The All will again be recreated in all its glory. We, like the earth God Brahma, will all participate." The being nodded to John and Genevieve. "Earthians have the best Gods and creation myths."

"I ain't buyin' it," Davey said stubbornly. He stood with his massive arms crossed on his big barrel chest, his legs rooted to the ground like tree stumps. "No one can convince me otherwise. If you wanna be dissolved into some big gloppy goo of Oneness, go right ahead. That's for airheads."

The small humanoid slapped his colleague on the back. "That's OK my friend. It will all turn out wonderful in the end."

After their return from the Eyrie John and Genevieve stayed up all night discussing the briefing and its ramifications. It just did not seem possible that a cosmic event was going to wipe out the universe. At two in the morning they walked outside in the cold to look at the stars. Nothing whatsoever seemed amiss. John said, "I don't believe it."

"Neither do I," Genevieve agreed.

Unspoken was the increased difficulty in negotiating the vibrational pathways back to earth upon their return from the Eyrie. In their robe and slippers the couple stood silently, alone with their thoughts.

"C'mon, let's get back inside," Genevieve said. "It's cold out here."

John thought about chasing her up the stairs but didn't want to wake Rachel and Robert. He satisfied himself with watching her graceful movements on the staircase. They got into bed.

"John, there's something that doesn't feel right about this. There's something we can do, I just feel it. It doesn't include Merging into One, like folding ourselves into some cake batter."

John laughed. But the anxious feeling in the pit of his stomach would not go away.

38

For the next week the Frankel household was in an uproar.

On the Sunday news telecasts Channel 5 ran the Tina Brooks interview with John. This time it was totally favorable. First the station showed the footage left out in the original broadcast. Tina Brooks apologized on the air for the slanted story. The new narrative showed a still picture of Genevieve, Robert, and Rachel and identified each. Tina explained Robert's actions as the natural anger of a man whose personal privacy was being invaded. The story also pointed out that Genevieve was a published author and mentioned the title of her book. Over a still shot of the family, the recording of her interview with John was played without alteration. Then John's explanation about the mysterious book. Tina showed stills of John's attempted book burning. Tina's voice-over said, "According to John Frankel, the pages are made from an unidentifiable substance. I have no idea whether this is true. I'm sure of one thing: it sure isn't paper. Here's me touching the page just after I torched it with my cigarette lighter for over a minute. The stuff wasn't even warm! When I tried to photograph the strange hieroglyphics on the pages all I got was this: " (shows blank picture).

"In my personal opinion Mr. Frankel is telling the truth. You'll have to make up your own mind. For Channel 5 news, this is Tina Brooks reporting."

"Shit on a stick," Robert said. "I can't believe what I just saw. A news reporter apologizing right on the air."

Later that day their phones overloaded with requests for interviews. "This is going to get intolerable," Robert complained.

"I'm afraid our quiet little family life will be no more," Rachel said. She felt discouraged.

"I have an idea," John said. He used his cell and called Richard Carlysle at his home.

"John! I've been trying to reach you all day. We sold out all our store copies in five hours yesterday. I'm getting orders faster than I can print books."

"That's great Richard. Listen, you have to help us out. We're being inundated by interview requests. You have to find me a publicist. We need to be able to refer all media requests to a single office so we can have our life back. Right now we can't even receive calls from our friends."

"Not to worry John," Carlysle said. "I've been thinking about that myself. I've already lined up a guy for you. He's my old school buddy who majored in media relations. I've arranged for him to organize the book tour. I'll just increase his responsibilities a little."

"Excellent. How do we get people from calling and texting?"

"You're always going to get a little of that, at least at first. Keep your published numbers. I'll have Darcy route your calls to a professional answering service. They'll screen your calls and send personal messages through. We'll do the same with your email. All you have to do is give Darcy a list of your friend's numbers and your personal address book. Darcy said he'd handle all that for you as soon as I give him the OK."

"OK. Tell him to get on it."

"Meanwhile, call that Tina Brooks and give her another interview. Give her the address, phone number, and email of the publicist's office. You can apologize to the viewers and say something like, 'I regret very much not being able to answer calls and email personally, but we're getting so many...etc. etc.'"

"Good idea."

"By the way, the book tour is almost finalized. You'll be hitting three in-state cities and four outside the state. After that we'll have to do a national one unless the momentum on your book dies down. I don't see that happening very soon."

"I guess we'll just have to go with the flow." John was not looking forward to the continued publicity.

"Yup. It can be a lot of fun or a pain in the ass. I'll have my friend Darcy Bledsoe give you a crash course in dealing with the media. Although you seem to do pretty well, John."

John wrote down all the details and hung up.

"OK gang. Richard Carlysle, our publisher, is getting everything set up. We're getting an office, a publicist, and a professional answering service to screen our calls and emails. I'll print off an information sheet for everyone. I'm going to call Tina right now and arrange another interview. Hopefully we can get this information out on the news first thing tomorrow."

John called Tina. She was only too happy to cooperate. "Our local ratings on that story were one of the highest ever recorded."

"This interview won't be so dramatic," John cautioned. "I'm willing to answer a few questions if you can think of any."

"I think I can do that. How about tomorrow morning around 9?"

"Sounds good." He was about to hang up but thought of something. "Did you ever call my publisher, Richard Carlysle?"

"Not yet," Tina said. "Been too busy."

"He's publishing both of our books and knows a lot about the technique. You might get some good information."

"Thanks. Anything to do with you is hot stuff right now."

John gave her Richard's phone number and hung up.

"We're all set." He turned to Genevieve. "Our dual book tour is just about ready to go."

She clapped her hands excitedly. "It might be fun!"

Over the next several days Darcy Bledsoe gave John and Genevieve a crash course in media relations. Darcy was a cheerful, rotund man of middle height, about 40, with thick glasses and a Beatles haircut.

"Don't say anything off the top of your head," he advised. "One of the most common tactics is to ask outrageous or provoking questions. Or present a lie as truth and ask you to respond. Just keep a smile on your face and say nothing, or something trivial, even if you feel like hitting the bastards."

The book tour was to kick off the following Monday morning. Darcy said they had several interview requests every day. "I'm going to recommend you talk with Sherry Grossman at NPR first off, and then Olga of NBC."

"Olga?"

Bledsoe stared at them disbelievingly. "Are you guys on a different planet? You know, the Olga show. A book recommendation from her and you're on the bestseller lists."

"Will she talk to us?" John asked.

Darcy shook his head. These people were *different*. "Let's say that she was very receptive."

John and Genevieve shrugged. John didn't know anything about the famous Olga, but he liked the idea of being interviewed by Sherry. "I feel that she's a personal friend of mine. Best interviewer out there."

"Olga will probably want you to make an appearance on her show," Darcy pointed out. "You'll have to decide how far you want to go with this media thing. I'd advise you to make a firm policy right now and not deviate from it. That way we're seen as fair."

"We're not publicity seekers. Deny all TV interviews. We'll use Tina Brooks for that. We're happy to speak on the phone with anyone you say is OK."

Over the next few weeks a couple more unflattering stories appeared on the major networks. Then the fireworks hit for real. Someone in Arizona interviewed Debra McGrady. She inadvertently let the cat out of the bag regarding Genevieve's origins.

The media had a field day. One headline in the *Star* said, "Outer Space Humans Counsel Mankind." Others read, "Genetically Engineered Robot?" and "Evil Alien Attempts Takeover of Earth." There were others just as bizarre.

One tabloid had a picture of Genevieve in a Superman costume. "Superwoman?" was the headline. A big debate followed about the ethics of genetic engineering and cloning. Genevieve was pilloried and praised from one end of the country to the other. Comedians made jokes about 'breathing your way to Nirvana.' Some religious groups and politicians portrayed Genevieve (and John) as "evil demons from hell."

Genevieve laughed it all off.

At a book signing at a suburban Philadelphia bookstore a young woman approached her. "How can you keep your sanity with all that criticism?"

"I just ignore it," Genevieve said. "I concentrate on the fun bits."

"Did you hear what Senator Smith called you on the news last night? Both of you? Threats to national security, he said. Potential terrorists."

"I didn't hear it because we don't follow the news," Genevieve replied.

The woman was amazed. "How can you know what to look out for if you stick your head in the sand and ignore important events?"

"Whatever you give your attention to in life will become more important to you. Events you experience then coalesce around those things."

The book signing had turned into a philosophy discussion. Dozens of people gathered around the double desk where John and Genevieve were seated.

"You can't ignore the negativity in the world. Senator Smith can make life very uncomfortable for you."

"How could he possibly do that?"

"Promoting extremist belief systems. You're getting the entire country agitated. Senator Smith has spoken against what you're doing many times. Many people agree with him."

Genevieve shrugged. "Let him bluster. We're doing nothing wrong."

The woman was amazed at their naiveté. Everyone in line was listening, or trying to listen. John spoke up. "I don't want negative things in my life. My life is 99% positive and the news is 99% negative."

A tall man at the back of the crowd spoke up. "You've been lucky so far. Eventually the odds will catch up with you."

"What do you mean?" Genevieve asked.

"It's not possible for life to be good all the time."

"Why not?" John asked.

The man looked at John as if he were crazy. "Because it just isn't! You have to take the bad with the good."

John smiled. "If you believe that your life can't always be good then it won't be. That will happen not because that's how life is, but because you have beliefs that guide your actions in that direction."

The man snorted his disgust.

A white-haired man to John's left was appalled at this philosophy. "How can you protect yourself against attacks if you don't know about them? We live in the real world, not some fantasy land."

"I'm just speaking from experience," John said. "The happier I get the better my life goes. I don't get negative events in my life. I've noticed this in other people as well. My old lab partner, Jimmy Callaghan, was a constant complainer. He always had bad things happen to him. His girlfriend left him, he got sick, he got into a car accident, then he lost his job. I used to think that Jimmy complained because his life was rotten. Now I realize his life was rotten because he complained all the time."

"That's crazy," the woman said. "You're saying that thoughts are more important than reality. By not protecting yourself you open yourself up to attack. You become totally vulnerable. Look at what happened on 9/11."

Another man seconded this. "History is filled with civilizations that were run over by more aggressive ones. If you don't protect yourself you get creamed."

There were murmurs of agreement among the crowd.

Genevieve responded. "When you protect against something you create it in your life. You give it power. Remember what Mother Teresa said. 'I was once asked why I don't participate in anti-war demonstrations. I said that I will never do that, but as soon as you have a pro-peace rally I'll be there.'"

"That's right," John said. "Create what you want. Don't protect against what you don't want."

The woman was unconvinced. "You could make a big stink about Smith's comments against you on social media. Politicians hate bad publicity."

"That would just be acknowledging the senator's viewpoint," Genevieve replied. "It would give credence to Senator Smith when he has none. It would begin a fight that would promote his hateful remarks."

John nodded. "If we pursued that line we would eventually become more like the thing we're trying to protect ourselves against."

"It's better than being pilloried in the media and being made fun of," a muscular man standing behind the woman said loudly.

A middle aged man to their right spoke up. "What you're saying is just what the Buddha said. The Buddha believed that a person's thoughts determined what happened to him. But that's a stretch in today's world. You just can't wish the bad stuff away."

Genevieve shrugged. "It works for us. Our lives keep getting better and better. I'm not too worried about Senator Smith and his threats."

A bald headed man in a tank top pushed forward. "I'm Max, pleased to meet you." He pointed his finger at John. "I don't care what you say. I always feel safer carrying a gun. If some scumbag is out there I can blow him away."

John smiled. "If you're looking for scumbags, or a fight, you're likely to find it."

The man was startled. Then he laughed. "Got into a big argument last night."

"I don't have anything against guns," John said. "I'd say that a person who is cheerfully living life is a lot less likely to encounter a scumbag, or hostility in general."

"That's not true!" a young man to Genvieve's left said. "Despite your happy lives you are attracting more and more hostility, not less. Look what happened to John at that debate. Now Senator Smith is threatening you."

John smiled. "Yet our lives are expanding and we are happier than ever. What appears to you as negative is just a natural reaction to something people don't understand yet."

"That's right," Genevieve said. "Our job is to continue to create our lives in a positive fashion. If we get sidetracked into fighting opposition we start resonating to that. We no longer create the energy of our goal. We become what we oppose."

"Got a point there," said the white-haired man. "It's like the old saying, 'birds of a feather flock together.' It's a hard way to live."

John smiled broadly. "Not at all my friend. Try it! As Johnny Mercer said, 'Accentuate the positive, eliminate the negative.'"

The young woman who originally asked the question smirked. "I'll be looking to see what happens to you two."

After another half hour or so the animated conversation had reached a lull. A young geeky kid with glasses stepped forward and placed his book in front of Genevieve. He gazed at her adoringly. "I've got to get going. Could you sign my book please?"

With that, everyone shuffled back into line. After another hour it was over.

The owner of the bookshop shook their hands and introduced herself. "I'm Jenine Black. Best day of business I've had in a long time. Can I take you out to dinner?"

"Sure!" John said. "Take us to the best Italian restaurant in Philadelphia."

"I know just the place."

At a bookstore in Detroit John and Genevieve were met by a large group of protesters. They held posters that read 'Spawn of Evil', 'Traitors', and 'Take Your Black Magic Out of Detroit.' Everywhere they went, crowds of people stood in line. John could tell that many of them were there for the drama. He was there for those who could look beyond the commonplace.

The readers of John's book were a mixed lot: athletes, new agers, and people looking for a way to ease stress. John did not have a picture of himself in his book. Many were surprised by his appearance, especially his wild looking hair. Some of the men would rib him about his goofy looks. But when he stood up to his full 6½feet they were a little taken aback. John's weightlifting had put a lot of muscle on his formerly thin frame.

Most of the fans of Genevieve's book were guys, especially young guys. She couldn't tell whether it was because of the picture of her on the back cover or because of the story itself. Some of them were pretty nerdy. They hovered around her at the desk asking dumb questions in an attempt to get her attention. John found it irritating. He told her so one night at the hotel. Genevieve was amused.

"They're just kids, John."

"A lot of them are as old as us."

That was true, she thought. John was 26, she was 25. "But look at all we've been through. We're battle-hardened veterans compared to almost anybody, regardless of their age."

"I don't care. I don't want you encouraging them."

"Oh you don't, do you? Even though we're trying to sell books?" She was enjoying his discomfiture. He was getting too full of himself lately.

"You can sell books without encouraging their advances!"

She laughed. "What's the matter? Are you jealous?"

"Yeah I'm jealous! You're my wife! I'm the only one who gets to put his hands on you. The way those guys paw at you sometimes..."

She tossed her head, tilted it sideways, and looked at him out of the corners of her eyes. "How exciting!"

John finally realized she was teasing him. "Why you little scamp. I'll get you for that." To punish her, John chased her around the room for ten minutes.

At their last stop in New York John was signing a book. He heard a booming voice behind him. "Hey white boy! Get your hair fixed!"

John looked up and saw Ja'Quan. The big giant, still proudly displaying his afro, strode toward the line. Immediately everyone made space.

"You're like Moses parting the Red Sea," John said with a smile. He stood up and shook the big man's hand. Then LaShawnda was beside him. Both John and Genevieve gave her a hug. She held out her hand to show off her wedding ring.

"You didn't even invite us!" Genevieve protested.

"We had a small private ceremony," she said. LaShawnda stuck her tongue out at her new husband. "Ja'Quan said that if you guys came it would turn into a circus."

John laughed. "So right my friend."

Ja'Quan glanced at LaShawnda for a second and spoke to John. "I heard something the other day that really rocked me." The buzz of conversation died down. LaShawnda said, "We heard that in a couple of years at most there's going to be a big explosion. Like a meteor hitting the earth or something. But even bigger than that."

"Where did you hear that?" Genevieve said sharply.

"On the Blythe Rogers Show."

A couple of people snickered. Blythe Rogers was a talk show host interested in the paranormal. His guests talked about UFOs and advanced ancient civilizations.

"I wouldn't put too much stock in that," John said.

Ja'Quan had noticed both their reactions.

"I heard it too," a woman said.

"Probably just another rumor," Genevieve said. "You know how fast stuff like that gets around."

That night at the hotel John was surfing the internet and came across an article in the science section of a national newspaper. It was titled, "Scientists Report Physical Abnormalities." The article stated that in experiments at the subatomic level unexplained anomalies were being recorded. "It seems as if the fundamental structure of matter is being stressed somehow. We can't explain it. We have observed changes in the strong nuclear force, which hold particles in the nucleus together. This force has become more unpredictable. Not enough to drastically affect atomic interactions, but there is a kind of pressure being exerted on the particles within the nucleus." The article concluded by saying, "Scientists are amazed because this phenomenon is very recent. The first reported observations occurred only four months ago."

John sat back in his chair with a feeling of dread. Was this direct physical evidence of the impending Event?

During the next several weeks John and Genevieve did two more successful book tours. The media attention gradually died down and the demands for interviews fell.

John called Richard's office one day. Tina Brooks answered.

"Tina? I'm looking for Richard."

"Rick went out. I'm watching the office for an hour."

It's Rick now is it? "Being as how you're a meddlesome newspaper reporter, I have no compunction about inquiring whether you and Richard have a thing going on."

She laughed. "Now who's being nosy?" There was a pause. "'Uh, yeah, we do. I went over to the office to ask him about his experiences with the technique. We hit it off right away. He's so calm and competent. And he's got money! I'm so tired of struggling financially." John heard some garbled talking.

"Hi John! It's Rick."

"Just checking in."

"I'm glad you did. There's been the usual quota of nuts and dissatisfied people demanding their money back," Carlysle said. "But there's also a strong minority requesting something more."

"How so?"

"They're saying that your book is only partially complete, that there's another step you're concealing. Frankly, I wondered about that myself."

John was taken aback. How could people have figured it out so quickly?

Of course it was impossible. He couldn't release steps three and four. It would blow the doors off. He and Genevieve would be subjected to the most intense and probably dangerous scrutiny. Performance enhancement was fine. Relieving stress and looking younger was perfectly natural. But altered states of consciousness? No way, he couldn't do it. No one would believe it anyway. A lot of bad publicity would result. People would get scared.

"...John? John? Are you there?"

"I'm here Richard."

"Call me Rick OK?"

"OK." John wasn't going to volunteer anything.

"Soooo, Johnnnnn, what about it?" Tina said, on another office phone.

He'd have to say something. "Yes, there are two more stages. It's too dangerous to release."

John heard Tina babbling excitedly on the other end. "John Frankel, don't you start holding out on me now! What is it?"

"It's something you can't understand until you have attained stage two."

"Give me a hint."

"I'm sorry Tina. No one who hasn't successfully used the technique can possibly understand. It will be misinterpreted. Wild, exaggerated stories will circulate. It'll be called black magic, devil worship, and evil. You know how the media is. I can't risk it."

Tina was concerned and it showed in her voice. "It's not bad is it?"

"Of course not!" John exclaimed. "It's incredible. It's the most awesome thing that could ever happen to anyone. But I can't release it to the general public."

"This is really big isn't it?" John could hear her excitement.

"It's the biggest thing imaginable."

"Then you can't hide it. You know it's going to come out John. Even if you only teach it to a few trusted people, someone is going to eventually spill the beans."

John thought that Tina was probably right. But right now the world wasn't ready for it. "Yeah. Eventually it's all going to come out. But not yet."

"Will you release it to those who have completed, uh, stage two?" Tina asked.

"I haven't even written it up yet. As far as I know there are only three people in the world who know it."

"Three?"

Damn! John thought. Sometimes being open and honest wasn't such a great idea.

"So there's another! Who is he?"

"Or she," John said, thinking that he should steer her away from Mats.

"John, Rick here. Come on buddy. It can't be worse than what we've already been through."

"Rick, it'll be a lot worse. A million times worse. Look what happened when we introduced a technique for relieving stress. This is so much bigger, it's like comparing the Pacific Ocean to a puddle of water. Like putting a match to gasoline. I'm afraid the consciousness of mankind is not even remotely ready to hear this."

"Playing God John?"

John laughed. He'd been taunted and baited too many times as a kid to even respond.

"I'm sorry. I just don't understand."

"I'll promise you something. Once you have mastered stage two I'll give you a personal, private lesson."

"Really? Can Tina come?"

"No," John said firmly. "It's out of the question. I'll bet she hasn't even tried the technique."

Tina grabbed the phone. "Goddammit John! I thought we were friends."

"We are friends Tina. That's why I won't even let you have a hint of this unless you have completed the second stage."

Click!

What should he do? John was painfully aware that it's not a good idea to have enemies in the media.

In that old movie "It's a Wonderful Life," young George Bailey has the poisoned prescription from Mr. Gower. He sees a sign that says, "Ask Dad, He'll Know." John knew that Robert couldn't help him. Or even Michael Walters.

Only Genevieve had the wisdom to counsel him.

That night he had a long talk with his wife.

"Eventually people will put the two together."

"Huh? The two what?"

She regarded him like a wise mentor to a child.

"No. No, it can't be."

She nodded sagely.

"My God. I never thought of it that way."

"Yes," she said. "Stages three and four have essentially been released in my novel."

"I wish I never asked. I could have maintained my innocence."

He rushed over to the library shelf in the living room and grabbed a copy of Genevieve's SF novel, *Fantastic Journey*. It was named after the classic Isaac Asimov story "Fantastic Voyage."

"For God's sake Genevieve. It's all right here. Or most of it."

"Enough for an intelligent reader once he or she makes the connection between the two books."

"Should I write up the rest of it and release it?"

Genevieve thought for several minutes. "Hold off for now. Let's see how the process unfolds. Maybe we'll never have to."

39

SENATOR Ralph Smith returned to his offices in the Hart Senate Office Building late one evening after a particularly trying day on the Hill. The debate on the Defense Appropriations bill was causing tempers to flare. His insertion of a provision in the bill to require more American made content in military hardware was meeting with stiff opposition from the Defense Department. Hell, he wasn't going to insist. But it sure made for some good publicity at home. One of his primary campaign contributors was being hit hard from competition from Asian contractors. His challenger was a soft-spoken graduate of the state university. Bradley Dunsmore was accusing him of being out of touch.

His wife Brenda wanted him to retire after his term ended. She'd been bugging him unmercifully and they'd had several fights recently.

"You promised Ralph," she had said yesterday. "Two terms, maximum. Then you're out."

"Honey, the party needs me. All the polls show we could lose the Senate in two years. The leadership has been on me hard to stay for one more term. The issues are too important to turn them down. There'll be two Supreme Court vacancies within the next five years. My vote is crucial."

Brenda Lauksonen Smith stood with her hands on her hips. "So your word means nothing."

"It means everything! My duty to my country is paramount."

"Even above your family?"

"Goddamit, yes! Don't make me choose, please, Brenda." She had made him swear. He hated that, but his volatile personality was difficult to control.

"The kids and I have already made plans. Now those are all down the drain. Your grandkids are growing up and you're missing all of it."

He hated when she used the club of family to beat him over the head. Women were so manipulative.

Senator Smith would have been shocked to hear many of his colleagues say the very same thing about him. Once Ralph Smith decided on something he would be right forevermore. Until he changed his mind of course.

Ralph took a deep breath and tried to regain control of his temper. "Brenda, the kids are proud of me and what I do."

"Of course they are. They want to see more of you."

"The Senate will recess for a couple of months at the end of this year. We'll go visit all the kids then."

"You promise?"

"I promise."

All these thoughts were running through his mind when he returned to the present and saw the book lying on his desk. That damn Frankel book. If there was any way to arrest this nutcase he'd do it by God. All investigations of the man showed he was squeaky clean. His hands were tied.

Ralph Smith didn't understand it. The Cob Tappelle forum should have put an end to this nonsense. Instead, this guy and his wife had finished their third book tour. Frankel had been cut to pieces but was still standing.

What was going on in this country? An explosion of insanity? He plopped down in the chair wearily. God, he was tired. He'd been pushing himself much too hard. There was also the difficulty with Lena.

When he thought of her his whole body shuddered with anticipation. A recent addition to the Senator's staff, Lena Watson had the hots for him. He couldn't resist. Ralph Smith couldn't remember the last time he'd had sex with Brenda. Lena was like a breath of fresh air. But it was getting complicated. If the affair became public now he'd lose in a landslide. Nobody in his conservative home state would have any tolerance for a 62-year- old senator making it with 23-year-old staffer.

His stupidity hit him like a ton of bricks.

My God, he had really screwed the pooch. Thinking with the little head. That's what Blair, his campaign coordinator, called it. If Blair ever found out...if anyone did...it would be the end of him and his reputation. His career would end in disgrace. Panicking, Ralph rose abruptly and banged his knee hard on the corner of the desk. He fell heavily to the floor, writhing in pain. It was too difficult to get up so he rested his head against the plush carpeting. He began to think about his life and where it was going.

Senator Ralph Smith did not have a lot of time for contemplation. He rose at 6 a.m. and worked all day. Chairing his committee and doing party work, which included sitting on a lot of boards. He attended policy meetings, did fundrasing, gave speeches, and dealt with the media. He was one of the chief party spokesmen for defense issues. There were lobbyists and contributors to massage. Most nights he was up till midnight and the next day it would start all over again. Ralph loved it but he was no longer a young man. His doctor was talking about heart bypass surgery if he didn't slow down.

The pain in his knee clarified his thinking. He would have to end the affair with Lena right away and tie up some of the loose ends of his life before the next campaign. He must get back to basics. How was he going to do that?

Ralph Smith hobbled back into his chair and looked at his watch. 10:30, and there were still two important committee reports to peruse. He glanced over at the Frankel book.

The senior senator from Nebraska never thought he'd see the day when this sort of garbage would become a best seller. For God's sake, even Brenda had tried it. For all he knew she was performing the rituals in her room right now. What was wrong with going to church, or consulting your minister? How had the world changed so quickly?

Ralph Smith had never read *Performance Enhancement Techniques for Athletes and Weekend Warriors*. Oh, he'd glanced through it. Enough to know that it contained a lot of new-age gibberish. The world was getting younger and he didn't understand the new generation. Many of them were on his own staff.

His hands found the book. It randomly opened to page 47: "The successful application of the techniques of stage one results in a feeling of total relaxation. You may feel like you're floating and even be unaware of your body sitting in the chair. A positive feeling of well being will permeate every cell of your body. Don't worry if you don't get there on the first few tries. It took me almost a year just to master these first few steps. You should notice some positive results right away IF you follow the directions."

Really? Sounds like something he could use himself.

What was he thinking? He didn't want any part of this nonsense. The book was halfway to the wastebasket beside the desk when something stopped the motion of his arm. An inner urge told him to flip back to page 47. As he grasped the book it opened to page 143. "When stage two is fully mastered an unshakable feeling of well being will fill your entire energy field."

Energy field? Oh yeah, something the snowflakes called a merkaba. Professor Flesch told him it was a crock of shit. Nevertheless, something inside him told him to keep reading.

"You know you have mastered stage two when there is a feeling of power within your entire being. You feel like you can do anything. There is no counter-intention, and a feeling of infinite possibility. It feels energizing but not aggressive. If you are a competitive athlete this might seem like a strange feeling unless you have gotten into the zone before. You may feel that time itself is slowing down or almost stopped altogether. This is where the performance enhancement aspect of the technique comes in. When competing, you can almost slow down the speed of the ball or the opponent and react very quickly. To your opponent it will seem that you have incredible anticipation. It will seem to him or her that you are there almost before he moves. In the highest mastery of stage two you will understand that there is really no opponent. Only you, and the joy of your movement. It will seem like the others are dancing with you, participating together, not opposing one another. Of course it is not necessary to reach this level of stage two to improve your performance dramatically. I only mention it as a possibility for you to consider."

Ralph Smith was horrified but intrigued. He had been a high school track star in the decathlon and played on the practice squad for his college football team. He had played against the top players and was amazed at their speed. Now he wondered. Was that speed generated solely from physical causes? Maybe this guy had something. Ralph was startled at his thought. No, it couldn't be. This man was a danger to society, that's what his advisors all told him.

Senator Smith read on...

Two hours later it was 12:30. Had Brenda called? Probably. He had heard no phones ringing. Dammit, he was going to prove to himself that this was a load of bunk. Senator Smith began the stage one exercises. Half an hour later he began to feel relaxed. The breathing felt good. It felt...right somehow, as if the procedures were tuned naturally to the rhythms of his body. After an hour he reached the state of floating described in the book. Ralph Smith had never felt so calm in his life. All his problems were melting away...

There was someone shaking his shoulder. It was Brenda, smiling down at him.

"I see you've tried the evil magic for yourself."

Ralph Smith didn't even hear the implied sarcasm because he was feeling too good. "Hello honey. How are you?"

"Ralph, you look ten years younger."

"Do I?" Senator Smith walked over to the full length mirror in the bathroom of his office suite. By God, she's right. I do look younger!

His reflection showed a noticeable glow coming from the inside of him. Ralph tried to tell himself it was wrong, scary, and evil.

He'd been wrong all along.

Ralph Smith was a stubborn man but not a foolish one. He could admit a mistake. He returned to his desk. With Brenda watching he turned to the back of the book, found the author's email address, and began to write:

"Dear Mr. Frankel,

As you know, I have been one of your most virulent critics. But I must tell you that today I tried your technique for the first time. I haven't felt this good in years..."

Looking over his shoulder, Brenda laid a hand gently upon his shoulder. "Ralph, you can change your mind faster than anyone ever I've ever met."

The next morning, after only four hours sleep, Ralph Smith woke up completely refreshed for the first time in ten years. He lay in bed for a second, pondering. Last night he had convinced himself it was all coincidence. "I'll feel back to normal tomorrow morning."

This morning he did not feel "normal." A warm feeling of relaxation permeated every cell of his body. Yet Ralph felt totally in control. How could relaxation lead to a feeling of control? To control something you had to be on top of it every minute. That's how he ran his life. That's why he was successful.

This was a new kind of control, a control that did not involve worry or anxiety. The problems that had loomed so large yesterday now seemed trivial. For example, what to do about Lena? That had been hounding his brain for the last several weeks. Now his path seemed clear. He would have a nice talk with her. They would both come to an agreement. He would tell Brenda all about it. No problem.

Why hadn't he thought of that before? He *had* thought about it before but it had seemed impossible.

Why should it be any different now? It didn't make sense.

There were two votes scheduled for today's session. He would not attend the posturing known as debate for these two; his opinions were well known and his votes as well. His first action was the staff meeting. After, he caught up with Lena as she made her way down the hallway. They chatted informally for a minute. On pretext of business he asked her to step inside a small conference room off the hall. After a few minutes he brought up the subject of their affair and how he was beginning to change his mind about their relationship. To his amazement, she breathed a sigh of relief.

"Oh sir, I do care for you! I've been feeling more and more guilty about the whole thing. I was trying to find a way to tell you I wanted to break it off."

"Well then, it'll be strictly business between us from now on."

She smiled in acknowledgment and turned toward the door. "Did something happen to you senator?"

"How do you mean Lena?"

"I don't know...you seem different. Different in a good way."

He raised his arms above his head. "Same old me!" he said, with a chuckle.

"Yes sir."

As Lena walked out of the room she turned her head toward the older man. There *was* something different about him.

Senator Smith decided that whatever was in that book wasn't so bad after all. During the day he met with media, lobbyists, public, and especially his conservative colleagues. Ralph noticed something curious. Almost every one of them made a comment. Most of them weren't complimentary. The senior senator from Texas said, "Ralph, are you sure you're ok?"

"Never better."

"You're not getting soft are you?"

Ralph was flabbergasted. "Now what in hell makes you say that Hal?"

"This morning I heard your comments on C-SPAN about the proposed anti-cult legislation. You already assured us of your full support. Today you didn't sound all that supportive."

"I didn't?" They were in a conference room off the senate floor. Hal Tyler pointed to the TV.

"Stay tuned for comments from Senator Ralph Smith about his views on the controversial anti-cult legislation. Some civil libertarians are up in arms. The conservative caucus assures the president of their full support. Coming up after this message."

Hal Tyler regarded him with a slightly pained expression. What the hell was the matter with the old coot anyway? Ralph thought.

"This is Odala Whitman. I'm with Senator Ralph Smith. Good morning senator."

"Good morning!" Ralph Smith looked like he really thought it was a good morning.

Tyler glanced over at his colleague.

Ralph was thinking to himself, "I look pretty good and it's only 8 a.m."

C-SPAN viewers saw a conservatively dressed man, a trim 6' 2", with a head of thick white hair. His eyes were wide set and deep, with bushy white eyebrows that crossed the bridge of his prominent nose. His square chin, high cheekbones, and leathery skin gave him the look of a bird of prey. He was formidable when roused to anger. This is the aspect he presented to the public, who knew him as an aggressive defender of conservative principles.

Ralph Smith's musings were cut short when he heard a voice coming from the TV. "Senator, as you know, Senate Bill S153 has been having a tough time these past two weeks. Senator Davenport of New York has called it a mean-spirited and unnecessary piece of legislation and a danger to civil liberties. Your conservative colleagues want to add even more stringent provisions to the bill. They want to give the Attorney General power to unilaterally assign a group cult status, thereby classifying it under the heading of dangerous to the national security of the United States. Your position on these new provisions senator?"

"Well," Hal Tyler drawled. "Here's a chance for ol' Pit-bull Smith to come in with guns blazing."

The Senator Smith on the TV was curiously amiable. "Ms. Whitman, I'm sure that cult groups are probably having enough trouble as it is just keeping their heads above water. We all know the nutcases who join them."

Odala Whitman was a little surprised. "You do not favor the new provisions? That would be quite an about-face."

"I'll say," Tyler said with dry sarcasm.

Senator Ralph Smith saw himself respond with a slight smile. "I've given my word to support them and I will."

"Ralph, you didn't sound too enthusiastic," Tyler said. The older man turned down the volume on the TV. "We all know how dangerous these organizations can be. We discussed that at the last caucus with your vehement support for the new provisions, if I recall."

Ralph Smith patted his older and taller friend on the shoulder. "Not to worry Hal. You have my vote." He walked away, whistling.

The feeling wore off as the day unfolded. At 8:30 that evening Hal Tyler stopped for a chat. "Well, back to normal I see," Hal said. "Good man."

As they parted Ralph wondered: What about me has changed from this morning? It must be something obvious. He went back to his office and scrutinized himself in the full length mirror. Yes, there was a hard edge about him. Something grating and aggressive. It showed in his face and the way he stood. He could feel it. This must be his "normal" state.

That hard edge meant power, didn't it? It meant toughness and the ability to stand up under pressure. Or did it? For the first time in his political life Ralph Smith felt confused. It was that damn book! Maybe it was truly sinful. Senator Smith remembered how good it made him feel last night and this morning.

Feeling a little guilty, Ralph sat down with the book and spent an hour reading the Frankel Method, trying to understand whether it was appropriate for a good Christian. A little voice (which sounded like his father) told him that the Frankel book may look good at first but would inevitably lead to evil. Could his soul become tainted using the Frankel Method?

"To hell with it. I'm just going to do this stuff and not worry about whether it's right or wrong." Half an hour later the senator floated in his chair and felt great. He opened his eyes and walked over to the mirror. What he saw was surprising and shocking. All of the hard edges were gone now. He had the same glow from within him as yesterday.

He was softer.

Now all of the guilt flooded through him again. He began to lose the good feeling. Ralph knew his father would disapprove. In Ralph's family soft was a dirty word: it meant being cowardly and weak. He had lived his whole life with this philosophy; it had landed him in the United States Senate. Now here he was, 62 years old, engaging in what could only be called a new-age cult ritual.

His father would have called the Frankel Method satanic. Ralph felt that the God he worshiped would say the same thing. He felt a flush of shame and saw his face turn red in the mirror. He thought he saw the image of his father looking over his shoulder, admonishing him, urging him back to the straight and narrow path.

Ralph recalled his father at age 62. The white haired figure of Albert Durant Smith was ramrod straight. He could outwork any of his sons. He went to church every Sunday and tithed more than his fair share. He was a tough but fair man; successful, courageous, a loving father. Ralph had tried to emulate him in everything he did. Now look at him! He recoiled from the mirror, grabbed the book, and threw it into the trash.

That night he got into another argument with Brenda over their weekend. They had planned to stay in town, take in a movie, and have dinner together. However, an important contributor needed help. He had promised to go back to Nebraska on Saturday to see his cattle operation. The Department of Environmental Quality (and neighboring farmers) were demanding that Lasco Inc. control the (alleged) severe runoff into the local river.

He had been on the phone yesterday talking to Bruce Mahorn and became immersed in the details of cattle operations.

"They're sayin' I'm polluting the river, and that just ain't so!" Bruce complained. "Ralph, I helped you get elected twice. It's time for me to call in some of those chips I'm holding."

Ralph's records showed that Lasco had contributed heavily during the last election cycle. He had known Bruce for over 20 years. He wouldn't let him down.

Ralph was boning up on water quality issues when Brenda interrupted with a question about the weekend. "I made dinner reservations for 6:30. Do you want to eat before the movie or after? I thought..."

"Brenda, we'll have to postpone our weekend. Bruce Lasco called. He's got an emergency."

"You said that it was all taken care of."

"That's what I thought. The DEQ has decided, for some reason, to come down hard on Bruce—" he stopped in mid-sentence. "Dunsmore. That's it. It's that rotten son-of-a-bitch fag Bradley Dunsmore!" Ralph's face was red. He was hollering.

"The family comes second again," Brenda said.

"Don't start with me honey. You knew what you were getting into when you married me."

"I didn't think it was going to be this bad." His wife slammed the door on the way out. Ralph groaned. He could handle high-stakes politics but couldn't keep the bridle on his own wife.

The next day was miserable. Lena told one of the female staffers about their brief relationship. Ralph had to spend the morning staff meeting putting out fires and explaining himself. He hated to have to justify his behavior to anyone. But he held his temper and used his considerable charm to smooth things over. After everyone left he read the Omaha Herald. Lasco Inc.'s dispute with the DEQ made the front page. Bradley Dunsmore again. With all of the party work he'd been neglecting his home territory lately. His challenger was making his play while the cat was away. Well, look out Bradley Dunsmore. Pit-bull Smith is coming back. I'll wipe that pansy-ass smile off your face, you bastard. Ralph felt his juices flowing again and that old aggressiveness coming back. It felt good.

An hour after that he got into a shouting match with the junior senator from New York outside the Senate floor. A couple of reporters picked up on it. Some very unflattering tape ran on C-SPAN. It was a slow news day. Ralph Smith was to be today's highlight: "...the famous Smith temper got the better of him as he cussed out New York Senator Clive Percy for his vote on the Defense Appropriations Bill rider..." The 'bleep' 'bleep' on the tape didn't look good.

What had happened to his equilibrium? Just yesterday he'd woken up refreshed and flown through the day. What was wrong with him?

It was late in the evening as he returned to the office, worn out. The book was still in the wastebasket beside the desk.

Ralph Smith felt totally confused. His upbringing and his beliefs told him the Frankel book was wrong. The softness he had seen in the mirror yesterday morning was wrong, even though it was accompanied by a good feeling. Soft was...not being up to the challenge. Soft was cowardice.

Yet he had gotten more done yesterday than in the two days sandwiched around it. It had been easy. Yesterday, in committee, Senator Percy was more than usually obnoxious. Even Percy's own colleagues had been admiring of how smoothly Pit-bull Smith had handled the man. Today he had argued with Percy in and out of session on exactly the same matters. The only difference in the outcome was his attitude.

Ralph Smith laughed out loud. "All right Mr. Liberal Frankel. I'm going to turn your new-age bullshit message to my own use." The senator retrieved the book and began to do the stage one exercises.

Two months later everyone in the Conservative Caucus noticed a change in Ralph Smith. The pit bull was no longer the same fiery, passionate advocate for their cause. Yet he was a much more effective leader. He had made the caucus' mark already on two important pieces of legislation. There was even talk of replacing Hal Tyler as chairman of the caucus. Tyler's term was expiring. A vote was scheduled for next week.

The big caucus vote was held behind closed doors at an exclusive Washington area club. No reporters were allowed, for there would be raised voices. Dirty laundry would be aired. Hal Tyler's supporters were furious with what they considered a stab in the back by supporters of Ralph Smith. Two months ago the election had been considered a formality. Now it was hotly contested. Ralph had not even considered challenging Hal Tyler until a groundswell of opinion within the membership convinced him to run.

On the day of the vote it was clear that Ralph Smith's victory was secure. At the last moment Tyler brought up the subject of the Frankel book.

"Ralph, you sure have changed over the last two months," Hal drawled. "Did you get a personality makeover?"

A question like this would have set off the old Ralph Smith like a bottle rocket. Ralph answered calmly. "Yes."

"Yes? Please enlighten us."

"I decided that I could be a far more effective spokesman by smoothing out some of my rough edges. I think it's made me much more effective." Murmurs of agreement were heard around the table.

"It's made you smoother. But you don't have the same fire you used to." Hal Tyler stood up to his full 6 feet 5. "I may be 71, but I've got more fire in my little finger than you do in your whole body." A few loud hoorays were heard.

Ralph didn't respond.

"I'm wondering Ralph. How could a firebrand like you have been for years suddenly get a personality transplant? It just doesn't make sense."

Ralph saw where things were going. "We all have the ability to change for the better."

"I'll let that pass for now. Did your sudden transformation from conservative firebrand to conservative wimp have anything to do with a certain book?" Tyler held up a copy of *Performance Enhancement for Athletes and Weekend Warriors*.

Most of the members were shocked; either at the accusation or the fact that it might be true.

"I was talking to Brenda the other day at the banquet. She had a few too many that night. She mentioned that she's been using this book." Tyler paused for effect and looked at everyone in the room, implying that no wife of his would be caught dead with it. "She even said you tried it and were so impressed that you wrote a letter to this new-age kook Frankel."

Now all eyes were turned on Ralph Smith. Most of his supporters were dumbfounded. They had expected him to vehemently deny the charge instantly.

"I have tried the techniques in the book. They help to relax me after a long day. My doctor says he's noticed an improvement in my heart condition."

There were a few sympathetic nods. Most in the group were angry.

"Do you mean to tell us that you've been personally using this nonsense?" said the junior senator from Alabama.

Ralph replied without rancor. "At first I thought it was black magic, even satanist. I threw the book in the trash can. After a particularly bad day I decided, what the hell. Only a simpleton criticizes something before he's even tried it. So I did. It worked."

"I can't believe what I'm hearing," said the senator from Idaho.

"I can't believe that intelligent people would be against something that can help us all more effectively promote the conservative cause," said Carson Jaworski, his friend from Nevada.

One of his closest colleagues, the senior senator from North Carolina, spoke up. "Ralph, using something like this violates every conservative principle we have. The fact that you don't even see it shows you are truly off base."

"That's right!" said another voice at the end of the conference table. "Conservatives stand for the traditional values which have made our country great. This doesn't include new age mumbo-jumbo and cultish ritual."

"You've read the booklet, I'm sure, from Professor Ari Flesch." Tyler waved it in the air vigorously. "Professor Flesch compares the so-called techniques in this book to the cant of the God's Light cult." Voices roared. Some of the members left their seats. Most of them agreed with Hal Tyler. "And—" Tyler tried to make himself heard above the din. "I wouldn't be surprised if this Frankel fellow copied his book right from the God's Light nonsense!" More yells of agreement.

"The book from which he claims to have gotten his ritual is also suspect," Dan Blackstone from Louisiana said. Blackstone pointed his finger at Ralph accusingly. "Some sort of book of hieroglyphics filled with strange symbols. There's no title, no ISBN number on the book. Even Frankel says he doesn't know where it comes from."

The room exploded. Shortly after the vote was taken. Hal Tyler won in a landslide.

Three days later Ralph Smith received two letters, both on Conservative Caucus stationery. The first one read:

Dear Senator Smith:

We, the undersigned, although appreciating your past dedication to conservative principles both in word and in deed...

Past dedication? He continued reading:

...must inform you of our strong objection to your support of cult books and cult ritual. You can't champion anti-cult legislation and then turn around and use it in your private life.

As conservatives we pride ourselves in the free exchange of ideas. We champion the ideals of liberty in public policy and in private life. However, we feel that the intimate connection with something so foreign to conservative ideals can only corrupt a true conservative. We do not wish our group to be tainted with a philosophy that strays too far from the Christian beliefs we all hold. We respectfully ask you to voluntarily resign your association with the Conservative Caucus until such time as you come to your senses.

We know that you are a good conservative at heart. We look forward to once again welcoming 'Pit-bull' Smith back to the most important group in America fighting to uphold the conservative agenda.

Yours Truly,

There were 23 handwritten signatures below, including his friends from North Carolina, Louisiana, Montana, and Tennessee.

He reread the letter again, feeling a slow burn rise within him. It was completely unwarranted. This technique of Frankel's had nothing to do with his conservative beliefs. If anything, it had strengthened them. For God's sake, he had almost single-handedly held the Senate's position during the House-Senate conference on HR1331, the liberal anti-gun bill.

Ralph tore open the next letter:

Dear Ralph:

We are dismayed at the action of the majority of our colleagues in asking you to resign from our caucus. We have noticed your increased effectiveness in promoting the conservative agenda. We wish to thank you on behalf of all clear thinking Americans for your tireless and steady work for our cause. In the strongest of terms we urge you not to buckle under to a confused majority who cannot seem to see the forest for the trees. We do have concerns about this crazy book and do not understand why you have chosen to follow its guidelines. Nevertheless, we cannot argue with the results you're getting. All of us have questioned you and observed you carefully over the last two months. We are impressed, as always, with your character and intelligence. Add to that a personal integrity which seems to have grown even stronger.

The majority has scheduled a vote of expulsion if you do not tender your resignation. We urge you not to do so. Fight this as hard as you can.

Sincerely,

There were 7 signatures, including the senator from Arizona, a Christian fundamentalist.

I'll be damned. You never know who your friends are until the going gets tough. Never in a million years would he have ever thought that Frank Faircloth would support him.

The Senate Conservative Caucus had bylaws which provided for the expulsion of a member deemed "a threat to conservative principles and the conservative agenda as outlined in the yearly Policy Statement" by a three-fourths vote of the membership. He grabbed the pocket calculator on his desk and divided 23 by 30. It read:

0.7666. He converted to percentage: 76.66%

So they already had enough votes to kick him out.

What should he do?

That night Senator Smith began to receive calls from the media. Like bloodhounds they were already on the scent. He made his decision that night just after doing the exercises. He would defend his integrity. If that meant no longer participating in the conservative caucus, then so be it.

The next morning all hell broke loose. Hal Tyler went to the networks denouncing Ralph Smith in the strongest terms. He was backed by five of his closest supporters. Surprisingly, Frank Faircloth defended him. Ralph rang him up on a video call that evening.

"Frank, this is Ralph Smith. I want to thank you for your support. I never would have thunk it."

Frank Faircloth looked like the straightlaced fundamentalist he was.

"Ralph, I can't condone what Tyler is doing. I do agree with him about that book of yours though. I'm supporting you because I don't believe it's anyone's business what you do in your private life. You're a good conservative Ralph. That's all that matters to me."

"I understand your reservations Frank. I appreciate your honesty and integrity. As far as I'm concerned you're the truest conservative in the country. If it was up to me I'd support you for president."

Frank Faircloth was surprised. He knew Smith wasn't terribly religious. "You would? Even though I'm what the liberals call a fundamentalist?"

"After today I would. I misjudged you Frank. I thought that because you disagreed with me and some of my policies that you weren't up to par. Now I see that you're a man who's willing to stick up for his principles, even if it is an unpopular position. That takes guts. It's the kind of character we need in a president."

Faircloth was pleased, even though the presidency was not one of his ambitions. "I'm glad you called Ralph. I've been noticing your work these past few months. I'm impressed. Being a hothead is all right sometimes. To be a true national leader you need to be more even tempered." Faircloth paused for a moment. "That counts me out." Another pause. "You know Ralph, you're just the kind of man this country needs. It's a little late, but I want you to consider putting your hat in the ring for the party's nomination for president."

Ralph Smith sat at his desk in silence, unable to respond. He had Frank Faircloth's support to be President of the United States?

Deep inside him a surge of excitement began to build. Then doubt. How could it possibly work if he was expelled from the caucus?

Frank Faircloth saw that he had struck home. "Well Ralph? What do you say?"

"Sorry Frank. You stunned me that's all."

"Make up your mind but do it quick. The field is already crowded. I don't see anyone I like yet."

"How do we work this expulsion vote?" Ralph wondered.

"Don't you worry about that Ralph. Let's just say that Hal Tyler has some skeletons in his closet, as does everyone else wanting to be president. That's another reason I like you. I've checked out your two previous campaigns and done a background examination. You're squeaky clean. I like that a lot. Don't care too much for the fact that you're not religious. But I'll take your honesty any time." There was another pause, and voices in the background. "By the way. Hal thinks he's some kind of party power broker but he doesn't know the half of it. Let me know in ten days what you've decided."

Ralph rang off, stupefied.

President of the United States!

By God, if his father were only alive to hear this.

He left the office and went home. His wife was there. Ralph broke the news to Barbara.

Her squeal of delight was the greatest reward he could have ever asked for. All of his past sins had been forgotten. "Oh Ralph, I always knew you had it in you. In the past three months I've been thinking the same thing myself. You're so calm and confident now! You inspired me. I've never thought that about you before. Your party credentials are impeccable. Oh, wait till I tell the kids!" And she was off. Just like that. His wife had big political ambitions herself and he hadn't even known it.

That was a good thing. He needed someone to stand beside him, not behind him. Someone to lean back on when the going got tough.

Brenda Lauksonen came from tough, hard-nosed Finnish stock. She was a stayer. Earlier in his political career he had used her often as a sounding board. How had he gotten away from that?

Three days later Ralph saw Hal Tyler in the hallway outside the committee room. The older man was all smiles. "Ralph! Sorry about our little misunderstanding. Sometimes in the heat of battle we go overboard a little." Tyler stuck out his hand. "No hard feelings?"

This guy has balls, Ralph thought. Three months ago he probably would have smacked him in the face. But the "new" Ralph Smith was more confident and more relaxed. Ralph took Hal Tyler's hand. "No hard feelings Hal."

They were out in the corridor. A camera flashed.

Oh boy, Ralph and Hal kiss and make up. There were rumors floating around the press corps about the caucus meeting and tension between the two men. Some speculated that Hal Tyler's attempted expulsion of Senator Smith from the Conservative Caucus had fizzled because of something in Tyler's past.

Ralph observed Tyler's sigh of relief. It was immediately replaced by an oily smile. "Frank Faircloth tells me you're going to throw your hat into the ring. Is that true?"

"Yes Hal. I thought I'd give it a shot."

Hal Tyler looked down searchingly into Ralph's eyes. He was three inches taller than Ralph. The look on his face was that of a disapproving father to a recalcitrant child.

"I'm disappointed in you Ralph. You have come to me several times in previous campaigns for advice. I've helped you no questions asked." Hal Tyler looked at Senator Smith questioningly. "Several months ago you responded positively to my candidacy. Now look at you! The presidential bug must have finally gotten to ol' pit bull."

"I believe it has Hal."

A slight sneer creased Hal Tyler's lips. Ralph Smith was just like him. He'd go back on his word if it meant political advancement. Of course Ralph hadn't explicitly given his support.

"Good luck," Tyler said. The older man turned quickly away and walked out of the building.

Ralph Smith smiled. He was going to announce his candidacy for president in two days.

When he told David Lawson of his thoughts, his chief of staff practically hit the roof in excitement. "If we don't win the nomination I'll walk backwards to Bourke with my pants down." That was an Aussie vote of confidence.

At the news conference announcing his candidacy, Ralph Smith faced some tough questions. Hal Tyler had already made his opposition known, as well as five others from the caucus.

"Senator, how can you realistically expect to secure your party's nomination when six of the most influential members of your own caucus oppose it?"

Ralph Smith was unruffled. "We feel we have a good chance. Otherwise I would not have entered." The media badgered him unmercifully, hoping to get a rise out of "Pit-bull" Smith. None was forthcoming.

Ralph's problems with Bradley Dunsmore disappeared. The senator would have to give up his seat. The race in the home state was now wide open, with Dunsmore the clear favorite. The slick bastard even called, personally congratulating him and wishing him good luck.

A week later things got rough again.

Ralph was frantically attempting to raise funds for the coming campaign. He was having almost nightly conferences with David Lawson and Brenda. Senator Smith continued his busy Senate schedule and his party work. A crowd of reporters surrounded him as he walked out of the Hart Senate building around 5 p.m.

"Senator Smith! Senator Smith! Your comments, sir, about the statements this morning from members of your party accusing you of inappropriate personal conduct?"

Ralph hadn't heard them because he hadn't checked in this morning with Lawson. There was probably a message on his cell. "I haven't heard them."

"Senator, they're accusing you of being a devotee of the Frankel cult book."

So that's what this was all about? Ralph was getting tired of the reaction to some simple techniques in a book. Suddenly, it all seemed so absurd. He burst out laughing.

"This book is on the *New York Times* bestseller list. It's #2 on the Amazon self-help EBook list. How can it be considered a cult book?"

"But senator, these are members of your own party whose support you will need for the nomination."

Ralph decided to deal with this here and now.

"Yes, I have read the Frankel book. And yes, I do some of the exercises to relieve stress and relax. I find that it's similar to yoga, which I investigated at the suggestion of Professor Flesch of Harvard University. I like this better. Is there anything else?"

"Senator! How will this admission affect support for you within the party, and ultimately with the voters?"

"I haven't the foggiest notion," he said calmly.

Some of their excitement was beginning to diffuse. His old self hated the media. His new self could see they were just doing a job. "Senator, this is a rather startling admission," one of the reporters said.

"Is it?" Ralph replied. "How many of you have read the book?"

"That's not the question, senator."

"I have," a woman said. "I've read the book and do the exercises every morning. It helps me to get going."

Suddenly there was confusion. One of their own had violated a fundamental rule: Never answer a question from the person being interviewed.

The senator smiled. "Well then. It's not so bad, is it?"

"Senator, the people who will vote for you are conservatives. Don't you think an admission like this will hurt your chances with these voters?"

"If telling the truth will hurt my chances for the presidency, we might as well get it over with quick. When I'm in the White House honesty will prevail."

Ralph Smith stood there, completely at ease. "Is there anything else?"

Some of the microphones pulled away. The interview was over.

The next day, one of the headlines in the *Washington Post* read, **Smith Endorses Frankel Book.** It was toward the bottom, one of those smallish one column stories used to fill out the front page.

That night he sat down with Brenda and Dave Lawson. "We've experienced a 25% drop-off in fund raising," Lawson said. "Privately, many of our contributors have read the book and don't see it as a big deal. They're afraid of the public reaction. Your friend from Lasco, Inc. pulled out yesterday. That guy doesn't know Christmas from Bourke Street."

Ralph was shocked. Bruce Mahorn had pulled the plug on him after all these years! And after he had fixed it with a few well placed phone calls to the state environmental office. He'd put his neck out for his friend and had been abandoned. The bastard! I'll give that son-of-a-bitch a piece of my mind...As Ralph reached for the phone Brenda spoke. "Forget him Ralph. We don't need quitters on the team."

That stopped him in mid-stride. That's just what his father always said. Dammit, she was right. Ralph looked at his wife and smiled. "Brenda, I'm sure glad you're back on the team."

She flushed with pride. "So am I."

"That's right," Lawson said. "Mahorn's just a show pony. Can't go the distance. Besides, we're getting feelers from some, ah, more moderate sources within the party. And even some feelers from the other side. You know how it goes. There are always blokes who want to hedge their bets."

Ralph Smith rubbed his hands. Maybe this could work after all.

40

ROBERT was watching the news when he called upstairs to John. "Son, come down here!"

John came down just in time to see the interview with Senator Ralph Smith. "Didn't I tell you about the letter he wrote?" John said.

Robert snorted. "That doesn't mean anything. Here he is on national TV admitting your book is OK." He looked up at his son. "Smith has changed. I've been watching him ever since he threatened to lock you up for exercising your first amendment rights. He's still a conservative but I'm almost beginning to like him."

That night, just as Genevieve turned out the light in the bedroom, something crashed to the floor.

"What the—" John jumped up and saw something glowing on the desk. It was a silvery color. He flipped on the light switch.

"Armondo! What are doing here?"

"Just a warning from Porniarsk. He says, "The situation is going to blow up again. I advise you release the final stages right away. Timing is just right. You'll have some helpers."

Armondo winked out.

"What was that all about do you think?" he asked Genevieve.

"It sounds like we're going to find out."

Two days later, on ABC News Tonight Cob Tappelle reported the following:

Strange stories coming from the world of Major League Baseball. You'll recall that two players from the Arizona Diamondbacks hit over

.400 last year. One of them claims he used the method in the controversial book, Performance Enhancement for Athletes and Weekend
Warriors, to travel to another planet. Here are two of his teammates
describing this wild story: "I think Carlos has finally gone off his nut.
Maybe that stuff he's doing has some kind of delayed reaction."

That was Brad Dahlgren, relief pitcher. The camera now showed a
thin, wiry player who talked with a Dominican accent. "I told you those
guys were crazy. What a stupid book! That's what you get for trying
to cheat. I get my hits the old fashioned way: with honest hard work."
He spit out some tobacco juice and faced the camera. "Anybody who
does this stuff is out of their mind."

That was Junior Gonzalez, the utility infielder on the Diamondbacks.

Cob Tappelle looked into the camera. With his most serious and authoritative voice he intoned, "It seems Mr. Frankel has quite a lot to
answer for."

What had happened before was only a prelude.

Emails, phone calls, and even snail-mail letters began pouring in to the office
and to the house.

The next day Carlos texted. "John, what is going on with this stuff you taught
us? I was going through the technique and all of a sudden the room disappeared!
It was incredible. I told Brad and then he told Junior and then somehow it got on
the news...call me back OK?"

Poor Carlos. He had experienced a shift in consciousness without any guidance at all. The fact he had done it was impressive. John was again amazed at the
power of this technique. Whoever wrote it had incredible insight into the physiol-
ogy, mind, and spiritual nature of human beings.

Richard Carlysle came over and showed John the latest sheaf of emails. In one
of them was another story just like Carlos'.

Carlysle said nothing, but he didn't have to. John was going to have to take
Armondo's advice. First he called Carlos.

Two weeks later John had a revised manuscript ready for Richard.

The third and fourth stages were presented as a personal memoir of a fictional
character.

The first page of the new section was a comprehensive legal disclaimer, ab-
solving the author and publisher of any responsibility for the actions of those who
applied the next two stages. John shuddered to think what would happen if people
began to "blue jaunt." John had applied the material and taught others for years.
He was almost certain that a "blue jaunt" was impossible. There was no mention of

such a thing in the codebook. The application of the technique either resulted in positive outcomes, or nothing.

"So far we haven't had any lawsuits," Richard Carlysle said. "By the way, do you think I'm ready for this next step?"

"It's up to you. Read the manuscript. Then try it."

"You're sure there's no harm? I mean, do you actually leave the earth? It sounds scary."

"Yes, I can't say for sure, and no. It appears subjectively that you leave here, go somewhere else, and have real experiences. It could also validly be called a very vivid dream because no time elapses while you're gone. You'll have to make that determination."

Richard read the introductory page:

"What I am about to say has no basis in reality unless you experience it yourself. Consider the rest of this book to be a delusional fantasy if you so choose. No possible harm can come to anyone who reaches stage two and proceeds beyond it.

"I believe the attainment of stages three and four are possible, eventually, for anyone who is able to open up to the awareness of their merkaba. The author does not guarantee success for you. I can only present this information as I have experienced it. Some would say imagined it. I am not far from agreeing with them. The rest is up to you.

"We have had reports of persons achieving stage four with no prior intimation that it even existed, or any guidance whatsoever. This section was added due to many reader requests."

That was it. They released a revised copy of the book and a 41 page booklet that could be purchased separately for previous readers.

"How many copies have we sold so far, Richard?" John asked.

"Almost 500,000," Richard replied.

"Wow! You owe me some more money." They both laughed. "Seriously, I didn't think it was that many."

"There'll be another spike soon if the media gets going like they did last time."

John realized that he and Genevieve were now financially well off. Their bank account had been swelling gradually. With the next check from Richard it would reach a very tidy sum. It had happened almost without effort.

Two weeks later Robert was flipping through the channels. He saw a promo for a network special entitled "Live: Proof of the Frankel Method."

"Join NBC News coverage of a live demonstration of the Frankel Method!" the TV blared. "A group of people who claim to have mastered the controversial procedures will manufacture an object out of thin air! Tuesday night at 7 p.m. Only on channel 4."

"Just like the news media to turn this into a circus," Robert said. "Nothing will happen. It's a joke, right John?"

"You're right, nothing will happen," John said. "I think. It's not part of the technique."

John had explained the last two stages to Robert more than once but his father's naturally skeptical turn of mind couldn't accept it. Robert was very bright but his intellect was far stronger than his intuition. He had never made it past stage one. The technique required both left and right brain aptitudes.

At 7 p.m. that Tuesday the Frankel family, along with the Walters', was in front of the TV set in the living room at 337 Magnolia. John expected to see a bunch of chanting space cadets putting on a dog and pony show. Instead the cameras showed a bunch of normal looking people standing in a big living room similar to the Frankel's. Each of the participants looked calm and confident. They were all glowing with an inner light that was typical of the end phenomenon for stage two. The moderator introduced the participants. A school teacher, two computer programmers, a banker, four college students, a high school student, a housewife, an engineer, and a professor of physics at the local university.

Rachel was amazed at the size of the group. "There are twelve of them."

John was confused. "Surely these people must know what's going to happen," he said to Genevieve. The failed demonstration to Michael Walters was uppermost in his mind. Walters was a trained scientist. He had observed nothing. A faint shimmering in the air perhaps.

Genevieve was excited. Her intuition told her that something unexpected was going to happen. "Watch closely. I think we're in for a surprise."

The physics professor, Dr. Richard Weisskopf, spoke for the group.

"Hey I know that guy!" Robert said. "He was my physics professor when I was in college. He's got to be 75 at least."

"Doesn't look it," Rachel said.

Dr. Weisskopf said, "We want to thank NBC news for their serious approach to this subject, and for giving us a half hour of commercial free airtime."

"For far too long this subject has been approached by our news media as either dangerous or ludicrous. It is neither. From the moment I read Mr. Frankel's book and mastered the first two stages of the technique, I saw further potential in it. I am presently writing a paper explaining the principles in Mr. Frankel's book. My paper will combine the rigor of hard science with metaphysics. For too long these subjects have been divorced from each other. Every particle in the universe is connected, immersed within an aether which is as yet undetectable to instrumentation. Mr. Frankel calls it the universal medium, and we will do the same."

He paused to take a drink of water from a glass lying on an end table.

"Tonight we will demonstrate that this aether exists. We interface directly with it. Instead of giving you a boring lecture we're going to show you."

The camera panned the room with a wide angle view, showing the arrangement of chairs. Taped to the dark carpeting was a hexagon with two interlocking triangles in the center, nodes enough for 12 chairs.

"In order to make this process work we have to position ourselves in a precise geometric arrangement," Weisskopf explained. "What you will see tonight is our basic protocol, which we call the Access Point. There are no gadgets or gizmos in this room other than the camera equipment NBC brought in to film us."

[Camera pans the room.]

"For those of you familiar with the Frankel Method, we need a little time to get ourselves ready. We have already brought ourselves to the middle of the second stage, which is the jumping off point for our procedure. It will take about five minutes for us to get up to speed. If you need to get a beer or go to the bathroom, now's the time to do it."

Everybody laughed, including the news crew off camera.

John and Genevieve looked at each other in amazement. John said, "These people are nutcases. What do they think they're doing?" Robert agreed. Genevieve was doubtful now.

They were both nervous, fearing that their credibility was about to be compromised by a bunch of publicity seekers.

The group members sat in their assigned chairs. The housewife, a large woman named Naima Brown, took the middle chair. The computer programmer, a rotund young man called Dobson Braithwaite, took the top chair. The professor took a chair on the bottom.

Dobson Braithwaite said, "Proceed. The Access Point."

Genevieve said, "Robert. Quick, get the laptop. I want you and John to make detailed observations, just as if you were in the lab. Rachel! Make sure we're recording this."

John observed carefully. He had quickly gone through his own routine and was attempting to observe the sphere of consciousness of each of the participants.

Robert observed and typed at the same time. At first he didn't see anything. After a few minutes the air around the group began to shimmer. He heard an off-camera exclamation from one of the crew. Something began to take shape above the heads of the group. It was a series of interlocking teardrops that met at a point and then went the other way. The image was faint but recognizable. It gradually grew stronger and stronger. The whole thing was pulsing.

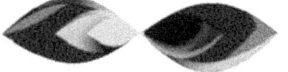

After two minutes the group relaxed and began laughing and smiling. "That felt like a good one." "Yeah, blues this time."

The crew were amazed. A voice was heard to say, in awed tones, "You got that recorded, right?" Everyone laughed. It was obvious this was an experienced group, and well drilled. The whole demeanor and tenor of the session was disciplined, professional, and positive. The air in the room was filled with good vibes.

Professor Weisskopf said, "Time?"

Someone off-camera said, "17 minutes professor."

"Do it again. I don't believe it really happened," said another voice.

"All right we will." The professor got everybody's agreement. Again, the teardrop appeared above the heads of the twelve, except larger this time.

Somebody swore off-camera. "This must be some kind of black magic, just like they say!"

"There's one way to find out," said the producer. Tentatively, he walked across the room and gingerly placed his hand within the glowing energy formation. Suddenly a smile broke across his face. "It feels great! What *is* this stuff?"

One of the cameramen abandoned his post and did the same. Everyone could see that both men stood there, grinning. Their hands were immersed in a soft, brightly glowing pattern of energy. Suddenly the teardrops collapsed. The group began talking excitedly amongst themselves.

The professor got up and faced one of the cameras, knowing that time was almost gone. "What did we do here tonight? We didn't create something from nothing, ladies and gentlemen! Only God can do that. What we did was access a subtle energy that lies all around us. We just amplified it. The people in this room are just regular people. There aren't any weirdos here. It is said that we only use 10% of our brain power. Well, it turns out that we're all a lot more powerful than we've been led to think. The next step in our investigations is a powerful new remote viewing procedure that lets us accurately look into the structure of matter itself—"

The broadcast ended abruptly. It was followed immediately by two drug commercials, a beer commercial, and an advertisement for a cleaning product. Robert switched off the TV as a prominent physicist pronounced the demonstration to be an elaborate hoax.

"Did that really happen?" Robert asked.

"I don't know," Rachel said.

John agreed. "Maybe it *was* a hoax. It sure looked real though."

Robert, Rachel, John, and Genevieve discussed the program far into the night. John wondered whether Mr. Weisskopf and his crew would receive a visit from Haliburton and Havel.

Genevieve laughed. "It's not a question of if, but when."

The next day Robert said that the program was now rated the highest of all time, with a 63 share and an 81 rating. It had gone viral in less than one hour on the WorldNet.

In Washington, Senator Ralph Smith sat watching with Brenda, David Lawson, and some of the campaign staff at their spacious Arlington home. Afterward, they all sat around in disbelief.

"A trick," Lena said. "Some kind of holographic manipulation." That's what Sag Carlson, the famous physicist, had said in his analysis. Everyone agreed. Ralph wasn't so sure. He hadn't made it to the end of stage two yet. But he was getting a glimmer of the power of the Frankel Method.

A mile away at his own home, Hal Tyler sat around with some of his colleagues. During the first demonstration, he snorted. "Smoke and mirrors." Everyone in the room echoed that sentiment, but not the senator from Louisiana. "Where's the smoke and where's the mirrors?" Dan Blackstone said. "You saw the thing yourself. Just a living room and a couple of cameras."

"Are you saying you believe this nonsense?" said Senator Keith Carswell from North Carolina.

"I'm not in the habit of pulling the wool over my eyes," Blackstone said. That shut most of them up. Dan Blackstone was a rough and ready character and known for his tell-it-like-it-is approach. That sort of thing went over well with Louisiana voters. During his last campaign he had been publicly accused by a hotel employee of adultery. The next night the senator stood in front of a statewide TV audience with his wife by his side and admitted the whole thing. A week later he won the election handily. Dan Blackstone had credibility among these men.

When the teardrops began to form a second time, Hal Tyler turned the TV off. "We don't have to put up with this crap," he said. "This is either black magic or a publicity stunt." Carson Jaworski grabbed the remote and turned it back on.

"Holy Christ, look at that," Blackstone said.

After it was over they all sat around, stunned. For once Hal Tyler had no words.

"Nothing like any special effects I ever saw," muttered Philoe Granger of West Virginia. It looked real. They all knew it.

Frank Faircloth was at his home in Arizona. His religious training told him it was all a fake. Something inside him said differently. When the teardrops began to form out of thin air he suddenly became dizzy and grabbed his head. He felt a sickening vertigo overtake him, as if the platform of his life had been whisked from underneath him. His wife was too stunned herself to even notice. He tried to dismiss it as a clever magic trick. A part of him knew it wasn't fake.

Frank Faircloth sat silently in front of the TV for half an hour as Sag Carlson dismissed the demonstration. A select panel of experts described how the hoax had been performed. Faircloth felt well enough recovered to pick up the phone. "Ralph, this is Frank Faircloth..."

Ralph Smith fielded many phone calls that night. He was up till 5 in the morning answering questions from colleagues on both sides of the aisle, and the media. Ralph thought that there were probably a lot of pols using the Frankel Method. He was the only one who had publicly admitted to it. He was a conservative, which somehow made his words more acceptable, like Nixon going to Red China back in 1972.

Ralph talked for over an hour with Frank Faircloth, soothing him. He hadn't understood the depth of Frank's religious beliefs until tonight. Ralph could tell he was shaken to the core. Ralph admired the man. At the end, Faircloth grabbed on to all the positive aspects of his Christianity. He reconciled the reality of what he had seen as a miracle of sorts. Ralph too was Christian but he was more a pragmatist, not wedded to dogma and ritual. Like his former friend Dan Blackstone, he considered himself to be someone who told the truth to others and to himself.

When Dan Blackstone called later that night Ralph received an apology. "I was wrong. It's clear to me that what we saw tonight was genuine."

"I agree. I have no idea how they did it though."

"When I'm wrong I say I'm wrong," Blackstone said firmly. "I hope there's no hard feelings."

Ralph understood the man completely. "You did what you thought was right. I've got no problems with that."

There was a little sigh at the other end of the line. "I'm getting sick of Tyler and his act. I always thought the man was a genius. Now I can see he's just a guy with a lot of strongly held opinions. He's not willing to change his mind even when the evidence is right in front of him. I still admire that, you know, stick to your guns and all that. What we saw tonight was incontrovertible as far as I'm concerned."

"I agree," Ralph responded. He felt like Blackstone was hinting at something. Ralph sat silently, waiting.

"Ralph, I've been thinking about your candidacy."

"And?"

Blackstone exhaled and the words came tumbling swiftly out, almost tripping on each other.

"I-Wondered-Whether-You-Had-Thoughts-Of-A-Vice-President."

Ralph Smith cleared his lungs as he leaned back against his chair, with the phone still in his hand. Things were looking up! People were beginning to jump on the Ralph Smith bandwagon. "My campaign manager and I have discussed it. In order to win the nomination we need a bona-fide conservative, preferably from a Southern state. We don't want someone too rigid. The Democrats won the popular vote last time."

Another sigh from the other end. Blackburn decided that he had gotten his message across. He didn't want to press any further. "OK Ralph."

The effect of Professor Weisskopf's demonstration caused another spike in the sale of John and Genevieve's books. It also lent a heightened respectability to consciousness studies. A few scientists began to come out of the woodwork supporting the Weisskopf protocols. Leading-edge researchers who had been formerly discredited or ignored by mainstream science began to find new interest in their work. Charlatans, marketers, and publicity seekers found the demonstration to be a gold mine. Several convincing hoaxes made their appearance on the WorldNet, strengthening the position of skeptics that Professor Weisskopf and his group were frauds.

A few universities began offering freshman level review courses in Metaphysics and Consciousness, compiling from the accepted literature. It became clear that the basis for the Weisskopf Protocols was the Frankel Method. Demands came in from all over the world for a rigorous teaching program. Darcy told John there were literally thousands of people wanting to be certified.

The office expanded. There were now half a dozen overwhelmed full-time staffers.

John and Genevieve had not anticipated such a spike in interest. John already had an outline for a certification course but it needed to be fleshed out.

A week later Darcy Bledsoe called. "Help! We need to tell these people what's happening. They're practically beating the doors down."

"Tell them that we are developing a certification course and it will be ready in three weeks," John said. "Take advanced registrations now and let me know how many sign up."

"How much will it cost?"

"I have no idea."

"Give me a ball park figure."

John thought out loud.

"Three hundred dollars for a basic course, which will teach up to the end of stage two. Five hundred for a teacher training course. Everybody has to do the basic course first. If they don't like that they don't have to attend. The courses will be three to four days, 9 a.m. to 6 p.m., but that could change. Tell them that we will personally certify a few hundred instructors and allow these to certify as they see fit. Don't register more than a thousand people. That's 20 courses, which will take 20 weeks. From there we'll have to certify the instructors. That's another 10 or 20 weeks. I think we can stand it that long. After that we're done."

"You should charge more. At that rate we'll have to turn away thousands."

"I don't want just the well-to-do to have a shot at this. Besides, $800 is a good chunk of change. A lot of people would have trouble coming up with that. If necessary, run a lottery."

"A lottery!" Darcy exclaimed. "Great idea. Then it'll be totally fair."

What had he done? Just committed himself and his wife (without asking her) to almost a year of full time teaching.

Genevieve was cool with it, even excited. "I'll quit my job at the high school. It'll be romantic, being together every single day in the same room."

"After teaching I can take you to bed and do amazing things to your body."

She snorted. "I'll be too tired."

"No you won't. It'll be fun. You know how being in crowds makes me horny."

She looked at him coyly. "We'll see."

After the news that Friday John went outside to look at the stars. He noticed a tension in the air. Years with the technique had sensitized his perceptions. John began to see something that frightened him. A hint of the chaotic roiling of the Unformed Potential was asserting itself into the fabric of space. Tentacles of half-formed potential were coming out of nowhere into the densely organized structure of matter and energy.

John walked back into the house. He tried to keep the fear out of his voice. "Gen, would you come out here for a second?"

"Hi sweetheart! Beautiful night for star gazing!"

"You're the brightest and most beautiful star I know."

She hugged him. "What's up?"

"Gen, do your thing like you were going out for Unformed Potential work. Tell me what you see."

"Any hints?"

"Nope. I may be seeing things that aren't there."

After several minutes Genevieve spoke. "Looks like the Unformed Potential is making its presence felt, even here."

"I knew it. Maybe our friends in the research division are right. Maybe these are the End Times. The end of the fucking universe."

Genevieve shook her head. "No, I don't believe it. It can't be John."

He gestured toward the heavens. "The evidence is all to the contrary."

"It's hard to believe in the end of everything when the methods necessary to even perceive it makes you feel so good," Genevieve pointed out.

"That's what I can't figure out."

41

"SIRE, the report from Earth." Tiriak Delnek entered the private chamber of Salat Toor, current ruler of the High Council of Orion. Toor was seated in the elaborately decorated ceremonial float in which he received his trusted personal aides. He took the message disc languidly and dismissed Delnek with a wave of an elegantly manicured hand. He then called in Melet Toor.

Salat Toor addressed his nephew. "Am I the first to read this report?"

Melet Toor smiled sardonically. "Oh yes sire. The first of any importance."

Salat laughed. "It has undoubtedly been read by every member of the Council."

Melet Toor shrugged. "It is traditional."

"A tradition I hope to eliminate very soon."

"The report, along with myself, has only arrived by transportal from earth less than one hour ago."

"Delnek would not dare to read it."

Melet Toor nodded affirmatively. "Only myself, the Council, and now you sire."

Salat Toor knew much of what was in the report and had already formulated his plans accordingly. He inserted the message disk into his reader and read through it.

"All right then. How has your Gyorgi Havel identity been holding up?"

"So far so good."

Salat Toor tapped his fingers upon the armrest of the royal float. "Things are getting rapidly out of control again, Melet! The unexpected discovery of the earthian Frankel is causing serious fissures in the Plan."

"I don't understand it sire. For thousands of years all has been well. In just two months the earthian socio-event matrix has been splintering. New memes are entering the human consciousness, placed there by the earthians themselves."

"Impossible! This rapid development is unprecedented."

"Everything about the planet is unusual sire."

Salat Toor ground his teeth. He thought out loud about their long association with this strange planet in Galaxy 6. "The first Orion scout ship discovered the earthian planet almost 10 million years ago. A beautiful blue water planet with an astonishing diversity of species. It lies like a jewel in a muddy back road in the Desert. The stellar neighborhood shows 106 stars of which all but 9 are orange, red, white, or brown dwarfs without intelligent life. Nowhere within the galaxy is there such a barren patch. The planet's little yellow dwarf is in the very center of the Desert, as if it had been placed there by a higher power. It is well-hidden, Melet. As the years passed we discovered that seed life forms from every sector in the galaxy are present upon the surface of the planet."

Melet Toot recalled the planet's bizarre history. "Several thousand years after its discovery Orion ships returned. The planet's oceans had convulsed, covering 90% of the land surface and destroying life on the surface. The planet was discovered to have a 26,000 year wobble, as a spinning top just before it falls to the floor. This wobble precipitates unpredictable geological and climactic events. After conditions stabilized we established a base upon the planet's surface and began to monitor conditions there."

Salat Toor swelled with pride. The Orion contribution was by far the greatest of all the galactic and intergalactic cultures that had participated in the shaping of earthian biology and the meme structure of humanity.

"A water planet such as earth could not have evolved in that solar system with its single sun. All of the other planets are either lifeless rocks or gas giants. Except perhaps for Mars. But Mars was never like the earthian planet. It more resembles humanoid planets in the rest of the galaxy."

Melet Toor shook his head. "The earthian planet is an astronomical anomaly, a square peg in a round hole."

"Correct! The Law of Binaries states that humanoid life everywhere in this galaxy originates under dual sun systems. Every humanoid species has one heart to pump the blood and the High Heart to distribute the prana that flows in from the top of the head." Salat thought of the single earthian heart, and the human head with its thick covering over the pineal. "It is impossible that such a leap in consciousness should occur in such a primitive biology."

"But it has, sire. Earthians are more than just unusual. The Council of Scientists says that it has the potential to be the most dynamic species in a billion years."

"Those who can insert the critical memes into human society stand to reap a large reward. Now, just as it is time to make ourselves known as the earthian planet's benign mentors and fathers, the Plan has fissured."

"It is as we feared, sire. We knew the earthians were gaining in wisdom as human civilization developed. It has just occurred faster than we thought."

"Go and do what you can, Melet. Oversee the new meme campaign. At all costs try to halt the acceleration of the Frankel and Weisskopf memes into human consciousness. Very often these new developments turn out to be mere fads. They can quickly disappear. The Plan can still be salvaged."

"Yes sire."

Salat Toor, now convulsed with anxiety, rose quickly from his float. He stared out of the transparency at the beautiful geometric display of lights that every ruling Toor had enjoyed for the past 20 million years.

Galactic culture had been stagnant for over a billion years. It had been foreseen by almost everyone that the earthian humans would eventually break loose from their overcrowded planet and reach for the stars. Their presence within a much slower-moving and moribund galactic culture would be profoundly felt. Humanity, with its melting pot of the best of galactic genetics, would be the catalyst his Traditionalist faction had hoped for. The earthians' dynamism and energy would help to transform the galaxy, guided by the Orion meme structure.

Over the last century and a half the preparation of humanity for their role had been accelerated. Their societies had been steadily ever more centralized, as well as their philosophies and their consciousness. They had been conditioned to hierarchical structures via meme insertion. It was now embedded in the consciousness of the species. When they moved out into the galaxy the earthians would be the willing arm of Orion, with the Toor family at its head.

It was perfect. Except for the unanticipated variables.

The new earthian movements had to be crushed before they gained any momentum with the masses. That was Melet Toor's job. It would be a difficult one. The speed with which the earthians could change was frightening. Like a bacterial culture growing out of control, new memes could destroy the carefully implanted ones growing in the mass consciousness. Even so, Orion and its earthian allies had plenty of time to extirpate the Frankel Method and the Weisskopf Protocols. Their previous attempts to discourage the Frankel Method had failed. However, the new campaign should handle all of that.

Two days later the following announcement was made on the national news networks: "Stay tuned for the most startling information you have ever received. The Truth about UFOs and extraterrestrial involvement on earth! The world-wide government cover-up exposed!"

The night of the broadcast almost every single TV in America, and the world, was tuned to the three major networks. The blogs had been rabid with anticipation.

Robert recorded the program, a two-hour special without commercial interruption. The program explained the existence of extra-terrestrials on earth and that several national governments knew of their existence. The overall impression of the show was to inform humanity that they were not alone. ETs had been interacting with earth for a very long time. An image of Melet Toor was shown, describing him as "a visitor form the Orion sector."

"That's Gyorgi Havel!" Genevieve said.

"I can't tell the difference," Rachel remarked. "He looks just like us."

John had to admit that the program lived up to its billing.

Attention and discussion now moved from Weisskopf's demonstration and the Frankel Method to the "ET Question," as the media was now calling it.

"Is the ET presence on earth right or wrong?"

"Should ETs be allowed to continue their association with mankind?"

"Have ETs benefited mankind or hurt us?"

In supermarkets, workplaces, and homes, the ET Question was on everyone's lips.

John called Darcy Bledsoe a week later, curious to see what had happened with the certification program.

"It's been a Godsend for us. We had over 200,000 inquiries in the first week alone. Now it's dropped off to a trickle. Two days ago we held the lottery drawing. We sent out confirmation emails yesterday. You'll start teaching next week."

John was relieved. They had made a big splash and now it was over. They would fade back into obscurity and no one would care what they did.

Salat Toor received the latest reports from earth. His nephew had done superb work.

The recent news was very good. Frankel and Weisskopf had disappeared from the lips of almost everyone. There were still thousands interested but the millions had turned away. The old memes had reasserted their primacy.

Humanity was so easy to manipulate! Decide on agenda item C. Create group A to promote C. Create group B to oppose group A and item C. Now all attention was on C, allowing its easy manifestation into the culture.

Salat Toor watched with glee as humans took one side of the "ET Question" or the other, never stopping to ask themselves whether the question itself had any validity. The ET Question would be posed over and over again in the mass media, in different formulations. The vast majority of earthians under the Bell curve would go with it.

Only one thought disturbed his equilibrium. What if another unexpected variable occurred?

Salat Toor shuddered, for it had been a very close call. The Frankel Method allowed its practitioners to rise above the inserted lower-level memes in mass consciousness and connect directly to the Unity Field. The Frankel Method was so good Toor had adopted it in his own meditations.

A much greater difficulty still loomed. The earthian Frankel had translated his meditation from a mysterious book of runes. Who had written that book? It had appeared just in time to derail their glorious Plan. A powerful counter-force was acting in opposition to Orion influence on the earthian planet. The origins of this counter-force had not been identified. He had some of his most able and trusted agents on it. They had discovered nothing.

Nevertheless, things were going quite well once more. Salat Toor leaned back in his float and smiled contentedly.

John and Genevieve began teaching their course, called the Frankel Method Certification Program. Darcy rented space at a downtown hotel right off the freeway. She made students come to them. Genevieve didn't want to go out on the road anymore.

Genevieve was glad to let John shoulder the responsibility and the publicity for the program. At heart she was a loner. At first it was difficult for her to face a roomful of people every day. After a week or so she began to enjoy it, although being around a crowd of people all day tired her out. The only difficulty was that John couldn't keep his hands off her. She really enjoyed his touch, but sometimes after a long day of work his attentions became irritating. They had a few arguments about that until she convinced him that sex twice a week was as much as she wanted.

John reluctantly agreed.

After a couple of weeks he looked forward eagerly to Saturday and Wednesday nights. He groaned when he got up on the other mornings.

"You know what day it is," he said to her on the first Saturday morning after their agreement.

"Yeah. It's Saturday."

John looked at her with goo-goo eyes. Despite herself she giggled. "God John, is that all you think about? The universe is collapsing. We're teaching the most important course in the history of the world. All you care about is sex!"

"It's not *all* I care about. But it's pretty high up on the list."

She threw a pillow at him and walked naked into the bathroom, feeling his eyes on her. She had to admit that she was satisfied with their arrangements.

The entity known to John and Genevieve as Porniarsk spoke to his five colleagues. The Elohim were assembled in the engineering section. They were observing events in the Twelve Galaxies in the outermost universe of the All. The group was concentrating particularly on events within Galaxy 6 and Galaxy 11. The earthian planet in Galaxy 6 and the Illirian planet of origin in Galaxy 11 were of particular interest.

"Our little plan seems to be working," Porniarsk said.

"My little plan, you mean," said another entity who might be called DaVinci. "You're always taking credit."

"My sublime attention to detail seems always to guarantee success, does it not?" Porniarsk countered.

"Without creativity nothing is possible," DaVinci retorted.

"Enough, you two," said Catherine the Great. "All of us participated. Although you two wrote the book of runes it was Planck and Bohr who devised the construction of the paper and ink. Our friend Hilbert designed all of those clever multidimensional links."

The Elohim who might be known to an earthian as Tesla spoke up. "Don't forget it was I who had the idea for our diminutive messengers."

Tesla was acknowledged.

Kurosawa laughed. "The Orions and their silly Plan will be swept aside by events. Nothing to worry about from that quarter."

All of the Elohim agreed.

"The timing is just right, is it not?" remarked Hitchcock. "Just as we have predicted, the Unformed Potential expansion is rapidly accelerating."

"Quite so," said Kurosawa. "All of the actors are in place for an exciting dénouement. I wager that this time the frontier will be fully prepared."

"Impossible," said Khufu. "The frontier is always last to ascertain the truth because of its position in the structure of reality."

"Not this time," Kurosawa said. "If the focal points are prepared, all else follows smoothly."

"Yes," agreed Porniarsk the Great Avatar. "Our calculations show conclusively that the earthian planet in sector 8802, cluster 237, region 12, Galaxy 6 will be the primary focus this time. The Symbol of All confirms it. Secondary focal point somewhere in the same region. All is in readiness."

"You are arrogant," Khufu objected. "There are too many variables. The earthian planet is not yet ready for the end of the Great Cycle and the Rebirth."

Porniarsk responded hotly. "When the time comes they will be."

"I wager 50 master builder points that they will not!" Khufu cried.

"I agree with Khufu," said Kurosawa. "I too wager 50 against."

"Thirty for Porniarsk!"

"Sixty against!"

In the back of Porniarsk's mind was the comment from that irritating earthian woman. Perhaps he and his colleagues did have a gambling problem...

42

A MONTH after the ET broadcast the initial excitement had worn off. People stopped arguing and began to question. Citizens realized their leaders had been lying to them about the ET Question. President Shrub and General Haverstam of the Joint Chiefs released a statement with the support of the National Security Council. "The ET Question involves national security issues. It was felt that acknowledging the alien presence on earth could cause a panic."

This caused more confusion as people looked at the image of Gyorgi Havel. (At this point Salat Toor removed his nephew from earth.)

One man on the news was heard to grumble. "What about patriotism? And terrorism? I was told we should defend our country against our enemies. Now it turns out we were all in bed with ETs."

Another woman said, "I always thought President Shrub was the enemy. He stole the election from Senator Brinson. What is our government up to? We know now we can't really trust them."

Slowly at first, then with growing vehemence, a bewildered public began demanding answers. Books on ancient cultures, UFOs, and the paranormal sold madly. A few new cults sprang up. To the consternation of many, the Blythe Rogers radio show became wildly popular.

The upcoming presidential election became a sounding board of blame for the past. Many citizens realized that their heads had been buried in the muck of untruth. Any politician with a tainted background was immediately suspect.

"Personal integrity" became the criteria by which all public officials were measured. Investigative reporters were all over the place, digging into the private lives of candidates. Several web sites were devoted to scrutinizing the background of news reporters. People all over the world were on the WorldNet, looking for answers and digging up hidden secrets.

Senator Ralph Smith sat in a frigid hotel room in Des Moines, Iowa late on a cold January night. It was past 10 after a long day of campaigning. His staff had left. Brenda was asleep in the double bed adjoining the office.

He had so far emerged unscathed from the media fixation on political integrity and transparency. Not a hint of his brief affair with Lena Watson had come out even though media types were running around his campaign like an overturned beehive.

Ralph had entered late in the race for the presidential nomination. He had not participated in the three-year scramble to amass a huge campaign war chest. Not by design of course, but it was working out in his favor. He was a decided underdog. Senator Smith didn't attract as much scrutiny as the big boys. But he was getting a growing following on social media sites. Brian Lawson made him write two or three posts every day. He would communicate directly to his followers, which included all of his big contributors.

Hal Tyler was far ahead in the money race. He was running an aggressive media campaign against every one of his rivals. Senator Smith was not spared. In Iowa, the first political test of the campaign, the Tyler campaign accused Senator Smith of being dishonest and abandoning conservative principles.

Ralph Smith is not a true conservative. He voted against S101, the anti-terrorist bill. He voted for stricter gun control. Vote Hal Tyler for President.

S101 was ostensibly anti-terrorist legislation. It contained a provision that would have required the military to buy more American oil. It had been promoted by a Texas oil magnate and a big Tyler contributor. Iowa would be a good test of his honesty policy. He could say that Hal Tyler was a liar in his accusation about voting for stricter gun control. But he would not engage in attack politics. If the voters fell for Tyler's negative crap, he was done for.

Ralph was about to go to bed when his phone rang.

"Ralph, Frank Faircloth. I'm trying to figure out just what's going on in this world. Have any ideas?"

"Hello Frank! I'd say that things are coming out which should have come out a long time ago. The more I think about it the more the idea of island earth seems preposterous. There's a big universe out there Frank. We're a part of it."

"It's tearing this country apart Ralph," Faircloth cried. "At our church we don't know what to tell people anymore. This thing is shaking people. Shaking their faith. Traditional values of God, country, and church are falling by the wayside. Conservative values that have kept this country strong."

"Frank, conservative values will never go out of style. Conservatives believe in the integrity of the human spirit. Loyalty, character, honesty, and hard work are never out of date. They're part of the fabric of life itself. That's what I'd tell my people if they came to me for advice."

There was a long pause at the other end of the line.

"I'm glad you're on our side Ralph. I look forward to calling on you in the White House."

Ralph sat at his desk after Frank rang off with the phone still in his hand. Frank Faircloth asking him for guidance! It beat all.

Ralph Smith was learning to rely on his own counsel. He was learning to trust himself. As his father would say...Ralph Smith started and the mobile fell from his hand onto the carpet.

Why did he admire his father so much? Because he was tough. Because Albert Durant Smith was his own man and kept his own counsel. And what had his son done? Tried to be Pit-bull Smith and be just like his father. It was the exact opposite of being your own man.

Ralph shook his head. Sixty-two years old and I finally got it! Ralph felt the presence of his father, smiling down on him, nodding.

Reaching down, he easily grabbed the phone and returned it to the desk. The arthritis that had begun to creep into his hands was now gone.

For the next two weeks Senator Smith crisscrossed the state. He spoke at Rotary club meetings, in churches, senior centers, convention centers, libraries, restaurants, and schools, telling the people his message. Not some bullshit written by a campaign staffer and motivated by focus-group results. Win or lose, his message would come from his own heart.

Ralph looked again at the primary schedule. Iowa, Jan 19th, New Hampshire on the 27th. Then on Feb 3rd, what he called the Boost. Six primaries all on the same day. None of the big states, but all six had voted Republican in the last election. Four were southern states. It would make or break his campaign.

The Michigan Primary on the 7th, then Virginia and Tennessee together, followed by Wisconsin. Then Super Tuesday on March 2nd. By that time it would probably be over.

Hal Tyler had been accused of vote rigging and illegal contributions. Numerous infidelities were uncovered in his personal life. In the new climate of honesty he had admitted to it all unapologetically. Tyler had modified his campaign of "America First" to include ET bashing. Tyler excoriated "those in power who have brought this alien menace to earth." He found a ready audience in those who were afraid of the new reality or who did not want to acknowledge its existence. A significant sector of society wanted to go back to the good old days. Hal Tyler desired to be their spokesman. At the present time he had a 7 point lead over Ralph Smith and a 15 point lead over Congressman Jokisch. The moderate Governor Rand of Maryland was 17 points back. The senator from California, Charlie Bateson, wasn't even on the map. Ralph was up in the polls only due to the influence of Frank Faircloth, who had legitimized him with religious conservatives. Third party candidates and their supporters were not a factor in Iowa.

The next day, at the Polk County Convention Center in Des Moines, Senator Smith said:

> Today we literally live in a new world. Recently we have learned that humanity is not alone in the universe. This should not be so startling. After all, the night sky shows us hundreds of stars. Now we know that the planets orbiting those faraway stars contain life, just as our beloved planet does. That life may look different but it is life created by God, and so it must be respected. The knowledge that ETs have been interacting with the governments of earth for several decades should be an exciting concept. The majority of our attention has been on finding fault with those who have not shared this knowledge with the rest of us. Certainly there is blame. Rather than focus on the past, let us look forward.
>
> Some have said that our hi-tech society has no use for conservative values, especially in light of recent events. Some say these values belong to an old, outdated world. I disagree. As I said to a friend of mine the other day, Senator Faircloth, conservative values will never go out of style. Conservatives believe in the integrity of the human spirit. Loyalty, character, honesty, and hard work are never out of date. They're part of the fabric of life itself.
>
> If I am elected I will always speak to you from my heart. I will never lie to you. In recent months I have undergone a personal transformation. I have become the person I always wanted to be since childhood. That person sees the value of each and every human being no matter what their status in society. That person sees that God is inside each one of us. That person sees a bright and positive universe, not a negative and dangerous one. We do not have to justify the goodness that lies inherently within each of us. We are, all of us, made in God's image—

Ralph Smith looked at what he had written and threw it away. He stood at the podium silently for a few seconds as the papers which contained his carefully thought out message fluttered to the ground.

> Why do I want to run for president? Some people say that you'd have to be a lunatic to want the job. [laughter]. I have asked myself that question over and over. I want to set an example of frankness and honesty in politics. Not the bullshit kind of honesty you always hear from politicians. Not the pat answers that come from speechwriters and focus groups. I want to talk about the affairs of our nation the way

my father used to talk to us about difficult family problems: openly, bluntly, and honestly.

I am a conservative because conservative values reflect the nature of life itself and because they are inspirational and can lead to true happiness. In my campaign I will detail my thinking on this subject as it develops. It will be a work in progress, just as I am a work in progress.

I am appealing to you as one human being to another. I don't have a lot of money in my campaign chest. I'd like to, but I don't. [laughter] I'm broke, as political campaigns go, so I won't be spewing campaign advertisements all over the place and interrupting your TV programs. [some cheers]

I don't know where our country is going. No one is smart enough to know that. No president is powerful enough to direct the lives of over 300 million people. So I will not be drawing up complicated policy papers for you all to study and debate. No one reads them except party insiders and political junkies. Real people are too busy to study them. I can hardly understand 'em myself! [laughter]

I want you to tell me what you want. I am setting up a web site at PresidentRalphSmith.org so you can tell me your vision for America, and for you personally. We'll tabulate the results as we go along.

I don't believe in getting bogged down in process and procedure. I believe in changing our policies with the times, guided by conservative principles. Let me know what you think. I'd appreciate your vote on January 17th.

Ralph Smith didn't wait for applause. He walked off the stage and was immediately surrounded by a crowd of people. Waving off security, he stood for an hour talking to reporters and the public. Then he left.

Hal Tyler was laughing as he saw the speech on TV.

"What about a strong defense? What about terrorism? What about illegal immigration? The economy? What about the core issues facing America? The guy sounds like a screaming new-age liberal! This is going to be so easy."

The next day in Iowa the Tyler campaign ran an ad. **Conservative or new-age liberal? Is Ralph Smith divorced from reality?** The ads then showed clips of his speech. "If you want a real conservative, vote for Hal Tyler. Hal Tyler stands for a strong America. Hal Tyler stands for real values people can understand."

Ralph didn't get it. Tyler was the frontrunner. He was spending an awful lot of time attacking the guy behind him. Maybe he was scared or angry. Ralph remembered the flare-up at the Conservative Caucus meeting last year.

David Lawson was worried. "Throwing away your speech was a nice gesture. Are we really not going to prepare policy papers? Ralph, you're taking an awful gamble."

"David, given our fundraising situation, what are our chances of winning the nomination?"

"About 1,000 to one," the campaign manager replied.

"That's right. I decided in the middle of that speech to be me. I'm not going to fake it David. Our only chance is for total openness. It's never been tried before I know. If we flop it'll be my fault. I meant it about speaking from the heart."

"Lawson was skeptical. "You'll have your chance at the debate on the 16th."

On the evening of January 16th John, Genevieve, Rachel, and Robert decided to watch the Iowa debate on C-SPAN.

Robert was especially keen to see Senator Smith, who had called his son a potential terrorist last year.

"Welcome ladies and gentlemen to the Republican presidential debate," said the moderator. On stage the five candidates for the Republican Party nomination stood in front of microphones. "Here we are at the Iowa Convocation Center in Des Moines. We are filled to capacity. This will be a moderated discussion. Questions will be asked by our distinguished panel of commentators. Each candidate will have five minutes to respond. At the end, if there is time, we will have an open mike discussion between the candidates. Without further ado let's introduce the panelists and the participants."

The camera panned to a table that had been set up in front of the stage, at which the five panelists were seated.

"You all know Cob Tapelle from ABC News. On his right, former national security advisor Lladislaw Kraynek. In the middle is Ari Flesch, Professor of Comparative Religion at Harvard University. To his right is Maryanne Holberg, director of the Reagan Public Policy Institute in Washington. Last but not least, Dr. Lucinda Prescott, director of the Iowa City Medical Center."

Robert was surprised. "Hey, Tapelle's on C-SPAN! And Kraynek, that nazi. Pretty big hitters for a lousy little debate before the Iowa caucuses."

"Someone must think it's important," Rachel responded. "Smith seems to have attracted a lot of attention."

"...and now for our candidates: from right to left, Governor Gerald Rand of Maryland, Congressman Walter Jokisch of Ohio, Senator Ralph Smith of Nebraska, Senator Hal Tyler of Texas, and on the right, Senator Charlie Bateson of California. Mr. Tapelle, your first question."

John and Robert were watching Tapelle and Flesch. "Any money they go after Smith right off the bat," Robert said.

"Senator Smith," Tapelle said. "In your speech last week in Des Moines you said you were a seat of your pants kind of guy. You also said that policy papers were a waste of time. You said you intended to be open and honest at all times. What I want to know, and I'm sure the American people want to know...,"

"Pompous bastard," Robert said.

"...is how you intend to direct the country without knowing where you're going?"

Ralph Smith had performed the technique just before coming onstage. Inside him Pit-bull Smith wanted to strangle that arrogant, toupee'd bastard. Ralph calmed himself down. "Excellent questions, Mr. Tapelle. 99% of the voters don't read policy papers. They're worded so that the average person can't understand them. What is their value in a democracy where the American people supposedly make the decisions?"

Ralph Smith smiled coolly at Cob and was gratified to see his irritation. "I'll be posting a document on my web site after the voting tomorrow. It will outline the important principles of my campaign in words that the average person can understand. I sat on several of the Congressional oversight committees so I'm well versed on national security and defense issues. My director of national security will be former Chairman of the Joint Chiefs of Staff, Darwin Kessinger. One of my platforms will be the declassification of many of our covert operations and black programs. General Kessinger and I agree that secretiveness leads to paranoia and bad decision making. We believe in openness and honesty with the public. The American people have a right to know what their government is doing!" [Cheers and applause from the audience].

"Senator Tyler, your response?" said Tapelle.

Hal Tyler sat for several moments, looking at his colleague with contempt. Ralph Smith sat calmly, returning his gaze. Tyler broke eye contact first. "Ralph Smith used to be a fine conservative, but look at him now." Tyler's voice dripped with sarcasm. "A new-age liberal. A very, very confused man. The Tyler Presidency will support a strong national defense. We will underscore the traditional values that built America and made her the most powerful nation in the world. The Tyler Presidency doesn't see what a bunch of outer space aliens has to do with that." (laughter) "It's all fine and good to be honest but there are times discretion must be the better part of valor. That's something that ol' Pit-bull Smith has never learned. Our campaign has already presented a complete set of policy papers to the media and on the web. We come prepared to guide America in the right direction. The direction of strength, prosperity, and traditional values." [applause]

"They're going to make Smith speak first all night so the others can attack him," Robert said.

Jokisch took a hard line, but was more concerned with the ****national debt. He spent his five minutes talking about that.

Senator Bateson talked about issues important to the California voters: water policy, education, illegal immigration, and the environment.

"Now for our next question," said the moderator, "from Lladislaw Kraynek, senior fellow at the prestigious Northampton Institute for Defense Policy."

"Senator Smith." Kraynek said the name harshly, without emotion. "What would you do in the event of a suspected terrorist attack against the United States using tactical nuclear weapons? Would you fly by the seat of your pants?"

Ralph Smith smiled. "Well sir, I have people a lot smarter than myself to figure all that out. The value of a president isn't what he knows. It's in his character."

Kraynek frowned. There were murmurs of agreement from the audience.

"The president will always be fully briefed by the finest minds in the country." Ralph changed his tone and addressed the former national security adviser as if he were a schoolboy. "A mind stuffed with policy options cannot necessarily make the wise choice. Only a wise man can do that, a man who has been through the mill. A man who understands himself. I have served my country proudly in the United States Air Force, and dealt with important issues of policy for the past 40 years. I have recently found an inner source of peace and strength which makes me as fit as anyone to deal with crisis situations."

Kraynek sneered. "And to what do we owe this new sense of enlightenment?"

"I'll be happy to answer that question, sir," said Ralph Smith calmly. "The other day I was thinking about my father, about how strong and sure of himself he was. I admired him deeply. All my life I would ask myself, 'What would dad do?' I realized one day that in that process I had lost myself. My father was able to make wise decisions because of his faith in himself and God. I realized that in order to be like my father I had to be myself. I had to trust myself to know the answers, just as my father had. We are all human and we will all make mistakes. If I make any mistakes while president I intend for them to be honest ones."

At the end of this speech you could hear a pin drop. A politician who revealed his innermost secrets! It was unheard of. Someone coughed. The moderator said, "Mr. Tyler, your response."

"Is this the same arsehole who threatened to put you in jail?" Rachel asked John.

"Same one. The guy has obviously had some kind of personal transformation."

"He speaks softly but powerfully," Genevieve said.

Hal Tyler began his response. "When I'm president and I'm told of an imminent terrorist attack on the United States, I immediately call a meeting of the National Security Council and we ensure the safety and security of the country. Then we hit the bastards responsible, hard. In my administration I hope to be so well prepared that we can stop the attacks before they even begin." [murmurs of approval]. "I'll tell you one thing. I'll take quick and decisive action. I'm not going to spend a lot of time philosophizing about it." [laughter and a few guffaws]

Jokisch tried to outdo Tyler, with some success. The Congressman wanted big reductions in immigration and large increases in the budget for Border Patrol,

Customs, and Coast Guard. "We can never do enough to stop terrorists," he said to a few cheers.

"Poor Jokisch!" Robert said. "He sees the arrangements. Always playing second fiddle to Tyler. It's not fair!"

"What do you care?" snorted Rachel. "You're not going to vote for him."

"It's rigged, that's all. I don't like it."

Bateson and Rand then said their bit.

"Oh no, that butthead Flesch is next," John said.

"About to take his pound of Flesch out of Smith I fear," Robert joked.

"I didn't know you were so into Republicans dad," Genevieve said.

"I'm not, usually. It helps to know who your enemy is. I've been watching this Smith guy carefully for over a year. I gotta say I like him even better than the Democrats or the third party candidates."

"Professor Flesch, your question," the moderator said.

"Is it true, Senator Smith, that you had an illicit affair with one of your staffers?"

For a split second the senator looked shell shocked. "It is true that for two weeks I had a sexual relationship with one of my staff. But it was broken off by mutual consent almost a year ago."

The audience broke into an excited babble. "Please ladies and gentlemen," the moderator said. "Quiet please."

"Oh-oh," Genevieve said to Robert. "Bad news for your guy."

"So much for integrity, eh senator?" Flesch said.

Ralph saw David Lawson, in the wings, place his hands on his head in dismay.

"Professor Flesch, the lady in question is here right now. Smith stood up and pointed to the back of the room. "Lena! Come up and tell us about it from your side."

Hal Tyler objected. "This is nonsense! Let the adulterer stew in his own juices!"

"My five minutes haven't expired yet Hal."

All eyes were on Lena Watson as she quickly walked up to the stage and grabbed the microphone. "About a year ago I had a crush on the Senator. I began to pursue him, I must admit. We slept together once. A week later he asked me to break it off. I agreed. I was having second thoughts anyway. I was a fool. It was a stupid thing to do and I regret it. But we're best of friends now." She handed the microphone back to the senator.

"I'll bet you are," Tyler responded. "I'm sure your wife is very happy, Ralph."

Suddenly Brenda Smith came roaring onto the stage. She grabbed the microphone away from Ralph. "A lot happier than your wife, Hal! And I can testify to that!"

There were hoots from the audience. Hal Tyler's indiscretions were well known.

"Hey this is better than a soap opera," Robert cracked.

Hal Tyler shrank back into his chair. Brenda Smith stood tall next to her husband. "Ralph told me about it as soon as it happened." She put her arm around him. "I was upset, of course, but it didn't last. In fact, it turned out to be the best thing that's happened in our marriage in 20 years. We had grown distant, you see, after 35 years of living together. It happens even to the most well-intentioned people. But we worked it out and we're stronger than ever. I'm a full-time member of the campaign team. I've never had so much fun in all my life. Y'all can say anything you want about my husband's moral standards. There probably isn't one person out there who hasn't sinned just as bad as Ralph." She pointed at Hal Tyler. "Including you, you philandering hypocrite! People in glass houses shouldn't throw stones." Hal Tyler blanched. Brenda replaced the microphone in its stand. She turned, put her arms around her husband, and gave him a kiss. There were hoots and jeers but some applause too.

"I'm not sure how well that little speech will go over with conservative Republican voters," Genevieve said.

"This guy doesn't do anything halfway does he?" Robert said. "Blackburn got away with that down in Louisiana but I don't think it will wash in Iowa."

"The media will crush him," John said. "This may be the last of Senator Smith."

After that it was all downhill. After the debate was over Governor Rand tried to attract some media attention. He had gone almost unnoticed during the event. The reporters all swarmed around Senator Smith and his wife.

"Senator! How do you think this affair will affect your chances with conservative voters?" a reporter for ABC asked.

"I have no idea. We'll just have to wait and see."

"Mrs. Smith! Are you bitter about your husband's infidelity?"

"Are you blind and deaf? Of course not. I said it was the best thing that had happened in our marriage in 20 years."

"Senator, how can the voters trust someone who has broken the most sacred vow one person can give to another?"

"That will be up to each individual voter. We'll find out tomorrow." For an hour Robert watched as Smith calmly fielded questions. He didn't try to duck anything. Finally, the reporters were talked out and everyone left. After a break C-SPAN played an interview with Hal Tyler. "I think we've seen who the real conservatives in this primary are. Myself and Congressman Jokisch."

"That's it," Robert said. "I'm going to vote Republican for the first time in my life."

"You're kidding!" Rachel exclaimed. It was the only heresy possible in Frankel family politics.

"Yup. There's something about this guy I like. Especially when he said that a mind full of facts is not guaranteed to make the best decisions. He's running on character issues. I think that's important."

"The guy just admitted to cheating on his wife," Genevieve said.

"I don't care. I like him."

On the morning of January 17th everyone in the Smith campaign sat around the TV sets, waiting for the final vote count. The mood was nervous anticipation.

When the results were finally tabulated Hal Tyler had won convincingly, 42% to 23% over Smith. Jokisch came in a close third at 19%.

Smith Big Loser in Iowa Caucuses read the headline in the *Des Moines Register*. The article said that Hal Tyler did much better than expected, and so did Congressman Jokisch. Senator Smith fell below analysts' projections.

It was just the opposite of what the Smith campaign had counted on. David Lawson was optimistic. "We thought we were under the radar. I guess not. They must think we're supposed to do better."

"We'll press on," Ralph said.

Three days later after dinner John heard the doorbell. He opened the front door to a very nervous elderly woman who lived four houses down. "Uh, Mr. Frankel. Would you come outside for a moment?"

John invited her in and went to the hallway closet for his winter coat. The woman peered out the window panel of the front door.

"Hello Mrs. Francis," Genevieve said as she walked into the hallway from the living room.

"Hello Genevieve. Maybe you should come out with us."

As they stepped onto the porch Mrs. Francis pointed to the clear black sky across the street and above the trees.

John noticed a very faint multicolored mist about ten times the diameter of the moon, with tendrils moving outward to cover about a third of the sky.

The woman spoke nervously. "What do you make of that?"

John tried to convince himself that the churning mist might be the aurora borealis. He said so.

"Doesn't look anything like it," the woman replied.

John had to admit that it didn't to him either. It was more like an algae bloom, but the patterns kept changing, morphing....

Genevieve said nothing but her stomach was roiling. 'It's here,' she thought. She had convinced herself that what was occurring in the Eyrie could have no relation to the real world. Obviously it did. She was an Unformed Potential technician with years of experience. One look at the sky told her all she needed to know.

"I read in the paper that there's something wrong with space, or matter, or something," the woman said. "Do you know anything about that?"

John and Genevieve calmed the woman, explaining that it was probably just a temporary atmospheric phenomenon.

After Mrs. Francis had gone Genevieve and John turned to each other with raised eyebrows.

"Well, here we go," John said. "For better or for worse."

During the weeks that followed a very faint mist appeared in the night sky. Some people said they saw rippling colors. Others said it looked like an algae bloom, except much more subdued. People pronounced the imminent end of the world, the dawning of a new age, or retribution on mankind from an angry God. The God's Light cult said it was the Second Coming of Jesus Christ.

On the evening news broadcasts, Sag Carlson explained it as an atmospheric phenomena due to a subtle change in the weak and strong nuclear forces. As time passed the phenomena persisted. It became obvious to everyone that something big was happening "out there."

On Beta Orionis, capital planet of the Orion sector in the Alnilam region, Salat Toor was bitter. Things had been progressing very well after their successful broadcast six weeks ago. Now earthians were again turning to the dangerous procedures of Frankel and Weisskopf. It was this crazy energy phenomenon. It was observable everywhere in the galaxy but particularly concentrated around the earthian planet!

Toor realized bitterly that their game might be over, through no fault of their own. Four million years of work down the drain. But they would not give up even though the best minds in the galaxy said that the disturbing phenomena presaged an upcoming event that was to be felt within all of the Twelve Galaxies.

Salat Toor was afraid. Even the new meditation didn't help much. He faced the fact that he was using the same technique he hoped the earthians would reject. "Yes," he told himself. "But earthians are barbarians. There is still hope."

The delegation from Deneb had just left his private chamber, invited by him for a personal consultation. The tall, dark skinned Denebians were known for their wisdom and grace under pressure. Toor could tell even they were nervous.

Olatida Ogunfatidime himself had asked his opinion. "Salat Toor, what is your assessment of this galactic phenomenon?"

Toor was shocked. Denebians never asked questions, they answered them. Their intuitive and psychic abilities were ranked the highest in the galaxy. Clearly, recent events were beyond the scope even of their vast predictive powers.

No! The Plan would continue, must continue. Salat Toor envisioned himself as one of his great ancestors; admired, respected, and consulted everywhere. Last night he looked over the historical records. In the holovid he had re-experienced the famous Council of Twelve over three billion years ago, when Rejak Toor had united the galaxy and formed the High Council and the Prefectorate. Ah, those were the good old days! And those days would come again. It was his job to make sure they did.

After Iowa Senator Ralph Smith had no time to mope. The New Hampshire primary was in eight short days. The campaign flew in to Concord, the state capitol, early in the morning of the 20th. They ensconced themselves in rented offices just outside the city limits. Ralph worked on his speech all day. After that he tried to get some rest. Hid mind was racing. Just as in Iowa, he would criss-cross the state, speaking in major cities and small towns. Lawson had made up the schedule and placed it in front of him before he had even had time to settle in his chair. "Read it and weep." There were luncheons, banquets, meetings with top political leaders and businessmen, field trips to schools, and a meeting with the VFW.

Ralph decided to have fun even though the pressure was on. The campaign must do well here. He must win or place a close second. Otherwise the media might write him off and so would most of the voters.

He was determined to run a campaign that was completely different from anything seen before. He would say what he had always wanted to say, but never had the guts. He might sink his campaign right here in New Hampshire. If he was going to go down it would be on his own terms.

Brenda came in to the private section of the suite. "How's it going?"

Ralph smiled. "I'm trying to put the pressure of expectations out of my mind."

"Let's get something to eat."

They drove into the city and found a nice restaurant. As they were seated a number of people recognized him and stopped to say a few words. "I really liked what you said in Iowa, "a man said. "About character and honesty. That took guts."

That evening Ralph Smith spoke at a citizen's forum in the lobby of a downtown hotel. A podium had been set up at the back. Several dozen people packed in around the speaker. Their boots and galoshes moistened the blue carpet, which had a fleur-de-lis pattern in gold. Ralph looked the crowd over. He received the distinct impression that many of them were looking to him for answers.

He said,

A politician's views on any issue are not as important as his character. Views and policies can be written by others and mouthed on stage like a parrot. Character cannot be faked. I am not here to talk to you about policies and statistics and data. I am not here to tell you that a Ralph Smith administration will solve all your problems. I am not here to lie to you and say that Ralph Smith has a superior vision for America, and that if you all follow me like some pied piper I will lead you to the promised land.

Today I want to tell you the things I have been thinking about for the past year. I want to tell you what is really in my heart. I have never had the guts to bare my soul to the people of this country. That is because I was afraid. Afraid of what others might think of me. Afraid of the ridicule. And mostly, afraid that being completely honest will lead to inevitable failure. That is what we politicians are told over and over. Ladies and gentlemen, I don't believe that anymore.

Senator Smith took the sheaf of papers in front of him and waved it in the air.

I was up all night writing this. People of New Hampshire, I have no idea where we are heading. When I first heard that extra-terrestrial beings have been working with the governments of earth for decades, it made me sick. Then I got really angry. Then I realized that I was a part of it. You see, I have sat on a number of government committees responsible for the security of our great country. During these private briefings we were told some strange things. I should have investigated. If I had done so I might have uncovered this story many years ago. I was afraid. I decided that to rock the boat could wreck my political career. So I did nothing. I am admitting to you that I am partly responsible for what has happened.

Ralph Smith wiped his brow.

There, that feels a little better. I feel like a kid who had to tell his father he's been raiding the bar downstairs." [laughter].

As in Iowa, the senior senator from Nebraska threw away his notes. He grabbed the front of the podium with both hands. He had everyone's attention.

The people always get the government they deserve. The majority of the people of earth have been misled throughout history by despots and dictators. America has been forced to step in, in 1917 and in 1941, to prevent global catastrophe by the forces of darkness. This darkness came from those like Hitler who lost touch with God.

This has happened because we have been too reliant on others. We have always been told to emulate this or that leader. We look to someone greater than ourselves for inspiration. But where did these great heroes and heroines get their own inspiration? If you study history, as I have, you understand that they all found courage inside their own soul.

Ladies and gentlemen, it is time for each of us to recognize our own self worth. To recognize that we have all been created by a wise, loving, and powerful God, and that within us lies a little piece of Him. As the Bible tells us, we have all been made in His image! It is time for each of us to recognize that inner light within each of us. My father, Albert Durant Smith, always told his children to become our own counselor. He wanted us to have the guts to make decisions based on what we feel is best.

As president I can promise you only one thing: that I will be honest with you. I do not promise you the sun, moon, and stars. I do not promise that a Ralph Smith administration will take all of the risk out of your lives and guarantee everyone in America prosperity and happiness. We all know government cannot do that. No one person or organization can do that. That is something which comes from within each of us. This is something that people in our great country have always instinctively understood. It is why America rose to a preeminent position upon the world stage.

In conclusion, ladies and gentlemen, I want to tell you why I am running for President of the United States. Because I really, really want the job! [laughter]. And because I want to see whether honesty is really the best policy. I know that I am being tested by you, the people, as you scrutinize my conduct and my past. But I am also testing you.

Are the people of the United States ready for true honesty? Are we ready for a president who thinks a little bit out of the box? Who isn't going to lie to you anymore? Who isn't going to give you a lot of stuff and nonsense? Are we ready for the next great evolution in American history? I believe we are on the threshold of something truly magnificent. Not just the people of America, but all the people of earth. My latest briefs tell me that we now have technology that can take us to the stars! We are on the threshold of a great dream. I believe that the great American Republic can and will lead the way into a glorious future not only for our people, but for all mankind.

Ralph Smith spread his arms out. "I'm asking for your vote on January 27th."

Robert saw the speech that evening as it was rebroadcast on C-SPAN. He made everyone sit down in front of the TV.

When it was all over Robert was in disbelief. "Who *is* this guy? This is not Ralph Smith. He has completely remade himself."

"Some in the media are saying that very thing," Rachel said. "They're saying it's a cynical attempt to take the high road, but that it won't work."

Robert snorted. "Typical." He rubbed his chin for a few seconds, a look of intense concentration on his face. "They're wrong this time. I hate conservatives and Republicans. But there's something about this guy that's genuine. I can feel it." He looked over at the women. "What do you think?"

"I like him too," Genevieve said. "I just don't know if I'm going to vote for him."

"I think he's cute," Rachel said.

"Cute?" Robert guffawed. "Women!"

"See if I make you anymore of that ravioli you like so much," Rachel said.

"I take it back!" Robert apologized.

Rachel looked at Genevieve. "Men!" she said

The women laughed together and left the room.

On January 28th the New Hampshire Primary results were in. 33% Jokisch, 32% Tyler, 24% Smith. The headline in the *Manchester Union Leader* read: **Smith's Quirky Campaign Barely Hangs in There**

"It wasn't as bad as in Iowa at least," Ralph said with a smile. "At least we can say we almost finished second."

Next stop: Arizona. Frank Faircloth said he would stump the state with him. "In your last speech you mentioned God three times and the Bible once," Frank said. "I think you're finally beginning to see the light Ralph."

Something strange occurred as Ralph Smith was making a last check of the hotel suite. He was supposed to meet Brenda in the lobby in 20 minutes. There was a knock on the door.

"Who is it?" Ralph shouted.

"A contributor."

Music to his ears. They had been scraping the bottom of the barrel just to get moving in Arizona. "Come on in."

A bald, stockily built man of medium height entered the room and stood at ease. Ralph looked, then looked again. There was something unusual about this guy. Didn't look like any contributor he ever saw; more of a military type. The man held out a beefy hand: "My name is Melvin Ruczinsky. My partners and I have been raising funds for your campaign."

Ralph laughed. "You could have fooled me. Never seen you before."

"I'm with a group that calls itself the Big Picture."

"Doesn't ring any bells with me I'm afraid."

"It shouldn't," Ruczinsky said. "We try to keep a low profile. Basically we're an investment club. About seven years ago we developed a sophisticated market analysis program that has enabled us to amass quite a lot of money. When you announced your candidacy last year we volunteered to be a fundraiser for your campaign. You probably don't even remember. I'm here to give you some very good news."

Ralph studied the man closely. Something didn't fit. His body was thick and muscular but the man's movements were unconsciously graceful, like a cat's. Training? Perhaps, but Ralph didn't think so.

"How much have you raised?" Ralph asked.

"Over 5 million dollars."

Ralph felt like a little kid with the tooth fairy. "Did I hear you correctly? Five million?" He began to get a little suspicious. "Wait a minute. Hal Tyler didn't send you here did he? Are you working for the FEC?"

Ruczinsky laughed. "We don't like Tyler at all. What's the FEC?"

Stranger and stranger. "Hey buddy, are you sure you're from this planet? A campaign contributor who doesn't know anything about the Federal Election Commission?"

Ruczinsky started for a split instant but recovered almost instantly. "I don't deal with the political end of things."

Ralph's old temper almost got the better of him. This guy must have been sent by Tyler or Jokisch to throw him off. "All of these contributions are hard money? $2,700 or less?"

"I don't know about that. I'm not involved in the fundraising. I'm here to ask you to meet with us at your headquarters in Arizona tomorrow morning at 11 a.m."

It didn't seem right. How did David Lawson miss out on five million dollars? They could have expanded their campaign much further in the Super Tuesday states already.

"Well sir, I certainly will meet with your people tomorrow morning. I'm flying in to Arizona in three hours. I just hope you guys are squeaky clean."

"We are. Everything we've done is by the books. We have documents to back it all up."

"Our campaign headquarters are in Flagstaff." Ralph gave him directions. "I'm really looking forward to meeting your partners."

As Ruczinsky left the room Ralph noticed he walked with a peculiar gliding motion.

He called David Lawson, who was flabbergasted. "Sorry mate I guess I let you down. Had no idea these guys were doing that well."

"Not to worry. If they check out we'll be in halfway decent shape again."

On the plane to Arizona Ralph got out Brenda's laptop and began looking into Ruczinsky's group. It was a specialty investment corporation, not listed on any exchange. The web site had a list of their stock transactions going back six years. Ralph examined the list carefully for evidence of insider trading or fraudulent finance. There were no big scores or big losses. Two steps forward and one step back, a gradual accumulation of net worth. That was good. Looked like they had some sort of system and stuck to it, even in the bad times. He checked six years ago during the last recession and found the same pattern. These people had lost almost all of their capital during a particularly bad stretch, but slowly recovered over the next three years. Excellent. Shows character. However, there were only 25 members of the group and no others had joined during the past three years.

Ralph got out his calculator and divided 5,000,000 by $2,700. It came out to 1,852. How did this small little club get that many people to donate that much money?

There was a section on Ruczinsky's site called, "Support the Smith Campaign." Underneath, a form to make a credit card contribution. Ralph saw a little counter at the bottom of the page. "You are the 225,678th visitor to this page." These guys must really be popular with the investment crowd.

Ralph did some quick calculating. If only half the people to the site donated, the average donation would be $45 to get to 5 million. It could happen.

Ralph leaned back in his chair and looked out the window. A few tufts of clouds floated in a bright blue sky. They were on their way to warm and sunny Flagstaff. His feet were still cold from tromping down frigid and snowy New Hampshire streets. He decided to do the exercises. After twenty minutes he felt a rush of well being go through his body. That was happening more and more often these days.

The next morning David Lawson checked in. "I can't find anything wrong with these guys. It sounds too good to be true."

"I want you here for the meeting Dave."

Two hours later himself, David Lawson, Brenda, and five of the Big Picture guys were sitting around a conference table. Ralph looked them over. Other than Ruczinsky, all seemed perfectly normal.

"We're very happy about the good news, " Ralph said. "We want to know how you raised all that money under our noses."

"We have 25 charter members of the investment club and over 200 other members," said Richard Tolliver, the club's financial manager. "We sell courses that teach our method and we do consulting work. We also sell a weekly newsletter called The Big Picture Investor. It has a wide circulation. You should know about us. You're on our mailing list."

Lawson snapped his fingers. "OK, I have you. I'm so busy I never have time to read it."

Tolliver laughed. "That's OK, neither do I." He continued with his explanation. "We are just as surprised as you are by the number of donations. Money just started pouring in. A lot of the people who contributed call themselves Democrats."

Ralph was flabbergasted. "Democrats donating to my campaign?"

Tolliver smiled. "Apparently many Democrats are not enamored of Governor Thompson."

Ralph snorted. Thompson was a traditional party-machine Democrat who had already sewn up the Democratic nomination. "How come we haven't seen any of this money? We could have used it."

"Most of it came in after your speech in Des Moines."

Brenda, Lawson, and Ralph stared at each other.

"You're kidding," Ralph said.

"Nope. We hardly believed it ourselves. The donations just started flooding in. Tony, check the database."

Tony Cavalleiro was a rotund little fellow with long blond hair tied back in a pony tail. "376 more donations totaling $35,234 since the speech in Concord on the 19th of January," he boomed.

"All hard money?" Brenda asked.

"All hard money. We only accept individual contributions of $2,700 or less. Most of the contributions are in the $50 – $100 range, but our club attracts many who can afford to donate $2,700."

And so it went. In Arizona, Frank Faircloth introduced him to all of the state bigwigs and made impassioned speeches in his favor. Ralph continued his unorthodox campaign. He wasn't sure if his message was getting across in this very conservative state.

Going into the voting the polls all showed Tyler with a slim lead over Jokisch and Smith trailing by 10 points. In five other states on what the Smith campaign called "Boost Day," they were leading only in Delaware.

And that's how it turned out in the voting on February 3rd. The *Phoenix Gazette's* headline read: **Smith's Message Not Hitting Home.** The subhead read: **Time for Senator Smith to Withdraw?**

"It seems we're always the center of attention anyway," Senator Smith said as he prepared for long days of campaigning in Michigan, Tennessee, and Virginia. Then on to the Super Tuesday states.

On February 7th the results of the Michigan Primary were in. On February 10th the primaries in Tennessee and Virginia concluded. The race for the Republican nomination for president was now a two man race between Congressman Jokisch of Ohio and Hal Tyler of Texas according to the established media. Some blogs pointed out that Ralph Smith trailed Hal Tyler by 307 delegates with 2,046 still to be decided. Congressman Jokisch was behind Tyler by only 30.

Ralph Smith had been written off by many as a former conservative who had turned a little goofy. He was called "New Age Ralph" by a political writer at the *Washington Times.* The *National Review* wondered whether "Senator Smith has lost his mind." In South Carolina, Senator Smith was advised to leave the Republican Party. "Ralph Smith will find himself more at home with adherents of the God's Light Party," opined an editorial in the *Columbia State.*

Now it was a week before Super Tuesday, when voters would go to the polls in twelve states. Over 750 delegates were up for grabs. "Funny thing about this campaign Ralph," Brenda said to him that night. "We've got money rolling in hand over fist from people all over the country. If we're so out of the mainstream, how come we have so much support?"

"It's probably Democratic and independent money," Ralph said a little gloomily. "Won't do us any good in closed primaries."

On Super Tuesday everyone in the Smith campaign sat riveted to their TV sets.

Ralph Smith had spent an equal amount of time in each of the Super Tuesday states. The Smith campaign was able to spend some of Ruczinsky's money on TV and radio spots, which showed excerpts from his speeches. At the end a simple text message: "Vote Smith for Honesty and Character." Fortunately, excerpts from every one of his speeches had been broadcast on the nightly news. Everything he said was immediately picked up. The news media followed him around like some celebrity going through a messy divorce. The media types were fascinated with his unorthodox campaign style. Therefore, Ralph Smith received more free publicity by far than any of his rivals. This caused charges of unfairness and demands for equal time from the Tyler and Jokisch campaigns.

The good thing about being a distant third was that Hal Tyler had focused his negative attacks on Congressman Jokisch. To his credit, Jokisch stuck to his campaign themes. The Congressman was by far the most conservative of the three. Ralph wanted to see how he'd do in the bigger states, especially New York and California.

To the consternation of many on Super Tuesday Senator Smith took most of California's delegates, Massachusetts, New York, and surprisingly, Georgia. Charlie Bateson's favorite son hope in California had been futile. Hal Tyler had sewn up Texas, Washington, Ohio, and Connecticut.

Walter Jokisch's surprisingly strong campaign had done well in the smaller states, but fell flat in the more populous ones. He almost won the Ohio delegation, but Hal Tyler prevailed. In his concession speech the Congressman urged Republicans in the remaining primaries to cast their votes for the senator from Texas. "Hal Tyler represents the only true conservative voice left in the party nomination process," Jokisch proclaimed.

When the final tallies were in, Ralph Smith had a 223 vote lead over the favorite of the party establishment, Hal Tyler. The victories in New York and California pushed the Smith campaign into the lead.

In an unprecedented move the Republican National Committee, in conjunction with the affected states, modified its rules. Any delegate who withdrew was able to transfer votes to the candidate of his choice. Jokisch immediately threw his 248 delegates to Tyler, and Governor Rand his 43 to Tyler. This gave Tyler a significant lead of 68 delegates after Super Tuesday.

The president, Walter Shrub III, was himself the impetus for this unheard of move. He claimed that "the integrity of the Republican Party is at stake. We must not allow a brokered national convention." The target of this statement was not lost on anyone. Political commentators proclaimed the Republican Party nominating process "a circus."

Ralph Smith refused to anger and issued strict orders to all campaign staff to say nothing. Paradoxically, the Smith campaign received high praise even from those conservative circles who hated him and were behind the rules change. "Ralph Smith, though completely misguided, has proved a loyal party supporter."

Hal Tyler could afford to be conciliatory after his rival's lead disappeared overnight. "Now it is a race to the wire. May the best man win."

Brenda Lauksonen, David Lawson, and many other Smith staffers were furious. "They're trying to steal the nomination from us!" When Ralph Smith arrived for the packed morning staff meeting he received an earful. His calm demeanor and confidence soon dissipated any anger. Lena Watson said it best. "Senator Smith is a sure-fire winner, no matter what the odds."

Senator Bateson's delegates were still up for grabs. In California, voting was proportional. Walter Shrub III and the RNC chairman were lobbying Senator Bateson hard to throw his delegates to Hal Tyler. If he did the race would be a slam dunk for the senator from Texas. The *Dallas Morning News* praised the RNC's action. "Senator Ralph Smith has no place in the Republican Party."

Hal Tyler got on the phone to Senator Bateson. "Charlie, what are you waiting for?"

"I haven't made up my mind yet Hal."

"There's that little matter of where your campaign money went."

"What are you talking about?"

"C'mon Charlie. We know all about the $200,000 you, ah, misappropriated."

"Fuck you Hal."

"For God's sake Charlie, I don't give a fuck what you did with that money. We can't allow this nutcase Smith to win the nomination."

"I'll think about it Hal." Senator Bateson clicked off.

Two days after the rules change Charlie Bateson held a press conference. "The attempt by President Shrub and the RNC to throw this election to Senator Tyler is disgusting," he said. "In the interest of fairness I hereby assign all of my 57 delegates to Senator Ralph Smith." During this recitation Charlie Bateson was gleefully thinking, "Up yours, Tyler." This sentiment was not expressed verbally, however.

Charlie Bateson's action sorely pissed off President Walter Shrub III, who accused the senator from California of being "a sore loser" and "a traitor to his party." Hal Tyler vowed to make Bateson pay if he lost the nomination.

The national media and the blogs went crazy. Instead of the race being over after Super Tuesday it was just beginning. After the readjustment Tyler now had a lead of only 11 delegates over Senator Smith. The smaller states, not the big ones, would decide the Republican presidential nomination.

After the June 8th primaries in Montana and New Jersey, Hal Tyler still had a razor-thin 3 delegate lead over Ralph Smith, 1,211 to 1,208. 90 delegates were up for grabs. 1,255 delegates were needed to nominate.

At the morning pow-wow David Lawson was optimistic. "The three states left are all a bit quirky. We have as good a shot as Tyler."

It would all come down to the primaries in Wyoming, Alaska, and Nevada.

The Republican Party nominating process had become as exciting as a horse race. Gambling services were busier than a termite in a lumberyard.

Governor Joe Thompson of Illinois, a liberal with a lot of special interest support, had already sewn up the Democratic nomination.

That summer, cosmic events again intruded into the world's consciousness.

Some people began to notice that objects had a very faint halo around them, even in bright daylight. It looked like a soft glow, composed of constantly changing colors. The quality of the light reminded John of Goldenrod's universe of light. Persons who could perceive the halos were a small minority. But in any group of fifty or more there would be at least one who did.

On social media people drew pictures of the halos and posted them. There was no explanation for the increasing strength of the churning mist in the night skies all over the planet. The mist had grown more intense as the weeks passed. Scientists were increasingly disturbed by the baffling phenomenon. Not even Sag Carlson had an explanation.

On August 17th, the Wyoming Presidential Caucuses ended in a dead heat. 14 for Smith and 14 for Tyler. Exit polls showed Wyoming voters responding to the character issue. They hadn't forgotten Ralph Smith's true-blue conservative past. Those who voted for Tyler were afraid and wanted things to go back to normal.

"Our hope has to be Alaska," David Lawson said. "Lots of independent thinkers up there. We don't want to go into Nevada behind."

"Lots of die-hard conservatives too," Brenda said despondently. She was looking at the latest polls that showed Hal Tyler with an almost insurmountable 13 point lead in the state.

Three days before the Alaska Presidential Primary a group of fringe third parties, including the God's Light Party, held a news conference. They all threw their support to Senator Smith.

Kooks for Smith, said the *Los Angeles Times* in a one inch headline.

Weirdos Urge Smith Presidency, the *New York Post* wisecracked.

The *Dallas Morning News* ran an editorial. "Senator Smith Go Home – You are an Embarrassment to the Republican Party."

Social media and the blogs were in a frenzy. Voter participation in the primaries was at an all-time high.

In Alaska all was quiet on the Nutsoid Front.

"Our surveys tell us we still have a chance here," David Lawson said at the morning staff meeting. "We've come too far to give up. Let's get out there and work our butts off."

In Juneau Hal Tyler said:

> The lines are clearly drawn in this campaign. On the one hand we have a former conservative, Mr. Ralph Smith, who seems to be more interested in UFOs and ETs than in finding solutions that make sense to ordinary people. In these times of drastic change we need to go back to our roots. We need to get back to the tried and true, not go off on some new-age philosophical rampage. As my father used to say, "Fancy talk always sounds good on paper. But it doesn't pay the bills." It's time for a little common-sense in America! I stand for a strong defense, lower tax rates, and education reform. By the way Ralph, the next time you talk to your ET buddies wear a crystal around your neck!

The night before election day something extraordinary occurred that threw the Tyler camp into a frenzy.

In the night skies over Juneau, Anchorage, Fairbanks, Homer, Seward, Whittier, Cordova, and Valdez, a spectacular display of UFOs was seen. An Anchorage resident said, "At first I thought it was the Northern Lights but these things were moving. I saw cigar shaped ones, triangular ones, and saucer shaped ones. There were eight of them making right angle turns at fantastic speeds. I've never seen anything like it."

Photographs of the objects were in all of the papers and social media that morning. Videos popped up all over the WorldNet.

It was the main topic all day on Alaskan talk radio. "Eight cities. No way this is coincidence," was the only thing on which all could agree. Some said it was a precursor to an alien invasion. Others said that the motherships were ready to land and take the Chosen away to a planet of peace and plenty. Most people were frustrated and fearful.

When the votes were counted Ralph Smith secured 16 to Hal Tyler's 13.

This was the most historic presidential nominating process in history. Coming in to the very last primary in Nevada, the race was dead even at 1,238 delegates apiece.

The later, smaller state primaries were supposed to be an afterthought. Two weeks before the Nevada Presidential Primary the scene resembled the week before the Super Bowl. Hordes of media and political junkies descended on the Las Vegas, Henderson, and Reno areas. Bookies took bets so fast they could hardly keep up. Every hotel in the area was booked two days after the Alaska voting. The casinos were full and it was standing room only at every nightclub in the state. Political commentators shook their literary heads at the carnival atmosphere. They said that the Republican nominee for president would be indelibly tainted with the stigma of it all during the general election. They predicted an easy Democratic victory, especially if Ralph Smith emerged as the winner.

Hal Tyler sat in his luxurious suite of offices in North Las Vegas, lounging on the sofa. With him were his wife Barbara, his chief of staff, and his speechwriter, Larry Noon.

"OK Larry, here is where you earn your money," Tyler said. "Find me something these people will love. I don't care whether it's positive or negative."

"Nevada is a very conservative state so we shouldn't have any problems," Noon replied. "Especially considering the nut we're running against."

Hal looked up sharply. "That's what you said in Alaska!" He privately agreed with his speechwriter.

"Don't worry," Larry said confidently. "I just have to figure the angle."

Hal looked at his chief of staff, Bobo Costello. Costello was a tried and true Texan, born and raised on a cattle ranch outside of Lubbock. He had been a foreman on a drilling rig, started a successful corporate consulting business, and played classical music on the piano. A well-rounded guy who understood people and could

smell bullshit a mile away. Bobo also had a mean streak. Once while walking on
the streets in DC, a disreputable looking man had quickly come forward, screaming obscenities. Before his bodyguard could even react Bobo had immobilized the
guy with a straight right to the jaw and a left to the solar plexus. His bodyguard had
nodded appreciatively.

"Nice work. Couldn't a done it better myself."

Hal Tyler liked tough guys. He liked to think he was one himself. Hal had
grown up in Plano, a north Dallas suburb. During his senior year he had been a
star receiver on the Plano East high football team.

He remembered Coach Cap Baskins' motto to his receivers: "We *like* to go
over the middle." He had done so during the Division I championship game and
got a concussion. In all honesty he hadn't liked to go over the middle. But he did it
anyway. From football he had learned the meaning of duty, loyalty, and toughness.
The thought of Ralph Smith as president made his stomach turn. Even Joe Thompson would be an improvement! At least he understood the governor of Illinois.

Bobo called Governor Thompson the Genie. "Wave enough money in front
of his face and you get your wish."

Larry Noon spoke. "Hal, it's your call. If you want to attack Smith I can write
a real hum-dinger. My opinion is to play it safe. Unless we get more UFOs you're
going to win hands down."

"I agree," Bobo said. "Stick with the tried and true."

Hal looked across the richly appointed suite and saw a decorative crystal bowl
on one of the end tables. Suddenly, he started.

"What's the matter?" Noon said.

Hal continued to stare at the object. "Holy Mother of God."

"What?" Barbara said.

Hal looked at her. "Barbara, look at that bowl and tell me what you see."

"It's a crystal bowl Hal. What, are you seeing fairies like that idiot Smith?"

Tyler glanced at Larry.

"It's a fuckin' bowl Hal."

"Bobo?"

"It's an empty bowl. Probably should be something in it, is that it?" Costello
was trying to be helpful.

Hal Tyler hesitated. "Yeah, that's it. I'm paying top dollar for this place. Should
at least be a little fruit in there."

The eyes of Larry, Barbara, and Bobo met briefly. Larry shrugged. "I'll go get
some."

"I'll come with you," Bobo said.

That wasn't it at all. Hal Tyler had seen a multicolored halo around that bowl
and it had shocked him to his core. "All right guys, meeting's over. I think I'm going
to lie down for a while."

"I'm going for a walk," Barbara said. "I need to stretch my legs."

Hal Tyler didn't sleep. He spent the next half hour tying to convince himself he wasn't hallucinating. Each time he looked at that bowl he could see a faint halo of rippling, impossibly rich colors. Suddenly he grabbed his cell phone. He walked through the suite of rooms, satisfying himself that they were empty.

"Tony? This is Hal Tyler...yes...yes, that's right. Can you get everything set at your end?...good. We're going ahead. No! After, not before...All right, half now. I'll have it at the drop tomorrow by 5 p.m."

Ralph Smith was a lucky bastard. But this time the stakes were too high. Hal Tyler wasn't going to leave anything to chance.

43

"Ｗʜᴀᴛ are you going to say today, Ralph?" Freddie Rodriquez asked. The Smith for President speechwriter was feeling neglected. The Senator wrote everything himself now, by hand on sheets of yellow lined tablet paper. His desk was covered with them. David Lawson, the campaign manager, peeked over his boss' shoulder.

Ralph looked at the metal lamp on his desk, which had a very faint multi-colored halo around it. "On the policy front we're going to continue to push the balanced budget theme. We all know how important it is. And the usual stuff."

"You mean the unusual stuff," Rodriquez corrected.

"I mean the things people are afraid of and don't want to talk about. The things that just made us five mil. Policy issues are becoming less and less important."

"Yet people are living their lives like nothing has changed. The race has been all about traditional values. The usual stuff. The things I'm good at writing about!"

"People are frightened, Freddie. They know something unusual is happening in nature but want it all to go away. At the same time they want reassurance that things will turn out OK. It's why I have been emphasizing the character issue and the connection to God. It's the most important stuff I talk about. I believe in it."

Freddie Rodriquez shook his head but said nothing. He just kept his blinds closed at night like most people. Life goes on. The normal stuff is what keeps people going. He hoped the senator wouldn't blow it.

David Lawson gave the older man a friendly slap on the shoulder. "I sure hope you're right senator. If Hal Tyler wins this election we're all in trouble. The man has no understanding except raw ambition."

In Henderson, Nevada's second-largest city, Ralph Smith said:

My fellow Republicans, there are only two days left before the nomination will be decided here in Nevada. I don't know about you, but I
am one of those who can see the halos around many of the everyday
objects in our world. Some say these halos represent the imminent
Second Coming of Christ. Some say they are the work of the devil
and indicate a great tribulation about to be inflicted upon our people
for our sins. Others say it is a mass hallucination. One thing is clear:
over twenty percent of persons in the United States now say they see
the halos. Everyone can see the strange but beautiful sky blooms at
night.

It is obvious that we are living in unusual times, historic times. Many
say that the old paradigm is going away and the 'new age' is upon
us. I do not believe that. Everything we have accepted about the nature of our physical reality seems turned upside down. But in times
like these the traditional values of integrity, character, courage, and
honesty assume even greater importance. These times of uncertainty
force us all to take a personal gut check. I have undergone that process myself and in my speeches I have tried to communicate that to
you, the voters of this great country—

The cameras clicked loudly in the big hotel lobby. Ralph Smith paused to look
at his papers.

"Scumbag!" A man screamed just behind and to the right of the stage. "You're
a traitor to your country!" Two quick shots rang out. Ralph Smith fell to the floor.
Two Secret Service agents, an instant too late, flung themselves on top of him.
Amidst the screams, security wrestled the man to the ground.

Ralph Smith got up slowly and resumed his stance at the podium. He stood
silently for ten minutes and observed the chaos around him. Most of the people
nervously resumed their seats. Media members were in a frenzy. They tried to rush
the stage and interview the senator. The two holes in his suitcoat were elegant testimony to an assassination attempt. At a gesture from Ralph, security pushed them
back.

"That's a pretty cool customer," one of the Secret Service agents remarked.

"Yeah," his partner replied. "I think this guy is for real."

After twenty minutes or so a semblance of order was reestablished. Ralph
Smith began speaking again.

"Not to worry ladies and gentlemen." He unbuttoned his suitcoat and revealed
a thin grey vest. "I was wearing a bullet-proof vest you see. We had word that an
attempt would be made on my life during my stay in Nevada. We came prepared."
Ralph continued with his speech, promising to balance the budget.

In conclusion, I want to repeat what I have said in every speech I have given over the past year. The time for leaders and followers is over. It is time to return to those true Republican values of individual independence, strength of character, and integrity which every one of you listening to me tonight possesses in abundance. It is time to recognize that we are each responsible for the conditions of our lives. It is time for all of us to stand up and claim our birthright as sovereign American citizens. It is time for us to put away our differences and work together!

Tomorrow I want you to turn off all media and think about what kind of person you really want to be. I don't care whether you are a CEO of a major corporation or one of our grass roots Republican supporters in the trenches. I want to you to think about the highest possible future for yourself and hold on to that dream all day. And the next day, when you turn on your media again, if you hear or read anything that disagrees with what you have begun to believe about yourself, I want you to ignore it.

I am asking each and every one of you to trust what is in your hearts. Ignore the nay-sayers and embrace your dreams.

I am asking each and every one of you who resonates to this message to go to the polls on September 14th and cast your vote for Ralph Smith for President of the United States!

Hal Tyler and his campaign war team listened unbelievingly to the speech.

"What a weirdo!" one of his staffers said. "The guy survives an assassination attempt. Instead of talking about his bravery and his ability to lead in a crisis, he gives us a bunch of liberal nonsense."

"How does he get away with that stuff in a REPUBLICAN party nomination process?" another staffer said.

"It's unfathomable," Barbara Tyler said.

This sentiment echoed around the room.

Hal Tyler sat with his head in his hands, depressed. He snuck a peek at the crystal bowl beside him, hoping this time he wouldn't see the halo. But there it was. A beautiful, multicolored mist. Every so often he'd look up at the TV and see his enemy talking about things that were just beginning to make sense to him.

Snap out of it! Hal thought to himself. It's time to go over the middle. The trigger had already been pulled.

In 48 hours the nomination would be his.

On the night of the voting the Smith for President campaign staff sat around their TV sets.

"...CBS exit polls show that as of 7:37 p.m., Mountain Standard time, Ralph Smith is the winner of the Nevada Presidential Primary by a 53 to 47 margin..."

An explosion of sound erupted in the room. Champaign bottles were uncorked. Somebody grabbed the remote and changed the channel.

"...ABC news predicts that Ralph Smith has won the Republican Presidential nomination with a convincing 55 to 45 percent victory over Senator Hal Tyler of Texas..."

The phone began to ring. There were shouts of "speech!" In the hotel lobby Smith supporters began clamoring for a personal appearance.

"...NBC news predicts a victory by Senator Smith in the Nevada Republican primary by a 54 to 46 margin..."

Gloom prevailed at the Tyler campaign headquarters. Bobo Costello shook his head. "I can't believe we lost to that nutcase." Barbara Tyler was angry. "That sonofabitch Smith pulled a fast one on us! There's no way we lose an honest election to that kook here in Nevada."

Hal Tyler stood up. "Ladies and gentlemen, the battle is not lost until the votes are actually counted."

Just then the phones started ringing. "No, we're NOT going to concede...No! ...In case you've forgotten, a winner has not been officially declared...Yes! We believe that when the votes are counted Senator Tyler will be the victor. Good bye."

"That's telling 'em Bobo," Barbara said. "We're not going to let a bunch of mealy-mouthed liberals in the news media determine this election!"

"That's right!" Larry Noon said defiantly.

Despite the bravado a sense of false optimism pervaded the atmosphere in the room.

"...Senator Smith says he will not give a victory speech until the results are in..."

"Give him credit for that at least," said a staffer. Barbara glared at him. "Give him nothing, the bastard."

Out of the corner of her eye she saw a mocking but confident sneer on the face of her husband. What was that about?

At 2:30 a.m. everybody went to bed.

At 5:30 a.m. Barbara Tyler got up and went online. She couldn't believe what she was reading. The headlines in the *Review-Journal*, the *Sun*, the *Gazette-Journal*, and the *Appeal* all screamed:

Tyler Victory in Nevada! – Dewey vs. Truman Revisited

Shocked, she read further:

Exit pollsters are confounded by the razor-thin Tyler victory in Nevada, by a 50.5 to 49.5 margin. Ananda Dev, chief statistician for NBC News, made a statement for NBC News. "I can't understand it. Mathematically it's impossible. We showed a comfortable 8 point victory for Senator Smith. Our results are accurate to plus or minus

3 percent. Even under the worst case scenario Smith should have won."

This sentiment was echoed by Paul Trybus, statistician at the University of Las Vegas. "All exit polling showed Smith with a 6 to 10 point victory. We've never been wrong before. I just can't understand it."

A spokesman for the Tyler campaign responded. "They got it wrong that's all. I've never had any confidence in pollsters and statistics. That old saw by Mark Twain came true."

For those of you who don't remember Twain said, "There are lies, there are damned lies, and there are statistics."

The old boy was right this time. The Republican presidential nominee is Senator Hal Tyler of Texas.

Barbara Tyler shrieked with joy, waking up everyone in the Tyler suite. Disbelief turned to joy as the team slowly assimilated the information. "It's true then," Larry Noon said. He had been up until 3 listening to the rumors on the podcasts and on the radio. "Incredible!"

Soon there were shouts and laughter. The champagne was dug out from its place of exile in the corner and uncorked. "To the next President of the United States!" was the cry all round.

Hal Tyler acknowledged their acclaim. With a slight sneer he said, "Victory!"

"Ain't it sweet!" Bobo exclaimed.

"Oh yes. Sweet." As the others partied Hal Tyler walked into his private suite and lay down on the bed.

"Is the senator ill?" someone asked.

"Probably just tired," a voice answered.

Barbara was ecstatic as she followed her husband into the bedroom. "Finally! All of our dreams have finally come true. The White House!"

"The White House." Hal spoke flatly but she was too excited to notice.

"I'm tired Barb. Could you keep 'em out of here for an hour or so?"

Twenty four hours later Senator Smith made a gracious concession speech. It was over. The media circus departed. Las Vegas, Reno, Henderson, and Carson City returned to a semblance of normalcy.

Two days after the Nevada primary a story appeared on page 7 of the *Las Vegas Sun:*

An election official last night charged voting irregularities at five North Las Vegas polling stations. The official, James McClelland, said, "There are votes counted that shouldn't be there." McClelland said he had called in a FEC representative to hear the charges. There is little Federal officials can do about the final results. State and county law enforcement officials are looking into the matter.

The Tyler campaign went back to Texas to prepare for the general election. The Smith campaign did not disband. Lena Watson burst into the office and pointed out the story to David Lawson. "Good girl," he said in his Australian accent. "Sharp as a tack." Their eyes met briefly. David Lawson felt a surge of electrical energy down his spine. He caught her eyes again. "Want to get some breakfast?"

Three days after the *Sun* story an article appeared on the left hand column of the front page of the *New York Times*.

Voting Irregularities Confirmed in Nevada Primary

State and county law enforcement officials in Nevada have confirmed voting abnormalities at 17 polling stations in North Las Vegas, Reno, and Henderson. A Federal Elections Commission official, Lucius Brown, told the New York Times yesterday that voting machine counts were altered when reported from local polling stations to district and county election officials. "Whoever did this forgot that the new machines we installed last year have a small backup storage capacity. We were able to find the correct tallies."

Indications are that the Tyler campaign had approximately 4,200 votes added to their total. Without these additions, the official said, the primary results would have resembled exit polling forecasts.

Bobo Costello walked into Hal Tyler's private office with his tablet. He pointed to a story in the *Dallas Morning News*. "Read that, look me in the eye, and deny it."

Hal Tyler saw the headline.

Tyler Campaign Election Violations Charged

Hal shrugged. "That's what they're saying. Bunch of damn liberals."

Bobo stood there, his eyes inspecting the man at the desk. Costello had not really observed the senator carefully since the morning of the startling turnaround in Vegas. Now he noticed the paunchy eyes, the haggard look, the rumpled clothing, and the slumped posture. Especially the uncombed hair and the scraggle of beard that covered his face.

Bobo Costello was shocked. His boss was a man careful about his appearance and his physical conditioning. Bobo had never seen Senator Tyler with so much as a hair out of place. Hal now looked like a wizened old man.

"Boss?"

Hal Tyler met his gaze. Something inside Bobo turned over and he felt sick. The eyes of the man before him were foreign, the being inside a shriveled husk of his former self.

"I had to do it," Tyler murmured blindly. "It was the only way. It's what we've worked for so hard all these years..." the words trailed off. Hal's campaign manager saw his boss idly twirling his finger along the rim of that damn crystal bowl, his eyes glazed over.

Bobo realized he had been holding his breath and he let it out all at once. Then he turned. Without a backward glance he, walked out of the room, got into his car, and began to drive.

Hal Tyler knew he wasn't coming back.

It had all gone wrong, terribly wrong. A few votes here and there, enough to put him over the top. The country couldn't take a Ralph Smith presidency. He had done it for the good of America....

Hal ripped his eyes off the crystal bowl. He regarded the heavy brass pen holder that had accompanied him on all his campaigns. It too began to ripple softly with color.

The blood left his face. He understood, completely, that Smith was right. He had been right all along. There was something grand about to happen. He could feel it now but he had missed his opportunity to be a part of it. Just one bad decision in a storied political career, that's all it was. Just one bad decision, motivated from ambition...

Hal Tyler's head was now on the desk. He was ruined. Finished. He'd be kicked out of the Senate in disgrace. The Tyler name would be forever stained.

There was plenty of money. What use was that now?

He couldn't bear to see the look on Barbara's face, on his son Hal Jr.'s face. He had let them all down.

Hal Tyler faced up to the fact that when the going really got tough, he hadn't had the guts to go over the middle. His life was a sham.

He'd been living a lie ever since the day he had woken up on that stretcher. The safety had been head-hunting all day. When Hal saw him coming his guts turned to water. He dropped the perfectly thrown pass that would have given Plano East the state title.

He was a failure, always had been.

With his right hand Hal Tyler slowly reached into the top desk drawer. His fingers felt for the comfort of his old Colt .45 revolver. There was always one bullet in the chamber, ready to fire. Funny, he thought, why only one?

Hal grasped the cool steel, placed the barrel to his temple, and pulled the trigger.

The next day Senator Ralph Smith, Republican nominee for President of the United States, called a news conference.

> It is with a very heavy heart that I speak to you today. The death of my friend Hal Tyler has been a great shock to me and my family, and to the country. Hal and I had our differences over the years but I always

respected him as a man of principle. The Republican Party has been deprived of a great conservative voice.

My friend Frank Faircloth called me today and read a passage from the Bible, a message of hope: "It was meet that we should make merry, and be glad: for this thy brother was dead, and is alive again; and was lost, and is found." (Luke 15:32).

Hal Tyler is not dead; only his body has gone. The soul of Hal Tyler lives on, safe in the arms of God.

As with the Prodigal Son God always welcomes us back into His arms, no matter what our transgressions. So let us take the opportunity to turn this tragedy into a blessing. During hard times my father always told us not to look to others, but deep inside for strength. Let us look inside to our innermost divine selves and find that kernel of wisdom, confidence, and well-being which is always there, given to us by God.

Let us be thankful for what we have, and hold within ourselves the idea of love. Love and compassion are the most important aspects of God, and all of us were made in His image. In that spirit let me send my own personal message of love to each and every one of you, and especially to the Tyler family and loved ones.

Today the Ralph Smith campaign will mourn. Tomorrow we will roll up our sleeves and get back to work. That is what Hal would have wanted us to do. As always, let us know your opinions at RalphSmithPresident.org.

Frank Faircloth was sitting at his home in Tucson, watching Senator Smith's acceptance speech. He had tears in his eyes, tears of happiness. He had picked a winner. Ralph Smith had finally seen the light of God.

Frank grabbed his handkerchief and wiped his eyes.

"Don't be embarrassed dear," his wife said. "I'm crying too."

"You're a woman," Frank replied.

John, Genevieve, Robert, Rachel, and Mats were sitting around the TV set at the Full Moon. A dozen others sat in the little cafe at the back of the store. All stared at Ralph Smith as he gave his speech.

Afterwards, Robert turned to one of the men. The speech had been delivered softly but with incredible power and conviction. It was more like a sermon. Or a benediction. "How can this guy be a Republican?"

"Look – the reporters are just sitting there," someone said.

"Usually they're screaming questions like a bunch of maniacs."

Mats said, "I might even vote this election."

They all laughed. Everyone could feel the love in the room.

Three weeks before the presidential election it appeared that the contest had already been decided.

During the presidential debates Joe Thompson was intelligent, soft spoken, and informed. But Ralph Smith had already taken his positions away. The political debate was turned on its head as Thompson took the traditional Republican lines of strong defense, national security issues, crime and drugs, and foreign affairs. The Thompson campaign was playing right into the hands of Smith. Thompson was a moderate at heart, not a conservative. Governor Thompson offered no clear alternative. Those who hated Smith had nowhere to go. The Smith campaign never varied from its targeted audience. His message seemed to strike a chord with a growing number of people.

The family sat around the TV after the last of the presidential debates. Rachel said, "Smith almost sounds like Swami Muktananda."

"Swami who?" Robert said.

"I agree," Michael Walters said. "Senator Smith has undergone a genuine spiritual awakening." He looked over at Alicia, took her hand, and smiled broadly. "Just as I have."

After the debate, those who could perceive the energy halos said they were able to see a similar halo of energy around Senator Smith's body.

Senator Smith had been talking about issues closer to Democratic hearts than Republican ones during the Republican nomination process. His name recognition was at 98%. About half of those who considered themselves true conservatives despised Ralph Smith as a dangerous radical. Supporters of the current administration of Walter Shrub III desperately tried to organize a third party candidacy in the form of Congressman Jokisch. The Congressman declined. He was looking toward the next election. The opposition to Senator Smith were bickering amongst themselves and could not get organized. They watched in dismay as Ralph Smith sewed up the election by the middle of October. Political commentators predicted the lowest turnout in history come November. Alienated voters vowed to abstain from casting a ballot.

Salat Toor of Orion was depressed. That damn earthian Smith! Ralph Smith, he had confidently predicted, would lead the United States and the world toward a centralized world government. He had been completely saturated with the correct memes. He had been groomed for this very election at this very time. Oh, the Plan's culmination would have been glorious! But just when victory was within their grasp Ralph Smith had done an about-face. He had broken free from his conditioning.

The earthian Smith had taken himself fully in hand and done the impossible. These humans seemed to mutate, like a bacterial culture, in odiously unpredictable ways.

Salat Toor thought of the beauty and sophistication of the Plan and how swiftly it had been derailed. Even at this late hour, however, there was still time to turn it around.

The key was repetition. After ten centuries Orion finally understood that even the stupidest and most illogical meme, if repeated often enough, could become accepted. Earthians simply didn't understand the importance of their own thoughts.

One day Salat Toor was bored and watched earthian TV all day, admiring his handiwork.

"Psoriasis sufferers! Get Blooger, with 'T-cell blocker'; fights the abnormal T cell activity that causes ugly skin patches."

What were the hidden memes? He listed them in order: Psoriasis, suffer, block, fight, abnormal, ugly. All in one innocent sentence.

"August is Psoriasis Awareness Month. Help us raise awareness about psoriasis and psoriatic arthritis." That's right. Raise awareness of it and get it activated in your consciousness. Then you too may become a psoriasis sufferer. See the advertisement and begin to resonate to psoriasis. Or cancer. Or war. The list was endless.

Every galactic citizen understood from infancy that physical abnormalities stemmed entirely from the misalignment of energy within the Vessel of Life that surrounded the body.

For just an instant Salat Toor felt a pang of guilt. In many ways he had more in common with earthians than with his own people. These earthians were devious, aggressive, and adventurous, with just the right amount of healthy paranoia thrown in.

The earthian planet was a galactic anomaly. It was a remarkable place, a horrible, dangerous, awful, beautiful, and exciting place! Like a powerful addiction it got into your blood and contaminated your very soul.

The heritage and history of humanity gave them a power that not even Orion scientists could calculate. Earthians appeared to be lowly mongrels but in reality they were like a huge volcano. Capped, but ready to explode at any moment. When that explosion occurred nothing in the galaxy could stop it.

Salat Toor's eyes narrowed and his lips firmed. Ralph Smith was perfectly positioned. For better or worse he was still their man. The earthian would have to be jolted back to reality. The assassination attempt had been a failure. The shock should have jolted Smith back to his old "pit bull" mentality. The power of the Frankel meditation was, apparently, still too strong.

He would have to intervene personally. He would personally confront this earthian. Toor smiled to himself. It was said that the hypnotic power of his gaze had a powerful effect.

"Prepare the 'Lord Toor' for departure to the earthian planet," he ordered his personal staff. "Gather the Court and assemble the best scientists and diplomats.

Allow embarkation only to those who cannot be distinguished from earthians. We arrive two weeks before the election in the United States."

The Court would be present to observe his success. They would travel in style, in Orion's finest and most luxurious ship. Until then, serious meditation would be necessary. To be exposed to the bombardment of earthian thought again would require all of his powers of concentration. He didn't know how earthians could take it.

They couldn't of course! Even the healthiest of them only lived 80 years or so.

Salat Toor laughed to himself as he thought of what was in store for Mr. Ralph Smith.

44

SALAT Toor might have been gravely concerned had he any inkling of the rapidly changing developments on Otone.

A coalition of civilizations from every culture that had contributed to earth developments over the last four million years had assembled. A specially prepared chamber had been prepared to house the various life forms. The conference gathered on one of the artificial moons that orbited Otone, the capital planet of the Deneb sector.

These conference moons were famous throughout the galaxy, as Deneb was the diplomatic hub of Galaxy 6. Disputes between sectors were often resolved here, with help from their friends from Sirius if the going got tough. Each conference chamber was situated within a bubble on the moon's surface, providing a breathtaking view of the starfield. The structure was dotted with landing areas for spacecraft, affording easy access in and out. In galactic diplomacy, abrupt departures were encouraged when tempers rose too high. Everyone knew that an angry delegate is an irrational one. It was understood that a successful outcome depended upon the satisfaction of all participants. Galactic diplomacy was often tedious. Cordial relations between sectors was deemed of ultimate importance. It was a formula that had worked for over 4 billion years.

On this day the conference bubble was filled with excited chatter. Lyrans, Vegans, the delegation of heavy planet beings from the Procyon sector, the beautiful and delicate creatures from Antares and Betelgeuse, the small brown-skinned Sirians, the light-skinned Pleiadians, were all represented. There were delegations from Arcturus, Pollux, Draco, Cassiopeia, Canopus, and the Zeta sector; from Fomalhaut, Altair, and dozens more.

Because genotypes varied widely, special arrangements were required. The delegates from Fomalhaut needed heated and irradiated spaces in order to feel comfortable. The facilities here were designed with these considerations in mind.

The discussions were led by the delegates from Deneb and Sirius, with assistance from Orion and Lyra. These were human genotypes most closely resembling earthians and whose consciousness could best cope with the earthian meme environment.

The great Olatida Ogunfatidime himself led the Denebian contingent and opened the proceedings. He stood next to the Lyran representative Arkyn Thorlief, with his fiery red hair, pale white skin, and impossibly blue eyes. The intensely black Denebian and the almost pure white Lyran made quite a contrast. Both races were tall by earthian standards, reaching an average height of 7 feet. Lyrans were muscular, with huge heads, gigantic barrel chests, and legs like tree trunks. The Denebians were lithe, slender, and graceful.

Olatida Ogunfatidime wore a headset, as did all of the delegates. The headsets sent his thought impulses to each of them. However, it was still correct protocol to speak in Galactic Standard. Some preferred it.

The musical voice of Olatida Ogunfatidime filled the conference space:

"Oh wonderful delegates from the far reaches of our beautiful galaxy and beyond, welcome! Welcome my friends, as we assemble here in Six Galactic Central to renew old acquaintances and re-establish community. Let us make this gathering a celebration of our great, collective heritage! Today we welcome some very distinguished guests, delegations from the entire Twelve Galaxies!"

[extended applause, greetings and introductions].

Many of the delegates were awed by the presence of the Illirian delegate.

This being came from Galaxy 11, where all of the planets containing life were gas giants. It arrived in an immense bubble of poisonous gases. A special container was reserved for It, because the space within must be radically cooled. Each of these great beings could easily pick up the thought transmissions of all present. This led to a little nervousness among some in attendance. Nothing whatsoever was known about Illlirian culture, for they kept to themselves. Illirians were asexual, reproducing or cloning themselves. They had the power to project their minds anywhere in the universe. Each of their planets had been seeded by mental projection, activating and molding the biological "soup" of their atmospheres into compatibility with their strange and bizarre form of life.

All of the assembled representatives were impressed. Representatives from all twelve galaxies were together in one room.

Olatida Ogunfatidime continued. "We have come here to discuss the situation known as the Event. And secondarily, the present situation upon the earthian planet. First we will deal with the earthian issue. That is mainly an internal affair within our own galaxy..."

Ogunfatidime stopped abruptly. A thought pulse of unimaginable clarity had come from the great Illirian and into his consciousness. It said, "The earthian issue also concerns us in Galaxy 11."

Ogunfatidime had never felt a thought of such power and crystalline purity. He continued.

"A faction of our brothers and sisters from Orion called the Traditionalists have been directly implementing a plan to control and direct earthian consciousness. It is the Denebian opinion that the situation on the earthian planet is intimately connected with what will happen during the cosmic event that is rapidly approaching."

[a buzz of voices erupted in the big conference room]

"Some are very concerned that our Orion friends will prevent the earthians from making an evolutionary leap forward, which could benefit a rather stagnant culture here in Galaxy 6. We know that there will be a demand for action at this gathering to foil the Orion plan. There is also a strong minority of sentiment the other way."

Kenet Toor, brother-in-law to Melet Toor, sat very close to the Denebian. He nodded his head in approval.

"Our prediction is that the conference will never come to unanimity of agreement. The issue is too important to act without full concordance. Our friends from Sirius concur with us."

Now the delegates broke out into excited chatter. After the hubbub died down, Ogunfatidime continued.

"Our suggestion is that a galactic delegation go to earth. In person we will place all before the earthians, acting upon the answers we receive from them."

An angry Kenet Toor demanded to be heard. He had orders not to allow anything that would interfere with events on the earthian planet. "This is outrageous. Are the entire Twelve Galaxies against us? We demand that this conference support the acknowledged doctrine of non-interference."

The attendees recognized this outburst as utterly self-serving. The Illirian delegate began pulsing to all attendees. Conversation stopped as the thought impulses of the great being resonated within the consciousness of all present.

"I am [Origin 0 (0, 0)]. I concur wholly with the Denebian," It said.

Now a startled gasp escaped the lips of many of the assembled delegates. [Origin 0 (0, 0)] was the legendary consciousness that had originated the entire Illirian race! A great honor indeed to be addressed by such a presence. It was well known in the Twelve that life developed in Galaxy 11 long before any of the others. This being was at least 10 billion galactic standard years old. The delegates listened with rapt attention as the Illirian pulsed. "None of you in the Twelve know that these earthians also have our essence within them."

Excited chatter again broke out in the room.

"Yes, conference delegates. Recall the global catastrophic event upon the earthian planet 60 million galactic standard years ago."

A multimedia template of thought pulsed into the consciousness of all present. It showed a gigantic meteor crashing into the planet. All higher life forms were destroyed.

"At that time templates from our galaxy and our life forms were inserted into the grids of the earthian planet. Our templates are of course necessarily subtle and latent, owing to our utterly opposite biology. Nevertheless, we are proud to also consider the earthians as our extrusions. We believe that when earthians break out of the imprisonment of their consciousness, our Illirian templates will provide tremendous power. You will see a merging of the abilities of the 11 galaxies with our own. Therefore, we can no longer allow anything to disturb their evolutionary progress. Our calculations [data stream sent] show that for optimum species growth, a meeting with the earthians is now required [sideband thought: intellectual satisfaction]."

An impression of tremendous power filled the minds of every delegate. Those with psychic abilities received a concentrated burst of symbolic logic and a complex matrix of mathematical data that accompanied Its statement. Each of them felt as if the Illirian carried a step-down transformer. Not for its convenience, but for their safety.

Nahimana, the famous intuitive from Galaxy 12, was seen to hold her head in agony.

Kenet Toor blanched. A hush settled over the room as each delegate began to consider the implications of the Illirian's decree. The Illirians were rumored to have the power to directly affect the universal field, which meant the power of action-at-great-distances. It was rumored that Illirians could combine their individual intelligences into a galaxy-wide Superbeing. It was said that Illirian thought was so powerful it could instantaneously destroy all life in the other 11 galaxies. Kenet Toor ground his teeth in frustration. Foiled again! Whether these rumors were true or not, no one wanted to test their validity.

The room was now entirely empty of sound and thought. All eyes were upon the sealed container holding the Illirian.

"We recommend that the conference follow the suggestion of the Denebian." It was said with such complete authority and intention that everyone understood it as a command. Suddenly, the Illirian container rose from its sealed enclosure and exited the conference area.

Kenet Toor was crushed, as were a number of other representatives who were in favor of no action. Olatida Ogunfatidime's face broke into a broad smile.

"Denebian, I demand an explanation," said Kenet Toor.

"I, too, echo that demand," said the big Lyran. "Its statement sounded tantamount to an order."

"My dear fellow delegates, I must share with you my realization during Its speech." Ogunfatidime paused for effect. "We have had the wrong impression of our neighbors from Galaxy 11. They are engaged in a grand experiment to create a new life form, to bridge our consciousness and physical format with theirs. It appears that Illirians have been searching the universe for compatible consciousness without success. For eons the Illirians have searched in vain for life who might understand their utterly unique perspective." He laughed. "Far from being a threat to us, these beings are like a lonely man seeking a lover."

Only the stature of the Denebian prevented an outburst of opposition. There were confused glances all around the room, and some disgruntled muttering.

"Perhaps you are reading too much into Its statement," said the representative from the Betelgeuse sector, a delicately built humanoid with translucent orange-red skin. These beings come from cool suns of spectral type M. Their planets exhibit the most homogenous environments of any in the galaxy. "The content of Its thought is very explicit with no sidebands."

Ogunfatidime merely smiled. "Very faint, to be sure."

All of the delegates understood the implied meaning.

"Perhaps we should get back to the subject," the delegate from Sirius gently suggested.

"Yes," said the Pleiadian representative, a delicately built humanoid with very light skin and black hair. The Pleidians, next to the Orions, were fairly close genetically to earthians except for their incredibly large liquid eyes and small mouths. "My sector has one of our great motherships ready to ferry all who wish to make the journey to earth. I think," he said with a smile, "that we should make the trip in style. There is no hurry. At a leisurely pace we may arrive on earth in two weeks from our present position. That will give us time to get reacquainted. We can discuss our common approach to the upcoming Event and formulate a common introduction to the earthians."

This suggestion was greeted by enthusiastic and unanimous agreement amongst all present.

Pleiadian hospitality was legendary, and their ships the finest in the galaxy. The volume of these pleasure craft are measured in cubic miles. They feature parks and gardens, beautifully sculptured plazas, courts, ball rooms, museums with galactic culture on display, gaming and sporting areas, intricately designed temples for meditation and relaxation, concert halls, large open dining spaces which encouraged beings to congregate, and a full complement of galactic chefs ready and eager to prepare even the most obscure delicacy for any visitor. And, of course, sumptuous living quarters. No one in the galaxy ever refused a Pleiadian invitation. To wangle an embarkation pass had become part of galactic diplomacy. Pleiadian boarding passes are bought and sold. They are an accepted form of galactic currency, reflecting their great value.

Even Kenet Toor was mollified. The unexpected presence of the Illirian delegate completely excused his failure to prevent galactic intervention on the earthian planet. Even Tiriak Delnek himself, much as he would desire to do so, could not poison the ear of Lord Toor against him. His butt, as the earthians would say, was covered. The Orion delegate smiled. He would bring his favorite concubine on the Pleiadian ship. The journey would now be quite an enjoyable one.

The ship was to depart in one galactic day.

Walter Shrub III, President of the United States, was having a difficult time dealing with the idea of the two term limitation. He sat in the Oval Office commiserating with his Attorney General, Bradley Tot.

"I can't imagine that fool Smith occupying this chair," the President said. "I can hardly get to sleep for the thought of it."

"I've been grinding my teeth for the last two months so badly I popped off my gold cap," Tot replied.

"What a jerk," Shrub said. "I watched the entire campaign and I still can't figure out how he did it."

"If you ever do, tell me. That bastard is going to ruin this country."

"If he thinks he's going to change anything he's crazy. He has no idea what he's dealing with," the president said.

Just then, the two men heard a crash. The room became pressurized. Both men swallowed, their ears popping.

"Sounded like a window just blew out," Tot said.

Shrub went to the long narrow window and looked out. "Oh my God."

"What's the matter?" Tot said. One good thing about a two term limitation: he wouldn't have to listen to this moron any longer. As much as he hated Democrats and liberals, they weren't far off in their portrayal of this guy.

Shrub stood at the window with his jaw open, a vacant stare on his face.

Tot moved over to the window and almost pissed his pants. Hovering 200 feet above the White House lawn was a monstrous glowing white craft. His eyes could not see the extent of it from his limited window view. Tot raced out to the lawn, leaving the president staring, slack-jawed.

"Armageddon," Shrub whispered to himself. "God's retribution." The President of the United States sank to his knees and cupped his hands together. "Forgive me O Lord. I am a sinner. We are not worthy. Our lives are forfeit, for we have failed You."

Security burst into the room. "Mr. President! Are you all right?" Agent Pastore observed the Commander in Chief on his knees with his head bowed in prayer, muttering.

"Come sir, see what is out front!" the Secret Service man said. "You won't believe it!"

The president was unresponsive.

Bradley Tot got outside and looked up. This time he really did piss his pants. A monstrous football shaped object literally filled the sky. At first he thought the moon had broken free from its orbit and had parked itself above the White House. Whatever it was, it was hovering absolutely motionless between the White House and the Ellipse. His knowledge of aircraft told him it was impossible, especially for something of this size. Tot's eyes travelled to the east and could barely discern the end of it, and similarly to the west. It must be several miles about its long axis. Standing underneath the belly of the ship, he could not determine its height. Tot only perceived a slow curve rising up to the north as the fuselage of the immense craft gradually curved upward. The ship's skin was creamy white, soft looking. The hull emitted a pleasant glow.

The realization of its presence hit him like a punch to the solar plexus. He lost his breath: A mothership!

As urine trickled down his leg, Tot understood somehow that the craft wasn't hostile. In fact, it was beautiful. His mind began to clear. He felt something funny tugging at his heart.

Bradley Tot's past flashed before his eyes. In an instant his life became meaningless. The political infighting, the struggle against evildoers, the attempt to mold society in the image of the Good. That was all bullshit now. Good Lord, a mothership! The kooks and the retards and the crazies were right! The goddammed softy liberals. How could it be?

Tot felt himself growing faint. The last thing he remembered as his body hit the ground was the fresh, sweet smell of grass.

A camera crew from one of the local TV stations raced to the scene. The guards at the gateways around the building abandoned their posts, staring upward. More and more camera crews stationed themselves around the White House. Tourists raced up from Pennsylvania Avenue, 15th, and 17th streets to fill the Ellipse. Traffic came to a standstill and people got out of their cars. The entire city came to a halt. The craft was visible for miles.

The word spread quickly across the planet.

In New Delhi, the Indian Prime Minister spoke with disgust. "Of course it had to happen in the United States. Why couldn't they have landed here?"

In Moscow, Russians were cheering. "Me first! Beam me up Scotty!"

In Lhasa, the Tibetan ruling council sat quietly, nodding their heads. "Now the planetary imbalances will be righted," they agreed.

In the Southwest desert, Hopi elders gathered around their TV. "It has come to pass," they said. "Now all that has been damaged will begin to be made whole again."

In Mali, the Dogon people were not surprised. Their legends said that another would follow the message of the first.

Billions watched as a tiny bubble emerged from the belly of the mothership.

John and Genevieve were teaching in their seminar room when someone burst in. "Turn on the TV, quick!" He raced to the television suspended from the ceiling and turned it on.

In the Full Moon, people were going crazy. The browsers all crowded around Mats' set. Others were watching on their mobiles.

The translucent bubble slowly reached the ground. Olatida Ogunfatidime stepped out. Wearing ceremonial white robes and decorative jewelry, the tall African-looking man beamed as he stood silently before the assembled multitudes for several minutes.

Demitrius Johnson was standing in 35th Street in a rundown DC neighborhood. He nudged Rodney White. "Hey Rodney, look at that."

"Whoo-whoo, look at that nigga! The first ET to walk out of a spaceship and he's a black man!"

"A real *black* black man. And what a ship. I love it!"

"What's he gonna do?"

"Maybe he's here to take all the white people away." Rodney nodded upward. "Looks like it's big enough."

"Uh-huh," Demitrius said. He envisioned the ship erupting with warriors, spilling onto the streets and establishing a new regime where everyone could get a fair deal.

"Nah, he gonna give them a lecture." Rodney looked at his friend. "White people are confused, everybody knows that. But what took them so long? This nigga is 300 years late!"

One hundred feet away William Buehler, a corporate lobbyist, turned to his friend Orson. "Oh-oh, we might be in trouble." Orson Kohl nodded his head seriously as he gazed at Ogunfatidime, looking like an African king.

Demitrius and Rodney were not far off in their assessment. In the backs of their minds, many of those who worked in DC felt a pang of fear in their gut and wondered whether the purpose of the giant craft was indeed a leveling of the playing field.

A minority of those gathered under the spacecraft simply rejoiced and felt a great release, as if a gigantic burden had been removed from their psyche. Here was living proof that the earth is not alone in the universe.

Ogunfatidime picked up on the joy, passion, fear, and worry. The polarity and intensity of emotions here was like nothing he had ever experienced.

Suddenly a voice was heard by the multitude. It seemed to be inside their heads and resonate through the air.

"Greetings, Earthians! I am Olatida Ogunfatidime, from the star you call Deneb. We have arrived with representatives from the Twelve Galaxies for a pow-wow. We would like you to assemble your delegates at the building you call the United Nations in one week's time, at noon on November the 4th. Until that time, 'memmalla ogonde pioritula.'"

The bubble reformed and carried the man back to the ship.

Not a sound could be heard except the slight rustle of what remained of the fall leaves. The ship continued to hang suspended, utterly silent and still.

For the next seven days no activity of any kind was observed from the craft. Air Force fighters inspected every inch of the ship but reported no doors, rivets, seams, or blemishes of any kind on the fuselage. Attempts to penetrate the hull were unsuccessful. Explosive devices failed to detonate when in close proximity to the ship.

After that, small airplanes began to land upon it. People had picnics on the hull. The glow of energy emitted from the ship was visible for about 100 feet. People reported that contact with it generated a feeling of well being. A Hindu holy man pronounced that the ship was giving Darshan.

Except for essential services like farming and food distribution, world commerce came to a halt. The planet held its collective breath.

President Walter Shrub III maintained his prayer vigil.

The Lord Toor arrived just in time to observe the proceedings. Salat Toor screamed with rage as he recognized the gigantic Pleiadian craft. He knew that any action on his part would now be impossible. But there was nothing he could do. Like all of humanity he had to wait and watch.

"Mr. President, are you going to New York?" said his Chief of Staff. The President was at his desk in the Oval Office. Every so often he would get up and look out the window. He still had not ventured outside. "No Barney. I'll be here in the White House, on duty, and praying for a peaceful outcome."

"A peaceful outcome sir?"

"The time of deliverance, or destruction, is now upon us. We are being judged. Only God knows how the scales will tip. I will be praying to God that within the hearts of mankind there is enough goodness to overcome our terrible sins."

Barney Schlesinger was confused. "Have you seen the ET, sir? He looks just like the president of Nigeria, except he's a foot taller. He just wants to talk with us."

"God works in mysterious ways," the president whispered. He returned to the papers on his desk, his hands folded upon it. "Ask the men in uniform to pray for me as I undertake this great responsibility," Walter Shrub III said.

"Yes sir," Schlesinger replied. He slowly closed the door.

On a warm November 4th, precisely at noon, a bubble arrived from the ship at the United Nations building in New York. Three humanoids stepped out. Olatida Ogunfatidime in his white robes was first, followed by a diminutive Sirian known to the Twelve Galaxies as Silla Oralie. The giant Arkyn Thorlief from Lyra was third. The crowds around the building oohed and ahhed. "That lady looks Indian!" someone said, pointing to the Sirian. It was true. Oralie wore the thin silk-like garments favored by her people. She wore them in layers and as she walked they changed color, reflecting her mood. Many of the women were openly admiring. "I want a dress like that honey!" one of them shouted.

"They look almost like us!" a man said.

"Wow, look at that hombre," Aurilio Rodriquez said, pointing to the Lyran giant. Well over 7 feet tall with flaming red hair and pale white skin, he resembled a massive oak tree. When he walked the ground practically vibrated.

The three ETs were smiling, evidently enjoying themselves. They stood for several minutes outside, allowing the crowds to get a good look. They probed the press of humanity in front of them, attempting to ascertain the precise characteristics of their consciousness. Then, slowly and majestically, they walked into the building. The three were greeted by a U.N. staff member. "Come this way," she said tentatively.

The corridors were lined with spectators, all of them silent and a little afraid. Sandwiched between the tall, lithe Denebian and the giant Lyran, Oralie would have gone unnoticed but for her beautiful robes, which shimmered in a fascinating pattern of blues, greens, and golds. The three were led to the General Assembly, where the heads of government were already assembled. Three chairs had been placed at the dais in front. Cameras were everywhere. The feed was broadcast live around the planet. Over the objections of the Shrub administration, it was agreed that the current president of the Security Council would greet the visitors and make the introductions for humanity.

The three ETs walked to the front and stood. Despite outward appearances all three were having a difficult time adjusting to psychic bombardment of the earthian meme structure.

Silla Oralie was shocked. She had not been on earth in over a hundred years. Her analysis of the mass consciousness revealed that certain negative memes were strongly amplified. She immediately recognized the influence of Orion. However, there was also a powerful stream of harmony within this ocean. Yes, and growing more dominant. She smiled. Ignoring the enturbulated thought and linking her consciousness to the beautiful, she regained her composure.

Thorlief was amazed. Since arriving one week ago he had felt immersed in a battle zone. As the gigantic Pleiadian ship approached the earth's solar system he felt a change in the fabric of space itself, a building of pressure. As they entered earthian space he felt like he had been immersed in a psychic high-G chamber.

Olatida Ogunfatidime was ecstatic. His consciousness floated over all of it. He sensed here an untapped, unrecognized, raw power about to explode. The poor Orions. He had not been here more than a few days before he was able to discern how hopeless was their silly Plan. They were trying to put a high energy plasma into a paper bag.

Ogunfatidime observed the hesitant approach of the little earthian toward the three. The room was utterly silent except for the click of cameras and an occasional cough. He could tell the assembled earthians were anxious and fearful.

Chiang Liu-Chen moved timidly toward the dais. He spoke nervously. "Welcome, visitors to earth." He was so nervous he dropped his papers. "You seem to have us at a disadvantage."

Everyone thought it was funny, thinking of the gigantic ship hovering over the White House. The assembled earthians were afraid to laugh for fear of offending the ETs. The big Lyran saw this and began to chuckle. He broke out in a belly laugh, his huge chest heaving up and down. This completely broke the ice. The humans began laughing as well, patting each other on the back and cracking jokes about 3 against 8 billion.

"Thank you Arkyn," Olatida sent mentally, smiling up at his Lyran counterpart. "Thank you earthians for coming," he said aloud. "For those of you watching on your WorldNet, our ship will broadcast on your frequencies all around the globe, in your own languages. Our Sirian friend, who speaks fluent English, will now give you a short briefing before we reveal our purpose for coming to your planet."

The earthians received a galactic primer. The briefing introduced the various galactic cultures and their locations within Galaxy 6. There was also a very brief summary of the other 11 galaxies in the Twelve. Then followed a brief history of ET interaction with earth. Humans learned about the Unity Field and how several dozen ET races had used this multidimensional component, and the grids of the planet, to alter the human genome. Humanity learned that some ETs looked enough like humans to pass for earthians. "The person next to you on the street may not even be from your planet," Silla Oralie concluded on the broadcast link.

Salat Toor was watching from his flagship in orbit around the planet. He was slightly mollified. Orion interference was not mentioned at all.

"Now we come to the purpose of our visit to your planet," Ogunfatidime continued. "We want to know whether you are prepared to cease your internal conflict and join the galactic community. It is not necessary to respond verbally. Our ship has been testing all life forms on the planet, especially the human ones, during our stay here. We needed to be physically present for this all important work. That is why we have brought our ship. Do not worry, you don't 'pass' or 'fail.' Your eventual entrance into the galactic community is an assured fact. However, the parameters and the scope of your membership will be decided by what we discover."

Ogunfatidime paused for a moment. "Now we are here to answer your questions as best we can. We know how excitable earthians can be. All that is necessary is to raise your hand quietly. We will determine the sequence of questioners based on the readings we take from you. We will choose in the order that will best present the material we want to share with you."

"There, on the aisle, you are first. Then you, in the back row. Yes, you. Then over here. Yes, the delegate from France will be third."

The first question was asked by the representative from Mali. "I am Azikiwe Mirembe. Sir, may I say that when you first stepped off the ship, all of Africa rejoiced. How is it that a black man leads a delegation from the Twelve Galaxies? We learned from your presentation that our genetic makeup is a combination of many ET cultures. Are your people our fathers? Was Africa the home continent for all of humanity? I ask these questions because there are at least 2 billion people of color on earth who are very interested in your response."

Ogunfatidime smiled. "We are well aware of the political and ethnic circumstances on your planet. However, race has very little meaning in the rest of the galaxy. There is so much diversity that such trivial distinctions as skin color and differences in physique or body type are irrelevant. Are we your fathers? Well, our contribution to your African biology is evident, is it not? We must tell you that earthians are almost identical genetically. You are literally all brothers and sisters."

The next to speak was the delegate from the United States. "Sir, we want to know why you have chosen this time to make yourselves known to us. If you have been interacting with us for millions of years, why did you wait so long?"

Arkyn Thorlief responded through a translation device. "We have not hidden our presence among you. The aggressive and conflicting meme structure on your planet makes it difficult for most of us to maintain our equilibrium on your planet for more than a couple of hours. Most importantly, we do not look at ourselves as 'ETs.' We are beings just like yourselves. We prefer to call ourselves visitors. We look at our presence here as you would an airplane trip to another country. If we have caused any mischief over the years, it is a direct reflection of your human consciousness. That is one thing you will learn very quickly when you join galactic society. The idea of 'they did it to us,' or 'he did it to me,' is a false one."

The French delegate was next. "Sir, there are five continents and five different types of human being on our planet. In Africa, the black man. In North America, the red man. In Asia, the yellow-skinned man. In Europe, the white man. And in the subcontinent, the brown-skinned man. I have always thought of earth like a board game called Risk, where each player gets some men and some defined territory and they all go at it. Have ETs... er, visitors... been performing a great sociological experiment on earth?"

Silla Oralie laughed, a musical sound that sounded like a flute.

"Dear Ones," she said, "that is not how it is at all. It is true that we have influenced events and even biology upon your planet. But this has been, as Arkyn already said, at your invitation." She paused for a moment and looked at Olatida Ogunfatidime. "There have been a series of cataclysmic events upon your planet (and within your solar system), over the past three billion years. Life on the surface has been periodically wiped out." She looked puzzled. "In all of the Twelve Galaxies, we do not know of another case like this. We have studied your solar system and the area around it for aeons and have not been able to discover the reason. It seems that Earth's history and geology, unlike every other planet in the universe, experiences growth in sudden and destructive leaps." She paused. "This is most unusual."

John Frankel, in his seminar room, nodded his head. That was exactly what Kjirsten said.

"Your solar system and the planets within it are also unusual. When you travel beyond it you will see for yourself." Silla Oralie smiled.

"Far from being a coordinated plan of action, the history of our involvement has been a fragmented and peripheral one. Your planet is isolated, in a practically uninhabited sector of the galaxy known as the Desert. It is off all galactic trade and communication routes and was discovered purely by accident. Whatever has happened here has been, from our view, a series of coincidences. As my Lyran friend pointed out, the earth human genotype is identical in almost all respects. So there are not really five different types of human. Only one, with superficial differences."

For several hours, the three were bombarded with questions. Every delegate was allowed to speak.

The delegate from Norway asked, "Where do UFOs come from?"

Thorlief laughed. "Everywhere." Everyone laughed.

"Are there evil ETs, excuse me, *visitors*, who dominate and control events on earth with their superior technology?" said the delegate from Australia.

Salat Toor, in his float in his private office on the Lord Toor, sat up sharply.

"Again," Silla Oralie said, "you misrepresent the true state of affairs. Every planetary culture has a certain consciousness, as do stellar sectors and even entire galaxies. What occurs on each planet is an accurate reflection of the consciousness of that planetary culture. Failure to understand this idea has resulted in a blame game. Some of you have found a new influence to blame for the unwanted conditions upon your planet: Us! Only when individuals begin to truly take responsibility for their lives can your civilization reach its glorious promise."

And so it went until 10 at night. The three visitors were exhausted. Never had they spent so much time in such a psychically challenging place.

Olatida Ogunfatidime made a concluding statement. "Now that your curiosity has been satisfied, there is one very important topic we want to bring up. Many of you have observed the halos of energy and have seen the unusual colors in the night sky. You are not alone, my friends. These phenomena have been observed everywhere in the Twelve Galaxies, although they are most exaggerated on your planet. That is why we believe that this little planet will play a vitally important role in whatever unfolds.

"Earthians, you may feel that we have come to help you. But we have actually come to seek your assistance. We have compiled a list of 33 people we feel can assist us to penetrate the parameters of the upcoming event. We request that the following beings meet us at the ship in precisely 38 hours from now, at noon eastern standard United States time. Thank you!"

Silla Oralie read the list. Most of them no one had ever heard of. Among them was the name of John Frankel and Ralph Smith.

"Was it all right, Sam?" the President asked his close friend and confidante, Samuel Jablonski.

"Didn't you see the TV broadcast Walter?"

"Oh no, I was busy with work. The summit with the Chinese is coming up next month. I need to prepare."

"Sir, all of the agreements are ready to sign. It'll just be a formality, as always. I want to know what you thought of the Iranian delegate's tirade."

"I didn't see it Sam. Was it all right?"

Jablonski felt like he was talking to his dog. "Yes sir, it was all right."

"Then it's working," said Walter Shrub III.

Back in the seminar room Genevieve was ecstatic. "Oh my God John, you've been invited to the party!" Not one of the fifty students had left. All were buzzing about in excited conversation.

"I'm not going without you. You should have been on that list."

"I'm touched by your loyalty sweetheart. It's irrelevant to me."

"If they want me they have to take you too. It's both of us or none at all."

Genevieve was secretly pleased. In truth, she would really like to step aboard the huge craft.

Every hotel room and flight to DC had been booked solid since the ship appeared. Fortunately John was able, from name recognition, to secure a flight for both of them that night. They arrived at 9 a.m. John was recognized immediately at the airport. He and Genevieve accepted accommodations at a local resident's house, half a mile from the White House. "We'll have to walk," their host said. "There are at least a million people camped out in every available space, except for the streets. It's a sanitation nightmare but somehow we're coping. People are eating canned food and are stacking and recycling. The DC garbage collectors are working crews 24 hours a day, as well as local food distributors. Residents are cooking food and selling it as fast as they can make it. It's pretty cool actually."

At the appointed time a large bubble descended from the ship. The 33 "chosen ones," plus Genevieve, stepped in. There were 17 from Asia, 5 from Africa, 4 from South America, 4 from Europe, and 3 from North America. The bubble was translucent and adjusted itself to fit its occupants. Inside, the humans felt a pleasant glow of energy suffuse through their bodies, as if going into a really comfortable sauna. Before they had even adjusted their positions they found themselves standing upon a gently curving platform suspended 1000 feet or so above the "floor" of the ship.

No one on the ground could figure out how the bubbles exited and entered the huge craft. A group of Georgetown University physicists had been studying the ship for over seven days. They were completely baffled. They could not understand the composition of the hull. Analysis of the "glow" revealed nothing to their instruments. Nevertheless, they carefully filmed the bubble's return to the ship. It appeared to have been extruded but no one could comprehend how something so solid could change state without a hull breach. It was a scientific mystery.

The humans looked about them, utterly astonished. They had not even noticed the mechanism of their arrival. Their bubble had simply vanished.

They were standing on a soft, creamy white surface that emitted a very fine, almost unnoticeable glow of energy. John felt it as a soft mist, or cloud. The ship had hundreds of levels arranged aesthetically, not in the typical cubic grid patterns their eyes were so used to seeing. Some of the levels were mere platforms while others ran as far as the eye could see. Each of the levels hung in space with no supporting beams or columns. John saw a beautiful marble grandstand with colored lights and a multi-tiered temple. He saw parks, gardens, and forests filled with flora and fauna, much of which he did not recognize. Birds of all shapes and sizes flew between them. The air was filled with their cries and their chirping. Subtle music filled the air, which contained a fascinating mixture of aromas and scents.

To their left a physical contest was in progress, played on a large platform the size of a football field. One of the participants, chasing a ball, ran headlong off the edge of the platform. John closed his eyes, imagining the man falling to his death. But there was no scream. Opening them again, he saw the figure running the other way.

There were lots of moving walkways, some going at a leisurely pace, others very quickly.

The sound of water in the distance came from a gigantic waterfall far below. The spray from it created a mist into which a rainbow appeared. Water was everywhere, streaming in rivers, pooling in small lakes, collecting in beautiful and ornate fountains. The light was uniform with no apparent point sources, and allowed clear visibility throughout the vessel.

Wherever John looked there was astonishing beauty. This ship was a floating city. A city of infinite variety, a city built for enjoyment. All of the structures were works of art. Nothing here was utilitarian. John let go of Genevieve's hand and sat for a few moments. Tears of joy ran down his face. Genevieve smiled down at him. John pulled himself back up to his feet.

Every breath energized his cellular structure. In the back of his mind he felt a peculiar calm; an absence of an irritating something that was a normal part of his subconscious. John remembered staying at a hotel in downtown Chicago. The traffic noises, the sounds of sirens, and the background rumbling had all become unnoticeable after a while. Until he returned to the big quiet house on Magnolia.

None of the humans had moved or made a sound, except for the soft intake and exhale of breath.

John walked slowly to the edge of the walkway and felt nauseous. He looked upward and felt vertigo. The lack of supporting columns or railings made him nervous.

A humanoid of medium height, fine black hair, and huge circular eyes approached them. "Do not worry," he said. "All of the levels are surrounded by fields of energy which prevent one from falling." He demonstrated by running off the walkway and bouncing easily off of it. John tried it. He was very hesitant at first, but then ran headlong and threw himself over the edge. Genevieve shrieked, but he was caught as if by gentle hands and deposited back on the surface.

"Come with me," the being said. "We will introduce you to the galactic delegation."

Out of the corner of his eye John noticed Ralph Smith, and nodded to him in recognition.

The walkway began to move slowly upward and then picked up speed. They passed by a museum of sculpture, an art gallery, conference rooms, living quarters (one of the very few enclosed spaces in this immense structure), concert halls, video centers with gigantic three dimensional displays, intricately designed gardens, a small forest, and another waterfall. They and finally came to rest inside a space demarcated by a double ellipse traced upon the cream colored floor.

A number of the beings in the room subtly acknowledged Genevieve. John wondered about that briefly because she had not been one of the invited 33. His eyes traveled to the floor. Next to the double ellipse was a beautiful and complex geometric design about 10 feet in length and 12 feet wide. John analyzed the patterns. Suddenly the design presented him with a thought package: the patterns leaped forward into a complete description of the room, its function, and background on its designers.

"This is the Celaeno conference room for newcomers to the ship. It exists to honor a great philosopher of the fourth planet orbiting the star of the same name," John said aloud.

An elephant-like humanoid with wrinkled skin and a short little trunk blasted an astonished response. Next to it and wearing her multicolored robes, John recognized Silla Oralie from the U.N. broadcast. "How could you possibly know that?" she asked.

John shrugged. "I have good pattern recognition skills." There was an excited buzz as their hosts spoke briefly among themselves.

An Indian woman standing beside Genevieve said, "This double ellipse represents the orbit of a planet around a binary star system." More excited chatter. John recognized Arkyn Thorlief. The Lyran gestured to a small, frail looking creature with a very large head as if to say: "I told you so."

"We have chosen well," Olatida Ogunfatidime said. A large smile covered his broad face.

There were over 2,000 beings in the space. Each was seated theater style all around them and suspended on little pillows of energy. John noticed one delegate stretched out, as if it were sleeping. The 34 earthians were at the bottom of the bowl.

Just as in the Eyrie, the assembled creatures made the bar in Star Wars I look like a meeting of the Aryan Racial Purity Institute. One of the beings resembled a spider. It had 8 legs, four of which were used for transport and four shorter ones for grasping. A long snake-like being with light green skin and a fascinating pattern etched upon it regarded him intensely. Its big head and large, expressive eyes indicated a broad intelligence. John began to receive from this being and knew that the skin patterns were a mark of social status in its culture. A rustling of feathers from the top row sent John's gaze upward. A gigantic black condor perched regally upon its cushion. It had beautiful wing feathers in brilliant hues of red, gold, and light blue. Its golden head was large. Like all ETs it had very large, expressive eyes. The being nodded its head toward John and Genevieve and raised a wickedly taloned but elegantly shaped leg toward them. This creature also had two short forelegs with flexible appendages, one of which it presently used for grooming itself. An amazing being resembling a pool of mercury flowed and unflowed. It suddenly sprouted an eye, which then lost its shape and returned to the pool of glop which formed its body. An intelligent amoeba? Immediately the creature formed itself into a very large eye, scrutinizing him carefully and startling him a little. John felt a warmth from the being that astonished him. John returned the love and saw the strange creature glowing with satisfaction, its malleable protoplasmic body rippling in pleasure.

About 20 feet above the others, isolated in a special chamber, floated a very large sphere. John felt an incredible coldness when he reached out to it with his energy field. Just then he felt a wave of recognition penetrate every nuance of his being. Something was alive in there! John's consciousness was overwhelmed by sensations he had never felt before. Here was a being that truly fit the definition of alien. In all his travels to other realities he had never encountered anything like this. These were entities that simply recreated themselves by splitting off from each other, as in cell division. They were completely asexual. The 'feel' of them was clinical, emotionless, and foreign.

John apprehended that this being called himself [2248, (6, 17)] and was in direct contact with another being called [Origin 0 (0, 0)]. [2248, (6, 17)] was one of 17 who came forth from the being [1263, (5,2)] who in turn had extruded from another being who in turn extruded from another...Everyone in this culture was intimately connected, a galaxy-wide intelligence that formed a completely transparent society. It was eerie to experience from such a viewpoint but John could see the advantages of it. From this being he felt an almost indistinguishable wave of excitement and relief, as if an aeons-long search might finally be over. Underneath this sterility of feeling John felt the love of a parent for his child. John's eyes opened wide. So they were not emotionless after all!

"The earthian is communing with the Illirian!" someone shouted.

John suddenly felt contact with the creature cease. He felt a little weak in the knees.

Genevieve steadied him. "Whew!" he said.

Olatida Ogunfatidime spoke to the group of humans. "Thank you so much for agreeing to come. We will, as earthians say, get right down to business. We have asked you here for two reasons. Firstly, we wish to understand more about you. We believe that your eclectic heritage has given each of you latent abilities we would like to test. We thought it prudent to meet you face to face and get to know you a little better."

"Secondly," Ogunfatidime continued, "we wish to understand more about the cosmic event and your relationship to it. There is a small but vocal minority of us who believe that you may be able to help us understand a little better what is about to occur to all of us."

One of the earthians asked a question. "I am Reinaldo Couto, from Brazil. We don't understand the selection process. If you want to know us a little better why didn't you invite the important people on our planet? The heads of state, the corporate leaders, the great scientists? The only person I recognize is the American senator." John wondered about that himself. He saw Ralph Smith smiling, enjoying himself. Unlike any politician he had ever seen the man was silent, but his eyes were missing nothing.

Silla Oralie said, "Dear ones, in our estimation you are the 33 most important people on your planet. Important not because of your perceived influence on earthian events but because each of you possesses a unique combination of latent capabilities."

Silla Oralie paused. "Let us begin."

For two hours the visitors were shown a variety of images. The earthians were presented with various sounds and music, from earth and other parts of the galaxy. All of it was connected to the unusual cosmic phenomena. The assembled galactics hung on every word the earthians spoke. The meeting resembled a collection of brilliant but uneducated young students being quizzed by a panel of distinguished professors.

"Now that you have exercised your minds a little take a look at these," Silla Oralie requested.

The last two images were of an ordinary object with a halo around it, and another of a spectacular 'sky bloom' taken from somewhere in space.

In the back of John's mind something spectacular suggested itself. He immediately rejected it. He tried to get it back...oh well. Maybe it would occur to him again sometime.

There were a number of suggestions which proved helpful to the galactics until John startled them with something he considered obvious. "Unformed Potential activity is seeping into, or becoming more visible, to our senses," he said.

"Unformed Potential?" said one of the galactics.

Oops! The odds were that no one here had ever reached the Eyrie, even if they knew how to travel using the sphere of consciousness.

Genevieve was amused but said nothing.

John launched into a brief explanation. Everyone was astonished.

The galactic with the spider-like body responded through a translation device. "John, we have monitored you very carefully and have seen no evidence of this so-called jaunting."

John had to explain about the causality of time between universes, and all the rest. When he was through everyone leaned back and contemplated for a while. "Genevieve's novel is all about that. An explanation is in my second book," he reminded them.

Olatida Ogunfatidime spoke. "John, I noticed a startled reaction when we first presented the last two images."

"Yes. It was somewhere in the back of my consciousness but I couldn't dig it out."

"Try to remember." After a few minutes John said, "Sorry, I can't." He shrugged.

Olatida Ogunfatidime exchanged glances with a few of the galactics seated in front. He turned on his float and looked out at the assembly. An exchange of some kind was occurring. After a couple of minutes the Denebian turned around to face the group of earthians.

"Thank you so much for all of your help. You have been of great service to us." He smiled broadly. "Now for some fun! Let me introduce you to your host. He will be giving you a tour of this magnificent vessel." The galactics were dismissing them but none of the 34 humans were insulted. Every one of them would have preferred to explore this awesome vessel since the moment of their arrival.

Their host for the tour was the large-eyed Pleiadian who had met them on their arrival.

"Did you build these ships?" one of the group asked.

"Please call me Asaelo," the being responded. He smiled, and his eyes twinkled. "We designed and supervised the construction of these ships but they are built in the Procyon sector. There are twelve of these vessels. Each one has a different theme."

John noticed how expressive were Asaelo's large eyes. The Pleiadian communicated the most subtle nuance with them. Gradually John was able to interpret his thoughts and moods. They played a little game together: Asaelo would show them something and John would try to read his expression. After a couple of hours both of them were laughing out loud. John knew one thing for sure: Cosmic Event or no, these people knew how to enjoy themselves. The entire ship was a cocoon for the expression of creative energies. People were having fun but there was none of the giggly, neurotic behavior that sometimes characterized human groups.

"Where's the bar?" John said. "I could go for a beer." Reinaldo Couto laughed. "Some wine my friend! And a nice plate of Bobó de Camarão!"

Asaelo chuckled. "We could handle your food request, but not the beer. There are no stimulants on this vessel."

"Why not?" Couto asked.

"None are needed. We find such chemicals too artificial."

"Well, my friend, you don't know what you're missing. There's nothing like a fine wine, good food, and a beautiful woman to keep you company."

John scrutinized Asaelo's countenance during this exchange. In his eyes John read amusement, good-natured condescension, and a startled surprise at the earthian's outburst. Asaelo's eyes widened and his small, thin mouth turned upward ever so slightly at the corners. When his eyes met John's they both burst into laughter.

Reinaldo Cuoto was a bit bewildered. "Did I say something?"

Soon the whole party was laughing together, including the Brazilian.

"Let us partake of some refreshment," their host said. "We do not cook flesh on this vessel. However, we can imitate the texture and flavor so closely you will not notice."

"You're on!" the earthians said. They stepped off the walkway into an area designated for food consumption. The food court had large pedestals, small- and medium-sized flat tables, and a number of intricately designed multi-level structures with flat areas and bowl-like depressions. There were chairs, futons, energy cushions and foot-sized bubbles in the floor. Asaelo touched one of these with his foot. A very large table with six curved leaves and a hole in the middle rose from the floor. Asaelo sat in the center. When all 34 humans were seated, each was easily able to have a conversation with any of the other 33, or with their host.

"This is a brilliant design," said one of the Europeans.

Asaelo beamed. "Thank you. I programmed it myself."

The refreshment area was just in front of a fantastic garden with many fountains circulating and spraying water in geometric patterns. John noticed how the water was made to turn in elegant spirals. It came together in small pools, to be shunted around and around between the fountains.

"Why do you spiral the water?" someone asked.

"Spiraling the water allows it to retain life giving properties. Like everything else water is conscious. When properly handled it has remarkable healing properties."

John looked out from their level and out into space. They were about two thirds of the way up. The height of the elliptical ship was at least two miles. The light here was a soft creamy color that illuminated perfectly. Anywhere he looked it felt as if he were outside, on the surface of a planet. John breathed deeply of the air. A fascinating combination of exotic and unrecognizable odors met his nostrils, all of them pleasant. The air itself was an elixir that refreshed and invigorated.

The humans were really into Asaelo's food challenge. Almost everyone ordered a meat dish.

Cuoto ordered the Brazilian dish "with lots of shrimp."

A South Korean named Jae-sun Kim ordered Peking Duck. "No one can fake the texture of duck," he said. It became a game to choose the most exotic and difficult dishes.

"General Tso's Chicken, with lots of hot sauce," someone else said.

Ralph Smith ordered Montreal smoked meat on rye with cole slaw, swiss cheese, and Russian dressing. "Had a taste of that on a trip to Quebec a few years ago."

"Coq au Vin," said another.

The humans made sure no dish was duplicated. Food from every major cuisine was ordered. Meanwhile, friendly banter was carried on amongst the 34 and their host, thanks to the translation devices. John was enjoying himself immensely. He said to Asaelo, "Is the food prepared by hand, or programmed?"

Asaelo chuckled. "It is prepared from scratch." John looked over at Genevieve. She had hardly said a word in the seven hours they had been aboard the ship. "Probably means it begins as pure energy."

When the food came the mix of aromas filled the food court. It was delivered all at once on a flying platform, shaped precisely to the geometry of the table and fitting snugly over it.

All agreed the food was indistinguishable from the 'real' thing.

"The flesh of an animal is simply an organization of energy. Anything that is organized can be duplicated," Asaelo said.

One of the humans snorted. "There's just the little problem of figuring that out."

Asaaelo smiled. John saw that he was not offended and didn't respond to the criticism. During the UN Q & A, a number of personal insults were delivered by hot-headed earthians worried about their answers to questions of religion. The three galactics never acknowledged anything negative.

"Why don't you guys ever get angry?" John asked.

"If nothing negative is inside you then there are no hot buttons to hit," Asaelo replied.

These beings are so far ahead of us, and they want our opinions? It didn't seem reasonable to John.

Asaelo responded calmly to the previous question. "When you join galactic society you will be shown all of these things. There's nothing new here. It's all been common knowledge for billions of years."

A Chinese woman spoke up. "I can't imagine a society existing for billions of years. We think it's a big deal to have been around for 5,000 years."

"It is a wonderful thing," Asaelo agreed. "Our people are for the most part very happy and prosperous. There is always an infusion of young, developing cultures. However, such a long history breeds an inevitable tendency toward sameness of thinking. It is in our natures, as conscious beings connected to the One, to become into harmony and understanding with each other. Therefore there are many in the galaxy who are ready to admit you now to full membership. Liven things up a little, they say."

"But you are not one of them," John said.

Asaelo regarded the earthians with his large and wonderfully expressive eyes. He communicated a feeling of love and apology. "No, I am not. But I believe that your admission is necessary anyway. If I had a vote I would vote yes. Your fiery and undisciplined natures will be ultimately beneficial to the whole."

Asaelo's eyes turned inward. "Our time is almost up. Soon it will be time for you to depart."

"Please tell us how the ship is propelled," an engineer asked.

"I am not a technician," Asaelo responded. "But I can tell you that it is similar to what happens when you take a watermelon seed and squeeze it on one end. It squirts out of your hand. Any medium can be treated like a fluid and compressed in such a way that the object inside of it is squirted forward. Space itself is such a medium. Many billions of years ago we learned how to manipulate the fabric of space so that we may physically travel swiftly from one end of the galaxy to the other in perfect safety. There is also transportal travel for those who dislike physical journeys."

Soon the 34 humans found themselves leaving the ship, and on the ground of earth once more. A few of them began to cry.

Three of the women and two of the men collapsed onto the ground, holding their heads. Media rushed all over the place, screaming questions. People were panicking.

"They hurt them!" said a news reporter.

"The Earth Firstians are right!"

"Call an ambulance!"

"911, quick!"

John and Genevieve went quickly to work calming the crowd. Others shielded those unable to rise. John held up his hands. "We have a statement! We'll answer all of your questions! Please, back off! Give us room!"

After several minutes a semblance of calm had been restored.

"Ladies and gentlemen," John said, "those who have collapsed are not sick. Our experience on the ship was so wonderful that a return to earth is almost too much to bear." John was bravely keeping it together himself. He felt empty inside. He had lost something perfect and magnificent, something he could never touch again.

Reinaldo Cuoto got up and addressed the cameras. "John is right. It was like going to heaven. Now we're back in hell. But it's a hell of our own making."

John realized Reinaldo was right. The negative thought streams were all humanly generated. There were no evil manipulative overlords. "We have met the enemy and he is us."

"What?" a reporter asked.

"Walt Kelly. Look it up."

Those who had fallen were now on their feet.

As they were being interviewed, someone pointed upward. "The ship is moving!"

It was true. The immense vessel was inching upward.

"If they want to go, why don't they just go?" someone in the crowd said.

One of the physicists in the 33 explained. "Because the ship displaces several cubic miles of air. If it were to leave all at once it would create a violent atmospheric disturbance."

Everyone went silent. All cameras were on the craft until it finally disappeared into the night sky. The crowds began to disperse.

John and Genevieve walked toward the Capitol Building. "I want to see the Senate and House floors," Genevieve said. Ralph Smith overheard and came over. "Let me give you a tour. Then we can go to my offices and talk. There's a few things I want to ask both of you."

President Walter Shrub III, deep in prayer, was informed of the ET vessel's departure. His personal secretary opened the door a crack. "Mr. President, the ship has left."

"Thank you O Lord," said Walter Shrub III in reverent tones. "In Your infinite compassion You have chosen to spare mankind."

The President of the United States held a news conference that evening. "The great ship has left," he said. "Humanity has avoided God's retribution, but only if we keep to the path of righteousness." Almost no one watched.

45

Senator Ralph Smith took the oath of office after the most polarized and bizarre election in U.S. history. Almost 100% of Democratic voters crossed party lines and cast their ballots for Smith. In October, Republicans had officially urged all of their voters to cast a ballot for Democratic Governor Thompson.

For once the left had united. Almost all left wing third parties had withdrawn from the race and thrown their support to Smith. The right was demoralized; many of them stayed home. Senator Smith barely won half the popular vote, and only a 17 vote majority in the Electoral College.

Walter Shrub III castigated those Republicans who failed to turn up at the polls. "You have ensured that the demon Smith will occupy this sacred chair," he said, speaking from the Oval Office.

Both major parties were in complete turmoil.

More and more people were beginning to see the halos. Psychic phenomena was increasing among the general population.

Fear dominated the consciousness of about half of the public. They could not understand a God-fearing Republican from Nebraska morphing into a peacenik Buddhist. If they perceived the strangeness occurring in the physical universe they did not acknowledge it. They utterly rejected a bunch of aliens traveling on a space-ship as big as a city, even though it had been on their TV sets for ten days. For them it had simply been a good science fiction story, a ten-day TV special. They longed for the good old days when life was simple: you grew up, got a job, got married, had kids, retired, and spoiled the grandkids. For many of them the whole world had gone crazy. Current events seemed not to be made by human beings but by powerful outside forces. A hard core believed it was the work of demonic forces, or satan himself. Many felt that Armageddon was just around the corner.

46

THROUGHOUT Galaxy 11 the Illirian Supermind assembled itself. This would be the most important council IT had undertaken since the last of their planets had been seeded over 10 billion years ago. On every planet of every star within Galaxy 11, all activity halted.

The call went out from the central core. "Illirians, assemble! New data has come to our attention which requires the full power of our Mind to analyze!"

[Origin 0 (0, 0)] opened the dialogue.

"Our analysis of the universal fabric shows an imminent large-scale change to the material of space itself. We have searched our Mind. Never in our history has such an event occurred."

[Origin 0 (0, 0) sighed mentally. "As you know, our search for compatible consciousness reached a dead-end 2.7335 billion orbits of the Origin planet in the past. It has been conclusively determined that the seeding of appropriate planets in other stellar environments has also been a complete failure."

The great Supermind expressed its intellectual disappointment and sadness.

"Nevertheless," [Origin 0 (0, 0)] streamed, "I am here to report that the earthian experiment is an unqualified success."

Now the great mind came apart in an explosion of what would, in Illirian terms, be classified as mental excitement, disbelief, and disagreement.

"Impossible! The noxious oxygen-breathers can have no connection to us whatsoever," was the dominant theme.

[Origin 0 (0, 0)] waited for the debate to subside and then commanded. "Assemble!"

Quickly, individual extrusions found their place within the whole.

"The earthian experiment, as I have just reported, has been successful. Because of the brilliant innovations of exobiologist [2248 (6, 17)], we have been able to create and insert patterns of subtle energy within the earthian planetary grid. Oxygen breathers are completely separate and disjointed entities. The earthian environment itself is confusing and almost haphazard, as millions of species and subspecies exist upon one tiny, compact world. [2248 (6, 17)]'s revolutionary advance was to precisely identify the species grid associated only with the resident humanoid species [data stream and a 3D map of the earthian planetary grids sent.] Then, the 3rd entity of the third bifurcation of [2248 (6, 17)] [data stream sent, an Illirian genealogy chart] discovered how to insert the patterns of our race consciousness into the human species grid."

The collective gasped.

[Origin 0 (0, 0)] paused for effect and intellectual approbation.

"After observing the evolution of these strange earthians for precisely 231,787 revolutions[1] of their noxious planet about their single sun, I have calculated[1] that we have successfully seeded the basic templates of our consciousness into the race mind of these unusual humanoid earthians [data stream sent]. Our consciousness is no longer alone in the universe!"

The great Supermind sighed in mental satisfaction.

The great Mind began to absorb this new data. IT's cogitations were interrupted by the 37th entity of the 23rd bifurcation of [Origin 0 (0, 0)] (a very recent extrusion). "What good will that do us!" It piped. "We can never associate with these alien life forms!"

The great race mind of Illir was prepared to agree when [Origin 0 (0, 0)] increased the amplitude of Its transmission. "Silence little one! Is it not the recent extrusions which demonstrate the most immaturity of thought?"

Almost all entities within the Supermind agreed with this statement.

"The two-digit DoublePrimes are always the most undisciplined," thought [Origin 0 (0, 0)].

At once all was stilled within the Supermind as each entity paid homage to the Origin and revered Its status as the seed consciousness. Each entity admired, so far as it was capable, the purity and clarity of Its thought.

The Origin calmed (when we say "calmed" we mean in Illirian terms).

"For a brief instant, I/we were in communication with one of the earthian humanoids. It is a profound but utterly unique pattern which I shall always keep in the forefront of my consciousness." [data stream sent of the encounter of [2248 (6, 17)] and [Origin 0 (0, 0)] with John Frankel on the Plieadian ship]

The character of the thought pattern of this encounter was soothing to the great mind. IT experienced, for the first time in millions of cycles, the most tenuous

---

[1] [Origin 0 (0, 0)] streamed, "I have calculated." The concept transmitted by these three words is the closest any Illirian comes to feeling a genuine emotion. It generates the intellectual satisfaction felt when a complicated series of calculations resolves to an elegant and consistent solution.

feeling of emotional pleasure. It was a delicious and shockingly forbidden fruit to which all elements of the great Mind subtly resonated.

[2248 (6, 17)] spoke. "It is as I have calculated.[2] There are certain heretofore unrecognized harmonic sidebands of thought within the earthian consciousness. These are consistent with our consciousness, and valuable."

Now the Mind rattled apart once more as the heretical nature of this proclamation was recognized by all entities.

"Impossible! Clarity and precision are paramount!" was the dominant concept that echoed within the vast collective consciousness.

[Origin 0 (0, 0)] expanded upon the assertion of [2248 (6, 17)], ignoring the intellectual clamor.

"Now we report on the observation bud we have created upon the fifth planet in the earthian solar system. The invasion of uncoordinated energy is most noticeable around only two nodes in Galaxy 6. Both are in the earthian solar system. We are monitoring the situation closely from the fifth planet. It is almost certain [data stream sent] that an uncalculatable event [intellectual frustration] affecting all portions of the known universe will originate there." [underlying fundamental assumption: any two-node system generates a potential]

The Illirian Supermind now collectively contemplated and integrated the new data. After a time there were many requests from the collective for a retransmission of the contact with the earthian.

The Supermind again shared the experience. From deep within its galactic consciousness, long forgotten sidebands were re-analyzed.

The end result of the conference was a subtle shift in Illirian awareness. For the first time in aeons a subtle emotion was expressed, acknowledged, and validated.

There was hope.

As the energy phenomenon became more visible, the Congress of the United States began its new session. A tax reform bill, an education decentralization bill, and a balanced budget proposal submitted by President Smith were on the agenda, along with a raft of other legislation. Both House and Senate were in turmoil. The people's representatives couldn't concentrate on business because the everyday mechanics of government seemed almost irrelevant. Nevertheless, human nature combined with political agendas assured that Congress stayed busy at the beginning of the new session.

Senator Bisbee of Oklahoma was attempting to drum up support for a bill that would make Bible study mandatory in public schools. "In this time of insanity and fear we need to get back to our roots. The word of God is a good place to start."

Representative Holcombe from Indiana introduced a bill in the House to expand the policing powers of Homeland Security. "The final battle is upon us and

---

[2] "It is as I have calculated." This is a phrase of even greater power than "I have calculated." It expresses the utmost feeling of intellectual exhilaration. It is never used without absolute certainty and verification of correctness.

the forces of evil are ascendant. Now is the time for all right thinking Americans to combat this threat. The enemy is known. Terrorists and fifth columnists have infiltrated our great country. Some of our own citizens and even some of our own public servants have gone astray. Crazy new-age thinking, irresponsible liberalism, and unbridled permissiveness are destroying this country. Now is the time to put a stop to it! No honest citizen has anything to fear. My fellow Americans, we cannot sit back and allow our great nation to rot from within."

Battle lines were being drawn among the nations of the world. Fearful governments tried to hang onto power and keep the status quo. In the Middle East and on the subcontinent, tactical nuclear weapons were used on civilian populations. In Angola, a bomb containing virulent biological agents exploded in the capital city, killing hundreds and necessitating evacuation of the entire population. The Russian government announced the unveiling of a new superweapon based on scalar wave technology, which could fry large sections of the earth from secure installations within the country.

Mass media spread the bad news quickly around the globe, causing panic.

On the other hand, a worldwide community of citizens, business leaders, NGO's, and government officials were coming together on a common agenda of peace and cooperation. Spurred by the WorldNet, this community was developing 'nodes of cooperation.' Like-minded people formed businesses, political organizations, and living associations they called community neighborhoods. Clean energy technologies got a much more serious look. Scientists and inventors began freely sharing their work. Funding for these projects was provided by enlightened entrepreneurs and venture capitalists.

Those who were healthy and abundant became more so. Those who were sick and poor were even worse off. The gap between the haves and have nots was at an all-time high, and growing worse.

On the night of April 8th John and Genevieve went outside to look at the stars. They had been doing this regularly for the past year. Kjirsten had given them their assignment before their teaching program began last year. "Stay within the earthian environment and detail your observations. I want a report at least once a week." Their sensitive inner sight enabled them to perceive both the zone of chaos around the planet and the subtle infiltration of Unformed Potential energy.

Robert and Rachel were sitting around a fire in the living room, reading. Genevieve burst into the room. "Mom, you have to come out and see this."

The older couple walked out the front door. Robert's mouth dropped open. "My God!" John's father now had many more requests for popular articles. It was a continual source of frustration to him that the scientific literature had no adequate explanation for the bizarre phenomenon.

The entire sky was now a chaotic riot of constantly changing colors. "It's beautiful," Rachel said. "But a little scary."

"What is it?" Robert said. "Not a sky bloom, too big. It seems to come from inside space itself."

"There's no more light though," Rachel said. "That's curious."

"What do you mean?" Genevieve asked.

"There seems to be more light in the sky but it's not reflected to earth."

"You're right mom," Genevieve responded. Even though the entire sky was filled with color it did not affect the usual pale glow cast by the moon, now 2/3rd's full, over the ground.

For the first time since the bizarre but beautiful lights appeared, Robert felt a pang of fear. Whatever it was it was growing stronger. He felt like a helpless pawn under the influence of powerful but unknown forces. "Armageddon," he mumbled.

John looked around and saw most of his neighbors on their front lawns. The children squealed with delight. A few of the adults walked over to talk, concerned about the expansion of the unexplained phenomenon.

"When is it going to stop?" a woman asked.

"What's happening to our world?" another added.

"I just want things to get back to normal," said a retired professor who lived across the street.

John reassured everyone that the universe was still in good working order. "Look at the animals and the children." He indicated a group of kids pointing excitedly at the sky, laughing and running about happily. "If something really was amiss they would feel it first." Just then one of the neighborhood dogs ran out to join the children at their play. A cat walked up to Genevieve and rubbed his head against her leg, purring. A squirrel chirruped in a tree.

"I just don't understand it," a man muttered. "What could be causing all of this?"

From that night forward the spectacular light show filled the night skies around the planet. Some said that God himself was showing His hand.

President Smith addressed the nation in an April 30th speech.

Tonight I address not only the people of the United States, but all the world. Some say we have a planetary crisis that will destroy human civilization. When we look about us, we can see the evidence of it.

But we also see evidence of unprecedented prosperity and community spirit. Ladies and gentlemen, it is clear that we are on the cusp of a very great change in human society. Unprecedented prosperity exists alongside poverty and despair. A mathematical friend of mine explained it this way: We are in a chaotic situation. In mathematics chaos does not mean random and purposeless destruction, but an explosion of possibility leading to a new state of affairs. In such an environment each of us must decide for ourselves where we are going with our lives. Those who focus on a positive outcome generate the conditions for rapid improvement. Attention on the negative will lead to a swift and uncomfortable regression. All of us understand what I'm saying. We have all seen how quickly events are unfolding. It seems that we now need only think of something to have it appear in our experience. We are all individually responsible for our own lives. At the same time we are intimately connected with our neighbors. The planet earth is now a global family.

The President paused to clear his throat and drink from a glass of water.

Now is not the time to give up hope. God has not abandoned us. On the contrary, we see the beautiful evidence of His handiwork when we look into the sky every night. All around the world we see the same Light surrounding our planet, as if God himself were sending angels to watch over us. We are being guided to a glorious future if only we will not abandon our faith in Him, and in ourselves.

The camera crew were listening with rapt attention. The speaker was delivering his lines with a calmness and a certainty that soothed internal disquiet and discomfort. His words were almost irrelevant.

We have no government program to make everything right. There are no economic proposals to fix the ills that beset so many of us. All of us understand that we are far beyond that now. There is no leader with all of the answers, no one who can tell us the perfect solution to our problems. Not even our extraterrestrial friends know what is happening in the universe at large.

There are two ways to approach the present situation. We can look at the dark side or we may look on the bright side. There is plenty of evidence to support both sides.

People of the United States and the world, there is nothing any of us can do to alter the amazing phenomena we are all observing. The very nature of matter and energy itself seems to be changing. If events in the universe at large are out of our control, what do we gain by gloom and doom? Like a cancer, our bad attitude infects those around us. There is no proof of our impending doom. There is no proof that what we are going through will turn out bad for us. All conclusions about the future are purely speculative. So why not make the best of it? Why not try to find as much joy in life as possible? Perhaps this is the lesson God wants us to learn.

The President smiled broadly.

I believe that the earth as a whole is about to experience something exciting, something glorious, something that is overwhelmingly positive. I can feel it.

In America there is a time-honored tradition of self-reliance combined with generosity of spirit. These principles will serve all of us in these turbulent times. Help your neighbors whenever you can. Share resources. Understand that God will not fail to provide a positive future if we will only keep faith in ourselves.

The camera crew could feel a warmth envelop them, as if they were basking in the rays of a human sun. Those watching could feel it too.

Don't give up the ship. Hang in there. Together, as a nation and as a planetary society, we will make it through to a wonderful future.

Two months after the President's speech the night skies around earth began to glow even brighter. Each night just after sunset the people of earth observed a beautiful, multicolored light show. Scientists called it an acceleration of the unexplained phenomena within matter and energy itself. This was scant comfort for the multitudes who regarded the scientific establishment as the repository for answers.

Doomsday cults sprang up like mushrooms. The God's Light cult, buoyed by the arrival of the great Pleiadian mothership, saw its membership increase dramatically. Its charismatic leader, Brian Buckholter, began to organize fringe groups and bring them into his political party.

War broke out in the subcontinent over Kashmir. In Europe the Czechs and Slovaks were fighting over borders. In China government institutions were under assault by groups demanding complete freedom of expression. The worldwide suicide rate jumped 5,000%.

Social scientists and social workers lamented increased crime rates in depressed areas and decried the unprecedented prosperity and abundance in other sectors of society.

"The social fabric of our great country is being ripped apart," said Simon Rogers, the noted political analyst. "There were more millionaires made last year than in the past fifty. Yesterday two people starved to death right in the middle of Washington DC."

On the news, a black and white graphic showed that the United States was becoming more and more a patchwork of prosperity and economic hardship. "The rich are getting very rich very fast and the poor are getting very poor very fast," the voice-over said. "It's accelerating more quickly every day."

The 33 who entered the ET craft did not lose touch with each other. Their shared experience created a strong bond of friendship. It had also profoundly altered their consciousness. Since returning from the great ship each of them had been talking with as many people as possible. Four had written books, three others had begun to lecture. All of the participants put up pictures of the inside of the Pleiadian ship on the WorldNet. This generated a sense of awe in those who saw the images.

Demand for the Frankel Method was again rising. John and Genevieve found time for two more book tours. They had been teaching seven days a week. The tours were like a vacation.

On a drive into Philadelphia, pockets of the city resembled war zones. Smoke rose from a high rise building.

"Another gang fight last night," their driver said. "It's all-out war for control of south Philly." A mile later construction crews crawled over a large new structure. "The new center for the performing arts. It's the largest construction project downtown in ten years." John was amazed. As they drove slowly through this section of the city he saw shiny new restaurants, clothing stores, art galleries, theaters, and lots of happy and affluent people.

"It's a downtown renaissance, that's what they're callin' it," Frank said. "Look around. Everybody's doin' real good here."

It was true. There was a liveliness and a bustling energy in this area. Pedestrians crowded the streets and shops. The sounds of happiness and prosperity were everywhere: the babble of conversation, the roar of trucks making deliveries. The atmosphere was filled with excitement.

"I don't get it," Genevieve said. "Just a mile away the city is smoking. But people are walking around here without a care in the world." She noticed a couple getting out of an expensive car in front of a luxurious downtown hotel, laughing as the keys were handed over to the parking attendant. "Aren't they worried about getting mugged, or their car stolen?" she asked.

Frank Rossovich frowned and looked at her through the rear view mirror. "That's the funny thing lady. All the crime stays in little pockets. They never come over here. People are startin' to leave their doors unlocked. It doesn't make any sense to me either."

John and Genevieve looked at each other, amazed. They weren't up on current events, having spent most of the last year in seminar rooms.

"Where is all this money coming from?" Genevieve asked.

"They say it's all comin' from the private sector, except for the new Arts Center. People are makin' money like crazy and actually payin' their taxes, so the city has a big surplus. The poor people don't pay nothing." Frank smiled. "That's the way it should be."

Frank swerved his vehicle to avoid a supply truck coming out of a blind alley. "Funny how it worked out. No law got passed. People just started doin' it."

"Do you consider yourself one of the rich guys or one of the poor guys?" Genevieve asked.

Frank looked offended. "Me? I'm one of the rich guys! Well, gettin' there anyway."

Rossovich waved his hand around the interior of the limousine. "This is mine now. Made the last payment two weeks ago."

They were pulling into the parking lot of Jenine Black's bookstore. "Wow," Genevieve said. "She's expanded!"

They got out of the car. John leaned in the open window and spoke to the driver. "Frank, do you see the halos?"

The man grinned. "Yeah I see 'em. But I don't worry no more about 'em. Not after what the president said last week." John and Genevieve exchanged glances. They waved to Frank, who had pulled his limo back out into traffic.

"Do you know what the president said last week?" John asked his wife.

"Haven't got a clue."

Holding hands, they walked in the front door of the bookstore. A crowd of people turned and a man pointed. "That's them!" Spontaneous applause broke out.

John and Genevieve stopped to take it all in. "This is fun!" she said, looking up at John from her position slightly in front of him. She had her neck craned slightly backward. Her jet black hair spilled onto his chest, revealing the beautiful earrings.

John saw the flash of a camera. One of the women gasped and stepped forward. "Those are lovely," she said, reaching a tentative finger toward Genevieve's ear.

Genevieve took off the earring and handed it to the woman. She carefully held it by the hook and watched it twirl and sparkle slowly in the light. Her mouth was slightly open and her eyes lit up. "This is the most beautiful thing I've ever seen in my life," she said softly. "Where did you get them?"

"From a master craftsman named Phillipe," John replied. Fortunately he was spared further explanation as Jenine clapped her hands excitedly. She motioned the crowd to a large room filled with chairs. In front were two desks and a large podium.

Jenine Black held out both hands to Genevieve. "It's nice to be back. We needed a break from our teaching."

"Thank you so much for coming. I'm afraid we've arranged a little Q & A session before the book signing. The last one you did was so successful we've had an ongoing discussion group here three nights a week." She pointed to the standing room only crowd. Two hundred people were crammed into every available space.

And so it went for every city on the tour. When they got to New York the pair were flabbergasted by what they saw. Parts of the city were fighting an all-out civil war. Other sections exuded an air of lightheartedness, gaiety, and prosperity.

Just as in Philadelphia, the blackened areas were self contained and did not spill out over their borders. "Like they were surrounded by a force field," John commented.

John and Genevieve had four stops in the city. One of them was in south Brooklyn, a place John expected to see in ruins. Instead they observed a racial melting pot of cooperation and peace. The neighborhoods were run-down but clean. New businesses were moving in. It was like a picture John once saw of a newly growing forest after a fire. New growth burst forth from the blackened husks of almost-dead trees. An air of quiet prosperity was beginning to settle in.

"Isn't it wonderful?" said their host, a short and stocky Dominican woman. She waved her hands around at the street. "A year ago this street had a bar, a strip joint, a couple of crack houses, and a broken down drug store. I almost can't believe it myself." The street now featured the bookstore, a small one-story affair with a brick façade, a grocery store, a small movie theater, and a gas station. Some recently renovated townhouses occupied the other half of the street. "Everyone in the neighborhood is employed, if you can believe it. All the bad apples just left. Last year I decided to open up the bookstore. It's been a great success. Our people are so very bright and so starved for knowledge. I'm selling books faster than I can get them in."

"You mean hardcopy is making a comeback?" Genevieve said.

"Oh yes. People want to come here to discuss ideas. They like having books in their hands. I also have an arrangement with an eBook supplier. I get half on all eBooks my customers buy from their store."

"One of our local boys just won the district chess championship," she said proudly.

John and Genevieve were pleased to be in this newly revitalized area. John was doubtful when Darcy Bledsoe put it on their list as a last second addition. "Why are we going to such a small place?" he asked.

"Because that's my old neighborhood." Darcy showed him a picture taken four years ago. "You wouldn't believe what's happened to it in such a short amount of time." He had looked John straight in the eyes. "You guys are too sheltered from the rest of the world. I want you to see a few things. It might open your eyes about what's really happening in this country."

Darcy was right.

Earlier they had taken a rather circuitous tour of Manhattan.

"Why don't we just go straight?" John asked.

"Gotta avoid the dangerous places," their driver said. "City's changing so fast it's hard to keep up. I want to keep my car."

In Boston the pair encountered a similar phenomenon. "It's like somebody programmed society with a big computer," John remarked. "Bad guys go there, good guys here."

On the plane to Detroit Genevieve felt a little nervous. She hadn't forgotten her earlier reception there.

They pulled up in front of the bookstore to cheering crowds. This section of the city was booming but earlier they had skirted a huge blighted area. "Most of the city is either dying or dead," the driver said. "The places that are living are like little suns blazing in the darkness. I've never seen anything like it."

When they stepped out of the car John felt an exhilarating energy, even more powerful than in Philadelphia and New York. It was standing room only inside the large downtown bookstore. Lines had formed outside the place. Everyone was cheerful and the space felt totally safe. As in New York, John saw people of all races and ethnicities laughing and conversing excitedly.

Genevieve's eyes were very large. "It feels wonderful here."

"Never would have expected it," John said.

Someone in the crowd overheard. "Everyone from the suburbs wants to come downtown now."

A man behind them spoke. "Can't you feel it? People in this town are finally coming together. This time we aren't going to let it slip away."

The two spent eight uninterrupted hours in the bookstore. When they had to leave to catch their plane the crowd gave them a rousing sendoff. It had been the best stop of the entire tour.

When John and Genevieve got home they were still keyed up, but exhausted. Both agreed that change was rapidly sweeping the country.

President Ralph Smith sat at his desk in the Oval Office and opened a red envelope with an airmail stamp. Inside was a letter.

Dear Mr. President:

We, the undersigned, have watched with approval and admiration at your journey to the presidency, and your subsequent actions as President of the United States.

We want to inform you of a permanent roundtable discussion group that your fellow 'mothership' participants have formed. A few of us got together shortly after our experience and began to dialogue on ways to improve the human condition. To our astonishment, we were able to recreate the feeling all of us experienced while aboard that amazing craft. When two or more of us brainstorm we notice an enhanced intelligence. Unlike most committees I have been associated with! We have found that the more of us gather, the more powerful is our focus and our results. Perhaps this is a special gift from our galactic friends, or perhaps it is one of those new abilities we humans are said to possess.

We are now missing only two of the original group. Yourself, and Mr. John Frankel. We are hoping you can spare a couple of hours each week from your busy schedule to meet with us at your convenience.

Sincerely, Chiang Tse-Hong

Underneath were the signatures of 31 of the original group of 33.

The President grinned. "Yes," he said aloud, "I think I can make time for that."

John received a similar letter. "Honey, they've invited me to roundtable discussion every week at the White House!"

"Who has invited you?"

"Our friends from the ship. They say that getting together somehow recreates the energy we experienced on the ship." He frowned. "They haven't invited you so I'm not going."

She smiled lovingly. "Don't let me stop you. If it's only for a few hours I won't miss you too badly."

John wondered again about Genevieve's presence on the mothership. During the hours they spent aboard she did not say a word. No questions were asked of her. Her presence was never acknowledged; she was invisible. Whenever he asked her about it she would just shake her head. "I was simply your consort. I played no part in the activities but I had a wonderful time anyway."

She seemed satisfied but John wasn't. Some part of him felt she was withholding something. Was she testing him again?

A week before the meeting of the 33 the light show became visible, faintly, even in broad daylight.

Many people were now truly frightened. Those who did not want to acknowledge the strange phenomena had been able to simply go through their day and stay home with curtains drawn in the evenings. Now it was different. A whole new wave of upset and discomfort rippled through society.

The first meeting of the group of 33 occurred in the White House, out of the eyes of the media. When the group came together everyone felt it. "Are we on the ship?" John asked. The president said, "I can't understand how this works, but it feels really good."

"We are now complete," said Rosa Cavellieri, a housewife from Milan, Italy. She directed her comments at President Smith. "None of us here can explain what's happening to our world so we don't even try. Scientists are stumped. Even galactic scientists have no idea what is happening to the universe, or why. What we are doing is using our network of 33 to...access a higher wisdom. That's the best we can describe it. When we come together we find that we are more intelligent. We can think of the right questions to ask. We get answers to those questions that make a lot of sense. We are all glad you could come Mr. President."

"So what are we going to do?" Ralph asked.

Chiang Tse-Hong smiled broadly. "We've got a lot of work to do, so let's get started. First..."

When the meeting was over all 33 walked out onto the White House porch for a meeting with the news media. Thousands of people lined the streets, hoping to catch a glimpse of the proceedings. Chiang Tse-Hong was the spokesman for the group. He stood in front while the others arranged themselves in a semicircle behind him. Some of the group members stood with arms about each others' shoulders. One happy man had his arms around a woman, who smiled shyly up at him.

The reporters quickly noticed the cheerful and excited demeanor of the group. They were amazed that the President of the United States would be standing in the back row next to that Frankel fellow. "This is no ordinary political meeting," one of them whispered to another. "These guys are genuinely happy." A number of the reporters laughed out loud.

"We have had a very fruitful and productive discussion," Tse-Hong began confidently. "We feel that we've got our hands on the pulse of what is happening. In a couple of months we hope to have a detailed report for the people of earth that will explain some things that right now seem a little confusing. We'll need time so don't expect miracles right away."

Cameras clicked away.

"What are your meetings like?"

Chiang thought for a moment. "Imagine your typical office meeting, with egos clashing and tempers flaring. It's just the opposite of that."

[laughter]

"All right ladies and gentlemen, that's all for now. We all have to get back to our lives, especially the president. From now on these discussions will be held virtually. We will keep you informed if there is any news."

The interview was over.

Robert watched on the TV at the Walters'. "There's something different about these guys. Maybe those ETs knew what they were doing."

"There's an energy around that group that's very interesting. I can feel it," Michael Walters said.

"Me too," Alicia said.

"Oooh-oooh!," said Amanda, the two year old.

Genevieve spoke to John one night shortly after John had completed one of the weekly meetings. "Lets go see Kjirsten. It's getting harder and harder to get to the Eyrie now. I want to see what's happening."

When they arrived after a very difficult passage, the place was in turmoil. The Eyrie resembled more an emergency room in a battle zone instead of a research facility. John noticed that the walls were shimmering and losing their stability, like a force field under attack from an energy weapon.

The two wandered about the place until they spotted a dejected Kjirsten and the gang. She didn't even look up as they approached.

"What's going on?" John asked.

"We have to abandon the Eyrie," Davey growled. "We're trying to save as many of the Records as we can."

Kjirsten finally looked up. "We lost. All our work was a total waste."

"Don't start on that subject again," the blue man said roughly. John could tell he was fighting back severe disappointment as well.

"I just thought of something," Bellerophon said. "Maybe the reason the Records are fragmented is because the same thing happened last time."

Kjirsten's head jerked up. Some of the old fire came back into her eyes. "Maybe you're right!" Then her head dropped again. "Ah, what difference does it make."

"All of the researchers are returning to their home universes before it's too late," Goliath said.

John raised his eyebrows at that.

"You may not have done much translating lately. It's getting almost impossible to negotiate the pathways anymore. Unformed Potential activity is simply too strong. It's exponentially worse in the outer universes."

"Where's Ivan?" Genevieve said.

"He had to leave a couple of days ago," Kjirsten said bitterly. "I didn't even get to say goodbye."

John was sad. He really liked the big griffon.

"What do we do now?" Davey said.

"We go back to our home planets and resume the remnants of our lives," Kjirsten said. She was still looking at the floor.

John sat down beside her on one of the benches. Slowly she raised her eyes to his, and he understood.

"What's left for me back there in Lyra?" she said, her eyes clouding. John took her in his arms and caressed the beautiful head. He felt her tears and tenderly wiped them away with his fingers. John said nothing, just gently rocked her back and forth.

After about ten minutes Genevieve sat down on the other side of her. "Why don't you come back to earth with us?"

There was no response from either of them. Genevieve repeated her question.

Kjirsten straightened abruptly and wiped the tears from her eyes. "What did you say?"

Genevieve smiled. "I said, why don't you come with us to earth?"

Kjirsten's mouth hung open for a second. Then she smiled broadly at Genevieve. "Oh, that would be wonderful!"

Kjirsten searched her friend's eyes. She wanted to make sure that Genevieve was making a genuine request. Kjirsten knew that Genevieve knew how much she loved John. "It's all right Kjirsten. Really it is." Now the redhead was jubilant.

Then she frowned. "Will I fit in?"

John laughed. "Well, you're 6½ feet tall, built like an amazon, have six fingers and six toes, and are stronger than 90% of the men on our planet. But yeah, you'll fit right in."

Kjirsten laughed too. She was beginning to get excited. From her Lyran training she knew how to handle men, how to manipulate them. Earth was a focal point for the coming crisis and she wanted to be where the action is. Earthians were different, but not that different. And the women, they would be child's play. She would have no trouble establishing herself, even on a planet as nutty as earth. She stood tall. "Let me get my things."

Genevieve and John were both delighted. "Kjirsten can stay with us until she gets her feet on the ground," John said.

"How will we introduce her to Robert and Rachel?" Genevieve asked John.

"Hmm, that's a good one. We'll have to think of something before we leave."

Meanwhile Davey and Bellerophon were shuffling their feet despondently. No one noticed them. Davey was putting a good face on things, but inside he was seething. They hadn't even said a word to him. After all these years battling together in the Unformed Potential, he was nothing to them...

Bellerophon was thinking along the same lines. He took the cigarette out of his mouth and stomped on it angrily. Didn't even know why he smoked the damn things anymore.

The eyes of the two males met briefly.

"They think I'm weird back on Orodani," Davey said.

"I'm an outcast in my society," Bellerophon replied.

Both men understood the other's pain.

"C'mon Davey, let's get the hell out of here." They began walking down the hall to their sleeping quarters.

John and Genevieve, chatting away, didn't notice.

Half an hour later Kjirsten appeared, dressed in a pair of jeans and a blouse. Her spectacular red hair was tied in a long braid and she wore a pair of black flats. She could easily pass for a very tall earth woman as long as no one noticed her hands.

John stared. No matter how you sliced it, she was a goddess.

Kjirsten was pleased. She twirled around. "Will I pass?"

Genevieve giggled. "You'll have people staring wherever you go." John said nothing. He hoped Kjirsten knew what she was doing. In Lyran society a woman had *carte blanche*. On earth she could get into trouble real fast with her quick Lyran temper and her enormous strength. What if she slugged someone and caused an injury? What if she got thrown in jail? Davey, Bellerophon, and Kjirsten were different than the ETs on the Pleiadian craft. They were more volatile, more like earthians. Maybe it was a necessary personality trait to survive in the Unformed Potential. Whatever it was she should be warned.

"Kjirsten..." he began.

Genevieve cut him off. "Kjirsten, we'll have to talk about our planet and some of its illogical customs."

"I understand," she said. Then she looked around. "Where's Davey and Bell?"

"Davey and Bell? Shit!!"

All three of them ran down the hallway, fighting through the crowds of beings getting ready to abandon their posts. Kjirsten hoped they were in time. For all she knew they had already translated out of the Eyrie and she'd never see them again.

Damn her vanity! Thinking about John and her new life on earth, teasing herself with the possibility of being near him, working with him....She wiped the tears away. Damn her! Where was her training?

Now she came to Davey's quarters, recognizing his room by the perfect circle he had drawn upon it one day with a blue colored pencil. Were they too late?

She thought she heard muttered conversation.

"Davey! Bell! Are you still here?"

The wall blurred and an aperture appeared. "Yeah we're still here," Davey's gruff voice responded from inside the room. "What do you care?"

"Is Bellerophon with you?" Kjirsten said anxiously. "Can I come in?"

"Yeah."

Kjirsten, John, and Genevieve walked into Davey's room. Upon the walls were images of Orodani; a dry desert world of browns, reds, and golds under a blue white sun. On the shelves were rock sculptures of animals, beautifully made. One of them depicted a four-legged creature that resembled a horse without a tail. Its head was thrown back in a gesture of defiance. The artist had captured its spirit perfectly; the sculpture was so lifelike it seemed ready to leap into the room. The other pieces were of equal quality, each capturing a beast frozen in time.

John was stunned. This man was a virtuoso, a genius. Not an intellectual genius perhaps. Just as with Goliath, he had misjudged Davey completely. He had let his petty prejudices dominate his assessment.

Kjirsten apologized for the three of them. "Davey, Bell, my sincerest apologies. I was so immersed in my own self-pity I forgot who my friends are. Along with Ivan and the three in this room, you two are the most important beings in the universe to me. I love both of you dearly."

Davey grunted his acknowledgment. Bellerophon had his back to them.

"Bell?"

The wiry man whirled around to face her. He spoke bitterly. "We just thought we merited a little more consideration."

Genevieve was about to interject but Kjirsten held up her hand. "And you do. What can I say? Sometimes we take for granted the ones we love the most."

"Why don't you two come to earth with us?" Genevieve asked.

John almost laughed out loud as he watched their emotions.

Davey's face broke out in an immediate grin, which he then quickly stifled. Bellerophon looked shocked at first, then angry, then pleased. Finally, he began to chuckle. "Well I'll be dipped in shit. That's just what I was hoping you'd say." Then he began to laugh, a loud deep laugh that no one who knew him had ever heard before. Bellerophon sat down on the bed and just let it all loose. It appeared to Kjirsten that he was releasing a lifetime's worth of rejection.

Davey's smooth blue metallic face was a study in contrast. He would look around at the images of his beloved Orodani, and sigh. Then he would gaze toward the others and a look of longing would cross his face. Then he would look back at his sculpture and his images again. Finally, he crossed his massive arms over his chest. "I accept," he said.

Kjirsten said, "You're sure you want to give up the dream of returning to Orodani?"

"Yes," the blue man said. "I have spent almost twenty years in this low G place. My muscles have atrophied and my bones have shrunk. I don't think I could go back now even if I wanted to." He paused for a moment and looked around the room. "But I must be allowed to take my sculpture and my pictures."

John said, "Are you kidding? You could sell any one of those on earth for a small fortune."

"Really? Then I won't have to work in a carnival or in a freak show?"

John walked over to one of the pieces. "I don't know about your planet, but on earth we can appreciate good art. Properly handled, you could sell your collection and be set for life."

Davey was pleased. He had visions of continuing his Unformed Potential research from earth. After all, it seemed to be the center of the action. He knew enough about earth to know there were plenty of hot, dry deserts. "You don't think my appearance is too unusual for earthians? No offense, but your planet is pretty backward."

John laughed. "We just had a bunch of ETs land on the White House lawn. You are certainly unusual. But if we present you as just another ET I don't think you'll have too many problems."

Davey brightened. "Good! It's settled then. When do we leave?"

"As soon as Bell gets his gear," Kjirsten replied.

"All right," Davey replied quickly. "I'll pack my stuff right now."

Bellerophon leaped off the bed and ran to his quarters.

As he gathered his pitifully few belongings, Bellerophon thought about what he would do on earth. He might pass for an earthian even though his eyes were overlarge like most humanoid galactics. He had very large ears which resembled conch shells (author's note: like a Ferengi, except of middle height, and a lot better looking). Oh well, he would find a way. He thought about his life and realized he could adapt to anything. His strong suit was his love of adventure and his iconoclastic worldview. Perhaps he could put that to good use. Become a comedian.

Earthians appreciated good humor but he'd have to learn about the culture. He had already studied the illogic in human society, he would capitalize on that. Bellerophon brightened. Earth was the nuttiest place in the galaxy! He came from a family of entertainers. It was in his blood.

Best of all, he could still hang out with the guys. Just to be with this group under any circumstances would be worth it. He'd miss the big mantis, but Goliath was longing for the Canopus sector and his hive.

Bellerophon realized he could joke about ETs and their interrelationships. Through his humor he would educate these backward humans about galactic life. While working with Goliath, Bellerophon had absorbed some of his teaching methods. He knew from the mantis that the most effective learning came when you didn't even know you were being taught. Humans were so limited in their thinking. But when they were laughing they were open to new ideas. He was good with words, maybe he could even write a few books. Yes, it was going to be exciting. Bellerophon threw his clothes and some personal effects, along with his dataset, into his ingeniously designed 'suitcase.' This device had secret compartments and could be rearranged to store any kind of object. In the wild days of his youth it had concealed many a stolen valuable.

Bellerophon raced back into Davey's room with a smile on his face.

The group returned to their cell in the great honeycomb. Goliath strode forward and clicked. "Now it is time for me to say farewell. It has been a wonderful experience working with all of you." He straightened his hat. "I am hopelessly behind in the latest fashions!"

Everyone laughed.

They said their goodbyes but there was no sadness. Such an emotion could not exist in the vicinity of Goliath's warm personality. No one could explain it, but each felt that somehow they would see their friend again.

Now the walls of the Eyrie began to fade in and out. There were only a few die-hards remaining.

"Not much time left," Davey said.

Kjirsten shook her head. "I can't believe we're going to lose this place."

Bellerophon said, "We better figure out where on the earthian planet we're going to translate. I don't want to do a blue jaunt."

John went over to one of the consoles and brought up the big bedroom on 357 Magnolia. "Right here. Gen and I will be in the two chairs. Follow us one at a time."

Half an hour later the group was deep in conversation. They didn't even notice the front door open, didn't hear the footfalls on the stairs. The bedroom door opened. Robert and Rachel stepped in.

"What the..." Kjirsten was standing. Robert looked her over, an awed expression on his face. Rachel stared at the thick blue bulk of Davey.

Bellerophon, an unlit cigarette dangling from his lips, looked on with a smirk of amusement. "What's the matter? Haven't you ever seen an ET before?"

"Holy shit," Robert said.

Rachel looked from one to the other. "These are your friends?" Rachel said.

"Yes mom," Genevieve replied. "Let me introduce our guests."

Genevieve did the introductions and gave the older couple a capsule summary of each.

Robert said, "How the hell did you get here?"

Bellerophon grinned. Davey grunted. John and Genevieve said nothing. Kjirsten came to the rescue. "We've been applying the techniques known on earth as the Frankel Method."

Robert was flabbergasted. He looked at his son resentfully. "Why didn't you *tell* me you could do stuff like that?"

"He did Robert," Rachel said. "You didn't believe him." Robert stood there not knowing what to say. He was torn between annoyance and fascination. John thought it was comical and hoped none of his friends would laugh.

"You mean you can travel between the stars with this method?"

"Oh yes, and much more," Bellerophon added. "Even between universes."

Robert's eyes widened in disbelief. "Between *universes*?"

Robert's scientific training simply did not allow him to accommodate such an assertion. His face reflected an inner battle between disbelief and the evidence of the ETs before him. He leaned against the door and muttered. "I don't believe it. You guys are all from some fantastic costume party." Robert's eyes kept glancing over at Davey, his blue skin shimmering in the light of the nearby lamp. Robert crossed the room slowly and hesitantly touched the blue man. "Feels real."

Davey just smiled.

"I want to learn how to do this translating thing," Robert said finally.

"Sorry dad," John said. "That's no longer possible."

"What do you mean it's not possible? They're here aren't they?"

Genevieve stepped in. "The same phenomena that is affecting the physical universe around earth has made inter-universal travel impossible. It's still possible, with great difficulty, to go between the stars. But even that is closing down now. The galactics use spacecraft. You see dad, even they don't know about the sort of consciousness altering we're doing."

Robert was stunned. "Then where did these people come from?"

"From a place we call the Eyrie," Genevieve said. "It's going to take way too long to explain. You can read my book if you want more of the details."

Now Robert was totally confused. He stared at Genevieve. "Are you telling me the stuff you wrote in that book is *real*?"

She nodded.

Robert turned his head and queried John silently. His son smiled back innocently. He looked at the three ETs again. Then he turned around and left the room.

Rachel giggled. "Men! They're not very flexible are they?"

Kjirsten burst out laughing. "I'll say not!"

"Hey that's not fair," Davey growled in his deep bass.

Bellerophon was having fun. Robert's reaction to their presence had already given him some ideas for a comedy routine. Maybe earth wasn't such a bad place after all.

Rachel spoke to Kjirsten. "Come over here dear. I want to have a look at you." She walked around the Lyran woman, amazed. "Are you from the same planet as Arkyn Thorleif?"

"Good guess. From the same sector of the galaxy."

Rachel looked up at the big Lyran. "You're the most magnificent creature I've ever seen."

Kjirsten was pleased. In the Eyrie, the diversity of species was so pronounced and the work so important that her feminine charms went unnoticed. Her position as group leader reinforced it. But here, among fellow humans, her feminine side would be recognized. That might not be a bad thing.

"My mom is a dress designer and a seamstress," Genevieve said. "I think she's contemplating a new creation for you."

Kjirsten clapped her hands together in excitement. "If it's anything like that dress you showed me before, I can't wait."

"So you know each other?" Rachel inquired.

"For almost 12 years."

Rachel was upset that her daughter hadn't seen fit to tell her of this amazing woman. But one more look at Kjirsten's figure made her forget all that. She was thinking of a dark plum colored dress, to show off that beautiful red hair.

"John, come over here and stand next to this goddess." Kjirsten came within a quarter inch of John's height. "My God girl, you're as tall as he is."

Kjirsten turned her head and the glance she exchanged with her son spoke volumes to Rachel. "She's in love with him," she thought to herself.

"On my planet I'm actually below average height," Kjirsten said. "Most of our men are over 7 feet tall, and the women average over 6½feet."

Soon the women were talking about clothes, men, and relationships.

Davey snorted. "Females are the same everywhere."

Bellerophon glanced at John and smiled. "Was that man your father?"

John nodded.

"I would like to speak with him. Perhaps I can make some sense out of all this for him."

John was doubtful but he led the way downstairs. Robert was seated at the desk in his study off the hall, his head in his hands. As the pair turned into the room he glanced up. "I'm not sure what to think anymore," Robert said. "The whole world has gone crazy."

Just then Davey came down the stairs. Even though he was only 5 feet tall they creaked under his enormous weight. Robert stared. "I guess I'll just have to believe it. I can't deny the evidence of my own eyes. I don't see any spaceships out on the lawn, and we've only been gone an hour."

Bellerophon pulled up a chair and sat next to Robert. "I'm here to try and answer any questions you might have." He wanted to start right away investigating these earthian people. Already he could see that their thinking was backwards, leading to tremendous confusion. Soon he had engaged Robert's attention completely.

Davey tried sitting on the sofa but he sank so far into it he almost broke one of the springs. John braced his feet against the bottom and helped him up. The man was as solid as a block of granite. "I'm gonna need some special furniture," he said, placing his bulk into what looked like a solidly built wooden chair.

"I'm also gonna have to find a place to stay, but I don't have any money yet." Davey spoke matter-of-factly. He knew that earthians placed prime importance on valuables like money. He also knew that their money was basically debt and had no intrinsic value whatsoever. It was one of the many paradoxes of this place that Bellerophon had pointed out to him. In the rest of the galaxy every being was looked upon as valuable. On earth, your value was measured by how much of something worthless you accumulated.

"You can stay here for a while," John said. "We want you to."

Davey said nothing, his thin lips creasing in a subtle smile. His student had turned out all right. A little weird and unpredictable, but he knew John had staying power. On Orodani you were nothing if you weren't persistent.

"...You and Bellerophon will have to room together," John was saying. "Kjirsten will have her own room. This is a big house so we can easily fit you all in."

Dinner was an adventure. None of the ETs would eat the flesh of animals. Davey shuddered at that idea. "Our planet is very hot and arid. Animal flesh decays very quickly. Besides, there isn't a lot of biomass on Orodani. Long ago our metabolisms became very efficient, adjusting to a minimalist diet of plants, roots, and tubers."

John noticed that Davey was well spoken when he wanted to be. Rachel went through the refrigerator and the cupboards with their guests until something satisfactory was found for each. Davey had a couple of small carrots, a few leaves of spinach, and a turnip. "This is good," he said biting into the bitter root vegetable.

Bellerophon was like a teenager; he could eat almost anything. He settled on an avocado, a piece of pumpernickel bread, a piece of tofu, and even tried some tuna fish. "Not bad," he said. "This has an interesting taste. It's very clean."

Kjirsten preferred pasta with tofu and some vegetables. When she tried the yogurt she flipped. "What is this substance? It's remarkable."

"From the milk of cows. These animals ingest grasses and digest them."

Davey liked grapefruit and went nuts over a lemon. He bit into the thing whole and swallowed it, skin and all. "Now this is what I call good food," he said. When Rachel got out an onion he liked that even better.

It seemed that there was enough diversity on earth to keep even ETs happy, John thought.

Rachel and Genevieve went to the supermarket to get supplies. When Bellerophon found out the price of cigarettes he was shocked. "I'm going to have to stop smoking. It's a bad habit anyway. Learned it from an old earth movie."

Rachel was relieved. Robert didn't like cigarette smoke and he might have gotten crabby, although he and Bellerophon had hit it off right away.

Robert liked Bellerophon because he seemed eager to listen to all of his opinions on every conceivable subject. Bellerophon wanted to find out the thought patterns of human beings. He couldn't have picked a better subject. Robert kept abreast of current events and seemed to reflect a lot of what the majority of earthians were concerned about.

And so things began to settle in quite nicely. John and Genevieve were still giving seminars but could now see light at the end of the tunnel. They were certifying the last batch of teachers. Both of them felt confident that the Frankel Method was in good hands. "It's pretty hard to mess it up," John told his wife. "If you don't get it, you don't get it."

Kjirsten, Davey, and Bellerophon were having a hard time adjusting psychically to earth. It was something they had all thought about. Now that they were completely immersed in earth's planetary consciousness it was more difficult than anticipated. The Eyrie was a community of highly evolved beings with a common purpose. Here there was so much conflict and competition. It appeared to the galactics that the natural reaction of an earthian to anything was opposition. None of them had ever experienced such strong thought streams of hatred, violence, and cruelty. The three ETs met the next evening when the household went out for dinner and a movie with the Walters'.

"Perhaps we should all go back to our home planets," Kjirsten suggested.

"That's out for me," Davey said, holding his head. "But I must admit that sometimes I'd almost rather get my bones crushed than put up with this psychic racket."

Bellerophon agreed. "We're here for some important purpose, I can just feel it. Look how it all fell into place."

"Interesting you should say that Bell," Kjirsten said. "I was thinking the same thing last night."

All three ETs brightened. "We have to keep practicing our technique faithfully every night," Davey asserted. "We still might need to get into action. It'll help us keep our sanity."

"Excellent Davey, that's perfectly correct," Kjirsten said. "We may yet be called upon to resume our former duties. Let's get ourselves established on this planet first. Then we can talk about reforming our group."

Davey slammed his palms onto his knees. "Now you're talkin' Kjirsten!"

The new visitors began to cause quite a stir in the neighborhood. The following Saturday Davey was out in the front yard, trying to discover how many species of life he could find. He had been digging in the dirt and just brought up a worm. One of the neighborhood kids came over.

"Hi, who are you?" she said, putting her thumb in her mouth.

'That's a good question,' he said to himself. 'What am I going to tell this little earthian?'

"I like your suit," she said. "Can I have one?" Davey roared with laughter, startling the little girl. He said, "This isn't a suit. It's my skin."

"Can I touch it?"

Davey let her put her little hand on his arm. He was amazed how fragile and soft it was. "Wow," she said. "It's hot."

"Yes that's right. On my planet it's very hot. Here it's a lot cooler so my skin compensates by keeping me warmer."

"It's pretty," she said, fascinated by the sunlight glinting off his blue body. Then she ran away.

These humans are interesting, he thought. The little ones were totally open and accepting. Why then was there so much misery and conflict here? Davey shook his head. Nutty, these earthians!

Bellerophon was out of doors a lot, roaming the neighborhood and curious to see everything he could. He thought nothing of stopping people on the street, introducing himself as an ET, and asking them about their lives. At first the neighbors were concerned. Rachel went over and introduced him to everyone. It wouldn't have been possible until the arrival of the great galactic vessel.

When the women saw Kjirsten for the first time they were all blown away.

"My God," one of them said. "How do you find clothes?" Kjirsten pointed to Rachel. "Oh." Rachel's outfits were the envy of the neighborhood, ever since Genevieve stole the show at John's high school graduation almost ten years ago.

Soon word spread and they began getting phone calls from the media. John called Tina Brooks.

"Tina, it's John Frankel."

Tina sniffed. "Are you calling to apologize?"

Tina still had not forgiven John for his refusal to tell her about the final stages of the Method. She tended to be a little possessive and liked to hold grudges.

"No. I'm calling to offer you an exclusive."

"Is it about those ETs people say are living at your house?"

"Yup."

"Oh boy! I'll be right over with a camera crew."

When Tina came she brought six others from Channel 5 with her.

"What's this, the entire news department?" Robert groused. Tina didn't take the bait. She knew John's father liked to complain.

Tina interviewed Kjirsten, Davey, and Bellerophon. Some of the neighbors came over and threw their two cents in. "Mommy look, there's the blue man. I like him." That provoked general laughter and cut the ice.

When the camera went up to the room Davey shared with Bellerophon, the men were agog at the sculpture. "This stuff is incredible," said the station manager, who had insisted at the last minute on being one of the party. "It's beautiful work. Has a real masculine feel to it." He examined a fierce predator that resembled a puma. Davey had captured its elegant body in a frontal view with its claws out-stretched and teeth bared. At the same time the piece showed the quintessential dignity of the animal's spirit. Like all of Davey's work it appeared to be a frozen snapshot of something actually real. The man could not take his eyes off it.

"This thing is alive!" he said wonderingly. "Is this an animal native to your home planet?"

"No, it's a puma," Davey said with a smile. "We don't have predators like this on our world."

"You've done this since arriving?"

"Yes. I've always loved to sculpt and carve."

By the time Tina left they had enough footage for a one hour special. On the porch she and John shook hands. "Thanks John."

"Am I forgiven?"

Tina scoffed. "Of course. It was you turned me on to Richard. I got promoted, my life is so much better now."

After the interview Bellerophon tried out some of his comedy routines on the neighbors. A couple of them were really funny and most of them were duds. Bell told himself he was still learning. He informed the earthians about the book he was writing, detailing galactic genotypes and cultures. Everyone was interested and demanded to know when it was coming out.

Kjirsten made the biggest splash of all. At an inter-cultural talk at the university (organized by Rachel) she wore an outfit of Rachel's making. Dark blue slacks with a pale blue belt and a plum colored blouse with dark lavender trim along the sleeves. Her hair flowed loosely. It reached almost to her waist, rippling with color whenever she moved. She emitted an air of confidence and command. None of the men could take their eyes off her. She tried not to stand too close to them for fear they would be intimidated. She exuded a magnetic feminine presence that attracted them anyway.

These earthian men were small and weak compared to Lyran males, Kjirsten thought. But they were unpredictable and she liked that. Lyran males were unsurprising. Their behavior patterns had been solidified long ago in Lyran society (a problem that existed among many galactic cultures).

She looked into the eyes of one who was only a couple of inches shorter than herself. This one had been inspecting her closely during most of her talk. He had dark hair and intense black eyes. As she met his gaze she felt a powerful presence and wisdom, just as when she looked into the eyes of the only man she had ever loved. Maybe coming here wasn't such a bad idea after all! Her musings were interrupted by a question.

"Do all the women on your planet look like you?" a woman asked.

"Pretty much. Actually, I'm a little below average height." All of the men gulped except Nicolas, the tall dark haired one.

Two days later Robert saw a promo for the interview Tina had done with the galactics. "Watch channel 5 on Sunday at 6 p.m. for a one hour special on the ETs living right here in Midland! Another Tina Brooks exclusive seen only on Channel 5."

The show was fascinating, Robert had to admit. Tina had done a good job of showing the ET personalities, although that was not very hard to do. Unlike most humans these ETs seemed to revel in their uniqueness. Especially that Bellerophon!

Less than a week later Davey had a number of flattering offers for his sculptures. Orders came in for as many as he could make. Bellerophon had five book contracts sitting on his desk. Kjirsten had offers from three modeling agencies at fantastic sums, but she scoffed at them. "These men get offers for their ability, I get requests to show off my body. Earthians have no idea what I'm capable of."

Rachel smiled. "Now you know what we women have to put up with dear."

The weeks progressed. The light displays grew even more intense and could easily be seen now in broad daylight. At night the skies were beautifully lit.

All objects emitted a soft glow. The continuing anomalies still made many afraid. Many others noticed a beneficial effect, especially those who had been near the gigantic ET craft in DC. A number of articles appeared in the *Washington Post* describing the calming and healing effect on those who had been exposed to the ship's energy field.

From the *Post* series of articles called "Mothership Diaries," a local resident named Luther Babcock wrote:

> Being the adventurous sort, I noticed the peculiar energy effect surrounding the ship right away. I decided to investigate. I placed myself

within its range on the very first day, camping out directly underneath it. People told me I was crazy because the ship appeared to be radioactive. I did not perceive anything harmful so I went ahead. The first day I noticed nothing, other than the fact that I didn't get hungry. That's not unusual because I'm a very light eater.

On the second day I noticed that my foot began to feel better. Ten years ago I was involved in a car accident and the bones in my right foot were crushed. The doctors did an amazing job of putting me back together, but I still experience constant pain. I ate a little food but still much less than normal. I noticed an increase in my energy. By this time many others of like mind had positioned themselves all along the length of the ship. That morning we were ordered off by the military. The Air Force shot off rockets at the thing and tried to drop explosives on it with absolutely no effect. All of their weapons were rendered harmless. This gave me even more confidence to continue.

On the third day my foot felt much better and the painful arthritis I occasionally experience in my hands was gone completely.

By the end of the fourth day my foot looked and felt completely normal. My energy level was higher than it's ever been. I felt no need to continue my vigil. I took my blanket, water bottle, and dried food, found my car, and drove home. I was curious about my foot so I went to my doctor for X-rays. The results showed a perfect bone structure and no evidence of my prior injury. I am beginning to doubt whether I was ever in a car accident at all. The physical damage has been completely restored, but it's like the past has been rewritten for me. I can hardly remember the details of the accident any more.

The group of 33 released a detailed report on the state of the world. The report concluded that the anomalies were benign, and the result of a subtle but highly refined energy that had permeated the fabric of space. There were no known intrinsically ill effects reported form these energies, other than fear of them. What about the bizarre and rigid compartmentalization of society into areas of haves and cells of have nots? The 33 concluded that the refined energies penetrated matter itself and somehow interfaced directly with thought. Therefore, the importance of choice and intent was magnified many fold.

All the evidence showed that those who were negatively focused congregated with those of like mind, and vice versa. The group speculated that this has always been so, but it is now more pronounced. Professor Hank Westruther, Dean of the School of Social Work at the University of Michigan, was quoted in the report. "We've seen well-off people literally abandon their lives and move into troubled areas. We've seen those in some traditionally poor areas suddenly come together and revitalize their neighborhoods and communities. Our analysis shows that even though there are rigidly defined sectors within our society, there is a surprising fluidity of movement of persons in and out of groups."

Prominent among the signatures was that of President Smith.

Academics, media analysts, and much of the scientific community pilloried the report. Sag Carlson called it "simplistic" and "much ado about nothing." Cob Tapelle compared it to the latest release of Winndoze, the computer operating system. "A junker masquerading as a Porsche," he opined. The report was read widely on the WorldNet. The official web site of the 33 was receiving over 50,000 hits per day.

John, Genevieve, Kjirsten, Davey, and Bellerophon were sitting around the house one evening. Bellerophon said, "I wonder what ever happened to the Eyrie?"

Davey dropped the piece of wood he'd been whittling. "Yeah. I wonder."

All eyes went to Kjirsten. "Why don't we try to find out?" she said.

Cheers went around the room. "It'll be just like the old days." Davey was fired up.

"We have to figure out how we're going to do this," John said.

Bellerophon scoffed. "What's there to figure out? We do what we've always done. It'll be good to get back in action again. This earth life is interesting but it's nothing compared to Unformed Potential work."

Davey agreed enthusiastically.

"What John means is that if the Eyrie isn't there anymore we might do a blue jaunt," Genevieve said.

"Whoops," Davey said. "Hadn't thought of that." From the chagrined look on Bellerophon's face, neither had he.

"Don't worry guys, I was with you too," Kjirsten said. She looked over at John. "For those of us who made the work our life, it is simply inconceivable that it no longer exists."

"Maybe it's still there," Davey said.

"There's a way to find out," John said.

Kjirsten looked at him admiringly. He always came up with the most brilliant suggestions. He was so deep and gentle, so warm, but yet so masculine. She wondered for the umpteenth time what it would be like to have him make love to her. "Yes John." She said this with a warmth everyone recognized. It was a subtle play that was enacted every time John, Genevieve, and Kjirsten were in the same room.

"All we have to do is access the guide symbol embedded within the universal medium," John said. "At the outermost point, adjacent to the tiny dot for earth, is an even tinier dot representing the Eyrie. We know this symbol is a dynamic representation in real time of the status and location of everything within the All. Therefore we should be able to determine the condition of the Eyrie without ever having to leave the vicinity of earth."

"Of course!" said Bellerophon.

John turned and saw Genevieve smiling at him. Genevieve felt his wave of love encompass her. She was satisfied. John understood that although his feelings for Kjirsten were powerful indeed, there was an inseparable bond between himself and his wife that reached to the very essence of his soul. Kjirsten was like a refreshing glass of water to a thirsty man. Genevieve was like breathing.

"Then let's get ready," Kjirsten said. "We'll all do our routines and access the guide symbol, comparing results after we're all back safely. Under no circumstances is anyone to send their merkaba outside the vicinity of this planet."

Fifteen minutes later everyone was ready to report.

There was unanimous agreement that the Eyrie was no more. Kjirsten was stunned, even though she had perceived it with her own senses. "I vote that we now attempt to make an independent analysis of the situation around earth, or as far out as we can go. Being stuck here and not knowing the big picture is driving me a little bit crazy."

Everyone responded enthusiastically.

She glanced nervously at John and Genevieve. "Please be careful."

John and Genevieve sent their combined merkabas outside the zone of chaos surrounding earth. They looked for the now familiar chaos of the Unformed Potential seeping into the reality of organized matter and energy.

"Look Gen, the leakage has stopped."

Genevieve peered out from within their little sphere of consciousness. She loved the feeling of John around her.

Genevieve saw that John was right. Either the Unformed Potential leakage had ceased or the chaotic nature of the energy had self-organized into something more subtle and refined.

He checked the vibrational pathways...still closed off. The universal medium seemed to be dampened, preventing communication and travel.

"All of the pieces on the cosmic chessboard are constrained to remain in place," Genevieve thought.

"That's right! It seems that we are approaching the Final Act."

"C'mon, let's get back. I'm anxious to hear what the others have to say."

With that they concluded their expedition and found their way back to the living room. They were the last to arrive.

"Report!" Kjirsten barked.

Genevieve summarized.

"Then we are all in observational agreement. Speculation?"

Bellerophon said, "There seems to be a lessening of energetic tension around the earthian planet."

"I observed a more benign character to the energy," Davey said. "Either the Unformed Potential has stopped seeping into the fabric of reality, or the character of the Unformed Potential energy is itself changing. Either way, a positive."

John and Genevieve concurred with Davey.

"I have to disagree with all of you," Kjirsten said. "But only because of something I happened to read in the Records. According to sketchy and fragmented reports about the last Event, the same pattern is repeating itself. A lessening of tension before the final explosion, like one of your cancerous tumors in regression suddenly going out of control."

Everyone was silent. They sat there for about 15 minutes until the front door opened. Michael Walters, Alicia, Robert, and Rachel entered, chatting merrily.

"Why all the long faces?" Michael said.

"Hi dad. We've, er, been talking about the future of the universe."

"Don't be so despondent. Come out and look! Everyone's been talking about it."

Half the neighborhood was out of doors in the cold. Tonight, the normal roiling but beautiful chaos was replaced by illumination in more subdued pastel colors. The phenomenon was even brighter than usual. "It's beautiful!" Alicia said.

John saw their chittering squirrel framed against the darkness of the tree bark. The field of energy around his body was particularly vivid tonight. The little guy didn't act like anything out of the ordinary was occurring.

They talked a bit with the neighbors. It was a little annoying to Robert because some of them knocked on the door at all hours of the day and evening, looking for advice. People thought that ETs were smarter than humans so they figured to take advantage.

ETs *are* smarter than humans, and wiser too, Robert thought. Except for Genevieve. She's the smartest of them all.

Robert looked up at the night sky. The moon was almost full, shining its creamy white light radially outward. The moonlight enhanced the colors from the light show. It was incredibly beautiful. How could things go wrong in the presence of such splendor? It made him feel good.

Finally they all trooped back inside. The older people were lighthearted and cheerful. The younger ones were thinking about what Kjirsten had said.

During the next several days it became apparent to everyone on earth that the dénouement was imminent. Whatever was going to happen would affect every living thing on earth. Planetary commerce ground to a halt as the ubiquitous luminescent glow accelerated in brightness every day. The light, normally multicolored, became more uniform and white. People saw inside the auras of each other, fascinated by the patterns and colors they observed. Those with a sense of humor enjoyed themselves. Those in fear warred with those of like mind, and within themselves. Emotions were heightened. Everyone felt far more intensely than ever before, both positive and negative.

People could read the thoughts of others, driving some insane. Gunshots were heard every night in the cities. People were jumping off bridges and rooftops. The authorities didn't even try to intervene because almost all of the trouble manifested in the peculiar patchwork pattern. People turned off their TV sets and their radios, for the latest news was always right in front of their eyes. Many barricaded themselves in fallout shelters or in their basements, convinced the end of the world was at hand.

In the final week an enhanced level of understanding was reached between human beings from every country. It was now possible to communicate telepathically with anyone in the world.

During the last three days the light grew more and more intense, whiter and whiter. It was not a blinding light, more like a glow. The light came from within the essence of matter itself.

Those who did not fear the light experienced spiritual awakenings. Those who already were awakened experienced a feeling of bliss and divine connection.

On the final day almost the entire neighborhood was crammed into the house on 337 Magnolia. It was very commodious and seemed to welcome all of its new guests. The five travelers were the center of all activity, telepathically informing the others of their experiences and their knowledge. It was a great help to those who were on the edge between fear and joy, tipping the scales in a positive direction.

At noon (or shall we say, noon by the clock, for 'time of day' now had no meaning) the five adventurers were holding hands in a circle. The figure of their old friend Goliath appeared. He wore one of the ludicrous hats he favored, an enormous thing with an absurd collection of colored feathers sticking out of it.

They all screamed in delight.

"Goliath!" "How did you get here?" "Is it you, or a projection?"

Goliath said he was in his hive thinking fondly of them, when suddenly they appeared in front of him.

"You have it backwards," Davey said. You're appearing in front of us."

"I haven't gone anywhere!" Goliath exclaimed. "You seem to be in the middle of my living quarters."

Everyone was amazed. The group had a long conversation. Goliath patiently answered the questions of the curious neighbors. "I think we'll be seeing more of each other," he said. Then the mantis disappeared.

"I saw grandma yesterday, just like that," one of the children said.

"Now all we need is Ivan," John said. But the griffon did not show. All five of the travelers tried contacting him without success.

"I hope nothing happened to him," Kjirsten said.

"That shapeshifter has more than nine lives," John soothed.

No one had eaten or drank in three days, but no one needed to. The white light seemed to fulfill all of the body's needs.

"Hey, my finger is growing back!" one of the men said. "I had it cut off in a farming accident when I was a child. Haven't had the use of it since I was ten."

As the 'day' passed, everyone felt the time was rapidly approaching.

The light refreshed everyone, there was no fear or apprehension. The children were running around screaming with delight, playing with one of the dogs. The cats were lounging about as if nothing was out of the ordinary. John saw one of them in what looked like a state of bliss, purring away. He and Genevieve had their arms around each other. Kjirsten had her head on John's shoulder. Robert and Rachel were locked arm in arm.

There was a feeling now as just before a thunderstorm: a clean fresh smell. Everyone waited for the thunderclap. The light became even brighter until it was brighter than the sun, yet it did not hurt the eyes. Still it became brighter, until – the group felt their consciousness effortlessly meld together. All those in the room were joined, including the animals. The assembled life forms became aware of everything in the neighborhood. Every life form, every tree, rock, and blade of grass were joined together. This awareness spread to the whole city, the state, the country, the planet – and beyond. John was aware of trillions of entities but he didn't feel overwhelmed. Parts of himself were being added, long lost loved ones he didn't even know he missed.

Genevieve felt the same way, as did every conscious entity. The squirrel out on the tree branch felt that *he* was the center of the universe and that it was all for his benefit. So did the tree on the front lawn, the insects in the earth, the animals in the zoo, the dolphins and whales in the sea, and the earth herself. Everywhere on planet earth, for a brief instant, unity consciousness prevailed as each merged with the universal field of consciousness.

But it did not end there.

The Illirian node on Jupiter was experiencing the same thing.

The expanding sphere of earth consciousness hit the expanding sphere from the Illirian node on Jupiter. In that instant only John Frankel in the earth sphere was consciously aware of it. He was the key to the smooth melding of two completely different spheres of consciousness: those of the practically disembodied, intellectually pure beings from Galaxy 11 and those of the emotionally charged physical beings from the planet earth. Here there was an impossible chasm of awareness. But one that had to be bridged.

When the edges of the two spheres hit each other the Illirians were ready. For billions of years they had perfected the mind melding. Their galaxy-wide awareness effortlessly came together into an even tighter consciousness as they eagerly reached out toward the earth sphere.

When the earthians contacted the Illirians there were screams of horror, for the Illirian thought patterns were totally alien. There was simply no common ground to promote even a glimmer of understanding.

Illirians were outcasts from all life they had ever come into contact with. They were loners who had decided, aeons ago, that the expression of any emotion or the acknowledgment of any feeling was an impediment to Truth. Their collective intelligence, through billions of years, had reached a state of such detachment from all emotion that the vibration of their consciousness made them incompatible with any civilization they interacted with. Beings exposed to full telepathic contact with Illirian consciousness experienced excruciating pain and an unbearable level of pure, cold, razor-sharp clarity. Human consciousness felt the Illirian consciousness as millions of impossibly sharp blades cutting them to pieces.

Deep within the Illirian Supermind the tiniest of emotional spores still lived. Within this spore of feeling, far beyond the conscious realization of any Illirian, were the emotions of abandonment, alienation, and loneliness.

The Illirian sphere, in its turn, became overwhelmed by the emotional intensity of the human reaction.

In the first femtosecond of contact with the human sphere a long lost vibration began to be activated within the Illirian sphere. Imperceptibly at first, then with greater volume, the Illirian consciousness began to experience a feeling. To a human this feeling would have been imperceptible. To an Illirian it was like a bomb exploding in a crowded church. As the two spheres came into fuller contact the Illirians were utterly overwhelmed.

If the unfeeling awareness of the Illirians was nightmarish for humans, think, dear reader, of the Illirian side. Imagine a hospital whose air has been filtered so fine that not even a microbe remains. Then deposit in that air a virulent influenza virus.

Like a peaceful valley under the onslaught of a bursting dam, the great Supermind was overmatched. Its component entities separated from the Whole. Each became utterly helpless before the fatal assault of human emotion!

[Origin 0 (0, 0)] felt the pure emotion of desperation and reached outward for the only human entity he had ever even remotely understood.

When John Frankel felt [Origin 0 (0, 0)] he rejoiced. Here was his friend from the Pleiadian ship, the one from whose immense mind he had felt a tendril of love. John saw instantly the plight of the Illirian group. He felt the love behind their alien-ness, a love that had been suppressed for eons.

John understood. From that understanding a bridge was instantly formed between those of earth and those from Galaxy 11. Earthians understood loneliness. They understood rejection, abandonment, and agony. When that common bond was forged the Illirian consciousness found an anchor to hold to. Something they had forgotten in the mists of time now became obvious: the value of faith and hope. To their logical minds such concepts had been pointless, but the earthians showed them the correct orientation. Illirians and earthians, outcasts both, were fellow brothers-in-arms. The subtle Illirian templates within human consciousness gave the earthians a logical platform for their own understanding.

All of this happened at the speed of thought. Which means that it happened in no time at all. But then again, it could have taken eons. Who is to judge?

Now the two spheres of consciousness were one. This expanded sphere now blossomed forth to meet all the others, from every galaxy in the universe. Uncounted trillions of individual spheres of consciousness came together into planetary consciousness. Billions of planetary spheres came together into galactic awareness and merged with each other to form a universal sphere of consciousness.

It began, as the Great Cycle always begins, on the leading edge of existence. At this moment it was the solar system of earth. The merging of the two diametrically opposing spheres of consciousness generated a tremendous spark which, like a flash of light illuminating the All, ignited expansion of awareness everywhere.

Chuang-Tzu observed it all, as he had almost since the beginning. To his comrades he pulsed. "It has begun. Behold, those in the outer universe have come together successfully, integrating the Strange Ones." His entire existence was based around these periodic universal events, when all consciousness everywhere would come together. The beings of Universe One were the most ancient in existence. They lived forever within the same identity, yet this identity expanded and grew every time Oneness was achieved during each Great Cycle.

Chuang-Tzu knew how necessary this process was for the maintenance of the structure of physicality, and for his own personal growth. He had participated so many times he lost count. For Chuang-Tzu and his kind, 15 billion years passed as did one century to an earthian.

The cosmic event was an opportunity for consciousness to touch base with the infinity of Its individual focused personalities and to create a synergy of Its component parts. It was a time to review and evaluate the new knowledge and experience It had gained in the previous cycle. Most important, it was a time to celebrate Itself. To allow each personality to experience the infinite vastness and magnificence of the whole. To become, for an instant, God.

And to once again birth a new part of Itself.

Now the outermost ring in the All was successfully integrated. Like dropping a stone into a pool, the pulsations would affect everything in its path.

Chuang-Tzu and his friends watched like little children anticipating Christmas as the integration of consciousness proceeded inward toward the indefinable Interface at the center of the All, which would now become activated.

"Soon we will all be united once more!" the beings in Universe One thought to each other. By the time the great pulse of consciousness reached their universe it would be at its maximum expansion and strength. It would contain the awareness of all life everywhere.

They would be the final pieces of the puzzle!

Now the great magnificent Pulse enveloped them. Or rather, they united with something so grand and glorious that the pitiful descriptions of language are woefully inadequate to express it.

The entirety of creation was united in a singularity of consciousness. As the great Pulse hit the center of creation it triggered the Interface between that which

IS and that which IS NOT. This created a potential Seed, a Seed that contained the combined knowledge and wisdom gained from the last 15 billion year Great Cycle of experience.

The Pulse would now flow outward again, birthing an entirely new universe! A universe that did not destroy the old.

Within the cocoon of Everything, each participant was fully aware of themselves as individuals. But now each had a hundred zillion new friends! It would be impossible to describe the conversations each had with the other because it happened outside of time. The moment of Singularity was eternal. Even Chuang-Tzu himself only completely understood this during these moments of complete unity.

The energy of the Unformed Potential, which had been building up for 15 billion years, was now organized and released. This singularity of matter and energy was a direct reflection of the Universal Consciousness that created it. The singularity contained the parameters for the new universe enfolded within it. It would now expand and eventually form the next glorious universe in the collection.

Kjirsten, John, Genevieve, Davey, Goliath, Bellerophon, Robert and Rachel, Michael Walters, and all the rest inspected their handiwork, and found that it was good.

47

THE glow of unity consciousness wore off more quickly for some than others, especially on earth. Much of global commerce resumed its course because people had to eat. Food distribution, energy, and finance were largely unchanged because a framework already existed.

The greatest changes were in health (medicine) and those industries associated with war.

Miraculously, everyone who survived the Event achieved perfect health. Grace Downing from across the street told this story:

> I went to the hospital very early in the morning after the Event to see my mother. She was in the IC unit and had been diagnosed with malignant cancer of the colon. When I walked in the door I saw people getting up out of their sickbeds and running down the hallways. Doctors and nurses were laughing and smiling with the patients. I saw my 83-year-old mom in the lobby, dancing with another white haired old lady.
>
> "Mom! Are you OK?"
>
> She turned to face me and threw both arms in the air, as if to say, 'ta-da.' There was no trace of the disease in her body.
>
> The hospital administrators said they might have to close the place down because there was no longer a need for their services.

Kjirsten, John, Genevieve, Bellerophon, and Davey resumed their activities. They found that the universal medium was responding as before. The vibrational pathways were open. Intra- and inter-universal translation was possible once more. The Eyrie was no more. The Unformed Potential was now as quiet and serene as the seas of Argelain. Its presence could barely even be detected.

The neighbors had all been present this evening, as they had been every evening for a week, talking, celebrating, and sharing experiences. The universal moment was so profound and exhilarating that it left an indelible impression on everyone. Tom Brubaker, a devout Christian, expressed this sentiment. "This is a high you can't come down from."

"We seem to have lost a few," someone else said.

On a two block area of Magnolia Street the population had been reduced from 123 to 75. Preliminary estimates showed a world population of 5.75 billion, down from 8.75 billion. No bodies were discovered. Those who died, apparently, had merged into Oneness and stayed there.

"So there *was* a Rapture!" Brubaker said. "It just didn't happen like we thought it would."

One night John and Genevieve were in their bedroom. Genevieve looked at her husband. "John, why don't we go to that beach I took you to on our first voyage together?"

"Yes, lets!"

Genevieve led the way. They translated onto the beautiful planet with its deep violet sky. A tiny purplish sun hovered just above the horizon. The light shone with a lavender tint, sparkling onto the water which lapped gently onto a pastel beach.

Suddenly they felt a strong breeze and heard the flapping of wings.

"Squawk! Hey kid, how are you?"

"IVAN!!!!!!"

The two humans rushed the startled griffon and threw their arms about him. "We thought you were gone forever!"

"Not me, silly earthians! I just stopped in to say hello. Now that the pathways are open again I'm going to visit every one of my old friends from the Eyrie."

Ivan told them that translation anywhere was now a piece of cake. "It's far easier than it ever was."

The three friends had a lively discussion, during which the big griffon chased John down the beach and knocked him into the water.

Genevieve laughed. "Oh John you looked so silly!" But she wasn't laughing so hard when Ivan picked her up in his big claws and dropped her in as well.

The two humans tried to gang up on him but he just flew into the air. "I have the advantage over you, ha-ha!"

After a time Ivan was ready to go. His restless nature would not allow him to stay in any one place for too long. "Please stay in touch old friend," John said.

Ivan raised himself into the air, almost knocking the two humans down. "Of course we'll stay in touch. The whole universe is available to us. You know how to find me."

Then he was gone.

John smiled. Of course! There would never again be any good-byes. The mechanism for attaining altered states of consciousness would now be easily received, even on earth. There were an infinity of universes to explore! A rush of joy coursed through every cell in his body.

John took Genevieve in his arms. She felt so wonderful against him. Over her head he observed the breathtaking colors of the risen sun and smelled the fragrant air, filled with the scent of this planet's life. John kissed Genevieve and whispered, "I love you."

Within the warm and life giving embrace of the man she loved, Genevieve's heart soared.

"I feel more like I do now than when I first got here," she said.

They both roared with laughter. John felt the lavender light from the purplish-red sun, now fully above the horizon, caress his face. A sudden breeze blew a strand of Genevieve's jet-black hair onto his shoulder.

Life was grand.

48 Afterword

THE all-that-is is multidimensional. The merkaba is a vehicle of consciousness that has the native capability to travel anywhere in the universe and even between dimensions. Of course human beings are thousands of years away from being able to do this, even though the Bible describes the Ascension of Eliza. (In garbled form. Basically what Eliza did was activate his merkaba and disappear in a sphere of light.) Right now many people believe that consciousness comes forth from matter, and that when you die, you're dead. So this book may seem wacko to that lot, but what the hell. I had fun writing it!

Beyond the Beginning is an attempt to bring forward metaphysical concepts that seem ridiculous and absurd right now. I have tried to put them in a framework based on present day references people will hopefully understand. I believe this is very important. If we don't know where we are headed we might not get there. The power of consciousness, as represented in the merkaba, is far beyond the common conception.

I hope you enjoyed this exploration into the potentials of consciousness. We are all more powerful than we have allowed ourselves to even imagine.

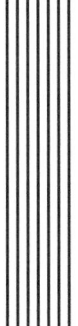

Author's Notes

The idea of travel without the use of machines or devices was, to my knowledge, first explored in Alfred Bester's *The Stars My Destination*. The end of the universe and the beginning of a new one was superbly handled from the current scientific framework by the great Poul Anderson in his classic *Tau Zero*. I have extended and expanded upon both of these ideas as the main theme of the book.

I have gratefully drawn upon both of these masters in the writing of this book, as well as the brilliant work of Gordon Dickson, my favorite SF writer, and E. E. "Doc" Smith.

The main characters are young because, frankly, by the time we reach thirty almost all of us are too set in our ways to accept radical new ideas. In my opinion our societies would be much better off if we listened more to our children. We're so busy trying to inculcate kids with the ideas we grew up with. These ideas have turned our planet into a polluted mess, with scarcity and conflict the order of the day. Generation after generation, we stifle their natural creativity and their remembrance of who they are. That connection to a higher consciousness is inherent in each one of us, but it is hammered out of almost all of us.

The suggestion that consciousness has a non-physical basis is rejected by science, and rightfully so. This assertion cannot now be tested, but it is coming. New inventions are on the horizon that will be able to observe quantum multi-dimensionality. This term sounds silly in today's scientific understanding. In the future I believe this will be well understood.

This book is dedicated to those of us who understand our spiritual origins and who can look beyond the commonplace.

Author's Notes to the First Edition

What is the origin of the universe? Is earth the only planet in the universe with intelligent life? What is consciousness, and is it dependent upon physical structure? Is the potential of the human race far greater than we have been led to believe? These questions, and the answers to them, are the topics of this book.

Beyond the Beginning was originally written as a kind of teaching manual for these concepts. I decided later to take out some of the more didactic material and make a novel out of it. Because the canvas is so large, I found this to be a much more difficult (but exciting) task than I had anticipated.

In *Beyond the Beginning* I have tried to present a view of life and the universe not just from the perspective of life on our tiny little planet, but from the much broader outlook of a universe teeming with intelligent life. The idea that a gigantic universe of over 10 million galactic superclusters containing billions of galaxies and 30 billion trillion stars was created for the exclusive use of one trivial planetary civilization in a nondescript galaxy is not only illogical, but ludicrous.

Acknowledging my SF writer heroes and heroines

Gordon Dickson
Dan Simmons
Poul Anderson
Roger Zelazny
Philip Jose Farmer
Alfred Bester
J. G. Ballard
Keith Laumer
Robert L. Forward
Andre Norton
Steven Baxter
Gregory Benford
David Brin
E. E. "Doc" Smith

Thanks to George Shearing, John Coltrane, Wolfgang Amadeus Mozart, Charles Lloyd, Tony Williams, Wayne Shorter, Miles Davis, Herbie Hancock, John McLaughlin, Kurt Rosenwinkel, and Brian Blade & Fellowship for the inspirational music that made some of the scenes in this book easier to write. Especially to the ECO and Murray Perahia for those superb Mozart piano concertos.

Thanks also to Lee Carroll, Esther Hicks, Drunvalo Melchizedek, Richard Feynman, Tom Bearden, Viktor Schauberger, Lyssa Royal, Robert Shapiro, Judith Merkle Riley, and Georgette Heyer for some crazy story ideas.

Thanks also to Peter Sobolev and his excellent website for the great pictures and descriptions of St. Petersburg, Russia.

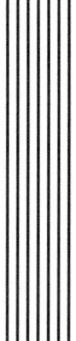

Appendix A – The Big Wide Universe

According to astronomical data, the radius of the visible universe is approximately 14 billlion light years. The universe has a cellular appearance, because galaxies collect into vast sheets and superclusters, arranged commonly in elongated bands or strings, sometimes called filaments. Intergalactic space between superclusters contain lower numbers of galaxies. The decrease is some regions can be described as "voids," referring to a scarcity of grouped galaxies. For a pictorial model of large scale structures in our universe, see the University of Chicago website at
http://cosmicweb.uchicago.edu/filaments.html.

Here are some facts about the composition of the known universe:

- Number of superclusters in the visible universe = 10 million

- Number of galaxy groups in the visible universe = 25 billion

- Number of large galaxies in the visible universe = 350 billion

- Number of dwarf galaxies in the visible universe = 3.5 trillion

- Number of stars in the visible universe = 30 billion trillion

For a wonderful and informative look at our universe, see the fantastic webpages of Richard Powell at
http://anzwers.org/free/universe/index.html.

Also check out the superb NASA website at
http://rst.gsfc.nasa.gov/Sect20/A2a.html.

Visible matter only accounts for 4% of the mass of the universe. 23% is dark matter, and 73% is dark energy, whatever that is!

An interesting fact about the expansion of the universe from the perspective of the "Big Bang" theory: Time and space is created on an "on-demand" basis. In other words, the matter and energy in our universe doesn't expand into the vast emptiness of an already created space; rather, space and time are created as the universe expands. If the universe is finite, it doesn't have an edge or a boundary; therefore the question, "What is outside the universe" is meaningless. Of course there may be other universes next to ours, as is postulated in this book.

What this means is that a spaceship traveling from one end of the universe to the other simply arrives back at the starting point. Topologically, such a structure is called a "three-torus." Moreover, there is no "origin" point that we can point to and say, "This is the place where the universe began," for the universe is expanding uniformly at all points within it.

Distance in Light Years from Sol

(See table on next page.)

Source: Stellar Brightness, from Chris Dolan at
http://www.astro.wisc.edu/~dolan/constellations/extra/brightest.html
And http://www.seds.org/Maps/Stars_en/

The Spectral Type indicates the internal temperature of the star. Stars are classified by their spectra (the elements that they absorb) and their temperature. There are seven main types of stars. In order of decreasing temperature, O, B, A, F, G, K, and M. O and B stars are uncommon but very bright; M stars are common but dim.

Spectral Types

Within each stellar type, stars are placed into subclasses (from 0 to 9) based on its position within the scale.

The Yerkes Luminosity Classes: (by William Wilson Morgan and Philip Keenan). Luminosity is the total brightness of a star (or galaxy). Luminosity is the total amount of energy that a star radiates each second (including all wavelengths of electromagnetic radiation).

The earthian sun is a yellow dwarf star, located within the Orion arm of the spiral galaxy we call the Milky Way. In the society of the Twelve it is known as Galaxy 6.

Star	Distance (light Years from Earth)	Apparent Magnitude	Absolute Magnitude	Spectral Type
Sol		26.72	4.8	G2V
Sirius	8.6	−1.46	1.4	A1Vm
Canopus	74	−0.72	−2.5	A9II
Alpha Centauri	4.3	−0.27	4.4	G2V+K1V
Arcturus	34	−0.04	0.2	K1.5IIIp
Vega	25	0.03	0.6	A0Va
Capella	41	0.08	0.4	G6III+G2III
Rigel	~1400	0.12	−8.1	B8Iae
Procyon	11.4	0.38	2.6	F5IV-V
Achernar	69	0.46	−1.3	B3Vnp
Betelgeuse	~1400	0.50 (var)	−7.2	M2Iab
Fomalhaut	25			A3V
Altair	16	0.77	2.3	A7Vn
Aldebaran	60	0.85 (var)	−0.3	K5III
Antares	~520	0.96 (var)	−5.2	M1.5Iab
Deneb	1500	1.25	−7.2	A2Ia
Regulus	69	1.35	−0.3	B7Vn
Pleiades	~365			
Casseopeia	~2500			
Draco (Eltanin)	147			
Zeta2 Reticuli	37			
M31 Andromeda (Galaxy 3)	2,900,000			

Spectral Type	Star
Ia	Very luminous supergiants
Ib	Less luminous supergiants
II	Luminous giants
III	Giants
IV	Subgiants
V	Main sequence stars (dwarf stars)
VI	Subdwarf
VII	White Dwarf

Appendix B – The Principles behind Jaunting and Portal Travel

World lines of John and Mats

Individual travel through the portals, or utilizing the sphere of consciousness from point A (source) to point B (destination) and then back again to point A results in no subjective elapsed time in the source frame of reference.

The causality of time is maintained between universes, and within universes. So portal travel must follow two simple rules:

1. Individual time lines are continuous in every frame of reference UNLESS this leads to a time paradox.

2. First in, last out.

Time is continuous; you don't get to jump around in time. This rule apparently exists to make the experiences of individual beings rational and consistent. Time jumping leads to paradoxes. Time "flows" or passes at a uniform rate no matter where you are.

First in, last out: Envision a container of 4 tennis balls. If you mark each one and place them in the can, #1 is at the bottom and #4 is at the top. When you remove the balls, they come out in reverse order.

A world line is a simplified diagram showing the path of an object in space-time. We put the "space" axis as a vertical line (y-axis) and the time axis as a horizontal line (x-axis). Here is how John and Mats' world lines look like as they traveled back and forth between the Full Moon and Argelain:

John and Mats start out at the Full Moon, at point D. Mats goes through the portal first, and arrives on the beach in Argelain at point H. Meanwhile, John takes

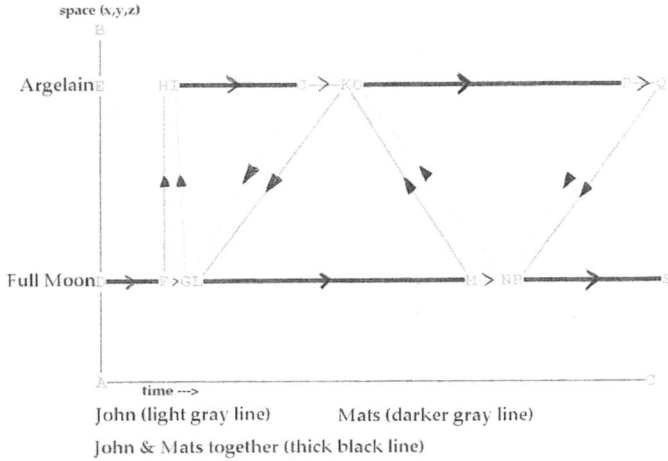

John (light gray line)   Mats (darker gray line)

John & Mats together (thick black line)

a few seconds to get himself into the portal, so he travels in time from point F to point G at the Full Moon. John arrives in Argelain at point I, an instant after Mats. John and Mats are together on Argelain for a bit, so they travel in time from I to J. John steps into the portal first and arrives back at the Full Moon at point G. No time has elapsed at the Full Moon. Mats follows him a few seconds later and meets John in the Full Moon at point L, an instant after John arrives at point G.

What would have happened if Mats tried to go through the portal first? Nothing! For that would have set up a paradox: Mats would have arrived at the same time he left, at point F, so he would have met John before John left. This situation violates rule (2), and leads to inconsistencies.

John's world line is continuous at point G (Full Moon), whereas Mats' world line jumps from F to L, in order to avoid experiential inconsistencies.

Here is where the concept of time traveling becomes complex. What if Mats entered the portal without John's knowledge? He could have spent a year on Argelain and returned to earth a split instant later, without a gap in his world line. But if John and Mats interact, if they each have conscious knowledge of their position in spacetime, different behavior is observed. Now we are coming very close to the famous double slit experiments with subatomic particles. Entangled particles demonstrate interesting behavior in such experiments, as they seemingly consciously interact with themselves and the experimenter. Experimentation has discovered that the position of a previously recorded entangled photon will change if, later, more information is learned about its twin! In other words, the first photon will be at one place if, later on in time, we learn more information about its twin, and it will be in another position if we don't have that information.

You can follow along the world lines of Mats and John in the rest of the diagram. Mats and John return to Argelain about a minute later and spend a few days there, then they arrive back at the Full Moon at point R, before the store opens. (Diagram is not to scale).

When Mats tries to enter Neptune's portal (in Chapter 16) after their visit, he cannot go through. Again, a time paradox is avoided. When John enters first, they both go through without difficulty.

Mats objects to John's insistence that they both return at the same time. Mats could have remained on Argelain as long as he liked, and he would have returned right after John, but John wasn't sure.

John discovered that using the Frankel Method always returns you to the same point in space relative to the source frame of reference. In other words, if John jaunts from his bedroom chair, he always returns to that chair, even if he intends to return somewhere else.

An objective observer could say, correctly, that the jaunter merely had a vivid dream and never went anywhere. Thus the "objective" observer is always correct and can invalidate the assertions of the traveler. Every observer is "correct" in his or her own frame of reference.

Multiverse jaunting may be explained if individual universes are superposed, or layered, like a digital photograph. In this case the consciousness altering procedure does not result in travel through space at all. It merely provides access to another interpreted reality within the same 'soup' of vibration.

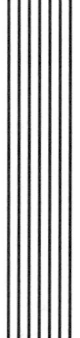

Appendix C – Additional Character Info

Bellerophon:

Bellerophon was (in his pre-Eyrie life) a maverick philosopher and activist. His ancestors came from a long line of free thinkers who questioned the idea of harmony in relationships. Bellerophon believed that harmony in groups leads to stagnation and that competition is a superior motivator to group members. Bell didn't have an off switch. He irritated even his family members. When he fell in love with the daughter of an important manager he began to turn her away from her family. He was permanently exiled to a planetoid that held persons like himself who would not conform to societal norms.

Bellerophon found his way to the Eyrie and spent as much time there as he could. No one missed him back home. He applied for candidate status but was immediately rejected because he was too impulsive and uncooperative. There were too many broken relationships with his former acquaintances.

It had taken Bell several years but he had patched things up. After that he passed his training with ease and was accepted into the small group led by Kjirsten. Bell's iconoclastic views were still sometimes irritating to his coworkers. Nevertheless, Bellerophon's enthusiasm and his daring contributed positively to the team.

Davey:

Davey comes from a heavy planet with a specific gravity 1.75 times that of earth. Davey's planet is dry and arid. Orodani is a world of rock and brownish-red sand with large mountains that reached almost ten miles above the planet's surface. Deserts abounded there. Smooth mesas, canyons, and outcroppings of hard stone dotted the surface of Orodani somewhat like the southwest desert of the United States. The planet has a thin atmosphere, a purplish-black sky, and a white-hot binary sun. The climate is hot and dry during the day and below freezing at night. Small underground caverns of water supplied what little moisture was needed to sustain life. The planet is sparsely populated, with very little biomass. The human population traveled the desert slowly in caravans, and were for the most part nomadic. There are two great cities on each of Orodani's three continents, which covered almost 97% of the planet's surface. It was a wild, free life. John picked up the excitement Davey felt for his home world. Only the fierce exhilaration of Unformed Potential work could surpass it.

Davey's massive physique evolved to support the increased gravitational attraction of Orodani. His blue skin evolved to ward off the intense heat and ultraviolet radiation, shielding him from the extreme temperatures and preventing evaporation. Davey hardly ever drank water. Once John saw Davey looking at earth, scowling at the oceans. "Waste of space," he said. Davey thought of Orodani as beautiful and earth as a freak show, a madman's canvas of haphazard and confusing variety. "Shoulda just stuck with one thing," he would say.

Kjirsten:

Kjirsten's home planet lies in the Lyran sector in his own galaxy. The Lyran peoples are tall and well made, with red hair, intense blue or green eyes, and very light skin. Their planets tend to be cold and icy, barren of physical resources. Earthian DNA contains Lyran genetics. The Viking is their legacy to earth. Lyrans are natural explorers and warriors. A Lyran on earth might do well in the armed forces, in athletics, or in a start-up business. A Lyran is comfortable anywhere on the leading edge because their personalities tend toward aggressiveness and passionate emotion.

Lyran women are almost as tall and strong as their men and are famous throughout the galaxy for their beauty. There aren't many human men on other planets capable of dealing with them on an equal basis.

On Lyran planets political leaders are women because the men are usually too volatile for diplomacy. Lyran women are able to cooperate whereas Lyran men felt the need to compete with one another. Lyran men trust their women implicitly and have a deep respect and love for them. Unlike on earth, assault on women is unheard of. For a man to attack a woman under any circumstances, even in self-defense, meant instant death from other men.

The relationship between men and women in Lyran society resembles that between a master and his dog. John had to stifle a laugh. He didn't want Genevieve to get any ideas but he heard her giggle within him.

A Lyran man will carry out the command of any woman, no matter how unreasonable. Even their slightest whim was treated as an important commission. As a result of this blind trust, girls were made cognizant of their enormous responsibilities to society. They were rigorously trained in mental and emotional discipline and the handling of males from the time they were able to stand on two feet. The female half of the Lyran genotype attained physical maturity quickly, at 12 or 13 years of age. Unfortunately, emotional maturity came later. Impulsive and ambitious girls sometimes created havoc within Lyran societies.

Because the race is so dynamic, diplomacy and conflict resolution are of the utmost importance. Girls who did not or could not excel in these areas were not allowed positions in society. These girls are not even allowed to have children. Lyran history goes awry when their women become uncooperative and amass power to themselves.

Lyran boys and men are allowed to find their areas of interest and pursue them without the slightest constraint. Men are the power sources within Lyran society but women are the harnessers and managers of that power. Lyrans are the earth equivalent of venture capitalists, entrepreneurs, explorers, and mercenaries of the galaxy. As a result, Lyran influence extends far beyond their little collection of barren planets. Like seed spores they travel all over the galaxy. They have established themselves on the frontiers in every galactic culture. Lyrans are sometimes looked upon as irritating children but their enthusiasm and vigor were widely admired.

Kjirsten came from an ancient ruling family, famous for their leadership abilities. She was a natural commander and on her home planet of Skjelgaard, a celebrated beauty. Even by Lyran standards Kjirsten was considered formidable.

John learned that there was a temperamental connection between Lyra and earth. However, even Kjirsten was shocked at the level of brutality, hatred, and psychosis that manifested upon the earthian planet. According to her, a good dose of feminine management would set things straight. Lyran history, in ancient times, was similar to that of present day earth.

Goliath:

Goliath's personality is like the rays of a warming sun. Like water in a rock fountain, the mantis fills the gaps with a sort of liquid love.

Goliath's civilization is prosperous, stable, and happy. It is oriented around the enjoyment of life and the nurturing and raising of children. Goliath's personality is open and tolerant, cheerful but not frivolous. He remains calm under pressure.

Ivan:

Ivan comes from an amazing universe of shapeshifters, halfway between the world of light and the outer rings. In his universe there are no rigidly defined structures. No galaxies, stars, or planets existed in Ivan's universe because its space is malleable and dynamic. Ivan's universe is constantly changing its character as beings altered the environment to suit the desires of the moment.

Change is so rapid that the word stability had no meaning.

Ivan is famous in his own universe. He is revered for his ability to travel the universal pathways. Like a guy who owns a gigantic hardware store, Ivan brought to his world new ways to mold and experience their reality.

Ivan is wide open and totally uninhibited. John was enthralled as he picked up on some of Ivan's experiences in his lively and vibrant world: A beautiful turreted castle set within a snow capped mountain and Ivan as a lady dressed in silks, holding a parasol and leaning upon a stone railing. Ivan as a bird settling on a plain of rapidly evolving plants, Ivan chasing the seeds as each one sprouted legs. Ivan diving into an ocean, becoming a dolphin, then a huge whale, then an otter. Suddenly he flew into into the clouds, bursting forth into a red sky, which then slowly changed its color into the blue, violet, and beyond. Diving now, he passed crystal cities floating thousands of feet in the air. Ivan spotted a creature standing upon a platform of glass and dissolved it, sending it plummeting and heard its cry of acknowledgment. Ivan changed form into a human, walking upon a beach when it suddenly became alive with poisonous serpents. Ivan quickly morphed into a hawk, soaring above the hissing creatures. Ivan soaring now above an orange sky, an orange sun just above the horizon...and on and on and on. Ivan considered the outer universes and their inhabitants dreadfully boring, useful only for finding new forms with which to amuse himself in his world.

Ivan is a loner, much more than John. His shapeshifting abilities makes him a whiz at Unformed Potential work.

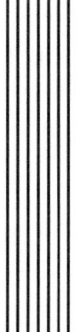

Definitions

Universal Medium : I am calling the universal medium a virtual field of subtle energy (thought) that fills the universe and composes all things in existence.

Consciousness: Consciousness is a static, massless, pure potential that has the ability to create and perceive what is has created. It is at one and the same time a pure potential, but also has the ability to create observable, perceivable quanta, through the vehicle of thought. The Bible refers to this when Jesus says, "I am the Alpha and the Omega."

Thought: The creation or product of consciousness. A thought is observable or perceivable by consciousness. It is the smallest quanta in any universe. All matter and energy is ultimately composed of thought.

We can say that a thought is a mapping between the pure potential of consciousness and the physical universe. Imagine a virtual function f that maps a thought T into the physical universe. We can write $f(T) \Rightarrow q$. Since both f and T are virtual and unobservable, it is not possible to say how this occurs. We simply say that the virtual function f, a property of consciousness, operates on a virtual thought T, translating it into a physical quantum, q.

Unformed Potential: A chaotic quasi-reality that acts as a buffer between the universal medium and any physical universe. The Unformed Potential provides all things with the opportunity and the space to grow and evolve. In the book, the Unformed Potential is the source of dark matter and energy.

About the Author

Kenneth MacLean is a freelance writer and book editor living in Ann Arbor, Michigan.

He can be reached at kmaclean@kjmaclean.com

Website at http://www.kjmaclean.com

and http://www.macleanediting.com

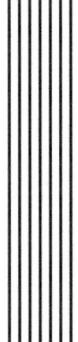

Other books by the author

(see complete list at
http://www.kjmaclean.com/Products/MainProductPage.php):

A Geometric Analysis of the Five Platonic Solids and Other Semi-regular Polyhedra – a meticulous mathematical analysis of some important polyhedra. For teachers, researchers, and the generally curious.

The Vibrational Universe – Harnessing the Power of Thought to Consciously Create Your Life – the relationship between consciousness and the physical universe.

The End of the Universe (SF novel) – What if the universe we see through our telescopes was merely a sophisticated holographic illusion?

Dialogues – Conversations with my Higher Self – A look at life, the universe and everything from a non-corporeal perspective.

The Manchild (SF novel) – A deadly bioenhancer is released by a rogue black program on an unsuspecting public.

Tesla's Lost Notebook – The long lost personal notebook of Nikola Tesla is discovered by a former Lockheed scientist, who uses it to create a device that can extract energy from the quantum vacuum.